WITHDRAWN

D1604870

EX LIBRIS

SOUTH ORANGE
PUBLIC LIBRARY

John Willis with Ben Hodges
THEATRE WORLD®

Volume 59
2002–2003

APPLAUSE
THEATRE & CINEMA BOOKS

792
THE

THEATRE WORLD
Volume 59

Copyright © 2005 by John Willis
All rights reserved

No part of this publication may be reproduced or transmitted in any form or by any means,
electronic or mechanical, including photocopy, recording or any other information storage
or retrieval system now known or to be invented, without permission in writing from the
publishers, except by a reviewer who wishes to quote brief passages in connection with
a review written for inclusion in a magazine, newspaper, or broadcast.

Art direction Mark Lerner
Book interior design Pearl Chang **Cover design** Kristina Rolander

ISBN (hardcover) 1-55783-634-5
ISBN (paperback) 1-55783-635-3
ISSN 1088-4564

Applause Theatre & Cinema Books
151 West 46th Street, 8th Floor
New York, NY 10036
Phone: (212) 575-9265
Fax: (646) 562-5852
Email: info@applausepub.com
Internet: www.applausepub.com

Applause books are available through your local bookstore, or you may order at
www.applausepub.com or call Music Dispatch at 800-637-2852

Sales & Distribution
North America:
    Hal Leonard Corp.
    7777 West Bluemound Road
    P. O. Box 13819
    Milwaukee, WI 53213
    Phone: (414) 774-3630
    Fax: (414) 774-3259
    Email: halinfo@halleonard.com
    Internet: www.halleonard.com
Europe:
    Roundhouse Publishing Ltd.
    Millstone, Limers Lane
    Northam, North Devon EX 39 2RG
    Phone: (0) 1237-474-474
    Fax: (0) 1237-474-774
    Email: roundhouse.group@ukgateway.net

In Memory of **IRENE WORTH**

Who, with her commanding contralto voice and emotional authority, captivated audiences around the world for over sixty years. One of the last of the generation of legendary actors of the English-speaking world, she was a founder of the Stratford Shakespeare Festival in Canada, as well as a member of the Old Vic Company and the Royal Shakespeare Company, where her many compatriots included Laurence Olivier, Ralph Richardson, John Gielguld, Alec Guinness, Paul Scofield, Noel Coward, Tyrone Guthrie, and Peter Brook, among many, many others. From Shakespeare to Shaw to Williams to Albee, she used her brilliance and penchant for artistic adventure to eventually embody most of the heroines in all of regularly performed dramatic literature.

She made her Broadway debut in 1943 in *The Two Mrs. Carrolls*, followed by *The Cocktail Party*, *Toys in the Attic* (Tony nomination, Best Actress in a Play), *Tiny Alice* (Tony Award, Best Actress in a Play), *Sweet Bird of Youth* (Tony Award, Best Actress in a Play), *The Cherry Orchard* (Tony nomination, Best Actress in a Play), *The Lady from Dubuque*, *John Gabriel Borkman*, *The Golden Age*, and *Lost in Yonkers* (Tony Award, Best Featured Actress in a Play). Off-Broadway productions include *Corialanus* with Christopher Walken, *The Gypsy and the Yellow Canary*, *The Chalk Garden* (Obie Award), and her solo *Irene Worth's Portrait of Edith Wharton*. Making London her primary residence much of her life, she appeared in many productions in London's West End, including as Lady Macbeth, Desdemona in *Othello*, Helena in *A Midsummer Night's Dream*, and Portia in *The Merchant of Venice* with the Old Vic. She also appeared as Goneril in Peter Brook's acclaimed *King Lear* with the Royal Shakespeare Company and as Jocasta with the National Theater of Great Britain. Other notable West End productions include *Native Son* and *The Cocktail Hour*. She also played in *All's Well That Ends Well* and *Richard III* at Canada's Stratford Festival. She won the British Academy Award for her film role in *The Scapegoat*, and made several other notable film appearances. She was renowned for her myriad solo performances later in her career, and was awarded an Obie in 1989 for Sustained Achievement.

CONTENTS

Acknowledgements   1

Broadway Highlights   3

BROADWAY

Productions that opened June 1, 2002 – May 31, 2003   19

Productions from past seasons that played through this season   63

Productions from past seasons that closed during this season   77

OFF-BROADWAY

Productions that opened June 1, 2002 – May 31, 2003   89

Productions from past seasons that played through this season   107

Productions from past seasons that closed during this season   113

Company Series   121

OFF-OFF-BROADWAY

Productions that opened June 1, 2002 – May 31, 2003   137

Company Series   165

PROFESSIONAL REGIONAL COMPANIES 181

AWARDS

2003 Theatre World Award Winners 237

Theatre World Awards: June 2, 2003 241

Previous Theatre World Award Recipients 245

Major Theatrical Awards 249

American Theatre Wing's Antoinette Perry "Tony" Awards and Past Tony Award Winners; Village Voice Obie Awards and Past Obie Best New Play Winners; Drama Desk Awards; Outer Critics Circle Awards; Pulitzer Prize Award Winners for Drama; New York Drama Critics Circle Award Winners; Lucille Lortel Awards and Past Lucille Lortel Award Winners; American Theatre Critics/Steinberg New Play Awards and Citations and ATCA/Steinberg New Play Award and Citations; Astaire Awards; Carbonell Awards; Clarence Derwent Awards; Connecticut Critics Circle Awards; Drama League Awards; Dramatist Guild Awards; Elliott Norton Awards; George Freedley Memorial Award; George Jean Nathan Award; George Oppenheimer Award; Helen Hayes Awards; Henry Hewes Design Awards; Joseph Jefferson Awards; Joseph Kesselring Prize; Kennedy Center Honors and Mark Twain Prize; M. Elizabeth Osborn Award; Musical Theatre Hall of Fame; National Medals of the Arts; New Dramatists Lifetime Achievement Award; Ovation Awards; Richard Rodgers Awards; Robert Whitehead Award; Susan Smith Blackburn Prize; Theater Hall of Fame and Margo Jones Citize of the Theater Medal; William Inge Theatre Festival Award

Longest Running Shows on Broadway 265

Longest Running Shows Off-Broadway 283

BIOGRAPHICAL DATA 291

OBITUARIES: JUNE 1, 2002 – MAY 31, 2003 311

INDEX 329

CONTRIBUTORS BIOGRAPHIES 373

PAST EDITOR   Daniel Blum (1945–1963)

EDITOR   John Willis (1964–present)

ASSOCIATE EDITOR   Ben Hodges

ACKNOWLEDGEMENTS:

Assistant Editors: Lucy Nathanson, Emmanuel Serrano, Rachel Werbel, Matt Wolf; **Assistants:** Herbert Hayward Jr., Tom Lynch, Barry Monush, John Sala, Huck Song; **Staff Photographers:** Aubrey Reuben, Michael Riordan, Laura Viade, Michael Viade, Jack Williams, Van Williams; **Applause Books Staff:** Pearl Chang, Mark Lerner, Kallie Shimek.

SPECIAL THANKS:

New York press agents, publicists, and photographers, who continue to be largely responsible for the production of this publication, Michael Messina, Kay Radtke, Glenn Young and Allison Levine at Applause Theatre and Cinema Books, Stanley Ackert and Robert Rems, Nicole Boyd and Aaron Goodfellow, Ron and Liz Briggs, Jason Cicci, Susan Cosson, Paddy Croft, Robert Dean Davis, Carol and Nick Dawson, Tim Deak and the Learning Theatre, Inc., Diane Dixon, Craig Dudley, Patricia Elliott, Ben Feldman and Epstein, Levinsohn, Bodine, Hurwitz, and Weinstein, LLP, Emily Feldman, Peter Filichia, Jason Bowcutt, Shay Gines, Nick Micozzi and the New York Innovative Theatre Awards, Mark Glubke and Back Stage Books, Helen Guditis and the Broadway Theater Institute, Jack Williams, Barbara Dewey, Blake Robison, and the University of Tennessee at Knoxville, Laura and Tommy Hanson, Esther Harriot, Patricia, Mike, Richie, and Jennifer Henderson, Al and Sherry Hodges, O. Alden James, Jason DeMontmorencey and the National Arts Club, Miriam Lee, Tom Lynch and Barry Monush, Jim Marks, Jonathan Harper and the Lambda Literary Foundation, Matthew Murray, Albert Bennett and the Morton Street Block Association, Virginia Moraweck, Bob Ost and Theatre Resources Unlimited, Angie and Drew Powell, Kate Rushing, Honor Scott, Hannah and Jason Slosberg, Barbara Steinberg, Susan Stoller, Chris Taruc, Marianne Tatum, Alan Thierman, Bob and Reneé Isely Tobin, Hugo Uys and staff of the Paris Commune, Wilson Valentin, Frederic B. Vogel and the Commercial Theatre Institute, Walter Willison, Zan Van Antwerp and Charlie Grant, Bill and Sarah Willis

The Associate Editor wishes to express special thanks to Emmanuel Serrano, without whose unwavering support, generosity, and dedication over the past year and a half to me both personally and professionally, the compilation and publication of this volume would not have been accomplished. I will be forever grateful and indebted.

BROADWAY HIGHLIGHTS

LONG DAY'S JOURNEY INTO NIGHT
Brian Dennehy, Vanessa Redgrave
PHOTO BY JOAN MARCUS

TAKE ME OUT
Left: Daniel Sunjata, Neal Huff, Frederick Weller
Below: Denis O'Hare, Daniel Sunjata
PHOTOS BY JOAN MARCUS

VINCENT IN BRIXTON
Clare Higgins, Jochum ten Haaf
PHOTO BY IVAN KYNCL

HAIRSPRAY
Left: Harvey Fierstein
Below: The Company
PHOTOS BY PAUL KOLNIK

MOVIN' OUT
Above: The Company
Left: John Selya
PHOTOS BY JOAN MARCUS

AMOUR
Melissa Errico, Malcolm Gets
PHOTO BY JOAN MARCUS

A YEAR WITH FROG AND TOAD
Left: Jay Goede, Mark Linn-Baker, Danielle Ferland, Frank Vlastnik
Below: Mark Linn-Baker, Jay Goedde

PHOTOS BY ROB LEVINE

GYPSY
Right: Tammy Blanchard
Below: Bernadette Peters
PHOTOS BY JOAN MARCUS AND T. CHARLES ERICKSON

GYPSY
Heather Tepe, Addison Timlin
PHOTO BY JOAN MARCUS

LA BOHEME
Chloe Wright and the Company
PHOTO BY SUE ADLER

MAN OF LA MANCHA
Mary Elizabeth Mastrantonio, Brian Stokes Mitchell
PHOTO BY JOAN MARCUS

NINE
Top to Bottom: Mary Stuart Masterson, Antonio Banderas, Jane Krakowski
PHOTO BY JOAN MARCUS

A DAY IN THE DEATH OF JOE EGG
Victoria Hamilton, Eddie Izzard
PHOTO BY JOAN MARCUS

DINNER AT EIGHT
Above: The Company
PHOTO BY JOAN MARCUS

FRANKIE AND JOHNNY IN THE CLAIR DE LUNE
Right: Stanley Tucci, Edie Falco
PHOTO BY JOAN MARCUS

ENCHANTED APRIL
Elizabeth Ashley
PHOTO BY CAROL ROSEGG

BROADWAY

Productions that opened **June 1, 2002 – May 31, 2003**

I'M NOT RAPPAPORT

Revival by Herb Gardner; Producers, Elliot Martin, Lewis Allen, Ronald Shapiro, Bud Yorkin, James Cushing, Roy Miller, Mari Nakachi, Tommy DeMaio, Zandu Productions; Director, Daniel Sullivan; Scenery, Tony Walton; Costumes, Teresa Snider-Stein; Lighting, Pat Collins; Sound, Peter Fitzgerald; Fight Direction, Rick Sordelet; Associate Producer, Sharon Fallon; Casting, Alison Franck; Production Stage Manager, Warren Crane; Stage Manager, Marlene Mancini; Press, Bill Evans and Associates, Jim Randolph. Opened at the Booth Theatre, July 25, 2002*

Judd Hirsch, Ben Vereen   PHOTO BY PATRICK FARRELL

Cast

Nat **Judd Hirsch**
Midge **Ben Vereen**
Danforth **Anthony Arkin**
Laurie **Tanya Clarke**
Gilley **Steven Boyer**
Clara **Mimi Lieber**
The Cowboy **Jeb Brown**

Understudies: Judd Hirsch (David S. Howard); Ben Vereen (Adam Wade); Anthony Arkin, Jeb Brown (Michael Pemberton); Mimi Lieber, Tanya Clarke (Nurit Koppel); Steven Boyer (Robert McClure)

Time: October 1982. Place: Central Park, New York City. Presented in two parts.

*Closed September 8, 2003

FRANKIE AND JOHNNY IN THE CLAIR DE LUNE

Revival by Terrence McNally; Producers, Araca Group, Jean Doumanian Productions, USA Ostar Productions, in association with Jam Theatricals, Ray and Kit Sawyer; Director, Joe Mantello; Scenery, John Lee Beatty; Costumes, Laura Bauer; Lighting, Brian MacDevitt; Sound, Scott Lehrer; Associate Producers, Clint Bond Jr./Aaron Harnick; Production Stage Manager, Andrea J. Testani; Stage Manager, Bess Marie Glorioso; Press, Boneau/Bryan-Brown, Adrian Bryan-Brown, Jackie Green, Amy Jacobs, Martine Sainvil. Opened at the Belasco Theatre, August 8, 2002*

Cast
Frankie **Edie Falco**†1
Johnny **Stanley Tucci**†2

Understudies: Edie Falco (Lisa Leguillou); Stanley Tucci (Tim Cummings)

Time: The present. Place: Frankie's small New York apartment in the West 50s. Presented in two parts.

*Closed March 9, 2003
†Succeeded by: 1. Rosie Perez 2. Joe Pantoliano

Stanley Tucci, Edie Falco

Joe Pantoliano, Rosie Perez PHOTOS BY JOAN MARCUS

The Company

HAIRSPRAY

Musical with book by Mark O'Donnell and Thomas Meehan; Music, Marc Shaiman; Lyrics, Marc Shaiman, Scott Wittman; Producers, Margo Lion, Adam Epstein the Baruch-Viertel-Routh-Frankel Group, James D. Stern/Douglas L. Meyer, Rick Steiner, Frederic H. Mayerson, SEL and GFO, New Line Cinema, in association with Clear Channel Entertainment, Allan S. Gordon, Elan V. McAllister, Dede Harris, Morton Swinsky, John and Bonnie Osher; Director, Jack O'Brien, Choreography, Jerry Mitchell; Scenery, David Rockwell; Costumes, William Ivey Long; Lighting, Kenneth Posner; Sound, Steve C. Kennedy; Orchestrations, Harold Wheeler, Music Direction, Lon Hoyt, Music Coordinator, John Miller, Assistant Director, Matt Lenz, Associate Choreographer, Michele Lynch; Associate Producers, Rhoda Mayerson, the Aspen Group, Daniel C. Staton; Casting, Bernard Telsey Casting; Production Stage Manager, Steven Beckler; Stage Manager, J. Philip Bassett; Press, Richard Kornberg and Associates, Richard Kornberg, Don Summa, Tom D'Ambrosio, Carrie Friedman. Opened at the Neil Simon Theatre, August 15, 2002*

Kerry Butler, Corey Reynolds

Harvey Fierstein

Marisa Jaret Winokur, Harvey Fierstein

The Company

(CONTINUED FROM PREVIOUS PAGE)

Cast

Tracy Turnblad **Marissa Jaret Winokur**
Corny Collins **Clarke Thorell**
Amber Von Tussle **Laura Bell Bundy**
Brad **Peter Matthew Smith**
Tammy **Hollie Howard**
Fender **John Hill**
Brenda **Jennifer Gambatese**
Sketch **Adam Fleming**
Shelley **Shoshana Bean**
IQ **Todd Michel Smith**
Lou Ann **Katharine Leonard**
Link Larkin **Matthew Morrison**
Prudy Pingleton; Gym Teacher; Matron **Jackie Hoffman**
Edna Turnblad **Harvey Fierstein**
Penny Pingleton **Kerry Butler**
Velma Von Tussle **Linda Hart**
Harriman F. Spritzer; Principal; Mr. Pinky; Guard **Joel Vig**
Wilbur Turnblad **Dick Latessa**
Seaweed J. Stubbs **Corey Reynolds**
Duane **Eric Anthony**
Gilbert **Eric Dysart**
Lorraine **Danielle Lee Greaves**
Thad **Rashad Naylor**
The Dynamites **Kamilah Martin, Judine Richard, Shayna Steele**
Little Inez **Danelle Eugenia Wilson**
Motormouth Maybelle **Mary Bond Davis**

Denizens of Baltimore: Eric Anthony, Shoshana Bean, Eric Dysart, Adam Fleming, Jennifer Gambatese, Danielle Lee Greaves, John Hill, Jackie Hoffman, Hollie Howard, Katharine Leonard, Kamilah Martin, Rashad Naylor, Judine Richard, Peter Matthew Smith, Todd Michel Smith, Shayna Steele, Joel Vig

Onstage Musicians: Matthew Morrison, guitar; Linda Hart, keyboard; Joel Vig, glockenspiel; Kerry Butler, harmonica

Marissa Jaret Winokur, Matthew Morrison PHOTOS BY PAUL KOLNIK

Understudies: Marissa Jaret Winokur (Shoshana Bean, Katy Grenfell); Harvey Fierstein, Dick Latessa (David Greenspa, Joel Vig); Linda Hart (Shoshana Bean, Jackie Hoffman); Laura Bell Buddy (Hollie Howard, Katharine Leonard); Mary Bond Davis (Danielle Lee Greaves, Kamilah Martin); Corey Reynolds (Eric Anthony, Eric Dysart); Matthew Morrison (Adam Fleming, John Hill); Clarke Thorell (John Hill, Peter Matthew Smith); Kerry Butler (Jennifer Gambatese, Hollie Howard); Danelle Eugenia Wilson (Judine Richard, Shayna Steele)

Orchestra: Lon Hoyt, conductor, keyboard; Keith Cotton, associate conductor, keyboard; Seth Farber, assistant conductor, keyboard; David Spinozza, Peter Calo, guitars; Francisco Centeno, electric bass; Clint de Ganon, drums; Walter "Wally" Usiatynski, percussion; David Mann, Dave Rickenberg, reeds; Danny Cahn, trumpet; Birch Johnson, trombone; Rob Shaw, Carol Pool, violins; Sarah Hewitt Roth, cello

Musical Numbers: Good Morning Baltimore, The Nicest Kids in Town, Mama, I'm a Big Girl Now, I Can Hear the Bells, (The Legend of) Miss Baltimore Crabs, The Madison, The Nicest Kids in Town (Reprise), Welcome to the '60s, Run and Tell That, Big, Blond and Beautiful, The Big Dollhouse, Good Morning Baltimore, Timeless to Me, Without Love, I Know Where I've Been, Hairspray, Cooties, You Can't Stop the Beat

Time: 1962. Place: Baltimore. A musical presented in two acts.

*Still playing May 31, 2003

THE BOYS FROM SYRACUSE

Revival by Nicky Silver; Music by Richard Rodgers; Lyrics by Lorenz Hart; Original Book by George Abbott; Artistic Director, Todd Haines; Managing Director, Ellen Richard; Executive Director of External Affairs, Julia C. Levy; Director, Scott Ellis; Choreography, Rob Ashford; Scenery, Thomas Lynch; Costumes, Martin Pakledinaz; Lighting, Donald Holder; Sound, Brian Ronan; Fight Direction, Rick Sordelet; Orchestrations, Don Sebesky; Music Direction and Vocal Arrangements, David Loud; Dance Music, David Kane; Music Coordinator, John Miller; Casting, Jim Carnahan; Production Stage Manager, Peter Hanson; Stage Manager, James Mountcastle; Press, Boneau/Bryan-Brown, Adrian Bryan-Brown, Matt Polk, Amy Dinnerman. Opened at the American Airlines Theatre, August 18, 2002*

Cast

A Sergeant **Fred Inkley**
The Duke **J.C. Montgomery**
Aegean **Walter Charles**
A Merchant **Scott Robertson**
A Soldier **Davis Kirby**
Antipholus of Syracuse **Jonathan Dokuchitz**
Dromio of Syracuse **Lee Wilkof**
Antipholus of Ephesus **Tom Hewitt**
Dromio of Ephesus **Chip Zien**
A Tailor **Joseph Siravo**
An Apprentice **Kirk McDonald**
Luce **Toni DiBuono**
A Sorcerer **George Hall**
Adriana **Lauren Mitchell**
Luciana **Erin Dilly**
Madam **Jackeé Harry**
Angelo **Jeffrey Broadhurst**
Courtesans **Sara Gettelfinger, Deirdre Goodwin, Milena Govich, Teri Hansen, Elizabeth Mills**

Understudies: Jonathan Dokuchitz, Tom Hewitt, Walter Charles, J.C. Montgomery (Tom Galantich); Toni Dibuono (Sara Gettelfinger); Jackee Harry (Deirdre Goodwin); Erin Dilly (Milena Govich, Teri Hansen); Lauren

Jonathan Dokuchitz, Erin Dilly

Mitchell (Teri Hansen, Allyson Turner); Jeffrey Broadhurst, Joseph Siravo, Kirk McDonald, George Hall, Scott Robertson (Tripp Hanson); Tom Hewitt (Fred Inkley); Fred Inkley (Tripp Hanson); Lee Wilkof, Chip Zien (Scott Robertson); Sara Gettelfinger, Deirde Goodwin, Milena Govich, Teri Hansen, Elizabeth Mills (Allyson Turner)

Orchestra: David Loud, conductor; Ethyl Will, associate conductor, keyboard; Paul Woodiel, Ella Rutkovsky, Liuh-Wen Ting, violin; Eddie Salkin, Jonathan Levine, Andrew Sterman, Mark Thrasher, reeds; Jon Owens, Matt Peterson, trumphet; Charles Gordon, trombone; R.J. Kelley, French horn; Brian Cassier, bass; Bruce Doctor, drums, percussion

Musical Numbers: Hurrah! Hurroo! (I Had Twins), Dear Old Syracuse, What Can You Do with a Man, Falling in Love with Love, A Lady Must Live, The Shortest Day of the Year, This Can't Be Love, This Must Be Love, You Took Advantage of Me, He and She, You Have Cast Your Shadows on the Sea, Big Brother, Come with Me, Oh, Diogenes, Hurrah! Hurroo! (Reprise), Sing for Your Supper, This Can't Be Love

Time: Thursday. Place: Ephesus, a city in ancient Greece. A musical presented in two acts.

*Closed October 20, 2002

Erin Dilly, Lauren Mitchell, Toni DiBuono PHOTOS BY JOAN MARCUS

SAY GOODNIGHT, GRACIE

By Rupert Holmes; Producers, William Franzblau, Jay H. Harris, Louise Westergaard, Larry Spellman, Elsa Daspin Haft, Judith Resnick, Anne Gallagher, Libby Adler Mages, Mari Glick, Martha R. Gasparian, Bruce Lazarus, Lawrence S. Toppall, Jae French; Director, John Tillinger; Scenery, John Lee; Lighting, Howard Werner; Sound, Kevin Lacy; Executive Producer, Mr. Franzblau; Production Stage Manager, Tina M. Newhauser; Press, Cromarty and Company, Peter Cromarty, Alice Cromarty. Opened at the Helen Hayes Theatre, October 10, 2002*

Cast
George Burns **Frank Gorshin**
Voice of Gracie Allen **Didi Conn**

Understudy: Mr. Gorshin (Joel Rooks)

Presented without intermission.

*Still playing May 31, 2003

Frank Gorshin PHOTO BY CAROL ROSEGG

FLOWER DRUM SONG

Revival by David Henry Hwang; Music by Richard Rogers, Lyrics by Oscar Hammerstein II; Original book by Oscar Hammerstein II, Joseph Fields; Novel by C.Y. Lee; Producers, Benjamin Mordecai, Michael A. Jenkins, Waxman Williams Entertainment, Center Theatre Group, Mark Taper Forum, Gordon Davidson, Charles Dillingham, in association with Robert G. Bartner, Robert Dragotta, Temple Gill, Marcia Roberts, Kelpie Arts, Dramatic Forces, Stephanie McClelland, Judith Resnick; arrangement by the Rodgers and Hammerstein Organization; Director and Choregraphy, Robert Longbottom; Scenery, Robin Wagner; Costumes, Gregg Barnes; Lighting, Natasha Katz; Sound, Acme Sound Partners; Orchestrations, Don Sebesky; Music Adaptation and Supervision, Mr. Chase; Music Coordinator, Seymour Red Press; Associate Director, Tom Kosis; Associate Choreographer, Darlene Wilson; Associate Producers, Dallas Summer Musicals, Inc.; Brian Brolly, Alice Chebba Walsh, Ernest De Leon Escaler; Casting, Tara Rubin Casting and Amy Lieberman; Production Stage Manager, Perry Cline; Stage Manager, Rebecca C. Monroe; Press, Boneau, Bryan-Brown, Adrian Bryan-Brown, Jim Byk, Susanne Tighe, Martine Sainvil. Opened at the Virginia Theatre, October 17, 2002*

Low Sandra Allen

Cast
Mei-Li **Lea Salonga**
Wang **Randall Duk Kim**
Chin **Alvin Ing**
Ta **Jose Llana**
Harvard **Allen Liu**
Linda **Low Sandra Allen**
Madame **Liang Jodi Long**
Chao **Hoon Lee**

Ensemble: Rich Ceraulo, Eric Chan, Marcus Choi, Ma-Anne Dionisio, Emily Hsu, Telly Leung, J. Elaine Marcos, Daniel May, Marc Oka, Lainie Sakakura, Yuka Takara, Kim Varhola, Ericka Yang

Understudies: Leah Salonga (Ma-Anne Dionisio, Yuka Takara); Alvin Ing (Eric Chan); Jose Llana (Rich Ceraulo, Hoon Lee, Telly Leung); Allen Liu (Marc Oka); Low Sandra Allen (Emily Hsu); Liang Jodi Long (Kim Varhola); Hoon Lee (Marcus Choi)

Swings: Susan Ancheta, Robert Tatad

Orchestra: David Chase, conductor; David Evans, associate conductor, keyboard; Jane A. Axelrod, flute, bamboo flute, dizi; Lou Bruno, bass; Claire Chan, violin; Raymond Grappone, drums; Richard Heckman, woodwinds; Ronald Janelli, woodwinds; Christian Jaudes, trumpet; Howard Joines, percussion; Stu Satalof, trumpet; Russel L. Rizner, horn; Clay Ruede, cello, erhu; Jack Schatz, trombone; Andrew Schwartz, guitar, pipa; Chuck Wilson, woodwind; Julius Rene Wirth, viola violin; Mineko Yajima, violin, mandolin

Musical Numbers: A Hundred Million Miracles, I Am Going to Like It Here, I Enjoy Being a Girl, You Are Beautiful, Grant Avenue, Sunday, Fan Tan Fannie, Gliding Through My Memoree, Chop Suey, My Best Love, Don't Marry Me, Love, Look Away, Like A God, A Hundred Million Miracles

Time: 1960. Place: Chinatown in San Francisco. A musical presented in two acts.

*Closed March 16, 2003

Jose Llana, Lea Salonga PHOTOS BY JOAN MARCUS

AMOUR

Musical with French Libretto by Didier van Cauwelaert; English Adaptation by Jeremy Sams; Music by Michel Legrand; Adapted from "Le Passe-Muraille" by Marcel Ayme; Producers, Shubert Organization, Jean Doumanian Productions, Inc., USA Ostar Theatricals; Director, James Lapine; Choreography, Jane Comfort; Scenery, Scott Park; Costumes, Dona Granata; Lighting, Jules Fisher, Peggy Eisenhauer; Sound, Dan Moses Schreier; Orchestrations, Michel Legrand; Musical Direction and Vocal Arrangement, Todd Ellison; Associate Choreographer, Lisa Shriver; Casting, Bernard Telsey Casting; Production Stage Manager, Leila Knox; Stage Manager, David Sugarman; Press, Bill Evans and Associates, Jim Randolph. Opened at the Music Box, October 20, 2002*

Cast
Dusoleil **Malcolm Gets**
Isabelle **Melissa Errico**
Claire; Whore **Nora Mae Lyng**
Bertrand; News vendor; Advocate **Christopher Fitzgerald**
Charles; Prosecutor **Lewis Cleale**
Madeleine **Sarah Litzsinger**
Painter **Norm Lewis**
Policemen **John Cunningham, Bill Nolte**
Doctor; Tribunal President **John Cunningham**
Boss **Bill Nolte**

Understudies: Malcolm Gets, Christopher Fitzgerald, Norm Lewis (Christian Borle); Melissa Errico (Jessica Hendy, Sarah Litzsinger); Lewis Cleale, Bill Nolte, John Cunningham (Matthew Bennett); Nora Mae Lyng, Sarah Litzsinger (Jessica Hendy)

Orchestra: Todd Ellison, conductor, pianist; Anthony Geralis, associate conductor, pianist; Bill Hayes, percussion; Ben Kono, woodwinds; Mark Vanderpoel, bass

Time: Shortly after World War II. Place: Paris. A musical presented without intermission.

*Closed November 3, 2002

Melissa Errico, Malcolm Gets

Sarah Litzsinger, Melissa Errico, Nora Mae Lyng

Malcolm Gets PHOTOS BY JOAN MARCUS

Jackie Mason

PRUNE DANISH

By Jackie Mason; Producers, Jyll Rosenfeld, Jill Stoll; Director, Jackie Mason; Lighting, Traci Klainer; Sound, Christopher T. Cronin; Stage Manager, Don Myers. Opened at the Royale Theatre, October 22, 2002*

Performed by Jackie Mason.

*Closed December 1, 2002

MOVIN' OUT

Dance Musical by Billy Joel; Music and Lyrics by Billy Joel; Conception by Twyla Tharp; Producers, James L. Nederlander, Hal Luftig, Scott E. Nederlander, Terry Allen Kramer, Clear Channel Entertainment, Emanuel Azenberg; Director and Choreographer, Twyla Tharp; Scenery, Santo Loquasto; Costumes, Suzy Benzinger; Lighting, Donald Holder; Sound, Brian Ruggles, Peter Fitzgerald; Additional Music Arrangements and Orchestrations, Stuart Malina; Music Coordinator, John Miller; Assistant Director and Choreographer, Mr. Wise; Casting, Jay Binder Casting, Sarah Prosser; Production Stage Manager, Tom Barlett; Stage Manager, Kim Vernace; Press, Barlow-Hartman, Michael Hartman, John Barlow, Bill Coyle. Opened at the Richard Rodgers Theatre, October 24, 2002*

Cast
Eddie **John Selya**
Brenda **Elizabeth Parkinson**
Tony **Keith Roberts**
Judy **Ashley Tuttle**
James **Benjamin G. Bowman**
Sergeant O'Leary; Drill Sergeant **Scott Wise**
Piano; Lead Vocals **Michael Cavanaugh**

Ensemble: Mark Arvin, Karine Bageot, Alexander Brady, Holly Cruikshank, Ron Dejesus, Melissa Downey, Pascale Faye, Scott Fowler, David Gomez, Rod McCune, Jill Nicklaus, Rika Okamoto

Wednesday and Saturday Matinees

Eddie **William Marrie**
Brenda **Holly Cruikshank**
Tony **David Gomez**
Judy **Dana Stackpole**
James **Benjamin G. Bowman**
Sergeant O'Leary; Drill Sergeant **Scott Wise**
Piano; Lead Vocals **Wade Preston**

Ensemble: Mark Arvin, Karine Bageot, Alexander Brady, Holly Cruikshank, Ron Dejesus, Melissa Downey, Pascale Faye, Scott Fowler, David Gomez, Rod McCune, Jill Nicklaus, Rika Okamoto

Understudies: Keith Roberts (Ron Dejesus, David Gomez); Elizabeth Parkinson (Karine Bageot, Holly Cruikshank); John Selya (Andrew Allagree); William Marrie (Lawrence Rabson); Ashley Tuttle (Meg Paul, Dana Stackpole); Scott Wise (John J. Todd); Benjamin G. Bowman (Scott Fowler, Alexander Brady)

Swings: Andrew Allagree, Aliane Baquerot; Laurie Kanyok, William Marrie, Meg Paul, Lawrence Rabson, Dana Stackpole, John J. Todd

Orchestra: Michael Cavanaugh, piano, lead vocals; Tommy Byrnes, leader, guitar, Wade Preston, keyboard; Dennis DelGaudio, guitar; Greg Smith, bass; Chuck Burgi, drums; John Scarpulla, lead sax, percussion; Scott Kreitzer, sax; Barry Danielian, trumpet; Kevin Osborne, trombone, whistler, vocals

Musical Numbers: It's Still Rock and Roll to Me, Scenes from an Italian Restaurant, Movin' Out (Anthony's Song), Reverie (Villa D'Este), Just the Way You Are, For the Longest Time, Uptown Girl, This Night, Summer, Highland Falls, Waltz #1 (Nunley's Carousel), We Didn't Start the Fire, She's Got A Way, The Stranger, Elegy (The Great Peconic), Invention in C Minor, Angry Young Man, Big Shot, Big Man on Mulberry Street, Captain Jack, Innocent Man, Pressure, Goodnight Saigon, Air (Dublinesque), Shameless, James, River of Dreams, Keeping the Faith, Only the Good Die Young, I've Loved These Days, Scenes from an Italian Restaurant (Reprise)

Time: 1960s. Place: Long Island, New York. A musical presented in two parts.

*Still playing May 31, 2003

Elizabeth Parkinson, Keith Roberts PHOTO BY JOAN MARCUS

Sara Niemietz, Linda Lavin   PHOTO BY JOAN MARCUS

HOLLYWOOD ARMS

By Carrie Hamilton and Carol Burnett; Producers, Harold Prince, Arielle Tepper; Director, Harold Prince; Scenery, Walt Spangler; Costumes, Judith Dolan; Lighting, Howell Binkley; Sound, Rob Milburn and Michael Bodeen; Music, Robert Lindsey Nassif; Associate Producer, Ostar Enterprises; Casting, Mark Simon; Production Stage Manager, Lisa Dawn Cave; Stage Managers, Brian Meister, Matthew Leiner; Press, Barlow-Hartman, John Barlow, Michael Hartman, Wayne Wolfe, Rob Finn. Opened at the Cort Theatre, October 31, 2002*

Cast
Older Helen **Donna Lynne Champlin**
Young Helen **Sara Niemietz**
Nanny **Linda Lavin**
Louise **Michele Pawk**
Dixie **Leslie Hendrix**
Malcolm **Nicolas King**
Bill **Patrick Clear**
Jody **Frank Wood**
Cop #1 **Christian Kohn**
Cop #2 **Steve Bakunas**
Alice **Emily Graham-Handley**

Understudies: Linda Lavin, Leslie Hendrix (Lucy Martin); Michele Pawk (Leslie Hendrix) Sara Niemietz (Sara Kapner); Nicolas King (Evan Daves); Patrick Clear (Steve Bakunas); Frank Wood (Christian Kohn); Christian Kohn, Steve Bakunas (Brian Meister); Donna Lynne Champlin (Lindsey Alley); Emily Graham-Handley (Sara Kapner, Lindsey Alley)

Time: 1941–1951. Place: Hollywood. Play presented in two parts.

*Closed January 5, 2003

Staceyann Chin PHOTO BY CAROL ROSEGG

RUSSELL SIMMONS' DEF POETRY JAM ON BROADWAY

Poetry performance conceived by Stan Lathan and Rusell Simmons; Producers, Rusell Simmons, Stan Lathan, in association with Kimora Lee Simmons, Island Def Jam Music Group, Brett Ratner, David Rosenberg; Director, Stan Lathan; Scenery, Bruce Ryan; Costumes, Paul Tazewell; Lighting, Yael Lubetzky; Sound, Elton P. Halley; Production Stage Manager, Alice Elliot Smith; Stage Manager, Steven Lukens; Press, Pete Sanders Group, Pete Sanders, Glenna Freedman, Terence Womble. Opened at the Longacre Theatre, November 14, 2002*

Performances by Beau Sia, Black Ice, Staceyann Chin, Steve Colman, Mayda Del Valle, Georgia Me, Suheir Hammad, Lemon, Poetri, Tendaji Lathan

Presented in two parts.

*Closed May 4, 2003

Mandy Patinkin

CELEBRATING SONDHEIM

Concert performance of songs by Stephen Sondheim; Producer, Dodger Stage Holding; Lighting, Eric Cornwell; Sound, Otts Munderloh; Arrangements, Paul Ford. Opened at the Henry Miller Theatre, December 2, 2002*

Performed by Mandy Patinkin, with Paul Ford (piano)

Presented without intermission.

*Closed January 6, 2003

WESTPORT COUNTRY PLAYHOUSE PRODUCTION OF OUR TOWN

Revival by Thornton Wilder; Artistic Director, Joanne Woodward; Associate Artistic Director, Anne Keefe; Executive Director, Alison Harris; Director, James Naughton; Scenery and Costumes, Tony Walton; Lighting, Richard Pillow; Sound, Raymond D. Schilke; Casting, Deborah Brown; Production Stage Manager, Katherine Lee Boyer; Stage Manager, Jenny Dewar; Press, Bill Evans and Associates, Jim Randolph. Opened at the Booth Theatre, December 4, 2002*

Cast

Stage Manager **Paul Newman**
Dr. Gibbs **Frank Converse**
Joe Crowell **T.J. Sullivan**
Howie Newsome **Jake Robards**
Mrs. Gibbs **Jayne Atkinson**
Mrs. Webb **Jane Curtin**
George Gibbs **Ben Fox**
Rebecca Gibbs **Kristen Hahn**
Wally Webb **Conor Donovan**
Emily Webb **Maggie Lacey**
Professor Willard **John Braden**
Mr. Webb **Jeffrey DeMunn**
Auditorium Women **Wendy Barrie-Wilson, Cynthia Wallace**
Auditorium Man **Reathel Bean**
Simon Stimson **Stephen Spinella**
Mrs. Soames **Mia Dillon**
Constable Warren **Stephen Mendillo**
Si Crowell **Travis Walters**
Baseball players **Kieran Campion, Patch Darragh**
Sam Craig **Carter Jackson**
Joe Stoddard **Tom Brennan**

Understudies: Jayne Atkinson, Mia Dillon, Jane Curtin (Wendy Barrie-Wilson, Lisa Reynolds); Frank Converse, Jeffrey DeMunn, Stephen Spinella (Reathel Bean, Malachy Cleary); Ben Fox, Carter Jackson (Kieran Campion, Patch Darragh); Maggie Lacey, Kristen Hahn (Erika Thomas); Jake Robards (Kieran Campion, Patch Darragh, Malachy Cleary); T.J. Sullivan, Travis Walters, Conor Donovan (Matthew Gusman); Wendy Barrie-Wilson, Cynthia Wallace (Lisa Richards, Erika Thomas); Reathel Bean, John Braden, Stephen Mendillo, Tom Brennan (Martin Shakar)

Time: The early years of the 20th century. Place: Grover's Corners, New Hampshire. Play presented in two parts.

*Closed January 26, 2003

The Company

Maggie Lacey, Paul Newman, Ben Fox PHOTOS BY JOAN MARCUS

MAN OF LA MANCHA

Revival of the musical with book by Dale Wasserman; Music by Mitch Leigh; Lyrics by Joe Darion; Producers, David Stone, Jon B. Platt, Susan Quint Gallin, Sandy Gallin, Seth M. Siegel, USA Ostar Theatricals, in association with Mary Lu Roffe; Director, Jonathan Kent; Choreography, Luis Perez; Scenery and Costumes, Paul Brown; Lighting, Paul Gallo; Sound, Tony Meola; Original Orchestrations, Carlyle W. Hall Sr.; Original Dance Music, Neil Warner; New Dance Music, David Krane; New Dance Orchestrations, Brian Besterman; Music Director, Mr. Billig; Music Coordinator, Michael Keller; Associate Director, Peter Lawrence; Executive Producers, Nina Essman, Nancy Nagel Gibbs; Casting, Bernard Telsey Casting; Production Stage Manager, Mahlon Kruse; Press, the Publicity Office, Bob Fennell, Marc Thibodeau, Candi Adams, Michael S. Borowski. Opened at the Martin Beck Theatre, December 5, 2002*

Cast

Dancer **Wilson Mendieta**
Opening Singer **Olga Merediz**
Cervantes; Don Quixote **Brian Stokes Mitchell**
Captain **Frederick B. Owens**
Sancho **Ernie Sabella**
Governor; Innkeeper **Don Mayo**
Duke; Carrasco **Stephen Bogardus**
Aldonza **Mary Elizabeth Mastrantonio**
Quito **Andy Blankenbuehler**
Tenorio **Timothy J. Alex**
Juan **Thom Sesma**
Paco **Dennis Stowe**
Anselmo **Bradley Dean**
Pedro **Gregory Mitchell**
Jose **Wilson Mendieta**
Maria **Michelle Rios**
Fermina **Lorin Latarro**
Antonia **Natascia Diaz**
Padre **Mark Jacoby**
Housekeeper **Olga Merediz**
Barber **Jamie Torcellini**
Guards **Michael X. Martin, Jimmy Smagula**
Gypsy Dancers **Lorin Latarro, Andy Blankenbuehler**
Prisoner **Allyson Tucker**
Onstage Guitarist **Robin Polseno**

Understudies: Brian Stokes Mitchell (Bradley Dean, Michael X. Martin); Ernie Sabella (Jimmy Smagula, Jamie Torcellini); Mary Elizabeth Mastrantonio (Natascia Diaz, Allyson Tucker); Stephen Bogardus (Michael X. Martin, Thom Sesma); Don Mayo (Michael X. Martin, Frederick B. Owens); Mark Jacoby (Bradley Dean, Jimmy Smagula); Natascia Diaz (Lorin Latarro, Allyson Tucker); Olga Merediz (Michelle Rios, Allyson Tucker); Jamie Torcellini (Carlos Lopez, Jimmy Smagula); Michelle Rios (Jamie Karen); Frederick B. Owens (Timothy J. Alex, Dennis Stowe)

Swings: Jamie Karen, Carlos Lopez, Richard Montoya.

Orchestra: Robert Billig, conductor; Cherie Rosen, associate conductor, guitar; Braden Toan, assistant conductor, bassoon; Wayne duMaine, lead trumpet; John Dent, trumpet; Dale Kirkland, trombone; Douglas Purviance, bass trombone; Eva Conti, Patrick Milando, French horns; Kathleen Nester, flute; Blair Tindall, oboe; Lino Gomez, clarinet; Steve Bartosik, drums, Randall Landau, bass; Robin Polseno, guitar; David Yee, percussion; Michael Hinton, tympani.

Musical Numbers: Man of La Mancha (I, Don Quixote), It's All the Same, Dulcinea, I'm Only Thinking of Him, The Missive, I Really Like Him, What Does He Want of Me?, Little Bird, Little Bird, Barber's Song, Golden Helmet of Mambrino, To Each His Dulcinea (To Every Man His Dream), The Impossible Dream (The Quest), The Combat, The Dubbing/Knight of the Woeful Countenance, The Abduction, The Impossible Dream (The Quest) (Reprise), Man of La Mancha (I, Don Quixote) (Reprise), Gypsy Dance, Aldonza, A Little Gossip, Dulcinea (Reprise), The Impossible Dream (The Quest) (Reprise), Man of La Mancha (I, Don Quixote) (Reprise), The Psalm, Finale

Time: 1594. Place: A prison in Seville, Spain, and in the imagination of Don Miguel de Cervantes. Musical presented without intermission.

*Still Playing May 31, 2003

Mary Elizabeth Mastrantonio, Brian Stokes Mitchell PHOTO BY JOAN MARCUS

LA BOHEME

Revival of the opera with libretto by Giuseppe Giacosa and Luigi Mica; Music by Giacomo Puccini; Based on stories from *Scenes de fa Vie de Boheme* by Henri Murger; Producers, Jeffrey Seller, Kevin McCollum, Emanuel Azenberg, Bazmark Live, Bob and Harvey Weinstein, Korea Pictures/Doyun Seol, Jeffrey Sine/Ira Pittelman/Scott E. Nederlander, Fox Searchlight Pictures; Directors Baz Luhrmann; Scenery, Catherine Martin; Costumes, Ms. Martin, Angus Strathie; Lighting, Nigel Levings; Sound, Acme Sound Partners; Orchestrations, Nicholas Kitsopoulos; Music Director and Principal Conductor, Constantine Kitsopoulos; Music Coordinator, John Miller; Associate Director, David Crooks; Executive Producers, Noel Staunton, Adam Silberman; Associate Producers, Daniel Karslake/Coats Guiles, Morton Swinsky/Michael Fuchs; Casting, Bernard Telsey Casting; Production Stage Manager, Frank Hartenstein; Stage Manager, Kelly Martindale; Press, Boneau/Bryan-Brown, Chris Boneau, Amy Jacobs, Juliana Hannett. Opened at the Broadway Theatre, December 8, 2002*

Jessica Comeau

The Company

Ben Davis, Chloe Wright

Cast

Marcello **Eugene Brancoveanu, Ben Davis**
Rodolfo **Alfred Boe, Jesus Garcia, David Miller**
Colline **Daniel Webb**
Schaunard **Daniel Okulitch**
Benoit **Adam Grupper**
Mimi **Lisa Hopkins, Wei Huang, Ekaterina Solovyeva**
Papignol **Dan Entriken**
Alcindoro **William Youmans**
Musetta **Jessica Comeau, Chloe Wright**
Customs Officer **Sean Cooper**
Sergeant **Graham Fandrei**

Ensemble: Enrique Abdala, Christine Arand, Janinah Burnett, Gilles Chiasson, Charlotte Cohn, Michael Cone, Vanessa Conlin, Sean Cooper, Patricia Corbett, Evangelia Costantakos, Lawrence Craig, Dan Entriken, Graham Fandrei, Bobby Faust, Katie Geissinger, Jennifer Goode, Paul Goodwin-Groen, Adam Grupper, Joy Hermalyn, Robb Hillman, Adam Hunter, Timothy Jerome, Katherine Keyes, Laurice Lanier, Peter Lockyer, Morgan Moody, Marcus Nance, Daniel Neer, Debra Patchell, Patricia Phillips, Jamet Pittman, Martin Sola, Radu Spinghel, Mark Womack.

Understudies: Eugene Brancoveanu, Ben Davis, Daniel Okulitch (Graham Fandrei, Joseph Kaiser, Mark Womack); Alfred Boe, Jesus

Wei Huang, Alfred Boe

Chloe Wright, the Company

David Miller, Ekaterina Solovyeva PHOTOS BY SUE ADLER

Garcia, David Miller (Peter Lockyer), Daniel Webb, Sean Cooper, (Morgan Moody); Adam Grupper (Dan Entriken, Timothy Jerome); Lisa Hopkins, Wei Huang, Ekaterina Solovyeva (Janinah Burnett); Jessica Comeau, Chloe Wright (Christine Arand, Jennifer Goode); William Youmans (Adam Grupper, Timothy Jerome)

Ensemble Swing: Joseph Kaiser

Children's Chorus: Ryan Andres, Ellen Hornberger, Joseph Jonas, Antonia Kitsopoulos, Alyson Lange, David Mathews, Suzanna Mathews, Luca Mannarino, Nathan Morgan, Jennifer Olsen, Ben Pakman, Samantha Massell Rakosi, Melissa Remo, Justin Robertazzi, Matthew Salvatore.

Lisa Hopkins, Jesus Garcia

Orchestra: Dale Stuckenbruck, concert master; Elizabeth Lim-Dutton, Vii Speth, Cecilia Hobbs Gardner, Robert Lubrycki, Sylvia D'Avanzo, Ming Yeh, Katherine Livolsi-Stern, John Connelly, violin; Sarah Adams, Maxine Roach, viola; Roger Shell, Chung Sun Kim, cello; Joe Bongiorno, bass; Bob Bush, flute, piccolo; Lynne Cohen, oboe, English horn; Jon Manasse, clarinet; Larry Guy, clarinet, bass clarinet; Jeff Marchand, bassoon; Carl Albach, Chuck Olsen, Kenny DeCarlo, trumpet; Matthew Ingman, trombone; Chris Komer, Zohar Schondorf, French horn; Dean Witten, timpani, percussion; Warren "Chip" Prince, Karl Mansfield, keyboard.

Time: 1957. Place: Paris. Presented in two parts.

*Still playing May 31, 2003

DANCE OF THE VAMPIRES

Musical with book by David Ives, Jim Steinman and Michael Kunze; Music and Lyrics by Jim Steinman; Original German book and lyrics by Mr. Kunze; Based on a film by Roman Polanski; Producers, Bob Boyett, USA Ostar Theatricals, Andrew Braunsberg, Lawrence Horowitz, Michael Gardner, Roy Furman, Lexington Road Productions, David Sonenberg; Directed by John Rando; Choreography, John Carrafa; Scenery, David Gallo; Costumes, Ann Hould-Ward; Lighting, Ken Billington; Sound, Richard Ryan; Fight Direction, Rick Sordelet; Orchestrations, Steve Margoshes; Music Supervision, Vocal and Dance Arrangements, Michael Reed; Music Direction, Patrick Vaccariello; Music Coordinator, Michael Keller; Associate Choreographer, Tara Young; Associate Producers, Michael Fuchs/Morton Swinsky, LFG Holdings, Clear Channel Entertainment, Kathryn Conway, Arielle Tepper, Norman Brownstein, William Carrick; Casting, Bernard Telsey Casting; Production Stage Manager, Bonnie Panson; Stage Manager, Michael J. Passaro; Press, Barlow-Hartman, John Barlow, Michael Hartman, Wayne Wolfe, Rob Finn. Opened at the Minskoff Theatre, December 9, 2002*

Mandy Gonzalez, Michael Crawford PHOTO BY PAUL KOLNIK

Cast

Sarah **Mandy Gonzalez**
Zsa-Zsa **Erin Leigh Peck**
Nadja **E. Alyssa Claar**
Count von Krolock **Michael Crawford**
Chagal **Ron Orbach**
Rebecca **Liz McCartney**
Magda **Leah Hocking**
Boris **Mark Price**
Professor Abronsius **Rene Auberjonois**
Alfred **Max Von Essen**
Mme. Von Krolock **Dame Edith Shorthouse**
Dream Sarah **Jennifer Savelli**
Herbert **Asa Somers**
Dream Alfred **Jonathan Sharp**
Dream Vampire **Edgar Godineaux**

Ensemble: David Benoit, E. Alyssa Claar, Jocelyn Dowling, Lindsay Dunn, Edgar Godineaux, Ashley Amber Haase, Derric Harris, Robin Irwin, Terace Jones, Larry Keigwin, Brendan King, Heather McFadden, Raymond McLeod, Erin Leigh Peck, Andy Pellick, Joye Ross, Solange Sandy, Jennifer Savelli, Jonathan Sharp, Asa Somers, Doug Storm, Jenny-Lynn Suckling, Jason Wooten

Understudies: Mandy Gonzalez (E. Alyssa Claar, Sara Schmidt); Erin Leigh Peck, E. Alyssa Claar (Heather McFadden, Sara Schmidt); Michael Crawford, Rene Auberjonois (Timothy Warmen); Ron Orbach (David Benoit, Raymond McLeod); Liz McCartney (Robin Irwin, Jenny-Lynn Suckling); Leah Hocking (Jenny-Lynn Suckling); Mark Price, Max Von Essen, Asa Somers (Doug Storm, Jason Wooten)

Standbys: Michael Crawford, Rene Auberjonois (Rob Evan)

Swings: Kerrin Hubbard, Nathan Peck, Sara Schmidt, Timothy Warmen

Orchestra: Patrick Vaccariello, conductor; Jim Laev, associate conductor; Ann Labin, concertmaster; Maura Giannini, Victor Heifets, Dana Ianculovici, Fritz Krakowski, Wende Namkung, violin; Peter Prosser, Danny Miller, Eileen Folson, cello; Tom Hoyt, lead trumpet; Larry Lunetta, trumpet; Morris Kainuma, bass trombone; Roger Wendt, Kelly Dent, Theo Primis, French horn; Helen Campo, flute, piccolo; Tuck Lee, oboe, English horn; Dennis Anderson, reeds; Ray Marchica, drums; Dave Kuhn, bass; Adam Ben-David, keyboard 1; T.O. Sterrett, Jim Laev, keyboard; J.J. McGeehan, guitar; David Rozenblatt, percussion.

Musical Numbers: Angels Arise, God Has Left the Building, Original Sin, Garlic Logic, There's Never Been a Night Like This, Don't Leave Daddy, A Good Nightmare Comes So Rarely, Death Is Such an Odd Thing, Braver Than We Are (additional lyrics by Don Black), Red Boots Ballet, Say a Prayer, Come With Me, Vampires in Love (Total Eclipse of the Heart), Books, Books, Carpe Noctem, For Sarah, Death Is Such an Odd Thing (Reprise), When Love Is Inside You, Eternity, Confession of a Vampire, The Ball: The Minuet, Never Be Enough, Come with Me, Braver Than We Are (Reprise) (additional lyrics by Don Black), The Dance of the Vampires

Time: 1880s. Place: Lower Belabartokovich, Carpathia. Musical presented in two parts.

*Closed January 26, 2003

Fiona Shaw PHOTO BY JOAN MARCUS

MEDEA

Revival of play by Euripides; Translated by Kenneth McLeish and Frederic Raphael; Producers, Roger Berlind, James M. Nederlander, Daryl Roth, Scott Rudin; Arrangement with Max Weitzenhoffer, Niea Burns, Old Vie Productions, Jedediah Wheeler; in association with Jean Stein, True Love Productions, Inc., Wendy vanden Heuvel; Director, Deborah Warner; Scenery, Tom Pye; Costumes, Jacqueline Durran; Lighting, Michael Gunning; Sound, David Meschter; Production Stage Manager, Nevin Hedley; Stage Managers, Patricia McGregor, Laurie Goldfeder; Press, Barlow-Hartman, Michael Hartman, John Barlow, Wayne Wolfe. Opened at the Brooks Atkinson Theatre, December 10, 2002*

Cast
Nurse **Siobhan McCarthy**
Medea **Fiona Shaw**
Tutor **Robin Laing**
Chorus **Kirsten Campbell, Joyce Henderson, Rachel Isaac, Pauline Lynch, Susan Salmon**
Kreon **Struan Rodger**
Jason **Jonathan Cake**
Aegeus **Joseph Mydell**
Messenger **Derek Hutchinson**
Children **Dylan Denton, Alexander Scheitinger, Michael Tommer**

Presented without intermission.

*Closed February 23, 2003

Swoosie Kurtz

Cherry Jones PHOTOS BY JOAN MARCUS

IMAGINARY FRIENDS

By Nora Ephron; Music by Marvin Hamlisch; Lyrics by Craig Carnelia; Producers, USA Ostar Theatricals; Director, Jack O'Brien; Choreography, Jerry Mitchell; Scenery, Michael Levine; Costumes, Robert Morgan; Lighting, Kenneth Posner; Sound, Jon Weston; Video Projection, Jan Hartley; Orchestrations, Torrie Zito; Music Direction and Dance Arrangements, Ron Melrose; Music Coordinator, Michael Keller; Casting, Tara Rubin Casting; Production Stage Manager, Evan Ensign; Stage Managers, Jim Woolley, Joel Rosen; Press, the Publicity Office, Bob Fennell, Marc Thibodeau, Michael S. Borowski, Candi Adams. Opened at Ethel Barrymore Theatre, December 12, 2002*

Swoosie Kurtz, Cherry Jones

Cast

Lillian Hellman **Swoosie Kurtz**
Mary McCarthy **Cherry Jones**
The Man **Harry Groener**
Abby Kaiser; others **Anne Allgood**
Leo; others **Bernard Dotson**
Mrs. Stillman; others **Rosena M. Hill**
Beguine Dancer; others **Gina Lamparella**
Fact; others **Dirk Lumbard**
Fiction; others **Peter Marx**
Vic; others **Perry Ojeda**
Fizzy; others **Karyn Quackenbush**
A Woman **Anne Pitoniak**

Standbys: Swoosie Kurtz, Cherry Jones (Susan Pellegrino); Harry Groener (Dirk Lumbard); Anne Pitoniak (Anne Allgood)

Swings: Jim Osorno, Melanie Vaughan

Orchestra: Ron Melrose, conductor, piano; Jonathan Smith, assistant conductor; Hollis Burridge, trumpet; Randy Andos, trombone, tuba; Charles Pillow, saxophone, woodwinds; Michael Keller, drums, percussion; Mary Ann McSweeney, bass; Brian Koonin, guitar, banjo, ukulele.

Presented in two parts.

*Closed February 16, 2003

DINNER AT EIGHT

Revival of play by George S. Kaufman and Edna Ferber; Artistic Director, Andre Bishop; Executive Producer, Bernard Gersten; Director, Gerald Gutierrez; Scenery, John Lee Beatty; Costumes, Catherine Zuber; Lighting, David Weiner; Sound, Aural Fixation; Music, Robert Waldman; Casting, Daniel Swee; Stage Manager, Karen Armstrong; Press, Philip Rinaldi, Barbara Carroll. Opened at the Vivian Beaumont, December 19, 2002*

Cast

Millicent Jordan **Christine Ebersole**
Gustave **Simon Jutras**
Dora **Enid Graham**
Oliver Jordan **James Rebhorn**
Paula Jordan **Samantha Soule**
Ricci **Mark Lotito**
Hattie Loomis **Ann McDonough**
Miss Copeland **Deborah Mayo**
Carlotta Vance **Marian Seldes**
Dan Packard **Kevin Conway**
Kitty Packard **Emily Skinner**
Tina **Charlotte Maier**
Dr. J.W. Talbot **John Doss**
Larry Renault **Byron Jennin**
Eddie, the Bellboy **Rhys Coiro**
Max Kane **Joe Grifasi**
Mr. Hatfield **Karl Kenzler**
The Waiter **Philip LeStrange**
Miss Alden **Anne Lange**
Lucy Talbot **Joanne Camp**
Mrs. Wendel **Sloane Shelton**
Joe Stengel **Peter Maloney**
Mr. Fitch **David Wohl**
Ed Loomis **Brian Reddy**
Musicians **Julian Gamble, Joseph Kamal, Mark LaMura, Philip LeStrange**

Marian Seldes, Christine Ebersole

Understudies: Christine Ebersole, Deborah Mayo, Anne Lange, Sloane Shelton (Sherry Skinker); James Rebhorn, Peter Maloney (Philip LeStrange); Enid Graham, Samantha Soule, Charlotte Maier (Christy Pusz); Marian Seldes (Sloane Shelton); Kevin Conway, Philip LeStrange, Brian Reddy (Julian Gamble); John Dossett, Byron Jennings, Karl Kenzler (Mark LaMura); Mark Lotito, Rhys Coiro, Joe Grifasi (Joseph Kamal); Emily Skinner, Charlotte Maier, Anne Lange (Natalie Griffith); Sloane Shelton (Deborah Mayo); Christine Ebersole (Anne Lange); Joanne Camp, Ann McDonough (Charlotte Maier); Julian Gamble, Joseph Kamal, Mark LaMura, Philip LeStrange (Rhys Coiro)

Time: November 1932. Place: Various locations in New York City. Presented in two parts.

*Closed January 26, 2003

The Company PHOTOS BY JOAN MARCUS

TARTUFFE

By Molière; Translation, Richard Wilbur; Artistic Director, Todd Haimes; Managing Director, Ellen Richard, Julia Levy; Executive Director of External Affairs; Director, Joe Dowling; Scenery, John Lee Beatty; Costumes, Jane Greenwood; Lighting, Brian MacDevitt; Sound and Music, Mark Bennett; Casting, Jim Carnahan, Production Stage Manager, Jane Pole; Stage Manager, Kevin Bertolacci; Press, Boneau/Bryan-Brown, Adrian Bryan-Brown, Matt Polk, Amy Dinnerman. Opened at the American Airlines Theatre, January 9, 2003*

Cast

Madame Pernelle **Rosaleen Linehan**
Cleante **John Bedford Lloyd**
Elmire **Kathryn Meisle**
Laurent **Erik Steele**
Dorine **J. Smith-Cameron**
Flipote **Virginia Louise Smith**
Damis **T.R. Knight**
Orgon **Brian Bedford**
Mariane **Bryce Dallas Howard**
Valere **Jeffrey Carlson**
Tartuffe **Henry Goodman**
Mons. Loyal **Philip Goodwin**
Officer **Erik Steele**

Ensemble: Alec Beard, John Nalbach, John Hayden, Melissa Miller, Brandy Mitchell, Robert Thompson

Understudies: Henry Goodman, Brian Bedford (Philip Goodwin); J. Smith-Cameron, Kathryn Meisle (Virginia Louise Smith); T.R. Knight, Jeffrey Carlson (Erik Steele); Bryce Dallas Howard, Virginia Louise Smith (Melissa Miller); Erik Steele (John Halbach)

Standbys: Roseleen Linehan (Patricia Kilgarriff); John Lloyd, Philip Goodwin, Brian Bedford (Anthony Newfield)

Time: 1669. Place: Orgon's house in Paris. Presented in two parts.

*Closed February 23, 2003

Rosaleen Linehan, Brian Bedford, Kathryn Meisle

Brian Bedford, Henry Goodman

Jeffrey Carlson, J. Smith-Cameron, Bryce Dallas Howard PHOTOS BY JOAN MARCUS

Charles S. Dutton, Carl Gordon

Charles S. Dutton, Whoopi Goldberg PHOTOS BY JOAN MARCUS

MA RAINEY'S BLACK BOTTOM

Revival of play by August Wilson; Producers, Sageworks, Benjamin Mordecai, Robert G. Bartner, Harriet N. Leve, Jennifer Manocherian, Kim Poster, Theatre Royal Haymarket Productions and Whoopi Goldberg, in association with Peg McFeeley Golden/Willa Shalit, Morton Swinsky/James D. Stern, Brian Brolly/Susan Dietz; By Special Arrangement with Robert Cole and Frederick Zollo; Director, Marion McClinton; Scenery, David Gallo; Costumes, Toni-Leslie James; Lighting, Donald Holder; Sound, Rob Milburn, Michael Bodeen; Fight Direction, David S. Leong; Music Director, Dwight Andrews; Associate Producers, Debbie Bisno/Alice Chebba Walsh; Casting, Janet Foster; Production Stage Manager, Diane DiVita; Stage Manager, Cynthia Kocher; Press, Barlow-Hartman, Michael Hartman, John Barlow, Jeremy Shaffer. Opened at the Royale Theatre, February 6, 2003*

Cast
Sturdyvant **Louis Zorich**
Cutler **Carl Gordon**
Irvin **Jack Davidson**
Toledo **Thomas Jefferson Byrd**
Slow Drag **Stephen McKinley Henderson**
Levee **Charles S. Dutton**
Ma Rainey **Whoopi Goldberg**
Policeman **Tony Cucci**
Dussie Mae **Heather Alicia Simms**
Sylvester **Anthony Mackie**

Understudies: Charles S. Dutton (Leland Gantt, Anthony Mackie); Whoopi Goldberg (Ebony Jo-Ann); Carl Gordon, Thomas Jefferson Byrd (Helmar Augustus Cooper); Stephen McKinley Henderson (Helmar Augustus Cooper, Leland Gantt); Heather Alicia Simms (Rochelle Hogue); Anthony Mackie (Leland Gantt); Louis Zorich, Jack Davidson, Tony Cucci (Joe Zaloom)

Time: Early 1927. Place: A band room and a recording studio in Chicago. Presented in two parts.

*Closed April 6, 2003

The Company

Daniel Sunjata

Denis O'Hare

Daniel Sunjata, Neal Huff, Frederick Weller

TAKE ME OUT

Transfer from Off-Broadway of the play by Richard Greenberg; Producers, Carole Shorenstein Hays and Frederick DeMann; Director, Joe Mantello; Scenery, Scott Pask; Costumes, Jess Goldstein; Lighting, Kevin Adams; Sound, Janet Kalas; Associate Director, Trip Cullman; Executive Producers, Greg Holland, Pilar DeMann; Casting, Jordan Thaler/Heidi Griffiths; Production Stage Manager, William Joseph Barnes; Stage Manager, CA. Clark; Press, Boneau/Bryan-Brown, Chris Boneau, Amy Jacobs, Juliana Hannett. Opened at the Walter Kerr Theatre, February 27, 2003*

Cast

Kippy Sunderstrom **Neal Huff**
Darren Lemming **Daniel Sunjata**
Shane Mungitt **Frederick Weller**
Skipper; William R. Danziger **Joe Lisi**
Martinez; Policeman **Robert M. Jimenez**
Rodriguez; Policeman **Gene Gabriel**
Jason Chenier **Kohl Sudduth**
Toddy Koovitz **David Eigenberg**
Davey Battle **Kevin Carroll**
Mason Marzac **Denis O'Hare**
Takeshi Kawabata **James Yaegashi**

Understudies: Neal Huff (Paul Sparks); Daniel Sunjata (Michael Ouvert); Frederick Weller (Jonno Roberts, Paul Sparks); Joe Lisi (John Schiappa); Robert M. Jimenez (Michael Ouvert, Jonno Roberts); Gene Gabriel (Michael Ouvert, Jonno Roberts); Kohl Sudduth (Paul Sparks, Jonno Roberts); David Eigenberg (John Schiappa); Kevin Carroll (Michael Ouvert); Denis O'Hare (Nat DeWolf); James Yaegashi (Musashi Alexander)

Presented in two parts.

*Still playing May 31, 2003

Denis O'Hare, Daniel Sunjata

The Company

Daniel Sunjata PHOTOS BY JOAN MARCUS

VINCENT IN BRIXTON

By Nicholas Wright; Artistic Director, Andre Bishop; Executive Producer, Bernard Gersten; By arrangement with the Royal National Theatre, Ambassador Theatre Group Ltd., Maidstone Productions, Robert Fox Ltd., Elliott F. Kulick, Incidental Colman Tod, the Shubert Organization; Director, Richard Eyre; Scenery and Costumes, Tim Hatley; Lighting, Peter Mumford; Sound, Neil Alexander; Projections, Wendall K. Harrington; Music, Dominic Muldowney; Casting, Daniel Swee; Stage Manager, Michael Brunner; Press, Philip Rinaldi, Barbara Carroll. Opened at the Golden Theatre, March 6, 2003*

Cast

Ursula Loyer **Clare Higgins**
Sam Plowman **Pete Starrett**
Vincent Van Gogh **Jochum ten Haaf**
Anna Van Gogh **Liesel Matthews**
Eugenie Loyer **Sarah Drew**

Understudies: Clare Higgins (Sandra Shipley); Jochum ten Haaf, Pete Starrett (Louis Cancelmi); Sarah Drew, Liesel Matthews (Maggie Baisch)

Time: 1873–76. Place: The kitchen at 87 Hackford Road, Brixton, South London. Presented in two parts.

*Closed May 4, 2003

Clare Higgins, Jochum ten Haaf

Clare Higgins PHOTOS BY IVAN KYNCL

Matt Cavenaugh (foreground), Mark Bove (background)   PHOTO BY PAUL KOLNIK

URBAN COWBOY

Musical with book by Aaron Latham and Phillip Oesterman; Music and Lyrics by composers listed below; Based on the film by Paramount Pictures; Producers, Chase Mishkin and Leonard Soloway, in association with Barbara and Peter Fodor; Director, Lonny Price; Choreography, Melinda Roy; Scenery, James Noone; Costumes, Ellis Tillman; Lighting, Natasha Katz; Sound, Peter Fitzgerald; Fight Direction, Rick Sordelet; Music Direction, Orchestrations, Arrangements, Jason Robert Brown; Music Coordinator, John Miller; Assistant Choreographer, Chad L. Schiro; Associate Producer, Barbara Freitag; Casting, Jay Binder/Jack Bowdan; Stage Manager, Heather Fields; Press, Pete Sanders Group, Pete Sanders, Terence Womble, Glenna Freedman. Songs by by Bob Stillman, Jeff Blumenkrantz, Ronnie Dunn, Mr. Brown, Danny Arena, Sara Light, Marcus Hummon, Martie Maguire, Wayland D. Holyfield, Bob Lee House, Carl L. Byrd, Pevin Byrd-Munoz, Roger Brown, Luke Reed, Lauren Lucas, Jerry Chesnut, Jerry Silverstein, Clint Black, James Hayden Nicholas, Tommy Conners, Skip Ewing, Rebekka Bremlette, Dorsey Burnette III, Annie L. Roboff, Charles Daniels, Tom Crain, Fred Edwards, Taz DiGregorio, Jim Marshall, Charlie Hayward, Wanda Mallette, Patti Ryan and Bob Morrison. Opened at the Broadhurst Theatre, March 27, 2003*

Cast
Bud **Matt Cavenaugh**
Jesse **Rozz Morehead**
Travis Williams **Michael Balderrama**
Marshall **Mark Bove**
Roadkill **Gerrard Carter**
J.D. Letterlaw **Justin Greer**
Baby Boy **Brian Letendre**
Trent Williams **Barrett Martin**
Luke "Gator" Daniels **Chad L. Schiro**
Bambi Jo **Lisa Gajda**
Bebe Baker **Michelle Kittrell**
Barbie McQueen **Kimberly Dawn Neumann**
Candi Cane **Tera-Lee Pollin**
Billie Wynette **Kelleia Sheerin**
Sam **Paula Wise**
Aunt Corene **Sally Mayes**
Uncle Bob **Leo Burmester**
Sissy **Jenn Colella**
Pam **Jodi Stevens**
"Tuff" Love Levy **Nicole Foret**
Wes **Marcus Chait**

Understudies: Jenn Colella (Nicole Foret, Michelle Kittrell); Jodi Stevens (Nicole Foret, Kimberly Dawn Neumann); Leo Burmester (Mark Bove); Sally Mayes (Kimberly Dawn Neumann)

Standbys: Matt Cavenaugh, Marcus Chait (Greg Stone); Rozz Morehead, Sally Mayes (Adinah Alexander)

Swings: Cara Cooper, Jennie Ford, Tyler Hanes, Josh Rhodes

Orchestra: Jason Robert Brown, conductor, keyboard; Dave Keyes, keyboard; Brian Brake, drums; Gary Sieger, guitar; Kermit Driscoll bass; Antoine Silverman fiddle; Gordon Titcomb, pedal steel guitar, banjo, electric and acoustic guitars.

Musical Numbers: Leavin' Home, Long Hard Day, All Because of You, Another Guy, Boot Scootin' Boogie, It Don't Get Better Than This, Dancin' the Slow Ones With You, Cowboy Take Me Away, Could I Have This Dance?, My Back's Up Against the Wall, If You Mess With the Bull, That's How She Rides, I Wish I Didn't Love You, That's How Texas Was Born, Take You for a Ride, Mr. Hopatong Heartbreak, T-R-O-U-B-L-E, Dances Turn Into Dreams, The Hard Way, Git It, Something That We Do, The Devil Went Down to Georgia, It Don't Get Better Than This (Reprise)/Lookin' for Love

Time: Late 1970s. Place: In and around Houston, Texas. Musical presented in two parts.

*Closed May 18, 2003

The Company

Hamish McColl, Sean Foley, Tobey Jones PHOTOS BY JOAN MARCUS

THE PLAY WHAT I WROTE

By Hamish McColl, Sean Foley and Eddie Braben; Producers, David Pugh, Joan Cullman, Mike Nichols, Hamilton South, Charles Whitehead, Stuart Thompson; Director, Kenneth Branagh; Choreography, Irving Davies, Heather Cornell; Scenery and Costumes, Alice Power; Lighting, Tim Mitchell; Sound, Simon Baker for Autograph; Songs, Gary Yershon; Musical Arrangements, Steve Parry, Casting, Juliet Taylor, Ellen Lewis, Patricia Kerrigan; Production Stage Manager, Nancy Harrington; Stage Manager, Julie Baldauff; Press, Boneau/Bryan-Brown, Adrian Bryan-Brown, Jackie Green, Adriana Douzos. Opened at the Lyceum Theatre, March 30, 2003*

Sean Foley, Hamish McColl

Cast
Sean **Sean Foley**
Hamish **Hamish McColl**
Arthur **Toby Jones**
Mystery Guest Star **Mystery Guest Star**
  Understudy: Toby Jones (Jay Russell)

Presented in two parts.

*Still Playing May 31, 2003

Brent Spiner, Helen Hunt PHOTO BY JOAN MARCUS

LIFE (X) 3

By Yasmina Reza; Translation by Christopher Hampton; Producers, Ron Kastner; Director, Manhew Warchus; Scenery, Mark Thompson; Lighting, Hugh Vanstone; Sound, Christopher T. Cronin; Music, Gary Yershon; Associate Producers, Jerome Swartz, Joseph Smith; Casting, Jim Carnahan; Production Stage Manager, David Hyslop; Stage Manager, James Mountcastle; Press, Boneau/Bryan-Brown, Adrian Bryan-Brown, Susanne Tighe, Joe Perrotta. Opened at the Circle in the Square, March 31, 2003*

Cast

Sonia **Helen Hunt**
Henry **John Turturro**
Hubert **Brent Spiner**
Inez **Linda Emond**

Standbys: Helen Hunt, Linda Emond (Charlotte Maier); John Turturro, Brent Spiner (Stephen Lee Anderson)

Time: The present. Place: Henry and Sonia's apartment, Paris. Presented in two parts.

*Still playing May 31, 2003

Victoria Hamilton, Eddie Izzard

A DAY IN THE DEATH OF JOE EGG

Revival of the play by Peter Nichols; Artistic Director, Todd Haimes; Managing Director, Ellen Richard; Executive Director of External Affairs, Julia C. Levy; Director, Laurence Boswell; Scenery and Costumes, Es Devlin; Lighting, Adam Silverman; Sound, Fergus O'Hare; Casting, Jim Carnahan; Production Stage Manager, Peter Hanson; Press, Boneau/Bryan-Brown, Adrian Bryan-Brown, Dennis Crowley, Matt Polk, Juliana Hannett. Opened at the American Airlines Theatre, April 3, 2003*

Cast

Bri **Eddie Izzard**
Sheila **Victoria Hamilton**
Joe **Madeleine Martin**
Pam **Margaret Colin**
Freddie **Michael Gaston**
Grace **Dana Ivey**

Standbys: Eddie Izzard (Tony Carlin); Victoria Hamilton (Tina Benko); Madeleine Martin (Erica Geno); Margaret Colin (Virginia Louise Smith); Michael Gaston (Rufus Collins); Dana Ivey (Lucy Martin)

Presented in two parts.

*Closed May 26, 2003

Victoria Hamilton, Eddie Izzard PHOTOS BY JOAN MARCUS

Yakov Smirnoff

AS LONG AS WE BOTH SHALL LAUGH

Solo performance by Yakov Smirnoff; Artistic Director, Todd Haimes; Managing Director, Ellen Richard; Executive Director of External Affairs, Julia C. Levy; Choreographer, Jennifer Werner; Scenery, Eric Renschler; Lighting, Mike Baldassari; Costumes, Robin L. McGee; Sound, Fitz Patton; Associate Producer, Lovely Jewsbury and Grant Niman; Casting, Jim Carnahan; Production Stage Manager, Jay Adler; Press, Boneau/Bryan-Brown, Adrian Bryan-Brown, Matt Polk, Juliana Hannett. Opened at the American Airlines Theatre, April 7, 2003*

Performed by Mr. Smirnoff.

Presented in two parts.

*Closed May 26, 2003

NINE

Revival of the musical with book by Arthur Kopit; Music and Lyrics by Maury Yeston; Adapted from the Italian by Mario Fratti, Artistic Director, Todd Haimes; Managing Director, Ellen Richard; Executive Director of External Affairs, Julia C. Levy; Director, David Leveaux; Choreography, Jonathan Butterell; Scenery, Scott Pask; Costumes, Vicki Mortimer; Lighting, Brian MacDevitt; Sound, Jon Weston; Orchestrations, Jonathan Tunick; Music Direction, Kevin Stites; Music Coordinator, John Miller; Executive Producer, Sydney Davolos; Casting, Jim Carnahan and Jeremy Rich; Production Stage Manager, Arthur Gaffin; Stage Manager, Laurie Goldfeder; Press, Boneau/Bryan-Brown, Adrian Bryan-Brown, Matt Polk, Amy Dinnerman. Opened at the Eugene O'Neill Theatre, April 10, 2003*

Antonio Banderas, Chita Rivera

Cast

Little Guido **William Ullrich**
Little Guido (Wed.; Sat. matinee) **Anthony Colangelo**
Guido Contini **Antonio Banderas**
Luisa **Mary Stuart Masterson**
Carla **Jane Krakowski**
Renata **Elena Shaddow**
Guido's Mother **Mary Beth Peil**
Stephanie Necrophorus **Saundra Santiago**
Diana **Rachel deBenedet**
Olga von Sturm **Linda Mugleston**
Maria **Sara Gettelfinger**
Lina Darling **Nell Campbell**
Sofia **Kathy Voytko**
Saraghina **Myra Lucretia Taylor**
Juliette **Rona Figueroa**
Annabella **Kristin Marks**
Claudia **Laura Benanti**
Our Lady of the Spa **Deidre Goodwin**
Liliane La Fleur **Chita Rivera**

Understudies: Chita Rivera (Nell Campbell); Laura Benanti (Elena Shaddow); Jane Krakowski, Saundra Santiago (Sara Gettelfinger); Mary

Mary Stuart Masterson (top), Antonio Banderas, Jane Krakowski (bottom)

Stuart Masterson (Linda Mugleston, Kristin Marks); Nell Campbell (Rona Figueroa); Deidre Goodwin (Kathy Voytko); Mary Beth Peil (Rachel deBenedet); Myra Lucretia Taylor (Linda Mugleston); Elena Shaddow, Gettelfinger, Figueroa, Marks (Stephanie Bast); Rachel deBenedet, Linda, Kathy Voytko (Jessica Leigh Brown)

Standby: Antonio Banderas (Paul Schoeffler)

Orchestra: Kevin Stites, conductor; Gregory J. Dlugos, associate conductor, keyboard; Martin Agee, concertmaster, violin; Conrad Harris, violin 2; Liuh-Wen Ting, viola; Sarah Seiver, cello; Brian Cassier, bass; Brian Miller, flute; Les Scott clarinet, sax; Marc Goldberg, bassoon; Theresa MacDonnell, French horn; Timothy Schadt, Raymond Riccomini, trumpet; Randy Andos, trombone; Barbara Biggers, harp; Bill Miller, drums, percussion

Musical Numbers: Overture Delle Donne, Spa Music, Not Since Chaplin, Guido's Song, Coda di Guido, My Husband Makes Movies, A Call From the Vatican, Only With You, The Script, Folies Bergeres, Nine, Ti Voglio Bene/Be Italian, The Bells of St. Sebastian, A Man Like You/Unusual Way, The Grand Canal, Simple, Be On Your Own, Waltz di Guido, I Can't Make This Movie, Getting Tall, My Husband Makes Movies, Nine (Reprise)

Time: The early 1960s. Place: A Venetian spa. Presented in two parts.

*Still playing May 31, 2003

The Company PHOTOS BY JOAN MARCUS

A YEAR WITH FROG AND TOAD

Musical with book and Lyrics by Willie Reale; Music by Robert Reale; Based on the children's books by Arnold Lobel; Producers, Bob Boyett, Adrianne Lobel, Michael Gardner, Lawrence Horowitz, Roy Furman, Scott E. Nederlander; Director, David Petrarca; Choreography, Daniel Pelzig; Scenery, Adrianne Lobel; Costumes, Martin Pakledinaz; Lighting, James F. Ingalls; Sound, Rob Milburn and Michael Bodeen; Orchestrations, Irwin Fisch; Musical Direction, Ms. Twine; Music Coordinator, Kimberlee Wertz; Assistant Director, Leland Patton, Assistant Choreographer, Ginger Thatcher; Casting, Cindy Tolan; Production Stage Manager, Michael J. Passaro; Stage Manager, Michelle Bosch; Press, Barlow-Hartman, John Barlow, Michael Hartman, Wayne Wolfe, Rob Finn. Opened at the Cort Theatre, April 13, 2003*

Mark Linn-Baker, Jay Goede PHOTOS BY ROB LEVINE

Musical Numbers: A Year with Frog and Toad, It's Spring, Seeds, The Letter, Getta Loada Toad, Underwater Ballet, Alone, The Letter, Cookies, A Year with Frog and Toad (Reprise), He'll Never Know, Shivers, The Letter (Reprise), Down the Hill, I'm Coming Out of My Shell, Toad to the Rescue, Merry Almost Christmas,

Presented in two parts.

*Still Playing May 31, 2003

Jay Goede, Mark Linn-Baker, Danielle Ferland, Frank Vlastnik

Cast
Birds **Danielle Ferland, Jennifer Gambatese, Frank Vlastnik**
Squirrels **Danielle Ferland, Jennifer Gambatese**
Frog **Jay Goede**
Young Frog; Mouse **Jennifer Gambatese**
Toad **Mark Linn-Baker**
Father Frog; Snail **Frank Vlastnik**
Mother Frog; Turtle **Danielle Ferland**
Moles **Danielle Ferland, Jennifer Gambatese, Frank Vlastnik**
Lizard **Frank Vlastnik**

Understudies: Jay Goede, Mark Linn-Baker, Frank Vlastnik (Jonathan Rayson); Danielle Ferland, Jennifer Gambatese (Kate Manning)

Orchestra: Linda Twine, conductor, piano; Linc Milliman, bass, tuba; James Saporito, drums, percussion; Brian Koonin, guitar, banjo; Eddie Salkin, Dan Block, woodwinds; Brian Pareschi, trumpet; Art Baron, trombone.

ENCHANTED APRIL

By Matthew Barber; From the novel by Elizabeth von Arnim; Producers, Jeffrey Richards, Richard Gross/Ellen Berman, Raymond J. and Pearl Berman Greenwald, Irving Welzer, Tonja Walker Davidson, Libby Adler Mages/Mari Glick, Howard R. Berlin, Jerry Frankel, Terry E. Schnuck, Frederic B. Vogel; Director by Michael Wilson; Scenery, Tony Straiges; Costumes, Jess Goldstein; Lighting, Rui Rita; Music and Sound, John Gromada; Associate Producers, Jack W. Batman, Lionel Goldfrank III, Samuel V. Goekjian; Casting, Bernard Telsey Casting; Production Stage Manager, Katherine Lee Boyer; Stage Manager, Matthew Aaron Stern; Press, Irene Gandy, Michelle Patrick, Michael Dressel, Alana O'Brien. Opened at the Belasco Theatre, April 29, 2003*

Elizabeth Ashley   PHOTO BY CAROL ROSEGG

Cast

Lotty Wilton **Jayne Atkinson**
Rose Arnott **Molly Ringwald**
Mellersh Wilton **Michael Cumpsty**
Frederick Arnott **Daniel Gerroll**
Lady Caroline Bramble **Dagmara Dominczyk**
Mrs. Graves **Elizabeth Ashley**
Antony Wilding **Michael Hayden**
Costanza **Patricia Conolly**
Servant **John Feltch**

Understudies: Michael Cumpsty, Michael Hayden, Daniel Gerroll (John Feltch); Elizabeth Ashley, Patricia Conolly, John Feltch (Jill Tanner)

Time: 1922. Place: London and the coast of Italy. Presented in two parts.

*Still playing May 31, 2003

SALOME

Revival of the play by Oscar Wilde; Producers, Robert Fox, Daryl Roth and Amy Nederlander; Director, Estelle Parsons; Scenery, Peter Larkin; Costumes, Jane Greenwood; Lighting, Howard Thies; Sound, Erich Bechtel and David Schnirman; Music, Yukio Tsuji; Production Stage Manager, Alan Fox; Press, Barlow-Hartman, John Barlow, Michael Hartman, Jeremy Shaffer. Opened at the Ethel Barrymore Theatre, April 30, 2003*

Dianne Wiest, Al Pacino, Marisa Tomei and the Company

Cast

The Young Syrian **Chris Messina**
The Page of Herodias **Timothy Doyle**
First Soldier **Timothy Altmeyer**
Second Soldier **Brian Delate**
A Cappadocian **Andrew Garman**
A Nubian **Daryl Mismond**
Jokanaan **David Strathairn**
Salome **Marisa Tomei**
A Slave **Jill Alexander**
Herod Antipas **Al Pacino**
Herodias **Dianne Wiest**
Tigellinus **Chris McGarry**
Ensemble **Robert Heller, Owen Hollander, Robert Lavelle, Ed Setrakian**
Musician **Yukio Tsuji**

Presented without intermission.

*Still playing May 31, 2003

David Strathairn, Marisa Tomei PHOTOS BY JOAN MARCUS

GYPSY

Revival of the musical with book by Arthur Laurents; Music by Jule Styne; Lyrics by Stephen Sondheim; Suggested by the memoirs of Gypsy Rose Lee; Producers, Robert Fox, Ron Kastner, Roger Marino, Michael Watt, Harvey Weinstein, WWLC; Director by Sam Mendes; Original Choreography, Jerome Robbins; Additional Choreography, Jerry Mitchell; Scenery and Costumes, Anthony Ward; Lighting, Jules Fisher and Peggy Eisenhauer; Sound, Acme Sound Partners; Musical Supervisor, Patrick Vaccariello; Orchestrations, Sid Ramin and Robert Ginzler; Additional Orchestrations, Bruce Coughlin; Original Dance Arrangements, John Kander; Music Direction, Additional Dance Music Arrangments, Mr. Laird; Music Coordinator, Michael Keller; Associate Director, Peter Lawrence; Associate Choreographer, Jodi Moccia; Casting, Jim Carnahan; Stage Managers, Richard Hester, Jim Woolley; Press, Boneau/Bryan-Brown, Adrian Bryan-Brown, Jim Byk, Jackie Green, Aaron Meier. Opened at the Shubert Theatre, May 1, 2003*

John Dossett

Heather Lee, Tammy Blanchard

Cast

Uncle Jocko **Michael McCormick**
Clarence **Stephen Scott Scarpulla**
Balloon Girl **Molly Grant Kallins**
Baby Louise **Addison Timlin**
Baby June **Heather Tepe**
Rose **Bernadette Peters**
Chowsie **Coco**
Pop **William Parry**
Newsboys **Eamon Foley, Stephen Scott Scarpulla, Jordan Viscomi**
Weber **MacIntyre Dixon**
Herbie **John Dossett**
Louise **Tammy Blanchard**
June **Kate Reinders**
Tulsa **David Burtka**
Yonkers **Matt Bauer**
L.A. **Brandon Espinoza**
Kansas **Benjamin Brooks**
Cohen Kringelein **William Parry**

Mr. Goldstone **Brooks Ashmanskas**
Miss Cratchitt **Julie Halston**
Farmboys **Matt Bauer, David Burtka, Benjamin Brooks Cohen, Joey Dudding, Brandon Espinoza, Tim Federle**
Cow **Sarah Jayne Jensen, Dontee Kiehn**
Agnes **Chandra Lee Schwartz**
Hollywood Blondes **Jenna Gavigan, Sarah Jayne Jensen, Dontee Kiehn, Ginifer King, Julie Martell**
Pastey **Brooks Ashmanskas**
Tessie Tura **Heather Lee**
Mazeppa **Kate Buddeke**
Cigar **Michael McCormick**
Electra **Julie Halston**
Rene **Cathy Trien**
Phil **MacIntyre Dixon**
Bougeron-Cochon **Tim Federle**

Ensemble: Matt Bauer, Benjamin Brooks Cohen, MacIntyre Dixon, Joey Dudding, Brandon Espinoza, Tim Federle, Eamon Foley, Jenna Gavigan, Sarah Jayne Jensen, Molly Grant Kallins, Dontee Kiehn, Ginifer King, Gina Lamparella, Julie Martell, Stephen Scott Scarpulla, Chandra Lee Schwartz, Cathy Trien, Jordan Viscomi

Understudies: Michael McCormick as Uncle Jocko, William Parry as Pop, Brooks Ashmanskas as Goldstone, (MacIntyre Dixon, Wally Dunn); Heather Tepe, Molly Grant Kallins (Alexandra Stevens); Addison Timlin (Molly Grant Kallins); Eamon Foley, Scott Scarpulla, Jordan Viscomi (Molly Grant Kallins); John Dossett (Michael McCormick, William Parry); Tammy Blanchard (Ginifer King, Julie Martell); Kate Reinders (Jenna Gavigan, Chandra Lee Schwartz); David Burtka (Matt Bauer, Tim Federle); William Parry as Kringelein, Michael McCormick as Cigar, Brooks Ashmanskas as Pastey (Wally Dunn); Chandra Lee Schwartz (Dontee Kiehn); Julie Halston, Heather Lee, Kate Buddeke (Gina Lamparella, Cathy Trien)

Standby: Bernadette Peters (Maureen Moore)

Swings: Graham Bowen, Wally Dunn, Pamela Remler

Orchestra: Marvin Laird, conductor; Ethyl Will, associate conductor, piano; Ann Labin, concertmaster; Maura Giannini, Dana Ianculovici, violin; Richard Brice, viola; Peter Prosser, Eileen Folson, cello; Grace Paradise, harp; Christian Jaudes, lead trumpet; Larry Lunetta, Hollis Burridge, trumpet; Bruce Eidem, Michael Seltzer, trombone; Morris Kainuma, bass trombone; Roger Wendt, French horn; Dennis Anderson, Mort Silver, Ralph Olsen, Charles Pillow, Ron Janelli, reeds; Cubby O'Brien, drums; Bill Ellison, bass; Deane Prouty, percussion.

Musical Numbers: May We Entertain You, Some People, Travelling, Small World, Baby June and Her Newsboys, Mr. Goldstone, I Love You, Little Lamb, You'll Never Get Away From Me, Dainty June and Her Farmboys, If Momma Was Married, All I Need Is the Girl, Everything's Coming Up Roses, Madame Rose's Toreadorables, Together, Wherever We Go, You Gotta Get a Gimmick, Small World (Reprise), Let Me Entertain You, Rose's Turn

Presented in two parts.

*Still playing May 31, 2003

Bernadette Peters

Heather Tepe, Addison Timlin   PHOTOS BY JOAN MARCUS AND T. CHARLES ERICKSON

THE LOOK OF LOVE

Musical Revue with Music by Burt Bacharach; Lyrics by Hal David; Conceived by David Thompson, Scott Ellis, David Loud and Ann Reinking; Artistic Director, Todd Haimes; Managing Director, Ellen Richard; Executive Director of External Affairs, Julia C. Levy; Director, Mr. Ellis; Choreography, Ms. Reinking; Scenery, Derek Mclane; Costumes, Martin Pakledinaz; Lighting, Howell Binkley; Sound, Brian Ronan; Orchestrations, Don Sebesky; Music Direction and Arrangements, Mr. Loud; Music Coordinator, John Miller; Associate Choreography, Debra McWaters; Associate Producer, James David; Casting, Jim Carnahan; Production Stage Manager, Lori M. Doyle; Stage Manager, Tamlyn Freund Yerkes; Press, Boneau/Bryan-Brown, Adrian Bryan-Brown; Dennis Crowley, Matt Polk, Joe Perrotta. Opened at the Brooks Atkinson Theatre, May 4, 2003*

The Company PHOTOS BY JOAN MARCUS

Performed by Liz Callaway, Kevin Ceballo, Jonathan Dokuchitz, Eugene Fleming, Capathia Jenkins, Janine la Manna, Shannon Lewis, Rachelle Rak, Desmond Richardson.

 Pit Singers: Farah Alvin and Nikki Renee Daniels
 Swings: Allyson Turner and Eric Jordan Young

Shannon Lewis, Janine la Manna, Rachelle Rak

Orchestra: Mr. Loud, conductor; Sue Anschutz, associate conductor, keyboard 2; Philip Fortenberry, assistant conductor, keyboard 1; Chuck Wilson, Kenneth Dybisz, Mark Thrasher, woodwinds; Jon Owens, Matt Peterson, trumpet; Stephen Benson, guitar; Benjamin Franklin Brown, bass; Dave Ratajczak, drums; Bill Hayes, percussion; Paul Woodiel, Ella Rutkovsky, Jonathan Dinklage, violin.

Musical Numbers: The Look of Love, (There's) Always Something There to Remind Me, You'll Never Get To Heaven (If You Break My Heart), I Say a Little Prayer, Promise Her Anything, I Just Don't Know What to Do With Myself, Raindrops Keep Falling on My Head, Are You There (With Another Girl), Another Night, Yo Nunca Volvere Acnar (I'll Never Fall in Love Again), She Likes Basketball, What's New Pussycat, Walk on By, A House Is Not a Home, One Less Bell to Answer, Casino Royale, Wishin' and Hopin, This Guy's in Love With You/This Girl's in Love With You, Alfie, Trains and Boats and Planes, Do You Know the Way to San Jose?, Eugene Fleming, Desmond Richardson, Twenty-Four Hours from Tulsa, Close to You, Anyone Who Had a Heart, Wives and Lovers, Make It Easy on Yourself, Knowing When to Leave, Promises, Promises, What the World Needs Now Is Love

Presented in two parts.

*Still playing May 31, 2003

BILL MAHER: VICTORY BEGINS AT HOME

Solo Performance by Mr. Maher; Producers, Eric Krebs, Jonathan Reinis, CTM Productions, Anne Strickland Squadron, in association with Michael Viner, David and Adam Friedson, Allen Spivak/Larry Magid, M. Kilburg Reedy; Scenery and Lighting Design by Peter R. Feuchtwanger; Sound, Jill B.C. DuBoff; Executive Producer, Sheila Griffith; Press, Bill Evans and Associates, Jim Randolph. Opened at the Virginia Theatre, May 5, 2003*

Presented without intermission.

*Closed May 18, 2003

Bill Maher

Bill Maher   PHOTOS BY BRUCE GLIKAS

LONG DAY'S JOURNEY INTO NIGHT

Revival of Play by Eugene O'Neill; Producers, David Richenthal, Max Cooper, Eric Falkenstein, Anthony and Charlene Marshall, Darren Bagert, in association with Kara Medoff, Lisa Vioni and Gene Korf; Director, Robert Falls; Scenery and Costumes, Santo Loquasto; Lighting, Brian MacDevitt; Sound, Richard Woodbury; Associate Producers, Entitled Entertainment, Ergo Entertainment, Anna Ryan Hansen, Toby Simkin; Casting, Bernard Telsey Casting; Production Stage Manager, Jane Grey; Press, Richard Kornberg, Don Summa, Tom D'Ambrosio, Carrie Friedman, Rick Miramontez. Opened at the Plymouth Theatre, May 6, 2003*

Cast

James Tyrone **Brian Dennehy**
Mary Cavan Tyrone **Vanessa Redgrave**
James Tyrone Jr. **Philip Seymour Hoffman**
Edmund Tyrone **Robert Sean Leonard**
Cathleen **Fiana Toibin**

Understudies: Brian Dennehy (Christopher Wynkoop); Philip Seymour Hoffman (C.J. Wilson); Robert Sean Leonard (Michael Dempsey); Fiana Toibin (Morgan Hallett)

Time: 1912. Place: The summer home of the Tyrone family. Play presented in three parts.

*Still playing May 31, 2003

Brian Dennehy, Vanessa Redgrave

Robert Sean Leonard, Philip Seymour Hoffman

Vanessa Redgrave, Brian Dennehy PHOTOS BY JOAN MARCUS

Brian Dennehy, Vanessa Redgrave

Productions from past seasons that **played through this season**

Taylor Dane

Adam Pascal, Heather Headley

Heather Headley, Members of the Company PHOTOS BY JOAN MARCUS

AIDA

Music, Elton John; Lyrics, Tim Rice; Book, Linda Woolverton, Robert Falls, David Henry Hwang; Suggested by the opera; Director, Robert Falls; Choreography, Wayne Cilento; Set/Costumes, Bob Crowley; Lighting, Natasha Katz; Sound, Steve C. Kennedy; Music Producer and Musical Direction, Paul Bogaev; Music Arrangements, Guy Babylon, Paul Bogaev; Orchestrations, Steve Margoshes, Guy Babylon, Paul Bogaev; Casting, Bernard Telsey; Production Stage Manager, Clifford Schwartz; Cast Recording, Buena Vista; Presented by Hyperion Theatricals (Peter Schneider and Thomas Schumacher); Press, Chris Boneau–Adrian Bryan-Brown/Jackie Green, Steven Padla. Previewed from February 25, 2000; Opened in the Palace Theatre on Thursday, March 23, 2000*

Cast

Amneris **Sherie René Scott** †1
Radames **Adam Pascal** †2
Aida **Heather Headley** †3
Mereb **Damian Perkins** †4
Zoser **John Hickok** †5
Pharaoh **Daniel Oreskes**
Nehebka **Schele Williams**
Amonasro **Tyrees Allen**

Ensemble: Robert M. Armitage, Troy Allan Burgess, Franne Calma, Bob Gaynor, Kisha Howard, Tim Hunter, Youn Kim, Kyra Little, Kenya Unique Massey, Corinne McFadden, Phineas Newborn III, Jody Ripplinger, Raymond Rodriguez, Eric Sciotto, Samuel N. Thiam, Jerald Vincent, Schele Williams, Natalia Zisa

Understudies: Franne Calma, Kelli Fournier (Amneris); Bob Gaynor, Raymond Rodriguez, Eric Sciotto (Radames); Schele Williams (Aida); Tim Hunter, Phineas Newborn III (Mereb); Troy Allan Burgess (Zoser); Robert M. Armitage (Pharaoh); Kyra Little, Endalyn Taylor-Shellman (Nehebka); Samuel N. Thiam, Jerald Vincent (Amonasro)

Standbys: Thursday Farrar (Aida); Neal Benari (Zoser, Pharaoh)

Swings: Chris Payne Dupré, Kelli Fournier, Timothy Edward Smith, Endalyn Taylor-Shellman

Musical Numbers: Every Story Is a Love Story, Fortune Favors the Brave, The Past Is Another Land, Another Pyramid, How I Know You, My Strongest Suit, Enchantment Passing Through, The Dance of the Robe, Not Me, Elaborate Lives, The Gods Love Nubia, A Step Too Far, Easy as Life, Like Father Like Son, Radames' Letter, Written in the Stars, I Know the Truth

A musical in two acts. The action takes place in Egypt. Winner of 2000 Tony Awards for Original Score, Actress in a Musical (Heather Headley), Scenic Design, and Lighting Design.

*Still playing May 31, 2003.
†Succeeded by: 1. Taylor Dane, Idina Menzel, Felicia Finley, Mandy Gonzalez 2. Richard H. Blake, Will Chase 3. Maya Days, Simone, Saycon Sembloh, Toni Braxton 4. Delisco 5. Donnie Kehr

BEAUTY AND THE BEAST

Music, Alan Menken; Lyrics, Howard Ashman, Tim Rice; Book, Linda Woolverton; Director, Robert Jess Roth; Orchestrations, Danny Troob; Musical Supervision/Vocal Arrangements, David Friedman; Musical Director/Incidental Arrangements, Michael Kosarin; Choreography, Matt West; Set, Stan Meyer; Costumes, Ann Hould-Ward; Lighting, Natasha Katz; Sound, T. Richard Fitzgerald; Hairstylist, David H. Lawrence; Illusions, Jim Steinmeyer, John Gaughan; Prosthetics, John Dods; Fights, Rick Sordelet; Cast Recording, Walt Disney Records; General Manager, Dodger Productions; Production Supervisor, Jeremiah J. Harris; Company Manager, Kim Sellon; Stage Managers, James Harker, John M. Atherlay, Pat Sosnow, Kim Vernace; Presented by Walt Disney Productions; Press, Chris Boneau/Adrian Bryan-Brown, Amy Jacobs, Steven Padla. Previewed from Wednesday, March 9, 1994; Opened in the Palace Theatre on Monday, April 18, 1994*

Cast

Enchantress **Wendy Oliver**
Young Prince **Tom Pardoe**
Beast **Steve Blanchard**
Belle **Andrea McArdle** †1
Lefou **Gerard McIsaac** †2
Gaston **Patrick Ryan Sullivan** †3
Three Silly Girls **Lauren Goler-Kosarin, Pam Klinger, Linda Talcott Lee**
Maurice **J.B. Adams**
Cogsworth **Jeff Brooks**
Lumiere **David deVries** †4
Babette **Louisa Kendrick** †5
Mrs. Potts **Barbara Marineau** †6
Chip **Jonathan Andrew Bleicher, Joseph DiConcetto**
Madame de la Grande Bouche **Judith Moore**
Monsieur D'Arque **Gordon Stanley**
Prologue Narrator **David Ogden Stiers**

Townspeople/Enchanted Objects: Ana Maria Andricain, Steven Ted Beckler, Kevin Berdini, Andrea Burns, Christophe Caballero, Sally Mae Dunn, Barbara Folts, Teri Furr, Gregory Garrison, Elmore James, Alisa Klein, Lauren Goler-Kosarin, Ellen Hoffman, Pam Klinger, Ken McMullen, Anna McNeely, Beth McVey, Bill Nabel, Wendy Oliver, Tom Pardoe, Raymond Sage, Joseph Savant, Sarah Solie Shannon, Matthew Shepard, Steven Sofia, Gordon Stanley, Linda Talcott Lee, David A. Wood, Wysandria Woolsey

Musical Numbers: Overture, Prologue (Enchantress), Belle, No Matter What, Me, Home, Gaston, How Long Must This Go On?, Be Our Guest, If I Can't Love Her, Entr'acte/Wolf Chase, Something There, Human Again, Maison des Lunes, Beauty and the Beast, Mob Song, The Battle, Transformation, Finale

Andrea McArdle, Steve Blanchard PHOTO BY EDUARDO PATINO

A musical in two acts. An expanded, live action version of the 1992 animated film musical with additional songs. *Beauty and the Beast* was the winner of 1994 Tony for Best Costume Design.

*Still playing May 31, 2003. The production moved to the Lunt-Fontanne Theatre on November 12, 1999.
†Succeeded by: 1. Sarah Litzsinger, Jamie-Lynn Sigler, Sarah Litzsinger, Megan McGinnis 2. Brad Aspel, Steve Lavner 3. Christopher Seilber, Chris Hoch 4. Rob Lorey, David deVries 5. Pam Klinger 6. Beth Fowler, Cass Morgan

CABARET

Music, John Kander; Lyrics, Fred Ebb; Book, Joe Masteroff; Based on the play *I Am a Camera* by John Van Druten and Stories by Christopher Isherwood; Director, Sam Mendes; Co-Director/Choreography, Rob Marshall; New Orchestrations, Michael Gibson; Musical Director, Patrick Vaccariello; Set/Club Design, Robert Brill; Costumes, William Ivey Long; Lighting, Peggy Eisenhauer, Mike Baldassari; Sound, Brian Ronan; Dance Arrangements, David Krane, David Baker; Company Manager, Denys Baker; Stage Manager, Peter Hanson; Cast Recording, RCA; Presented by Roundabout Theatre Company (Todd Haimes, Artistic Director; Ellen Richard, General Manager; Gene Feist, Founding Director); Press, Chris Boneau–Adrian Bryan-Brown/Erin Dunn, Jackie Green, Andrew Palladino, Amy Nieporent. Previewed from Friday, February 13, 1998; Opened in the Kit Kat Club (the Henry Miller Theatre) on Thursday, March 19, 1998*

Cast

Emcee **Matt McGrath** †1
Kit Kat Girls:
  Rosie **Christina Pawl**
  Lulu **Victoria Lecta Cave**
  Frenchie **Nicole Van Giesen**
  Texas **Leenya Rideout**
  Fritzie **Victoria Clark**
  Helga **Kristin Olness**
Kit Kat Boys:
  Bobby **Michael O'Donnell**
  Victor **Brian Duguay**
  Hans **Richard Costa**
  Herman **Fred Rose**
Sally Bowles **Joley Fisher** †2
Clifford Bradshaw **Michael Hayden** †3
Ernst Ludwig **Martin Moran** †4
Customs Official; Max **Fred Rose**
Fraulein Schneider **Carole Shelley** †5
Fraulein Kost **Candy Buckley** †6
Rudy **Richard Costa**
Herr Schultz **Dick Latessa** †7
Gorilla **Christina Pawl**
Boy Soprano (recording) **Alex Bowen**

Understudies: Linda Romoff, Victoria Lecta Cave (Sally); Brian Duguay, Michael O'Donnell (Cliff); Fred Rose, Manoel Felciano (Ernst); Vance Avery, Michael Arnold (Emcee); Maureen Moore (Schneider); Scott Robertson (Schultz); Leenya Rideout, Victoria Lecta Cave (Kost)

Swings: Linda Romoff, Penny Ayn Maas, Vance Avery, Manoel Felciano, Michael Arnold

A newly revised production of the 1966 musical in two acts. The action takes in Berlin, Germany, 1929–30. Winner of 1998 Tony Awards for Actor in a Musical (Alan Cumming), Actress in a Musical (Natasha Richardson), Featured Actor in a Musical (Ron Rifkin), and Best Revival of a Musical. For original Broadway production with Joel Grey, Jill Haworth, and Lotte Lenya, see *Theatre World* Vol. 23.

Gina Gershon

*Still playing May 31, 2003. The production moved to Studio 54 on November 12, 1998.
†Succeeded by: 1. Raúl Esparza, John Stamos, Raúl Esparza, Neil Patrick Harris 2. Lea Thompson, Katie Finneran, Gina Gershon, Kate Shindle, Brooke Shields, Molly Ringwald, Jane Leeves, Molly Ringwald, Heather Laws, Deborah Gibson 3. Matthew Greer, Rick Holmes 4. Peter Benson 5. Polly Bergen, Carole Shelley, Alma Cuervo, Mariette Hartley 6. Penny Ayn Maas, Jane Summerhays 7. Larry Keith, Hal Linden, Tom Bosley

The Company PHOTOS BY JOAN MARCUS

CHICAGO

Music, John Kander; Lyrics, Fred Ebb; Book, Mr. Ebb, Bob Fosse; Script Adaptation, David Thompson; Based on the play by Maurine Dallas Watkins; Original Production Directed and Choreographed by Bob Fosse; Director, Walter Bobbie; Choreography, Ann Reinking in the style of Bob Fosse; Music Director, Rob Fisher; Orchestrations, Ralph Burns; Set, John Lee Beatty; Costumes, William Ivey Long; Lighting, Ken Billington; Sound, Scott Lehrer; Dance Arrangements, Peter Howard; Cast Recording, RCA; General Manager, Darwell Associates and Maria Di Dia; Company Manager, Scott A. Moore; Stage Managers, Clifford Schwartz, Terrence J. Witter; Presented by Barry & Fran Weissler in association with Kardana Productions; Press, Pete Sanders/Helen Davis, Clint Bond Jr., Glenna Freedman, Bridget Klapinski. Previewed from Wednesday, October 23, 1996; Opened in the Richard Rodgers Theatre on Thursday, November 14, 1996*

Cast

Velma Kelly **Sharon Lawrence** †1
Roxie Hart **Belle Calaway** †2
Fred Casely **Gregory Mitchell**
Sergeant Fogarty **Michael Kubala**
Amos Hart **P.J. Benjamin** †3
Liz **Michelle M. Robinson**
Annie **Mamie Duncan-Gibbs**
June **Donna Marie Asbury**
Hunyak **Mindy Cooper**
Mona **Caitlin Carter**
Matron "Mama" Morton **Roz Ryan** †4
Billy Flynn **Brent Barrett** †5
Mary Sunshine **R. Bean** †6
Go-To-Hell-Kitty **Mary Ann Hermansen**
Harry **Sebastian LaCause**
Aaron **David Warren-Gibson**
Judge **Gregory Butler**
Martin Harrison; Doctor **Denis Jones**
Court Clerk **John Mineo**
The Jury **Michael Kubala**

Understudies/Standbys: Nancy Hess, Amy Spanger, Donna Marie Asbury (Velma, Roxie); Caitlin Carter (Roxie); John Mineo, Randy Slovacek (Amos); Mamie Duncan-Gibbs (Mama, Velma); Michael Berresse (Billy); Michael Kubala (Billy, Amos); J. Loeffelholz (Mary); Luis Perez, Gregory Butler (Billy, Fred); Denis Jones (Amos, Fred); Michelle M. Robinson, Deidre Goodwin (Mama); Eric L. Christian, Rocker Verastique, Mark Anthony Taylor, Sebastian LaCause (Fred)

Musical Numbers: All That Jazz, Funny Honey, Cell Block Tango, When You're Good to Mama, Tap Dance, All I Care About, A Little Bit of Good, We Both Reached for the Gun, Roxie, I Can't Do It Alone, My Own Best Friend, Entr'acte, I Know a Girl, Me and My Baby, Mister Cellophane, When Velma Takes the Stand, Razzle Dazzle, Class, Nowadays, Hot Honey Rag, Finale

Brent Barrett and the Merry Murderesses PHOTO BY CAROL ROSEGG

A new production of the 1975 musical in two acts. This production is based on the staged concert presented by City Center Encores. The action takes place in Chicago, late 1920s. Winner of 1997 Tony Awards for Revival of a Musical, Leading Actor in a Musical (James Naughton), Leading Actress in a Musical (Bebe Neuwirth), Direction of a Musical, Choreography, and Lighting. For original Broadway production with Gwen Verdon, Chita Rivera, and Jerry Orbach, see *Theatre World* Vol. 32.

*Still playing May 31, 2003. Moved to the Shubert Theatre on February 12, 1997.
†Succeeded by: 1. Vicki Lewis, Jasmine Guy, Bebe Neuwirth, Donna Marie Asbury, Deidre Goodwin, Vicki Lewis, Deidre Goodwin, Anna Montanero, Deidre Goodwin, Donna Marie Asbury, Roxane Carrasco, Deidre Goodwin, Stephanie Pope, Roxane Carraasco, Caroline O'Connor, Brenda Braxton 2. Charlotte d'Amboise, Belle Calaway, Nana Visitor, Petra Nielsen, Nana Visitor, Belle Callaway, Denise Van Outen, Belle Calaway, Amy Spanger, Belle Calaway, Tracy Shayne 3. Tom McGowan, P.J. Benjamin, Ray Bokhour, P.J. Benjamin, Rob Bartlett, P.J. Benjamin 4. Marcia Lewis, Jennifer Holliday, Marcia Lewis, Roz Ryan, Michele Pawk, Alix Korey, B.J. Crosby, Angie Stone 5. Chuck Cooper, Clarke Peters, George Hamilton, Eric Jordan Young, Ron Raines, George Hamilton, Michael C. Hall, Destan Owens, Taye Diggs, Billy Zane, Kevin Richardson, Clarke Peters, Gregory Harrison 6. J. Loeffelholz, R. Bean, A. Saunders, J. Maldonado, R. Bean, A. Saunders, R. Bean, M. Agnes, D. Sabella

42ND STREET

Music, Harry Warren; Lyrics, Al Dubin; Book, Michael Stewart, Mark Bramble; Based on a Novel by Bradford Ropes; Director, Mark Bramble; Musical Staging/New Choreography, Randy Skinner; Musical Director, Todd Ellison; Musical Adaptation/Arrangements, Donald Johnston; Orchestrations (original), Philip J. Lang; Set, Douglas W. Schmidt; Costumes, Roger Kirk; Lighting, Paul Gallo; Sound, Peter Fitzgerald; Hair/Wigs, David H. Lawrence; Company Manager, Sandra Carlson; General Manager, Robert C. Strickstein, Sally Campbell Morse; Production Stage Manager, Frank Hartenstein; Stage Manager, Karen Armstrong; Casting, Jay Binder; Original Direction/Dances, Gower Champion; Presented by Dodger Theatricals, Joop Van Den Ende and Stage Holding; Press, Chris Boneau–Adrian Bryan-Brown/Susanne Tighe, Amy Jacobs, Adriana Douzos. Previewed from Wednesday, April 4, 2001; Opened in the Ford Center for the Performing Arts on Wednesday, May 2, 2001*

The Company

Cast

Andy Lee **Michael Arnold**
Maggie Jones **Mary Testa**
Bert Barry **Jonathan Freeman**
Mac **Allen Fitzpatrick**
Phyllis **Catherine Wreford**
Lorraine **Megan Sikora**
Diane **Tamlyn Brooke Shusterman**
Annie **Mylinda Hull**
Ethel **Amy Dolan**
Billy Lawlor **David Elder**
Peggy Sawyer **Kate Levering** †1
Oscar **Billy Stritch**
Julian Marsh **Michael Cumpsty** †2
Dorothy Brock **Christine Ebersole** †3
Abner Dillon **Michael McCarty**
Pat Denning **Richard Muenz**
Waiters **Brad Aspel, Mike Warshaw, Shonn Wiley**
Thugs **Allen Fitzpatrick, Jerry Tellier**
Doctor **Allen Fitzpatrick**

Ensemble: Brad Aspel, Becky Berstler, Randy Bobish, Chris Clay, Michael Clowers, Maryam Myika Day, Alexander de Jong, Amy Dolan, Isabelle Flachsmann, Jennifer Jones, Dontee Kiehn, Renée Klapmeyer, Jessica Kostival, Keirsten Kupiec, Todd Lattimore, Melissa Rae Mahon, Michael Malone, Jennifer Marquardt, Meredith Patterson, Darin Phelps, Wendy Rosoff, Megan Schenck, Kelly Sheehan, Tamlyn Brooke Shusterman, Megan Sikora, Jennifer Stetor, Erin Stoddard, Yasuko Tamaki, Jonathan Taylor, Jerry Tellier, Elisa Van Duyne, Erika Vaughn, Mike Warshaw, Merrill West, Shonn Wiley, Catherine Wreford

Understudies/Standbys: Beth Leavel (Dorothy Brock, Maggie Jones); Brad Aspel (Andy Lee, Bert Barry); Becky Berstler (Annie); Randy Bobish (Andy Lee); Amy Dolan (Annie, Maggie Jones); Allen Fitzpatrick (Abner Dillon, Pat Denning); Renée Klapmeyer (Diane); Jessica Kostival (Dorothy Brock); Richard Muenz (Julian Marsh); Meredith Patterson (Peggy Sawyer); Darin Phelps, Luke Walrath (Doctor, Mac, Thug); Erin Stoddard (Lorraine, Peggy Sawyer); Jerry Tellier (Julian Marsh, Pat Denning); Elisa Van Duyne (Phyllis); Shonn Wiley (Billy Lawlor)

Musical Numbers: Overture, Audition, Young and Healthy, Shadow Waltz, Go into Your Dance, You're Getting to Be a Habit with Me, Getting Out of Town, Dames, Keep Young and Beautiful, Dames, I Only Have Eyes for You (not in orig production), We're in the Money, Keep Young and Beautiful (not in orig production), Entr'acte, Sunny Side to Every Situation, Lullaby of Broadway, Getting Out of Town, Montage, About a Quarter to Nine, With Plenty of Money and You (not in orig. production), Shuffle Off to Buffalo, 42nd Street, Finale

A revival of the original 1980 musical in two acts. The action takes place in New York City and Philadelphia, 1933. *42nd Street* was the winner of 2001 Tony Awards for Best Revival/Musical and Best Actress in a Musical (Christine Ebersole). For original Broadway production with Jerry Orbach and Tammy Grimes, see *Theatre World* Vol. 37.

Variety tallied 11 favorable, 1 mixed, and 4 negative reviews. *Times* (Brantley): "…premature revival…a faded fax of the last musical staged by the fabled Gower Champion…" *News* (Kissel) "…loaded with talent. And you know it as soon as the curtain rises on 24 pairs of tap-dancing feet." *Post* (Barnes): "…cast with exquisite care…everyone is superb…" *Variety* (Isherwood): "…gaudy, relentless production…pays tribute to the Gower Champion original…"

*Still playing May 31, 2003
†Succeeded by 1. Meredith Patterson, Kate Levering, Nadine Isenegger 2. Michael Dantuono, Tom Wopat 3. Beth Leavel, Christine Ebersole, Beth Leavel

Christine Ebersole PHOTOS BY JOAN MARCUS

THE LION KING

Music, Elton John; Lyrics, Tim Rice; Additional Music/Lyrics, Lebo M, Mark Mancina, Jay Rifkin, Julie Taymor, Hans Zimmer; Book, Roger Allers and Irene Mecchi adapted from screenplay by Ms. Mecchi, Jonathan Roberts and Linda Woolverton; Director, Julie Taymor; Choreography, Garth Fagan; Orchestrations, Robert Elhai, David Metzger, Bruce Fowler; Music Director, Joseph Church; Set, Richard Hudson; Costumes, Julie Taymor; Lighting, Donald Holder; Masks/Puppets, Julie Taymor, Michael Curry; Sound, Tony Meola; Vocal Arrangements/Choral Director, Lebo M; Cast Recording, Disney; Company Manager, Steven Chaikelson; Stage Manager, Jeff Lee; Presented by Walt Disney Theatrical Productions (Peter Schneider, President; Thomas Schumacher, Executive VP); Press, Chris Boneau–Adrian Bryan-Brown/Jackie Green, Patty Onagan, Colleen Hughes. Previewed from Wednesday, October 15, 1997; Opened in the New Amsterdam Theatre on Thursday, November 13, 1997*

Cast
Rafiki **Sheila Gibbs** †1
Mufasa **Samuel E. Wright**
Sarabi **Denise Marie Williams** †2
Zazu **Tony Freeman** †3
Scar **Derek Smith**
Young Simba **Mykel Bath**
Young Nala **Leovina Charles**
Shenzi **Vanessa S. Jones** †4
Banzai **Leonard Joseph** †5
Ed **Timothy Gulan** †6
Timon **John E. Brady** †7
Pumba **Tom Alan Robbins**
Simba **Christopher Jackson** †8
Nala **Sharon L. Young** †9

Ensemble Singers: Eugene Barry-Hill, Gina Breedlove, Ntomb'khona Dlamini, Sheila Gibbs, Lindiwe Hlengwa, Christopher Jackson, Vanessa A. Jones, Faca Kulu, Ron Kunene, Anthony Manough, Philip Dorian McAdoo, Sam McKelton, Lebo M, Nandi Morake, Rachel Tecora Tucker

Ensemble Dancers: Camille M. Brown, Iresol Cardona, Mark Allan Davis, Lana Gordon, Timothy Hunter, Michael Joy, Aubrey Lynch II, Karine Plantadit-Bageot, Endalyn Taylor-Shellman, Levensky Smith, Ashi K. Smythe, Christine Yasunaga

Understudies/Swings: Sheila Gibbs, Lindiwe Hlengwa (Rafiki); Eugene Barry-Hill, Philip Dorian McAdoo (Mufasa); Camille M. Brown, Vanessa A. Jones (Sarabi); Kevin Cahoon, Danny Rutigliano (Zazu, Timon); Kevin Bailey (Scar); Kai Braithwaite (Young Simba); Jennifer Josephs (Young Nala); Lana Gordon, Vanessa A. Jones (Shenzi); Philip Dorian McAdoo, Levensky Smith (Banzai); Frank Wright II (Ed); Philip Dorian McAdoo, Danny Rutigliano (Pumba); Timothy Hunter, Christopher Jackson (Simba); Lindiwe Hlengwa, Sonya Leslie (Nala)

Musical Numbers: Circle of Life, Morning Report, I Just Can't Wait to Be King, Chow Down, They Live in You, Be Prepared, Hakuna Matata, One by One, Madness of King Scar, Shadowland, Endless Night, Can You Feel the Love Tonight, King of Pride Rock/Finale

A musical in two acts. Winner of 1998 Tony Awards for Best Musical, Direction of a Musical, Scenic Design, Costume Design, Lighting, and Choreography.

Sheila Gibbs PHOTO BY JOAN MARCUS

*Still playing May 31, 2003
†Succeeded by: 1. Nomvula Dlamini 2. Meena T. Jahi, Denise Marie Williams, Meena T. Jahi, Robyn Payne 3. Adam Stein 4. Lana Gordon, Marlayna Sims 5. Curtiss I' Cook 6. Thom Christopher Warren 7. Danny Rutigliano 8. Josh Tower 9. Rene Elise Goldsberry

MAMMA MIA!

Book by Catherine Johnson; Music and Lyrics, Benny Andersson, Björn Ulvaeus, some songs with Stig Anderson; Director, Phyllida Lloyd; Sets and Costumes, Mark Thompson; Lighting, Howard Harrison; Sound, Andrew Bruce, Bobby Aitken; Choreography, Anthony Van Laast; Musical Supervision, Martin Koch; Musical Direction, David Holcenberg; Musical Coordination, Michael Keller; Associate Director, Robert McQueen; Associate Choreographer, Nichola Treherne; Produced by Judy Craymer, Richard East and Björn Ulvaeus for LittleStar, in association with Universal Casting, Tara Rubin; Press, Boneau/Bryan-Brown, Adrian Bryan-Brown, Steven Padla, Jackie Green, Karalee Dawn. Opened at the Winter Garden Theatre October 18, 2001*

Tina Maddigan, Joe Machota

Cast

Sophie Sheridan **Tina Madigan**
Ali **Sara Inbar**
Lisa **Tonya Doran**
Tanya **Karen Mason** †1
Rosie **Judy Kaye**
Donna Sheridan **Louise Pitre**
Sky **Joe Machota**
Pepper **Mark Price**
Eddie **Michael Benjamin Washington**
Harry Bright **Dean Nolan** †2
Bill Austin **Ken Marks** †3
Sam Carmicheal **David W. Keeley**
Father Alexandrios **Bill Carmichael**

Understudies: Ms. Madigan (Meghann Dreyfuss, Somer Lee Graham); Ms. Inbar (Kim-e J. Balmilero, Kristin McDonald); Ms. Doran (Meredith Atkins, Yuka Takahara); Ms. Pitre (Marsha Waterbury); Ms. Mason (Leslie Alexander, Marsha Waterbury); Ms. Kaye (Robin Baxter, Marsha Waterbury); Mr. Machota (Adam Monley, Peter Matthew Smith); Mr. Price (Stephan Alexander, Jon-Erik Goldberg); Mr. Washington (Chris Prinzo, Peter Matthew Smith); Mr. Nolen (Tony Carlin, Bill Carmichael); Messers. Marks, Keeley (Brent Black, Tony Carlin)

Louise Pitre and the Company

Orchestra: David Holcenberg, conductor, keyboard; Rob Preuss, associate music director, keyboard 3; Steve Marzullo, keyboard 2; Myles Chase, keyboard 4; Doug Quinn, guitar 1; Jeff Campbell, guitar 2; Paul Adamy, bass; Gary Tillman, drums; David Nyberg, percussion

Musical Numbers: Chiquitita, Dancing Queen, Does Your Mother Know?, Gimme! Gimmie! Gimmie!, Honey, Honey, I Do, I Do, I Do, I Do, I Have a Dream, Knowing Me Knowing You, Lay All Your Love on Me, Mamma Mia, Money Money Money, One of Us, Our Last Summer, Slipping Through My Fingers, S.O.S., Super Trouper, Take a Chance on Me, Thank You For the Music, The Name of the Game, The Winner Takes All, Under Attack, Voulez-Vous

A musical in two acts. Time: A wedding weekend. Place: A tiny Greek island. Songs of the 1970s group ABBA strung together in a story of baby boomer wistfulness and a girl's search for her unknown father.

*Still playing May 31, 2003
†Succeeded by: 1. Jeanine Morick 2. Richard Binsley 3. Adam LeFevre

Karen Mason, Louise Pitre, Judy Kaye PHOTOS BY JOAN MARCUS

THE PHANTOM OF THE OPERA

Music, Andrew Lloyd Webber; Lyrics, Charles Hart; Additional Lyrics, Richard Stilgoe; Book, Mr. Stilgoe, Mr. Lloyd Webber; Director, Harold Prince; Musical Staging/Choreography, Gillian Lynne; Orchestrations, David Cullen, Mr. Lloyd Webber; Based on the novel by Gaston Leroux; Design, Maria Björnson; Lighting, Andrew Bridge; Sound, Martin Levan; Musical Direction/Supervision, David Caddick; Conductor, Jack Gaughan; Cast Recording (London), Polygram/Polydor; Casting, Johnson-Liff & Zerman; General Manager, Alan Wasser; Company Manager, Michael Gill; Stage Managers, Steve McCorkle, Bethe Ward, Richard Hester, Barbara-Mae Phillips; Presented by Cameron Mackintosh and The Really Useful Theatre Co.; Press, Merle Frimark, Marc Thibodeau. Previewed from Saturday, January 9, 1988; Opened in the Majestic Theatre on Tuesday, January 26, 1988*

Leila Martin, Gary Maurer

Cast

The Phantom of the Opera **Howard McGillin** †1
Christine Daae **Sarah Pfisterer, Adrienne McEwan (alternate)** †2
Raoul, Vicomte de Chagny **Gary Maurer** †3
Carlotta Giudicelli **Liz McCartney**
Monsieur Andre **Jeff Keller**
Monsieur Firmin **George Lee Andrews**
Madame Giry **Leila Martin**
Ubaldo Piangi **Larry Wayne Morbitt**
Meg Giry **Geralyn Del Corso**
M. Reyer **Richard Poole**
Auctioneer **Richard Warren Pugh**
Porter; Marksman **Maurizio Corbino**
M. Lefevre **Kenneth H. Waller**
Joseph Buquet **Joe Gustern**
Don Attilio **John Kuether**
Passarino **Thomas Sandri**
Slave Master **Daniel Rychlec**
Solo Dancer **Paul B. Sadler Jr.**
Flunky; Stagehand **Jack Hayes**
Hairdresser; Marksman **Gary Lindemann**
Policeman **Thomas Sandri**
Page **Patrice Pickering**
Porter; Fireman **Maurizio Corbino**
Spanish Lady **Wren Marie Harrington**
Wardrobe Mistress; Confidante **Mary Leigh Stahl**
Princess **Elizabeth Southard**
Madame Firmin **Melody Johnson**
Innkeeper's Wife **Johanna Wiseman**
Ballet Chorus of the Opera Populaire **Emily Addona, Teresa DeRose, Nina Goldman, Elizabeth Nackley, Erin Brooke Reiter, Christine Spizzo, Kate Wray**

Understudies: Jeff Keller (Phantom); James Romick (Phantom, Raoul, Firmin, Andre); Elizabeth Southard (Christine); John Schroeder, Jim Weitzer (Raoul); Richard Warren Pugh (Firmin, Piangi); John Kuether (Firmin); George Lee Andrews, Richard Poole (Andre); Wren Marie Harrington, Johanna Wiseman, Melody Johnson (Carlotta); Susan

The Phantom of the Opera PHOTOS BY JOAN MARCUS

Russell, Patrice Pickering, Mary Leigh Stahl (Giry); Maurizio Corbino (Piangi); Teresa DeRose, Kate Wray (Meg); Paul B. Sadler Jr. (Master); Daniel Rychlec (Dancer)

Swings: Susan Russell, James Romick, Jim Weitzer

Musical Numbers: Think of Me, Angel of Music, Little Lotte/The Mirror, Phantom of the Opera, Music of the Night, I Remember/Stranger Than You Dreamt It, Magical Lasso, Notes/Prima Donna, Poor Fool He Makes Me Laugh, Why Have You Brought Me Here?/Raoul I've Been There, All I Ask of You, Masquerade/Why So Silent?, Twisted Every Way, Wishing You Were Somehow Here Again, Wandering Child/Bravo Bravo, Point of No Return, Down Once More/Track Down This Murderer, Finale

A musical in two acts with nineteen scenes and a prologue. The action takes place in and around the Paris Opera House, 1881–1911. Winner of 1988 Tony Awards for Best Musical, Leading Actor in a Musical (Michael Crawford), Featured Actress in a Musical (Judy Kaye), Direction of a Musical, Scenic Design, and Lighting Design. The title role has been played by Michael Crawford, Timothy Nolen, Cris Groendaal, Steve Barton, Jeff Keller, Kevin Gray, Marc Jacoby, Marcus Lovett, Davis Gaines, Thomas J. O'Leary, Hugh Panaro, and Howard McGillin.

*Still playing May 31, 2003
†Succeeded by: 1. Hugh Panaro 2. Sandra Joseph, Adrienne McEwan, Sarah Pfisterer, Beth Southard, Lisa Vroman 3. Jim Weitzer, Michael Shawn Lewis. John Cudia

THE PRODUCERS

Music/Lyrics, Mel Brooks; Book, Mr. Brooks, Thomas Meehan; Based on the 1967 film; Director/Choreography, Susan Stroman; Director, Patrick S. Brady; Musical Arrangements/Supervision, Glen Kelly; Orchestrations, Douglas Besterman, Larry Blank (uncredited); Musical Director/Vocal Arrangements, Patrick S. Brady; Set, Robin Wagner; Costumes, William Ivey Long; Lighting, Peter Kaczorowski; Sound, Steve Canyon Kennedy; Hair/Wigs, Paul Huntley; General Manager, Richard Frankel/Laura Green; Company Manager, Kathy Lowe; Production Stage Manager, Steven Zweigbaum; Stage Manager, Ira Mont; Cast Recording, Sony; Casting, Johnson-Liff Associates; Advertising, Serino Coyne, Inc.; Presented by Rocco Landesman, SFX Theatrical Group, The Frankel-Baruch-Viertel-Routh Group, Bob and Harvey Weinstein, Rick Steiner, Robert F.X. Sillerman and Mel Brooks, in association with James D. Stern/Douglas L. Meyer; Press, John Barlow–Michael Hartman/Bill Coyle, Shellie Schovanec. Previewed from Wednesday, March 21, 2001; Opened in the St. James Theatre on Thursday, April 19, 2001*

Cast

The Usherettes **Bryn Dowling, Jennifer Smith**
Max Bialystock **Nathan Lane** †1
Leo Bloom **Matthew Broderick** †2
Hold-me Touch-me **Madeleine Doherty**
Mr. Marks **Ray Wills**
Franz Liebkind **Brad Oscar** †3
Carmen Ghia **Roger Bart** †4
Roger De Bris **Gary Beach** †5
Bryan; Judge; Jack Lepidus **Peter Marinos**
Scott; Guard; Donald Dinsmore **Jeffry Denman**
Ulla **Cady Huffman** †6
Lick-me Bite-me **Jennifer Smith**
Shirley; Kiss-me Feel-me; Jury Foreman **Kathy Fitzgerald**
Kevin; Jason Green; Trustee **Ray Wills**
Lead Tenor **Eric Gunhus**
Sergeant; Baliff **Abe Sylvia**
O'Rourke **Matt Loehr**
O'Houlihan **Robert H. Fowler**

Ensemble: Jeffry Denman, Madeleine Doherty, Bryn Dowling, Kathy Fitzgerald, Robert H. Fowler, Ida Gilliams, Eric Gunhus, Kimberly Hester, Naomi Kakuk, Matt Loehr, Peter Marinos, Angie L. Schworer, Jennifer Smith, Abe Sylvia, Tracy Terstriep, Ray Wills

Understudies: Jim Borstelmann (Franz Liebkind, Roger De Bris); Jeffry Denman (Franz Liebkind, Leo Bloom); Ida Gilliams, Angie L. Schworer (Ulla); Jamie LaVerdiere (Carmen Ghia, Leo Bloom); Brad Musgrove (Carmen Ghia, Roger De Bris); Brad Oscar (Max Bialystock, Roger De Bris); Ray Wills (Max Bialystock)

Swings: Jim Borstelmann, Adrienne Gibbons, Jamie LaVerdiere, Brad Musgrove, Christina Marie Norrup

Musical Numbers: Opening Night, The King of Broadway, We Can Do It, I Wanna Be a Producer, In Old Bavaria, Der Guten Tag Hop Clop, Keep It Gay, When You Got It Flaunt It, Along Came Bialy, Act One Finale, That Face, Haben Sie Gehoert das Deutsche Band?, You Never Say "Good Luck" On Opening Night, Springtime for Hitler, Where Did We Go Right?, Betrayed, 'Til Him, Prisoners of Love, Leo and Max, Goodbye!

Nathan Lane, Matthew Broderick PHOTO BY PAUL KOLNIK

A musical comedy in two acts. The action takes place in New York City, 1959. Winner of 2001 Tony Awards for Best Musical, Best Score, Best Book of a Musical, Best Actor in a Musical (Nathan Lane), Best Featured Actor in a Musical (Gary Beach), Best Featured Actress in a Musical (Cady Huffman), Best Director/Musical, Best Choreography, Best Sets, Best Costumes, Best Lighting, Best Orchestrations

Variety tallied 18 favorable and 1 mixed review. *Times* (Brantley): "…the real thing: a big Broadway book musical that is so ecstatically drunk on its powers to entertain that it leaves you delirious, too….Mr. Lane and Mr. Broderick…have the most dynamic stage chemistry since Natasha Richardson met Liam Neeson in Anna Christie…" *News* (Kissel): "Nathan Lane does his funniest work in years…Matthew Broderick sings and dances with suitably forlorn charm…No new musical in ages has offered so much imagination, so much sheer pleasure." *Post* (Barnes): "…a cast-iron, copper-bottomed, super-duper, mammoth old-time Broadway hit." *Variety* (Isherwood): "…the material is inherently terrific. But Brooks and his collaborators go further, capitalizing on the new medium in ways that add immensely to its appeal…the first Broadway smash of the new century."

*Still playing May 31, 2003
†Succeeded by: 1. Ray Wills (during illness), Henry Goodman, Brad Oscar, Lewis J. Stadlen 2. Jamie LaVerdiere (during illness), Steven Weber, Roger Bart, Don Stephenson 3. John Treacy Egan, Peter Samuel 4. Sam Harris, Brad Musgrove 5. John Treacy Egan 6. Sarah Cornell

RENT

Music/Lyrics/Book by Jonathan Larson; Director, Michael Greif; Arrangements, Steve Skinner; Musical Supervision/Additional Arrangements, Tim Weil; Choreography, Marlies Yearby; Original Concept/Additional Lyrics, Billy Aronson; Set, Paul Clay; Costumes, Angela Wendt; Lighting, Blake Burba; Sound, Kurt Fischer; Cast Recording, Dreamworks; General Management, Emanuel Azenberg, John Corker; Company Manager, Brig Berney; Stage Managers, John Vivian, Crystal Huntington; Presented by Jeffrey Seller, Kevin McCollum, Allan S. Gordon, and New York Theatre Workshop; Press, Richard Kornberg/Don Summa, Ian Rand; Previewed from Tuesday, April 16, 1996; Opened in the Nederlander Theatre on Monday, April 29, 1996*

Cast

Roger Davis **Norbert Leo Butz** †1, **Richard H. Blake (alternate)**
Mark Cohen **Trey Ellett** †2
Tom Collins **Alan Mingo Jr.** †3
Benjamin Coffin III **Stu James** †4
Joanne Jefferson **Natalie Venetia Belcon** †5
Angel Schunard **Jai Rodriguez** †6
Mimi Marquez **Loraine Velez** †7
Maureen Johnson **Cristina Fadale** †8
Mark's Mom; Alison; Others **Maggie Benjamin**
Christmas Caroler; Mr. Jefferson; Pastor; Others **Byron Utley**
Mrs. Jefferson; Woman with Bags; Others **Aisha de Haas**
Gordon; The Man; Mr. Grey; Others **Chad Richardson**
Steve; Man with Squeegee; Waiter; Others **Owen Johnston II**
Paul; Cop; Others **Robert Glean**
Alexi Darling; Roger's Mom; Others **Kim Varhola**

Understudies: Dean Balkwill (Roger); Richard H. Blake, Will Chase (Roger, Mark); Byron Utley (Tom); Calvin Grant, Robert Glean (Tom, Benjamin); Darryl Ordell (Benjamin); Shelly Dickinson, Aisha de Haas (Joanne); Shayna Steele, Sharon Leal (Joanne, Mimi); Juan Carlos Gonzalez, Mark Setlock, Jai Rodriguez (Angel); Jessica Boevers, Maggie Benjamin (Maureen); Kristen Lee Kelly (Maureen); Owen Johnston II (Roger, Angel); Chad Richardson, Peter Matthew Smith (Roger, Mark); Yassmin Alers, Karen Olivo, Julie P. Danao (Mimi, Maureen)

Swings: Mr. Blake, Ms. Danao, Mr. Gonzalez, Mr. Grant, Ms. Leal, Ms. Steele

Musical Numbers: Tune Up, Voice Mail (#1–#5), Rent, You Okay Honey?, One Song Glory, Light My Candle, Today 4 U, You'll See, Tango: Maureen, Life Support, Out Tonight, Another Day, Will I?, On the Street, Santa Fe, We're Okay, I'll Cover You, Christmas Bells, Over the Moon, La Vie Boheme/I Should Tell You, Seasons of Love, Happy New Year, Take Me or Leave Me, Without You, Contact, Halloween, Goodbye Love, What You Own, Finale/Your Eyes

A musical in two acts. The action takes place in New York City's East Village. Winner of 1996 Tony Awards for Best Musical, Best Original Score, Best Book of a Musical and Featured Actor in a Musical (Wilson Jermaine Heredia). Tragedy occurred when the 35-year-old author, Jonathan Larson, died of an aortic aneurysm after watching the final dress rehearsal of his show on January 24, 1996.

Manley Pope, Loraine Velez PHOTO BY JOAN MARCUS

*Still playing May 31, 2003
†Succeeded by: 1. Manley Pope, Sebastian Arcelus 2. Matt Caplan, Joey Fatone, Matt Caplan 3. Mark Leroy Jackson, Mark Richard Ford 4. Stu James 5. Myiia Watson-Davis, Merle Dandridge, Kenna J. Ramsey 6. Andy Senor, Jai Rodriguez, Andy Senor 7. Karmine Alers, Krystal L. Washington 8. Maggie Benjamin, Cristina Fadale

THOROUGHLY MODERN MILLIE

Book by Richard Morris and Dick Scanlan; Based on the Story and Screenplay by Richard Morris (Universal Pictures production); Director, Michael Mayer; Sets, David Gallo; Lighting, Donald Holder; Costumes, Martin Pakledinaz; Sound, Jon Weston; New Music, Jeanine Tesori; New Lyrics, Dick Scanlan; Choreography, Rob Ashford; Orchestrations, Doug Besterman, Ralph Burns; Music Coordination, John Miller; Casting, Jim Carnahan; Produced by Michael Leavitt, Fox Theatricals, Hal Luftig, Stewart F. Lane, James L. Nederlander, Independent Presenters Network, Libby Adler Mages/Marian Glick, Dori Berinstein/Jennifer Manocherian, Dramatic Forces, John York Noble, Whoopi Goldberg; Associate Producers, Mike Isaacson, Krisitin Caskey, Clear Channel Entertainment; Press, Barlow-Hartman Public Relations, John Barlow, Michael Hartman, Jeremy Shaffer. Opened at the Marquis Theatre April 18, 2002*

Cast

Millie Dillmount **Sutton Foster**
Ruth **Megan Sikora**
Gloria **JoAnn M. Hunter**
Rita **Jessica Grové**
Alice **Alisa Klein**
Ethel Peas **Joyce Chittick**
Cora **Catherine Brunell**
Lucille **Kate Baldwin**
Mrs. Meers **Harriet Harris**
Miss Dorothy Brown **Angela Christian**
Ching Ho **Ken Leung**
Bun Foo **Francis Jue**
Miss Flannery **Anne L. Nathan**
Mr. Trevor Graydon **Marc Kudisch** †1
Speed Tappists **Casey Nicholaw, Noah Racey**
The Pearl Lady **Roxane Barlow**
Jimmy Smith **Gavin Creel**
The Letch **Noah Racey**
Officer **Casey Nicholaw**
Muzzy Van Hossmere **Sheryl Lee Ralph** †2
Kenneth **Brandon Wardell**
Mathilde **Catherine Brunell**
George Gershwin **Noah Racey**
Dorothy Parker **Julie Connors** †3
Rodney **Aaron Ramey**
Dishwashers **Aldrin Gonzalez, Aaron Ramey, Brandon Wardell**
Muzzy's Boys **Gregg Goodbrod, Darren Lee, Dan LoBuono, John MacInnis, Noah Racey, T. Oliver Reid**
Daphne **Kate Baldwin**
Dexter **Casey Nicholaw**
New Modern **Jessica Grové**

Ensemble: Kate Baldwin, Roxane Barlow, Catherine Brunell, Joyce Chittick, Julie Connors, David Eggers, Gregg Goodbrod, Aldrin Gonzalez, Jessica Grové, Amy Heggins, JoAnn M. Hunter, Alisa Klein, Darren Lee, Dan LoBuono, John MacInnis, Casey Nicholaw, Noah Racey, Aaron Ramey, T. Oliver Reid, Megan Sikora, Brandon Wardell

Understudies: Ms. Foster (Catherine Brunell, Susan Haefner); Mr. Creel (Aaron Ramey, Brandon Wardell); Ms. Christian (Kate Baldwin, Jessica Grové); Mr. Kudisch (Gregg Goodbrod, Aaron Ramey); Mr. Leung (Fancis Jue, Darren Lee); Mr. Jue (JoAnn M. Hunter, Darren Lee) Ms. Nathan (Julie Connors, Susan Haefner)

Orchestra: Michael Rafter, conductor, music director; Lawrence Goldberg, associate conductor and piano; Charles Descarfino, assistant conductor, percussion; Lawrence Feldman, Walt Weiskopf, Dan Willis, Allen Won, woodwinds; Craig Johnson, Brian O'Flaherty, Glenn Drewes, trumpet; Larry Farrell, Jeff Nelson, trombone; Brad Gemeinhardt, French horn; Belinda Whitney, Eric DeGioia, Laura Oatts, Karl Kawahara, Mary Whitaker, violin; Stephanie Cummins, Anik Oulianine, cello; Emily Mitchell, harp; Ray Kilday, bass; Jack Cavari, guitar; Warren Odze, drums

Musical Numbers: Not For the Life of Me, Thoroughly Modern Millie, How the Other Half Lives, The Speed Test, They Don't Know, The Nuttycracker Suite, What Do I Need With Love?, Only in New York, Jimmy, Forget About the Boy, I'm Falling in Love With Someone, I Turned the Corner, Muqin, Long As I'm Here With You, Gimme Gimme

A musical in two acts. Time: 1920s. Place: New York City. Based on a 1967 movie about a kid from Kansas who struggles to survive amid adversity in the big city. Winner of six Tony Awards, 2002: Best Actress, Featured Actress, Choreography, Musical, Orchestrations, Costumes.

*Still playing May 31, 2003
† Succeeded by: 1. Christopher Sieber 2. Leslie Uggams 3. Christian Borle

The Company PHOTO BY JOAN MARCUS

URINETOWN

Book and Lyrics by Greg Kotis; Director, John Rando; Music and Lyrics, Mark Hollman; Sets, Scott Pask; Lighting, Brian MacDevitt; Choreography, John Carrafa; Costumes, Jonathan Bixby; Sound, Jeff Curtis, Lew Meade; Fight Direction, Rick Sordelet; Orchestrations, Bruce Coughlin; Musical Direction, Edwin Strauss; Music Coordination, John Miller; Casting, Jay Binder, Cindi Rush, Laura Stanczyk; Production Stage Manager, Julia P. Jones; Stage Manager, Matthew Lacey; Press, Boneau/Bryan-Brown, Adrian Bryan-Brown, Jim Byk, Jackie Green, Martin Sainvil; Produced by the Araca Group and Dodger Theatricals, in association with TheaterDreams, Inc. and Lauren Mitchell. Opened at the Henry Miller Theatre, September 20, 2001*

The Company PHOTO BY JOAN MARCUS

Cast

Officer Lockstock **Jeff McCarthy**
Little Sally **Spencer Kayden** †1
Penelope Pennywise **Nancy Opel** †2
Bobby Strong **Hunter Foster** †3
Hope Cladwell **Jennifer Laura Thompson** †4
Mr. McQueen **David Beach**
Senator Fipp **John Deyle**
Old Man Strong; Hot Blades Harry **Ken Jennings**
Tiny Tom; Dr. Billeaux **Rick Crom**
Soupy Sue; Cladwell's Secretary **Rachel Coloff**
Little Becky Two-Shoes; Mrs. Millenium **Jennifer Cody**
Robbie the Stockfish; Business Man #1 **Victor Hawks**
Billy Boy Bill; Business Man #2 **Lawrence Street**
Old Woman; Josephine Strong **Kay Walbye**
Officer Barrell **Daniel Marcus**
Cladwell B. Cladwell **John Cullum**

Understudies: Mr. McCarthy (Don Richard, Peter Reardon); Ms. Kayden (Jennifer Cody, Erin Hill); Mr. Foster (Peter Reardon, Victor W. Hawkes); Mses. Thopmson, Walbye (Erin Hill, Rachel Coloff); Mr. Cullum (Don Richard, Daniel Marcus); Ms. Opel (Kay Walbye, Rachel Coloff); Mr. Beach (Rick Crom, Lawrence Street); Mr. Marcus (Victor W. Hawkes, Don Richard); Mr. Deyle (Rick Crom, Don Richard); Messers. Crom, Hawkes (Peter Reardon, Lawrence Street); Ms. Cody (Erin Hill); Ms. Coloff (Erin Hill); Mr. Street (Peter Reardon)

Orchestra: Ed Goldschneider, conductor, piano; Paul Garment, clarinet, bass clarinet, alto sax, soprano sax; Ben Herrington, tenor trombone, euphonium; Tim McLafferty, drums, percussion; Dick Sarpola, bass

Musical Numbers: Urinetown, It's a Privilege to Pee, It's a Privilege to Pee (Reprise), Mr. Cladwell, Cop Song, Follow Your Heart, Look at the Sky, Don't Be the Bunny, Act 1 Finale, What Is Urinetown?, Snuff That Girl, Run Freedom Run, Follow Your Heart (Reprise), Why Did I Listen to That Man?, Tell Her I Love Her, We're Not Sorry, We're Not Sorry (Reprise), I See a River

A musical presented in two acts. A town with a water shortage finds itself paying dearly for one of the most basic human needs in this eco-satire and spoof of Broadway musicals; winner of three Tony Awards (for Book, Score and Director). Originally presented as part of the 1999 New York International Fringe Festival before a 2001 Off-Broadway engagement.

*Still playing May 31, 2003
†Succeeded by: 1. Megan Lawrence, Spencer Kayden 2. Victoria Clark, Carolee Carmello 3. Charlie Pollack, Tom Cavanaugh 4. Anastasia Barzee

Productions from past seasons that **closed during this season**

CONTACT
Above: The Company
1,010 performances
Opened March 30, 2000
Closed September 1, 2002
PHOTO BY PAUL KOLNIK

THE CRUCIBLE
Right: Liam Neeson, Brian Murray,
Laura Linney, Jack Willis
101 performances
Opened March 7, 2002
Closed June 9, 2002
PHOTO BY JOAN MARCUS

THE ELEPHANT MAN
Left: Billy Crudup, Rupert Graves, Kate Burton
57 performances
Opened April 14, 2002
Closed June 2, 2002
PHOTO BY JOAN MARCUS

FORTUNE'S FOOL
Above: Enid Graham, Alan Bates
127 performances
Opened April 2, 2002
Closed July 21, 2002
PHOTO BY CAROL ROSEGG

THE FULL MONTY
Left: John Ellison Conlee, Marcus Neville,
Romain Frugé, Jason Danieley, André De Shields
770 performances
Opened October 26, 2000
Closed September 1, 2002
PHOTO BY CRAIG SCHWARTZ

THE GOAT OR, WHO IS SYLVIA?
Below: Mercedes Ruehl, Bill Pullman, Jeffrey Carlson
309 performances
Opened March 10, 2002
Closed December 15, 2002
PHOTO BY CAROL ROSEGG

THE GRADUATE
Above: Alicia Silverstone, Jason Biggs
380 performances
Opened April 4, 2002
Closed March 2, 2002
PHOTO BY JOAN MARCUS

LES MISÉRABLES
Left: The Company
6,680 performances
Opened March 12, 1987
Closed May 18, 2003
PHOTO BY JOAN MARCUS

THE MAN WHO HAD ALL THE LUCK
Right: Chris O'Donnell, James Reborn, Samantha Mathis
70 performances
Opened May 1, 2002
Closed June 30, 2002
PHOTO BY JOAN MARCUS

METAMORPHOSES
Below: Doug Hara, Erik Lochtefeld
400 performances
Opened March 4, 2002
Closed February 16, 2003
PHOTO BY JOAN MARCUS

MORNING'S AT SEVEN
Above: William Biff McGuire, Estelle Parsons
112 performances
Opened April 21, 2002
Closed July 28, 2002
PHOTO BY JOAN MARCUS

MOSTLY SONDHEIM

Below: Barbara Cook
26 performances
Opened January 14, 2002
Closed August 25, 2002

PHOTO BY MIKE MARTIN

NOISES OFF

Above: Patti Lupone
348 performances
Opened November 1, 2001
Closed September 1, 2002

PHOTO BY JOAN MARCUS

OKLAHOMA!

Left: The Company
388 performances
Opened March 21, 2002
Closed February 23, 2003

PHOTO BY MICHAEL LEPOER TRENCH

PRIVATE LIVES
Left: Lindsay Duncan, Alan Rickman
127 performances
Opened April 28, 2002
Closed September 1, 2002
PHOTO BY JOAN MARCUS

QED
Left: Alan Alda
40 performances
Opened November 18, 2001
Closed June 20, 2002
PHOTO BY CRAIG SCHWARTZ

PROOF
Above: Mary-Louise Parker
917 performances
Opened October 24, 2000
Closed January 5, 2003
PHOTO BY JOAN MARCUS

SWEET SMELL OF SUCCESS
Above: John Lithgow
109 performances
Opened March 14, 2002
Closed June 15, 2002

PHOTO BY PAUL KOLNIK

THE TALE OF THE ALLERGIST'S WIFE
Right: Tony Roberts, Linda Lavin, Michelle Lee
777 performances
Opened November 2, 2000
Closed September 15, 2002

PHOTO BY JOAN MARCUS

TOPDOG/UNDERDOG
144 performances
Opened April 7, 2002
Closed August 11, 2002

Left, top: Jeffrey Wright, Don Cheadle
Left, bottom: Mos Def, Jeffrey Wright
Right: Mos Def

PHOTOS BY MICHAL DANIEL

OFF-BROADWAY

Productions that opened **June 1, 2002 – May 31, 2003**

Dennis Michael Hall, Gerard Canonico in *The Prince and the Pauper* PHOTO BY CAROL ROSEGG

THE PRINCE AND THE PAUPER

Musical with book by Bernie Garzia and Ray Roderick; Music by Neil Berg; Lyrics by Neil Berg and Bernie Garzia; Based on the novel by Mark Twain; Producers, Carolyn Rossi Copeland, Marian Lerman Jacobs and Leftfield Productions; Director, Ray Roderick; Scenery, Dana Kenn; Costumes, Sam Fleming; Lighting, Eric T. Haugen; Sound, One Dream Sound; Fight Direction, Rick Sordelet; Orchestrations, Music Supervision and Arrangements, John Glaudini; Press, Cromarty and Company, Peter Cromarty. Opened at the Lamb's Theatre, June 16, 2002*; Reopened November 27, 2002**

Cast
Prince Edward **Dennis Michael Hall**
Tom Canty, the Pauper **Gerard Canonico**
Miles; Charlie; Patch **Rob Evan**
Hugh Hendon; Stache **Stephen Zinnato**
Lady Edith; Karyn **Rita Harvey**
Lady Jane; Jamie; Nan **Allison Fischer**
John Canty; King Henry; Castle Cook **Michael McCormick**
Pike; Guard Sergeant **Wayne Schroeder**
Father Andrew; Woody; Soldier; Me. Ferguson; Richard; Guard
Aloysius Gigl
Mary Canty; Maggie **Sally Wilfert**
Hermit; Grammer; Dresser **Robert Anthony Jones**
Annie **Kathy Brier**

Presented in two parts.

*Closed October 21, 2002
**Closed January 5, 2003

THUNDER KNOCKING ON THE DOOR

Musical with book by Keith Glover; Music and Lyrics by Keb' Mo' and Anderson Edwards; Additional Music and Lyrics by Keith Glover; Producers, Ted Tulchin and Benjamin Mordecai, in association with Mari Nakachi and Robert G. Bartner/Stephanie McClelland; Director, Oskar Eustis; Musical Staging, Luis Perez; Scenery, Eugene Lee; Costumes, Toni-Leslie James; Lighting, Natasha Katz; Sound, Acme Sound Partners; Music Supervision, Linda Twine; Musical Direction, George Caldwell; Arrangements and Orchestrations, Zane Mark, Linda Twine, George Caldwell; Production Stage Manager, Diane DiVita; Press, Barlow-Hartman, Jeremy Shaffer. Opened at the Minetta Lane Theatre, June 20, 2002*

Cast
Good Sister Dupree **Leslie Uggams**
Jaguar Senior; Dregster Dupree **Chuck Cooper**
Marvell Thunder **Peter Jay Fernandez**
Glory Dupree **Marva Hicks**
Jaguar Dupree **Michael McElroy**

Musicians: George Caldwell, keyboard; Billy Thompson, Billy "Spaceman" Patterson, guitar; Toby Williams, drums; Anderson Edwards, bass; Messrs. Cooper and Fernandez, harmonica

Musical Numbers: This House is Built, Believe Me, Big Money, Hold On, Stranger Blues, Hurt Somebody, See Through Me, Way Down on the Inside, I'm Back, I Wish I Knew, Motor Scooter, Even When You Win, Sometimes You Lose, Rainmaker, That Ain't Right (Cuttin' Contest), Take On the Road, Willing to Go, Movin' On

Presented in two parts.

*Closed July 28, 2002

Michael McElroy, Marva Hicks, Leslie Uggams in *Thunder Knocking on the Door*
PHOTO BY JOAN MARCUS

ENDPAPERS

By Thomas McCormack; Producers, Benjamin Mordecai and Griffin Productions; Director, Pamela Berlin; Scenery, Neil Patel; Costumes, Amela Baksic; Lighting, Rui Rita; Sound, Ken Travis; Production Stage Manager, Pamela Edington; Press, Cohn Davis Associates, Helene Davis. Opened at the Variety Arts Theatre, June 23, 2002*

Cast

Griff **Bruce McCarty**
Cora McCarthy **Pippa Pearthree**
Grover Shively **Neil Vipond**
Joshua Maynard **William Cain**
Sara Maynard **Maria Thayer**
Sheila Berne **Shannon Burkett**
Kay Carson **Beth Dixon**
John Hope **Alex Draper**
Ted Giles **Tim Hopper**
Ram Spencer **Gregory Salata**
Peter Long **Oliver Wadsworth**

Presented in two parts.

*Closed October 27, 2002

THE COMEDY OF ERRORS

Revival of the play by William Shakespeare; Adapted by Robert Richmond; Artistic Director, Peter Meineck; Director, Mr. Richmond; Scenery, David Coleman and Owen Collins; Costumes, Lisa Martin Stuart; Lighting, Peter Meineck; Composer and Musical Director, Anthony Cochrane; Press, Pete Sanders Group, Rick Miramontez. Opened at the East 13th Street Theatre, July 11, 2003*; Reopened at the Harold Clurman Theatre, September 3, 2002**

Cast

Egeon; Balthasar; Pinch **Alex Webb**
Solinus, Duke of Ephesus **William Kwapy**
Both Antipholuses **David Caron**
Adriana **Lisa Carter**
Luciana **Mira Kingsley**
Emilia; Nell **Marci Adilman**
Both Dromios **Louis Butelli**

Presented in two parts.

*Closed September 1, 2002
**Closed November 17, 2002

Bruce McCarty, Pippa Pearthree, Neil Vipond in *Endpapers* PHOTO BY JOAN MARCUS

HARLEM SONG

Musical revue by George C. Wolfe; Music by Zane Mark and Daryl Waters; Producers John Schreiber, Margo Lion/Jay Furman, Daryl Roth, Morton Swinsky, Color Mad Inc. and Charles Flateman, in association with Sony Music, Arielle Tepper, Whoopi Goldberg, the Apollo Theater Foundation and Herb Alpert; Director, George C. Wolfe; Choreography, Ken Roberson; Scenery, Riccardo Hernandez; Costumes, Paul Tazewell; Lighting, Jules Fisher and Peggy Eisenhauer; Sound, Acme Sound Partners; Projections, Batwin and Robin Productions; Orchestratrions, Mr. Waters; Arrangements and Music Supervision, Messrs. Mark and Waters; Production Stage Manager, Fred D. Klaisner; Press, Carol R. Fineman, Leslie Baden. Opened at the Apollo Theater, August 6, 2002*

Performed by Rosa Evangelina Arredondo, Renee Monique Brown, Gabriel A. Croom, B.J. Crosby, Rosa Curry, Randy A. Davis, Queen Esther, DeLandis McClam, Sinclair Mitchell, Zoie Morris, DanaShavonne Rainey, Stacey Sargent, David St. Louis, Keith Lamelle Thomas, Charles E. Wallace

Orchestra: Zane Mark, conductor, keyboard; John Gentry Tennyson, associate conductor, keyboard; Benjamin Franklin Brown, bass; Rodney Jones, guitar; Jason Jackson, brass; Bill Easley, Jimmy Cozior, reeds; Brian O. Grice, drums

Musical Numbers: Well Alright Then, Drop Me Off in Harlem, Connie's Inn Kids, Tarzan of Harlem, Shakin' the Africann, For Sale, Drop Me Off in Harlem (Reprise), Take the "A" Train, Doin' the Niggerati Rag, Hungry Blues, Miss Linda Brown, Here You Come With Love, Time Is Winding Up, King Joe, Fable of Rage in the Key of Jive, Dream Deferred, Shake, Tree of Life

Presented without intermission.

*Closed December 29, 2002

Ty Burrell, Catherine Keener, Dallas Roberts in *Burn This* PHOTO BY SUSAN JOHAN

BURN THIS

Revival by Lanford Wilson; Founding Artistic Director, James Houghton; Director, James Houghton; Scenery, Christine Jones; Costumes, Jane Greenwood; Lighting, Pat Collins; Sound, Robert Kaplowitz; Fight Direction, J. Steven White; Music, Loren Toolajian; Casting, Jerry Beaver and Associates; Production Stage Manager, Michael McGoff; Press, the Publicity Office, Bob Fennell, Marc Thibodeau, Candi Adams. Opened at the Union Square Theatre, September 19, 2002*

Cast
Anna **Catherine Keener**
Burton **Ty Burrell**
Larry **Dallas Roberts**
Pale **Edward Norton**

Understudies: Ty Burrell, Dallas Roberts, Edward Norton (Quentin Mare); Catherine Keener (Christa Scott-Reed)

Time: Mid-October and the following three months. Place: New York City. Presented in two parts.

*Closed January 5, 2003; Production hiatus November 10–19, 2002

LITTLE HAM

Musical with book by Dan Owens; Music by Judd Woldin; Lyrics by Richard Engquist and Judd Woldin; Based on the play by Langston Hughes; Producers, Eric Krebs, in association with Ted Snowdon, Martin Hummel, Entitled Entertainment; Director, Eric Riley; Choreography, Leslie Dockery; Scenery, Edward T. Gianfrancesco; Costumes, Bernard Grenier; Lighting, Richard Latta; Sound, Jens Muehlhausen; Orchestrations and Arrangements, Luther Henderson; Additional Orchestrations and Arrangements, Mr. Bunn; Associate Producer, M. Kilburg Reedy; Casting, Jessica Gilburne, Edward Urban; Production Stage Manager, Brenda Arko; Press, Origlio Public Relations, Tony Origlio, Joel Treick, Deena Benz, Richard Hillman, Kip Vanderbilt, Yufen Kung, Amas Musical Theatre; Opened at the John Houseman Theatre, September 26, 2002*

Cast
Clarence **Christopher L. Morgan**
Hamlet Hitchcock Jones **Andre Garner**
Lucille **Cheryl Alexander**
Tiny Lee **Monica L. Patton**
Opal **Joy Styles**
Louie "The Nail" Mahoney **Richard Vida**
Larchmont **D'Ambrose Boyd**
Rushmore **Jerry Gallagher**
Leroy **Lee Summers**
Jimmy **Joe Wilson Jr.**
Mrs. Dobson **Venida Evans**
Sugar Lou Bird **Brenda Braxton**
Amanda **Julia Lema**
Policeman; Bradford **Howard Kaye**

Understudies: Richard Vida, Jerry Gallagher (Howard Kaye); Lee Summers (D'Ambrose Boyd); Andre Garner, Christopher L. Morgan, Joe Wilson Jr., D'Ambrose Boyd, Howard Kaye (Steven Ward); Christopher L. Morgan, Joe Wilson Jr., D'Ambrose Boyd, Howard Kaye, Lee Summers (Donnell Aarone); Monica L. Patton, Julia Lema, Venida Evans, Joy Styles (Daria Hardeman); Brenda Braxton, Joy Styles, Julia Lema, Venida Evans (Stacey Haughton)

Orchestra: David Alan Bunn, musical director, piano; Warren Smith, percussion; Marcus McLaurine, bass; Patience Higgins, reeds; Reggie Pittman, trumpet.

Musical Numbers: I'm Gonna Hit Today, Stick With Me, Kid, No, Get Yourself Some Lovin', That Ain't Right, Cuttin' Out, Room for Improvement, Get Back, Harlem, You're My Girl, Angels, Big Ideas, It's a Helluva Big Job, Wastin' Time, Say Hello to Your Feet

Time: 1936. Place: Harlem. Presented in two parts.

*Closed December 1, 2002

Members of the company of *Little Ham* PHOTO BY CAROL ROSEGG

JOLSON AND COMPANY

Musical with book by Stephen Mo Hanan and Jay Berkow; Music and Lyrics by various artists listed below; Producers, Ric Wanetik and Crimson Productions; Direction and musical staging by Jay Berkow; Scenery, James Morgan; Costumes, Gail Baldoni; Lighting, Annmarie Duggan; Musical Direction, Peter Larson; Production Stage Manager, Scott DelaCruz; Press, Rubenstein Associates Inc., Thomas Chiodo. Opened at the Century Center for the Performing Arts, September 29, 2002*

Performed by Stephen Mo Hanan, Robert Ari, Nancy Anderson

Musical Numbers: Swanee, A Bird in a Gilded Cage, I'm Sitting on Top of the World, The Little Victrola, You Made Me Love You, Where Did Robinson Crusoe Go With Friday on Saturday Night?, California, Here I Come, Sonny Boy, When the Red, Red Robin Comes Bob-Bob-Bobbin' Along, My Mammy, Toot, Toot, Tootsie Goodbye, Hello, Central, Give Me No Man's Land, Rock a Bye Your Baby with a Dixie Melody, April Showers, You Made Me Love You (Reprise)

Presented in two parts.

*Closed December 22, 2002

Nancy Anderson, Stephen Mo Hanan in *Jolson and Company* PHOTO BY RAHAV SEGEV

Siân Phillips in *My Old Lady* PHOTO BY CRAIG SCHWARTZ

MY OLD LADY

By Israel Horovitz; Producers, Richard Frankel, Tom Viertel, Steven Baruch, Marc Routh, Amy Danis/Mark Johannes, Center Theatre Group/Mark Taper Forum/Gordon Davidson; Director, David Esbjornson; Scenery, John Lee Beatty; Costumes, Elizabeth Hope Clancy; Lighting, Peter Kaczorowski; Sound, Jon Gottlieb and Matthew Burton; Music, Peter Golub; Associate Producers, Pamela Cooper, Judith Marinoff, Ira Pittelman; Casting, Jay Binder and Jack Bowdan; Production Stage Manager, John M. Atherlay; Press, Barlow-Hartman, John Barlow, Michael Hartman, Jeremy Shaffer. Opened at the Promenade Theatre, October 3, 2002*

Cast

Mathilde Giffard **Siân Phillips**
Mathias Gold **Peter Friedman**
Chloe Giffard **Jan Maxwell**

Standbys: Sian Phillips (Betty Low); Peter Friedman (Sam Guncler); Jan Maxwell (Rebecca Nelson)

Time: The present. Place: An apartment in Paris. Presented in two parts.

*Closed December 8, 2002

THE EXONERATED

By Jessica Blank and Erik Jensen; Producers, The Culture Project, Dede Harris, Morton Swinsky, Bob Balaban, Allan Buchman, in association with Patrick Blake and David Elliott; Director, Bob Balaban; Scenery, Tom Ontiveros; Costumes, Sara J. Tosetti; Music and Sound, David Robbins; Casting, Eve Battaglia, Nina Pratt, Kim Moarefi; Production Stage Manager, Thomas J. Gates; Press, the Jacksina Company Inc., Judy Jacksina, Shawyonia Pettigrew, Jacquie Phillips. Opened at 45 Bleecker Street, October 10, 2002*

Cast

Delbert Tibbs **Charles Brown**
Male Ensemble #2 **Philip Levy**
Robert Earl Hayes **David Brown Jr.**
David Keaton **Curtis McClarin**
Sunny Jacobs **Jill Clayburgh**
Gary Gauger **Jay O. Sanders**
Kerry Max Cook **Richard Dreyfuss**
Sue Gauger; Sandra **Sara Gilbert**
Male Ensemble #1 **Bruce Kronenberg**
Georgia Hayes; Judge; Paula; Prosecutor **April Yvette Thompson**

Understudies: Charles Brown Jr., Curtis McClarin (Ed Blunt)

Presented without intermission.

*Still playing May 31, 2003

WATER COOLERS

Musical revue by Thomas Michael Allen, Joe Allen, Marya Grandy, David Nehls and E. Andrew Sensenig; Producers, Steven Baruch, Marc Routh, Richard Frankel, Tom Viertel, Pete Herber, Ross Meyerson, Rodger Hess, Ken Gentry at Dmons; Director, William Wesbrooks; Choreography, Timothy Albrecht; Scenery, Michael Schweikardt; Costumes, Jeffrey Johnson Doherty; Lighting, John-Paul Szczepanski; Sound, T. Richard Fitzgerald; Musical Direction and Arrangements, Mr. Nehls and Fiona Santos; Production Stage Manager, Jason Brantman; Press, Barlow-Hartman, John Barlow, Jeremy Shaffer. Opened October 14, 2002*

Cast

Judy **Marya Grandy**
Frank **Peter Brown**
Steve **Adam Mastrelli**
Brooke **Elena Shaddow**
Glen **Kurt Robbins**

Standbys: Marya Grandy, Elena Shaddow (Barbara Helms); Adam Mastrelli, Kurt Robbins, Peter Brown (Mitchell Jarvis)

Musical Numbers: Gather 'Round, Panic Monday, In My Cube, The Paranoia Chorus, PC, The Great Pretender, A Song of Acceptance, And Hold Please, The IT Cowboy, In Windows 2525, Who Will Buy, One Rung Higher, Chat Room, A Love Song, What You Want, Just Another Friday, Many Paths

Presented in two parts.

*Closed December 22, 2002

Elena Shaddow, Adam Mastrelli, Marya Grandy in *Water Coolers* PHOTO BY CAROL ROSEGG

DUDU FISHER: SOMETHING OLD, SOMETHING NEW

Musical revue by Richard Jay-Alexander; Based on Mr. Fisher's life; Producers, Elie Landau, Yeeshas Gross, Donny Epstein, in association with Ergo Entertainment; Director, Mr. Jay-Alexander; Scenery, Michael Brown.

Opened at the Mazer Theatre, October 15, 2002*

Performed by Mr. Fisher with Jason DeBord (piano) and Michael Blanco (bass)

*Closed December 8, 2002

Dudu Fisher in *Dudu Fisher: Something Old, Something New* PHOTO BY CAROL ROSEGG

THE RESISTIBLE RISE OF ARTURO UI

Revival by Bertolt Brecht; Adapted by George Tabori; Founder and Artistic Director, Tony Randall, in association with Complicite; Director, Simon McBurney; Scenery, Robert Innes Hopkins; Costumes, Robert Innes Hopkins and Christina Cunningham; Lighting, Paul Anderson; Sound, Christopher Shutt; Projections, Ruppert Bohle; Executive Producer, Manny Kladitis; Casting, Cindy Tolan; Production Stage Manager, Doug Hosney; Stage Managers, Andrew Neal and Christine Catti; Press, Springer/Chicoine Public Relations, Gary Springer, Susan Chicoine, Ann Guzzi, Joe Trentacosta, Michelle Moretta. Opened National Actors Theatre, October 21, 2002*

Cast

The Barker; Court Physician; Shorty; Bowl **Ajay Naidu**
Goodwill **Sterling K. Brown**
Flake; The Defense Counsel **Billy Crudup**
Gaffles **Robert Stanton**
Caruther; Greenwool **Chris McKinney**
O'Casey; Sheet; Judge **William Sadler**
Butcher; Crocket **John Ventimiglia**
The Actor **Tony Randall**
Mulberry **Jack Willis**
Giuseppe Givola **Steve Buscemi**
Clark **Dominic Chianese**
Arturo Ui **Al Pacino**
A Wounded Woman **Novella Nelson**
Ernesto Roma **Chazz Palminteri**
The Defendant Fish; Young Inna **Lothaire Bluteau**
Old Dogsborough; Ted Ragg; Ignatius Dullfeet **Charles Durning**
Prosecutor **Paul Giamatti**
Young Dogsborough; Pastor **Tom Riis Farrell**
Dockdaisy **Jacqueline McKenzie**
Arturo Ui's Bodyguards **Michael Goldfinger, Matte Osian**
Betty Dullfeet **Linda Emond**
Emanuele Giri **John Goodman**
Reporters; Gunmen; Grocers **Ensemble**

Time: Early 1930s. Place: Chicago, Illinois. Presented in two parts.

*Closed November 10, 2002

Steve Buscemi, Michael Goldfinger, Matte Osian, Tony Randall, Al Pacino in *The Resistible Rise of Arturo Ui* PHOTO BY JOAN MARCUS

Members of the company of *Debbie Does Dallas* PHOTO BY MEGAN MALOY

DEBBIE DOES DALLAS

Musical with book by Erica Schmidt; Music by Andrew Sherman; Additional Music and Lyrics by Tom Kitt and Jonathan Callicutt; Conceived by Susan L. Schwartz; Adapted from the film; Producers, the Araca Group, Jam Theatricals and Waxman Williams Entertainment, by special arrangement with VCX Ltd.; Director, Erica Schmidt; Choreography, Jennifer Cody; Scenery, Christine Jones; Costumes, Juman Malouf; Lighting, Shelly Sabel; Sound, Laura Grace Brown; Music Supervision, Tom Kitt; Associate Producers, Susan L. Schwartz, Clint Bond Jr., Aaron Harnick; Production Stage Manager, Megan Schneid; Press, Boneau/Bryan-Brown, Adrian Bryan-Brown, Jackie Green. Opened at the Jane Street Theatre, October 29, 2002*

Cast

Hardwick; others **Paul Fitzgerald**
Greenfelt; Biddle; Kevin **Del Pentecost**
Lisa **Mary Catherine Garrison**
Debbie **Sherie René Scott**
Tammy **Caitlin Miller**
Rick; Hamilton; Bigtime **Jon Patrick Walker**
Donna **Tricia Paoluccio**
Roberta **Jama Williamson**

*Closed February 15, 2003

ANTIGONE

Revival by Sophocles; Modern Greek translation by Nikos Panayotopoulos; Producers, the National Theater of Greece, in association with ICM Artists, Ltd. and Kritas Productions; Director, Niketi Kontouri; Choreography, Vasso Barboussi; Scenery and Costumes, Yorgos Patsas; Lighting, Lefteris Pavlopoulos; Music, Takis Farazis; Assistant Director, Yiannis Anastassakis; Assistant Choreographer, Nina Alkalae. Opened at City Center, October 30, 2002*

Cast

Antigone **Lydia Koniordou**
Ismene **Maria Katsiadaki**
Creon **Sophoclis Peppas**
Guard **Kostas Triantaphyllopoulos**
Haemon **Nikos Arvanitis**
Tiresias **Kosmas Fondoukis**
Messenger A **Themistoklis Panou**
Eurydice **Miranta Zafiropoulou**
Messenger B **Thodoros Katsafados**

*Closed November 3, 2002

BEWILDERNESS

Revival by Bill Bailey; Producers, WestBeth Entertainment, Islington Entertainment, Jam Theatricals and BBC America Comedy Live; Lighting, Josh Monroe; Sound, Gregory Kostroff; Press, the Jacksina Company Inc., Judy Jacksina, Shawyonia Pettigrew. Opened at the 47th Street Theatre, November 7, 2002*

Performed by Bill Bailey.

Presented in two parts.

*Closed December 29, 2002

Margaret Colin, Chad Allen, Robert Cuccioli in *Temporary Help* PHOTO BY JOAN MARCUS

TEMPORARY HELP

By David Wiltse; Producers, Revelation Theater, in association with Eileen T' Kaye, Director, Leslie L. Smith; Scenery, Troy Hourie; Costumes, Mattie Ullrich; Lighting, Chris Dallos; Sound, David A. Arnold; Production Stage Manager, Jana Llynn; Press, Barlow-Hartman, Michael Hartman, Joe Perrotta. Opened at the Women's Project Theatre, November 17, 2002*

Cast

Faye Streber **Margaret Colin**
Vincent Castelnuovo-Tedesco **Chad Allen**
Karl Streber **Robert Cuccioli**
Ron Stucker **William Prael**

Presented in two parts.

*Closed December 8, 2003

Jon Tenney, Alvin Epstein in *Tuesdays With Morrie* PHOTO BY CAROL ROSEGG

TUESDAYS WITH MORRIE

By Jeffrey Hatcher and Mitch Albom; Based on the book by Mitch Albom; Producers, David S. Singer, Elizabeth Ireland McCann, Joey Parnes, Amy Nederlander and Scott E. Nederlander, Harold Thau, Moira Wilson, ShadowCatcher Entertainment; Director, David Esbjornson; Scenery, Robert Brill; Costumes, Valerie Marcus; Lighting, Brian MacDevitt; Sound, John Kilgore; Casting, Jerry Beaver; Production Stage Manager, Mo Chapman; Press, Barlow-Hartman, Michael Hartman, John Barlow, Jeremy Shaffer. Opened at the Minetta Lane Theatre, November 19, 2002*

Cast

Morrie **Alvin Epstein**
Mitch **Jon Tenney**

Understudies: Alvin Epstein (Yusef Bulos); Jon Tenney (Daniel Cantor)

Presented without intermission.

*Closed February 23, 2003

BARTENDERS

Solo performance by Louis Mustillo; Producers, Louis S. Salamone, Janice Montana, Christopher Wright, Edgewood Productions and Jeff Murray; Director, Janis Powell; Press, the Jacksina Company Inc., Judy Jacksina. Opened at the John Houseman Studio Theatre, November 22, 2002*

Performed by Mr. Mustillo.

*Still playing May 31, 2003

Louis Mustillo in *Bartenders*   PHOTO BY STEFAN HAGEN

Cast
Christopher **Harold Perrineau Jr.**
Bruce **Glenn Fitzgerald**
Robert **Zeljko Ivanek**

Presented in two parts.

*Closed January 12, 2003

Harold Perrineau Jr., Glenn Fitzgerald in *Blue/Orange*   PHOTO BY CAROL ROSEGG

BLUE/ORANGE

By Joe Penhall; Artistic Director, Neil Pepe; Producing Director, Beth Emelson; Director, Neil Pepe; Scenery, Robert Brill; Costumes, Laura Bauer; Lighting, Brian MacDevitt; Sound, Scott Myers; Casting, Bernard Telsey Casting/William Cantler; Dramaturg, Christian Parker; Production Stage Manager, Darcy Stephens; Press, Boneau/Bryan-Brown, Chris Boneau, Susanne Tighe, Adriana Douzos. Opened November 24, 2002*

ADULT ENTERTAINMENT

By Elaine May; Producers, Julian Schlossberg, Roy Furman, Ben Sprecher, Jim Fantaci, Bill Ronnick and Nancy Ellison, Ted Lachowicz, in association with Aaron Levy; Director, Stanley Donen; Scenery, Neil Patel; Costumes, Suzy Benzinger; Lighting, Phil Monat; Sound, T. Richard Fitzgerald; Music, Bryan Louiselle; Associate Producer, Jill Furman; Casting, Stuart Howard, Amy Schecter, Howard Meltzer; Production Stage Manager, Jane Grey, Stage Manager, Marc Schlackman; Press, the Publicity Office, Bob Fennell, Marc Thibodeau, Candi Adams, Michael S. Borowski. Opened at the Variety Arts Theatre, December 11, 2002*

Cast
Guy Akens **Danny Aiello**
Gerry DiMarco **Brandon Demery**
Frosty Moons **Jeannie Berlin**
Jimbo J **Eric Elice**
Vixen Fox **Mary Birdsong**
Heidi-the-Ho **Linda Halaska**

Understudies: Danny Aiello (Alfred Karl); Brandon Demery, Eric Elice (Reese Madigan); Jeannie Berlin, Mary Birdsong, Linda Halaska (Jen Cooper Davis)

Time: The present; a few weeks later. Presented in two parts.

*Closed April 13, 2003

Eric Elice, Mary Birdsong, Linda Halaska, Jeannie Berlin, Danny Aiello in *Adult Entertainment*   PHOTO BY NANCY ELLISON

Tommy Tune: White Tie and Tails

TOMMY TUNE: WHITE TIE AND TAILS

Musical revue featuring the works of Fred Astaire, Peter Allen, Irving Berlin, Cole Porter, George Gershwin and others; Producers, Chase Mishkin, Leonard Soloway, Roy Furman, Julian Schlossberg, in association with James M. Nederlander; Lighting, Natasha Katz; Sound, Peter Fitzgerald; Projections, Wendall K. Harrington; Arrangements, Wally Harper; Orchestrations, Peter Matz, Randall Biagi, Larry Blank, Don Sebesky, Andy Stein; Music Director, Michael Biagi; Press, Pete Sanders Group, Glenna Freedman. Opened at the Little Shubert Theatre, December 18, 2002*

Performed by Tommy Tune with the Manhattan Rhythm Kings, Marc Kessler, Brian Nalepka, Hal Shane.

Musical Numbers: Same Old Song and Dance, Tap Your Troubles Away, Everything Old Is New Again, Puttin' on the Ritz, When I'm 64, I'm My Own Grandpa, Shanghai W, I Can't Be Bothered Now, Fascinatin' Rhythm, It's You, When That Midnight Choo-Choo Leaves for Alabama, Nice Work If You Can Get It, Shall We Dance, They Can't Take That Away From Me, Nowadays/Honey Rag

Musical revue featuring Tommy Tune and others performing well-known musical works.

Presented without intermission.

*Closed January 5, 2003

THE LOVE HUNGRY FARMER

By Des Keogh; Based on the writings of John B. Keane; Artistic Director, Charlotte Moore; Producing Director, Ciaran O'Reilly; Director, Ms. Moore; Costumes, David Toser; Lighting, Sean Farrell; Production Stage Manager, Andrew Theodorou; Press, Barlow-Hartman, Joe Perrotta. Opened at the Irish Repertory Theatre, January 22, 2003*

Performed by Mr. Keogh.

*Closed February 16, 2003

SLEEPING WITH STRAIGHT MEN

By Ronnie Larsen; Producer, Great Scott Productions; Director, Mr. Larsen; Scenery, Scott Aronow; Lighting, Russel Drapkin and Aaron J. Mason; Production Stage Manager, Lauren A. Oliva; Press, KPM Associates, Kevin P. McAnarney, Grant Lindsey. Opened at the Maverick Theatre, February 16, 2003*

Performed by Joanna Keylock, Mink Stole, Paul Tena, Leila Babson, Jared Scott, Hedda Lettuce, Dia Shepardson, Aaron Wimmer.

Presented without intermission.

*Closed March 23, 2003

Jim Norton, Keith Nobbs in *Dublin Carol* PHOTO BY CAROL ROSEGG

DUBLIN CAROL

By Conor McPherson; Artistic Director, Neil Pepe; Producing Director, Beth Emelson; Director, Conor McPherson; Scenery, Walt Spangler; Costumes, Kaye Voyce; Lighting, Tyler Micoleau; Sound, Scott Myers; Production Stage Manager, Darcy Stephens; Press, Boneau/Bryan-Brown, Chris Boneau, Susanne Tighe, Adriana Douzos. Opened at the Atlantic Theater Company, February 20, 2003*

Cast

John **Jim Norton**
Mark **Keith Nobbs**
Mary **Kerry O'Malley**

Presented without intermission.

*Closed April 6, 2003

ONE MILLION BUTTERFLIES

By Stephen Belber; Executive Producer, Casey Childs; Artistic Director, Ciaran Leynse; Director, Tyler Marchant; Scenery, Narelle Sissons; Costumes, Olivera Gajic; Lighting, Jane Cox; Production Stage Manager, Nina Iventosch; Press, Jeffrey Richard. Opened February 24, 2003*

Cast
Mike **Matthew Mabe**

Presented without intermission.

*Closed March 16, 2003

Matthew Mabe in *One Million Butterflies*

John Pankow, Julie White in *Barbra's Wedding* PHOTO BY JOAN MARCUS

SHOWTUNE: THE WORDS AND MUSIC OF JERRY HERMAN

Musical revue by Paul Gilger; Words and Music by Jerry Herman; Producers, Jenny Strome and David Brown; Director and Choreographer, Joey McKneely; Scenery, Klara Zieglerova; Costumes, Tracy Christensen; Lighting, Brian Nason; Sound, Peter Fitzgerald; Musical Arrangements, James Followell; Press, Keith Sherman and Associates, Brett Oberman. Opened at the Theatre at Saint Peter's Church, February 27, 2003*

Performed by Sandy Binion, Paul Harman, Russell Arden Koplin, Thomas Korbee Jr., Karen Murphy, Bobby Peaco, Martin Vidnovic.

Musical Numbers: Shalom, Before the Parade Passes By, Hello, Dolly!, It Only Takes a Moment, It Takes a Woman, Put on Your Sunday Clothes, Ribbons Down My Back, So Long Dearie, Bosom Buddies, If He Walked Into My Life, It's Today, Mame, The Man in the Moon, My Best Girl, Open a New Window, That's How Young I Feel, We Need a Little Christmas, What Do I Do Now?, And I Was Beautiful, Kiss Her Now, I Don't Want to Know, One Person, Big Time, Hundreds of Girls, I Promise You a Happy Ending, I Won't Send Roses, Look What Happened to Mabel, Movies Were Movies, Tap Your Troubles Away, Time Heals Everything, Wherever He Ain't, I'll Be Here Tomorrow, Just Go to the Movies, Nelson, A Little More Mascara, The Best of Times, I Am What I Am, Song on the Sand, With You on My Arm

Presented in two parts.

*Closed April 13, 2002

BARBRA'S WEDDING

By Daniel Stern; Producers, Dodger Stage Holding, Manhattan Theatre Club; Director, David Warren; Scenery, Neil Patel; Costumes, David C. Woolard; Lighting, Jeff Croiter; Sound, Fitz Patton; Fight Direction, Rick Sordelet; Executive Producer, Dodger Management Group; Associate Producer, Lauren Mitchell; Casting, Jay Binder; Production Stage Manager, Scott Allen; Press, Boneau/Bryan-Brown, Adrian Bryan-Brown, Susanne Tighe, Adriana Douzos. Opened at the Westside Theatre, March 5, 2003*

Cast
Jerry Schiff **John Pankow**
Molly Schiff **Julie White**

Understudies: John Pankow (Tony Freeman); Julie White (Deirdre Madigan)

Presented without intermission.

*Closed June 15, 2003

Melissa Feldman, Portia, Liza Colón-Zayas in *Our Lady of 121st Street* PHOTO BY JOAN MARCUS

OUR LADY OF 121ST STREET

By Stephen Adly Guirgis; Producers, John Gould Rubin, Ira Pittelman, Robyn Goodman, Ruth Hendel, Daryl Roth, in association with the LAByrinth Theater Company; Director, Philip Seymour Hoffman; Scenery, Narelle Sissons; Costumes, Mimi O'Donnell; Lighting, James Vermeulen; Sound, Eric DeArmon; Assistant Director, Brian Roff; Associate Producers, Jack Thomas, Michael Filerman; Casting, Bernard Telsey Casting; Production Stage Manager, Monica Moore, Stage Manager, Jacki O'Brien; Press, Barlow-Hartman, John Barlow, Michael Hartman, Wayne Wolfe, Rob Finn. Opened at the Union Square Theatre, March 6, 2003*

Cast

Victor **Richard Petrocelli**
Inez **Portia**
Balthazar **Felix Solis**
Norca **Liza Colón-Zayas**
Rooftop **Ron Cephas Jones**
Edwin **David Zayas**
Father Lux **Mark Hammer**
Pinky **Al Roffe**
Flip **Russell G. Jones**
Marcia **Elizabeth Canavan**
Gail **Scott Hudson**
Sonia **Melissa Feldman**

Presented in two parts.

*Still playing May 31, 2003

TEA AT FIVE

By Matthew Lombardo; Producers, Daryl Roth, David Gersten, Paul Morer, Michael Filerman, Amy Nederlander and Scott E. Nederlander, in association with Hartford Stage; Director, John Tillinger; Scenery, Tony Straiges; Costumes, Jess Goldstein; Lighting, Kevin Adams; Sound, John Gromada; Production Stage Manager, Christine Cani; Press, David Gersten. Opened at the Promenade Theatre, March 9, 2003*

Cast

Katharine Hepburn **Kate Mulgrew**

Presented in two parts.

*Still playing May 31, 2003

Kate Mulgrew in *Tea at Five* PHOTO BY CAROL ROSEGG

FOLEY

By Michael West; Artistic Director, Charlotte Moore; Producing Director, Ciaran O'Reilly, in association with Richard Wakely and the Corn Exchange; Director, Annie Ryan; Costumes, Suzanne Cave; Lighting, Eamon Fox; Music, Vincent Doherty; Production Stage Managers, Colette Morris and John Brophy; Press, Barlow-Hartman. Opened March 13, 2003*

Cast
George Foley **Andrew Bennett**

Presented without intermission.

*Closed April 19, 2003

Andrew Bennett in *Foley* PHOTO BY CAROL ROSEGG

ZANNA, DON'T!

Musical with book, Music and Lyrics by Tim Acito; Additional book and lyrics by Alexander Dinelaris; Producers, Jack M. Dalgleish, in association with Stephanie Joel; Director and Choreographer, Devanand Janki; Scenery and Costumes, Wade Laboissonniere and Tobin Ost; Lighting, Jeff Nellis; Sound, Robert Killenberger; Orchestrations, Arrangements and Musical Supervision, Edward G. Robinson; Associate Producers, Susan R. Hoffman and Lisa Juliano; Production Stage Manager, Jenifer Shenker; Press, Origlio Public Relations, Tony Origlio, Richard Hillman, Philip Carrubba. Opened at the John Houseman Theatre, March 20, 2003*

Cast
Zanna **Jai Rodriguez**
Paige Mike **Enrico Rodriguez**
Roberta **Anika Larsen**
Tank **Robb Sapp**
Buck **Darius Nichols**
Kate **Shelley Thomas**
Candy **Amanda Ryan**
Steve **Jared Zeus**

Musical Numbers: Who's Got Extra Love?, I Think We Got Love, I Ain't Got Time, Ride 'Em, Zanna's Song, Be a Man, Don't Ask, Don't Tell, Fast, I Could Write Books, Don't You Wish We Could Be in Love?, Whatcha Got?, Do You Know What It's Like?, Zanna's Song (Reprise), 'Tis A Far, Far Better Thing I Do/Blow Winds, Straight to Heaven, Someday You Might Love Me, Straight to Heaven (Reprise)

Presented without intermission.

*Still playing May 31, 2003

Jai Rodriguez in *Zanna, Don't!* PHOTO BY JOAN MARCUS

MIDNIGHT'S CHILDREN

By Salman Rushdie, Simon Reade and Tim Supple; Based on Salman Rushdie's novel; President, Lee C. Bollinger, in association with the University of Michigan Musical Society; Director, Tim Supple; Choreography, Scenery, Costumes and Video Direction, Melly Still; Lighting, Bruno Poet; Sound and Video Design, John Leonard; Dramaturg, Simon Reade; Stage Manager, Jondon; Press, Boneau/Bryan-Brown, Adrian Bryan-Brown, Dennis Crowley. Opened at the Apollo Theater, March 24, 2003*

Performed by Ravi Aujla, Antony Bunsee, Pushpinder Chani, Kammy Darweish, Meneka Das, Neil D'Souza, Mala Ghedia, Kulvinder Ghir, Anjali Jay, Alexi Kaye Campbell, Shaheen Khan, Ranjit Krishnamma, Syreeta Kumar, Selva Rasalingam, Tania Rodrigues, Sirine Saba, Kish Sharma, Zubin Varia, Antony Zaki, Sameena Zehra.

Presented in two parts.

*Closed March 30, 2003

Michael W. Howell, Jason Petty in *Lost Highway*

GOLDA'S BALCONY

By William Gibson; Artistic Director, David Fishelson; Managing Director, Sandra Garner; Director, Scott Schwartz; Scenery, Anna Louizos; Costumes, Jess Goldstein; Lighting, Howell Binkley; Music and Sound, Mark Bennett; Projection Design, Batwin and Robin Productions; Dramaturg, Aaron Leichter; Production Stage Manager, Charles M. Turner III; Press, Bradford Louryk. Opened at Manhattan Ensemble Theatre, March 26, 2003*

Cast

Golda Meir **Tovah Feldshuh**

*Closed July 13, 2003

Zubin Varia, Sameena Zehra in *Midnight's Children*   PHOTO BY MANUEL HARLAN

Jason Petty, Stephen G. Anthony, Drew Perkins, Myk Watford in *Lost Highway*
PHOTOS BY AARON EPSTEIN

LOST HIGHWAY

Transfer of the Off-Off-Broadway musical with book by Randal Myler and Mark Harelik; Music and Lyrics based on the work of Mr. Illiams; Producers, Cindy and Jay Gutterman, Kardana-Swinsky Productions Inc., Jerry Hamza, Sony/A TV Music Publishing LLC, in association with Manhattan Ensemble Theater; Director, Randal Myler; Scenery, Beowulf Boriu; Costumes, Robert Blackman; Lighting, Don Damutzer; Sound, Randy Hansen; Musical Direction, Dan Wheetman; Production Stage Manager, Antonia Gianino; Press, Carol R. Fineman, Leslie Baden. Opened at the Little Shubert Theatre, March 26, 2003*

Cast

Hank Williams **Jason Petty**
Jimmy (Burrhead) **Myk Watford**
Tee-Tot **Michael W. Howell**
Leon (Loudmouth) **Drew Perkins**
Waitress **Juliet Smith**
Fred "Pap" Rose **Michael P. Moran**
Mama Lilly **Margaret Bowman**
Audrey Williams **Tertia Lynch**
Hoss **Stephen G. Anthony**
Shag **Russ Wever**

Musical Numbers: This Is the Way I Do, Message to My Mother, Thank God, WPA Blues, Long Gone Lonesome Blues, Settin' the Woods on Fire, Sally Goodin, Honky Tonk Blues, I'm Tellin' You, I Can't Help It (If I'm Still in Love With You), I'm So Lonesome I Could Cry, Jambalaya (On the Bayou), Move It on Over, Mind Your Own Business, Lovesick Blues, The Blood Done Sign My Name, Happy Rovin' Cowboy, I'm Gonna Sing, Sing, Sing, Long Gone Lonesome Blues (Reprise), Way Downtown, I'm So Lonesome I Could Cry (Reprise), I'm a Run to the City of Refuge/A House of Gold, Hey, Good Lookin', I Saw the Light, Lost Highway, Your Cheatin' Heart, I Saw the Light (Reprise)

Presented in two parts.

*Still playing May 31, 2003

Kathleen Chalfant in *Talking Heads*

THE JACKIE WILSON STORY

Musical revue by Jackie Taylor; Based on the work of Jackie Wilson with additional songs by Jackie Taylor; Producers, Jackie Taylor and Brian Kabatznick, in association with the Black Ensemble Touring Company; Director, Jackie Taylor; Musical Arrangements, George Paco Patterson; Musical Direction, Jimmy Tillman and Rick Hall; Associate Producer, Douglas Gray; Production Stage Manager, Ore Robinson; Press, Carol R. Fineman, Leslie Baden. Opened at Apollo Theater, April 6, 2003*

Cast

Jackie Wilson **Chester Gregory II**
Eliza **Melba Moore**
BB **Rueben D. Echoles**
Freda **Katrina Tate**
Roquel "Billy" Davis **Mark D. Hayes**
Carl Davis **Robert L. Thomas**
Father; William Davis **Elfeigo N. Goodun III**
Shaker; Sam Cooke; Clyde McPhatter **Lyle Miller**
Shaker; Billy Ward; Reporter **Tony Duwon**
Etta James; Harlene **Valarie Tekosky**
LaVern Baker; Barbara Acklin **Eva D.**

Musical Numbers: My Heart Is Crying, I Am the Man, We Are the Shakers, I Ain't Had Your Woman, When The Sun Refused to Shine, You Can't Keep a Good Man Down: Little-Bitty Pretty One, Move to the Outskirts of Town, Tweedle Dee, Reet Petite, I Can't Help It, That's Why I Love You So, To Be Loved: Tennessee Waltz, Something's Got a Hold on Me, Lonely Teardrops, Shake, Shake, Shake, Doggin' Me Around, A Woman, A Lover, A Friend, Oh, Danny Boy, Whispers (Getting Louder), The Closer I Get, (Your Love Keeps Lifting Me) Higher and Higher, To Be Loved (Reprise), Baby Workout, Nightshift, Higher and Higher (Reprise)

Presented in two parts.

*Closed April 27, 2003

TALKING HEADS

By Alan Bennett; Producers, Tom Hulce and Julia Rask, Ron Kastner, Daryl Roth, Cheryl Wiesenfeld, Margaret Cotter, Amy Nederlander, Scott E. Nederlander, by special arrangement with Roundabout Theatre Company; Director, Michael Engler; Scenery, Rachel Hauck; Costumes, Candice Donnelly; Lighting, Chris Parry; Music and Sound, Michael Roth; Projections, Wendall K. Harrington; Associate Producers, Jerry Meyer, Joseph Smith; Casting, Jim Carnahan; Production Stage Manager, Martha Donaldson; Press, Barlow-Hartman, John Barlow, Michael Hartman, Bill Coyle. Opened at the Minetta Lane Theatre, April 6, 2003*

Cast

MISS FOZZARD FINDS HER FEET
Miss Fozzard **Lynn Redgrave**
WAITING FOR THE TELEGRAM
Violet **Frances Sternhagen**
THE HAND OF GOD
Celia **Brenda Wehle**
BED AMONG THE LENTILS
Susan **Kathleen Chalfant**
A CHIP IN THE SUGAR
Graham **Daniel Davis**
A LADY OF LETTERS
Miss Ruddock **Christine Ebersole**
HER BIG CHANCE
Lesley **Valerie Mahaffey**

Presented in two parts.

*Still playing May 31, 2003

Lynn Redgrave in *Talking Heads* PHOTOS BY CAROL ROSEGG

THE LAST SUNDAY IN JUNE

Transfer of the Off-Off-Broadway play by Jonathan Tolins; Producer, Ted Snowdon, in association with Rattlestick Theatre; Director, Trip Cullman; Scenery, Takeshi Kata; Costumes, Alejo Vietti; Lighting, Paul Whitaker; Sound, Jeffrey Yoshi Lee; Production Stage Manager, Lori Ann Zepp; Press, Origlio Public Relations, Tony Origlio. Opened at the Century Center for the Performing Arts, April 9, 2003*

Cast

Brad **Arnie Burton**
James **Mark Setlock**
Charles **Donald Corren**
Tom **Peter Smith**
Michael **Johnathan F. McClain**
Joe **David Turner**
Susan **Susan Pourfar**
Scott **Matthew Wilkas**

*Still playing May 31, 2003

Arnie Burton, Matthew Wilkas, Johnathan F. McClain, Donald Corren, Peter Smith, David Turner in *The Last Sunday in June* PHOTOS BY ROBERT CAREY

BROAD CHANNEL

By Anna Theresa Cascio and Doc Dougherty; Producer, Helen Maier; Director, Molly Fowler; Scenery, Michelle Malavet; Lighting, Greg MacPherson; Sound, Elizabeth Rhodes; Press, Boneau/Bryan-Brown, Chris Boneau, Juliana Hannett. Opened at the Phil Bosakowski Theatre, April 13, 2003*

Performed by Doc Dougherty.

Presented without intermission.

*Closed May 4, 2003

MARY TODD . . . A WOMAN APART

By Carl Wallnau; Producer, Centenary Stage Company; Director, Carl Wallnau; Scenery, Gordon Danielli; Costumes, Brenda Lightcap; Lighting, Ed Matthews; Sound, Joseph Langham. Opened at the Samuel Beckett Theatre, April 29, 2003*

Performed by Colleen Smith Wallnau.

*Closed May 17, 2003

DOWN A LONG ROAD

By David Marquis; Producer, Long Road Productions; Director, Doug Jackson; Choreography, Deanna Deck; Costumes, Giva Taylor; Lighting, Linda Blase; Musical Direction, Mr. Mohmed; Press, KPM Associates, Kevin P. McAnarney, Grant Lindsey. Opened at the Lamb's Theatre, May 14, 2003*

Performed by Mr. Marquis.

Musicians: Buddy Mohmed guitar, bass; Gale Hess violin; Kenny Grimes percussion.

Presented without intermission.

*May 18, 2003

Susan Pourfar, David Turner, Donald Corren, Arnie Burton in *The Last Sunday in June*

Skipp Sudduth, Paul Reiser in *Writer's Block* PHOTO BY CAROL ROSEGG

WRITER'S BLOCK

By Woody Allen; Artistic Director, Neil Pepe; Producing Director, Beth Emelson, in association with Letty Aronson; Director, Woody Allen; Scenery, Santo Loquasto; Costumes, Laura Bauer; Lighting, James F. Ingalls; Sound, Scott Myers; Casting, Bernard Telsey Casting/William Cander; Production Stage Manager, Janet Takami; Press, Boneau/Bryan-Brown, Chris Boneau, Susanne Tighe, Joe Perrotta. Opened at Atlantic Theater Company, May 15, 2003*

Cast
RIVERSIDE DRIVE
Jim **Paul Reiser**
Fred **Skipp Sudduth**
Barbara **Kate Blumberg**
OLD SAYBROOK
Sheila **Bebe Neuwirth**
Norman **Jay Thomas**
Jenny **Heather Burns**
David **Grant Shaud**
Hal **Christopher Evan Welch**
Sandy **Clea Lewis**
Max **Richard Portnow**

Presented in two parts.

*Still playing May 31, 2003

BOOBS! THE MUSICAL (THE WORLD ACCORDING TO RUTH WALLIS)

Musical revue with book by Steve Mackes and Michael Whaley; Music and Lyrics by Ruth Wallis; Producers, SRU Productions LLC, Lawrence Leritz and Michael Whaley; Director, Donna Drake; Choreography, Lawrence Leritz; Costumes, Robert Pease and J. Kevin Draves. Opened at the Triad Theater, May 19, 2003*

Performed by Kristy Cates, Robert Hunt, Max Perlman, J. Brandon Savage, Jenny-Lynn Suckling, Rebecca Young.

*Still playing May 31, 2003

Rebecca Young, Robert Hunt in *Boobs! The Musical (the world according to Ruth Wallis)* PHOTO BY CAROL ROSEGG

Productions from past seasons that **played through this season**

De La Guarda: Villa Villa

DE LA GUARDA: VILLA VILLA

Created/Directed by Pichon Baldinu and Diqui James; Music/Musical Director, Gabriel Kerpel; Presented by Kevin McCollum, Jeffrey Seller, David Binder, Daryl Roth; Press, Richard Kornberg/Don Summa. Opened in the Daryl Roth Theatre on Tuesday, June 9, 1998*

Cast
Valerie Alonso
Pichon Baldinu
Gabriela Barberio
Martin Bauer
Mayra Bonard
Carlos Casella
Fabio D'Aquila
Julieta Dentone
Rafael Ferro
Ana Frenkel
Alejandro Garcia
Diqui James
Tomas James
Gabriel Kerpel
Maria Ucedo

Performance art presented (in an old bank) without intermission. "Villa Villa" translates roughly, as "by the seat of your pants."

*Still playing May 31, 2003.

THE DONKEY SHOW

Created/Directed by Diane Paulus and Randy Weiner; Conception, Mr. Weiner; Set, Scott Pask; Costumes, David C. Woolard; Lighting, Kevin Adams; Sound, Brett Jarvis; Specialty Dances, Maria Torres; Stage Manager, Jim Atens; Press, Karpel Group/Bridget Klapinski, Brian Carmody; Judy Jacksina/Aryn DeKaye, Molly Shaffer; Presented by Jordan Roth. Opened August 10, 1999, at Club El Flamingo*

Cast
Oberon, club owner **Rachel Benbow Murdy**
Tytania, disco-diva girlfriend **Anna Wilson**
Rollerena, Puck on Roller Skates **Roman Pietrs**
Helen, in love with Dimitri **Jordin Ruderman**
Dimitri, in love with Mia **Emily Hellstrom**
Mia, beloved of Sander **Rachel Benbow Murdy**
Sander, beloved of Mia **Anna Wilson**
Vinnie 1, a rude mechanical **Jordin Ruderman**
Vinnie 2, a rude mechanical **Emily Hellstrom**
Mustard Seed, Tytania's Fairy **Oscar Estevez**
Cob Web, Tytania's Fairy **Luke Miller**
Moth, Tytania's Fairy **Dan Cryer**
Peasebottom, Tytania's Fairy **Quinn**
Rico Suave, bouncer **Orlando Santana**
Disco Lady **Barbara Resstab**
DJ Hernando Pacheski **Kevin Shand**

Musical Numbers: A Fifth of Beethoven, Also Sprach Zarathustra, Car Wash, Dance with Me, Disco Circus, Don't Leave Me This Way, I Love the Nightlife, Never Knew Love Like This Before, I'm Your Boogie Man, Knock on Wood, Ring My Bell, Salsation, That's the Way of the World, You Sexy Thing, We Are Family

A disco adaptation of Shakespeare's *A Midsummer Night's Dream* performed in a dance club.

*Still playing May 31, 2003.

FORBIDDEN BROADWAY: 20TH ANNIVERSARY CELEBRATION

Created/Written/Directed by Gerard Alessandrini; Co-director, Philip George; Costumes, Alvin Colt; Set, Bradley Kaye; Musical Director/Pianist, Brad Ellis; Choreographer, Philip George; Consultant, Pete Blue; General Manager, Jay Kingwell; Stage Manager, Jim Griffith; Cast Recordings, DRG; Presented by John Freedson, Harriet Yellin, Jon B. Platt; Press, Pete Sanders/Glenna Freedman. Opened at the Douglas Fairbanks Theatre February 7, 2002*

Cast
Donna English
Michael West
Ben Evans
Valerie Fagan

Current program includes: Selections from Mamma Mia!, The Producers, Aida, The Lion King, Chicago, Les Misérables

Performed in two acts. The twentieth anniversary edition of the long-running revue which first

Premiered in 1982.

*Still playing May 31, 2003

I LOVE YOU, YOU'RE PERFECT, NOW CHANGE

Music/Arrangements, Jimmy Roberts; Lyrics/Book, Joe Dipietro; Director, Joel Bishoff; Musical Director, Tom Fay; Set, Neil Peter Jampolis; Costumes, Candice Donnelly; Lighting, Mary Louise Geiger; Sound, Duncan Edwards; Cast Recording, Varese Sarabande; Production Supervisor, Matthew G. Marholin; Stage Manager, William H. Lang; Presented by James Hammerstein, Bernie Kukoff, Jonathan Pollard; Press, Bill Evans/Jim Randolph; Previewed from July 15, 1996. Opened in the Westside Theatre/Upstairs on Friday, August 1, 1996*

Cast
Andrea Chamberlain
Jordan Leeds
Kevin Pariseau
Cheryl Stern
Succeeding Cast: Lori Hammel, Andrea Chamberlain, Amanda Watkins, Karyn Quackenbush, Marissa Burgoyne, Sandy Rustin, Mylinda Hull, Melissa Weil, Evy O'Rourke, Marylee Graffeo, Cheryl Stern, Janet Metz, Anne Bobby, Bob Walton, Adam Hunter, Sean Arbuckle, Frank Baiocchi, Colin Stokes, Evy O'Rourke, Danny Burstein, Adam Grupper, Gary Imhoff, Darrin Baker

Swings: Ray Roderick, Karyn Quackenbush

Erin Leigh Peck, Cheryl Stern, Jordan Leeds, Kevin Pariseau in *I Love You, You're Perfect, Now Change* PHOTO BY CAROL ROSEGG

Musical Numbers: Cantata for a First Date, Stud and a Babe, Single Man Drought, Why Cause I'm a Guy, Tear Jerk, I Will Be Loved Tonight, Hey There Single Guy/Gal, He Called Me, Wedding Vows, Always a Bridesmaid, Baby Song, Marriage Tango, On the Highway of Love, Waiting Trio, Shouldn't I Be Less in Love with You?, I Can Live with That, I Love You You're Perfect Now Change

A two-act musical revue for hopeful heterosexuals. On January 7, 2001, the production played its 1,848th performance and became the longest running musical revue in Off-Broadway history (besting *Jacques Brel Is Alive and Well and Living in Paris*).

*Still playing May 31, 2003.

MENOPAUSE: THE MUSICAL

Book and Lyrics by Jeanie Linders; Director, Kathleen Lindsey; Sets, Jesse Poleshuck; Lighting, Michael Gilliam; Costumes, Martha Bromelmeier; Sound, Johnna Doty; Musical Direction, Corinne Aquilina; Choreographer, Patty Bender; Production Stage Manager, Christine Catti; Producers, Mark Schwartz and TOC Productions; in association with Brent Peek; Press, Shirley Herz Associates. Opened at Theatre Four on April 4, 2002*

Carolanne Page, Lynn Eldredge, Joy Lynn Matthews, Sally Ann Swarm in *Menopause: The Musical* PHOTO BY CAROL ROSEGG

Cast

Power Woman **Joy Lynn Matthews**
Soap Star **Mary Jo McConnell** †1
Earth Mother **Joyce A. Presutti** †2
Iowa Housewife **Carolann Page**

Understudies: Marnee Hollis, Sally Ann Swarm

Orchestra: Corinne Aquilina, piano, keyboard; Diana Herald, drums; Audrey Terry, bass guitar

A musical presented without intermission. The action takes place in Bloomingdale's department store, in the present.

*Still playing May 31, 2003
†Succeeded by: 1. Sally Ann Swarm 2. Lynn Eldredge

NAKED BOYS SINGING!

By Stephen Bates, Marie Cain, Perry Hart, Shelly Markham, Jim Morgan, David Pevsner, Rayme Sciaroni, Mark Savage, Ben Schaechter, Robert Schrock, Trance Thompson, Bruce Vilanch, Mark Winkler; Conceived/Directed by Robert Schrock; Choreography, Jeffry Denman; Musical Direction/Arrangements, Stephen Bates; Set/Costumes, Carl D. White; Lighting, Aaron Copp; Stage Manager, Christine Catti; Presented by Jamie Cesa, Carl D. White, Hugh Hayes, Tom Smedes, Jennifer Dumas; Press, Peter Cromarty; Previewed from Friday, July 2, 1999. Opened in the Actors' Playhouse on Thursday, July 22, 1999*

Cast

Glenn Allen †1
Jonathan Brody †2
Tim Burke †3
Tom Gualtieri
Patrick Herwood
Daniel C. Levine †4
Sean McNally †5
Adam Michaels †6
Trance Thompson †7

The Company of *Naked Boys Singing!* PHOTO BY JOAN MARCUS

James Farrell, Catherine Russell in *Perfect Crime* PHOTO BY JOE BLY

Musical Numbers: Gratuitous Nudity, Naked Maid, Bliss, Window to Window, Fight the Urge, Robert Mitchum, Jack's Song, Members Only, Perky Little Porn Star, Kris Look What You've Missed, Muscle Addiction, Nothin' but the Radio on, The Entertainer, Window to the Soul, Finale/Naked Boys Singing!

A musical revue in two acts.

*Still playing May 31, 2003.
†Succeeded by: 1. Trevor Richardson, Eric Dean Davis 2. Richard Lear, Steve Sparagen 3. Kristopher Kelly 4. George Livengood 5. Luis Villabon 6. Glenn Allen, Patrick Herwood 7. Dennis Stowe, Ralph Cole Jr., Stephan Alexander, Eric Potter

PERFECT CRIME

By Warren Manzi; Director, Jeffrey Hyatt; Set, Jay Stone, Mr. Manzi; Costumes, Nancy Bush; Lighting, Jeff Fontaine; Sound, David Lawson; Stage Manager, Julia Murphy; Presented by The Actors Collective in association with the Methuen Company; Press, Debenham Smythe/Michelle Vincents, Paul Lewis, Jeffrey Clarke. Opened in the Courtyard Playhouse on April 18, 1987*

Cast

Margaret Thorne Brent **Catherine Russell**
Inspector James Ascher **Michael Minor**
W. Harrison Brent **Don Leslie** †1
Lionel McAuley **Chris Lutkin** †2
David Breuer **Patrick Robustelli**

Understudies: Lauren Lovett (Females); J.R. Robinson (Males)

A mystery in two acts. The action takes place in Windsor Locks, Connecticut.

*Still playing May 31, 2003. After opening at the Courtyard Playhouse, the production transferred to the Second Stage, 47th St. Playhouse, Intar 53 Theater, Harold Clurman Theatre, Theatre Four, and currently, The Duffy Theatre.
†Succeeded by: 1. Peter Ratray 2. Brian Hotaling

STOMP

Created/Directed by Luke Cresswell and Steve McNicholas; Lighting, Mr. McNicholas, Neil Tiplady; Production Manager, Pete Donno; General Management, Richard Frankel/Marc Routh; Presented by Columbia Artists Management, Harriet Newman Leve, James D. Stren, Morton Wolkowitz, Schuster/Maxwell, Galin/Sandler, and Markley/Manocherian; Press, Chris Boneau/Adrian Bryan-Brown, Jackie Green, Bob Fennell; Previewed from Friday, February 18, 1994. Opened in the Orpheum Theatre on Sunday, February 27, 1994*

Cast
Taro Alexander
Morris Anthony
Maria Emilia Breyer
Marivaldo Dos Santos
Mindy Haywood
Raquel Horsford
Stephanie Marshall
Keith Middleton
Jason Mills
Mikel Paris
Raymond Poitier
Ray Rodriguez Rosa
R.J. Samson
Henry W. Shead Jr.
Mario Torres
Davi Vieira
Sheilynn Wactor
Fiona Wilkes

An evening of percussive performance art. The ensemble uses everything but conventional percussion to make rhythm and dance.

*Still playing May 31, 2003.

TUBES

Created and Written by Matt Goldman, Phil Stanton, Chris Wink; Director, Marlene Swartz and Blue Man Group; Artistic Coordinator, Caryl Glaab; Artistic/Musical Collaborators, Larry Heinemann, Ian Pai; Set, Kevin Joseph Roach; Costumes, Lydia Tanji, Patricia Murphy; Lighting, Brian Aldous, Matthew McCarthy; Sound, Raymond Schilke, Jon Weston; Computer Graphics, Kurisu-Chan; Stage Manager, Lori J. Weaver; Presented by Blue Man Group; Press, Manuel Igrejas. Opened at the Astor Place Theatre on Thursday, November 7, 1991*

Blue Man Casts
Chris Bowen
Michael Cates
Wes Day
Jeffrey Doornbos
Gen. Fermon Judd Jr.
Matt Goldman
John Grady
Randall Jaynes
Pete Simpson
Phil Stanton
Pete Starrett
Steve White
Chris Wink

An evening of performance art presented without intermission.

*Still playing May 31, 2003.

Tubes PHOTO BY MARTHA SWOPE

Productions from past seasons that **closed during this season**

BOYS AND GIRLS
Left: Robert Sella, Malcolm Gets
16 performances
Opened May 28, 2002
Closed June 9, 2002
PHOTO BY JOAN MARCUS

CAPITOL STEPS: WHEN BUSH COMES TO SHOVE
124 performances
Opened May 16, 2002
Closed August 31, 2002

THE CARPETBAGGER'S CHILDREN
Left: Jean Stapleton
112 performances
Opened March 25, 2002
Closed June 30, 2002
PHOTO BY T. CHARLES ERICKSON

CRISS ANGEL: MINDFREAK
600 performances
Opened December 13, 2001
Closed January 6, 2003

THE GODFADDA WORKOUT
Below: Seth Isler
80 performances
Opened March 25, 2002
Closed June 2, 2002

PHOTO BY JOAN MARCUS

HOUSE AND GARDEN
Nicholas Woodeson, Veanne Cox
80 performances
Opened May 21, 2002
Closed July 28, 2002

LATE NIGHT CATECHISM
Left: Patti Hannon
1,268 performances
Opened October 3, 1996
Closed May 18, 2003
PHOTO BY CAROL ROSEGG

LOVE, JANIS
Below: Andra Mitrovich and band
713 performances
Opened April 22, 2001
Closed January 5, 2003

MR. GOLDWYN
Lauren Klein, Alan King
104 performances
Opened March 12, 2002
Closed June 9, 2002
PHOTO BY CAROL ROSEGG

THE ODYSSEY (not pictured)
33 performances
Opened May 5, 2002
Closed June 2, 2002

ONE SHOT, ONE KILL (not pictured)
40 performances
Opened May 20, 2002
Closed June 23, 2002

OUR SINATRA
Left: Eric Comstock, Hilary Kole, Christopher Gines
1,096 performances
Opened December 19, 1999
Closed July 28, 2002
PHOTO BY JAMES J. KIEGSMANN

PUPPETRY OF THE PENIS
Below: Simon Morley, David Friend
452 performances
Opened October 5, 2001
Closed November 3, 2002

RED HOT MAMA
Left: Sharon McKnight
91 performances
Opened May 8, 2002
Closed August 4, 2002
PHOTO BY LARRY LAZLO COMEDIA

RICKY JAY ON THE STEM (not pictured)
81 performances
Opened May 2, 2002; Closed June 9, 2003
Opened June 18, 2003; Closed July 14, 2003
Opened September 17, 2003; Closed October 20, 2003

SURVIVING GRACE (not pictured)
112 performances
Opened March 12, 2002
Closed June 16, 2002

THE SYRINGA TREE
Right: Pamela Gien
586 performances
Opened September 14, 2000
Closed June 2, 2002

PHOTO BY MICHAEL LAMONT

TONY 'N' TINA'S WEDDING
4,914 performances
Opened February 6, 1988
Closed May 18, 2003

21 DOG YEARS: DOIN' TIME @AMAZON.COM
Right: Mike Daisey
127 performances
Opened May 9, 2002
Closed August 31, 2002

UNDERNEATH THE LINTEL
Left: T. Ryder Smith
400 performances
Opened October 23, 2001
Closed January 5, 2003
PHOTO BY GILLES DECAMPS

THE VAGINA MONOLOGUES
Right: Eve Ensler
1,381 performances
Opened October 3, 1999
Closed January 26, 2003
PHOTO BY JOAN MARCUS

VIENNA: LUSTHAUS (REVISITED) (not pictured)
111 performances
Opened May 8, 2002
Closed August 11, 2002

Company Series

BROOKLYN ACADEMY OF MUSIC

FOUNDED IN 1861

Chairman of the Board, Bruce C. Ratner; President, Karen Brooks Hopkins; Executive Producer, Joseph V. Melillo

MARIA STUART In association with the Royal Dramatic Theatre of Sweden; Revival by Friedrich von Schiller; English translation by Michael Feingold; Swedish translation by Britt G. Hallqvist; Director, Ingmar Bergman; Choreography, Donya Feuer; Scenery, Goran Wassberg; Costumes, Charles Koroly; Lighting, Hans Akesson; Music, Daniel Bortz; press, Sandy Sawotka, Melissa Cusick, Fateema Jones, Tamara McCaw, Kila Packett Cast: Maria Stuart (Pernilla August), Lena Endre (Elizabeth), Gunnel Lindblom (Hanna Kennedy), Mikael Persbrandt (Lord Leicester), Borje Ahlstedt (Lord Burleigh), Per Myrberg (Lord Talbot), Ingvar Kjellson (Lord Paulet), Erland Josephson (Melvil), Stefan Larsson (Mortimer)

Presented in two parts; Howard Gilman Opera House; June 12–16, 2002; 5 performances

UNCLE VANYA Revival by Anton Chekhov; A presentation of a Donmar Warehouse production; Adapted by Brian Friel; Director, Sam Mendes; Scenery, Anthony Ward; Costumes, Mark Thompson; Lighting, Hugh Vanstone, David Holmes; Sound, Paul Arditti; Music, George Stiles; Musical Director, Ms. Humphris; Assistant Director, Aria O'Loughlin; Casting, Anne McNulty; stage manager, Marian Spon; Press, Sandy Sawotka, Melissa Cusick, Fatima Kafele, Tamara McCaw, Kila Packett Cast: David Bradley (Alexander Serebryakov), Anthony O'Donnell (Illya Telegin), Selina Cadell (Marya Voynitsky), Simon Russell Beale (Vanya), Luke Jardine (Yefim), Gyuri Sarossy (Petrushka), Helen McCrory (Yelena), Mark Strong (Mikhail Astrav), Cherry Morris (Marina), Emily Watson (Sonya); Orchestra: Caroline Humphris, piano; Peter Sachon, cello; Frederic Hand, guitar

Time: Late 1800s; summer and early September. Place: The Serebryakov Estate. Presented in two parts; Harvey Theater; January 17–March 9, 2003; 25 performances

TWELFTH NIGHT Revival by William Shakespeare; A presentation of a Donmar Warehouse production; Director, Sam Mendes; Scenery, Anthony Ward; Costumes, Mark Thompson; Lighting, Hugh Vanstone, David Holmes; Sound, Paul Arditti; Music, George Stiles; Musical Director, Ms. Humphris; Assistant Director, Orla O'Loughlin; Casting, Anne McNulty; Stage Manager, Marian Spon; Press, Sandy Sawotka, Melissa Cusick, Fatima Kafele, Tamara McCaw, Kila Packett Cast: David Bradley (Sir Andrew Aguecheek), Anthony O'Donnell (Feste), Selina Cadell (Maria), Gary Powell (Antonio), Luke Jardine (Fabian), Simon Russell Beale (Malvolio), BelchPaul Jesson (Sir Toby), Gyuri Sarossy (Sebastian), Helen McCrory (Olivia), Mark Strong (Orsino), Cherry Morris (Lady), Emily Watson (Viola)

Presented in two parts; Harvey Theater; January 18–March 8, 2003; 30 performances

HASHIRIGAKI Music-theater piece with book by Gertrude Stein; Music by Brian Wilson; Additional Music by Heiner Goebbels; Based on Ms. Stein's *The Making of Americans* and Mr. Wilson's *Pet Sounds*; Director, Mr. Goebbels; Scenery and Lighting, Klaus Grunberg; Costumes, Florence von Gerkan; Sound, Willi Bopp; Press, Sandy Sawotka, Melissa Cusick, Fatima Kafele, Tamara McCaw, Kila Packett Cast: Charlotte Engelkes, Marie Goyette, Yumiko Tanaka

Presented without intermission; The Harvey Theater; March 19–23, 2003; 5 performances

THE ISLAND Revival of the play by Athol Fugard, John Kani and Winston Ntshona; A Royal National Theatre and the Market Theatre of Johannesburg production; Director, Athol Fugard; Lighting, Mannie Manim; Press, Sandy Sawotka, Melissa Cusick, Fatima Kafele, Tamara McCaw, Kila Packett Cast: John Kani, Winston Ntshona

Presented without intermission; Harvey Theater; April 1–13, 2003; 13 performances

CITY CENTER ENCORES!

TENTH SEASON

President and Executive Director, Judith E. Daykin; Artistic Director, Jack Viertel

HOUSE OF FLOWERS Concert version of the musical with book by Truman Capote; Music by Harold Arlen; Lyrics by Mr. Arlen and Mr. Capote; Musical Director, Rob Fisher; Director in Residence, Kathleen Marshall; Director and choreographer Kathleen Marshall; Scenery, John Lee Beatty; Costumes, Toni-Leslie James; Lighting, Peter Kaczorowski, Sound, Bruce Cameron; Orchestrations, Jonathan Tunick; Concert Adaptation, Kirsten Childs; Music Coordinator, Seymour Red Press; Guest Musical Director, David Chase; Associate Choreographer, Vince Pesce; Casting, Jay Binder; Production Stage Manager, Beverley Randolph; Press, Rubenstein Associates Inc. Cast: Tonya Pinkins, Armelia McQueen, Maurice Hines, Roscoe Lee Browne, Nikki M. James, Brandon Victor Dixon, Brenda Braxton, Stacy Francis, Alexandra Foucard, Peter Francis James, Desmond Richardson, Wayne W. Pretlow, Everett Bradley Ensemble: Sondra M. Bonitto, Lloyd Culbreath, Duane Martin Foster, Darren Gibson, Amy Hall, Francesca Harper, Derric Harris, Danielle Jolie, C. Mingo Long, Monique Midgette, Mayumi Miguel, Maia A. Moss, Herman Payne, Solange Sandy, Laurie Williamson, Michael-Leon Wooley. February 13–16, 2003; 5 performances

THE NEW MOON Concert Version of Musical with Book and Lyrics by Oscar Hammerstein II, Frank Mandel and Laurence Schwab; Music by Sigmund Romberg; Musical Director, Rob Fisher; Director in Residence, Kathleen Marshall; Director, Gary Griffin; Choreography, Daniel Pelzig; Scenery, John Lee Beatty; Costumes, Michael Krass; Lighting, Ken Billington; Sound, Scott Lehrer; Orchestrations, Emil Gerstenberger, Alfred Goodman, Hans Spialek; Musical Director, Mr. Fisher; Concert Adaptation, David Ives; Musical Coordinator, Mr. Red Press; Associate Music Director and Choral Preparation, Ben Whiteley; Casting, Jay Binder/Laura Stanczyk; Production Stage Manager, Karen Moore; Press, Rubenstein Associates Inc. Cast: Lauren Ward (Julie), Christiane Noll (Marianne Beaunoir), Simon Jones (Monsieur Beaunoir), David Masenheimer (Fouchette), Ravil Atlas (Butler), John Wilkerson (Doorkeeper), Burke Moses (Captain George Duval), Brandon Jovanovich (Philippe L'Entendu), F. Murray Abraham (Le Vicomte Ribaud), Anne Allgood (Girl), Rodney Gilfry (Robert Mission), Mary Ann Lamb (Rosita), Peter Benson (Alexander), Jason Mills (Innkeeper), Danny Rutigliano (Besac), Alix Korey (Clotilde Lombaste), Alex Sanchez (Jaques), Simon Jones (Admiral de Jean); Ensemble: Anne Allgood, Ravil Atlas, Christopher Eaton Bailey, Tony Capone, Marie Danvers, Colm Fitzmaurice, Ann Kittredge, David Masenheimer, Jason Mills, Morgan Moody, Karyn Overstreet, Devin Richards, Vale Rideout, Rebecca Robbins, Margaret Shafer, Rebecca Spencer, Susan Wheeler, John Wilkerson; Chorus: Jennifer Chase, Julie Cox, Alexandra de Suze, Cherry Duke, Sherrita Duran, David Gagnon, Cara Johnston, Daniel Judge, Sara Lerch, Kenneth Overton, John Pickle, Douglas Purcell, Katherine Schmidt, Sam Smith, Keith Spencer, J.D. Webster; Orchestra: Rob Fisher, conductor; Suzanne Ornstein, concertmistress, violin; Belinda Whitney, Mineko Yajima, Katherine Livolsi-Stern, Kristina Musser, Eric DeGioia, Robert Zubrycki, Lisa Matricardi, Laura Seaton, Mia Wu, Susan Shumway, violin; Jill Jaffe, Ken Burward-Hoy, David Blinn, Crystal Garner, viola; Clay Ruede, Lanny Paykin, cello; John

Beal, Richard Sarpola, double bass; Sheryl Henze, flute, piccolo; Seymour Red Press, flute; William Blount, Lino Gomex, clarinet; Blair Tindall oboe, English horn; Russ Rizner, Dan Culpepper, French horn; Domenic Derasse, Lowell Hershey, trumpet; Jack Gale, trombone; John Redsecker, drums; Joseph Passaro, percussion; Lise Nadeau, harp; Musical Numbers: Marianne, The Girl on the Prow, Gorgeous Alexander, An Interrupted Love Song, Tavern Song, Rosita's Tango, Softly, as in a Morning Sunrise, Stouthearted Men, One Kiss, Ladies of the Jury, The New Cotillion Dance, Wanting You, Funny Little Sailor Men, Lover, Come Back to Me, Love is Quite a Simple Thing, Try Her Out at Dances, Softly, as in a Morning Sunrise (Reprise), Never for You, Lover, Come Back to Me (Reprise), One Kiss (Reprise)

Presented in two parts; March 27–30, 2003; 5 performances

NO STRINGS Concert version of musical with book by Samuel Taylor; Music and Lyrics by Richard Rodgers; Musical Director, Rob Fisher; Director in Residence, Kathleen Marshall; Director and Choreographer, Ann Reinking; Scenery, John Lee Beatty; Costumes, Candice Donnelly; Lighting, Ken Billington; Sound, Scott Lehrer; Music Director, Mr. Fisher; Orchestrations, Ralph Burns; Concert Adaptation, David Thompson; Music Coordinator, Mr. Red Press; Associate Choreographer, Debra McWaters; Casting, Jay Binder; Production Stage Manager, Karen Moore; Press, Rubenstein Associates Inc. Cast: Maya Days (Barbara Woodruff), Marc Kudisch (Mike Robinson), James Naughton (David Jordan), Len Cariou (Louis de Pounal), Caitlin Carter (Jeanette Valmy), Emily Skinner (Comfort O'Connell), Casey Biggs (Luc Delbert), Mary Ann Lamb (Gabrielle Bertin), Penny Fuller (Molie Plummer), Denis Jones (Marcello Agnolotti); Ensemble: Harry Bayron, Kristine Bendul, John Carroll, Alessandra Corona Lamm, Dylis Croman, Lloyd Culbreath, Naleah Dey, Joey Dowling, Darren Gibson, Melissa Hillmer, Ashley Hull, Darren Lorenzo, Abbey O'Brien, Alex Sanchez, Jennifer Savelli, Patricia Tuthill, Darlene Wilson; Orchestra: Rob Fisher, conductor; Andrew Sterman, piccolo, flute, alto flute, clarinet, tenor sax; Roger Rosenberg, flute, clarinet, bass clarinet, bassoon, baritone sax; Richard Heckman, piccolo, flute, oboe, clarinet, alto sax; Steven Kenyon, flute, clarinet, bass clarinet, alto sax; Seymour Red Press, flute, clarinet, alto sax; Lawrence Feldman, flute, clarinet, alto sax; Alva Hunt, flute, clarinet, bass clarinet, tenor sax; John Campo, clarinet, bass clarinet, bassoon, baritone sax; John Frosk, Stu Satalof, Kamau Adilifu, Glenn Drewes, trumpet; Jack Gale, Jason Jackson, Jack Schatz, trombone; Susan Jolles, harp; Lawrence Yurman, piano; Jay Berliner guitar; John Beal acoustic bass; John Redsecker, drums; Erik Charlston, percussion; Musical Numbers: The Sweetest Sounds, How Sad, The Sweetest Sounds (Reprise), Loads of Love, The Man Who Has Everything, Be My Host, La, You Don't Tell Me, Love Makes the World Go, Nobody Told Me, Look No Further, Maine, An Orthodox Fool, Eager Beaver, No Strings, Maine (Reprise), The Sweetest Sounds

Presented in two parts; May 8–11, 2003; 5 performances

LINCOLN CENTER THEATER

EIGHTEENTH SEASON

Artistic Director, André Bishop; Executive Producer, Bernard Gersten

A MAN OF NO IMPORTANCE Musical with book by Terrence McNally; Music by Stephen Flaherty; Lyrics by Lynn Ahrens; Director, Joe Mantello; Musical Staging, Jonathan Butterell; Scenery, Loy Arcenas; Costumes, Jane Greenwood; Lighting, Donald Holder; Sound, Scott Lehrer; Vocal Arrangements, Stephen Flaherty; Music Direction, Ted Sperling; Music Coordinator, John Miller; Orchestrations, William David Brohn and Christopher Jahnke; Stage Manager, Michael Brunner; Press, Philip Rinaldi Publicity; Cast: Roger Rees (Alfie Byrne), Martin Moran (Ernie Lally), Jarlath Conroy (Father Kenny), Jessica Molaskey (Mrs. Patrick), Katherine McGrath (Mrs. Grace; Kitty Farrelly), Luther Creek (Peter; Breton Beret), Sean McCourt (Sully O'Hara), Barbara Marineau (Miss Crowe), Faith Prince (Lily Byrne), Patti Perkins (Mrs. Curtin), Charles Keating (Carney; Oscar Wilde), Ronn Carroll (Baldy O'Shea), Steven Pasquale (Robbie Fay), Michael McCormick (Rasher Flynn; Carson), Sally Murphy (Adele Rice); Orchestra: Rob Berman, conductor, keyboard; Shawn Gough, associate conductor, keyboard, accordion; Kevin Kuhn, guitar; Antoine Silverman, violin, mandolin; Brian Miller, flute; Peter Sachon cello; David Phillips, bass; Musical Numbers: A Man of No Importance, The Burden of Life, Going Up, Princess, First Rehearsal, The Streets of Dublin, Books, Man in the Mirror, The Burden of Life (Reprise), Love Who You Love, Our Father, Confession, The Cuddles Mary Gave, Art, A Man of No Importance (Reprise), Confusing Times, Love Who You Love (Reprise), Man in the Mirror (Reprise), Tell Me Why, A Man of No Importance (Reprise), Love Who You Love (Reprise), Welcome to the World

Time: Early 1960s. Place: Dublin. Presented in two parts; Mitzi E. Newhouse Theater; October 10–December 29, 2002; 93 performances

OBSERVE THE SONS OF ULSTER MARCHING TOWARDS THE SOMME Frank McGuinness; Director, Nicholas Martin; Scenery, Alexander Dodge; Costumes, Donald Holder; Sound, Jerry Yager; Music, Shaun Davey; Casting, Amy and Christopher Swee; Stage Manager, Leila Knox; Press, Philip Rinaldi Publicity, Barbara Carroll; Cast: Richard Easton (Kenneth Pyper in his 80s), Justin Theroux (Kenneth Pyper in his 20s), Jason Butler Harner (David Craig), Scott Wolf (John Millen), Dashiell Eaves (William Moore), Jeremy Shamos (Christopher Roulston), Christopher Fitzgerald (Martin Crawford), Rod McLachlan (George Anderson), David Barry Gray (Nathaniel McIlwaine); Understudies: Justin Theroux, Jeremy Shamos (Barnaby Carpenter); Rod McLachlan (Tom O'Brien); Richard Easton (Geddeth Smith); Scott Wolf, Rod Fitzgerald, David Barry Gray (Seth Ullian)

Time: 1969; 1915; 1916. Place: Ulster; the Somme. Presented in two parts; Mitzi E. Newhouse Theater; February 24–April 13, 2003; 56 performances

ELEGIES Song cycle by William Finn; Director, Graciela Daniele; Costumes, Toni-Leslie James; Lighting, Donald Holder; Sound, Scott Stauffer; Music Director, Vadim Feichtner; Vocal Arranger, Gihieh Lee; Stage Manager, Patty Lyons; Press, Philip Rinaldi; Cast: Christian Borle, Betty Buckley, Carolee Carmello, Keith Byron Kirk, Michael Rupert

Roger Rees in *A Man of No Importance*   PHOTO BY PAUL KOLNIK

Scott Wolf, Justin Theroux, Dashiell Eaves in *Observe the Sons...*   PHOTO BY CAROL ROSEGG

Presented in two parts; Mitzi E. Newhouse Theater; March 24–30, 2003, Reopened April 14–19, 2003; 9 performances

MANHATTAN THEATRE CLUB

THIRTY-FIRST SEASON

Artistic Director, Lynne Meadow; Executive Producer, Barry Grove

IN REAL LIFE Charlayne Woodard; In association with the Mark Taper Forum; Director, Daniel Sullivan; Scenery, John Lee Beatty; Costumes, James Berton Harris; Lighting, Kathy A. Perkins; Sound, Chris Walker; Music, Daryl Waters; Production Stage Manager, Denise Yaney; Press, Boneau/Bryan-Brown, Chris Boneau, Jim Byk, Jackie Green, Aaron Meier

Performed by Charlayne Woodard; Standby: Angela Lockett

Presented in two parts; City Center Stage II; October 8–November 10, 2002; 34 performances

YELLOWMAN Dael Orlandersmith;Director, Blanka Zizka; Scenery, Klara Zieglerova; Costumes, Janus Stefanowicz; Lighting, Russell H. Champa; Music, Elliott Sharp; Casting, Nancy Piccione and David Caparelliotis; Production Stage Manager, Alex Lyu Volckhausen; Press, Boneau/Bryan-Brown, Chris Boneau, Jim Byk, Jackie Green, Aaron Meier; Cast: Dael Orlandersmith (Alma), Howard W. Overshown (Eugene); Understudies: Dael Orlandersmith (Michael Hyatt), Howard W. Overshown (Cornell Womack)

Presented without intermission; City Center Stage I; October 22–December 15, 2002

GONE HOME John Corwin; Director, David Warren; Scenery, James Youmans; Costumes, Laura Bauer; Lighting, Jeff Croiter; Sound, Fitz Patton; Casting, Nancy Piccione, David Caparelliotis; Production Stage Manager, Kelley Kirkpatrick; Press, Boneau/Bryan-Brown, Chris Boneau, Jim Byk, Jackie Green, Aaron Meier; Cast: Chelsea Altman (Kate), Kellie Overbey (Anne), Rob Campbell (Del), Callie Thorne (Suzie), Josh Hamilton (Jack)

Presented in two parts; City Center Stage II; December 17, 2002–January 26, 2003; 48 performances

Charlayne Woodard in *In Real Life* PHOTO BY CHRIS BENNION

Howard W. Overshown in *Yellowman* PHOTO BY JOAN MARCUS

Josh Hamilton, Chelsea Altman in *Gone Home* PHOTO BY JOAN MARCUS

John Gallagher Jr., Ana Gasteyer, Marylouise Burke in *Kimberly Akimbo* PHOTO BY JOAN MARCUS

Paul Hecht, Blair Brown in *Humble Boy* PHOTO BY JOAN MARCUS

KIMBERLY AKIMBO by David Lindsay-Abaire; Director, David Petrarca; Scenery, Robert Brill; Costumes, Martin Pakledinaz; Lighting, Brian MacDevitt; Sound, Bruce Ellman; Music, Jason Robert Brown; Casting, Nancy Piccione and David Caparelliotis; Production Stage Manager, Jason Scott Eagan; Press, Boneau/Bryan-Brown, Chris Boneau, Jim Byk, Jackie Green, Aaron Meier; Cast: Marylouise Burke (Kimberly), John Gallagher Jr. (Jeff), Ana Gasteyer (Debra), Jodie Markell (Pattie), Jake Weber (Buddy); Understudies: Jodie Markell, Ana Gasteyer (Antoinette LaVecchia); Marylouise Burke (Patti Perkins); Jake Weber (Gareth Saxe); John Gallagher Jr. (Daniel Zaitchik)

Time: The Present. Place: Bogota, New Jersey. Presented in two parts; City Center Stage I; February 4–April 6, 2003; 72 performances

Nancy Bell, Nancy Opel, Walter Bobbie, Malcolm Gets (seated) in *Polish Joke*
PHOTO BY JOAN MARCUS

POLISH JOKE by David Ives; Director, John Rando; Scenery, Loy Arcenas; Costumes, David C. Woolard; Lighting, Donald Holder; Sound, Bruce Ellman; Production Stage Manager, Heather Cousens, Press, Boneau/Bryan-Brown, Chris Boneau, Jim Byk, Aaron Meier; Cast: Malcolm Gets (Jaslu), Richard Ziman (Uncle Roman; others), Walter Bobbie (Wojtek; others), Nancy Opel (Magda; others), Nancy Bell (Helen; others)

Presented in two parts; City Center Stage II; March 18–April 20, 2003; 40 performances

HUMBLE BOY by Charlotte Jones; Director, John Caird; Scenery and Costumes, Tim Hatley; Lighting, Paul Pyant; Sound, Christopher Shutt; Music, Joe Cutler; Production Stage Manager, Roy Harris; Press, Boneau/Bryan-Brown, Chris Boneau, Jim Byk, Aaron Meier; Cast: Jared Harris (Felix Humble), Bernie McInerney (Jim), Mary Beth Hurt (Mercy Lott), Paul Hecht (George Pye), Blair Brown (Flora Humble), Ana Reeder (Rosie Pye)

Presented in two parts; City Center Stage I; May 18; Still playing May 31, 2003; 18 performances

Jimmy Smits, Julia Stiles, Kathryn Meisle, Zach Braff in *Twelfth Night* PHOTO BY MICHAL DANIEL

Kate Burton, Martha Plimpton in *Boston Marriage*

NEW YORK SHAKESPEARE FESTIVAL/JOSEPH PAPP PUBLIC THEATRE

FORTY-SEVENTH SEASON

Producer, George C. Wolfe; Executive Director, Mara Manus; Artistic Producer, Rosemarie Tichler

TWELFTH NIGHT Revival by William Shakespeare; Director, Brian Kulick; Scenery, Walt Spangler; Costumes, Miguel Angel Huidor; Lighting, Michael Chybowski; Sound, Acme Sound Partners; Music, Duncan Sheik; Production Stage Manager, James Latus; Press, Carol R. Fineman, Tom Naro; Cast: Jimmy Smits (Orsino), Michael Potts (Feste), Al Espinosa (Curio), Kathryn Meisle (Olivia), Andre McGinn (Valentine), Christopher Lloyd (Malvolio), Julia Stiles (Viola), Sterling K. Brown (Antonio), Bill Buell (Captain), Zach Braff (Sebastian), Oliver Platt (Sir Toby Belch), Kevin Isola (Fabian), Kristen Johnston (Maria), Stephanie Blake (Servant Marsha), Michael Stuhlbarg (Sir Andrew Aguecheek), Craig Baldwin (Priest)

Presented in two parts; Delacorte Theater; July 21–August 11, 2003; 19 performances

TAKE ME OUT by Richard Greenberg; Executive Director, Mara Manus, in association with the Donmar Warehouse; Director, Joe Mantello; Scenery, Scott Pask; Costumes, Jess Goldstein; Lighting, Kevin Adams; Sound, Janet Kalas; Associate Director, Trip Cullman; Associate Producers, Bonnie Metzgar and John Dias; Casting, Jordan Thaler/Heidi Griffiths; Production Stage Manager, CA. Clark; Press, Carol R. Fineman, Elizabeth Wehrle; Cast: Neal Huff (Kippy Sunderstrom), Gene Gabriel (Rodriguez; TV Interviewer), Daniel Sunjata (Darren Lemming), Frederick Weller (Shane Mungin), Kohl Sudduth (Jason Chenier), Joe Lisi (Skipper; William R. Danziger), Kevin Carroll (Davey Battle), Dominic Fumusa (Toddy Koovitz), Robert M. Jimenez (Martinez; Stadium Announcer), James Yaegashi (Takeshi Kawabata), Denis O'Hare (Mason Marzac)

Presented in three parts; Anspacher Theater; September 5–November 24, 2002; 94 performances

BOSTON MARRIAGE by David Mamet; Director, Karen Kohlhaas; Scenery, Walt Spangler; Costumes, Paul Tazewell; Lighting, Robert Perry; Production Stage Manager, James Latus; Press, Carol R. Fineman, Elizabeth Wehrle; Cast: Martha Plimpton (Claire), Arden Myrin (Catherine, the maid), Kate Burton (Anna)

Presented in two parts; Martinson Hall; November 20–December 22, 2002; 39 performances

RADIANT BABY Musical with book by Stuart Ross; Music by Debra Barsha; Lyrics by Ira Gasman and Stuart Ross; Based on Keith Haring: The Authorized Biography by John Gruen; Director, Mr. Wolfe; Choreography, Fatima Robinson; Scenery, Riccardo Hernandez; Costumes, Emilio Sosa; Lighting, Howell Binkley; Sound, Dan Moses Schreier; Projections, Batwin and Robin Productions; Orchestrations, Zane Mark; Music Director, Kimberly Grigsby; Production Stage Manager, Rick Steiger; Press, Carol R. Fineman, Elizabeth Wehrle; Cast: Anny Jules (Mikayla), Daniel Reichard (Keith

Daniel Reichard, Aaron Lohr, Keong Sim in *Radiant Baby* PHOTO BY MICHAL DANIEL

Haring), Gabriel Enrique Alvarez (Jake; Maurice), Aaron Lohr (Carlos), Remy Zaken (Rini), Michael Winther (Mr. Haring; Johnny Lounge), Kate Jennings Grant (Amanda), Keong Sim (Tseng Kwong Chi), Julee Cruise (Mrs. Haring; Andy Warhol); Ensemble: Curtis Holbrook, Billy Porter, Angela Robinson, Tracee Beazer, Celina Carvajal, Christopher Martinez, Rhett G. George, Christian Vincent, Christopher Livsey, Jermaine Montell; Musicians: Kimberly Grigsby, conductor, synthesizer; John Roggie, James Sampliner, synthesizer; Vincent Henry, guitar, saxophone; Konrad Adderley, bass; John Clancy, drums

Time: 1988. Presented in two parts; Newman Theater; March 2–23, 2003; 25 performances

FUCKING A by Suzan-Lori Parks; Director, Michael Greif; Scenery, Mark Wendland; Costumes, Ilona Somogyi; Lighting, Kenneth Posner; Sound, Obadiah Eaves; Music Direction, Arrangements and Orchestrations, Tim Weil; Associate Producer, Bonnie Metzgar; Casting, Jordan Thaler/Heidi Griffiths; Production Stage Manager, Kristen Harris; Press, Carol R. Fineman, Elizabeth Wehrle; Cast: S. Epatha Merkerson (Hester Smith), Daphne Rubin-Vega (Canary Mary), Bobby Cannavale (The Mayor), Michole Briana White (The First Lady), Susan Blommaert (Freedom Fund Lady), Mos Def (Monster), Peter Gerety (Butcher), Susan Blommaert (Scribe) Jojo Gonzalez (First Hunter), Manu Narayan (Second Hunter), Jesse Lenat (Third

Hunter), Chandler Parker (Jailbait), Bobby Cannavale (Prison Guard), Manu Narayan (Waiting Woman #1), Susan Blommaert (Waiting Woman #2), Full Company (Freshly Freed Prisoners), Chandler Parker (Hunter); Orchestra: T.O. Sterrett, conductor, piano, synthesizer, accordion; Nathan Durham, euphonium, trumpet, trombone; Jojo Gonzalez, guitar, percussion; Jesse Lenat, guitar; Manu Narayan, alto, soprano saxophone.

Place: A small town in a small country in the middle of nowhere. Presented in two parts; Anspacher Theater; March 16–April 6, 2003; 25 performances

AS YOU LIKE IT Revival by William Shakespeare; Producer, George C. Wolfe, Executive Director, Maca Manus; Direction and costumes by Erica Schmidt; Lighting, Shelly Sabel; Casting, Jordan Thaler/Heidi Griffiths; Associate Producer, Bonnie Metzgar; Production Stage Manager, Buzz Cohen; Press, Carol R. Fineman, Elizabeth Wehrle; Cast: Drew Cortese (LeBeau; Duke Frederick; Duke Senior; Silvius), Johnny Giacalone (Touchstone; Jaques), Bryce Dallas Howard (Rosalind), Jennifer Ikeda (Adam; Phebe; Audrey), Lethia Nail (Celia; William), Lorenzo Pisoni (Orlando; Oliver)

Presented without intermission; Martinson Hall; April 14–May 4, 2003; 24 performances

Mos Def, Daphne Rubin-Vega in *Fucking A* PHOTO BY MICHAL DANIEL

Members of the Company of *As You Like It* PHOTO BY MICHAL DANIEL

NEW YORK THEATRE WORKSHOP

TWENTY-SECOND SEASON

Artistic Director, James C. Nicola; Managing Director, Lynn Moffat

PLAY YOURSELF by Harry Kondoleon; Director, Craig Lucas; Scenery, John McDermott; Costumes, Catherine Zuber; Lighting, Ben Stanton; Music and Sound, David Van Tieghem; Production Stage Manager, Antonia Gianino; Press, Richard Kornberg and Associates, Don Summa; Cast: Ann Guilbert (Selma), Elizabeth Marvel (Yvonne), Juan Carlos Hernandez (Harmon), Marian Seldes (Jean)

Presented in two parts; Century Center for the Performing Arts; July 10–August 4, 2002; 31 performances

FAR AWAY by Caryl Churchill; Director, Stephen Daldry; Scenery, Ian MacNeil; Costumes, Catherine Zuber; Lighting, Rick Fisher; Sound, Paul Arditti; Associate Director, Michael Sexton; Production Stage Manager, Martha Donaldson; Press, Richard Kornberg and Associates, Don Summa; Cast: Frances McDormand (Harper), Marin Ireland (Joan), Alexa Eisenstein, Gina Rose (Joan as child), Chris Messina (Todd)

Presented without an intermission; November 11, 2002–January 18, 2003; 79 performances

BEXLEY, OH(!) OR, TWO TALES OF ONE CITY by Prudence Wright Holmes; Director, Lisa Peterson; Scenery, Riccardo Hernandez; Costumes, Gabriel Berry; Lighting, Ben Stanton; Sound and Music, Robert Kaplowitz; Production Stage Manager, Erika Timperman; Press, Richard Kornberg and Associates, Don Summa; Cast: Wright Holmes

Presented in two parts; March 10–30, 2003; 24 performances

CAVEDWELLER by Kate Moira Ryan; Based on a novel by Dorothy Allison; Director, Michael Greif; Scenery, Riccardo Hernandez; Costumes, Ilona Somogyi; Lighting, Jennifer Tipton; Sound, Jerry Yager; Projections, Jan Hartley; Music, Stephen Trask and Julia Greenberg; Production Stage Manager, Michael McGoff; Press, Richard Kornberg and Associates, Don Summa; Cast: Deirdre O'Connell (Delia Byrd), Adriane Lenox (Rosemary), Merritt Wever (Cissy Pritchard), Lynne McCollough (Waitress, Louise Windsor, Marcia Pearlman, Nadine Reitower, Gillian Wynchester, Mrs. Caidenhead, Bartender), Carson Elrod (Grandaddy Byrd, Nolan Reitower), Jenny Maguire (Dede Windsor), Shannon Burkett (Amanda Windsor), Stevie Ray Dallimore (Clint Windsor, Deputy Emmet Tyler, Michael Graham, Billy Tucker), Julia Greenberg (Vocals)

May 8, 2003; Still playing May 31, 2003; 28 performances

PLAYWRIGHTS HORIZONS

THIRTY-SECOND SEASON

Artistic Director, Tim Sanford; Managing Director, Leslie Marcus; General Manager, William Russo

THE WORLD OVER by Keith Bunin; Director, Tim Vasen; Scenery, Mark Wendland; Costumes, Ilona Somogyi; Lighting, Michael Chybowski; Sound and Music, David Van Tieghem; Fight Direction, J. Allen Suddeth; Casting, James Calleri; Production Stage Manager, Jared T. Carey; Press, the Publicity Office, Bob Fennell, Marc Thibodeau, Michael S. Borowski; Cast: James Urbaniak (The Geographer, Tobias, High Priest, Lorenzacchio, Mamillus, Mapmaker), Kevin Isola (Xavier, a sailor, The Gryphon, Prince Wilhelm, Nicholeaus), Stephen Largay (Vincitore, Prince Bartholomew, Prince Anselm, Johannes, Sultan Saturnius, Red-Winged Hawk), Mia Barron (Empress Oleandra, Queen Amarantha, Princess Isobel), Rhea Seehorn (Nurse, Princess Euralie, Old Crone in a cave, Ulrike, Cindra, Marguerite, Ruselka), Justin Kirk (Adam), Matthew Maher (King Ferdinand, Hanif, Root, Otto, Darkly Jack, Crown Prince Leocad, Karl)

Presented in two parts; The Duke Theater; October 1–13, 2002; 16 performances

Justin Kirk, Rhea Seehorn, Kevin Isola in *The World Over* PHOTO BY JOAN MARCUS

T. Ryder Smith, E. Katherine Kerr, Marissa Copeland, David Greenspan in *She Stoops to Comedy* PHOTO BY JOAN MARCUS

WHAT DIDN'T HAPPEN by Christopher Shinn; Director, Michael Wilson; Scenery, Jeff Cowie; Costumes, David C. Woolard; Lighting, Howell Binkley; Music and Sound, John Gromada; Production Stage Manager, Susie Cordon; Press, the Publicity Office, Bob Fennell, Michael S. Borowski; Cast: Steven Skybell (Dave), Chris Noth (Peter), Robert Hogan (Alan), Matt Cowell (Jeff), Suzanne Cryer (Emily), Matt McGrath (Scott), Annalee Jefferies (Elaine)

Time: 1999; 1993. Place: A country house. Presented in two parts; The Duke Theater; December 10–22, 2002; 16 performances

MY LIFE WITH ALBERTINE Musical with book and lyrics by Richard Nelson; Music by Ricky Ian Gordon; Based on sections from Remembrance of Things Past by Marcel Proust; Artistic Director, Tim Sanford; Managing Director, Leslie Marcus; General Manager, William Russo; Director, Richard Nelson; Choreography, Seán Curran; Scenery, Thomas Lynch; Costumes, Susan Hilferty; Lighting, James F. Ingalls; Sound, Scott Lehrer; Orchestrations, Bruce Coughlin; Music Direction, Charles Prince; Music Coordinator, John Miller; Associate Producer, Ira Weitzman; Production Stage Manager, Matthew Silver; Press, the Publicity Office, Bob Fennell, Michael S. Borowski; Cast: Brent Carver (Narrator), Caroline McMahon (Andree), Chad Kimball (Marcel), Brooke Sunny Moriber (Rosemonde), Kelli O'Hara (Albertine), Paul Anthony McGrane (Pianist), Donna Lynne Champlin (Grandmother, Francoise), Laura Woyasz (Mlle Lea's Girlfriend), Nicholas Belton, Jim Poulos, Paul A. Schaefer (Three Young Men), Emily Skinner (Mlle. Lea)

Presented in two parts; March 13–30, 2003; 22 performances

Brooke Sunny Moriber, Kelli O'Hara, Caroline McMahon in *My Life With Albertine*
PHOTO BY JOAN MARCUS

SHE STOOPS TO COMEDY by David Greenspan; Director, David Greenspan; Scenery, Michael Brown; Costumes, Miranda Hoffman; Lighting, Matthew Frey; Production Stage Manager, Beth Stiegel Rohr; Press, the Publicity Office, Bob Fennell, Michael S. Borowski; Cast: Mr. Greenspan (Alexandra Page), E. Katherine Kerr (Kay Fein, Jayne Summerhouse), Philip Tabor (Hal Stewart), Mia Barron (Eve Addaman), Marissa Copeland (Alison Rose), T. Ryder Smith (Simon Lanquish)

Presented without intermission; April 13–27, 2003; 17 performances

Matt McGrath, Suzanne Cryer in *What Didn't Happen* PHOTO BY JOAN MARCUS

I AM MY OWN WIFE by Doug Wright; Director, Moises Kaufman; Scenery, Derek McLane; Costumes, Janice Pytel; Lighting, David Lander; Sound, Andre Pluess and Ben Sussman; Casting, James Calleri, Production Stage Manager, Andrea J. Testani; Press, the Publicity Office, Bob Fennell, Marc Thibodeau, Michael S. Borowski, Candi Adams; Cast: Jefferson Mays (Charlotte von Mahlsdorf; others)

Time: The Nazi Years; the Communist Years. Place: Various locations in the US and Germany. Presented in two parts; May 27–Still playing May 31, 2003; 6 performances

Jefferson Mays in *I Am My Own Wife* PHOTO BY JOAN MARCUS

John Carter, Michael Learned, Bill Moor, Patrick Garner, Rosemary Harris in *All Over*

ROUNDABOUT THEATRE COMPANY

THIRTY-SEVENTH SEASON

Artistic Director, Todd Haimes; Managing Director, Ellen Richard; Executive Director of External Affairs, Julia C. Levy

ALL OVER Revival by Edward Albee; In association with the McCarter Theatre; Director, Emily Mann; Scenery, Thomas Lynch; Costumes, Jennifer von Mayrhauser; Lighting, Allen Lee Hughes; Casting, Bernard Telsey Casting; Production Stage Manager, Jay Adler; Stage Manager, Richard Costabile; Press, Boneau/Bryan-Brown, Adrian Bryan-Brown, Matt Polk, Amy Dinnerman; Cast: Rosemary Harris (The Wife), Pamela Nyberg (The Daughter), Michael Learned (The Mistress), Bill Moor (The Doctor), Richard Cottrell, Keith Dixon, Chuck McMahon (Newspapermen), Patrick Garner (The Son), John Carter (The Best Friend), Myra Carter (The Nurse); Understudies: Rosemary Harris, Myra Carter (Mikel Sarah Lambert); Michael Learned, Pamela Nyberg (Alison Edwards); John Carter, Bill Moor (Fred Burrell); Patrick Garner (Richard Cottrell)

Time: 1971. Place: The private quarters of a townhouse. Presented in two parts; Gramercy Theatre; June 27–September 1, 2002

Michael Learned, Rosemary Harris in *All Over* PHOTOS BY JOAN MARCUS

SECOND STAGE THEATRE

TWENTY-THIRD SEASON

Artistic Director, Carol Rothman; Managing Director, Carol Fishman

SPANISH GIRL by Hunt Holman; Director, Erica Schmidt; Scenery, Michelle Malavet; Lighting Shelly Sabel; Costumes, Juman Malouf; Sound, Bart Fasbender; Production Stage Manager, Jennifer O'Byrne; Press, Richard Kornberg and Associates, Don Summa; Cast: Ari Graynor (Skyler), Nate Mooney (Chet), Joey Kern (Bucky), Jama Williamson (Jolene)

Presented without intermission; McGinn/Cazale Theatre; July 28–August 4, 2002; 9 performances

CROWNS by Regina Taylor; Based on a book by Michael Cunningham and Craig Marberry; In association with the McCarter Theatre; Director Regina Taylor; Choreography, Ronald K. Brown; Scenery, Riccardo Hernandez; Costumes, Emilio Sosa; Lighting, Robert Perry; Sound, Darron L. West; Musical Direction and Arrangements, Linda Twine; Production Stage Manager, Alison Cote; Press, Richard Kornberg and Associates, Tom D'Ambrosio; Cast: Janet Huber (Wanda), Ebony Jo-Ann (Mother Shaw), Lilias White (Velma), Lawrence Clayton (Man), Carmen Ruby Floyd (Yolanda), Hariett D. Foy (Jeanette), Lynda Gravatt (Mabel); Musicians: David Pleasant, percussion; Michael Mitchell, piano

Presented without intermission; Second Stage Theatre; December 22, 2002–January 5, 2003; 40 performances

LITTLE FISH Musical with Book, Music and Lyrics by Michael John LaChiusa; Based on stories by Deborah Eisenberg; Director and Choreographer, Graciela Daniele; Scenery, Riccardo Hernandez; Costumes, Toni-Leslie James; Lighting, Peggy Eisenhauer; Sound, Scott Lehrer; Music Coordinator, Seymour Red Press; Production Stage Manager, Lisa Iacucci; Stage Manager, Thomas Borchard; Press, Richard Kornberg and Associates, Tom D'Ambrosio; Cast: Jennifer Laura Thompson (Charlotte), Lea DeLaria (Cinder), Marcy Harriell (Kathy), Eric Jordan Young (John Paul), Jesse Tyler Ferguson (Marco), Celia Keenan-Bolger (Young Girl), Hugh Panaro (Robert), Ken Marks (Mr. Bunder; Bodega Man)

Presented without intermission; February 13–March 9, 2003; 29 performances

Walter Willison in *Two by Two* PHOTO BY MICHAEL RIORDAN

THE JEWISH REPERTORY THEATRE

TWO BY TWO: THE RICHARD RODGERS CENTENNIAL CONCERT

Music by Richard Rodgers; Lyrics by Martin Charnin; Book by Peter Stone; Based on *The Flowering Peach* by Clifford Odets; A revival of the musical which opened on November 10, 1970 at the Imperial Theatre. Director, Walter Willison; Musical Director, Lanny Meyers; Orchestrations, Eddie Sauter; Dance and Vocal Arrangements, Trude Rittman; Production Stage Manager, Jack Gianino; Lighting and Sound Robin Grant; Sound Design, Chip M. Fabrizi; Special Consultants, Bruce Pomahac, Michael Buckley; Presented by the Jewish Repertory Theatre and Ron Avni; Cast: Walter Willison (Noah), Pat Suzuki (Esther), Ryan Driscoll (Japheth), Gregory Zaragoza (Shem), Buck Dietz (Ham), Jo Anna Rush (Leah), Christina Seymour (Rachel), Hallie Brown (Goldie), Douglas Holmes (Narrator); Musical Numbers: Why Me?, Put Him Away, Something, The Gitka's Song, Something, Somewhere, You Have Got to Have a Rudder on the Ark, Something Doesn't Happen, An Old Man, Ninety Again, Two by Two, I Do Not Know a Day I Did Not Love You, Reprise: Something, Somewhere, When It Dries, You, Forty Nights, The Golden Ram, Poppa Knows Best, Reprise: I Do Not Know a Day I Did Not Love You, As Far As I'm Concerned, Hey, Girlie, The Covenant

A musical in two acts. The action takes place before, during and after the Flood. Act I: In and around Noah's home; Act II: An ark, and atop Mt. Ararat; the Center for Jewish History; April 10–14, 2002; limited engagement, 4 performances

MINNIE'S BOYS IN CONCERT: THE MARX BROTHERS MUSICAL

Music by Larry Grossman; Book by Arthur Marx and Robert Fisher; A new concert adaptation of the musical which opened at the Imperial Theatre on March 26, 1970. Adapted and Directed by Walter Willison; Musical Direction, New Vocal Arrangements by Fred Barton; Additional Musical Staging by Joanna Rush; Vocal Arrangements, John Berkman; Dance Arrangements and Incidental Music, Marvin Hamlisch, Peter Howard; Lighting and Sound Design, Jaesun Celebre; Video Design, Stephen Treadway; Maxie's Hair Design, Stephen Bishop; Production Stage Manager, Jack Gianino; Presented by the Jewish Repertory Theatre and Ron Avni; Press, Pete Sanders. Cast: Douglas Holmes (Narrator; Samuel "Frenchie" Marx; Maxie), Fred Barton (Piano Man; Cop; Western Union Boy; Robwell), Joanna Rush (Showgirl One; Mrs. Flanagan; Southern Belle; Mrs. McNish), Corinne Melancon (Showgirl Two; Mrs. Krupnik; Cindy; Miss Murdock), Henry Grossman (Hockmeister; Heckler; Sidebark; E.F. Albee), Sam Reni (Al Shean), Francis Kelly (Miltie Marx, Gummo), James Donegan (Herbie Marx, Zeppo), Stephen Brockway (Leonard Marx, Chico), Jamison Stern (Adolph Marx, Harpo), Gary Littman (Julie Marx, Groucho), Diane J. Findlay (Minnie Marx); Musical Numbers: Prologue, Five Growing Boys, Rich Is, More Precious Far, Four Nightingales, Underneath It All, Mama, A Rainbow, You Don't Have To Do It For Me, Where Was I?, Hello, Big Time, You Remind Me of You, Minnie's Boys, They Give Me Love, The Act, Minnie's Boys Finale

James Donegan, Stephen Brockway, Diane J. Findlay, Jamison Stern, Gary Littman in *Minnie's Boys* PHOTO BY STEPHEN TREADWAY

A musical comedy in two acts. The action centers around the lives of the Marx family, between 1909 and 1923. The Center for Jewish History; October 31–November 4, 2002; limited engagement, 4 performances

OFF-OFF-BROADWAY

.002.

Productions that opened **June 1, 2002 – May 31, 2003**

ABINGDON THEATRE COMPANY

SUCKER FISH MESSIAH by Ryan Michael Teller; Director, Taylor Brooks; June 6, 2002; Cast: Lori Gardner, Richard Edward Long, Julia Klein, Nicholas Piper

TEDDY TONIGHT! by Laurence Luckinbill; Director, Kim T. Sharp; October 18, 2002; Cast: Laurence Luckinbill

UNCLE DAN by Joe Byers; Director, William Lipscomb; December 12, 2002; Cast: Alice Barden, David Rockwell Miller, Mark Willett

GOD'S DAUGHTER by Barton Bishop; Director, Alex Dmitriev; Janaury 23, 2003; Cast: Peter Brouwer, Anne DuPont, Susanne Marley, William Prael

DAISY IN THE DREAMTIME by Lynne Kaufman; Director, Kim T. Sharp; March 12, 2003; Cast: Molly Powell, Jerome Preston Bates, Jodie Lynne McClintock

ACCESS THEATER

3 O'CLOCK IN BROOKLYN by Israela Margalit; Director, Margarett Perry; October 10, 2002; Cast: Jordan Charney, Louisa Flaningam, Jesse Doran, Erica Piccininni, Kim Zimmer, Jeremy Webb

THAT DAMN DYKSTRA (The Boxed Set) by Brian Dykstra; Director, Margarett Perry; February 10, 2003; Cast: Cynthia Babak, Sarah Baker, Matthew Boston, Brian Dykstra, Patrick Frederick, Vickie Tanner

THE ACTING COMPANY

AMERICAN DREAMS: LOST AND FOUND by Studs Terkel; Adapted by Peter Frisch; Director, Rebecca Guy; May 13, 2003; Cast: Paul Cosentino, Peter Zazzali, Lamont Stephens, Joe Osheroff, Jaime St. Peter, Michael Lluberes, Jessica Bates, Siobhan Juanita Brown, Glenn Peters, Fletcher McTaggart, Christen Simon, Kevin Kraft, Evan Zes

THE ACTORS COMPANY THEATRE (TACT)

HAPPY BIRTHDAY by Anita Loos; Director, Scott Alan Evans; October 13, 2002; Cast: Cynthia Darlow, Cynthia Harris, Larry Keith, Jack Koenig, Darrie Lawrence, Margaret Nichols, Scott Schafer, Lynn Wright, Alexander Alioto, James DeMarse, Colton Green, Richard Fromm, Richard Ferrone, Elizabeth Moser, James Prendergast, Kim Sykes, Jenn Thompson, Ashley West

THE RIVALS by Richard Brinsley Sheridan; Director, Scott Alan Evans; November 24, 2002; Cast: James Murtaugh, Jack Koenig, Rob Breckenridge, Kyle Fabel, Gregory Salata, Scott Schafer, Jamie Bennett, Delphi Harrington, Margaret Nichols, Mary Bacon, Eve Michelson

THE POTTING SHED by Graham Greene; Director, Scott Alan Evans; January 26, 2003; Cast: James Prendergast, Stina Nielsen, Jenn Thompson, Darrie Lawrence, Jack Koenig, Kyle Fabel, Nicholas Krepos, Jamie Bennett, Paddy Croft, Laurinda Barrett, Simon Jones

EURYDICE by Jean Anouilh; Director, Kyle Fabel; March 3, 2003; Cast: Kevin Henderson, James Murtaugh, Scott Shafer, Richard Ferrone, Cynthia Darlow, Margaret Nichols, Cynthia Harris, Simon Jones, Denis Butkus, Sean Arbuckle, Gregory Salata, Nick Toren, Richard Ferrone

USA: A READING by Paul Shyre; Adapted from the work of John Dos Passos; Director, Scott Alan Evans; May 5, 2003; Cast: Greg McFadden, Nora Chester, Jamie Bennett, Lynn Wright, Rachel Fowler, Larry Keith

THE ACTOR'S PLAYGROUND THEATRE

VICTIMS! TRUST by David Yee; Director, Matthew Landfield; August 3, 2002; Cast: Heather Aldridge, Mary Holmstrom, Larry Mitchell, April Peveteaux, Nicole Seymour, Guido Venitucci

ALMOST BLUE by Keith Reddin; Director, Hal Brooks; May 11, 2003; Cast: Joe Passaro, Kurt Everhart, James Biberi, Antoinette la Vecchia

ACTORS PLAYHOUSE

RHAPSODY IN SETH by Seth Rudetsky; Director, Seth Rudetsky; March 11, 2003; Cast: Seth Rudetsky

Seth Rudetsky in *Rhapsody in Seth*   PHOTO BY DAVID COOLIDGE

ALTERED STAGES

LAST DAY by Daniel Roberts; Director, Samuel Roberts; November 10, 2002; Cast: Scott Duffy, Michael Hogan, Robert McKay, Heather Raffo, Kate Roe, Alexa Zee

AMERICAN MAGIC by Gil Kofman; Director, Matthew Wilder; May 8, 2003; Cast: Lyndsay Rose Kane, Walter Murray, Sonny Perez, Indrajit Sarkar

AMERICAN GLOBE THEATRE

LOVE'S LABOURS LOST: THE MUSICAL Based on William Shakespeare's play; Adapted by Kenneth Mitchell; Music and Lyrics by Bob McDowell; Director, John Basil and Kenneth Mitchell; March 15, 2003; Cast: Trent Dawson, Geoffrey Barnes, Julia Cook, Deborah S. Craig, Elizabeth Keefe, Kelley McKinnon, Rainard Rachele, Alyson Reim, Basil Rodericks, Graham Stevens, Ross Stoner, Andrew Thacher, Justin Ray Thompson, Carey Urban

THE AMERICAN THEATRE OF ACTORS

JUST US BOYS by Frank Stancati; Director, Thomas Morrissey; June 20, 2002; Cast: Joe Gulla, Davis Kirby, Gerard Gravellese, Ludis Schnore, Jeffrey Todd

ARC LIGHT THEATRE

BIG AL by Bryan Goluboff; Director, Evan Bergman; November 5, 2002; Cast: Juan Carlos Hernandez, David Thornton, Frank Whaley

ARS NOVA THEATER

JULIA SWEENEY: GUYS AND BABIES, SEX AND GODS by Julia Sweeney; Director, Mark Brokaw; January 29, 2003; Cast: Julia Sweeney

BANK STREET THEATRE

UNITY FEST 2002: GROWING UP

OVER ANALYSIS by Gabriel Shanks; Director, Dennis Smith; December 3, 2002; Cast: Caitlin Barton, John Jay Buol, Matt Gorrek, Bekka Lindstrom, Jack Merlis, Lawrence Merritt, Karen Stanion

THE HOURGLASS by Ryan Mark; Director, Dennis Smith; December 3, 2002; Cast: Moe Bertran, Ivan Davila

COME LIGHT THE MENORAH by Rich Orloff; Director, Courtenay Wendell; December 3, 2002; Cast: Bekka Lindstrom, Karen Stanion

THE MUTANT FACTOR OF RECONCILIATION by Jess Carey; Director, Donna Jean Fogel; December 3, 2002; Cast: John Jay Buol, Bekka Lindstrom, Nicole Longchamp

CHRISTOPHER T. WASHINGTON LEARNS TO FIGHT by Jordan Seavey; Director, Keith Lorrel Manning; December 3, 2002; Cast: Caitlin Barton, Moe Bertran, John Jay Buol, Matt Gorrek, Karen Stanion

THE BEGINNING by Dan Clancy; Director, James McLaughlin; December 3, 2002; Cast: Jack Merlis, Lawrence Merritt

THE SEED by David Pumo; Director, Donna Jean Fogel; December 3, 2002; Cast: Moe Bertran, Bekka Lindstrom, Tom Johnson, Maxx Santiago

THE GENERATIONS

MADONNA AND CHILD by Kenneth Pressman; Director, Keith Lorrel Manning; December 4, 2003; Cast: Lynn Battaglia, Maxx Santiago

ACT OF CONTRITION by Dan Bacalzo; Director, Nicholas Warren-Gray; December 4, 2003; Cast: Moe Bertran, Matt Gorrek

BY HER SIDE by Steve Willis; Director, Donna Jean Fogel; December 4, 2003; Cast: Ardes Quinn

PADDING THE WAGON by Gary Garrison; Director, Courtenay Wendell; December 4, 2003; Cast: Donna Jean Fogel, Keith Lorrel Manning, Gisele Richardson

PERHAPS by David Pumo; Director, Karin Bowersock; December 4, 2003; Cast: Donna Jean Fogel, Mikeah Ernest Jennings, Bekka Lindstrom

WHAT I MISSED IN THE '80s by David DeWitt; Director, James McLaughlin; December 4, 2003; Cast: Matt Gorrek, Tony Hamilton

TRAFFIC

IT'S A WONDERFUL LIE by Tony Hamilton; Director, Joan Evans; December 5, 2002; Cast: Tony Hamilton

TRAFFICKING IN BROKEN HEARTS by Edwin Sanchez; Director, Dennis Smith; December 5, 2002; Cast: Moe Bertran, Ivan Davila, Philip Estrera, Heland Lee, Gisele Richardson, Maxx Santiago, Karen Stanion, Nicholas Warren-Gray

RED AND TAN LINE by Peter Mercurio; Director, Chuck Blasius; March 6, 2003; Cast: Patrick Davey, Tony Hamilton, Carson Hinners, James McLaughlin

THE LADIES OF THE CORRIDOR by Dorothy Parker and Arnaud d'Usseau; Director, Dan Wackerman; May 5, 2003; Cast: Kelly AuCoin, Ron Badgen, Hal Blankenship, Patrick Boyd, Peggy Cowles, Jo Ann Cunningham, Dawn Evans, Libby George, Astrit Ibroci, Susan Jeffries, Patricia Randell, Andy Phelan, Carolyn Seiff, Susan Varon

AUNTIE MAYHEM by David Pumo; Director, Donna Jean Fogel; May 29, 2003; Cast: Moe Bertran, Ivan Davila, Jimmy Hurley, Randy Aaron, Isaac Calpito, Henry Alberto

THE BARROW GROUP

LAST TRAIN TO NIBROC by Arlene Hutton; Director, Seth Barrish and Michael Connors; December 5, 2002; Cast: Jenny Eakes, Emory Van Cleve

OFF THE MAP by Joan Ackerman; Director, Eric Paeper; February 13, 2003; Cast: Lee Brock, Reade Kelly, Rick Pepper, Michael Warren Powell, Melissa Russell, Julie Shain, Wendy vanden Heuvel

BLUE HERON ARTS CENTER

VALPARAISO by Don Delillo; Director, Hal Brooks; July 24, 2002; Cast: Matthew Lawler, Elizabeth Sherman, Kate Nowlin, Andrew Benator, David Fitzgerald, Carla Harting, Julie Fitzpatrick

HARLEM DUET by Djanet Sears; Director, Djanet Sears; November 13, 2002; Cast: Oni Faida Lampley, Gregory Simmons, Walter Borden, Barbara Barnes Hopkins, Nyjah Moore Westbrooks

HOLD, PLEASE by Annie Weisman; Director, Connie Grappo; February 28, 2003; Cast: Laura Esterman, Kathryn Rossetter, Emma Bowers, Jeanine Serralles

ALMA AND MRS. WOOLF by Anne Legault; Translated by Daniel Libman; Director, Jim Pelegano; March 10, 2003; Cast: Joan Grant, Nicole Orth-Pallavicini

THE ONTOLOGICAL DETECTIVE by Kenneth Heaton; Director, Kenneth Heaton; April 10, 2003; Cast: Christopher Mattox, Michael Luz, Romi Dias, Mark Sage Hamilton, Charles Paul Holt, Johnny Sparks

Oni Faida Lampley, Gregory Simmons in *Harlem Duet* PHOTO BY RICHARD TERMINE

Nicole Orth-Pallavicini, Joan Grant in *Alma and Mrs. Woolf* PHOTO BY RICHARD TERMINE

THE BOTTLE FACTORY THEATER COMPANY

ROOM 314 by Michael Knowles; Director, Michael Knowles; March 20, 2003; Cast: J. Malia Hawley, Mr. Knowles, Anna Lodej, Kate Lunsford, Jared Michalski, Donald Silva, Jennifer Smith, Christopher Trunell

TERRITORY by Lawrence Levine; Director, Lawrence Levine; May 21, 2003; Cast: John Good, Amanda Gruss, Grant Varjas

BOWERY POETRY CLUB

DOOR WIDE OPEN by Joyce Johnson; Director, Tony Torn; May 17, 2003; Cast: Amy Wright, John Ventimiglia, Adira Amram, Meg Brooker

Top Row: Jonathan Todd Ross, Noah Weisberg, Lance Olds; Middle: Doug Kreeger, Meyer deLeeuw; Bottom kneeling: Adrienne Young, Ann Hu; Front with radio: Nicole Martone in *Beach Radio* PHOTO BY CAROL ROSEGG

CAFE A GO GO THEATRE

CAFÉ A GO GO Musical by the Heather Brothers; Director, John Hadden; June 5, 2002; Cast: Jessica Aquino, Jessica Cannon, Wade Fisher, Zachary Gilman, Stacie May Hassler, Matthew Knowland, Jasika Nicole Pruitt, Stephanie St. Hilaire, Juson Williams

CAP 21 THEATER

BEACH RADIO Musical with book and lyrics by Drey Shepperd; Music by Gerard Kenny; Directed and choreographed by Larry Fuller; October 29, 2002; Cast: Meyer deLeeuw, Ann Hu, Doug Kreeger, Nicole Martone, Meredith McCasland, Rosemary McNamara, Lance Olds, Jonathan Todd Ross, Noah Weisberg, Adrienne Young

KILLING LOUISE by Carol Galligan; Director, Michael Montel; March 4, 2003; Cast: Alexandra Geis, Rosemary Prinz, Brenda Thomas, Eliza Ventura, Van Zeiler

THE BARBARA WOLFF MONDAY NIGHT READING SERIES

WAITING FOR MY MAN (WORLD WITHOUT END) by Tony DiMurro; Director, Anthony Patellis; April 7, 2003

SIX OF ONE MUSICAL with book and lyrics by Scott Burkell; Music by Paul Loesel; Director, Lynne Shankel; April 14, 2003

MINNESOTA FATS IS RIGHT AROUND THE CORNER by Tony DiMurro; May 12, 2003

THE PLAYWRIGHT OF THE WESTERN WORLD by L.J. Schneiderman; May 19, 2003

CASTILLO THEATRE

HAMLET MACHINE by Heiner Muller; Translated by Carl Weber; Music and Lyrics by Fred Newman; Director, Fred Newman; Cast: Jeremy Black, Dave DeChristopher, I. Thecia Farrell, Roger Grunwald, Kenneth Hughes, Gabrielle Kurlander, Marian Rich, Anne Suddaby

CENTER STAGE

NIGHT ETHER by J. Grawemeyer; Director, Don Jordan; February 27, 2003; Cast: Gyda Arber, Rosanna Canonigo, Kristina Carroll, Peter Philip Clarke, Paul Daily, Nathan DeCoux, Jeff Pagliano, Malinda Walford

EATFEST: MENU A

ALMOST FULL CIRCLE AT THE GUGGENHEIM by Dee Sposito; Director, Tim Herman; April 2–6, 2003; Cast: Jeffrey Bateman, Kristin Dubrowsky

DANGER OF STRANGERS by Glenn Alterman; Director, Wesley Apfel; April 2–6, 2003; Cast: Ashley Green, Michael Silva, Walker Richards, Tara Perry, Terri Girvin, Johnathan Cedano, Stephanie Ila Silver, Richard Ezra Zekaria, Ellen Reilly, Brian Letscher, Rochele Tillman, Tim Barke, Chris Lucas, Peter Levine, Amy Bizjak, Bryan McKinley

V-DAY by Nancy Pothier; Director, Dawn Copeland; April 2–6, 2003; Cast: Ashley Green, Michael Silva, Walker Richards, Tara Perry, Terri Girvin, Johnathan Cedano, Stephanie Ila Silver, Richard Ezra Zekaria, Ellen Reilly, Brian Letscher, Rochele Tillman, Tim Barke, Chris Lucas, Peter Levine, Amy Bizjak, Bryan McKinley

EATFEST: MENU B

THE KING AND QUEEN OF PLANET POOKIE by Eric Alter; Director, Rebecca Kendall; April 2–6, 2003; Cast: Jason Hare, Linda Horwatt

GLIMMER OF HOPE by Joan Ross Sorkin; Director, Eric Chase; April 2–6, 2003; Cast: Peter Herrick, Lue McWilliams, Jeff Riebe

THE MOMENT by Gregg Pasternack; Director, Chris Wojyltko; April 2–6, 2003; Cast: Hal Blankenship, Daniel Gurian, EC Kelly, Sara Kramer, Philippe Cu Leong, Grant Machan, Vivian Meisner

EATFEST: MENU C

COUNTER GIRLS by Jonathan Reuning; Director, Paul Adams; April 9–13, 2003; Cast: Jane Altman, Blanche Cholet, Nicola Sheara

NIGHT BLOOMERS by Sarah Morton; Director, Maryna Harrison; April 9–13, 2003; Cast: Marnie Andrews

OEDIPUS FOR DUMMIES by Jack Rushen; Director, Gregory Fletcher; April 9–13, 2003; Cast: Jessica Calvello, Jason Cornwell, Bill Dyszel, Glory Gallo, Wayne Henry, Cree Monique, Jason Moreland, Kami Rodgers, Erez Rose, Dayna Steinfeld

EATFEST: MENU D

WOMEN IN HEAT by Rich Orloff; Director, Laurissa James; April 9–13, 2003; Cast: Wendy Allyn, Daniel Kaufman, Callie Mauldin, Kathy McCafferty

NIETZSCHE ATE HERE by Roy Berkowitz; Director, Christopher Borg; April 9–13, 2003; Cast: Wynne Anders, Benjamin Howes

SALLY SMELLS by Ted LoRusso; Director, Ian Marshall; April 9–13, 2003; Cast: Scott Clarkson, Margaux Laskey, Jason O'Connell

CENTURY CENTER FOR THE PERFORMING ARTS

WHEN WE DEAD AWAKEN by Henrik Ibsen; Director, J.C. Compton; June 9, 2002; Cast: Tami Dixon, Bruce Barton, Carl Palmer, Tom Knutson

CHASHAMA

THE OTHER SIDE OF THE CLOSET by Edward Roy; Director, Mark Cannistraro; September 9, 2002; Cast: Vincent Briguccia, Melissa Carroll, Charlene Gonzalez, Willie Mullins, Richard Tayloe

STONE COLD DEAD SERIOUS by Adam Rapp; Director, Carolyn Cantor; April 7, 2003; Cast: Betsy Aidem, Guy Boyd, Gretchen Cleevely, Matthew Stadelmann, Anthony Rapp

CIRCLE EAST

2003 SHORT PLAY FESTIVAL MAY 8–25, 2003

YOUR CALL IS IMPORTANT TO ME by Craig Lucas

THIS WILL BE THE DEATH OF HIM by David DeWitt

THE LONG SHOT by Richard Cottrell; Director, Peg Denithorne

MERMAIDS ON THE HUDSON by Anastasia Traina; Director, Mary Monroe

LILY OF THE VALLEY by Lisa Humbertson; Director, Erma Duricko

CLIMATE by Joe Pintauro; Director, Jude Schanzer

LOVE by Betty Shamieh; Director, Janice Goldberg

INFORMED CONSENT by Paul Knox; Director, Keith Greer

SOOOO SAD by Ty Adams; Director, Barbara Bosch

THE FUQUA SLONE REISENGLASS APPRAISAL by Lawrence Harvey Shulman; Director, Guy Giarrizzo

VERT-GALANT by Jon Fraser

CHERRY LANE THEATRE

GRASMERE by Kristina Leach; Director, Joseph Arnold; June 8, 2002; Cast: Darcy Blakesley, Annie Di Martino, Aaron Gordon, Logan Sledge

YOUNG PLAYWRIGHTS FESTIVAL 2002

AN ICE CREAM MAN FOR ALL SEASONS by Molly Lambert; Director, Jeremy Dobrish; September 26, 2002; Cast: Keith Davis, Jonathan Sale

PARTS THEY CALL DEEP by Lauren Gunderson; Director, Brett W. Reynolds; September 26, 2002; Cast: Shannon Emerick, Cynthia Hood, Celia Howard, Nathan Darrow

TRADE by Caroline V. McGraw; Director, Valentina Fratti; September 26, 2002; Cast: Shannon Emerick, Nathan Darrow, Ryan Rentmeester, Adriana Gaviria, Gina Hirsch, Jonathan Sale

HAPPY DAYS by Samuel Beckett; Director, Joseph Chaikin; September 29, 2002; Cast: Joyce Aaron, Ron Faber

Joyce Aaron in *Happy Days* PHOTO BY CAROL ROSEGG

IT JUST CATCHES by Carol Hemingway; Based on stories by Ernest Hemingway; Songs by Cole Porter; Director, Edward Hastings; February 9, 2003; Cast: David Ackroyd, Ann Crumb, Marsh Hanson, Ryan Shively, Daniel Freedom Stewart, Jessica D. Turner

MENTOR PROJECT 2003

URGENT FURY by Allison Moore (Marsha Norman, mentor); Director, Richard Caliban; March 12, 2003; Cast: Patrick Boll, Halley Feiffer, Carol Halstead, Kathryn A. Layng, Peter Scanavino, John Speredakos, Lindsay Wilson

SLAG HEAP by Anton Dudley (Ed Bullins, mentor); Director, Erica Schmidt; April 9, 2003; Cast: Brienan Bryant, Caroline Clay, Nina Zoie Lam, Andy Powers, Yvonne Woods

THE PARENTS EVENING by Bathsheba Doran (Michael Weller, mentor); Director, Irina Brown; May 7, 2003; Cast: Lisa Emery, Ken Marks

KIKI & HERB: COUP DE THEATRE Musical by Justin Bond and Kenny Mellman; book by Justin Bond; Musical Direction by Kenny Mellman; Director, Scott Elliott; May 7, 2003; Cast: Justin Bond and Kenny Mellman

CLASSICAL THEATRE OF HARLEM

KING LEAR by William Shakespeare; Director, Alfred Preisser; July 12, 2002; Cast: Paul Butler, Arthur French, April Yvette Thompson, Lawrence Winslow

MA RAINEY'S BLACK BOTTOM by August Wilson; Director, Arthur French; October 4, 2002; Cast: Leopold Lowe, Charles Turner, Allie Woods, Jerry Matz, Ben Rivers, Henry Bradley, Ronald Rand, Roz Davis, Tamela Aldridge

THE BLACKS: A CLOWN SHOW by Jean Genet; Director, Christopher McElroen; January 31, 2003; Cast: Ty Jones, J, Kyle Manzay, Jammie Patton, Maechi Aharanwa, Yusef Miller, Gwendolyn Mulamba, Erin Cherry, Cherise Boothe, Ron Simons, A-men Rasheed, John-Andrew Morrison, Neil Dawson, Oberon

THE CRAZY LOCOMOTIVE by Stanislaw Ignacy Witkiewicz; Director, Christopher McElroen; March 28, 2003; Cast: Alfred Preisser, Leopold Lowe, Erica Ball, Maria Oliveras, Ross Williams, Michael O'Day, Marissa Tiamfook, Roland Garcia, Yves Rene, Roger Hendricks Simon, Dan Hendricks Simon

CLEMENTE SOTO VELEZ CULTURAL CENTER (CSV)

A GIRL OF 16 by Aya Ogawa; Director, Aya Ogawa; April 30, 2003; Cast: Karmenlara Brownson, Drae Campbell, Erika Hildebrandt, Peter Lettre, Magin Schantz, Dario Tangelson, Saori Tsukuda, Aaron Mostkoff Unger, Deborah Wallace

CLUBBED THUMB

THE TYPOGRAPHER'S DREAM by Adam Bock; Director, Drew Barr; February 9, 2003; Cast: Kate Hampton, Meg MacCary and Dan Snook

SPRINGWORKS 2003

SOMEWHERE SOMEPLACE ELSE by Ann Marie Healy; Director, Annie Dorsen; April 11–May 3, 2003; Cast: Mara Stephens, Laura Heisler, Todd Cerveris, Andrew Weems

DESIGN YOUR KITCHEN by Kate Ryan; Director, Robert Davenport; April 11–May 3, 2003

LATE (A COWBOY SONG) by Sarah Ruhl; Director, Deborah Saivetz; April 11–May 3, 2003

CONNELLY THEATRE

LEONCE AND LENA by Georg Buchner; Director, Lenard Petit; July 11, 2002; Cast: Jonathan Fielding, Carman Lacivita, Keirin Brown, Almeria Campbell, Dalane Mason, Jason Lambert, Drew Hayes, Bryan Fenkart, Leslie Powers, Karen Freer, Alicia Avery, Nick Greco, Lauren Kleiman, Christopher Klinger, Aimee McCabe, Mitchell McEwan, Reyna Decourcy O'Grady, Sebastian Stan, Sylvia Yntena

LA MUSICA by Marguerite Duras; Director, Caroline Nastro; September 12, 2002; Cast: Diana Ruppe, John Sharp, Mercedes Herrero

CATCALL by Rebeca Ramirez; Director, Rebeca Ramirez; October 8, 2002; Cast: Laine D'Souza, Timothy Hawkinson, Omar Jerrnaine, Paola Mendoza, Thelma Medina, Rachael Roberts, Jamie Velez, Rolando Zuniga

REQUIEM FOR WILLIAM Based on short plays by William Inge; Director, Jack Cummings III; February 8, 2003; Cast: Dean Alai, Nicole Alifante, Toni DiBuono, Madeleine Jane DoPico, Corinne Edgerly, Taina Elg, Lovette George, Robyn Hussa, Samantha Jumper, Joe Kolinski, Mark Ledbetter, Tom Ligon, Michael Mags, Barbara Marineau, Richard Martin, Sean Maclaughlin, Marni Nixon, Monica Russell, Katie Scharf, Cheryl Stern, Diane Sutherland, Jonathan Uffelman, James Weber, John Wellman, Matt Yeager

THE LUCKY CHANCE by Aphra Behn; Director, Rebecca Patterson; April 25, 2003; Cast: Virginia Baeta, Gretchen S. Hall, Jennifer Larkin, Valentina McKenzie, Shauna Miles, Jena Necrason, Shanti Elise Prasad, Jill Repplinger, Gisele Richardson, Ami Shukla and DeeAnn Weir

THE ACCIDENTAL ACTIVIST by Kathryn Blume; Director, Michaela Hall; April 30, 2003; Cast: Kathryn Blume and live music by Eliza Ladd

CREATIVE ARTISTS LABORATORY THEATRE

THE FUTURE? by Tanya Klein; Director, Tanya Klein; October 26, 2002; Cast: Laurie Ann Orr, Stephen Kelly, Ryan Freeman, Jaime Sheedy, Gayle Pazerski, Michael Fife, Nicholas John Mazza, Tim Loftus

CULTURE CLUB

BIRDY'S BACHELORETTE PARTY by Mark Nassar, Suzanna Melendez and Denise Fennell; Director, Suzanna Melendez; June 7, 2002; Cast: Maria Baratta, Wass M. Stevens, Melissa Short, Jamie Sorrentini, Alice Moore, Michael Gargani, Frank Rempe, Ms. Fennell, Christopher Campbell, Scott Bilecky, Reid Hutchins

DANCE THEATER WORKSHOP

SON OF DRAKULA by David Drake; Director, Chuck Brown; October 24, 2002; Cast: David Drake

ANTIGONE by Sophocles; Adapted by Mac Wellman; Director, Paul Lazar; December 15, 2002; Cast: Didi O'Connell, Molly Hickok, Rebecca Wisocky, Tricia Brouk, Leroy Logan

DARYL ROTH THEATRE

ROMAN NIGHTS by Franco D'Alessandro; Director, Bick Goss; September 12, 2002; Cast: Franca Barchiesi, Roy Miller

DIMSON THEATRE

SHOPPERS CARRIED BY ESCALATORS INTO THE FLAMES by Denis Johnson; Director, David Levine; June 25, 2002; Cast: Gretchen Cleevely, Kevin Corrigan, Emily McDonnell, Betty Miller, Will Patton, Michael Shannon, Adam Trese, James Urbaniak, Kaili Vernoff

THE DIRECTORS COMPANY

ADDICTIONS by Tricia Walsh-Smith; Director, Pamela Berlin; October 2, 2002; Cast: Laila Robins, Robert Cuccioli, Orlagh Cassidy, Julie White, Bernadette Quigley, Redman Maxfield

LOVE IN THE AGE OF NARCISSISM by Brad Desch; Director, Chris Smith; November 1, 2002; Cast: David Alan Basche, Maddie Corman, Richmond Hoxie, Amy Landecker, Amber McDonald, Alysia Reiner, William Severs

BLUE HEAVEN by Raymond Hardie; Director, Judith Dolan; December 16, 2002; Cast: Colm Meaney, Laila Robins, Mary Bacon, Peter Gerety, Melinda Page Hamilton, James Kennedy

MINNESOTA FATS IS RIGHT AROUND THE CORNER by Tony DiMurro; Director, Nancy S. Chu; March 7, 2003; Cast: John Speredakos, Richard Leighton, Tricia Paoluccio, Amy McKenna, Peter Appel

Stephen Rowe, Priscilla Shanks in *O Jerusalem* PHOTO BY PETER JACOBSEN

DOUGLAS FAIRBANKS THEATRE

ALMOST LIVE FROM THE BETTY FORD CLINIC by Michael West; Director, Michael West; January 16, 2003; Cast: Michael West

DR2 THEATRE

IT'S BEGINNING TO LOOK A LOT LIKE MURDER! by Kurt Kleinmann; Director, Blake Lawrence; December 6, 2002; Cast: A. Raymond Banda, Steve Borowka, Darren Capozzi, Tarissa Day, James Gilbert, Shay Gines, Tim Honnoll, Robert Lehrer, Leslie Patrick, Ellen Reilly, John Weigand

WORM DAY by Matthew Calhoun; Director, Tom Herman; February 18, 2003; Cast: Miriam Shor, Kelly AuCoin, Will Swenson

THE FLEA THEATER

ANYTHING'S DREAM by Mac Wellman; Director, Beth Schachter; January 3, 2003; Cast: Stephen Soroka, Alison Hinks, Jamie McKittrick, Jessica Ball, Jess Barberry, David Bish, Madeline Hoak, Phil Kimble, Goron Ivanovski, Lance Bankerd, Jordan Ahnquist, Liliana Andreano, Justin Brehm, DyShaun Burton, Kevin Cvitanov, Matt Dibiasio, Jared Franzman, Frank Grande-Marchione, Kieran Maroney, Charlotte McIvor, Adam Pinti, Keiko Yoshida

O JERUSALEM by A.R. Gurney; Director, Jim Simpson; March 18, 2003; Cast: Priscilla Shanks, Stephen Rowe, Rita Wolf, Mercedes Herrero, Chaz Mena

45TH STREET THEATRE

PRINCE HAL by Bennett Windheim; Director, Elysabeth Kleinhans; March 8, 2003; Cast: Bruce Sabath, Deborah Ludwig, Diane Landers, Marc Geller, Simon Feil, Donna Dimino, Jennifer Jiles

45 BLEECKER

EVOLUTION by Jonathan Marc Sherman; Director, Lizzie Gottlieb; September 30, 2002; Cast: Josh Hamilton, Keira Naughton, Peter Dinklage, Iona Skye, Armando Riesco, Larry Block

RAPT by Roland Tec; Director, Mr. Tec; December 9, 2002; Cast: Chris Arruda, Lisa Barnes, Tom Bozell, Cori Lynn Campbell, Carl Palmer, Bill Tobes, Kate Weiman

EINSTEIN'S DREAMS by Alan Lightman; Adapted by Kipp Erante Cheng; Director, Rebecca Holderness; January 10, 2003; Cast: Jason Asprey, Amanda Barron, Dunia Bogner, Daniel Brink-Washington, H. Clark, Jared Coseglia, Rebecca DuMaine, Jessma Evans, Tom Knutson, Kate Kohler Amory, Alison Hanson, Puy Navarro, Barrett Ogden, Edward O'Blenis, Malinda Walford

THE BROTHERS KARAMAZOV, PART 1 by Fyodor Dostoevsky; Adapted by Alexander Harrington; Director, Alexander Harrington; February 9, 2003; Cast: Lisa Altomare, Frank Anderson, Stephen Reyes, Steven L. Barron, Ken Schactman, Joel Carino, David Fraioli, Ken Fuchs, Jennifer Gibbs, Robert Molossi, Gregory Sims, Greta Storace, Yaakov Sullivan, Sorrel Tomlinson, Jim Williams

AMERICAN MA(U)L by Robert O'Hara; Director, Robert O'Hara; April 14, 2003; Cast: Richarda Abrams, Chad Beckim, Colman Domingo, Susan Greenhill, Suzette Gunn, Charles Karel, Greg Keller, Maurice McRae, Lloyd Porter, Ariel Shafir

PERICLES by William Shakespeare; Director, Jesse Berger; June 9, 2002; Cast: Dale Soules, Raphael Nash Thompson, Daniel Breaker, Margot White, Wayne Scott, Carol Halstead, Addie Brownlee, Aysan Celik, Angela Ai, Grant Goodman, Zachary Knower, Alvaro Mendoza, A-men Rasheed, Ashley Strand, Price Waldman

47TH STREET THEATRE

CORNER WARS by Tim Dowlin; Director, Mel Williams; January 19, 2003; Cast: David Shaw, Warren Merrick III, Eric Carter, Joel Holiday, Omar Evans, Christopher Williams, Ray Thomas

14TH STREET Y

LADY, BE GOOD Musical with book by Guy Bolton and Fred Thompson; Music by George Gershwin; Lyrics by Ira Gershwin; Director, Thomas Mills; May 14, 2003; Cast: Amy Barker, Jennifer Bernstone, Todd Buonopane, Lindsey Chambers, Jeffry Denman, Kurt Domoney, Jennifer Dunn, Leo Ash Evans, Brian Hedden, Nancy Lemenager, Malina Linkas, David McDonald, Andrew Rasmussen, Ginette Rhodes, Tom Sellwood, Doug Shapiro, Jennifer Taylor, Doug Wynn

GLORIA MADDOX THEATRE

PRELUDE TO A KISS by Craig Lucas; Director, Glenn Krutoff; November 16, 2002; Cast: Gene Fanning, Rachel Feldman, Lawrence Garello, Eric Hottinger, Elizabeth Hayes, Eric Ilijevich, John Lisanti, Andrea Marshall-Money, Heidi E. Philipsen, Tania Santiago, Peter Sloan

GROUND FLOOR THEATRE
FAT CHANCE PRODUCTIONS, INC.

PART-TIME GODS by Noah Klein; Director, Ben Hodges; October 14, 2002; Cast: Michael Connors, Renata Hinrichs, Ben Hodges, Peter Lewis, Nicole Severine, Brant Spencer

Ben Hodges, Michael Connors in *Part-Time Gods* PHOTO BY MERRY YAN

HAROLD CLURMAN THEATRE

CLASS MOTHERS '68 by Eric H. Weinberger; Director, Jeremy Dobrish; December 9, 2002; Cast: Priscilla Lopez

HERE ARTS CENTER

QUEER @ HERE FESTIVAL

TOUCHSCAPE by James Scruggs; June 17–30, 2002

IN THE REALM OF THE UNREAL by Travis Chamberlain and Kyle Jarrow; June 17–30, 2002

LESBIAN PULP-O-RAMA! Created and performed by Heather de Michele, Anna Fitzwater, Gretchen M. Michelfeld, Beatrice Terry; June 17–30, 2002

THE MYSTIQUE OF FLY by Leslie Duprey; June 17–30, 2002

A PAIR OF HANDS by Raymond Luczak; June 17–30, 2002

CORNHOLED! by Daniel Nardicio; June 17–30, 2002

BAD WOMEN by Sidney Goldfarb; Director, Tina Shepard; June 20, 2002; Cast: Will Badgett, Purva Bedi, Rosemary Quinn, Sonja Rzepski, Jack Wetherall, Connie Winston, Alana Harris, Erica Kelly, Anya Maddow-Zimet, Ruthie Marantz, Tamara Rosenblum

THE AMERICAN LIVING ROOM

NINE ELEVEN by Susanna Speier; Director, Susanna Speier; July 13–September 1, 2002

THE FRANKLIN THESIS by Bradley Bazzle; Director, Alex Timbers; July 13–September 1, 2002

SNOW ANGEL by David Lindsay-Abaire; Director, Jake Hart; July 13–September 1, 2002

ALOHA FLIGHT 243 by Sophia Chapadjiev and Allison Leyton-Brown; Director, Pamela Seiderman; July 13–September 1, 2002

THE KINGDOM OF LOST SONGS by Abhijat Joshi; Director, Broke Brod; July 13–September 1, 2002

PUBLIC RELATIONS by Jeff Kellner; Director, Anthony Castellano; July 13–September 1, 2002

NOISES AND VOICES by Michael Schuval; Director, Hyunjung Lee; July 13–September 1, 2002

EIGHTEEN by Allison Moore; Director, Maryann Lombardi; July 13–September 1, 2002

EXCELSIOR by Jay Bernzweig; Director, Kevin Vavasseur; July 13–September 1, 2002

MOTHERGUN by Christine Evans; Director, Heidi Howard; July 13–September 1, 2002

TUMOR by Sheila Callaghan; Director, Catherine Zambri; July 13–September 1, 2002

DUG OUT by Nicholas Gray; Director, Mark Armstrong; July 13–September 1, 2002

WHITE RUSSIAN by Joseph Goodrich; Director, Isis Saratial Misdary; July 13–September 1, 2002

BOCHENSKI'S BRAIN by Gabriel Shanks and Tim Brown; Director, Gabriel Shanks and Tim Brown; July 13–September 1, 2002

OUT OF MY MIND by Suzanne Weber; Director, Christopher Duva; July 13–September 1, 2002

MISOGAMY, OR YOU'RE SO PRETTY WHEN YOU'RE UNFAITHFUL TO ME by Bronwen Bitetti; Director, Heather de Michele; July 13–September 1, 2002

THE DEATH OF TINTAGILES by Maurice Maeterlinck; Director, Joseph Rosswog; July 13–September 1, 2002

BRONX CASKET COMPANY by Andrea Lepcio; Director, Andrea Lepcio; July 13–September 1, 2002

FIELD OF FIREFLIES by Jason Mills; Director, Anna D'Agrossa; July 13–September 1, 2002

THE BASSET TABLE by Susannah Centlivre; Director, Rachel Ford; July 13–September 1, 2002

LAST CHILD by Rebecca Sharp; Director, Michele Travis; July 13–September 1, 2002

VOYAGE OF THE CARCASS by Dan O'Brien; Director, Alyse Leigh Rothman; July 14, 2002; Cast: Michael Anderson, Rebecca Harris, Chris Mason

PSYCHOTHERAPY LIVE! by Lisa Levy; July 22, 2002; Cast: Lisa Levy

MR. GALLICO by Sam Carter; Director, Henry Caplan; August 8, 2002; Cast: Jason Howard, Karl Herlinger, Tate Henderson

RAY ON THE WATER by Edward Allan Baker; Director, Ed Bianchi; September 28, 2002; Cast: Jessica Alexander, Suzanne Di Donna, Bruce MacVittie, Kirsten Russell, Georgia Strauss

THE SKY OVER NINEVEH by Mac Rogers; Director, Boris Kievsky; October 18, 2002

OR POLAROIDS (VERSION 2.1) by Ken Urban; Director, Ken Urban; November 1, 2002; Cast: Anni Bluhm, Andrew Breving, Kristin Stewart Chase, Maggie Cino

FUNDAMENTAL Multimedia work created by the company; Director, Brian Rogers; November 8, 2002; Cast: David Green, Gary Hennion, Mami Kimura, Sheila Lewandowski, James Morss, Stephane Penn

IPHIGENIA IN TAURIS by Euripides; Translated by Witter Bynner; Director, Veronica Newton; November 13, 2002

CULTUREMART

BLUE FLOWER by Ruth Bauer and Jim Bauer; January 3–11, 2003

INTIMATE SHIFT by Daniel Levy

RADIO WONDERLAND by Joshua Fried; January 3–11, 2003

THE DAKOTA PROJECT by Noah Haidle and Davis McCallum; January 3–11, 2003

PHENOMENON by Alyse Leigh Rothman; January 3–11, 2003

ELEGY by Tiffany Mills; Music by John Zorn; January 3–11, 2003

ERENDIRA by Gabriel Garda Marquez; Director, Kristin Marting; February 24, 2003; Cast: Ching Valdes-Aran, Elisa Terrazas, Alex Endy, Janio Marrero, Marc Petrosino

WHAT'S INSIDE THE EGG? by Lake Simons; Director, Lake Simons; March 19, 2003; Cast: Ms. Simons, Harold Lehmann, Erin Eagar, Chris Green, Matthew Acheson

SATURN'S WAKE by Deke Weaver and Michael Farkas; Director, Jill Samuels; March 23, 2003

Aviva Jane Carlin in *Almost Grown Up* PHOTO BY AMY FEINBERG

HYPOTHETICAL THEATRE COMPANY

ALMOST GROWN UP by Aviva Jane Carlin; Director, Amy Feinberg; September 9, 2002; Cast: Aviva Jane Carlin

INTAR 53

FUNTEOVEJUNA by Lope de Vega; adapted by Mia Katigbak; Director, David Herskovits; October 17, 2002; Cast: Konrad Aderer, Yoko Akashi, Pun Bandhu, Joel Carino, Deborah S. Craig, Joel de la Fuente, Andrew Eisenman, Siho Ellsmore, Lydia Gaston, Mel Gionson, Paul Juhn, Ms. Katigbak, C.S. Lee, Tina Lee, Timothy Ford Murphy, Tomi Peirano, Felice Yeh, Aaron Yoo

IRISH ARTS

POOR BEAST IN THE RAIN by Billy Roche; Director, Terence Lamude; November 13, 2002; Cast: Bernadette Quigley, Steve Brady, Tracy Coogan, John Keating and Mickey Kelly

THE GALLANT JOHN-JOE by Tom Mac Intyre; March 17, 2003; Cast: Tom Hickey

JEAN COCTEAU REPERTORY

HENRY V by William Shakespeare; Director, David Fuller; September 22, 2002; Cast: Harris Berlinsky, Christopher Black, Christopher Browne, Stafford Clark-Price, Abe Goldfarb, Edward Griffin, Brian Lee Huynh, Amanda Jones, Marlene May, Rebecca Robinson, Michael Surabian, Jason Crowl

THE IMPORTANCE OF BEING EARNEST by Oscar Wilde; Director, Ernest Johns; September 26, 2002; Cast: Harris Berlinsky, Jason Crowl, Abe Goldfarb, Amanda Jones, Angela Madden, Marlene May, Michael Surabian, Carey Van Driest

UNCLE VANYA by Anton Chekhov; Director, Eve Adamson; January 10, 2003; Cast: Harris Berlinsky, Christopher Black, Eileen Glenn, Angus Hepburn, Brian Lee Huynh, Amanda Jones, Marlene May, Craig Smith, Elise Stone

THE EFFECT OF GAMMA RAYS ON MAN-IN-THE-MOON MARIGOLDS by Paul Zindel; Director, Ernest Johns; March 7, 2003; Cast: Kate Holland, Angela Madden, Elsie James, Rebecca Robinson, Stefanie Varveris

THE TRIUMPH OF LOVE by Pierre Marivaux; Translated by Rod McLucas; Director, David Fuller; March 21, 2003; Cast: Amanda Jones, Kate Holland, Michael Surabian, Christopher Black, Edward Griffin, Marlene May, Bill Fairbairn

JOHN HOUSEMAN THEATRE

A "PURE" GOSPEL CHRISTMAS by Leslie Dockery and David A. Tobin; Directed and choreographed by Leslie Dockery; December 17, 2002; Cast: Richard Bellazzin, Ken Boyd, Diane Michelle Buster, Kim Crawford, Brian Dickerson, Arlene Frink, Damon Horton, Sandra Keel-Huff, Delise Jones, Darin Myers, Cypriana Okuzu, Deborah E. Oatman, Kim Pacheco, Romel Robinson, David A. Tobin

JOSE QUINTERO THEATRE

JOE AND BETTY by Murray Mednick; Director, Guy Zimmerman; June 2, 2002; Cast: Annabelle Gurwitch, John Diehl, Shawna Casey, Tom McCleister, Edith Fields, Sharron Shayne, Drago Sumonja. (Transferred with cast changes to the Kirk Theatre in the Theatre Row complex on February 15, 2002 for a limited run)

SHAKESPEARE UNPLUGGED: THE HISTORY CYCLE

HENRY V by William Shakespeare; Director, Joanne Zipay and Ivanna Cullinan; November 12, 2002; Cast: Laurie Bannister-Colon, Grant Mudge, Jane Titus, Kevin Scott Till, Gail Kay Bell, David Huber, Miriam Lipner, Eileen Glenn, Richard Simon, Eric Aschenbrenner, Joseph Capone, Jovinna Chan, Omri Schein, Irma St. Paule, Jennifer Sherron Stock, Hilary Ward

HENRY VI: PARTS 1, 2 AND 3 by William Shakespeare; Director, Ivanna Cullinan and Joanne Zipay; March 27, 2003; Cast: Susan Ferrara, Carey Van Driest, Hilary Ward, Mary Hodges, Miriam Lipner, Michelle Kovacs, Dacyl Acevedo, Alyssa Simon, Lynn Kanter, Corrie McCrea, Angela Liao, Kristen Harlow, Lisa Preston, Sheila Ostadazim, Marie Bridget Dundon, Joseph Capone, Jovinna Chan, Ari Barbanell, Laurie Bannister-Colon, Renee Bucciarelli, John Kinsherf

THE METAMORPHOSIS by Franz Kafka; Adapted by E. Thomalen; Director, Francine L. Trevens; January 9, 2003; Cast: Peter J. Coriaty, Brandon deSpain, Marcalan Glassberg, David Kornhaber, David Lamberton, Ozlem Turhal, Kevin Whittinghill, Loretta Guerra Woodruff, Alexis Wickwire

NURSE! by Lisa Hayes; Director, Annie Levy; May 6, 2003; Cast: Lisa Hayes

KEEN COMPANY

MUSEUM by Tina Howe; Director, Carl Forsman; June 9, 2002; Cast: Maxwell L. Anderson, Susan Blackwell, Brennan Brown, Elizabeth Bunch, Jimmon Cole, Teddy Coluca, Chris Denzer, Katie Firth, Jennifer Gibbs, Robyn Goodman, Nathan Guisinger, Tony Hale, Kate Hampton, Chris Hutchinson, Tim Kang, Lael Logan, Jenny Maguire, Marilyn Moore, Christina Parker, Dina Pearlman, Christa Scott-Reed, Jordin Ruderman, Andrew Schulman

Lisa Hayes in *Nurse!*

THREE-CORNERED MOON by Gertrude Tonkonogy; Director, Carl Forsman; September 8, 2002; Cast: Denis Butkus, Christopher Duva, Yetta Gottesman, Kathleen Kaefer, Maggie Lacey, Mikel Sarah Lambert, Greg McFadden, Andrew McGinn, Nick Toren

KIRK THEATRE

TEXARKAN WALTZ by Louis Broom; Director, Allison Narver; November 13, 2002; Cast: Tina Benko, Caroline Bottle, Doug Cote, Adrian LaTourelle, Jesse Lenat, Denise Lute, Chuck Montgomery, Annie Parisse, Tom Wiggin

HEAT LIGHTNING Musical with book by George Griggs and Paul Andrew Perez; Music and Lyrics by George Griggs; Director, Mr. Perez; March 5, 2003; Cast: Laura Marie Duncan, Sean Fri, Nicolette Hart, Jackie Seiden, Coleen Sexton, Will Swenson, Jennifer Waldman

MESHUGAH by Emily Mann; adapted from the novel by Isaac Bashevis Singer; Director, Loretta Greco; May 15, 2003; Cast: Barbara Andres, Ned Eisenberg, Ben Hammer, Ted Koch, Elizabeth Marvel

KRAINE THEATER

THE MAYOR'S LIMO by Mark Nassar; Director, Santo Fazio; September 25, 2002; Cast: Kevin Alexander, Sharon Angela, Patrick Michael Buckley, James J. Hendricks, Mark Nassar, Michael Perri, Robert Stevens, Rebecca Weitman, James Wormsworth

LABYRINTH THEATER COMPANY

OUR LADY OF 121ST STREET by Stephen Adly Guirgis; Director, Philip Seymour Hoffman; September 29, 2002; Cast: Elizabeth Canavan, Liza Colón-Zayas, David Deblinger, Melissa Feldman, Mark Hammer, Ron Cephas Jones, Richard Petrocelli, Portia, Al Roffe, Felix Solis, David Zayas. First presented as a LAByrinth Theater Company workshop (August 20–October 12, 2002; 15 performances from the September 28, 2002 press opening). Transferred to Off-Broadway's Union Square Theatre (March 6, 2003; 100 performances through May 31, 2003)

DIRTY STORY by John Patrick Shanley; Director, John Patrick Shanley; March 2, 2003; Cast: David Deblinger, Florencia Lozano, Chris McGarry, Michael Puzzo

LION THEATRE

SPLIT by Michael Weller; Director, Drew DeCorleto; September 16, 2002; Cast: Teresa L. Goding, Leo Lauer, Stephen Brumble Jr., Nina Edgerton, Andrew J. Hoff, Jeremy Koch, Veronica Mittenzwei

SOAR LIKE AN EAGLE Musical with book by Adam Dick; Music and Lyrics by Paul Dick; Director, Daniel T. Lavender; Cast: Carrie A. Johnson, Nicholas Dalton, Mary Ann Hannon, Paul Straney, Jaye Maynard, Michael Minarik, Seth Golay, Stephanie Girard, Javier Munoz, Patrick Bodd, Michael Shane Ellis

A RITUAL OF FAITH by Brad Levinson; Director, Igor Goldin; March 2, 2003; Cast: Michael Cruz, Laura Fois, Ryan Hilliard, Aaron Feldman, Marilyn Sanabria, Tibor Feldman, Marc Krinsky, Matthew Boston

NEW BOY by William Sutcliffe; Adapted by Russell Labey; Director, Russell Labey; April 24, 2003; Cast: Neil Henry, Todd Swenson, Lisa Barnes, Dana Powers Acheson, Peter Russo

MANHATTAN ENSEMBLE THEATER

DEATH IN VENICE by Robert David MacDonald; Adapted from the novella by Thomas Mann; Translation by David Luke; Director, Giles Havergal; June 6, 2002; Cast: Giles Havergal

HANK WILLIAMS: LOST HIGHWAY by Randal Myler and Mark Harelik; Director, Randal Myler; December 19, 2002; Cast: Jason Petty, Michael W. Howell, Juliet Smith, Margaret Bowman, Stephen G. Anthony, Myk Watford, Drew Perkins, Michael P. Moran, Tertia Lynch, Russ Wever. (Transferred to the Off Broadway's Little Shubert Theatre March 26, 2003; 65 performances through May 31, 2003)

MA-YI THEATRE

THE ROMANCE OF MAGNO RUBIO by Lonnie Carter; adapted from a story by Carlos Bulosan; Direction and scenery by Loy Arcenas; October 26, 2002; Cast: Art Acuna, Ramon de Ocampo, Ron Domingo, Jojo Gonzalez, Orlando Pabotoy

DEAD MAN'S SOCKS by Ralph B. Pena; Director, Ralph B. Pena; March 6, 2003; Cast: Chris Thorn, Rodney To, John Wernke

LAST OF THE SUNS by Alice Tuan; Director, Chay Yew; April 27, 2003; Cast: Ching Valdes-Aran, Mia Katigbak, Kathy Kuroda, Tess Lina, Ron Nakahara, Eric Steinberg

MCGINN/CAZALE THEATRE

THE NOTEBOOK by Wendy Kesselman; Director, Evan Yionulis; June 23, 2002; Cast: Lisa Harrow, Miles Purinton, Portia Reiners, Peter Van Wagner

MONSIEUR IBRAHIM AND THE FLOWERS OF THE KORAN by Eric-Emmanuel Schmitt; Translated by Stephane Laporte; Director, Maria Mileaf; January 26, 2003; Cast: Ed Vassallo

BUICKS by Julian Sheppard; Director, Brian Kulick; March 9, 2003; Cast: Olivia Birkelund, Lucia Brawley, Bill Buell, Norbert Leo Butz

MELTING POT THEATRE COMPANY

COOKIN' AT THE COOKERY by Marion J. Caffey; Director, Marion Caffey; January 22, 2003; Cast: Ann Duquesnay, Debra Walton

John Tedeschi in *I Love Myself*

METROPOLITAN PLAYHOUSE

SUN-UP by Lula Vollmer; Director, Mahayana Landowne; March 7, 2003; Cast: Ruthanne Gereghty, Sarah Dandridge, Roy Bacon, John Summerour, Joe Plummer, Scott Ebersold, Tom Richter, T.I. Moore

FASHION by Anna Cora Mowatt; Director, Alex Roe; April 10, 2003; Cast: Henry Afro-Bradley, Erika Bailey, Matt Daniels, Sean Dill, Stephanie Dorian, Jon-Michael Hernandez, Olivia Keister, Sean Kenin, Tod Mason, Sylvia Norman, Karl Williams

IS THERE A DOCTOR IN THE HOUSE? by Joel Jeske; Director, Joel Jeske; May 7, 2003; Cast: Laura Dillman, Bill Edwards, Mr. Jeske, Jeremiah Murphy, Rob Pedini, Juliet Schaefer-Jeske

MIDTOWN INTERNATIONAL THEATRE FESTIVAL

ALL THE WORLD'S A STAGE by Donna Stearns

APPLE by Vern Thiessen; Director, Randy White

BELLES OF THE MILL Musical with book by Rachel Rubin Ladutke; Music and Lyrics by Jill Marshall-Work; Director, Arlene Schulman

BEYOND THE VEIL by John Chatterton; Director, Linda Burson

BOULEVARD X by Susan N. Horowitz; Director, Rajedra Ramoon Maharaj

BUON NATALE, BRUNO by Terianne Falcone; Director, Gary Austin

CIRRIUS, NEBRASKA by Nick Vigorito

CITY OF DREAMS Musical with book and lyrics by David Zellnik; Music by Joseph Zellnik; Director, Michael Alltop

DIRTY LAUNDRY by Deborah Louise Ortiz

THE DURANG PROJECT: FIVE SHORT PLAYS by Christopher Durang; The Doctor Will See You Now; DMV Tyrant; Funeral Parlor; Kitty the Waitress; Business Lunch in the Russian Tea Room; Director, Michael Klimzak

FAUSTUS by Christopher Marlowe; Adaptation by Jay Michaels; Director, Jay Michaels

FLACK by Tina Posterli

HEAVY METTLE by Richard Hoehler

HEROES by Jonathan Brady; Director, Mark Steven Robinson

I LOVE MYSELF and **WHO ARE THE PEOPLE IN YOUR NEIGHBORHOOD?** Two one-man shows with John Tedeschi

I LOVE NEW YORK—WHAT'S YOUR EXCUSE? by David Kosh; Director, Ann Bowen

MORE BITCH THAN A BITCH by John Paul

MUSTARD—IT'S A GAS! by Ben Murphy

MY LIFE IN THE TRENCHES by Jill Dalton

RUBBER by Tom Sleigh; Director, Dyana Kimball

SAINTS AND SINGING by Gertrude Stein

STAR-CROSSED LOVERS by Charles Battersby; Director, Valentina Cardinalli

TIME MACHINE 2.0 Musical with book, Music and Lyrics by Mark Weiser; Director, Daniella Topol

WILL AND THE GHOST by Aoise Stratford and Conal Condren; Director, Christian Ely

WOMAN VS. SUPERMAN by Kelly Jean Fitzsimmons

MINT SPACE

PADDYWACK by Daniel Magee; Director, Herman Babad; November 3, 2002; Cast: Mary Jasperson, Kelly Miller, Declan Mooney, Frank Shattuck, Allan Styer, Carla Tassara

THE UNINVITED GUEST by Michael R. Murphy; Director, Daniel Kuney; January 12, 2003; Cast: Jane Altman, Jack Garrity, Michael Graves, Rachel Lee Harris, Ryan Hilliard, Sean Matic, Kittson O'Neill, David Runco

HALLELUJAH BREAKDOWN by Ted LoRusso; Director, Gregory Fletcher; January 12, 2003; Cast: Wynne Anders, David Bell, TJ Gambrel, Jack Garrett, Lue McWilliams, Casey Weaver, Nicholas Wuehrmann

GOD AND MR. SMITH by Travis Baker; Director, Marshall Mays; March 20, 2003; Cast: Brigit Darby, Todd Allen Durkin, Daryl Lathon, Lucy McMichael, Susan Molloy, Marc Moritz, Michael Nathanson, Najla Said, Jim Wisniewski, Jeffrey C. Wolf, Daniel Snow

SINFULLY RICH by Rich Orloff; Director, Todd Allen Durkin, Nolan Haims, Catherine Baker Steindler, Joseph Ward and Jeffrey C. Wolf; March 24, 2003; Cast: Ilene Bergelson, Annie Edgerton, William Green, Gavin Hoffman, Daniel Kaufman, Larissa Kiel, Cynthia Posillico, Kim Reed, Sarah Saltzberg, Matty D. Stuart, Jamie Watkins, Gregg Weiner, Marshall York

OF MICE AND MEN by John Steinbeck; Director, Harvey Perri; April 11, 2003; Cast: John Topping, K. Winston Osgood, Caroline Luft, Paul Barry, Jefferson Slinkard, James Edward Lee, Jason Edwards

THE NOVELIST by James Bosley; Director, Rebecca Kendall; May 11, 2003; Cast: Troy Schremmer, Francisco Lorite, Marilyn Sanabria, Jason Hare, Sean Matic

SCREAMING IN THE WILDERNESS by Vanda; Director, Steven McElroy; May 12, 2003; Cast: Cynthia Brown, Gerald Downey, Barbara J. Spence, Danielle Quisenberry, Tom Dusenbury, Aimee Howard, Marianne Mackenzie, Mark Mears, Billy Rosa, Vanessa Villalobos

NATIONAL ASIAN AMERICAN THEATRE COMPANY

AIR RAID by Archibald MacLeish; Director, Stephen Stout; March 23, 2003; Cast: Michi Barall, Jodi Lin, Han Ong, Eileen Rivera, Joel de la Fuente, Mel Gionson, Jennifer Chang, Gita Reddy, Siho Ellsmore, Geeta Citygirl

NEW GEORGES

NONE OF THE ABOVE by Jenny Lyn Bader; Director, Julie Kramer; March 19, 2003; Cast: Alison Pill, Kel O'Neill

Alison Pill, Kel O'Neill in *All of the Above* PHOTO BY CAROL ROSEGG

NEW VICTORY THEATER

THE JUNEBUG SYMPHONY by James Thierree; Director, James Thierree; October 9, 2002; Cast: James Thierree, Vma Ysamat, Raphaelle Boitel, Magnus Jakobsson

A YEAR WITH FROG AND TOAD Musical with book and lyrics by Willie Reale; music by Robert Reale; based on the children's books by Arnold Lobel; Director, David Petrarca; November 15, 2002; Cast: Jay Goede, Mark Linn-Baker, Danielle Ferland, Kate Reinders, Frank Vlastnik

THWAK! by David Collins and Shane Dundas; Director, Philip Wm. McKinley; April 6, 2003; Cast: David Collins, Shane Dundas

A MIDSUMMER NIGHT'S DREAM by William Shakespeare; Adapted by Robert Richmond; Director, Robert Richmond; May 2, 2003; Cast: Kenn Sabberton, Gabriela Fernandez-Coffey, Guy Oliver-Watts, Ryan Conarro, Lindsay Rae Taylor, Andrew Schwartz, Renata Friedman

NEW YORK THEATRE WORKSHOP

DETAILS by Lirs Noren; Director, Bille August; January 23, 2003; Cast: Ole Lemmeke, Benedicte Hansen, Helle Fragalid, Nicolai Dahl Hamilton

NEW YORK INTERNATIONAL FRINGE FESTIVAL

SCHEDULE INCLUDED: MATT AND BEN by Mindy Kaling and Brenda Withers. Director, Mindy Kaling and Brenda Withers; August 9–25, 2002; Cast: Mses. Kaling and Withers

MARGINAL SAINTS by Lee Gundersheimer; Director, Donna Sue de Guzman; August 9–25, 2002

LOVE IN PIECES by Sarah Morton; August 9–25, 2002; Cast: Ryan Brack, Lisa Gardner

THE BIZARRO BOLOGNA SHOW by Dan Piraro; Additional material by Lee Ritchey; Music by Steve Powell and Ernie Myers; Director, Lee Ritchey; August 9–25, 2002

MEDEAMACHINE by Ian Belton

SELMA'S BREAK AND RX by Matthew Swan; Directors, Matthew Swan and Carlo Vogel; August 9–25, 2002; Cast: Jessie Hutcheson, Lisa M. Perry, Jonathan Marc Sherman, Matthew Swan, Linda S. Nelson

NOT HERSELF LATELY by Neil Genzlinger; August 9–25, 2002

SHERLOCK HOLMES AND THE SECRET OF MAKING WHOOPEE by Sean Cunningham; August 9–25, 2002

FIVE FROZEN EMBRYOS by David Greenspan; Director, Jon Schumacher; August 9–25, 2002; Cast: Ilka Saddler Pinheiro, Ellen Shanman

THE SLEEPERS by Christopher Shinn; Director, Jon Schumacher; August 9–25, 2002; Cast: Laura Marks, Russel Taylor, Paul Juhn

THE WAY OUT by Timothy Nolan; Director, Vincent Marano; August 9–25, 2002; Cast: Shiek Mahmud-Bey, Tod Engle

DEATH OF FRANK by Stephen Belber; Director, Nancy S. Chu; August 9–25, 2002; Cast: Raymond James Hill, Alexa Dubreuil, Paul Keany, Tessa Gibbons

RESA FANTASTISKT MYSTICK by Lars Mattsun; Adapted by Carolyn Almos, Matt Almos, Jon Beauregard, Joel Marshall, Todd Merrill, Katharine Noon, Victor Ortado, Laura Otis and Selina Smith; Director, Carolyn Almos; August 9–25, 2002; Cast: Jon Beauregard, Todd Merrill, Victor Ortado, Selina Smith, Laura Otis, Daniel Stewart

BEAT by Kelly Groves; Based on the life and writing of Allen Ginsberg and others; Director, Kelly Groves; August 9–25, 2002; Cast: Dan Pintauro, Andrew Cruse, Todd Kovner, John Jeffrey Martin, Geoffrey Molloy, Ezra Nanes and Glenn Peters

HIM AND HER Musical with book, Music and Lyrics by Paul Scott Goodman; Director, Miriam Gordon; August 9–25, 2002; Cast: Paul Scott Goodman, Liz Larsen

OHIO THEATER

RUM AND VODKA by Conor McPherson; Director, Samuel Buggeln; October 7, 2002; Cast: Mark Alhadeff

KOLTES NEW YORK 2003: NEW AMERICAN TRANSLATIONS.

WEST PIER by Bernard Marie Koltes; Translated by Marion Schoevaert and Theresa Weber; Director, Jay Scheib; May 8, 2003; Cast: Tom Day, Marina Garcia-Gelpe, Dan Lilian, Krassin Iordanov, Ryan Justeson, Aimee Phelan, Michael Stumm, Zishan Ugurlu

ROBERTO ZUCCO by Bernard Marie Koltes; Translated by Daniel Safer; Director, Daniel Safer; May 11, 2003; Cast: Aubrey Chamberlin, Sean Donovan, Jessma Evans, Emmitt C. George, Jason Lew, Jennie Marytai Liu, Katie Lowes, Mike Mikos, Micki Pellerano, Laura Berlin Stinger. E. Randy Thompson, Raina von Waldenburg, Wendy Meiling Yang, David Cale

BATTLE OF BLACK AND DOGS by Bernard Marie Koltes; Translated by Michael Attias; Director, Doris Mirescu; May 14, 2003; Cast: Joan Jubett, Matt Landers, Leopold Lowe, Eric Dean Scott

IN THE SOLITUDE OF COTTON FIELDS by Bernard Marie Koltes; Translated by Lenora Champagne; Director, Marion Schoevaert; May 16, 2003; Cast: Terrence Bae, Shaun O'Neil

ONTOLOGICAL THEATRE

OTHER LOVE by Bill Talen; Director, Tony Torn and Savitri Durkee; June 7, 2002; Cast: Reverend Billy

PANIC! (HOW TO BE HAPPY!) by Richard Foreman; Directed and designed by Richard Foreman; January 9, 2003; Cast: D.J. Mendel, Elina Lowensohn, Tea Alagic, Robert Cucuzza

THE AUTOBIOGRAPHY OF GOD AS TOLD BY MEL SCHNEIDER by Marv Siegel; Director, Donovan Dolan; May 22, 2003; Cast: Ron Palillo, Joseph Lee Gramm, Genna Brocone, Rainey Welch, Ward Horton

PANTHEON THEATRE

ETTA JENKS by Marlane Meyer; Director, Robert Funaro; March 8, 2003; Cast: Ruth Aguilar, Neil Barsky, Richard Boccato, Heather Hanemann, Tony Hitchcock, John Koprowski, Ernest Mingione, Susan Mitchell, John Prada, Chesney Snow

SEALED FOR FRESHNESS by Doug Stone; Director, Doug Stone; April 2, 2003; Cast: Jeanne Hime, Nancy Hornback, Elissa Olin, Kate VanDevender, J.J. Van Name, Shawn Curran

THAT DAY IN SEPTEMBER by Artie Van Why; Director, Richard Masur; April 9, 2003; Cast: Artie Van Why

PARADISE THEATER COMPANY

PETER AND VANDY by Jay DiPietro; Director, Jay DiPietro; September 12, 2003; Cast: Monique Vukovic, Jay DiPietro

I WANT YOU TO by Eric Maierson; March 2, 2003; Cast: Ken Forman, Monique Vukovic

FEAR AND FRIDAY NIGHTS by Lawrence Levine; Director, Lawrence Levine; March 2, 2003; Cast: Jicky Schnee, Grant Varjas

LOSING GROUND by Bryan Wizemann; Director, Bryan Wizemann; March 27, 2003; Cast: Kendall Pigg, Mark Meyer, Eileen O'Connell, Monique Vukovic, Rhonda Keyser, John Good

Reverend Billy in *Other Love*

THE PEARL THEATRE COMPANY

SHE STOOPS TO CONQUER by Oliver Goldsmith; Director, Chuck Hudson; September 22, 2002; Cast: John Camera, Stewart Carrico, Celeste Ciulla, Dominic Cuskern, Sally Kemp, Mary Molloy, Christopher Moore, John Livingstone Rolle, Edward Seamon, Jay Stratton, Scott Whitehurst, Eunice Wong

NATHAN THE WISE by Gotthold Lessing; Adapted by Richard Sewell; Director, Barbara Bosch; October 20, 2002; Cast: John Camera, Celeste Ciulla, Dominic Cuskern, Sally Kemp, Christopher Moore, John Livingstone Rolle, Edward Seamon, Jay Stratton, Scott Whitehurst, Eunice Wong

THE TEMPEST by William Shakespeare; Director, Padraic Lillis; December 8, 2002; Cast: Rachel Botchan, Jonathan Brathwaite, Stewart Carrico, Celeste Ciulla, Dominic Cuskern, Dan Daily, Flannery Foster, Robert Hock, Amy Hutchins, Sean McNall, Christopher Moore, John Newton, Andy Prosky, Edward Seamon, Scott Whitehurst, Brenda Withers

HEARTBREAK HOUSE by George Bernard Shaw; Director, Gus Kaikkonen; February 16, 2003; Cast: Russ Anderson, Rachel Botchan, Robin Leslie Brown, Joanne Camp, Dominic Cuskern, Dan Daily, Robert Hock, George Morfogen, Nada Rowand, Edward Seamon

DAISY MAYME by George Kelly; Director, Russell Treyz; April 13, 2003; Cast: Rachel Botchan, Robin Leslie Brown, Joanne Camp, Dominic Cuskern, Robert Hock, Sean McNall, Carol Schultz, Samantha Soule

PECCADILLO THEATER COMPANY

VERONIQUE by John O'Hara; Director, Dan Wackerman; July 14, 2002; Cast: Jim Iorio, Jennifer Erin Roberts, Susan Jeffries, Richard Leighton, Meg Brooker, Benjamin Howes, Elizabeth Elson, Jason Cicci

THE SHANGHAI GESTURE by John Colton; revised by Joanna Chan; Director, Dan Wackerman; October 27, 2002; Cast: Richard Bekins, Gerald Blum, Nick Bosco, Robert Lee Chu, Briana Davis, Elizabeth Elson, Camilla Enders, Catherine Jhung, Janie Kelly, Brian Linden, Jackson Ning, Frank Perich, Ron Piretti, Jade Wu

PELICAN THEATRE

NOT FOOL THE SUN OR FESTER 'N SEXX by Peter Florax; Director, Peter Florax; December 9, 2002; Cast: Jason Altman, Randee Barrier, Mike Bocchetti, Dave Durkin, Chris O'Neil, Brian Rush, Steve Tresty

PHIL BOSAKOWSKI THEATRE

BAPTIZING ADAM by David Allyn; Director, Kevin Lee Newbury; August 22, 2002; Cast: Vince Gatton, Megan Hollingshead, Andrew Glaszek, Philip James Sulsona, Henry Glovinsky

THE ONE FESTIVAL

LOVE ARM'D by Karen Eterovich; October 31–November 5, 2002

THIEVES IN THE TEMPLE: THE RECLAIMING OF HIP HOP by Aya DeLeon; October 31–November 5, 2002

BANG! by C.C. Seymour; October 31–November 5, 2002

SHOES by Tim Douglas Jensen; October 31–November 5, 2002

THE POETICS OF BASEBALL by Neil Bradley; October 31–November 5, 2002

CIRQUE JACQUELINE by Andrea Reese; October 31–November 5, 2002

DONNA PARADISE by Matthew Wells; Director, Rob O'Neill; November 9, 2002; Cast: Elissa Lash, Krish Batnagar, Candy Simmons, Jennifer Ward

LOST AND FOUND by Paul Harris; Director, Fred Barton; May 11, 2003; Cast: Leila Martin, Stu Richel, John Kevin Jones

THE PRODUCERS CLUB

WHAT'S YOUR KARMA? by Lilith Dove; July 23, 2002

JOHNNY 23 Musical by Jim Doyle; Director, GW Reed; October 5, 2002; Cast: Bill Tatum, Gerrianne Raphael, Leslie Feagan, Andrew Fitzsimmons, Andrew Horwitz, Jill Kotler, Annie Lee Moffett, Ellen Saland

CUBAN OPERATOR PLEASE AND FLOATING HOME by Adrian Rodriguez; Director, Arian Blanco; October 9, 2002; Cast: Jose Antonio, John C. Cunningham, Emilio Delgado, Omar Hernandez, Mercy Valladares

CHRISTMAS WITH THE CRAWFORDS Musical by Mark Sargent and Richard Winchester; Directed and choreographed by Donna Drake; November 22, 2002; Cast: Joey Arias, Kate Botello, Trauma Flintstone, Brant Kaiwi, Joe Levesque, Chris March, Sade Pendarvis, Mark Sargent, Jason Scott

KEROUAC by Tom O'Neil; Director, Anthony P. Pennino; January 26, 2003; Cast: Tim Cox, Deanne Dawson, John Kwiatkowski, Kyle Pierson, Gavin Walker, Deirdre Schwiesow, Peter Stewart

MARATHON by Edoardo Erba; Translated by Israel Horovitz; Director, Weylin Symes; March 7, 2003; Cast: Eric Laurits, Adam Paltrowitz

PROSPECT THEATER COMPANY

SPRING AWAKENING by Frank Wedekind; Translated by Ted Hughes; Director, Jackson Gay; November 2, 2002; Cast: Blake Hackler, Bridget Flanery, Austin Jones

TAXI CABERET by Peter Mills and Cara Reichel; Director, Cara Reichel; November 5, 2002; Cast: Alison Cimmet, Christopher Graves, Jason Mills, Katie O'Shaughnessey, Simone Zamore

EXODE

THE BUCCANEER by Jacob Grigolia-Rosenbaum; November 11–13, 2002

CORN CORN by Cara Reichel; November 11–13, 2002

PERSIANS by Andrew Case; November 11–13, 2002

DIDO (AND AENEAS) by Roxane Heinze and Cara Reichel; Adapted from Virgil; Music and Arrangements by Daniel Feyer, Richard Hip-Flores and Peter Mills; Director, Cara Reichel; February 8, 2003

THE ALCHEMISTS Musical with book by Peter Mills and Cara Reichel; Music and Lyrics by Peter Mills; Director, Cara Reichel; April 26, 2003; Cast: Benjamin Eakeley, Damian Long, Tony Valles, Blake Hackler, Kelly Snyder, Jordan Wolfe, Joshua Marmer, Seamus Boyle, Jonathan Demar, Danielle Melanie Brown, Larry Brustofski, Richard Todd Adams, Carol A. Hickey, Erica Wright, Navida Stein, Peter Maris, Greg Horton

PULSE ENSEMBLE THEATRE

ALEXANDRA'S WEB by H. Richard Silver; Director, Alexa Kelly; June 13, 2002; Cast: Heather Berman, David Winton, Ezra Nanes, Bill Barnett

RATTLESTICK THEATRE

MY SPECIAL FRIEND Musical with book and lyrics by Philip Courtney; Music by P.J. Cacioppo; Director, R.J. Tolan; July 4, 2002; Cast: Eric Axen, Andrew Fetherolf, Lisa Raymond

FASTER by Adam Rapp; Director, Darrell Larsen; September 8, 2002; Cast: Robert Beitzel, Mtume Gant, Chris Messina, Fallon McDevitt Brooking, Roy Thinnes

Garth T. Mark, Kristin Stewart Chase in *Dear Prudence* PHOTO BY DAVID GOCHFIELD

BLISS by Ben Bettenbender; Director, Julia Gibson; with Johanna Day, Peter Jay Fernandez, Rob Sedgwick; November 17, 2002

THE LAST SUNDAY IN JUNE by Jonathan Tolins; Director, Trip Cullman; February 9, 2003; Cast: Arnie Burton, Matthew Wilkas, Johnathan F. McClain, Donald Corren, Mark Setlock, Peter Smith, Susan Pourfar, David Turner. Transferred to Off Broadway's Century Center for the Performing Arts (April 9, 2003; 61 performances through May 31, 2003)

DEAR PRUDENCE by Susan Kathryn Hefti; Director, Rosemary K. Andress; March 27, 2003; Cast: Kristin Stewart Chase, Jerusha Klemperer, Lynn Antunovich, Natasha Piletich, Garth T. Mark, Jim Conroy

THE RED ROOM

MATCH AND BEEP by Marc Chun; Director, Steven Gridley; September 2, 2002; Cast: Jessica Calvello, James Mack, Andres Munar, Erin Treadway, Stephen Douglas Wood

Mtume Gant, Chris Messina in *Faster* PHOTO BY CAROL ROSEGG

SAMUEL BECKETT THEATRE

BURNING BLUE by D.M.W. Greer; Director, John Hickok; October 16, 2002; Cast: Jerome Preston Bates, P.J. Brown, Bill Dawes, Matthew Del Negro, Mike Doyle, Sherri Parker Lee, Chad Lowe, Susan Porro

SANDE SHURIN THEATRE

STAR-CROSSED: A QUINTET OF FIVE SHORT PLAYS

> **SINGLISH** by Sloan MacRae; October 11–18, 2002

> **THE TREE** by Eric J. Polsky; October 11–18, 2002

> **MATCH** by John Cassel; October 11–18, 2002

> **SALOME SINGS THE BLUES** by Sloan MacRae; October 11–18, 2002

> **THE MYTH OF MOON AND MORNING STAR** by John Cassel; Director, Stuart Carden and Julie Fei-Fan Balzer; October 11–18, 2002

JANE'S EXCHANGE AND NORTH OF PROVIDENCE by Edward Allan Baker; Director, Russell Treyz; November 3, 2002; Cast: Joe Capozzi, Amorika M. Armoroso, Julie Karlin, Tonya Cornelisse, Judy Del Guidice, Mark Belasco

UNRESOLVED:
ONE-ACT PLAYS ON LOSS, GRIEF AND RECOVERY

> **ELLIPSIS** by Steven Fechter; November 21–December 15, 2002

> **FLOATING WORLD** by Laren Stover; November 21–December 15, 2002

> **CODA** by Romulus Linney; November 21–December 15, 2002

> **ROSEN'S SON** by Joe Pintauro; November 21–December 15, 2002

> **BLESS ME, FATHER** by Jeff Baron; November 21–December 15, 2002

> **COCOONING** by R. David Robinson; Director, Richard Mover; November 21–December 15, 2002; Cast: Wendy Bilton, Ann Carr, Nathan Cline, Eric D'Entrone, Ann Farrar, Alice Gold, Michael J. Lombardi, Allan Mirchin, Mr. Mover, Patricia Randell, Mr. Robinson, Erik Sher

MUCH ADO ABOUT NOTHING by William Shakespeare; Director, Jonathan Hadley; March 28, 2003; Cast: Bill Weeden, Carolyn Younger, Amanda Bruton, Ben Cherry, Todd Faulkner, Sean Griffin, Bob Harbaum, Laura Johnston, Sean Kent, Kasey Mahaffy, Michael Menger, Joey Monacelli, Robyne Parrish, Alex Smith, PJ Sosko, Katrina Thomas

78TH STREET LAB

INSIDE A BIGGER BOX by Trish Harnetiaux; Director, Jude Domski; January 10, 2003; Cast: Caroline Cromelin, Janaki, Nathan Guisinger, Melanie Rey

MARK OF CAIN by Morti Vizki; Translated by Jens Svane Boutrup; Director, Jens Svane Boutrup; February 7, 2003; Cast: Vincent Sagona, Michael Evans Lopez, Sarah Gifford

THE CHINESES ART OF PLACEMENT by Stanley Rutherford; Director, Jessica Bauman; March 3, 2003; Cast: T. Scott Cunningham

SOURCEWORKS THEATRE

A QUEER CAROL by Joe Godfrey; Director, Mark Cannistraro; December 2, 2002; Cast: Dan Pintauro, Tim Cross, Kip Driver, Valerie Hill, Michael Lynch, Marc Moritz, Greg Parente, Cynthia Pierce, David Weincek

STUDIO 42

REDBIRD by Clay Mcleod Chapman; Director, Isaac Butler; March 20, 2003; Cast: Hannah Bos, Abe Goldfarb, Bradford Louryk, Alexa Scott-Flaherty, Paul Thureen, Phoebe Ventouras

NOTHING OF ORIGINS by Devon Berkshire, Jackie Kristel, Laura Roemer, Ashley Salmon-Wander and Tella Storey; adapted from Aeschylus; Director, Kate Marks; May 1, 2003; Cast: Devon Berkshire, Jackie Kristel, Ashley Salmon-Wander, Tella Storey

STUDIO THEATRE

ANNA CHRISTIE by Eugene O'Neill; Director, Mary Catherine Burke; September 15, 2002; Cast: Barry J. Hirsch, Ben Upham, Duncan Nutter, Craig Rising, Bill Dealy, Dale Fuller, Rebecca Hoodwin, Caroline Strong, William Peden

SYNAPSE THEATRE

SILENCE by Moira Buffini; Director, Ginevra Bull; June 3, 2002; Cast: Matthew Maher, Abby Savage, Jessica Claire, Jessica Chandlee Smith, Chan Casey, Jens Martin Krummel

THE PHOENICICAN WOMEN by Euripides; Adapted by David Travis; Director, David Travis; November 13, 2002; Cast: Michael Arnov, Aysan Celik, Keith Davis, Will Davis, Curt Hostetter, Robert Kya-Hill, Sybil Lines, Chris Thorn

THEATRE AT ST. PETER'S

MODIGLIANI by Dennis McIntyre; Director, Robert Castle; September 22, 2002; Cast: William Abadie, Panos Makedonas, Jacob Battat, Amadeo Riva, Marcel Simoneau, Jack Michel-Bernard, Nandana Sen, Bruno Gelormini

THEATRE 3

TIME AND THE CONWAYS by J.B. Priestley; Director, Ron Russell; June 13, 2002; Cast: Melissa Friedman, James Wallert, Lisa Rothe, Abigail Lopez, Jenny Sterlin, Tom Butler, Craig Rovere, Nilaja Sun

ONLY THE END OF THE WORLD by Jean-Luc Lagarce; Translated by Lucie Tiberghien; Director, Lucie Tiberghien; August 5, 2002; Cast: Michael Emerson, Jennifer Mudge, Stephen Belber, Sandra Shipley, Katie Firth

THE FLASHING STREAM by Charles Morgan; Director, Miranda d'Ancona; April 17, 2003; Cast: Thomas Barbour, Michael Bastock, Glynis Bell, Cameron Francis, L.J.Ganser, Scott Glascock, Steve Groff, Davis Hall, Robert Sonderskov, Jennifer Dorr White

HABITAT by Judith Thompson; Director, Julia Gibson; May 22, 2003; Cast: Melissa Friedman, Teri Lamm, Michael Reid, Craig Rovere, Rebecca Schull, James Wallert

LITTLE EYOLF by Henrik Ibsen; adapted by Ron Russell; Director, Ron Russell; May 29, 2003; Cast: Melissa Friedman, Teri Lamm, Michael Reid, Craig Rovere, Rebecca Schull, James Wallert

13TH STREET REPERTORY THEATRE

3 WEEKS AFTER PARADISE by Israel Horovitz; Director, Stanley Harrison; with Mel England; September 11, 2002

TIMES SQUARE THEATRE

BLESSING IN DISGUISE by Larry Pellegrini; Music by Jason Howland; Director, Larry Pellegrini; October 19, 2002; Cast: Patrick Quinn, Ken Prymus, Julio Augustin, Jeffrey Drew, James Grimaldi, Jacob Harran, Allen Hidalgo, Andrew Pang

TOWN HALL: BRAVE NEW WORLD

THE OTHER LINE by Alfred Uhry; Director, Doug Hughes; September 9, 2002; Cast: Dana Ivey

A SONG FOR LACHANZE by Lynn Ahrens and Stephen Flaherty; Sung by LaChanze; September 9, 2002

ALIVE A song by John Patrick Shanley and Daniel Harnett; Director, John Gould Rubin; September 9, 2002; Cast: Orfeh

NINE TEN by Warren Leight; Director, Randal Myler; September 9, 2002; Cast: Christopher McCann, Jenny McGuire, Brennan Brown, Harriet Harris, Jenna Stern, Timothy McCracken

I AM STRONG IN THE FACE OF EVERYTHING EXCEPT NUCLEAR WAR A poem by Eve Ensler; Read by Isabella Rossellini; September 9, 2002; Read by Marlo Thomas; September 11, 2002

EXCERPT FROM RETURN TO THE UPRIGHT POSITION by Caridad Svich; September 9–11, 2002

CASSANDRA SONG A song by Ellen Mclaughlin; Music by Peter Foley; Performed by Melissa Errico; September 9, 2002

2001: AN ORAL HISTORY by Lillian Ann Slugocki; Director, Erica Gould; September 9 and 11, 2002; Cast: Judith Hawking, Catherine Curtin, Brian Carter, Saidah Arrika Ekulona, Carolyn Baeumler, Steven Rattazzi

GIVE THEM WINGS An excerpt from 110 Stories by Sarah Tuft; Director, Barry Edelstein; September 9, 2002, Performed by Elias Koteas; September 11, 2002, Performed by Chita Rivera

IMPACT by Jose Rivera; Director, Barry Edelstein; September 9, 2002, Cast: Kristin Davis, Jason Patric; September 11, 2002, Cast: Marisa Tomei, Jason Patric

LAND OF THE DEAD by Neil LaBute; Director, Neil LaBute; September 9, 2002, Cast: Kristin Davis, Paul Rudd; September 11, 2002, Cast: Kristin Davis, Liev Schreiber

A BROKEN HEAD by Andrew Solomon; Director, Jack Wrangler; September 9, 2002; Cast: Len Cariou

SKYLAB by Christopher Durang; Director, Walter Bobbie; September 9 and 11, 2002; Cast: Dana Ivey

NO ONE YOU KNOW by Neal Bell; Director, Mark Wing-Davey; September 9, 2002; Cast: Peter Gallagher, Lorraine Bracco

THE CRAZY GIRL by Frank Pugliese; Director, Me. Pugliese; September 9, 2002; Cast: Jill Clayburgh, Lily Rabe

THERE WILL BE A MIRACLE A song by Michael John LaChiusa; Performed by Donna Murphy; September 9, 2002

CLIMATE by Joe Pintauro; Director, Damian Gray; September 9, 2002; Cast: Marsha Mason, Austin Pendleton, Peggy Lipton

TERROR EYES by OyamO; Director, Marion McClinton; September 9, 2002; Cast: Reg E. Cathey

ADOPT A SAILOR by Charles Evered; Director, Craig Carlisle; September 9, 2002, Cast: Bebe Neuwirth, Michael Nouri, Neil Patrick Harris; September 10, 2002, Cast: Eli Wallach, Anne Jackson, Craig Williams; September 11, 2002, Cast: Liev Schreiber, Sam Waterston, Amy Irving; September 11, 2002

ELEVATOR by Rinne Groff; Director, Edward Stern; September 9, 2002

A PRAYER by Terrence McNally; Performed by Frances Sternhagen; September 9, 2002

AND MY FRIEND A choral by David Simpatico and Will Todd; September 9, 2002

FIRST DAY OF SCHOOL by Lynn Nottage; Director, Matthew Penn; September 10, 2002; Cast: Kenajuan Bentley, Catherine Curtin, Judith Hawking, Elias Koteas, Timothy Britten Parker

THE LAST ONE by Ed Seebald; Performed by Alec Baldwin; September 10, 2002

NUN DANKET ALLE GOTT Song by Rinde Eckert; September 10, 2002

EXODUS by J. Dakota Powell; Director, Stephen Wisker; September 10–11, 2002; Cast: Maya Gabrielle, Robert Neill, Laura Flanagan, Ninon Rogers, Christen Clifford, Kenajuan Bentley, Ivan Davila, Randy Ryan, Sarah Hayon

SEPTEMBER MORNING A poem by Kathryn Stern; Performed by Frances Sternhagen; September 10, 2002

BLACK ALERT IN SARAJEVO by Ruth Margraff; Director, Molly Smith; September 10, 2002

AUNT PITTI-PAT IN THE TOWER by David Simpatico; Director, Steven Williford; September 10, 2002; Cast: Mario Cantone

THROW by Brian Silberman; Director, James D. Stern; September 10, 2002; Cast: Trudie Styler, Matt Servitto, David Bennett

THE BALLAD OF MARY O'CONNOR A song by Greg Kotis and Mark Hollman; Performed by Rich Krueger; September 10, 2002

PASSENGERS by Betty Shamieh; Director, Billy Hopkins; September 10, 2002; Cast: Rosie Perez, Christen Clifford, Jenny Maguire, Sarah Hayon

SECOND SKIN by Chay Yew; Director, John Ruocco; September 10, 2002

HAITI by Keith Reddin; Director, Mark Brokaw; September 10, 2002; Cast: Amy Irving, Michael Potts, Boris McGiver

7–11 by Kia Corthron; Director, Michael John Garces; September 10, 2002; Cast: Rosie Perez, Kenajuan Bentley, Dariush Kashani

REDESIGN by Beth Henley; Performed by Holly Hunter, Elias Koteas, Bud Cort; September 10, 2002

THAT'S HOW I SAY GOODBYE A song by Marvin Hamlisch and Craig Cornelia; Performed by Kelli O'Hara; September 10, 2002

HIS WIFE by Romulus Linney; Director, Penelope Cherns; September 10, 2002; Cast: Jessica Hecht, Jason Patric, Boris McGiver

AFTER by Nicole Burdette; Director, Nicole Burdette; September 10, 2002; Cast: Jason Patric

HANDS HOLDING HANDS A song by Gilles Chaisson and Chris Roberts; Performed by Idina Menzel; September 10, 2002

WOMAN AT A THRESHOLD, BECKONING by John Guare; Director, Michael Wilson; September 9–11, 2002; Cast: John Turturro

ANTHEM A song by John Patrick Shanley; September 10, 2002

THE MOON PLEASE by Diana Son; Director, Chris Smith; September 11, 2002; Cast: Gloria Reuben, Frank Wood; September 11, 2002

STOP ALL THE CLOCKS by Erin Cressida Wilson; Director, Steve Lawson; September 11, 2002; Cast: Joel Grey, Ann Reinking

3 WEEKS AFTER PARADISE by Israel Horovitz; Performed by Israel Horovitz; September 11, 2002

I'M STILL HERE A song by Stephen Sondheim; Performed by Polly Bergen; September 11, 2002

STRONG AS A LION, SOFT AS SILK A poem by Tyler Wallach; Performed by Eli Wallach; September 11, 2002

WE NEVER KNEW THEIR NAMES by John Henry Redwood; Director, Amy Saltz; September 11, 2002; Cast: Brennan Brown, Gina Bardwell, Kate Rigg, James Ascher, James Martinez

ANTIGONE'S RED by Chiori Miyagawa; Director, Mary B. Robinson; September 11, 2002; Cast: Christina Chang, Michi Barall, Brian Nishii, Andrew Garman, George Sheffey

SOME OTHER TIME A song by Adolph Green and Leonard Bernstein; Performed by Phyllis Newman

4/19(/95) by John Pielmeier; Director, Shepard Sobel; September 11, 2002

THE MARRIOTT by Jacquelyn Reingold; Director, Michael Warren Powell; September 11, 2002; Cast: Michael Nouri, Louise Pitre

STRANGE FISH by Jaye Austin-Williams; Director, Monika Gross; Cast: Robert McKay, Mylika Davis, Sue Jin Song, Jeff Breckfield, Jeanine Carter, Craig Williams, Haythem Noor, Carl Vitali, Louis Menken

THE GRAND DESIGN by Susan Miller; Director, Cynthia Croot; September 11, 2002; Cast: Marlo Thomas, Scott Cohen

COMING TOGETHER A song by Jason Robert Brown; September 11, 2002

RIBBON IN THE SKY by Jonathan Marc Sherman; Director, Michael Wilson; September 11, 2002; Cast: Ethan Hawke, Amanda Peet

POPS by Edwin Sanchez; Director, Dennis Smith; September 11, 2002; Cast: Ivan Davila

LAKEERA by Christopher Shinn; Director, Mark Brokaw; September 11, 2002; Cast: Armando Riesco

LAST YEAR A song by Michael John LaChiusa; September 11, 2002

9–19 by Eric Mendelsohn; Performed by Edie Falco, Stanley Tucci; September 11, 2002

THE NEW RULES by Laurence Klavan; Director, Robert Knopf; September 11, 2002; Cast: Erik Jensen, Danny Zorn

HANDS by Erin Cressida Wilson; Director, Nela Wagman; September 11, 2002; Cast: Julianna Margulies

STEVE by Bill Leavengood; Director, Lawrence Sacharow; September 11, 2002; Cast: Fisher Stevens, Dariush Kashani

THIRTY-FOURTH AND DYER by Lee Blessing; Director, Nela Wagman; September 11, 2002; Cast: Cynthia Nixon, Keith Nobbs

LULLABY Music by Geoffrey Menin; Performed by Geoffrey Menin; September 11, 2002

ANONYMOUS REMAILERS by Constance Congdon; September 11, 2002

WILL THE SUN EVER SHINE AGAIN? A song by Alan Menken and Glenn Slater; Performed by Alan Menken; September 11, 2002

SPECIAL PRICE FOR YOU, OKAY? by Leah Ryan; Performed by Kate Rigg; September 11, 2002

LATE NIGHT, EARLY MORNING by Frank Pugliese; Director, Frank Pugliese; September 11, 2002; Cast: Marisa Tomei, Scott Cohen

DISORDERLY CONDUCT by Tina Howe; Director, George C. White; September 11, 2002; Cast: Lorinne Towler, Ned Eisenberg, Kate Rigg, Blake Robbins, Mylika Davis, Charles Montgomery, Kalimi Baxter, Kenajuan Bentley, Ivan Davila, Rana KazKaz, Mather Zickel

TRIBECA PLAYHOUSE

LOVE'S LABOUR'S LOST by William Shakespeare; Director, Kit Thacker; March 20, 2003; Cast: Katrin Macmillan, Sarah Megan Thomas, Joy Barrett, Amy Groeschel, Michael X. Izquierdo, George Burich, Jordan Dyck, Michael Craig Patterson, Natalie Gold, Vivia Font, Corey Tazmania Stieb, Jessica Chandlee Smith, Nicole Stewart, Matthew R. Wilson

T. SCHREIBER STUDIO

THE WOMAN FROM THE SEA by Spence Porter; Director, Terry Schreiber; February 1, 2003; Cast: Pete Byrne, Sterling Coyne, Margaret Dawson, A.J. Handegard, Debbie Jaffe, Fred Rueck, Tatjana Vujosevic, David Winton

29TH STREET REP

HIGH PRIEST OF CALIFORNIA by Charles Willeford; Director, Leo Farley; February 19, 2003; Cast: Tim Corcoran, Paula Ewin, Jerry Lewkowitz, David Mogentale, Carol Sirugo, James E. Smith

URBAN STAGES

MIDWESTERN CHUM by Sarah Bewley with Cathleen Miller; Director, T.L. Reilly; August 5, 2002; Cast: Vanessa Quijas, Sam Guncler, Cherene Snow, Maria Cellario, Gabor Morea

ROSES IN DECEMBER by Victor L. Cahn; Director, T.L. Reilly; February 25, 2003; Cast: Keira Naughton, Victor Slezak

THE VILLAGE THEATRE

DREAM A LITTLE DREAM by Denny Doherty and Paul Ledoux; Director, Randal Myler; April 23, 2003; Cast: Denny Doherty, Richard Burke, Angela Gaylor, Doris Mason

WESTSIDE THEATRE DOWNSTAIRS

TRUMBO by Christopher Trumbo; Director, Peter Askin; March 31, 2003; Cast: Christopher Trumbo

James Naughton in *Roses in December* PHOTO BY CAROL ROSEGG

WHITE BIRD PRODUCTIONS

BORO TALES: BROOKLYN

TWELVE BROTHERS by Jeffrey M. Jones and Camila Jones; Director, Page Burkholder; March 8–23, 2003

THE LITTLE MATCHGIRL by Lynn Nottage; Director, Miriam Weiner; March 8–23, 2003

SNOW WHITE by Onome Ekeh; Director, Page Burkholder; March 8–23, 2003

LUCKY HANS by Marjorie Duffield; Director, Jean Wagner; March 8–23, 2003

THE DANCING PRINCESSES by Creative Theatrics' Performance Team and Marjorie Duffield; Director, Welker White; March 8–23, 2003; Cast: Arnie Bermowitz, April Mathis, Robert Hatcher, Joseph Jamrog, C. Andrew Bauer, Corinne Edgerly, Kathryn Velvel

THE WORKSHOP THEATER COMPANY

FROM THE TOP by Scott C. Sickles; Director, Max Mantel; January 31, 2003; Cast: Christopher Burke, Rob Cameron, Lori Faiella, Roger Dale Stude, Stephen Zinnato

IPHIGENIA by P. Seth Bauer; Based on Euripides; Director, Elysa Marden; March 21, 2003; Cast: Shamika Cotton, Carrie Edel, Katherine Freedman, Mark Hofmaier, Brian Homer, Marinell Madden, Greg Skura, Pauline Tully

LAST STAND by Timothy Scott Harris; Director, Timothy Scott Harris; May 7, 2003; Cast: Shoshana Ami, Christopher Burke, Dee Dee Friedman, Allan Knee, Gerrianne Raphael, GW Reed, Bill Tatum

SUBWAY SERIES—THE SUBWAY by Craig Pospisil; Director, Keith Teller; May 28–31, 2003

QUICK AND DIRTY (A SUBWAY FANTASY) by David Reidy; Director, Greg Skura; May 28–31, 2003

THE LOCAL by Michael Rhodes; Director, Darleen Jaeger; May 28–31, 2003

SILENT PIECE by P. Seth Bauer and Michael Rhodes; May 28–31, 2003

THE ATTRACTIVE WOMEN ON THE TRAIN by P. Seth Bauer; Director, Keith Teller; May 28–31, 2003

DOWN IN THE DEPTHS by Michael Rhodes; Director, Keith Teller; with Sophie Acadine, Barbara Helms, Mark Hofmaier, Lois Markle, Paul Molnar, Michael Rhodes, Greg Skura, Jill Van Note, Hilary Ward; May 28–31, 2003

WORTH STREET THEATER COMPANY

AS YOU LIKE IT by William Shakespeare; Director, Jeff Cohen; July 23, 2002; Cast: Dan Ahearn, Sally Wheeler, Virginia Williams, Dwight Ewell, Devin Haqq, Keith Davis, David Brown Jr., Ron Simons, James Martinez, Matt Conley, Liza Lapira

THE MYSTERY OF ATTRACTION by Marlane Meyer; Director, Jeff Cohen; January 12, 2003; Cast: Dan Ahearn, Richard Bekins, Kendra Leigh Landon, Barry Del Sherman, Jefferson Slinkard, Deirdre O'Connell

ZIPPER THEATER

ELLE by Jean Genet; Adapted by Alan Cumming; Translation by Terri Gordon; Director, Nick Philippou; July 24, 2002; Cast: Stephen Spinella, Anson Mount, Chad L. Coleman, Mr. Cumming, Brian Duguay

Company Series

Fiona Shaw, Jonathan Cake in *Medea* PHOTO BY CAROL ROSEGG

AMAS MUSICAL THEATRE

Producing Artistic Director, Donna Trinkoff

ZANNA, DON'T! Musical with book, Music and Lyrics by Tim Acito; with additional book and lyrics by Alexander Dinelaris; Director and Choreographer, Devanand Janki; Scenery, Wade Laboissonniere and Tobin Ost; Lighting, Jeffrey Lowney; Sound, Robert Killenberger; October 17, 2002; Cast: Adam Michael Kookept, Anika Larsen, Darius Nichols, Amanda Ryan Paige, Robb Sapp, Shelley Thomas, Gregory Treco, Jared Zeus

LATIN HEAT by Ovi Vargas, Maria Torres, Oscar Hernandez, David Coffman; Director and Choreographer, Maria Torres; February 18, 2003

ATLANTIC THEATER COMPANY

Artistic Director, Neil Pepe; Producing Director, Beth Emelson

THE BUTTER AND EGG MAN by George S. Kaufman; Director, David Pittu; Scenery, Anna Louizos; Costumes, Bobby Frederick Tilley II; Lighting, Robert Perry; Music and Sound, Fitz Patton; Production Stage Manager, Stephen M. Kaus; October 2, 2002; Cast: David Turner, Rosemarie DeWitt, Tom Mardirosian, Julie Halston, Michael McGrath, Amelia White, Todd Buonopane, David Cromwell, David Brummel, Robin Skye, Amanda Davies, John Ellison Conlee

BROOKLYN ACADEMY OF MUSIC—

Next Wave Festival

Chairman, Alan H. Fishman; President, Karen Brooks Hopkins; Executive Producer, Joseph V. Melillo

GALILEO GALILEI An opera with libretto by Mary Zimmerman with Philip Glass and Arnold Weinstein; Music by Philip Glass; Director, Mary Zimmerman; Scenery, Daniel Ostling; Costumes, Mara Blumenfeld; Lighting, T.J. Gerckens; Sound, Michael Bodeen, Projections, John Boesche; Conductor, William Lumpkin; October 1, 2002; Cast: John Duykers, Andrew Funk, Alicia Berneche, Eugene Perry, Elizabeth Reiter

MEDEA by Euripides; Translated by Kenneth McLeish and Frederic Raphael; Director, Deborah Warner; Scenery, Tom Pye; Costumes, Tom Rand; Lighting, Peter Mumford; Sound, Mel Mercier; October 2, 2002; Transferred to Broadway's Brooks Atkinson Theatre, December 10, 2002; Cast: Siobhan McCarthy, Robin Laing, Fiona Shaw, Struan Rodger, Jonathan Cake, Joseph Mydell, Derek Hutchinson, Dylan Denton

WOYZECK by Georg Buchner; Adapted by Wolfgang Wiens and Ann-Christin Rommen; Music and Lyrics by Tom Waits and Kathleen Brennan; Direction and Scenery by Robert Wilson; Codirection, Ann-Christin Rommen; Costumes, Jacques Reynaud; Lighting, A.J. Weissbard and Robert Wilson; October 29, 2002; Cast: Jens Jorn Spottag, Kaya Bruel, Morten Eisner, Marianne Mortensen, Ole Thestrup, Ann-Mari Max Hansen, Morten Lutzhoft, Benjamin Boe Rasmussen, Tom Jensen, Troels Il Munk, Joseph Driffield, Jeppe Dahl Rordam, Morten Thorup Koudal, Ivana Catanese, Ryan Hill, Maria Pessino, Matthew Shattuck, Carlow Soto, Kameron Steele

MERCY Music-theater work by Meredith Monk and Ann Hamilton; Developed in collaboration with Theo Bleckmann, Ellen Fisher, Katie Geissinger, Ching Gonzalez, Lanny Harrison, John Hollenbeck, Louise Smith, Allison Sniffin; Music by Meredith Monk; Lighting, Noele Stollmack; Costumes, Gabriel Berry; Sound, David Meschter; December 3, 2002

MACBETH by William Shakespeare; Director, Yukio Ninagawa; Scenery, Tsukasa Nakagoshi; Costumes, Lily Komine; Lighting, Tamotsu Harada; Sound, Masahiro Inoue; Fight Choreography, Masahiro Kunii; December 4, 2002

CLASSIC STAGE COMPANY

Artistic Director, Barry Edelstein; Producing Director, Anne Tanaka

GHOSTS by Henrik Ibsen; Translation by Lanford Wilson; Director, Daniel Fish; Scenery, Christine Jones; Costumes, Kaye Voyce; Lighting, Scott Zielinski; Music and Sound, Eric Shim; November 10, 2002; Cast: Amy Irving, Daniel Gerroll, Lisa Demont, David Patrick Kelly, Ted Schneider

THE WINTER'S TALE by William Shakespeare; Director, Barry Edelstein; Scenery, Narelle Sissons; Costumes, Mattie Ullrich; Lighting, Jane Cox; Sound, Elizabeth Rhodes; Music, Michael Torke; January 30, 2003; Cast: David Strathairn, Barbara Garrick, Michel Gill, Mary Lou Rosato, Teagle F. Bougere, Tom Bloom, David Costabile, Angel Desai, Mark H. Dold, Gene Farber, Andrew Guilarte, Larry Paulsen, Elizabeth Reaser, Michael Reid, Elizabeth Sherman, Joaquin Torres

DRAMA DEPT.

Artistic Directors, Douglas Carter Beane, Michael S. Rosenberg

SHANGHAI MOON by Charles Busch; Director, Carl Andress; Scenery, B.T. Whitehill; Costumes, Michael Bottari and Ronald Case; Lighting, Kirk Bookman; Sound, Laura Grace Brown; Fight Director, Rick Sordelet; Stage Manager, John Handy; January 17, 2003; Cast: Charles Busch, Becky Ann Baker, Sekiya Billman, Daniel Gerroll, Marcy McGuigan, B.D. Wong

ENSEMBLE STUDIO THEATRE

Artistic Director, Curt Dempster

MARATHON 2002 (SERIES C)

HOPE BLOATS by Patricia Scanlon; Director, David Briggs; June 10, 2002; Cast: Dave Simonds, Patricia Scanlon

UNION CITY, NEW JERSEY, WHERE ARE YOU? by Rogelio Martinez; Director, Randal Myler; June 10, 2002; Cast: Rosie Perez, Felix Solis, Julien A. Carrasquillo

MY FATHER'S FUNERAL by Peter Maloney; Director, Beatrice Terry; June 10, 2002; Cast: Peter Maloney, Griffith Maloney

THE MOON BATH GIRL by Graeme Gillis; Director, Eliza Beckwith; June 10, 2002; Cast: Michael Esper, Alicia Goranson

CITY OF DREAMS Musical with book and lyrics by David Zellnik; Music by Joseph Zellnik; Director, Michael Alltop; Choreography, Janet Bogardus; Scenery, Mark Fitzgibbons; Costumes, Randall E. Klein; Lighting, Hideaki Tsutsui; Sound, Ryan Streber; July 15, 2002; Cast: Ben Nordstrom, Kristin Griffith, D. Michael Berkowitz, Sharron Bower, Alison Fraser, Megan McGinnis, Paul Anthony Stewart, Stephen Bel Davies, Michael Mendiola, John Hellyer

MASHA NO HOME by Lloyd Suh; Director, Nela Wagman; Scenery, Jennifer Varbalow; Costumes, Nan Young; Lighting, Greg MacPherson; Sound, Robert Gould; Music, David Rothenberg; November 30, 2002; Cast: Cindy Cheung, Kevin Louie, James Saito, Eddie Shin, Samantha Quan

STRING FEVER by Jacquelyn Reingold; Director, Mary B. Robinson; Scenery, David P. Gordon; Costumes, Michael Krass; Lighting, Michael Lincoln; Sound, Rob Gould; March 3, 2003; Cast: Cynthia Nixon, Cecilia deWolf, Evan Handler, David Thornton, Tom Mardirosian, Jim Fyfe

FULL SPECTRUM: A TECHNO-THEATRE EXPERIMENT Featuring plays by Sarah Ruhl and Susan Kim; Director, Brenda Bakker Harger; March 27, 2003; Cast: Nate Jones, Serena Lam, Patrick McKiernan, Timothy Price, Christopher M. Spiller, Jennifer R. Spiller

MARATHON 2003 (SERIES A)

OF TWO MINDS by Billy Aronson; Director, Jamie Richards; May 11, 2003; Cast: Geneva Carr, Annie Campbell, Ian Reed Kesler, Brad Bellamy, Conor White

THE HONEY MAKERS by Deborah Grimberg; Director, Tom Rowan; May 11, 2003; Cast: Thorn Rivera, Cori Thomas, Bill Cwikowski, Jake Myers

CODA by Romulus Linney; Director, Julie Boyd; May 11, 2003; Cast: Thomas Lyons, Joseph Siravo, Helen Coxe, Jane Welch

A BLOOMING OF IVY by Garry Williams; Director, Richmond Hoxie; May 11, 2003; Cast: James Rebhorn, Phyllis Somerville

MEMENTO MORI by Susan Kim; Director, Abigail Zealey Bess; May 11, 2003; Cast: Cecilia deWolf, Amy Staats

INTAR

Producing Artistic Directors, Max Ferra, Michael John Garces

HAVANA UNDER THE SEA by Abilio Estevez; Director, Max Ferra; Scenery, Van Santvoord; Costumes, Willa Kim; Lighting, Ed McCarthy; Sound, David M. Lawson; March 6, 2003; Cast: Doreen Montalvo, Meme Solis

DRAWN AND QUARTERED by Maggie Bofill; Director, Louis Moreno; Costumes, Meghan Healey; Lighting, Shawn Kaufman and Kevin Hardy; Sound, David M. Lawson; April 18, 2003; Cast: Yetta Gottesman, Carlos Valencia

MEMORIES OF OUR WOMEN by Arthur Giron; Developed in collaboration with Perry Garcia and the actors; Director, Angel David; Costumes, Meghan Healey; Lighting, Shawn Kaufman and Kevin Hardy; Sound, David M. Lawson; April 25, 2003; Cast: Raul Castillo, AnaMaria Correa, Annie Henk, Ana Tulia Ramirez, Joselin Reyes, Letty Soto

WHISPER by Oscar A. Colon; Director, Jesse Ontiveros; Costumes, Meghan Healey; Lighting, Shawn Kaufman and Kevin Hardy; Sound, David M. Lawson; May 2, 2003; Cast: Melissa Delaney Del Valle, Carlos Molina, Larilu Smith, Michelle Torres

N.E. 2ND AVENUE by Teo Castellanos; Director, Michael John Garces; May 9, 2003; Cast: Teo Castellanos

IRISH REPERTORY THEATRE

Artistic Director, Charlotte Moore; Producing Director, Ciaran O'Reilly

THE PLAYBOY OF THE WESTERN WORLD by J.M. Synge; Scenery, David Raphel; Lighting, Kirk Bookman; Costumes, David Toser; Sound, Murmod Inc.; Music, Larry Kirwan and Black 47; July 2, 2002; Cast: Clodagh Bowyer, Dara Coleman, David Costelloe, Laura James Flynn, James Gale, Christopher Joseph Jones, John Keating, John Leighton, Aedin Moloney, Heather O'Neill, Derdriu Ring

BAILEGANGAIRE by Tom Murphy; Director, Tom Murphy; Scenery, David Raphel; Lighting, Brian Nason; Costumes, David Toser; Sound, Murmod Inc.; October 10, 2002; Cast: Pauline Flanagan, Terry Donnelly, Babo Harrison

Babo Harrison, Terry Donnelly, Pauline Flanagan in *Bailegangaire* PHOTO BY CAROL ROSEGG

A CELTIC CHRISTMAS Musical adapted from Dylan Thomas's *A Child's Christmas in Wales*; Director, Charlotte Moore; Costumes, Linda Fisher; Lighting, Sean Farrell; Musical Direction, Eddie Guttman; December 8, 2002; Cast: Rebecca Bellingham, Peter Cormican, Eddie Guttman, Kenny Kosek, Jayne Ackley Lynch, Joyce A. Noonan, Joshua Park

BEDBOUND by Enda Walsh; Director, Enda Walsh; Scenery, Klara Zieglerova; Lighting, Kirk Bookman; Sound, Zachary Williamson; January 23, 2003; Cast: Brian F. O'Byrne, Jenna Lamia

PEG O' MY HEART by J. Hartley Manners; Songs by Charlotte Moore; Director, Charlotte Moore; Scenery, James Morgan; Costumes, David Toser; Lighting, Mary Jo Dondlinger; Sound, Zachary Williamson; Musical Direction, Eddie Guttman; May 22, 2003; Cast: Melissa Hart, Jody Madaras, Rita Harvey, James A. Stephens, Jonathan Hadley, Kathleen Early, Don Sparks, J. Kennedy

THE JOSEPH PAPP PUBLIC THEATER/ NEW YORK SHAKESPEARE FESTIVAL—
Special Projects

Producer, George C. Wolfe; Executive Director, Mara Manus

ANNA IN THE TROPICS Written and directed by Nilo Cruz; April 26, 2003

MARIELA IN THE DESERT by Karen Zacarias; Director, Tom Prewitt; April 27, 2003

BLIND MOUTH SINGING by Jorge Ignacio Cortinas; Director, Ruben Polendo; April 28, 2003

A CHINESE TALE by Aravind Enrique Adyanthaya; Director, Bob McGrath; April 29, 2003

TWO LOVES AND A CREATURE by Gustavo Ott; Translated by Heather McKay; Director, Steve Cosson; April 30, 2003

EXPAT/INFERNO by Alejandro Morales; Director, Trip Cullman; May 1, 2003

DEMON BABY by Erin Courtney; Director, Ken Rus Schmoll; May 2, 2003

HILDA by Marie Ndiaye; Translated by Erika Rundle; Director, Jo Bonney; May 3, 2003

BIRO Written and directed by Ntare Guma Mbaho Mwine; May 4, 2003

THE LADIES by Anne Washburn and Anne Kauffman; May 5, 2003

JOEY SHAKESPEAR by Brendan Cochrane and Joseph Assadourian; Director, Michael John Garces; May 6, 2003

BODEGA LUNG FAT by Mike Batistick; Director, Jo Bonney; May 7, 2003

IGGY WOO by Alice Tuan; Director, Mark Wing-Davey; May 8, 2003

THE NEXT EPISODE by Chris Papagapitos; Director, Robert Milazzo; May 9, 2003

THE ARGUMENT by David Greenspan; Director, Brian Mertes; May 10, 2003

ACCIDENTAL NOSTALGIA by Cynthia Hopkins; George C. Wolfe, Producer; Mara Manus, Executive Director; May 11, 2003

TAKING STEPS THREE THIRTEEN Book, music and lyrics by Matthew Doers; Musical Direction by Luqman Brown; May 11, 2003

NO GOD BUT YEARNING Book by Donna Di Novelli; music by David Rodwin and others; May 12, 2003

THE STRANGER Book and Lyrics.by Micah Schraft; music by Michael Friedman; Director, Trip Cullman; May 12, 2003

LA MAMA EXPERIMENTAL THEATRE CLUB (ETC)

Founder and Director, Ellen Stewart

THE BRONX WITCH PROJECT by Alba Sanchez; Directed and designed by Gary Dini; September 19, 2002; Cast: Alba Sanchez

SLUTFORART A.K.A. AMBIGUOUS AMBASSADOR by Ping Chong and Muna Tseng; Director, Ping Chong; Costumes, Han Feng; Lighting, Mark London; Sound, Brian Hallas; Projections, Jan Hartley; October 3, 2002; Cast: Muna Tseng, and the voices of Timothy Greenfield-Sanders, Kristoffer Haynes, Bill T. Jones, Ann Magnuson, Richard Martin, Kenny Scharf, Jenny Yee

BILLIE by Roz Nixon; Director, Roz Nixon; October 10, 2002; Cast: Madame Pat Tandy

Ping Chong in *UE92/02* PHOTO BY STEPHEN GARRETT

UE92/02 (a new work in the Undesirable Elements/Secret History series) by Ping Chong and Talvin Wilks; Director, Ping Chong; October 17, 2002; Cast: Luanne Edwards, Angel Gardner, Leyla Modirzadeh, Zohra Saed, Tania Salmen, Michelle van Tonder, Ping Chong

SURVIVAL OF THE FETUS Musical with book by Coby Koehl; Music and Lyrics by Coby Koehl and Sean Dibble; Director and Choreographer, Vic DiMonda; Musical Direction, Jonah Spidel; Arrangements, Jonah Spidel, Erik Reyes and Ken Kincaid; October 24, 2002; Cast: Coby Koehl, Cherie Hannouche, Natalie Joy Johnson, Matthew R. Wilson

CURVE by Nicholas Devine; Director, Jeffrey Dewhurst; October 30, 2002; Cast: Nicholas Devine

SPECTACLE OF SPECTACLES: THE CLAIRVOYANT CABARET by Deirdre Broderick; Director, Deirdre Broderick; Scenery, Brian P. Glover; November 14, 2002; Cast: Bill Connington, Brian P. Glover, Katherine Gooch

GENEVA by Nicholas von Hoffman; Director, Mary Fulham; Scenery, Gregory John Mercurio; Costumes, Ramona Ponce; Sound, Tim Schellenbaum; November 14, 2002; Cast: Brigitte Barnett, Ari Benjamin, Todd Davis, Steve Hauck, Carol London, John Otis, Michael Quinlan, Kerry Sullivan

ORPHAN ON GOD'S HIGHWAY by Josh Fox; Director, Josh Fox; Scenery, David Esler; Lighting, Charles Foster; November 16, 2002; Cast: Sophie Amieva, Josh Fox, Connie Hall, Gina Hirsch, Ravi Jain, Peter Lettre, Alanna Medlock, Jason Quarles, Bob Saietta, Magin Schantz, Dario Tangelson, Aaron Mostkoff Unger

STAR MESSENGERS by Paul Zimet; Music by Ellen Maddow; Director, Paul Zimet; Choreography, Karinne Keithley; Scenery, Nic Ularu; Costumes, Kiki Smith; Lighting, Carol Mullins; December 2, 2002; Cast: Will Badgett, David Greenspan, Christine Ciccone, Ryan Dietz, Court Dorsey, Marcy Jellison, Ms. Keithley, Ms. Maddow, Randy Reyes, Michelle Rios

H.A.M.L.E.T. by Linda Mussman; in collaboration with Claudia Bruce and Gerald Stoddard; Directed by Linda Mussman; Scenery, Jun Maeda; Lighting, Linda Mussman; Video, Linda Mussman and Gerald Stoddard; Music, Claudia Bruce and Gerald Stoddard; December 5, 2002; Cast: Claudia Bruce and Gerald Stoddard

BLUE SKY TRANSMISSION: A TIBETAN BOOK OF THE DEAD by Raymond Bobgan and contributing writers Mike Geither, Patricia Harusame Leebove and Ray McNiece; Director, Raymond Bobgan; Scenery, Michael Guy James; Costumes, Karen Young; Lighting, Trad A. Burns; December 8, 2002; Cast: Lisa Black, Tracy Broyles, Kishiko Hasegawa, Holly Holsinger, Brett Keyser, Amy Kristina, Karin Randoja, Sophia Skiles, Rebecca Spencer, Chi-wang Yang

THE DEVILS OF LOUDUN by Matt Mitler; Adapted from Aldous Huxley; Director and Designer, Matt Mitler; Costumes, Karen Hatt; Musical Direction, Bob Strock; January 2, 2003; Cast: Matt Mitler

SSS-T-O-N-E-DDD by Arthur Maximillian Adair; Director and Designer, Arthur Maximillian Adair; Music, S-Dog; January 16, 2003; Cast: Arthur Maximillian Adair

PAINTED SNAKE IN A PAINTED CHAIR by Ellen Maddow; Director, Paul Zimet; Choreography, Karinne Keithley; Scenery, Nic Ularu; Costumes, Kiki Smith; Lighting, Carol Mullins; January 18, 2003; Cast: Diane Beckett, Gary Brownlee, Randolph Curtis Rand, Steven Rattazzi, Tina Shepard, Louise Smith, "Blue" Gene Tyranny (keyboard)

BAD BUGS BITE by Andrea Paciotto; Based on a fairytale by Ivo Andric and stories by Andrea Paciotto; Director, Andrea Paciotto; Lighting, Jasper Buurman; Music, Jan Klug; January 23, 2003; Cast: Charlotte Brathwaite, Monika Haasova, Jelena Jovanovic

MARGA GOMEZ'S INTIMATE DETAILS by Marga Gomez; Director, David Schweizer; Scenery, Gary Baura; Lighting, Arthur Maximillian Adair; Sound, Alfredo D. Troche; January 30, 2003; Cast: Marga Gomez

(CONTINUED ON NEXT PAGE)

Matt Mitler, Nun in foreground: Yvonne Brecht in *Devils of Loudon* PHOTO BY ARTURO CUBRIA

(CONTINUED FROM PREVIOUS PAGE)

PHILOKTETES by John Jesurun; February 10, 2003; Cast: Ruth Maleczech

HELEN: QUEEN OF SPARTA by Theodora Skipitares; Director and Designer, Theodora Skipitares; Music, Arnold Dreyblatt; Additional Music, Tim Schellenbaum; Lighting, Pat Dignan; Video, Kay Hines; February 13, 2003

A STREET CORNER PIERROT by Terrell Robinson; Director, Sheila Kaminsky; Scenery, Mark Tambella; Lighting, Federico Restrepo; Music and Sound, Joshua Camp; February 20, 2003; Cast: Terrell Robinson

THE LAST TWO JEWS OF KABUL by Josh Greenfeld; Director, George Ferencz; Scenery, Tom Lee; Costumes, Sally Lesser; Lighting, Jeff Tapper; Sound, Tim Schellenbaum; February 27, 2003; Cast: Jerry Matz, George Drance

BREAD AND CIRCUS 3099 by Jack Shamblin and Nicole Zaray; Choreography, Paulo Henrique; Scenery, Carlos Diaz; Costumes, Tania Sterl and Marika Dadiani; Lighting, David Overcamp; February 27, 2003; Cast: Jack Shamblin, Nicole Zaray, Hadas Gil Bar

YOKASTAS by Saviana Stanescu and Richard Schechner; Director, Saviana Schechner; Choreography, Kilbane Porter; Scenery and Lighting, E.D. Intemann; March 20, 2003; Cast: Rachel Bowditch, Chris Healy, Tracey Huffman, Ms. Porter, Suzi Takahashi

THE MOTHER by Stanislaw Ignacy Witkiewicz; Director, Brooke O'Harra; Costumes, Audrey Robinson; Lighting, Michael Phillips; Music, Brendan Connelly; March 27, 2003; Cast: Tina Shepard, Jim Fletcher, Suli Holum, Nicky Paraiso, Wilson Hall, Zakia Babb, Barb Lanciers

THE BOOK OF JOB Musical with Book, Music and Lyrics by Danny Ashkenasi; April 8, 2003; Cast: Julie Alexander, Mr. Ashkenasi, Ian August, Joel Briel, Ryan Connolly, Allison Easter, Darra Herman, Anita Hollander, Jennie Im, Jamie Mathews

DIPTERACON, OR SHORT LIVED S*%T EATERS by Raine Bode; Music and Lyrics by Felicia Carter Shakman; Director, Raine Bode; Scenery and Lighting, Arthur Maximillian Adair; April 17, 2003; Cast: Kristin Atkinson, John Benoit, Ann Bonner, Antonio Cerezo, Eveleena Dann, Kaori Fujiyabu, Sara Galassini, Mark Gallop, Denise Greber, Nicky Paraiso, Lars Preece, Ramona Pula, Stephanie Rafferty, Peter Schuyler, Shannan Shaughnessy, Shigeko Suga, Mary Ann Walsh

THE EARTH'S SHARP EDGE by Thaddeus Phillips; Director, Thaddeus Phillips; May 1, 2003; Cast: Tatiana Mallarino, Gareth Saxe, Michael Fegley, Gina E. Cline, Muni Kulasinghe, Kent Davis Packard, Thaddeus Phillips

George Drance, Jerery Matz in *The Last Two Jews of Kabul* PHOTO BY JONATHAN SLAFF

PRIVATE JOKES, PUBLIC PLACES by Oren Safdie; Director, Craig Carlisle; May 4, 2003; Cast: M.J. Kang, Fritz Michel, Graeme Malcolm, David Chandler

GOD'S COMIC by Oleg Braude; Inspired by a novel by Heinrich Boll and Siava Polunin; Director, Oleg Braude; Costumes, Kaori Onodera; Lighting, Oleg Braude; Sound, Tim Schellenbaum; May 22, 2003; Cast: Amy Kirsten, Daniel Logan, David Tyson, Douglas Allen, Johanna Weller-Fahy, Margaret Norwood, Rachel Diana, Zarah Kravitz

SLANTY EYED MAMA RE-BIRTH OF AN ASIAN by Kate Rigg and Leah Ryan; Director, Dave Mowers; May 22, 2003; Cast: Kate Rigg, Lyris Hung (violinist)

IT'S A . . . MEXICAN-MORMON by Elna Baker; Director, Liz Swados; May 26, 2003; Cast: Elna Baker

LINCOLN CENTER FESTIVAL 2003

PACIFIC OVERTURES Musical with book by John Weidman; Music and Lyrics by Stephen Sondheim; Translated by Kunihiko Hashimoto; Director, Amon Miyamoto; Choreography, Rino Masaki; Scenery, Rumi Matsui; Costumes, Emi Wada; Lighting, Yasutaka Nakayama; Sound, Kunio Watanabe; Fight Direction, Akinori Tani; Music Direction, Kosuke Yamashita; July 9, 2003; Cast: Takeharu Kunimoto, Norihide Ochi, Ben Hiura, Haruki Sayama, Usaburo Oshima, Shintaro Sonooka, Atsushi Haruta, Yuji Hirota, Akira Sakemoto, Masaki Kosuzu, Kanjiro Murakami, Shuji Honda, Kirihito Saito, Makoto Okada, Shinichiro Hara, Takanori Yamamoto, Kyoko Donowaki, Urara Awata, Shunpo, Mayu Yamada, Takeshi Ishikawa

THE TA'ZIYEH OF HOR Director, Mohammad Ghaffari; July 12, 2002; Cast: Hassan Nargeskhani, Deligani Alaeaddin Ghassemi, Mohammadreza Ghassemi, Hassan Aliabbasi Jazi, Kamal Aliabbasi Jazi, Majid AliabbasiJazi, Esmaeil Arefian Jazi, Asadollah Momenzadeh Khoulenjani, Mohammadali Momenzadeh Khoulenjani, Mahmood Moini, Morteza Saffarianrezai

THE MUTE DREAM by Attila Pessyani; Director and Designer by Mr. Pessyani; July 17, 2002; Cast: Fatemeh Naghavi, Setareh Pessyani, Khosrow Pessyani and Attila Pessyani

MABOU MINES

Artistic Directors include Lee Breuer, Sharon Fogarty, Ruth Maleczech, Frederick Neumann, and Terry O'Reilly

CARA LUCIA by Sharon Fogarty; Additional Text by Lee Breuer; Director, Sharon Fogarty; Choreography, J'aime Morrison; Scenery and Lighting, Jim Clayburgh; Projections, Julie Archer; Music, Carter Burwell; Artistic Directorate, Lee Breuer, Sharon Fogarty, Ruth Maleczech, Frederick Neumann and Terry O'Reilly; April 23, 2003; Cast: Ruth Maleczech, Rosemary Fine, Clove Galilee

MCC THEATER

Artistic Directors, Robert LuPone and Bernard Telsey; Associate Artistic Director, William Cantler

THE MERCY SEAT by Neil LaBute; Director, Neil LaBute; Scenery, Neil Patel; Costumes, Catherine Zuber; Lighting, James Vermeulen; Sound, David Van Tieghem; December 18, 2002; Cast: Liev Schreiber, Sigourney Weaver

SCATTERGOOD by Anto Howard; Director, Doug Hughes; Scenery, Hugh Landwehr; Lighting, Clifton Taylor; Costumes, Linda Fisher; Music, David Van Tieghem; February 26, 2003; Cast: Brian Murray, T.R. Knight, Tari Signor

Lisa Bostnar, Hans Tester in *Far and Wide* PHOTO BY RICHARD TERMINE

MINT THEATER COMPANY

Artistic Director, Jonathan Bank

THE CHARITY THAT BEGAN AT HOME by St. John Hankin; Director, Gus Kaikkonen; Scenery, Charles F. Morgan; Costumes, Henry Shaffer, Lighting, William Armstrong; Music, Ellen Mandel; October 7, 2002; Cast: Christopher Franciosa, Kristin Griffith, Benjamin Howes, Karl Kenzler, Becky London, Lee Moore, Troy Schremmer, Harmony Schuttler, Michele Tauber, Pauline Tully, Bruce Ward, Alice White

FAR AND WIDE by Arthur Schnitzler; Adapted by Jonathan Bank; Director, Jonathan Bank; Scenery, Vicki R. Davis; Lighting, Josh Bradford; Costumes, Theresa Squire; Sound, Stefan Jacobs; February 17, 2003; Cast: Ezra Barnes, Lisa Bostnar, Rob Breckenridge, Lee Bryant, Ann-Marie Cusson, Kurt Everhart, Ken Kliban, James Knight, Victoria Mack, Matt Opatrny, Allen Lewis Rickman, Hans Tester, Pilar Witherspoon

NEW DRAMATISTS THEATRE

Artistic Director, Todd London; Executive Director, Joel K. Ruark

THE TRIPLE HAPPINESS by Brooke Berman; Director, David Goldstein; September 9, 2002; Cast: Michael Chernus, Julie Boyd, Chris McKinney, Susan Pourfar, Jack Wetherall

WAVE by Sung Rno; Director, Linsay Firman; September 9, 2002; Cast: Ron Domingo, Cindy Cheung, Ralph B. Peiia

PAPER ARMOR by Eisa Davis; Director, David Levine; September 9, 2002; Cast: Eisa Davis, Duane Boutte, Yvette Ganier

KIT MARLOWE by David Grimm; Director, David Grimm; September 9, 2002; Cast: Michael Stuhlbarg, Ron Riley, Zach Shaffer, Michael Chernus

BYE, BYE by Victor Lodato; Director, Tyler Marchant; September 9, 2002; Cast: Dion Graham, John McAdams

THUNDERBIRD by Joe Fisher; Director, Randy White; September 9, 2002; Cast: Marin Ireland, Michael Stuhlbarg

YELLOWMAN by Dael Orlandersmith; Director, Dael Orlandersmith; September 9, 2002; Cast: Dael Orlandersmith

LUSCIOUS MUSIC by Matthew Maguire; Director, Michael John Garces; September 13, 2002; Cast: Lourdes Martin, Peter Mele, Edward O'Blenis, Clea Rivera, Donald Silva, Ed Vassallo

THE ARGUMENT by David Greenspan; Directed by David Greenspan; September 30, 2002; Cast: David Chandler, Ted Schneider, John McAdams

DANCING ON MOONLIGHT by Keith Glover; Director, Keith Glover; October 1, 2002; Cast: Cherise Boothe, Chuck Cooper, Yvette Ganier, Leland Gantt, Bryan Hicks, Mike Hodge, Keith Randolph Smith, Stacey Robinson

CLUBLAND by Roy Williams; Director, Jo Bonney; October 10, 2002; Cast: Akili Prince, Leslie Elliard, Yvette Ganier, David Deblinger, Michael Chernus

BAG OF MARBLES by Kathryn Ash; Director, Leah Gardiner; October 15, 2002; Cast: Larry Block, Lynn Cohen, Mia Dillon, Gretchen Lee Krich, Leslie Lyles

BLOOD WEDDING by Caridad Svich; Director, Deborah Saivetz; October 16, 2002; Cast: Jenny Sterlin, Molly Powell, Stacey Robinson, Mercedes Herrero, Gretchen Lee Krich, Lizzy Cooper Davis, Jesse Perez, Robert Alexander Owens, George Heslin, Michael Ray Escamilla, Michael J.X. Gladis

RAREE by K.C. Davis; Director, Randy White; October 17, 2002; Cast: Maria Thayer, Autumn Dornfeld, Florencia Lozano, Siobhan Mahoney, Christopher Evan Welch, Jack Wetherall, Lars Hanson

SANS CULLOTES IN THE PROMISED LAND by Kirsten Greenidge; Director, Seret Scott; November 4–16, 2002; Cast: Erika Tazel, Michael Potts, Sandra Daley, Brenda Thomas, Eisa Davis, Cherise Boothe

THE STREET OF USEFUL THINGS by Stephanie Fleischmann; Director, Julie Anne Robinson; November 4–16, 2002; Cast: Jenny Sterlin, Patrick Husted, Leslie Lyles, Addie Johnson, Molly Powell, Gretchen Lee Krich

SARCOXIE AND SEALOVE by Sander Hicks; Director, Peter Hawkins; November 4–16, 2002; Cast: Roderick Hill, Sarah Lord, Charles Hyman, Ron Riley, Joseph Goodrich, Ed Vassallo, Gary Perez, John McAdams

PENETRATE THE KING by Gordon Dahlquist; Director, David Levine; November 4–16, 2002; Cast: Joseph Goodrich, Mary Bacon, Molly Powell, John McAdams, Patrick Husted, Addie Johnson

JUMP/CUT by Neena Beber; Director, Leigh Silverman; November 4–16, 2002; Cast: Christopher Evan Welch, Mary Bacon, Christopher Duva

EXPAT/INFERNO by Alejandro Morales; Director, Scott Ebersold; November 19, 2002; Cast: Ramon de Ocampo, Justin Bond, Stephen St. Paul, Alma Cuervo, Nathan White, Jeff Bond

CATARACT by Lisa D'Amour; Director, Katie Pearl; November 20, 2002; Cast: Brennan Brown, Brandy Zarle, Paul Sparks, Mia Barron

UP (THE MAN IN THE FLYING LAWN CHAIR) by Bridget Carpenter; Director, Peter DuBois; November 21, 2002; Cast: Matthew Maguire, Babo Harrison, Rufus Tureen, Alicia Goranson, Judith Hawking, Ron Riley

ILLUMINATING VERONICA by Rogelio Martinez; Director, Lou Jacob; Opened at the New Dramatists Theatre, December 10, 2002; Cast: Lucia Brawley, Gary Perez, Judith Delgado, Ramon de Ocampo, Felix Solis, Vivia Font, Chris DeOni, Joanna Liao

UNTIL WE FIND EACH OTHER by Brooke Berman; Director, Randy White; December 10, 2002; Cast: Michael Chernus, Lennon Parham, Mia Barron, Robert Beitzel, Heather Goldenhersh

CLEVELAND RAINING by Sung Rno; Director, Linsay Firman; December 12, 2002; Cast: Eunice Wong, Louis Galindo, Paul Jun, Deborah S. Craig

IN LOVE AND ANGER by Michael Henry Brown; Director, Gordon Edelstein; January 6, 2003; Cast: Keith David, Curtis McClair, Harriett D. Foy, Linda Powell

HOMEWRECKER by Kelly Stuart; Director, Melissa Kievman; January 10, 2003; Cast: David Chandler, Pamela Gray, Jan Leslie Harding, Ron Riley

WHORES by Lee Blessing; Director, Ed Herendeen; January 13, 2003; Cast: Elizabeth Reaser, Carrie Preston, Karen Ziemba, Jayne Houdyshell, Shawn Elliott

MESSALINA by Gordon Dahlquist; Director, David Levine; January 23, 2003; Cast: Michael Stuhlbarg, Molly Powell, Addie Johnson, John McAdams, Alana Jerins, Robert Alexander Owens

THE SAVAGES OF HARTFORD by David Grimm; Director, David Grimm; February 6, 2003; Cast: Buzz Bovshow, Charles Parnell, Tom Mardirosian, Leslie Lyles, Dan Pintauro, Christopher Duva, Leslie Elliard, Keira Naughton, Martin Rayner

LOST IN TRANSLATION by Rogelio Martinez; Director, Ted Sod; February 18, 2003; Cast: Mimi Lieber, Yul Vazquez, Joseph Siravo, K.J. Sanchez, Ron Riley, Gloria Garayva, Rebecca White

THE LYSISTRATA PROJECT Director, Linsay Firman; March 3, 2003; Cast: Sander Hicks, Arlene Hutton, Honour Kane

PYRETOWN by John Belluso; Director, Tim Farrell; March 11, 2003; Cast: Melissa Leo, Jessica Hecht, Christopher Thornton

NITA AND ZITA by Lisa D'Amour; Director, Lisa D'Amour; March 12, 2003; Cast: Katie Pearl, Kathy Randals

MAGNIFICENT WASTE by Caridad Svich; Director, David Levine; March 18, 2003; Cast: Jennifer Morris, Nina Hellman, Jonathan Tindle, Jack Ferver, Juliana Francis, Joanna P. Adler, Trevor Williams, John McAdams

PRECIOUS STONE by Morgan Allen; Director, Linsay Firman; March 20, 2003; Cast: David Engel, Mitch Montgomery, Justin Pappas

MOTHERBONE Musical with Book by Karen Hartman; Music by Graham Reynolds; Director, Jason Neulander; March 27, 2003; Cast: Patricia Phillips, Elan Rivera, Ken Prymus, Adam Michael Kaokept, Olivia Oguma, Rena Strober, Craig Feser, Paul Goodwin-Groen

SCHOOL FOR GREYBEARDS by Hannah Cowley; Director, Randy White; April 3, 2003; Cast: Harding Lemay, Aurora Nonas-Barnes, Caridad Svich, Catherine Filloux, Paul Zimet, Jono Hustis, Mark Bazzone, David Grimm, Dominic Taylor, Karen Hartman, Qui Nguyen, Eisa Davis, Zakiyyah Alexander

THE ZERO HOUR by Madeleine George; April 7, 2003; Cast: Colleen Werthmann, Aysan Celik

CLANDESTINE CROSSING by Keith Glover; Director, Keith Glover; April 8, 2003; Cast: Michelle Dawson, Trent Dawson, Benim Foster, James Judy, Nicole Orth-Pallavicini, Mark Pinter, Michelle R. Six

FAIR GAME by Karl Gajdusek; Directed by Robert Milazzo; April 14, 2003; Cast: Gerry Bamman, Judith Light, Michele Monaghan, Ty Burrell, Jenna Stern

MEDIA MEDEA by Tara Welty; Director, Lauren Rosen; Opened at the New Dramatists Theatre, April 22, 2003; Cast: Marin Ireland, Jack Phillips, April Sweeney, David Gravens, David Bennett, Elowyn Castle, Amanda Plattsmier

TONGUE TIED AND DUTY FREE by Jim Nicholson; Director, Sturgis Warner; April 22, 2003; Cast: Yetta Gottesman, Steven Boyer, Christopher Innvar, Molly Powell, Karl Herlinger, Mercedes Herrero, Oliver Wadsworth, Sturgis Warner

ASCENDING LULU by Caridad Svich; Director, Linsay Firman; April 23, 2003; Cast: Carolyn Baeumler, Jennifer Morris, Armando Riesco, Chris Wells, Alfredo Narciso, T.R. Knight

PHAEDRA IN DELIRIUM by Susan Yankowitz; Director, Kirsten Brandt; May 1, 2003; Cast: Shawn Elliott, Maggie Reed, Fiona Scoones, Michael Severence

THE TROJAN WOMEN by Ellen Mclaughlin; Music by Katie Down; Director, Rachel Dickstein; May 27, 2003; Cast: Jane Nichols, Maggie Gyllenhaal, Seth Kanor, Elena McGhee, Vivienne Benesch, Denis O'Hare, Kerry Chipman, Ruth Coughlin, Stephanie DiMaggio, Tara Good, Briana Mandel, Maria McConville, Concetta Rose Rella, Satomi Yamauchi, Julia Prud'homme

NEW FEDERAL THEATRE

Woodie King, Jr., Producing Director

AMERICAN MENU by Don Wilson Glenn; Director, Ajene Washington; April 23, 2003; Cast: Patricia R. Floyd, Sharon Hope, Benja K., Kimberly "Q" Purnell, M. Drue Williams

WHOSE FAMILY VALUES! by Richard Abrons; Director, Philip Rose; Scenery, Robert Joel Schwartz; Costumes, Gail Cooper-Hecht; Lighting, Shirley Prendergast; Sound, Sean O'Halioran; May 22, 2003; Cast: Glynis Bell, Rosalyn Coleman, Chris Hutchison, Clayton LeBouef, Martha Libman, Ted Rodenborn, Herb Rubens, Gammy Singer

NEW GROUP

Artistic Director, Scott Elliott; Geoffrey Rich, Executive Director; Ian Morgan, Associate Artistic Director

COMEDIANS by Trevor Griffiths; Director, Scott Elliott; Scenery; Derek Mclane; Costumes, Mimi O'Donnell; Lighting, Jason Lyons; Sound, Ken Travis; January 15, 2003; Cast: Jim Dale, Raul Esparza, Max Baker, Ismail Bashey, James Beecher, Gordon Connell, Allen Corduner, William Duell, Jamie Harris, David Lansbury, David McCallum, Marcus Powell

THE WOMEN OF LOCKERBIE by Deborah Brevoort; Director, Scott Elliott; Scenery, Derek Mclane; Costumes, Mattie Ullrich; Lighting, Jason Lyons; Sound, Ken Travis; April 6, 2003; Cast: Larry Pine, Jenny Sterlin, Angela Pietropinto, Kristen Sieh, Judith Ivey, Adam Trese, Kathleen Doyle; Presented in association with Women's Project and Productions

PERFORMANCE SPACE 122

Artistic Director, Mark Russell

JOE by Richard Maxwell; Director, Mr. Maxwell; Scenery, Gary Wilmes; Costumes, Tory Vazquez; Lighting, Jane Cox; September 8, 2002; Cast: Richard Zhuravenko, Matthew Stadelmann, Brian Mendes, Mick Diflo, Gene Wynne

MIGHTY NICE! by Paul Zaloom; Additional Text by Sean Forrester; Director, Randee Trabitz; Scenery, Paul Zaloom; Costumes, Betsey Potter; Lighting, Sean Forrester; January 3, 2003; Cast: Paul Zaloom

BITTER BIERCE, OR THE FRICTION WE CALL GRIEF by Mac Wellman; Director, Mac Wellman; Scenery and Lighting, Kyle Chepulis; Costumes, Barb Mellor; February 6, 2003; Cast: Stephen Mellor

NOTES FROM UNDERGROUND by Eric Bogosian; Director, Eric Bogosian; May 1, 2003; Cast: Jonathan Ames

PRIMARY STAGES

Executive Director, Casey Childs; Artistic Director, Andrew Leynse

CALL THE CHILDREN HOME Musical with Book by Thomas Babe; Music and Lyrics by Mildred Kayden; Additional Material by J.D. Myers; Director, Kent Gash; Choreography, Tanya Gibson-Clark; Scenery, Emily Beck; Costumes, Austin K. Sanderson; Lighting, William H. Grant III; Sound, Johnna Dory; Musical Direction, William Foster McDaniel; September 23, 2002; Cast: Tamara Tunie, Eugene Fleming, Angela Robinson, Sophia Salguero, Julian Gamble, Caesar Samayoa, Christiane Noll, Sean McDermott

THE FOURTH WALL by AR Gurney; Director, David Saint; Scenery, James Youmans; Costumes, David Murin; Lighting, Jeff Croiter; Sound, Christopher J. Bailey; November 13,2002; Cast: Susan Sullivan, Charles Kimbrough, Sandy Duncan, David Pittu

ROMOLA AND NIJINSKY by Lynne Alvarez; Director, David Levine; Choreography, Robert laFosse; Scenery, Michael Byrnes; Costumes, Claudia Stephens; Lighting, Lap-Chi Chu; Sound, Jane Shaw; Music, Brendan Connelly; May 15, 2003; Cast: David Barlow, Kelly Hutchinson, Allen Fitzpatrick, Michelle Lookadoo, Laura Martin, John McAdams, Daniel Oreskes, Janet Zarish

Charles Kimbrough, Sandy Duncan in *The Fourth Wall* PHOTO BY MARVIN EINHORN

Christiane Noll, Caesar Samayoa in *Call the Children Home* PHOTO BY MARVIN EINHORN

PUERTO RICAN TRAVELING THEATER

Founder and Producer, Miriam Colon Valle

BECOMING BERNARDA by Oscar A. Colon; Director, Sturgis Warner; Scenery, Robert Culek; Costumes, Karen Flood; Lighting, Ben Stanton; June 11, 2002; Cast: Annie Henk, Nina Polan, Silvia Brito, Blanca Camacho, Adriana Sananes, Maggie Bofill, Lourdes Martin, Carlos Molina, Carlos Orizondo, Chaz Mena

THE MISTRESS OF THE INN (LA POSADERA) by Carlo Goldoni; Director, Dean Zayas; Costumes, Elizabeth Wittlin Lipton; Sound, Christophe Pierre; August 12, 2002; Cast: Emanuel Loarca, Hemky Madera, Fior Marte, Coco Nunez, Frank Perozo, Osvaldo Placencia, Pablo Tufino, Fulvia Vergel

SIGNATURE THEATRE COMPANY

Artistic Director, James Houghton

BOOK OF DAYS by Lanford Wilson; Director, Marshall W. Mason; Scenery, John Lee Beatty; Costumes, Laura Crow; Lighting, Dennis Parichy; Sound, Chuck London and Stewart Werner; November 3, 2002; Cast: Alan Campbell, Hope Chernov, Jim Haynie, Jonathan Hogan, Susan Kellermann, John Lepard, Kelly McAndrew, Boris McGiver, Tuck Milligan, Matthew Rauch, Miriam Shor, Nancy Snyder

FIFTH OF JULY by Lanford Wilson; Director, Jo Bonney; Scenery, Richard Hoover; Costumes, Ann Hould-Ward; Lighting, James Vermeulen; Music and Sound, John Gromada; Fight Direction, J. Steven White; February 3, 2003; Cast: Robert Sean Leonard, Michael J.X. Gladis, David Harbour, Parker Posey, Jessalyn Gilsig, Sarah Lord, Pamela Payton-Wright, Ebon Moss-Bachrach

RAIN DANCE by Lanford Wilson; Director, Guy Sanville; Scenery, Christine Jones; Costumes, Daryl A. Stone; Lighting, James Vermeulen; Sound, Kurt Kellenberger; May 20, 2003; Cast: Randolph Mantooth, Suzanne Regan, James Van Der Beek, Harris Yulin

Harris Yulin, James Van Der Beek in *Rain Dance* PHOTO BY JOAN MARCUS

Alan Campbell, Matthew Rauch in *Book of Days* PHOTO BY RAHAV SEGEV

Parker Posey, Sarah Lord, Jessalyn Gilsig, Robert Sean Leonard in *Fifth of July*
PHOTO BY RAHAV SEGEV

SOHO REP

Artistic Director, Daniel Aukin; Executive Director, Alexandra Conley

SIGNALS OF DISTRESS by the Flying Machine; Based on the novel by Jim Crace; Director, Joshua Carlebach; Scenery, Marisa Frantz; Costumes, Theresa Squire; Lighting, Josh Bradford and Raquel Davis; Sound, Bill Ware; November 15, 2002; Cast: Richard Crawford, Jessica Green, Kathryn Phillip, Kevin Varner, Gregory Steinbruner, Jason Linder, Tami Stronach, Matthew Gray

MOLLY'S DREAM by Maria Irene Fornes; Music by Maury Loeb; Artistic Director, Daniel Aukin; Executive Director, Alexandra Conley; Director, Daniel Aukin; Choreography, David Neumann; Scenery and Costumes, Louisa Thompson; Lighting, Marcus Doshi; Sound, Ken Travis; Musical Direction, Michael Friedman; May 16, 2003; Cast: Bo Corre, Dominic Bogart, Erin Farrell, Shannon Fitzgerald, Jessica Heney, Debra Wassum, Casey Wilson, Matthew Maher, Patrick Boll, Toi Perkins

THEATER FOR THE NEW CITY

Executive Director, Crystal Field

CONNECTIONS by Vernon Church; Director, Larry Shanet; Scenery, Fay Torres-Yap; Lighting, Mark Hankla; Music, Sean Altman; September 24, 2002; Cast: Rich Egan, Shellee Nicols, Michael S. Rush, Max Goldberg, Sean Devine, Kina Bermudez, Cristy Piccini, Jennifer Maturo, Sonya Tsuchigane, Suzie Moon, Amanita Heird, Franca Vercelloni, Jenny Moss

AT A PLANK BRIDGE by Kannan Menon; Director, Tina Chen; January 10, 2003; Cast: Mano Maniam, Jackson Loo

THE VOLUNTEER by Paulanne Simmons; Director, Mary Catherine Burke; Choreography, Mary Ann Wall; Scenery, Michael V. Moore; Costumes, Becky Lasky; Lighting, K.J. Hardy; Sound, Jake Hall; January 30, 2003; Cast: Rebecca Hoodwin, Shannon Bryant, Justin Aponte, Victor Barranca, Bill Dealy, Kim Gardner, Frieda Lipp, Amy Silver, Leni Tabb

THE GOLDEN BEAR by Laurel Hessing; Lyrics by Laurel Hessing; Music by Arthur Abrams; Based on *Jews Without Money* by Michael Gold; Director, Crystal Field; Scenery and Lighting, Donald L. Brooks; Costumes, Myrna Duarte and Terry Leong; Sound, Joy Linscheid; March 13, 2003; Cast: Alexander Bartenieff, Elizabeth Ruf, Primy Rivera, Mira Rivera, Frank Biancomano, Elizabeth Barkan

–1 (MINUS ONE) by Gyavira Lasana; Director, David Willinger; May 3, 2003; Cast: Aja M. Yamagata, Monica Stith, Christopher King, Angelique Orsini, Robert Hatcher, Robert Colston, Shannon Bryant, Robert Lehrer, Jennifer McCabe, Daniel Hicks

Michael Martinez, Clara Ruf-Maldonado, Elizabeth Ruf, Mira Rivera, Primy Rivera, Elizabeth Barkan in *The Golden Bear*   PHOTO BY JONATHAN SLAFF

Shannon Bryant, Rebecca Hoodwin in *The Volunteer*   PHOTO BY GREGORY P. MANGO

THEATRE FOR A NEW AUDIENCE

Founding Artistic Director, Jeffrey Horowitz

THE GENERAL FROM AMERICA by Richard Nelson; Director, Jeffrey Nelson; Scenery, Douglas Stein; Costumes, Susan Hilferty, Lighting, James F. Ingalls; Sound, Scott Lehrer; Fight Direction, Brian Byrnes; November 21, 2002; Cast: Corin Redgrave, Alice Cannon, Sean Cullen, Jon DeVries, Thomas M. Hammond, Kate Kearney-Patch, Nicholas Kepros, Paul Anthony McGrane, Jesse Pennington, Thomas Sadoski, Yvonne Woods

JULIUS CAESAR by William Shakespeare; Director, Karin Coonrod; Scenery, Douglas Stein; Costumes, Catherine Zuber; Lighting, David Weiner; Music and Sound, Mark Bennett; Fight Direction, B.H. Barry; January 19, 2003; Cast: Earl Hindman, Justin Campbell, Hope Chernov, Curzon Dobell, Michael Ray Escamilla, Kristin Flanders, Thomas M. Hammond, Andy Hoey, David Don Miller, Nicholas Mongiardo-Cooper, Simeon Moore, Daniel Oreskes, Michael Rogers, Matt Saldivar, Jacob Garrett White, Graham Winton

DON JUAN by Moliere; Translated by Christopher Hampton; Director, Bartlett Sheri; Scenery and Lighting, Christopher Akerlind; Costumes, Elizabeth Caitlin Ward; Sound, Peter John Still; Fight Direction, J. Steven White; March 23, 2003; Cast: Byron Jennings, John Christopher Jones, Liam Craig, Nicholas Kepros, Sherri Parker Lee, Nicole Lowrance, Dan Snook, Price Waldman, Graham Winton, David Wohl, Anne Louise Zachry

THE VINEYARD THEATRE

Artistic Director, Douglas Aibel; Managing Director, Bardo S. Ramirez; Executive Director for External Affairs, Jennifer Garvey-Blackwell

THE FOURTH SISTER by Janusz Glowacki; Director, Lisa Peterson; Scenery, Rachel Hauck; Costumes, Mattie Ullrich; Lighting, Kevin Adams; Sound, Jill B.C. DuBoff; Music, Gina Leishman; Fight Direction, Rick Sordelet November 21, 2002; Cast: Jase Blankfort, Bill Buell, Alicia Goranson, Jessica Hecht, Marin Hinkle, Daniel Oreskes, Lee Pace, Steven Rattazzi, Suzanne Shepherd, Louis Tucci

AVENUE Q Musical with book by Jeff Whitty; Music and Lyrics by Robert Lopez and Jeff Marx; Director, Jason Moore; Choreography, Ken Roberson; Scenery, Anna Louizos; Costumes, Mirena Rada; Lighting, Frances Aronson; Sound, Brett Jarvis; Puppets, Rick Lyon; March 19, 2003; Cast: Ann Harada, Natalie Venetia Belcon, Jordan Gelber, Stephanie D'Abruzzo, Rick Lyon, John Tartaglia, Jen Barnhart

WOMEN'S PROJECT AND PRODUCTIONS

Artistic Director, Julia Miles; Managing Director, Georgia Buchanan

CHEAT by Julie Jensen; Director, Joan Vail Thorne; Scenery, David P. Gordon; Costumes, Gail Cooper-Hecht; Lighting, Michael Lincoln; Music and Sound, Scott Killian; October 16, 2002; Cast: Lucy Deakins, Shayna Ferm, Kevin O'Rourke and Karen Young

BIRDY by Naomi Wallace, Adapted from the novel by William Wharton; Director, Lisa Peterson; February 17, 2003

ELEANORE AND ISADORA: A DUET OF SORROWS by Diane Kagan; Director, Diane Kagan; March 10, 2003

BEFORE DEATH COMES FOR THE ARCHBISHOP by Elaine Romero; Director, Deborah Saivetz; March 17, 2003

BOX OF PEARLS by Marcie Begleiter; Director, Passion; March 24, 2003

YORK THEATRE COMPANY

Artistic Director, James Morgan; Consulting Managing Director, Louis Chiodo; Company Administrator, Scott DelaCruz

PORTERPHILES Musical revue with book by Judy Brown and James Morgan; Music and Lyrics by Cole Porter Artistic Director, James Morgan; Consulting Managing Director, Louis Chiodo; Company Administrator, Scott DelaCruz; Direction and Scenery by James Morgan; Musical Staging, Barry McNabb; Costumes, Margiann Flanagan; Lighting, Mary Jo Dondlinger; December 12, 2002; Cast: Lynne Halliday, Ricky Russell, Stephen Zinnato

Walter Willison, Mary Rodgers, Marcy DeGonge Manfredi from *Wall to Wall Richard Rodgers* PHOTO BY RICK MANFREDI

WALL TO WALL RICHARD RODGERS

In celebration of the centennial of the Broadway legend. A gala twelve-hour celebration of Richard Rodgers centennial featuring 18 musical segments; mini-musical comedies and solo acts climaxing in an evening concert in two acts.

Music by Richard Rodgers; Lyrics, Oscar Hammerstein II, Lorenz Hart, Martin Charnin, Sheldon Harnick, Stephen Sondheim; Artistic Director, Isaiah Sheffer; Conductor, Elliot Lawrence; Musical Directors, Abba Bogin, Lanny Meyers; Musical Coordinator, John Kroner; Special Orchestrations, Bruce Pomahac, Wayne Blood; Assistant Producer, John Tighe; Lighting, Brian Aldous; Sound, Hear No Evil, LLC; Production Manager, Jamie Spear; Tech Director, Denis Heron; Tech Crew, Mike Duffy, Michael Casanova; Vice President, Joanne Cossa; Managing Director, Peggy Wreen; Cast Recording *Fynsworth Alley*; Press, Two-Five Media, Amy Paternite; Symphony Space; March 23, 2002.

OH, WHAT A BEAUTIFUL MORNIN' *Introduction*: Douglas Webster, Hon. Kate Levin, Commissioner, Dept. of Cultural Affairs, NYC; *Victory at Sea*: InterSchool Orchestras of New York Symphonic Band, Brian P. Worsdale, Conductor; Dr. David Winkler

CAROUSEL Director, Arthur Bartow; Musical Director, Jack Lee; Choreographer, Lori Leshner; Stage Manager, Elisa R. Kuhar; Costumes, Kitty Leech, Gregg Barnes. Cast: Aileen Goldberg (Carrie Pipperidge), Jamie Kirchner (Julie Jordan), Greg Kata (Billy Bigelow), Christina E. Morrell (Nettie Fowler), J. Austin Eyer (Enoch Snow), P.J. Griffith (Jigger Craigin), Sergia Anderson, Chris Aniello, Monica Anselm, Cristin Boyle, Christina Bianco, J. Claude Deering, Cheryl Dowling, Thayules K. Floyd, Alexander Crowder Gaines, Jennifer Long, Kiera Mickiewicz, Michael Miller, Ben Nahum, Eric Neher, Gabriel Paez, Billy Rosa, Sarah Shahinian, Byron St. Cyr

SWINGING RODGERS I, II, III Terrie Richards Alden, Howard Alden, Tovah Feldshuh, Bob Goldstone, Melba Joyce, Barbara Carroll, Jay Leonhart, Fred Hersch, Mary Cleere Haran, Maureen McGovern

DEAREST ENEMY Deborah Litwak (Mrs. Murray), Thomas Lucca (John Copeland), Stacy Baer (Betsy Burke), Jennifer Luers (Jane Murray), Brian Charles Rooney (Harry Tryon), Village Light Opera Chorus, Michael Thomas (piano)

RODGERS & DAUGHTERS Mary Rodgers Guettel, Linda Rodgers Emory

A HAMMERSTEIN MATINEE: A GRAND NIGHT FOR SINGING Director, Jonathan Bernstein; Musical Director, Steven Freeman; Original Director, Walter Bobbie; Cast: Victoria Clark, James Hindman, Connie Kunkle, Joseph Mahowald, Lynne Wintersteller, Jonathan Bernstein

WITH A SONG IN MY HEART Nora York, Charles Giordano, Greg Cohen, Steve Ross, Jo Sullivan Loesser, Colin Romoff, Betty Comden, Adolph Green, Paul Trueblood, KT Sullivan, Larry Woodard

MANHATTAN MADCAPS OF 1924 World Premiere; Music, Richard Rodgers; Lyrics, Lorenz Hart; Book, Jerzy Turnpike; Musical Direction, Arrangements, Lanny Meyers; Musical Staging, Eleanor Reissa; Decors, Ruth Priscilla Kirstein; Lighting, Brian Aldous, Allison Eggers; Cast: Sidney J. Burgoyne (Casey), Garrett Long (Cassie), Don Stephenson (Gary), Emily Loesser (Gracie), Ivy Austin (Jeanette), David Staller (Johnny), Walter Willison (Stonewall Moskowitz), Marcy DeGonge-Manfredi (Manhattan Mamie)

LATER LYRICS Walter Willison (*Two By Two*), Sheldon Harnick, KT Sullivan, Larry Woodard (*Rex*), Loni Ackerman, Marcy DeGonge-Manfredi, Stephanie Vitale (*Do I Hear a Waltz*)

TODAY'S BROADWAY Spencer Kayden, Billy Stritch, Molly Ringwald, Raul Esparza, Judy Kaye, Schuler Hensley

RODGERS IN YIDDISH Saymour Rexite, Zalmen Mlotek

SOME ENCHANTED EVENING Conductor, Elliot Lawrence; Loni Ackerman, Ivy Austin, Sidney J. Burgoyne, Victoria Clark, Marcy DeGonge-Manfredi, Melissa Errico, Debbie Gravitte, David Green, Jonathan Hadary, Celeste Holm, Melba Joyce, Garrett Long, James Naughton, Christiane Noll, Patrick Quinn, Mary Rodgers Guettel, David Staller, Richard White, Douglas Webster, Walter Willison

PROFESSIONAL REGIONAL COMPANIES

ALLEY THEATRE

Houston, Texas

FIFTY-SIXTH SEASON

Artistic Director, Gregory Boyd; Managing Director, Paul Tetreault

THE GENERAL FROM AMERICA by Richard Nelson; Director, Richard Nelson; Scenic Design, Douglas Stein; Costume Design, Susan Hilferty; Lighting Design, James F. Ingalls; Sound Design, Scott Lehrer; October 11–November 9, 2002; Cast: Alice Cannon (Lady Clinton), Sean Cullen (Joseph Reed and Robinson), Jon DeVries (George Washington), Thomas Hammond (Stephen Kemble and Van Wart), Nicholas Kepros (Sir Henry Clinton), Paul Anthony McGrane (John Andre), Kate Kearney-Patch, Jesse Pennington (Alexander Hamilton), Corin Redgrave (Benedict Arnold), Thomas Sadoski (Timothy Matlack and Pauling), Yvonne Woods (Peggy)

FRAME 312 by Keith Reddin; Director, Peter Masterson; Scenic Design, Kevin Rigdon; Costume Design, Linda Ross; Lighting Design, Rui Rita; Sound Design, Joe Pino; October 25–November 24, 2002; Cast: Elizabeth Bunch (Lynette in her 60s), Carlin Glynn (Lynette in her 90s), Jenny Maguire (Stephanie), Stephanie Kurtzuba (Margie, Marie, Doris), Jeffrey Bean (Tom, Roy, Agent Barry), James Black (Graham)

A CHRISTMAS CAROL by Charles Dickens; Director and Adaptation by Stephen Rayne; Scenic Design, Douglas W. Schmidt; Costume Design, Esther Marquis; Lighting Design, Rui Rita; Sound Design, Malcolm Nicholls; November 29–December 29, 2002; Cast: James Belcher (Ebenezer Scrooge), Bettye Fitzpatrick (Miss Goodleigh, Mrs. Dilber), John Tyson (Bob Cratchit), Paul Hope (Coutts, Fezziwig), Jeffrey Bean (Marley, Old Joe), Charles Krohn (Priest), Jovan Jackson (Ghost of Christmas Future, Labourer, Fezziwig Guest), Philip Lehl (Fred), David Rainey (Poor Man, Ghost of Christmas Present), Sarah Prikryl (Ghost of Christmas Past, Mrs. O'Mally), Laura Hooper (Moll, Miss 1, Fred's Sister, Poor Woman), David Born (Undertaker, Fezziwig Guest, Fred Guest), Anne Quackenbush (Miss Bumble, Miss 3, Mrs. Fred), Joel Sandel (Phizz, Belle's Husband, Fezziwig Guest), Jennifer Cherry (Belle, Martha), Shelly Calene-Black (Mrs. Cratchit, Mrs. Fezziwig), Richard Carlson (Topper), K. Todd Freeman (Deedles), Richard Ramsey (Royal Exchange, Turkey Boy)

WHO'S AFRAID OF VIRGINIA WOOLF? by Edward Albee; Director, Gregory Boyd; Scenic Design, Tony Straiges; Costume Design, Andrea Lauer; Lighting Design, John Ambrosone; Sound Design, Joe Pino; January 10–February 8, 2003; Cast: Judith Ivey (Martha), James Black (George), Elizabeth Bunch (Honey), Ty Mayberry (Nick)

THE GOAT OR WHO IS SYLVIA? by Edward Albee; Director, Pam MacKinnon; Scenic Design, Tony Straiges; Costume Design, Daryl A. Stone; Lighting Design, Kevin Rigdon; Sound Design, Joe Pino; January 17–February 16, 2003; Cast: James Belcher (Ross), Elizabeth Heflin (Stevie), Matt Hune (Billy), Todd Waite (Martin)

YOU CAN'T TAKE IT WITH YOU by Moss Hart and George S. Kaufman; Director, Sanford Robbins; Scenic Design, Linda Buchanan; Costume Design, Judith Dolan; Lighting Design, Kevin Rigdon; Sound Design, Rob Milburn and Michael Bodeen; February 28–March 29, 2003; Cast: Annalee Jefferies (Penelope Sycamore), Robin Terry (Essie), Ann C. James (Rheba), James Black (Paul Sycamore), James Belcher (Mr. De Pinna), Jeffrey Bean (Ed), David Rainey (Donald), Charles Krohn (Martin Vanderhof), Victoria Adams (Alice), Todd Waite (Henderson), Ty Mayberry (Tony Kirby), John Tyson (Boris Kolenkhov), Elizabeth Heflin (Gay Wellington), Paul Hope (Mr. Kirby), Anne Quackenbush (Mrs. Kirby), Bettye Fitzpatrick (Olga)

THE TRIP TO BOUNTIFUL by Horton Foote; Director, Michael Wilson; Scenic Design, Jeff Cowie; Costume Design, David C. Woolard; Lighting Design, Rui Rita; Sound Design, John Gromada; April 11–May 10, 2003; Cast: Dee Maaske (Mrs. Carrie Watts), Devon Abner (Ludie Watts), Hallie Foote (Jessie Mae Watts), Robin Terry (Thelma)

STONES IN HIS POCKETS by Marie Jones; Director, Joe Brancato; Production Design, Kevin Rigdon; Sound Design, Elizabeth Rhodes; April 18–May 18, 2003; Cast: Jeffrey Bean (Charlie Conlon), Todd Waite (Jake Quinn)

HAMLET by William Shakespeare; Director, Gregory Boyd; Scenic Design, Neil Patel; Costume Design, Constance Hoffman; Lighting Design, Chris Parry; Sound Design, Rob Milburn and Michael Bodeen; May 23–June 22, 2003; Cast: Ty Mayberry (Hamlet), James Black (Claudius, The Ghost), Elizabeth Heflin (Gertrude), Philip Lehl (Horatio), John Tyson (Polonius), Daniel Magill (Laertes), Jennifer Cherry (Ophelia), Paul Hope (Reynaldo, Osric), Pablo Bracho (Rosencrantz), Joel Sandel (Guildenstern, Francisco), James Belcher (Player King, The Priest), Sarah Prikryl (Player Queen), David Rainey (Marcellus) Charles Krohn (The Grave Digger)

Judith Ivey, James Black in *Who's Afraid of Virginia Woolf* PHOTO BY JIM CALDWELL

Paul Whitworth, T. Edward Webster, Marco Barricelli in *Night and Day* PHOTO BY KEVIN BERNE

AMERICAN CONSERVATORY THEATRE

San Francisco, California
THIRTY-SIXTH SEASON

Carey Perloff, Artistic Director; Heather M. Kitchen, Managing Director

NIGHT AND DAY by Tom Stoppard; Director, Carey Perloff; Scenic Design, Annie Smart; Costume Design, Judith Anne Dolan; Lighting Design, Peter Maradudin; Sound Design, Garth Hemphill; Dramaturg, Paul Walsh; Dialect Consultant, Deborah Sussel; Fight Direction, Gregory Hoffman; Casting, Meryl Lind Shaw; Wigs and Makeup, Rick Echols; Assistant Director, Rona Waddington; Stage Manager, Kimberly Mark Webb; Assistant Stage Manager, Julie Haber; Intern, K. Mauldin; Cast: Paul Whitworth (George Guthrie), Gregory Wallace (Francis), René Augesen (Ruth Carson), Harley Grandin, Zachary Lenat (Alastair Carson), Marco Barricelli (Dick Wagner), T. Edward Webster (Jacob Milne), Anthony Fusco (Geoffrey Carson), Steven Anthony Jones (President Mageeba) Understudies: Tommy A. Gomez (George Guthrie, Dick Wagner), Emily Ackerman (Ruth Carson), Rod Gnapp (Geoffrey Carson), Rhonnie Washington (President Mageeba, Francis)

LACKAWANNA BLUES Written and performed by Ruben Santiago-Hudson; Accompanied by Bill Sims, Jr.; Director, Loretta Greco; Scenic Design, Myung Hee Cho; Lighting Design, James Vermeulen; Sound Design, Garth Hemphill; Stage Manager, Julie Haber; Assistant Stage Manager, Kimberly Mark Webb; Cast: Ruben Santiago-Hudson

A CHRISTMAS CAROL by Charles Dickens; Adapted by Dennis Powers and Laird Williamson; Director, Craig Slaight; Original Direction, Laird Williamson; Scenic Design, Robert Blackman; Lighting Design, Peter Maradudin; Costume Design, Robert Morgan; Additional Costumes and Design Supervision, David F. Draper; Original Music, Lee Hoiby; Original Lyrics, Laird Williamson; Sound Design, Garth Hemphill; Music Direction, Peter Maleitzke; Assistand Director and Choreographer, Christine Mattison; Wigs and Makeup, Production Stage Manager, Francesca Russell; 1st

Assistant Stage Manager, Shona Mitchell; 2nd Assistant Stage Manager, John W. Sugden; Intern, K. Mauldin; Rick Echols; Cast: Forrest Fraser Tiffany II (Boy Caroler), Tommy A. Gomez (Charles Dickens), Steven Anthony Jones (Ebenezer Scrooge), Brud Fogarty (Bob Cratchit), Ali Baker, Margaret Schenck (Charitable Gentlewomen), Tyler McKenna (Fred), Judy Butterfield, Jacob Ming-Trent, Victoria Thompson (Carol Sellers), Daniel Patrick Kennedy, Gabriel Kenney, Chase Macauley Maxwell, Nicholas Perloff-Giles, Christopher Ward (Sled Boys), Allison Schubert (Woman in the Street), Devon Charisse Hadsell (Daughter of Woman in the Street), Scout Katovich, Charlotte Locke (Beggar Girls), Adam Brooks (Mistletoe Carrier) Camila Borrero, Amanda Hastings-Phillips, John Patrick Higgins, Lizzi Jones, Edward Nattenberg, Elizabeth Raetz, Jay Randall, Chara Riegel, Michelle Roginsky, Brian Keith Russell, Rachel Scott, Nathan Thomas Wheeler, D. Matt Worley (Christmas Eve Walkers), Rhonnie Washington (Marley's Ghost), John Patrick Higgins, D. Matt Worley (Chain Bearers), David Ryan Smith (Ghost of Christmas Past), Candice McKoy (Wife of Christmas Past), Colin Todd Woodell, Keelin Shea Woodell (Children of Christmas Past), Daniel Patrick Kennedy, Gabriel Kenney, Chase Macauley Maxwell, Nicholas Perloff-Giles, Christopher Ward (School Boys), Adam Brooks (Boy Scrooge), Lizzi Jones (Little Fan), Allison Schubert (Belle Cousins), Jacob Ming-Trent (Young Scrooge), Brian Keith Russell (Mr. Fezziwig), D. Matt Worley (Dick Wilkins), Margaret Schenck (Mrs. Fezziwig), Ali Baker, John Patrick Higgins, Edward Nattenberg, Elizabeth Raetz, Jay Randall, Chara Riegel, Rachel Scott (Fezziwig Guests), Lizzi Jones (Toy Ballerina), Devon Charisse Hadsell (Toy Clown), Michelle Roginsky (Toy Cat), Nicholas Perloff-Giles (Toy Monkey), Christopher Ward (Toy Bear), Tommy A. Gomez (Ghost of Christmas Present), Charlotte Locke (Sally Cratchit), Gabriel Kenney (Ned Cratchit), Nathan Thomas Wheeler (Peter Cratchit), Scout Katovich (Belinda Cratchit), Rachel Scott (Mrs. Cratchit), Camila Borrero (Martha Cratchit), Chase Macauley Maxwell (Tiny Tim Cratchit), Amanda Hastings-Phillips (Mary), D. Matt Worley (Jack), John Patrick Higgins (Topper), Ali Baker (Beth), Elizabeth Raetz (Meg), Jay Randall (Ted), Rhonnie Washington (Miner), Candice McKoy (Miner's Wife), Allison Schubert, Colin Todd Woodell, Keelin Shea Woodell (Miner's Family), Brian Keith Russell (Helmsman), Forrest Fraser Tiffany II (Cabin Boy), Adam Brooks, Jacob Ming-Trent, Edward Nattenberg, Chara Riegel, Margaret Schenck, David Ryan Smith (Carolers), Judy Butterfield, Victoria Thompson (Celebrants), Michelle Roginsky (Want), Daniel Patrick Kennedy (Ignorant), Jay Randall (Ghost of Christmas Future), John Patrick Higgins, Tyler McKenna, Brian Keith Russell, David Ryan Smith, Rhonnie Washington (Businessmen), Elizabeth Raetz (Mrs. Filcher), Chara Riegel (Mrs. Dilber), D. Matt Worley (Undertaker's Boy), Edward Nattenberg (Old Joe), Forrest Fraser Tiffany II (Boys in the Street) Understudies: Robert Ernst (Dickens, Marley's Ghost, Mr. Fezziwig, Male Fezziwig Guests, Ghost of Christmas Present), Rhonnie Washington (Scrooge, Old Joe), Edward Nattenberg (Bob Cratchit, Topper), Chara Riegel (Mary, Charitable Gentlewomen), D. Matt Worley (Fred), Jay Randall (Chain Bearers), Tyler McKenna (Ghost of Christmas Past), Amanda Hastings-Phillips (Wife of Christmas Past), Elizabeth Raetz (Belle Cousins), John Patrick Higgins (Young Scrooge, Ghost of Christmas Future), Nathan Thomas Wheeler (Dick Wilkins), René Augensen (Mrs. Fezziwig, Female Fezziwig Guests, Mrs. Cratchit), Jacob Ming-Trent (Jack, Helmsman, Businessmen), Candice McKoy (Meg, Beth, Mrs. Filcher), David Ryan Smith (Ted, Miner), Ali Baker (Mrs. Dilber)

AMERICAN BUFFALO by David Mamet; Director, Richard E. T. White; Scenic Design, Kent Dorsey; Costume Design, Christine Dougherty; Lighting Design, Peter Maradudin; Sound Design, Garth Hemphill; Assistant Director, Dylan Russell; Dialect Consultant, Deborah Russell; Fight Direction, Gregory Hoffman; Casting, Meryl Lind Shaw; Wigs and Makeup, Rick Echols; Dramaturgical Assistance, Hannah Knapp; Stage Manager, Julie Haber; Assistant Stage Manager, Katherine Riemann; Intern, Les Reinhardt; Cast: Matt DeCaro (Don Dubrow), Damon Seawell (Bob), Marco Barricelli (Walter Cole, called "teach") Understudies: Tommy A. Gomez (Don Dubrow), Jonathan Rhys Williams (Bob), Rod Gnapp (Teach)

THE COLOSSUS OF RHODES Written and Directed by Carey Perloff; Music composed by Catherine Reid; Musical Direction, Peter Maleitzke; Scenic Design, Hisham Ali; Costume Design, Cassandra Carpenter; Lighting Design, Nancy Schertler; Sound Design, Jake Rodriguez; Dramaturg, Paul Walsh; Dialect Consultant, Deborah Russell; Casting, Meryl Lind Shaw; Wigs and Makeup, Rick Echols; Assistand Director, C. Dianne Manning; Production Stage Manager, Nicole Dickerson; Production Assistant, Ritz Gray; Scenic Design Associate, Dustin O'Neill; Lighting Design Associate, Kimberly J. Scott; Cast: Allyn Burrows (Cecil Rhodes), Paul Vincent Black (Barney Barnato), Robert Parsons (Ruskin, Jameson, Anderson), Kathleen Antonia (Fanny Bees), David Adkins (Randall Pickering), Rufus Collins (Charles Rudd), David Stewart Hudson, Sidney Burrows, Jr. (Ensemble)

Damon Seawell, Marco Barricelli in *American Buffalo* PHOTO BY PHOTOWORKS

THE DAZZLE by Richard Greenberg; Director, Laird Williamson; Scenic Design, Robert Mark Morgan; Costume Design, Sandra Woodall; Lighting Design, Don Darnutzer; Sound Design, Garth Hemphill; Musical Direction, Peter Maleitzke; Dramaturg, Paul Walsh; Casting, Meryl Lind Shaw; Choreography, Francine Landes; Wigs and Makeup, Rick Echols; Stage Manager, Kimberly Mark Webb; Assistant Stage Manager, Shona Mitchell; Intern, K. Mauldin; Cast: Greggory Wallace (Langley Collyer), Steven Anthony Jones (Homer Collyer), René Augesen (Milly Ashmore) Understudies: Mark A. Phillips (Langley Collyer), Tommy A. Gomez (Homer Collyer), Jenny Lord (Milly Ashmore)

THE CONSTANT WIFE by W. Somerset Magham; Directed by Kyle Donnelly; Scenic Design, Kate Edmunds; Costume Design, Anna R. Oliver; Lighting Design, Nancy Schertler; Sound Design, Garth Hemphill; Dramaturg, Paul Walsh; Casting, Meryl Lind Shaw; Wigs and Makeup, Rick Echols; Assistant Director, Elizabeth Williamson; Stage Manager, Julie Haber; Assistant Stage Manager, Katherine Riemann; Intern, Les Reinhardt; Cast: Beth Dixon (Mrs. Culver), Tom Blair (Bentley), Emily Ackerman (Martha Cutler), Stacy Ross (Barbara Fawcett), Ellen Karas (Constance Middleton), Ashley West (Marie-Louise Durham), Jonathan Fried (John Middleton, F.R.C.S.), Mark Elliot Wilson (Bernard Kersal), Charles Dean (Mortimer Durham), Rachel Scott (Maid) Understudies: Emily Ackerman (Constance Middleton), James Carpenter (Bentley, John Middleton, Bernard Kersal), Rachel Scott (Martha Culver, Marie Louise Durham), Tom Blair (Mortimer Durham), Trish Mulholland (Mrs. Culver, Barbara Fawcett, Maid)

THE THREE SISTERS by Anton Chekov; Translated by Paul Schmidt; Directed by Carey Perloff; Scenic Design, Ralph Funicello; Costume Design, Beaver Bauer; Lighting Design, James F. Ingalls; Sound Design, Garth Hemphill; Music Direction and Arrangements, Peter Maleitzke; Dramaturg, Paul Walsh; Speech and Text Coaching, Deborah Sussel; Choreographer, Francine Landes; Casting Director/Assistant Director, Meryl Lind Shaw; New York Casting, Bernard Telsey; Wigs and Makeup, Rick Echols; SDCF (Stage Directors and Choreographers Foundation) Observer, Dave Sikula; Stage Manager, Elisa Guthertz; Assistant Stage Manager, Shona Mitchell; K. Mauldin, Intern; Cast: Tommy A. Gomez (Andréi Prøzorov), Lorri Holt (Olga), René Augesen (Másha), Katherine Powell (Irína), Mirjana Jokovic (Natàsha), Gregory Wallace (Kulýgin), Marco Barricelli (Vershínin), Anthony Fusco (Baron Túzenbach), John Keating (Solyóny), Steven Anthony James (Chebutykin), Jacob Ming-Trent (Fedótik), Brud Fogarty (Róhde), Frank Ottiwell (Ferapónt), Joan Mankin (Anfísa), David Ryan Smith (Orderly/Musician), Jenny Lord (Nurse/Maid) Understudies: Jacob Ming-Trent (Andréi Prózorov), Jeri Lynn Cohen (Ólga Másha, Anfísa, Nurse/Maid), Jenny Lord (Irína, Natásha), David Mendelsohn (Kulýgin, Baron Túzenbach, Solyóny, Orderly/Musician), Brud Fogarty (Vershínin), Robert Ernst (Chebutykin, Ferapónt), David Ryan Smith (Fedótik, Róhde)

URINETOWN Book and Lyrics by Greg Kotis; Music and Lyrics by Mark Hollman; Director, John Rando; Musical Staging, John Carrafa; Scenic Design, Scott Pask; Costume Design, Gregory A. Gale and Jonathan Bixby; Brian MacDevitt; Cast: Tom Hewitt, Ron Holgate, Beth McVey

AMERICAN REPERTORY THEATRE

Loeb Drama Center at Harvard University
Cambridge, Massachusetts
TWENTY-FOURTH SEASON

Robert J. Orchard, Executive Director; Robert Woodruff, Artistic Director; Gideon Lester, Associate Artistic Director/Dramaturg; Robert Brustein, Founding Director and Creative Consultant

UNCLE VANYA by Anton Chekov; Director, János Szász; Scenic Design, Riccardo Hernandez; Costume Design, Edit Szücs; Lighting Design, Christopher Akerlind; Sound Design, David Remedios; Production Stage Manager, Chris DeCamillis; Assistant Stage Manager, Amy James; Voice and Speech Coach, Laura Wayth; Movement Director, Andrei Droznin; November 30–December 28, 2002; Cast: Karen MacDonald (Marina), Arliss Howard (Mikhail Lvovich Astrov), Thomas Derrah (Ivan Petrovich, Vanya), Will LeBow (Alexander Serebriakov), Remo Airaldi & Benjamin Evett (Ilya Ilych Telegin), Phoebe Jonas (Sonya), Linda Powell (Yelena), Elbert Joseph (Yeffim), Genna Ravvin (the bartender), Jonathan Mirin, Paul DiMilla, John Michael Dupuis, Jason Grossman (bar patrons) Understudies: Deborah Cooney (Marina), Curtis August (Astrov), Dan Domigues (Vanya), Jason Kaufman (Serebriakov), Jay Klaitz (Telegin), Jennifer Mackey (Sonya), Georgia Hatzis (Yelena)

THE CHILDREN OF HERAKLES by Euripides; Staged by Peter Sellars; Costume Design, Brooke Stanton; Lighting Design, James F. Ingalls; Sound Design, Shahrokh Yadegari; English translation, Ralph Gladstone; Casting, Will Cantler, Bernard Telsey Casting; Producer on behalf of the Ruhr-Triennale, Diane J. Malecki; Production Stage Manager, Nancy Harrington; Assistant Stage Manager, Julie Baldauff; Assistant Stage Manager, Amy James; Assistant Director, Robert Casto; January 4–25, 2003; Cast: Jan Triska (Ioalus), Elaine Tse (Copreus), Brenda Wehle (President of Athens), Julyana Soelistyo (Macaria), Albert S. (attendant), Julyana Soelistyo (Alcmene), Cornel Gabara (Eurystheus & Mycenae), Ulzhan Baibussynova (Music performed and sung), Christopher Lydon (moderator), Boston area refugee youth (the children of Herakles)

LA DISPUTE by Marivaux; Translated by Gideon Lester; Adapted and directed by Anne Bogart; Scene Design, Neil Patel; Costume Design, James Schuette; Lighting Design, Christopher Akerlind; Soundscape, Darron L. West; Production Stage Manager, Elizabeth Moreau; Assistant Stage Manager, Chris De Camillis; Production Associate, Elizabeth Kegley; Voice and Speech Coach, Karen Kopryanski; Dance Movement, Barney O'Hanlon; Prologue Music, Calexico; Dramaturg, Barbara Whitney Feb 1–22, 2003; Cast: Frank Raiter (The Prince), Lynn Cohen (Hermione), Ellen Lauren (Églé), Stephen Webber (Azor), Lizzy Cooper Davis (Carise), Remo Airaldi (Mesrou), Kelly Maurer (Adine), Will Bond (Mesrin), Barney O'Hanlon (Meslis), Akiko Aizawa Ensemble: Curtis August, Dan Domingues, Benjamin Evett, Mark Alexandre Fortin, Donei Hall, Georgia Hatzis, Jason Kaufman, Jennifer Mackay, Mindy Woodhead, Ashley Wren Collins Understudies: Benjamin Evett (The Prince, Azor), Georgia Hatzis (Hermione), Ashley Wren Collins (Églé), Donei Hall (Carise), Mark Alexandre Fortin (Mesrou), Mindy Woodhead

(Adine), Dan Domingues (Mesrin), Jason Kaufman (Meslis), Jennifer Mackay (Dina), Rebekah Maggor (ensemble), Rory Kozoll (ensemble)

HIGHWAY ULYSSES Written and Composed by Rinde Eckert; Director, Robert Woodruff; Set and Costume Design, David Zinn; Lighting Design, David Weiner; Sound Design, David Remedios; Movement, Doug Elkins; Music Director/Keyboards, Peter Foley; Stage Manager, M. Pat Hodge; Assistant Stage Manager, Amy James; Voice and Speech Coach, Nancy Houfek; Dramaturg, Ryan McKittrick; March 1–22, 2003; Cast: Nora Cole (Bride), Thomas Derrah (Ulysses), Dana Marks (Son), Heather Benton, Rinde Eckert, Will LeBow, Karen MacDonald, Michael Potts (Ensemble), Dianne Chalifore, Alison Clear, Lisa P. Miller Gilliespie, Seth Reich, Josh Wright, Holly Vanasse (Wedding Guests); David Curry viola, theremin, homemade instruments, digital loop samples, singing saw, horn; Chris Brokaw guitar, percussion; Jonah Sacks cello, guitar

PERICLES by William Shakespeare; Direction and Movement, Andrei Serban; Set and Video Design, Dan Nutu; Costume Design, Gabriel Berry; Lighting Design, Beverly Emmons; Sound Design, David Remedios; Casting, Cindy Tolan Casting; Production Stage Manager, Chris De Camillis; Assistant Stage Manager, Amy James; Assistant Stage Manager, Thomas Kaufmann; Dramaturg, Gideon Lester; Voice and Speech Coach, Nancy Houfek; Advertising Consultants, Stevens Advertising; May 10–June 27 2003; Cast: Yolande Bavan (Gower), Robert Stella (Pericles), Thomas Derrah (King Antiochus), Georgia Hatzis (Daughter of Antiochus), Curtis August (Thailliard), Jason Beaubier (messenger), Jeremy Geidt (Helicanus), Will LeBow (Cleon), Karen MacDonald (Dionyza), Gilbert Owuor (Leonine), Curtis August Thomas Piper (pirates), Zoë King (young Philoten), Jasmine Jackson (young Marina), Remo Airaldi, Jeremy Geidt, Thomas Piper (fishermen), Thomas Derrah (King Simonides), Mia Yoo (Thaisa), Dan Cozzens, Oliver Henzler (lords), Jason Beaubier (marshal), Curtis August, Jason Kaufman, Doug Lockwood (knights in the tournament), Jason Beaubier, Jason Kaufman (sailors), Emily Knapp (Lychorida), Yolande Bavan (Cerimon), Curtis August (Philemon), Georgia Hatzis (Diana) Alison Clear, Emily Knapp, Katarina Morhacova (temple dancers), Pascale Armand (Marina), Will LeBow (Pandar), Thomas Derrah (Boult), Remo Airaldi (Bawd), Dan Cozzens, Doug Lockwood (brothel clients), Emily Knapp, Katarina Morhacova (whores), Oliver Henzler (Lysimachus), Andrei Serban (messenger)

THE SOUND OF A VOICE Music by Philip Glass; Text by David Henry Hwang; Director, Robert Woodruff; Scenic Design, Robert Israel; Costume Design, Kasia Walicka Maimone; Lighting Design, Beverly Emmons; Sound Design, David Remedios; Music Director/Conductor, Alan Johnson; Fight Director, Doug Elkins; Film Projection Design, Burt Sun & Shalom Buberman; Production Stage Manager, Thomas M. Kauffman; Production Associate, Elizabeth Kegley; Dramaturg, Ryan McKittrick; Advertising Consultants, Stevens Advertising; May 24–June 28, 2003; Cast: The Sound of a Voice: Suzan Hanson (Woman), Herbert Perry (Man); Hotel Of Dreams: Janice Felty (Woman), Eugene Perry (Yamamoto), Musicians: Wu Man pipa; Rebecca Patterson cello; Susan Gall flute, bamboo flute, piccolo; Robert Schulz percussion; Kurt Crowley rehearsal pianist

ARDEN THEATRE COMPANY

Philadelphia, Pennsylvania
FIFTEENTH SEASON

Producing Artistic Director, Terrence J. Nolen; Managing Director,
Amy L. Murphy

DAEDALUS: A FANTASIA OF LEONARDO DA VINCI by David
Davalos; Director, Aaron Posner; Scenic Design, Tony Cisek; Costume
Design, Margaret K. McCarty; Lighting Design, James Leitner; Sound
Design, James Sugg; World premiere; September 12–November 3, 2002;
Cast: Julie Czarnecki, Grace Gonglewski, Scott Greer, Monica Koskey, Peter
Pryor, Buck Schirner, Greg Wood

ALL MY SONS by Arthur Miller; Director, Terrence J. Nolen; Scenic
Design, Bob Phillips; Costume Design, KJ Gilmer; Lighting Design, Drew
Billiau; Sound Design, Kevin Francis; October 17–November 17, 2002; Cast:
Amy Acchione, Carla Belver (Kate Keller), John Francis Brown, David
Corenswet, Lenny Haas, E. Ashley Izard, Tracey Maloney, Tom McCarthy
(Joe Keller), Ian Merrill Peakes, William Zielinski

THE BOXCAR CHILDREN Adapted by Barbara Field from the book by
Gertrude Chandler Warner; Director, Whit MacLaughlin; Scenic Design,
Lewis Folden; Costume Design, Richard St. Clair; Lighting Design, Drew
Billiau; Sound Design, Doug Smullens; December 4, 2002–January 12, 2003;
Cast: Sarah Doherty, Bill Dooley, Maggie Lakis, Anthony Lawton, Sally
Mercer, Matt Mezzacappa, Karen Elizabeth Peakes, Matt Pfeiffer, Tom Teti

NORTHEAST LOCAL by Tom Donaghy; Director, Terrence J. Nolen;
Scenic Design, Christopher Pickart; Costume Design, Alison Roberts;
Lighting Design, James Leitner; Sound Design, Jorge Cousineau; January
30–March 23, 2003; Cast: Raphael Peacock (Jesse), Catharine K. Slusar (Gi),
Dale Soules (Mair), William Zielinski (Mickey)

TWELFTH NIGHT by William Shakespeare; Director, Whit MacLaughlin;
Scenic Design, David P. Gordon; Costume Design, Rosemarie McKelvey;
Lighting Design, James Leitner; Sound Design, Jorge Cousineau; March
13–April 13, 2003; Cast: Bev Appleton (Feste), Nancy Boykin (Olivia), Patrick
Brinker (Orsino), Aaron Cromie (Fabian), Scott Drummond (Aguecheek),
Arnold Kendall (Valentine, Antonio), Jeb Kreager (Seaman, Officer), Mary
Martello (Maria), Karen Elizabeth Peakes (Viola), Tobias Segal (Sebastian),
Steve Tague (Malvolio), Gene Terruso (Toby)

Rich Ceraulo, Jorge E. Maldonado in *Pacific Overtures* PHOTO BY MARK GARVIN

PACIFIC OVERTURES Music and Lyrics by Stephen Sondheim; Book by
John Weidman; Additional Material by Hugh Wheeler; Director, Terrence J.
Nolen; Scenic Design, James Kronzer; Costume Design, Marla Jurglanis;
Lighting Design, Daniel MacLean Wagner; Sound Design, Jorge Cousineau;
Choreographer, Myra Bazell; May 22–June 22, 2003; Cast: Arthur T. Acuna
(Reciter), Bev Appleton, Billy Bustamante, Rich Ceraulo, Derrick Cobey,
Scott Greer, Adam Michael Kaokept, C. Mingo Long, Jorge E. Maldonado,
Steve Pacek, Glenn Townsend, Rob Tucker

BARTER THEATRE

Abingdon, Virginia
SEVENTIETH SEASON

Producing Artistic Director, Richard Rose; Associate Directors, John Hardy, Evalyn Baron; Business Manager, Joan Ballou; Development Dirctor, Lisa Aldermann; Marketing Director, Debbie L. Addison; Assistant to Mr. Rose, Carrie Clark; Accounting Assistant, Nellie Trivett; Development Assistant, Diana H. Haynes; Campaign Associate Director, Melissa Massengill; Assistant Marketing Director, Stacy N. Fine; Marketing Associate, Callie Harrill; Marketing Assistant, Tommy Bryant; Group Sales Reservationist. Linda Pruner; Group Sales Assistant, Shirley Henderson; Stage Managers, John Keith Hall, Karen N. Rowe; Production Intern, Scot Atkinson; Production Assistants, Stevie Ford, Brian Duff; Resident Musical Director, William Perry Morgan; Resident Scenic Designer, Cheri Prough DeVol; Technical Director, Mark J. DeVol; Assistant Technical Director, Glenn Stratakes; Master Carpenter, Greg Owens; Main Stage Carpenter, Roy Fisher; Stage 2 Carpenter, Tim Bruneau; Carpenter, Darin Cralle; Scenic Artist, D.R. Mullins; Assistant Scenic Artist, Tessa Hammel; Properties Master, Helen Stratakes; Assistant Properties Master, Stephen Vess; Props Intern, William Denley; Resident Costume Designer, Amanda Aldridge; Costume Shop Manager, Krista Guffey; Draper, Lynae Vandermeulen; Shop Assistant, Rebecca Reed; Head Stitcher, Judy Pickle; Stitcher, Jamie Grace; Main Stage Wardrobe Supervisor, Theresa Heinmann; Main Stage Wardrobe Intern, Eileen Sanders; Wardrobe Intern, Nathan Coleman; Craftsperson, Melissa Davidson; Master Electrician, Trevor Maynard; Assistant Master Electrician, Craig Zemsky; Stage 2 Electrician, Rose Nuchims; Resident Sound Designer/Chief Sound Engineer, Bobby Beck; Sound Engineers, Jacob Krimbel, Sean Platt

AROUND THE WORLD IN 80 DAYS by Mark Brown; Adapted from the novel by Jules Verne; Director, Katy Brown; Scenic Designer, Cheri Prough DeVol; Costume Designer, Amanda Aldridge; Lighting Designer, Trevor Maynard; Sound Designer, Bobby Beck; Properties Master, Helen Stratakes; Technical Director, Mark J. DeVol; Stage Manager, John Keith Hall; February 13–April 19 2003; Cast: Frank Green, Josephine Hall, Richard Major, Michael Poisson, Karen Sabo, Alice White

Michael Poisson, Richard Major in *Around the World*

THE TEMPEST adapted by Richard Rose, written by William Shakespeare; Director, Richard Rose; Original Music, Peter Yonka; Scenic Designer, Mark J. DeVol; Costume Designer, Amanda Aldridge; Lighting Designer, Trevor Maynard; Sound Designer, Bobby Beck; Properties Master, Helen Stratakes; Technical Director, Mark J. DeVol; Stage Manager, John Keith Hall; New York Casting, Paul Russell Casting, NYC; February 20–May 10 2003; Cast: Derek Davidson, Kathryn Foster, Frank Green, John Hedges, JJ Musgrove, Mike Ostroski, Michael Poisson, Chris Ross, Peter Yonka

SUNDOWN by Joe Bravaco and Larry Rosler; Music by Peter Link; Lyrics by Larry Rosler; Director and Choreographer, Richard Rose; Musical Director, William Perry Morgan; Scenic Designer, Cheri Prough DeVol; Costume Designer, Amanda Aldridge; Lighting Designer, E. Tonry Lathroum; Sound Designer, Bobby Beck; Properties Master, Helen Stratakes; Technical Director, Mark J. DeVol; Stage Manager, Karen N. Rowe; New York Casting, Paul Russell Casting, NYC; March 7–May 17 2003; Cast: Evalyn Baron, Derek Davidson, Kathryn Foster, John Hardy, John Hedges, JJ Musgrove, Mike Ostroski, Nicholas Piper, Chris Ross, Eugene Wolf, Peter Yonka

Peter Yonka (foreground), John Hardy in *Sundown*

Josephine Hall, Elizabeth P. McNight in *Steel Magnolias* PHOTOS BY BARTER THEATRE PHOTOS

DIVORCE SOUTHERN STYLE by Jennifer Jarrett; Director, John Hardy; Scenic Designer, Cheri Prough De Vol; Costume Designer, Amanda Aldridge; Lighting Designer, E. Tonry Lathroum; Sound Designer, Bobby Beck; Technical Director, Mark J. DeVol; Properties Master, Helen Stratakes; Stage Manager, Karen N. Rowe; New York Casting, Paul Russell Casting, NYC; March 19–May 17 2003; Cast: Evalyn Baron, Josephine Hall, Richard Major, Nicholas Piper, Karen Sabo, Alice White, Eugene Wolf

STEEL MAGNOLIAS by Robert Harling; Director, Karen Sabo; Scenic Designer, Cheri Prough De Vol; Costume Designer, Amanda Aldridge; Lighting Designer, Trevor Maynard; Sound Designer, Bobby Beck; Technical Director, Mark J. DeVol; Properties Master, Helen Stratakes; Stage Manager, John Keith Hall; May 1–August 24 2003; Cast: Mary Lucy Bivins, Kimberly Cole, Josephine Hall, Janine Kyanko, Elizabeth P. McKnight, Alice White

1776 by Peter Stone; Music and Lyrics by Sherman Edwards; Director, Evalyn Baron; Musical Director, William Perry Morgan; Choreographer, Amanda Aldridge; Scenic Designer, Dale Jordan; Costume Designer, Amanda Aldridge; Lighting Designer, Dale Jordan; Sound Designer, Bobby Beck; Technical Director, Mark J. DeVol; Properties Master, Helen Stratakes; Stage Manager, Karen N. Rowe; May 22–August 23 2003; Cast: Scot Atkinson, Evalyn Baron, Derek Davidson, Frank Green, Roger Dean Grubb, John Hardy, John Hedges, Richard Major, Jeffrey Spence McGullion, Greg McMillan, Rick McVey, JJ Musgrove, Mike Ostroski, Nicholas Piper, Michael Poisson, Miles Polaski, Eric Pope, Chris Ross, M. Ryan Smith, Willoughby Smith, Terry Sneed, A Michael Tilford, Pamela Turpin, Richard Neal Williams, Eugene Wolf, Peter Wonka

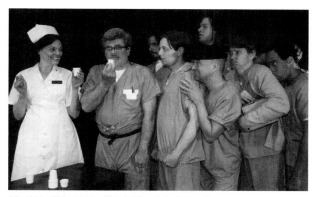

Alice White, Richard Major, Nicholas Piper, John Hedges, Derek Davidson, Frank Green, Peter Yonka, (bottom, background), Mike Ostroscki (top, background) in *One Flew Over the Cuckoo's Nest*

ONE FLEW OVER THE CUCKOO'S NEST by Dale Wasserman; Adapted from the novel by Ken Kesey; Director, John Hardy; Scenic Designer, Dale Jordan; Costume Designer, Melissa Davidson; Lighting Designer, Dale Jordan; Sound Designer, Bobby Beck; Technical Director, Mark J. DeVol; Properties Master, Helen Stratakes; Stage Manager, John Keith Hall; June 11–August 16, 2003; Cast: Mary Lucy Bivins, Derek Davidson, Frank Green, Josephine Hall, John Hedges, Richard Major, Jeffrey Spence McGullion, Elizabeth P. McKnight, Mike Ostroski, Nicholas Piper, Chris Ross, M. Ryan Smith, Willoughby Smith, Alice White, Eugene Wolf, Peter Yonka

PIRATES & PINAFORES: A CELEBRATION OF THE MUSIC AND LYRICS OF GILBERT AND SULLIVAN by Richard Rose; Adapted from the works of Gilbert and Sullivan; Director, Karen Sabo; Musical Director, William Perry Morgan; Scenic Designer, Cheri Prough DeVol; Costume Designer, Amanda Aldridge; Lighting Designer, Trevor Maynard; Sound Designer, Bobby Beck; Technical Director, Mark J. DeVol; Stage Manager, Karen N. Rowe; June 17–August 10, 2003; Cast: Evalyn Baron, Roger Dean Grubb, Janine Kyanko, Wm. Perry Morgan, Michael Poisson, Terry Sneed, A. Michael Tilford, Pamela Turpin, Amber Wiley, Richard Neal Williams

BAY STREET THEATRE

Sag Harbor, New York
ELEVENTH SEASON

Co-Artistic Directors, Sybil Christopher, Emma Walton; Executive Director, Stephen Hamilton; Producer, William Buford; Director of Development, Julie Fitzgerald; Director of Marketing, Christina L. Warner; Production Manager, Gary N. Hygom; Company Manager, Wendy Leonard; Technical Director, Eric Schlobohm; Facilities Manager In Memoriam, William Pharaoh; Box Office Manager, Kristina Saumanis; Costumer, Greg Wilson; Comptroller, Christina Reina; Artistic Associate/Education Coordinator, Michael J. Desanti; Educational Program Administrator, Marilyn Koch; Operations Associate, Hilary McDonald; Marketing and Development Associate, Mindy Washington; Literary Manager, Mia Grosjean; Teaching Artists, John Beuscher, Bill Buford, Michael Desanti, Stephen Hamilton, Susan Merrell, Christine Murphy, Emma Walton, Mindy Washington; Assistant House Manager, Elizabeth Sudler; Assistant Box Office Manager, Tamara Aldrich; Ticket Sales, Christine Murphy; Volunteer Coordinator, Dolores Cooleen; Ticket Sales, Bonnie Murphy

Twiggy in *Blithe Spirit* PHOTO BY GARY J. MAMAY

BLITHE SPIRIT by Noël Coward; Director, Daniel Gerroll; Set Design, Dan Kuchar; Costume Design, Tony Walton; Lighting Design, Eric Schlobohm; Sound Design, Janet Kalas; Production Stage Manager, Bradley McCormick; Production Manager, Gary Hygom; Associate Costume Design, Rachel Gruer; Cast: Kerrie Blaisdell, Herb Foster, Daniel Gerroll, Dana Ivey, Patricia Kalember, Angela Thornton, Twiggy. This production made possible in part by a generous gift from Lizabeth and Michael Pandolfell.

OUR TOWN by Thornton Wilder; Director, Jack Hofsiss; Set Designer, Gary Hygom; Costume Designer, Willa Kim; Lighting Designer, Beverly Emmons; Music Written and Arranged by Edward Barnes; Sound Designer, Randall Freed; Production Stage Manager, Brian Meister; Production Manager, Gary Hygom; Cast: Mark Baker, Noah Bean, Michael B. Downing, John Fiedler, Catherine Gaffigan, Sophie Hayden, Bryan Hicks, Pat Hingle, Bryce Dallas Howard, Adriane Lenox, Raphael Odell Shapiro, Haley Willis, B.D. Wong, Frank Wood

TALLEY'S FOLLY by Lanford Wilson; Director, Ron Lagomarsino; Set Design, Ted Simpson; Costume Design, Michael Krass; Lighting Design, Brian Nason; Sound Design, Tony Melfa; Production Stage Manager, Bradley McCormick; Production Manager, Gary Hygom; Cast: Matthew Arkin, Jessica Hecht

THE WEST END HORROR by Anthony Dodge and Marcia Milgrom Dodge; Adapted from the novel by Nicholas Meyer; Director, Marcia Milgrom Dodge; Set Design, Troy Hourie; Costume Design, Christianne Myers; Lighting Design, Brian Nason; Sound Design, Randall Freed; Music Archivist and Arrangements, Matt Kovich; Production Stage Manager, Chris Clark; Production Manager, Gary Hygom; World premiere; Cast: Terrence Mann, Anthony Dodge, Wynn Harmon, Martin Hillier, Matt Kovich, Dennis Ryan, Mark Shanahan, Jennifer Waldman

Jessica Hecht, Matthew Arkin in *Talley's Folly* PHOTO BY GARY J. MAMAY

BERKELEY REPERTORY THEATRE

Berkeley, California
THIRTY-FIFTH SEASON

Artistic Director, Tony Taccone; Managing Director, Susan Medak

THE HOUSE OF BLUE LEAVES by John Guare; Director, Barbara Damashek; Scenic Design, William Bloodgood; Costume Design, Beaver Bauer; Lighting Design, York Kennedy; Sound Design, Matthew Spiro; Dialect Coach, Lynne Soffer; Fight Coordinator, Gregory Hoffman; September 6–October 20, 2002; Cast: Jarion Monroe (Artie), Adam Ludwig (Ronnie), Jeri Lynn Cohen (Bunny), Rebecca Wisocky (Bananas), Susannah Schulman (Corrinna), Wilma Bonet (Head Nun), Margaret Schenck (Second Nun), Mollie Stickney (Little Nun), Craig Neibaur (Military Policeman), Jeffrey Hoffman (Man in White), Bill Geisslinger (Billy)

MENOCCHIO by Lillian Groag; Director, Lillian Groag; Scenic and Lighting Design, Alexander V. Nichols; Costume Design, Beaver Bauer; Sound Design, Jeffrey Mockus; November 1–December 22, 2002; Cast: Charles Dean (Menocchio), Jeri Lynn Cohen (His Wife, Faustino, Brother Paolo), Robert Sicular (Merchant, Bookseller, Count Orazio de Montereale, Odorico), Dan Hiatt (Bastian, Ensemble), Peter Van Norden (Father Daniele Melchiore), Ken Ruta (Inquisitor of Aquileia and Concordia, Fra Felice de Montefalco, Pasqualina Fasseta, Panfilo Crespino)

HAROUN AND THE SEA OF STORIES by Salman Rushdie; Adaptation, Dominique Serrand and Luan Schooler from the play by Tim Supple and David Tushingham; Director, Dominique Serrand; Scenic Design, Dominique Serrand and Will Leggett; Costume Design, Sonya Berlovitz; Lighting Design, Marcus Dilliard and Jennifer Setlow; Sound Design, Bill Williams; Video Composition, Kimberlee Koym; November 15, 2002–January 7, 2003; Cast: Russ Appleyard (musician), Myla Balugay (Mali, Blabbermouth, Chupwala), Colman Domingo (Storyteller, Mr. Sengupta, Princess Eek; Walrus; Khattam-Shud), Nora El Samahy (Haroun Khalifa), David Kelly (Iff, Prince Bolo), Katie Kreisler (Oneeta Sengupta; Mr. Butt; Goopy; storyteller; Ambassador), Jarion Monroe (Snooty Buttoo, Hoopoe, Princess Batcheat), Jennifer Baldwin Peden (Soraya, Mudra's Shadow, Chupwala), Jennifer Riker (Bagha, Mudra, Chupwala), Dominique Serrand (Rashid Khalifa)

SUDDENLY LAST SUMMER by Tennessee Williams; Director, Les Waters; Scenic Design, Annie Smart; Costume Design, Meg Neville; Lighting Design, Chris Parry; Composer/Sound Designer, Michael Roth; Dialect Coach, Lynne Soffer; February 7–March 23, 2003; Cast: Randy Danson (Mrs. Venable), Joey Collins (Dr. Sugar), Jeri Lynn Cohen (Miss Foxhill), T. Edward Webster (George), Anne Darragh (Mrs. Holly), Michelle Duffy (Catharine), Deborah Black (Sister Felicity)

FRAULEIN ELSE from the novella by Arthur Schnitzler; Adaptation and Translation, Francesca Faridany; Director, Stephen Wadsworth; Scenic Design, Thomas Lynch; Costume Design, Anna Oliver; Lighting Design, Joan Arhelger; Sound Design, Bill Williams; February 28–March 30, 2003; Cast: Francesca Faridany (Fraulein Else), Michael Tisdale (Paul), Lauren Lovett (Cissy), Mary Baird (Mother), Julian Lopez-Morillas (Herr Von Dorsday), Ornid Abtahi (Porter)

SURFACE TRANSIT by Sarah Jones; Director, Tony Taccone; Scenic and Lighting Design, Alexander V. Nichols; Costume Design, Donna Marie; Sound Design, Bill Williams; Original Director, Gloria Feliciano; Music Director, Jimmie Lee Patterson; April 18–June 1, 2003; Cast: Sarah Jones

THE GUYS by Anne Nelson; Director, Robert Egan; Scenic Design, Will Leggett; Lighting Design, York Kennedy; Sound Design, Bill Williams; Projection Design, Alexander V. Nichols; Costume Coordinator, Maggie Yule; May 16–July 5, 2003 Cast (rotating): Sharon Lawrence, Keith David, Lorraine Toussaint, Dan Lauria, Joe Spano, Linda Purl, Jimmy Smits and Wanda De Jesus

Joey Collins, Michelle Duffy in *Suddenly Last Summer* PHOTO BY KEVIN BERNE/KEN FRIEDMAN

BERKSHIRE THEATRE FESTIVAL

Stockbridge, Massachusetts
SEVENTY-FOURTH SEASON

Associate Director, James Warwick

ZORBA Adapted from Nikos Kazantzakis' novel by Joseph Stein; Music, John Kander; Lyrics, Fred Ebb; Director, James Warwick; June 19–July 6, 2002; Main Stage; Cast: Thom Christopher (Alexis Zorba), Mark Edgar Stephens (Niko), Gerianne Raphael (Hortense), Maree Johnson (The Widow), Melissa Hart (The Leader), Walter Hudson (Mavrodani), Ramzi Khalaf (Pavli), Robert McDonald (Manolako), Tony Spinosa (Lukas), Richard Gould (Father Zahoria), Howard Kaye (Katapolis), Lee Zarret (Mimiko), Susan Buchholtz (Sofia), Rachel Siegel (Efterpi), Isadora Wolfe (Athena, Dancer), Diedra Friel (Katina), Alexander Hill, Ruslan Sprague, Nora McCloskey (Children)

QUARTET by Ronald Harwood; Director, Vivian Matalon; Main Stage; Cast: Kaye Ballard (Cecily Robson), Robert Vaughn (Reginald Paget), Paul Hecht (Wilfred Bond), Elizabeth Seal (Jean Horton)

A SAINT SHE AIN'T Book and Lyrics by Dick Vosburgh; Music by Denis King; Director, Eric Hill; July 30–August 10, 2002; Main Stage; Cast: P.J. Benjamin (Snaveley T. Bogle), Roland Rusinek (Willoughby Dittenfeffer), Kate Levering (Anna Bagalucci), Jason Gillman (Danny O'Reilly), Jay Russell (Skip Watson), Joel Blum (Ray Bagalucci), Allison Briner (Faye Bogle), Lovette George (Trudy McCloy)

THE FOREIGNER by Larry Shue; Director, Scott Schwartz; August 13–31, 2002; Main Stage

BACK STORY by Joan Ackermann; Director, Michael Dowling; May 23–June 8, 2002; Unicorn Theater; Cast: Amanda Byron, Janice Rowland, David Polanski, Erin Gorski, Ryan O'Shaughnessy, Brian Sell

DIMETOS by Athol Fugard; Director, Peter Wallace; June 12–June 29, 2002; Unicorn Theater; Cast: Eric Hill (Dimetos), Tara Franklin (Lydia), Annie O'Sullivan (Sophia), Jeremy Davidson (Danilo)

MISS JULIE by August Strindberg; English Adaptation by Craig Lucas (based on a literal translation by Anders Cato); Director, Anders Cato; July 3–20, 2002; Unicorn Theater; Cast: Marin Hinkle (Miss Julie), Mark Feuerstein (Jean), Rebecca Creskoff (Christine)

INSURRECTION: HOLDING HISTORY by Robert O'Hara; Director, Timothy Douglas; July 24–August 17, 2002; Unicorn Theater; Cast: Tymberlee Chanel (Mutha Wit, Mutha), Richard T. Johnson (T.J.), Shane Taylor (Nat Turner, Ova Seea Jones), Wayne Scott (Ron), Cherise Boothe (Octavia, Katie Lynn), Nedrah Banks (Gertha, Mistress Mo'tel), Sekou Campbell (Hammet), Jake Goodman (Buck Naked), Dana Wilson (Izzie Mae), Chris Bolden (Ensemble)

BROWNSTONE by Josh Rubins, Peter Larson, and Andrew Cadiff; Director, James Warwick; August 21–30, 2002; Unicorn Theater; Cast: James Barry (Howard), Susan Schuld (Mary), Stephanie Girard (Joan), Sheila Vasan (Claudia), Kevin Reed (Stuart)

THE MAGIC FLUTE Adapted from Motzart by E. Gray Simons, III; Director, E. Gray Simons III; June 26–July 20, 2002; Theatre for Young Audiences

MONKEY Written by E. Gray Simons, III; Director, Tara Franklin; July 26–August 17, 2002; Theatre for Young Audiences

CALDWELL THEATRE COMPANY

Boca Raton, Florida
TWENTY-EIGHTH SEASON

Artistic & Managing Director, Michael Hall

MASTER CLASS by Terrence McNally; Director, Michael Hall; Scenic Design, Tim Bennett; Lighting Design, Thomas Salzman; Costume Design, Estela Vrancovich; Sound Design, Steve Shapiro; Stage Manager, Marcia A. Glotzer; October 21–December 15, 2002; Cast: Eric Alsford (Manny), Lisa Bansavage (Maria Callas), Kristen Hertzenberg (Sophie), Tom Wahl (Stagehand), Tami Swartz (Sharon), Nicholas Rodriguez (Tony)

PARK YOUR CAR IN HARVARD YARD by Israel Horovitz; Director, Bruce Lecure; Scenic Design, Tim Bennett; Lighting Design, Thomas Salzman; Sound Design, Steve Shapiro; Costume Design, Patricia Burdett; Stage Manager, Dan Zittel; December 29, 2002–February 9, 2003; Cast: Dennis Creaghan (JacobBrackish), Cary Anne Spear (Kathleen Hogan), George Merner (Byron Weld)

Nicholas Rodriduez, Lisa Bansavage in *Master Class*   PHOTO BY CALDWELL THEATRE COMPANY

THE COUNTESS by Gregory Murphy; Director, Michael Hall; Scenic Design, Tim Bennett; Lighting Design, Thomas Salzman; Costume Design, Estela Vrancovich; Sound Design, M. Anthony Reimer; Stage Manager, Marcia A. Glotzer. February 16–March 30, 2003; Cast: Brian Quirk (John Ruskin), Lanie MacEwan (Effie Ruskin), George Merner (John Ruskin, Sr.), Harriet Oser (Margaret Ruskin),Terrell Hardcastle (Frederick Crawley), Pat Nesbit (Lady Eastlake), Eric Sheffer Stevens (John Everett Millais)

FORTUNE'S FOOL by Ivan Turgenev; Adaptation by Mike Poulton; Director, Michael Hall; Scenic Design, Tim Bennett; Lighting Design, Thomas Salzman; Costume Design, Estela Vrancovich; Sound Design, Steve Shapiro; Stage Manager, Dan Zittel; April 6–May 18, 2003; Cast: Pat Nesbit (Praskovya), George Merner (Trembinsky), Michael Turner (Pyotr), John Felix (Kuzovkin), Dan Leonard (Ivanov), Lanie MacEwan (Olga), Terrell Hardcastle (Yeletsky), Geoffrey Wade (Tropatchov), Brian Quirk (Karpatchov), Kathleen Emrich, Norma Dobrikow-O'Hep, Paula Villar (Servants)

THE LAST SUNDAY IN JUNE by Jonathan Tolins; Director, Michael Hall; Scenic Design, Tim Bennett; Lighting Design, Thomas Salzman; Costume Design, Patricia Burdett; Sound Design, Steve Shapiro; Stage Manager, Heather Loney; June 20–August 3, 2003; Cast: Jeff Meacham (Tom), Nate Clark (Michael), John Bixler (Joe), Jack Garrity (Brad), Steve Hayes (Charles), Tim Burke (James), Dean Strange (Scott), Beth Bailey (Susan)

HEARTBEATS Book, Music and Lyrics by Amanda McBroom; Created by Amanda McBroom and Bill Castellino; Additional Music by Gerald Sternbach, Michele Brourman, Tom Snow and Craig Safan; Director, Michael Hall; Choreography, Barbara Flaten; Musical Director, Eric Alsford; Scenic Design, Tim Bennett; Lighting Design, Thomas Salzman; Costume Design, Estela Vrancovich; Sound Design, Steve Shapiro; Stage Manager, James Danford; September 5–28, 2003; Cast: Lourelene Snedeker (Annie), Martin Vidnovic (Steve), Stephanie Lynge (Woman #1; Young Annie; Jennifer; others), Elizabeth Dimon (Woman #2; Annie's best friend; others); Benjamin Schrader (Man #1; Young Steve; others); Todd Alan Crain (Man #2; Jeff; the waiter; others)

Lourelene Snedeker, Stephanie Lynge, Benjamin Schrader, Martin Vidnovic, in *Heartbeats*   PHOTO BY CALDWELL THEATRE COMPANY

CAPITAL REPERTORY THEATRE

Albany, New York
TWENTY-FIRST SEASON

Producing Artistic Director, Maggie Mancinelli-Cahill; Managing Director, Jeff Dannick

SONG OF SINGAPORE Book, Music and Lyrics by Alan Katz, Erick Frandsen, Michael Garin, Robert Hipkens, Paula Lockheart; Directed by Gordon Greenberg; Scenic Design, Alexander Dodge; Costume Design, Thom Heyer; Lighting Design, Jeff Croiter; Sound Design, Christopher St. Hilaire; Production Stage Manager, Diane McLean; Casting Director, Stephanie Klapper, CSA; Cast: Lisa Capps (Rose), Samuel Cohen (Spike), Marsh Hanson (Freddy S. Lyme), Erik Scharf (Hans), Mia Tagano (Chah Li), Ron Wisniski (Kurland, Hindu, Piolt, Noonan); Musicians Adrian Cohen, Mike Del Prete, Kris Farrow, Chad Ploss

Lisa Capps, Marsh Hanson, Ron Wisniski, Erik Schark, Samuel Cohen in *Song of Singapore* PHOTO BY JOE SCHUYLER

2 PIANOS, 4 HANDS by Ted Dykstra and Richard Greenblatt; Directed by Bruce K. Sevy; Scenic Design, Carol Beckley; Lighting Design, Don Darnutzer; Production Stage Manager, Beatrice Campbell; Cast: Mark Anders (Ted), Carl J. Danielsen (Richard)

FULLY COMMITTED by Becky Mode; Directed by Martha Banta; Scenic Design, Donald Eastman; Costume Design, Denise Dygert; Lighting Design, Rachel Budin; Sound Design, Christopher St. Hilaire; Production Stage Manager, Diane McLean; Casting Director, Stephanie Klapper, CSA; Cast: Oliver Wadsworth (Sam)

Mary Bacon, Richard Mawe in *Proof* PHOTO BY JOE SCHUYLER

PROOF by David Auburn; Directed by Maggie Mancinelli-Cahill; Scenic Design, Ted Simpson; Costume Design, Denise Dygert; Lighting Design, Deborah Constantine; Sound Design, Jane Shaw; Production Stage Manager, Margaret A. Currier; Casting Director, Stephanie Klapper, CSA; Cast: Mary Bacon(Catherine), Matthew J. Cody (Hal), Krista Hoeppner (Claire), Richard Mawe (Robert)

Mark Anders, Carl J. Danielsen in *2 Pianos, 4 Hands* PHOTO BY JOE SCHUYLER

BEGUILED AGAIN: THE SONGS OF RODGERS AND HART

Music Richard Rodgers, Lyrics by Lorenz Hart, Conceived by J. Barry Lewis, Lynnette Barkley & Craig D. Ames, Musical Arrangements by Craig D. Ames; Directed by J. Barry Lewis; Scenic & Costume Design, Austin K. Sanderson; Lighting Design, William H. Grant III; Sound Design, Christopher St. Hilaire; Musical Director, Bryan L. Wade; Choreographer, Lynnette Barkely; Casting Director, Stephanie Klapper, CSA; Production Stage Manager, Christopher Sadler; Cast: Tamra Hayden (Woman #1), Tom Kenaston (Man #3), James Patterson (Man #2), Abe Reybold (Man #1), Erica Schroder (Woman #3), Peggy Taphorn (Woman #2, Assistant Choreographer); Musicians: Bryan L. Wade, Michael Wicks, Rob Cenci

Lois Markle, Larry Marshall in *Driving Miss Daisy* PHOTO BY JOE SCHUYLER

Erica Schroeder, Tamra Hayden in *Beguilded Again* PHOTO BY JOE SCHUYLER

DRIVING MISS DAISY by Alfred Uhry; Directed by Regge Life; Scenic Design, Ruben Arana-Downs; Costume Design, Barbara A. Bell; Lighting Design, Michael Giannitti; Sound Design, Christopher St. Hilaire; Production Stage Manager, Leanna Lenhart; Casting Director, Stephanie Klapper, CSA; Cast: Lois Markle (Miss Daisy), Jay Edwards (Boolie), Larry Marshall (Hoke)

THE BLUE ROOM Freely adapted from Arthur Schnitzler's *La Ronde* by David Hare; Directed by Maggie Mancinelli-Cahill; Scenic Design, Donald Eastman; Costume Design, Thom Heyer; Lighting Design, Stephen Quandt; Sound Design, Christopher St. Hilaire; Production Stage Manager, Diane McLean; Casting Director, Stephanie Klapper, CSA; Cast: Dan Cordle (Man), Amy Landecker (Woman)

Amy Landecker, Dan Cordle in *The Blue Room* PHOTO BY JOSEPH SCHYLER

CENTER THEATRE GROUP/AHMANSON THEATRE

Los Angeles, California
THIRTY-SIXTH SEASON

Artistic Director/Producer, Gordon Davidson; Managing Director, Charles Dillingham; General Manager, Douglas C. Baker; Press Director, Tony Sherwood; Press Associate, Ken Werther; Associate Manager, Jennifer Oliver; Assistant Producer, Susan Obrow; Director of Marketing & Communications, Jim Royce; Advertising and Promotions Director, Michael Anderson; Casting Director, Amy Lieberman, C.S.A.; Development Director, Yvonne Carlson Bell; Chief Financial Officer, Edward L. Rada

MAMMA MIA! Music and Lyrics by Benny Andersson and Björn Ulvaeus; Some songs with Stig Anderson; Book by Catherine Johnson; Director, Phyllida Lloyd; Choreographer, Anthony Van Laast; Production Design, Mark Thompson; Lighting Design, Howard Harrison; Sound Design, Andrew Bruce, Bobby Aitken; Musical Supervisor, Additional Material and Arrangements, Martin Koch; Tour Music Supervisor, Edward G. Robinson; Musical Director, Boko Suzuki; Associate Choreographer, Nichola Treherne; Associate Director, Robert McQueen; Production Stage Manager, Ray Gin; Stage Manager, Niesa D. Silzer; Assistant Stage Manager, Jennifer Marik; Casting, Stephanie Gorin, C.D.C., Tara Rubin Casting; Casting Consultant, David Grindrod; Technical Supervisor, Arthur Siccardi, Theatrical Services, Inc.; Executive Producer, Nina Lannan Associates. Produced by Judy Craymer, Richard East and Björn Ulvaeus for Littlestar in association with Universal and David & Ed Mirvish; September 19–November 23, 2002; Cast: Dee Hoty (Donna Sheridan), Gary P. Lynch (Sam Carmichael), Michelle Aravena (Sophie), Ryan Silverman (Sky), Gabrielle Jones (Rosie, understudy Donna), Mary Ellen Mahoney (Tanya), Craig Bennett (Bill Austin), Mark Zimmerman (Harry Bright), Emy Baysic (Alí), Karen Burthwright (Lisa), Mike Erickson (Pepper), Joe Paparella (Eddie, understudy Sky), Charlie Brady (Ensemble, understudy Sky, Eddie), Kim Craven (Dance Captain, Swing), Jennifer DiNoia (Ensemble, understudy Alí), Cody Green (Ensemble), Lori Haley Fox (Ensemble, understudy Donna, Tanya, Rosie), Chilina Kennedy (Ensemble, understudy Sophie, Alí), Melanie Merkosky (Swing, understudy Lisa), Daniel Jason O'Keefe (Swing), Nadine Roden (Ensemble, understudy Tanya, Rosie), Ambere Rogers (Ensemble, understudy Lisa), Elizabeth Share (Ensemble, understudy Sophie, Lisa), Milo Shandel (Father Alexandrios, understudy Bill, Harry), Ian Simpson (Ensemble, understudy Harry, Bill, Sam, Father Alexandrios), Jason Snow (Swing, understudy Pepper), Devon Tullock (Ensemble, understudy Pepper, Eddie), Astrid Van Wieren (Ensemble, understudy Rosie), Shawn Wright (Ensemble, understudy Sam, Bill)

MORNING'S AT SEVEN by Paul Osborn; Director, Daniel Sullivan; Set Design, John Lee Beatty; Costume Design, Jane Greenwood; Lighting Design, Brian MacDevitt; Sound Design, Scott Myers; Wigs and Hair, Paul Huntley; Production Stage Manager, Roy Harris; Casting, Daniel Swee, C.S.A., Amy Lieberman, C.S.A. Center Theatre Group/Ahmanson presents the Lincoln Center Theater production; December 4, 2002–January 26, 2003; Cast: Paul Dooley (Carl Bolton), Elizabeth Franz (Aaronetta Gibbs), Julie Hagerty (Myrtle Brown), Buck Henry (David Crampton), Piper Laurie (Esther Crampton), William Biff McGuire (Theodore Swanson), Frances Sternhagen (Ida Bolton), Stephen Tobolowsky (Homer Bolton), Mary Louise Wilson (Cora Swanson), Tom Carey (Understudy Carl, David, Thor), Maree Cheatham (Understudy Esther, Cora), Linda Marie Larson (Understudy Myrtle Brown), David Manis (Understudy Homer, Carl), Lorraine Michaels (Understudy Aaronetta, Ida)

Frances Sternhagen, Piper Laurie in *Morning's at Seven* PHOTO BY JOAN MARCUS

BRING IN 'DA NOISE, BRING IN 'DA FUNK Conceived and Directed by George C. Wolfe; Choreographer, Savion Glover; Book &Lyrics, Reg E. Gaines; Music, Daryl Waters, Zane Mark, Ann Duquesnay; Scenic Design, Riccardo Hernandez; Costume Design, Paul Tazewell; Lighting Design, Jules Fisher/Peggy Eisenhauer; Sound Design, Shannon Slaton; Projection Design, Batwin + Robin; Music Supervision & Orchestrations, Daryl Waters; Musical Director, Tommy James; Vocal Arrangements, Ann Duquesnay; On-Stage Percussion, Jared Crawford; Dramaturg, Shelby Jiggetts-Tivony; Production Stage Manager, Ed De Shae; Technical Supervisor, Tech Production Services, Inc.; General Management, Columbia Artists Theatricals; Casting, Barry Moss, C.S.A., Bob Kale; National Press Representative, Rubenstein Public Relations; Tour Press & Marketing, TOURture Press & Marketing; Executive Producer, Aldo Scrofani. Produced by Columbia Artists Theatricals. This tour presented in association with Alliance Theatre Company, Atlanta, Georgia, Susan V. Booth, Artistic Director; January 28–February 15, 2003; Cast: Savion Glover ('da Beat), Lynette Dupree ('da Singer), Thomas Silcott ('da Voice), Maurice Chestnut (Performer), Marshall L. Davis Jr. (Performer), Dormeshia Sumbry-Edwards (Performer, understudy 'da Beat), Cartier A. Williams "Big Coop" ('da Kid), Jared "Choclatt" Crawford (Drummer), Raymond A. King (Drummer), Arnell Powell (Understudy 'da Voice), Carolyn Saxon (Understudy 'da Singer), Troy Swanigan (Grin, Swing)

BARBARA COOK IN MOSTLY SONDHEIM Musical Director, Tex Arnold; Production Design, D. Martyn Bookwalter; Production Sound, Jon Gottlieb and Philip G. Allen; Piano, Tex Arnold; Bass, Dave Carpenter. Presented by Center Theatre Group/Ahmanson Theatre. February 28–March 9, 2003; Cast: Barbara Cook

Elaine Stritch in *Elaine Stritch At Liberty* PHOTO BY MICHAL DANIEL

SEXAHOLIX...A LOVE STORY Written by and starring John Leguizamo; Director, Peter Askin; Lighting Design, Kevin Adams; Sound Design, T. Richard Fitzgerald; Costume Consultant, Santiago; Music Consultant, Tony Touch; Contributing Editor, Stephen Chbosky; Production Stage Manager, Arabella Powell. Produced by Tate Entertainment Group, Inc. March 11–23, 2003; Cast: John Leguizamo

ELAINE STRITCH AT LIBERTY Directed by George C. Wolfe; Constructed by John Lahr; Reconstructed by Elaine Stritch; Scenic Design, Riccardo Hernández; Costume Design, Paul Tazewell; Lighting Design, Jules Fisher & Peggy Eisenhauer; Sound Design, Acme Sound Partners; Orchestrations, Jonathan Tunick; Music Director, Rob Bowman; Music Coordinator, Seymour Red Press; Technical Supervisor, Fred Allen; Marketing, TMG The Marketing Group; Production Stage Manager, Larry Baker; General Manager, Columbia Artists Theatricals; Producer, Bruce H. Weinstein; Executive Producer, Scott Sanders; Produced by Creative Battery in association with John Schreiber. April 8–27, 2003; Cast: Elaine Stritch

THE SEARCH FOR SIGNS OF INTELLINGENT LIFE IN THE UNIVERSE Written and Directed by Jane Wagner; Set Design, Klara Zieglerova; Lighting Design, Ken Billington; Sound Design, Mark Bennett, Tom Clark; Production Supervisor, Co-producer, Janet Beroza; General Manager, Frier McCollister; Technical Supervision, Theatersmith, Inc.; Sound Engineer, Candice Nelms; Stage Manager, Nevin Hedley. Produced by Tomlin and Wagner Theatricalz in association with The Seattle Repertory Theatre and McCarter Theatre Center. May 13–July 6, 2003; Cast: Lily Tomlin

The Company of *42nd St.* PHOTO BY JOAN MARCUS

42ND STREET Directed by Mark Bramble; Book by Michael Stewart & Mark Bramble; Music by Harry Warren; Lyrics by Al Dubin; Based on the novel by Bradford Ropes; Musical Staging and New Choreography by Randy Skinner; Original Direction and Dances by Gower Champion; Scenic Design, Douglas W. Schmidt; Costume Design, Roger Kirk; Lighting Design, Paul Gallo; Sound Design, Peter Fitzgerald; Production Stage Manager, Renée Rimland; Casting, Jay Binder; Wigs & Hair Design, David H. Lawrence; Musical Supervision, Todd Ellison; Musical Adaptation, Arrangements & Additional Orchestrations, Donald Johnston; Conductor, Jeff Rizzo; Orchestrations, Philip J. Lang; Music Coordinator, John Miller; Technical Supervisor, Peter Fulbright; National Marketing and Press Representative, Catherine Major; Produced by Dodger Stage Holding and Joop van den Ende; July 9–August 31, 2003; Cast: Blair Ross (Dorothy Brock), Patrick Ryan Sullivan (Julian Marsh), Catherine Wreford (Peggy Sawyer), Patti Mariano (Maggie Jones), Frank Root (Bert Barry), Robert Spring (Billy Lawlor), Paul Ainsley (Abner Dillon), Suellen Estey (Standby for Dorothy Brock, Maggie Jones), Michael Fitzpatrick (Mac, Thug, Doctor, understudy Julian Marsh, Bert Barry, Abner Dillon), Dexter Jones (Andy Lee), Tom Judson (Oscar), Daren Kelly (Pat Denning, understudy Julian Marsh, Abner Dillon), Alana Salvatore (Annie, understudy Dorothy Brock, Maggie Jones)

CENTER THEATRE GROUP/MARK TAPER FORUM

Los Angeles, California
THIRTY-SIXTH SEASON

Artistic Director, Gordon Davidson; Managing Director, Charles Dillingham

NICKEL AND DIMED by Joan Holden; Based on Barbara Ehrenreich's book Nickel and Dimed: On (Not) Getting by in America; Director, Bartlett Sher; Artistic Associate, Anna Deavere Smith; Scenic Design, John Arnone; Costume Design, Rose Pederson; Lighting Design, Mary Louise Geiger; Sound Design, Jon Gottlieb; Dramaturg, Mame Hunt; Casting, Kate Godman and Amy Lieberman, CSA; The Intiman Theatre World Premiere production; September 8–October 27, 2002; Cast: Jason Cottle, Kristin Flanders, Cynthia Jones, Sharon Lockwood (Barbara), Cristine McMurdo-Wallis, Olga Sanchez, composer/musician Michael McQuilken, Waitress Riffs: Sophia Chumley

BIG RIVER: THE ADVENTURES OF HUCKLEBERRY FINN Music and Lyrics, Roger Miller; Book, William Hauptman; Adapted from the novel by Mark Twain; Director and Choreographer, Jeff Calhoun; Music Director, Steven Landau; Scenic Design, Ray Klausen; Costume Design, David R. Zyla; Lighting Design, Michael Gilliam; Sound Design, Jon Gottlieb and Philip G. Allen; Hair and Wig Design, Carol F. Doran; Associate Director, Coy Middlebrook; Associate Choreographer, Patti D'Beck; Head ASL Master Freda Norman; ASL Masters, Linda Bove, Betsy Ford, Anthony Natale; Production Interpreter, Catherine Richardson Kiwitt; Casting, Amy Lieberman, CSA, and Bruce H. Newberg, CSA; The Deaf West Theatre production; November 5–December 29, 2002; Cast: Chuck Baird (Judge Thatcher), Michelle A. Banks (Alice's Daughter), Rufus Bonds Jr. (Slave Jim), Gibby Brand (Preacher), Michael Davis (Tom Sawyer), Phyllis Frelich (Miss Watson), Tyrone Giordano (Huck), Lyle Kanouse (Papp), Rod Keller (Voice of Tom), Carol Kline (Widow Douglas), Troy Kotsur (Papp), Jarret LeMaster (Ben Rogers), William Martinez (Voice of Duke), Ryan Schlecht (Dick Simon), Gwen Stewart (Alice), Melissa van der Schyff (Mary Jane), Scott Waara (Mark Twain), Alexandria Wailes (Joanna)

Christine McMurdo-Wallis, Kristin Flanders, Sharon Lockwood in *Nickel and Dimed*
PHOTO BY CRAIG SCHWARTZ

Rufus Bonds Jr., Tyrone Giordano in *Big River* PHOTO BY CRAIG SCHWARTZ

Zilah Mendoza, Amy Aquino in *Living Out* PHOTO BY CRAIG SCHWARTZ

LIVING OUT by Lisa Loomer; Director, Bill Rauch; Scenic Design, Christopher Acebo; Costume Design, Candice Cain; Lighting Design, Lap-Chi Chu; Sound Design, Jon Gottlieb; Original Music Composition, Joe Romano; Dramaturgs, Corey Madden and John Glore; Hair and Wig Design, Carol F. Doran; Casting, Amy Lieberman, CSA; World premiere; January 18–March 9, 2003; Cast: Amy Aquino (Nancy), Richard Azurdia, Carlos Gomez (Bobby), Daniel Hugh Kelly (Richard), Dihlon McManne, Zilah Mendoza (Ana), Kate A. Mulligan (Wallace), Maricela Ochoa (Sandra), Diane Rodriguez (Zoila), Elizabeth Ruscio (Linda)

Richard Montoya, Herbert Siguenza, Ric Salinas in *Chavez Ravine* PHOTO BY CRAIG SCHWARTZ

Phylicia Rashad, Anthony Chisholm in *Gem of the Ocean* PHOTO BY CRAIG SCHWARTZ

Jonathan M. Woodward, Stacy Keach in *Ten Unknowns* PHOTO BY CRAIG SCHWARTZ

TEN UNKNOWNS by Jon Robin Baitz; Director, Robert Egan; Scenic Design, David Jenkins; Costume Design, Joyce Kim Lee; Lighting Design, Michael Gilliam; Sound Design, Jon Gottlieb; Paintings, Conor Foy; Casting, Amy Lieberman, CSA; West Coast premiere; March 15–May 4, 2003; Cast: Patrick Breen (Trevor Frabricant), Stacy Keach (Malcolm Raphaelson), Klea Scott (Julia Bryant), Jonathan M. Woodward (Judd Sturgess)

CHAVEZ RAVINE by Culture Clash (Richard Montoya, Ric Salinas, Herbert Siguenza); Director, Lisa Peterson; Scenic Design, Rachel Hauck; Costume Design, Christopher Acebo; Lighting Design, Anne Militello; Sound Design, Dan Moses Schreier; Music Director/Arranger John Avila; Original Music and Lyrics, Scott Rodarte, Randy Rodarte, John Avila and Richard Montoya; Dramaturg, John Glore; Casting, Amy Lieberman, CSA; World premiere; May 17–July 12, 2003; Cast: Roberto Alcaraz, John Avila, Eileen Galindo, Minerva Garcia, Edgar Landa, Richard Montoya, Randy Rodarte, Scott Rodarte, Ric Salinas, Herbert Siguenza.

AUGUST WILSON'S GEM OF THE OCEAN Director, Marion McClinton; Scenic Design, David Gallo; Costume Design Constanza Romero; Lighting Design, Donald Holder; Sound Design, Dan Moses Schreier; Music Composer and Arranger, Kathryn Bostic; Wigs, John Aitchison; Fight Director, Steve Rankin; Casting, Harriet Bass, Amy Lieberman, CSA; World premiere; July 20–September 7, 2003; Cast: Anthony Chisholm (Solly Two Kings), Yvette Ganier (Black Mary), Peter Francis James (Caesar), John Earl Jelks (Citizen Barlow), Phylicia Rashad (Aunt Ester), Raynor Scheine (Rutherford Selig), Al White (Eli)

CINCINNATI PLAYHOUSE IN THE PARK

Cincinnati, Ohio
FORTY-THIRD SEASON

Producing Artistic Director, Edward Stern; Executive Director, Buzz Ward

AH, WILDERNESS! by Eugene O'Neill; Director, Edward Stern; Set Design, Joseph P. Tilford; Costume Design, David Kay Mickelsen; Lighting Design, Phil Monat; Composer, Fabian Obispo; Dialect Coach, Rocco Dal Vera; September 3–October 4, 2002; Cast: Lynn Milgrim (Essie Miller), Mike Heffron (Tommy Miller), Joneal Joplin (Nat Miller), Keri Setaro (Mildred Miller), Eric Sheffer Stevens (Arthur Miller), Carol Schultz (Lily Miller), Robert Elliott (Sid Davis), Daniel Talbott (Richard Miller), Richard Russell Ramos (Mr. McComber), Kathy McCafferty (Norah), Eric Altheide (Wint Selby), Katherine Scholl (Belle), Drew Fracher (Bartender), Jerry Vogel (Salesman), Winslow Corbett (Muriel McComber)

HAVANA IS WAITING by Eduardo Machado; Director, Ron Daniels; Set Design, Riccardo Hernandez; Costume Design, Miguel Angel Huidor; Lighting Design, Scott Zielinski; September 21–October 20, 2002; Cast: Chaz Mena (Federico), Paolo Andino (Fred), Antonio Edwards Suarez (Ernesto), Sheila Tapia (Pregnant Girl), Richard Marquez (Musician)

A FLEA IN HER EAR by Georges Feydeau; Translation, Douglas Johnson; Director, John Going; Set Design, James Wolk; Costume Design, Elizabeth Covey; Lighting Design, Dennis Parichy; October 20–November 22, 2002; Cast: Jeffries Thaiss (Camille Chandebise), Patricia Dalen (Antoinette Plucheux), David Diaz (Etienne Plucheux), Paul DeBoy (Dr. Finache), Andrea Cirie (Lucienne de Histangua), Deanne Lorette (Raymonde Chandebise), Anderson Matthews (Victor-Emmanuel Chandebise/Poche), R. Ward Duffy (Romain Tournel), Thom Rivera (Carlos Homenides de Histangua), Thomas Carson (Augustin Ferraillon), Alisha McKinney (Eugenie), Lisa McMillan (Olympe), T. Doyle Leverett (Helmut Krause), A. Jackson Ford (Hotel Guest), Autumn Gentile (Hotel Guest), Sheila Tapia (Hotel Guest), Collin Worster (Hotel Guest)

THE BIBLE: THE COMPLETE WORD OF GOD (ABRIDGED) by Adam Long, Reed Martin and Austin Tichenor; Director, Reed Martin; Set Design, David A. Centers; Costume Design, Rebecca Senske; Lighting Design, Susan Terrano; November 9–December 31, 2002; Cast: Todd Cerveris (Todd), Jeffrey Kuhn (Jeffrey), Greg McFadden (Greg)

A CHRISTMAS CAROL by Charles Dickens; Adaptation, Howard Dallin; Director, Michael Evan Haney; Set Design, James Leonard Joy; Costume Design, David Murin; Lighting Design, Kirk Bookman; Sound Design and Composition, David B. Smith; Lighting Contractor, Susan Terrano; Costume Coordinator, Cindy Witherspoon; Musical Director, Rebecca N. Childs; Choreographer, Dee Anne Bryll; December 4–30, 2002; Cast: Joneal Joplin (Ebenezer Scrooge), Mark Mocahbee (Mr. Cupp, Percy), Larry Bates (Mr. Sosser, Dick Wilkens, Topper, Man with Shoe Shine), Bruce Cromer (Bob Cratchit, Schoolmaster Oxlip), Jake Storms (Fred), Gregory Procaccino (Jacob Marley, Old Joe), Dale Hodges (Ghost of Christmas Past, Rose, Mrs. Peake), Nathan Wallace (Boy Scrooge, Boy at Fezziwig's), Ali Breneman (Fan), Mark Mineart (Mr. Fezziwig, Ghost of Christmas Present), Amy Warner (Mrs. Fezziwig, Patience), Jeremiah Wiggins (Young and Mature Scrooge, Ghost of Christmas Future), Kelly Mares (Belle, Catherine Margaret), Regina Pugh (Mrs. Cratchit, Laundress), Dustin M. Hicks (Peter Cratchit, Gregory), McKenzie Miller (Belinda Cratchit), Sloan Thacker (Martha Cratchit), Evan Martin (Tiny Tim), Leanne Robinson (Rich Caroler, Maid at Fezziwig's), Jim Ward (Rich Caroler, Accountant at Fezziwig's), Amber K. Browning (Poor Caroler, Rich Wife at Fezziwig's), Damon Gravina (Poor Caroler, Tailor at Fezziwig's), Alec Shelby Bowling (Matthew, Ignorance), Aaron Mayo (Charles, George), Kathryn A. Winternitz (Want, Guest at Fezziwig's), Robin Benson (Mrs. Dilber, Guest at Fezziwig's), Sheila Tapia (Scrubwoman at Fezziwig's), Autumn Gentile (Guest at Fezziwig's, Poulterer), Todd Frugia (Lawyer at Fezziwig's, Man with Pipe), Ric Sechrest (Constable at Fezziwig's, Undertaker), A. Jackson Ford (Rich Father at Fezziwig's)

PROOF by David Auburn; Director, Michael Evan Haney; Set Design, Paul Shortt; Costume Design, Gordon DeVinney; Lighting Design, Kirk Bookman; January 12–February 22, 2003; Cast: Robert Elliott (Robert), Michelle R. Six (Catherine), Christopher Kelly (Hal), Rachel Fowler (Claire)

AN INFINITE ACHE by David Schulner; Director, Greg Leaming; Set Design, Marjorie Bradley Kellogg; Costume Design, Claudia Stephens; Lighting Design, Dan Kotlowitz; Composer, Fabian Obispo; February 1–March 9, 2003; Cast: Eunice Wong (Hope), Mark Alhadeff (Charles)

PACIFIC OVERTURES Music and Lyrics, Stephen Sondheim; Book, John Weidman; Additional Material by Hugh Wheeler; Director, Kent Gash; Choreographers, Darren Lee and Francis Jue; Musical Director/Conductor, M. Michael Fauss; Set Design, Neil Patel; Costume Design, Paul Tazewell; Lighting Design, Michael Philippi; Sound Consultant, Abe Jacob; Cultural Advisor/Movement Coach, Yuriko Doi; Fight Director, Drew Fracher; March 5–April 5, 2003; Cast: Ronald M. Banks (Second Councilor, Soothsayer, Thief, British Sailor, Russian Admiral, Assassin), Eric Bondoc (Fisherman, American Officer, Kanagawa Girl, Lord of the South, Priest, Ensemble), Miyoko Conley (Kurogo), Steven Eng (Kayama, Ensemble), Mikio Hirata (Shogun's Mother, Old Man, Lord of the South, Old Samurai Master, Merchant's Grandmother), Kenway Hon Wai K. Kua (Samurai, Assassin, Commodore Perry, Kanagawa Girl, Samurai's Daughter, Noble, Sword Craftsman, Ensemble), Jason Ma (Manjiro, Observer One, Dutch Admiral, Ensemble), Allan Mangaser (Tamate, Shogun's Companion, French Admiral, Assassin, Ensemble), Tony Marinyo (Lord Abe, American Officer, Ensemble), Alan Muraoka (Third Councilor, Merchant, British Admiral, Madam, Old Man, Physician, British Valet, Assassin, Ensemble), Randy Reyes (Priest One, Boy, Kanagawa Girl, British Sailor, Merchant's Son, Female Servant, Ensemble), James Saito (Reciter, Shogun, Storyteller), Erwin G. Urbi (Shogun's Wife, Kanagawa Girl, Merchant, Samurai Warrior, American Admiral, British Sailor, Observer Two, Ensemble), Melissa Urriquia (Kurogo)

THE LOVE SONG OF J. ROBERT OPPENHEIMER by Carson Kreitzer; Director, Mark Wing-Davey; Set Design, Douglas Stein; Costume Design, Catherine Zuber; Lighting Design, David Weiner; Sound Design, Marc Gwinn; Video Design, Ruppert Bohle; Dramaturgy, Kathleen Tobin; World Premiere winner of the Lois and Richard Rosenthal New Play Prize; March 22–April 20, 2003; Cast: Curzon Dobell (J. Robert Oppenheimer), Judith Hawking (Lilith), Jason Bowcutt (Young Scientist, British Envoy, Strauss), Michael Pemberton (Scientist One, Rabi, Security One, General Groves, Scientist Voice, J. Edgar Hoover, Committee Voice), Steven Rattazzi (Teller, Security Two, Lansdale, Scientist Voice), Blaire Chandler (Kitty Oppenheimer), Carolyn Baeumler (Jean Tatlock, Censor, Reporter, Nurse, Mother)

THE SMELL OF THE KILL by Michele Lowe; Director, Edward Stern; Set Design, Klara Zieglerova; Costume Design, Gordon DeVinney; Lighting Design, Thomas C. Hase; Fight Director, Rick Sordelet; April 27–May 30, 2003; Cast: Suzanne Grodner (Debra), Cheryl Gaysunas (Molly), Nancy Hess (Nicky), Andy Prosky (Jay), Kevin Orton (Danny, Marty)

THE SYRINGA TREE by Pamela Gien; Director, Michael Evan Haney; Set Design, Narelle Sissons; Costume Design, Elizabeth Eisloeffel; Lighting Design, James Sale; Sound Design, Chuck Hatcher; May 17–June 15, 2003; Cast: Stephanie Cozart and Shannon Koob (Elizabeth—Ms. Cozart and Ms. Koob appeared in alternating performances.)

CITY THEATRE

Pittsburgh, Pennsylvania
TWENTY-EIGHTH SEASON

Artistic Director, Tracy Brigden; Managing Director, David Jobin

INVENTING VAN GOGH by Steven Dietz; Director, Neel Keller; Set Design, Anne Mundell; Lighting Design, Rand Ryan; Sound Design, Joe Pino; Costume Design, Lorraine Venberg; Hair Design, Elsen Associates, Inc.; Production Stage Manager, Patti Kelly; September 19–October 20, 2002; Cast: Lee Sellars (Patrick Stone), Larry John Myers (Dr. Jonas Miller, Dr. Paul Gachet), Martin Giles (René Bouchard, Paul Gauguin), Kelly Boulware (Vincent van Gogh), Janelle Baker (Hallie Miller, Marguerite Gachet)

LA DOLCE VITA: MOVIE SONGS OF THE 1960S Created and Performed by Jilline Ringle; Director, Robert Gilbo; Musical Director, Thomas Wesley Douglas; Set Design, Tony Ferrieri; Lighting Design, Richard Currie; Sound Design, Elizabeth Atkinson; Costume Design, Venise St. Pierre; Production Stage Manager, Marianne Montgomery; October 17, 2002–January 19, 2003; Cast: Jilline Ringle; Musicians: Thomas Wesley Douglas, Dave Flodine, Pasquale Vincenzo Macioce

Kelly Boulware in *Inventing Van Gogh* PHOTO BY RIC EVANS

MRS. BOB CRATCHIT'S WILD CHRISTMAS BINGE by Christopher Durang; Original Music, Michael Friedman; Lyrics, Christopher Durang; Director, Tracy Brigden; Choreographer, Scott Wise; Music Director, Douglas Levine; Scenic Design, Jeff Cowie; Costume Design, Elizabeth Hope Clancy; Lighting Design, Rick Martin; Sound Design, Elizabeth Atkinson; Hair Design, Elsen Associates, Inc.; Production Stage Manager, Patti Kelly; World premiere; November 7–December 22, 2002; Cast: Lauren Rose Gigliotti and Allison Hannon (Young Jacob Marley), Shane Jordan and Matt Lang (Young Ebeneezer Scrooge), January Murelli (The Ghost of Christmas Past, Present and Future), Douglas Rees (Ebeneezer Scrooge), Darren E. Focareta (Tiny Tim, Fezziwig's Daughter), Martin Giles (Bob Cratchit), Kristine Nielsen (Mrs. Bob Cratchit), Jeff Howell (Mr. Fezziwig, Mr. Beadle), Matthew Gaydos (Edvar, George Bailey, Serena), Larry John Meyers (Jacob Marley's Ghost, Clarence the Angel), Sheila McKenna (Mrs. Fezziwig, Mrs. Beadle, Little Nell), Elena Passarello (Hedwig, Nice Mrs. Cratchit, Monica)

Jilline Ringle in *La Dolce Vita* PHOTO BY RIC EVANS

Jeff Howell, Kristine Nielsen in *Mrs. Bob Cratchit's Wild Christmas Binge* PHOTO BY RIC EVANS

Helena Ruoti, Conan McCarty in *Sorrows and Rejoicings* PHOTO BY RIC EVANS

John Shepard, Chandler Vinton in *Fair Game* PHOTO BY RIC EVANS

SORROWS AND REJOICINGS by Athol Fugard; Director, Timothy Douglas; Scenic Design, Tony Ferrieri; Costume Design, Cletus Anderson; Lighting Design, Thom Weaver; Sound Design, Elizabeth Atkinson; Hair Design, Elsen Associates, Inc.; Production Stage Manager, Patti Kelly; Dialect Coach, Don Wadsworth; Dramaturg, Carlyn Ann Aquiline; January 16–February 16, 2003; Cast: Helena Ruoti (Allison), Kelly Taffe (Marta), Rebecca Utt (Rebecca), Conan McCarty (Dawid)

FAIR GAME by Karl Gajdusek; Director, Tracy Brigden; Scenic Design, Scott Bradley; Lighting Design, Jeff Croiter; Costume Design, Michael Olich; Sound Design, Dave Bjornson; Production Stage Manager, Patti Kelly; March 6–April 12, 2003; Cast: Ron Menzel (Simon Werthman), Chandler Vinton (Miranda Carter), Christine Ryndak (Elizabeth Rain), Cary Anne Spear (Governor Karen Werthman), John Shepard (Senator Bill Graber)

BIRDIE BLUE by Cheryl L. West; Director, Leah C. Gardiner; Sound Design and Choreography, Elizabeth Atkinson; Scenic Design, Tony Ferrieri; Lighting Design, Andrew David Ostrowski; Costume Design, Pei-Chi Su; Production Stage Manager, Marianne Montgomery; March 20–May 11, 2003; Cast: Irma P. Hall (Birdie), Ernest Perry, Jr. (Jackson, Ensemble)

HEDWIG AND THE ANGRY INCH Text, John Cameron Mitchell; Music and Lyrics, Stephen Trask; Director, Brad Rouse; Scenic Design, Michael Olich; Costume Design, Miguel Angel Huidor; Lighting Design, Howell Binkley; Sound Design, Keith Bates and Elizabeth Atkinson; Hair Design, Lair Paulsen; Production Stage Manager, Patti Kelly; May 1–June 27, 2003; Cast: Anthony Rapp (Hedwig), Sarah Siplak (Yitzak), Brandon Lowry (Skszp), John Purse (Krzyzhtoff), Daniel Tomko (Jacek), A.T. Vish (Schlatko)

Ernest Perry Jr., Irma P. Hall in *Birdie Blue* PHOTO BY RIC EVANS

Anthony Rapp in *Hedwig and the Angry Inch* PHOTO BY RIC EVANS

David Alley, John Forrest Ferguson, Guiesseppe Jones in *"Art"* PHOTO BY ERIC SMITH

CLARENCE BROWN THEATRE AT THE UNIVERSITY OF TENNESSEE

Knoxville, Tennessee

TWENTY-EIGHTH SEASON

Artistic Director, Blake Robison; Managing Director, Thomas Cervone; Production Manager, Laura Sims; Company Manager, Betty Tipton; Marketing/Development Director, Whitney Lawson; Public Relations Director, Rachael Fugate; Education/Outreach Director, Kim Midkiff; Box Office Manager, Roger Hoover; Assistant Box Office Manager, Laura Starratt; House Manager, James Brimer; Business Manager, Sharon Ward; Senior Accountant, Kelli Blair; Program Resource Specialist, C. Sue Dodd; Staff Technical Director, Marty Cooke; Scene Shop, Bryan C. Jones, Don Conard; Properties Master, Mary Murdie; Costume Shop Manager, Jeffrey Todhunter; Costume Shop, Ann Knight, Allison Steadman; Electrics Shop Manager and Resident Lighting Designer, John Horner; Master Electrician; Joshua P. Hamrick Sound Engineer and Resident Sound Designer, Mike Ponder; Stage Supervisor, John Gann; Production Stage Manager, Marta Stout

"ART" a new play by Yasmina Reza, translation by Christopher Hampton; Produced on Broadway by David Pugh, Sean Connery and Joan Cullman, March 1, 1998; Directed by Bruce Speas; Scenic Design, Michael Heil; Costume Design, Stephen Brown; Lighting Design, Joshua P. Hamrick; Sound Design, Mike Ponder; Stage Manager, Marta Stout; Fight Choreographer, Bruce Speas; August 30–September 14, 2002; Cast: John Forrest Ferguson (Marc), Guiesseppe Jones (Serge), David Brian Alley (Yvan)

NORA Stage version by Ingmar Bergman, Based on Henrik Ibsen's *A Doll House*, translated by Frederick J. and Lise-Lone Marker. Directed by Frank Hanig, Dramaturg, Klaus van den Berg; Scenic Design, Biff Edge and Britton Lynn; Costume Design, Leah Barnes; Courtney Burt, Masha Kamyshkova, and Jessica Wegener, Lighting Design, Weston Wilkerson, Sound Design, Mike Ponder, Stage Manager, Michael Jones; October 11–27, 2002; Cast: Jeremy Fischer (Torvald Helmer), Alecia White (Nora), Rebecca Eddy (Mrs. Linde), Forrest D. Martin (Nils Krogstad), Juan Salvati (Doctor Rank)

OLIVER! Music, Lyrics, and book by Lionel Bart, Produced for the Broadway Stage by David Merrick and Donald Albery, Directed by Blake Robison, Music Director, James Brimer, Choreography, Casey Sams, Scenic Design, Jeff Modereger, Costume Design, Leah Noel Barnes, Lighting Design, Kenton Yeager, Sound Design, Mike Ponder, Dialect Coach Terry Weber, Stage Manager, Marta Stout; November 22–December 8, 2002; Cast: John Forrest Ferguson (Fagin), Jarron Edward Vosburg (Oliver), Joseph

Jeremy Fischer, Alecia White in *Nora* PHOTO BY ERIC SMITH

Members of the Company of *Oliver!* PHOTO BY ERIC SMITH

Beuerlein (Artful Dodger), Nicole Begue (Nancy), Harmony Livingston (Bet), Steven Biggs (Bill Sykes), Carroll Freeman (Mr. Bumble), Anne Thibault (Widow Corney), David Brian Alley (Mr. Sowerberry, Dr. Grimwig), Meghan McCoy (Mrs. Sowerberry, Mrs. Bedwin), Jessenia She (Charlotte), Collin Martin (Noah Claypole), James T. Kirk (Mr. Brownlow), Caroline Addinall (Old Sally); Pickpockets: Michael Boris (Charlie), Daviel Evans, Christiane Frith, Christopher Frith, Chelsea Jacobs, Jess Milewicz, Garrett Montgomery, Reedy Swanson, Rob Tatgenhorst; Chorus, Vendors: Christopher M. Szyz (Knives, Bow Street Runner), Mandy Lawson (Roses), Jeannine Souder (Milk), Robin Watson (Strawberries), Grant Collins (Bow Street Runner), Rebecca Hillson, Michael Turner; Orphans: Lee Bryant, Christiane Frith, Chelsea Jacobs, Garrett Montgomery, Emily Poulsen, Alyssa Scott, Reedy Swanson, Rob Tatgenhorst, Alaina Woodall, April Woodall

THE BACCHAE OF EURIPIDES: A COMMUNION RITE by Wole Soyinka; Directed by Elizabeth Craven; Choreography by Alia Curchak; Musical Direction by Mike Ponder and Nancy Prebilich; Scenic Design, Jaroslav Malina; Costume Design, Courtney Burt; Lighting Design, Penny Remsen; Sound Design, Mike Ponder; Stage manager, Marta Stout; Dramaturg, Nkechi Ajanaku; This adaptation of The Bacchae of Euripides: A Communion Rite by Wole Soyinka is based on two versions by Gilbert Murray, published by Allen and Unwin, London, and Oxford University Press, New York, and William Arrowsmith, published in Euripides Fire: Three Tragedies, edited by David Grene and Richard Lattimore, by University of Chicago Press; February 7–22, 2003; Cast: Starr Releford (Slave Leader); Rene Thornton Jr. (Dionysos); Forrest Martin (Pentheus); Candace Taylor (Agave); Collin Martin (Herdsman); Jeremy Fischer (Officer); Steven Biggs (Kadmus); John Forrest Ferguson (Tiresius); Faezah Jalali (1st Bacchante);

Bonnie Gould in *Midwives* PHOTO BY ERIC SMITH

Ensemble: Mike Pittman, Zakiah Modeste, Nancy Prebilich, Christian Scott, Roshaunda Ross, Shamicka Benn, Dametria Mustin, Marissa Weaver, Rebecca Eddy, Jessenia She, Alecia White, Anne Thibault, Walter Hayes, Juan Salvati, Doug James, William Revill III, Nicole Franklin, Effay Tio Smith, Umar Tate; Musicians: Simba Smith, Brandon Beavers

MIDWIVES by Dana Yeaton, based on the best-selling novel *Midwives* by Chris Bohjalian; Directed by Kathryn Long; Scenic Design, Vladimir Shpitalnik; Costume Design, Clinton O'Dell; Lighting Design, Keith Kirkland; Sound Design, Mike Ponder; Stage Manager, Dawn Wagner; New York Casting, Stephanie Klapper; This adaptation had its world premiere at Vermont Stage Company in Burlington, Vermont, as part of the Catherine Filene Shouse New Play Series; February 28–March 15, 2003; Cast: Bonnie Gould (Sibyl Danforth), Christina Apathy (Connie Danforth); Amy Hubbard (Charlotte Bedford); Connan Morrissey (Anne Austin, Lori Pine, Patty); Carol Mayo-Jenkins (Louise, Dr. Gerson, Reconstructionist); Harrison Long (Stephen Hastings); Stephen Bradbury (Bill Tanner); David Brian Alley (Asa Bedford, Physician); Tony Cedeno (David Pine, Road Crew Man, Dr. Lang, Barton Hewitt)

ROMEO AND JULIET by William Shakespeare; Directed by Paul Barnes; Assistant Director, Michael Shipley; Scenic Design, Bill Clarke; Costume Design, Bill Black; Lighting Design, John Horner; Sound Design, Mike Ponder; Choreography, Denise Gabriel; Fight Director, Scot Mann; Text/Dialect Coach, Nancy Houfek; Stage Manger, Maggie Haun; April 11–26, 2003; Cast: Rene Thornton, Jr. (Escalus, Prince of Verona); Joshua Eleazer (County Paris, Kinsman to the Prince); Charlie Effler (Mercutio, Kinsman to the Prince, friend of Romeo); James Francis (Lord Montague, Father to Romeo); Marissa Weaver (Lady Montague, Mother to Romeo); John Ulen (Romeo); John Forrest Ferguson (Lord Capulet, Father to Juliet); Lindsey Andrews (Lady Capulet, Mother to Juliet); Candace Taylor (Angelica, Nurse to Juliet); Paige Cannon (Juliet); Terry Weber (Friar Laurence, A Franciscan); Ben Srok (Friar John); Jacob Bell (Benvolio, Friend to Romeo); Casey Payne (Tybalt, Nephew to Capulet); Grant Collins (Sampson, Servingman to the Capulets); Chris Czyz (Gregory, Servingman to the Capulets); Doug James (Peter, Servant to the Capulets); Travis Flatt (Potpan, Servant to the Capulets, an Apothecary); Chris Palmer (Attendant to Escalus); Walter Hayes (Bartolomeo, Page to Tybalt); Fisher Neal (Balthasar, Page to Romeo); Josh Lay (Abram, Page to Benvolio); Ben Srok (Angelo, Page to Mercutio); Larry Williams, Jr. (Attendant to Escalus); Chris Palmer (Attendant to Escalus); Bora Ercan (Attendant to Escalus); Travis Flatt (An Apothecary); Women of Verona: Lauren Houston (Isabella); Tricia Holman (Katerina); Tara Taylor (Luciana); Sarah Campbell (Emilia)

PUMP BOYS AND DINETTES Conceived and written by John Foley, Mark Hardwick, Debra Monk, Cass Morgan, John Schimmel and Jim Wann; Original stage production by Dodger Productions; Directed by Jason Edwards, Set Design, Biff Edge; Costume Design, Amanda Jenkins; Lighting Design, John Horner; Sound Design, Mike Ponder; Stage Manager, Marta Stout; New York Casting, Stephanie Klapper; May 30–June 14, 2003 Musicians: Jason Edwards (Jim, Rhythm Guitar); Steve Rust (Eddie, Bass); Barry Tarallo (Jackson, Lead Guitar); Guy Strobel (L.M., Piano); Linda Edwards (Prudie Cupp, Percussion); Allison Briner (Rhetta Cupp, Percussion)

CLEVELAND PLAY HOUSE

Cleveland, Ohio
EIGHTY-SEVENTH SEASON

Artistic Director, Peter Hackett; Managing Director, Dean R. Gladden

TEA AT FIVE by Matthew Lombardo; Director, John Tillinger; Scene Design, Tony Straiges; Costume Design, Jess Goldstein; Lighting Design, Kevin Adams; Music and Sound Design, John Gromada; Stage Manager, Christa Bean; Assistant Stage Manager, Janine Wochna; Assistant Lighting Design, Stephen A. Brady; Bolton Theatre; August 20–September 3, 2002; Cast: Kate Mulgrew (Katharine Hepburn)

Mike Hartman, Darrie Lawrence in *On Golden Pond* PHOTO BY ROGER MASTROIANNI

LOST HIGHWAY: THE MUSIC AND LEGEND OF HANK WILLIAMS by Randal Myler and Mark Harelik; Director, Randal Myler; Scenic and Costume Design, Robert Blackman; Lighting Design, Don Darnutzer; Sound Design, Robin Heath; Stage Manager, Corrie E. Purdum; Casting, Elissa Myers, Paul Fouquet; Bolton Theatre; September 24–October 20, 2002; Cast: Jason Petty (Hank Williams), Michael Howell (Tee-Tot), Juliet Smith (The Waitress), Margaret Bowman (Mama Lilly), Stephen G. Anthony (Hoss), Myk Watford (Jimmy, Burrhead), Drew Perkins (Leon, Loudmouth), Mike Hartman (Pap), Tertia Lynch (Audry Williams), Russ Wever (Shag)

BRIGHT IDEAS by Eric Coble; Director, David Colacci; Scene and Lighting Design, Pavel Dobrusky; Costume Design, Amanda Whidden; Sound Design, Robin Heath; Stage Manager, John Godbout; Drury Theatre; October 15–November 10, 2002; Cast: Susan Ericksen (Genevra), Andrew May (Joshua), Chip DuFord (Parent #3, Steward, Mr. Angus, Ross), Kate Hodge (Parent #2, Denise, Miss Caithness, Ms. Lennox), Elizabeth Rainer (Mrs. Menteith, Mrs. Malcom, Bix the Beaver)

ON GOLDEN POND by Ernest Thompson; Director, Carol Dunne; Scene Design, Bill Clarke; Costume Design, Kristine A. Kearney; Lighting Design, Matthew Frey; Sound Design, Jonathan Erwin; Stage Manager, Corrie Purdum; Casting, Elissa Myers, Paul Fouquet; Bolton Theatre; November 12–December 8 2002; Cast: Mike Hartman (Norman Thayer, Jr.), Darrie Lawrence (Ethel Thayer); Steve McCue (Charlie Martin), Kate Levy (Chelsea Thayer Wayne), Adam Siciliano (Billie Ray), Peter Hackett (Bill Ray)

A TUNA CHRISTMAS by Jaston Williams, Joe Sears and Ed Howard; Director, William Hoffman; Scene Design, Bill Clarke; Costume Design, Kristine A. Kearney; Lighting Design, Richard Winkler; Sound Design, Robin Heath; Stage Manager, John Godbout; Drury Theatre; November 26–December 22, 2002; Cast: Chuck Richie (Thurston Wheelis, Elmer Watkins, Bertha Bumiller, R.R. Snavely, Aunt Pearl Burras, Sheriff Givens, Ike Thompson, Inita Goodwin, Leonard Childers, Pheobe Burkhalter, Joe Bob Lipsey), Dana Snyder (Arles Struvie, Didi Snavely, Jody Burmiller, Charlene Burmiller, Stanley Burmiller, Vera Carp, Dixie Deberry, Helen Bedd, Farley Burkhalter, Garland Poteet)

PROOF by David Auburn; Director, Seth Gordon; Scene Design, Michael Ganio; Costume Design, Jeffrey Van Curtis; Lighting Design, Derek Duarte; Sound Design, Robin Heath; Stage Managers, Corrie Purdum, Olivia Goldsberry; Casting, Elissa Myers, Paul Fouquet; Baxter Stage; January 7–February 2, 2003; Cast: Derdriu Ring (Catherine), Mike Hartman (Robert), Chad Willett (Hal), Carol Dunne (Claire)

CRUMBS FROM THE TABLE OF JOY by Lynn Nottage; Director, Chuck Patterson; Scene Design, Felix E. Cochren; Costume Design, Myrna Colley-Lee; Lighting Design, William H. Grant III; Sound Design, Robin Heath; Stage Manager, John Godbout; Drury Theatre; February 4–March 9, 2003; Cast: Aynna Siverls (Ernestine Crump), Zainab Jah (Ermina Crump), Terry Alexander (Godfrey Crump), Vivian Reed (Lily Ann Green), Meg Kelly Schroeder (Gerte Schulte)

Ivy Vahannian, Andrew May in Dr. Jekyll and Mr. Hyde PHOTO BY ROGER MASTROIANNI

DR. JEKYLL AND MR. HYDE Adapted by David Edgar from the novel by Robert Louis Stevenson; Director, Peter Hackett; Scene Design, Michael Ganio; Costume Design, David Kay Mickelsen; Lighting Design, Rick Paulsen; Sound Design, Robin Heath; Stage Managers, Corrie E. Purdum, Olivia Goldsberry; Casting Elissa Myers, Paul Fouquet; Composer Larry Delinger; Fight Choreographer, Ron Wilson; Bolton Theatre; February 25–April 6, 2003; Cast: Curt Karibalis (Gabriel John Utterson), Jonathan Partington (Richard Enfield, a parson), Liz DuChez (Lucy, a Maid, a Woman on the platform), Kyle Blackburn, J.P. Gagen (Charles), Anna Cody (Katharine Urquart), Ivy Vahanian (Annie Loder), Andrew May (Dr. Henry Jekyll, Edward Hyde), Lee Moore (Poole), Craig Bockhorn (Dr. Hastie Lanyon, Sir Danvers Carew), Paul Bender, Stephen D. Hood, Michael Roache (Citizens)

DIRTY BLONDE by Claudia Shear; Conceived by Claudia Shear and James Lapine; Director, Peter Hackett; Scene Design, Vicki Smith; Costume Design, David Kay Mickelsen; Lighting Design, Richard Winkler; Sound Design, Robin Heath; Music Director, Lee Stametz; Choreographer, Ron Wilson; Stage Manager, John Godbout; Casting, Elissa Myers, Paul Fouquet; Drury Theatre; April 8–May 4, 2003; Cast: Tom Frey (The Man), Elizabeth Meadows Rouse (Jo, Mae), Nick Sullivan (Charlie)

BLUE ROOM Adapted by David Hare from *La Ronde* by Arthur Schnitzler; Director, Edward Payson Call; Scene and Lighting Design, Kent Dorsey; Costume Design, Christine Dougherty; Music and Sound Design, Bruce Odland; Stage Manager, Corrie Purdum; Casting, Elissa Myers, Paul Fouquet; Baxter Stage; April 29–May 25, 2003; Cast: Bradford Cover (The Cab Driver, the Student, the Politician, the Playwright, the Millionaire), Emily Frankovich (the Girl, the Au Pair, the Married Woman, the Model, the Actress)

COURT THEATRE

Chicago, Illinois
FORTY-EIGHTH SEASON

Charles Newell, Artistic Director; Diane Claussen, Executive Director

PHÉDRE by Jean Racine; Adapted by Paul Schmidt; Directed and Further Adapted by JoAnne Akalaitis; Scenic Design, Gordana Svilar; Costume Designer, Kaye Voyce; Lighting Designer, Joel Moritz; Sound Designers, Andre Pluess and Ben Sussman; September 5–October 13, 2002; Cast:Jenny Bacon (Phèdre), De Anne N. J. Brooks (Ismene), Chaon Cross (Aricia), James Elly (Hippolytus), James Krag (Theseus), Elizabeth Laidlaw (Enone), Scott Parkinson (Theramenes), Nicole Wiesner (Panope)

SCAPIN by Molière; Adapted by Shelley Berc and Andrei Belgrader; Music and Lyrics, Rusty Magee; Director, Christopher Bayes; Musical Director, Jeff Caldwell; Choreographer, by David Silverman; Scenic Design, Michael Sommers; Costume Design, Elizabeth Caitlin Ward; Lighting Design, Diane D. Fairchild; October 24–November 24, 2002; Cast: Jeff Caldwell (Nérine), Chaon Cross (Hyacinte), Jason Denuszek (Porter), Sean Fortunato (Sylvestre), Allen Gilmore (Argante), Chester Gregory II (Octave), Kimberly Hébert-Gregory (Zerbinette), Matthew Krause (Carle, musician), Ned Noyes (Léandre), Jeremy Shamos (Scapin), David Silverman (Géronte)

JAMES JOYCE'S THE DEAD Book, Richard Nelson; Music, Shaun Davey; Lyrics conceived and adapted by Richard Nelson and Shaun Davey; Director, Charles Newell; Musical Director, Jeff Lewis; Choreographer, Mark Howard; Scenic Design, Brian Sidney Bembridge; Costume Design, Linda Roethke; Lighting Design, Joel Moritz; Sound Design, Bruce Holland; November 21–December 29, 2002; Cast: McKinley Carter (Mary Jane Morkan), Christopher Cordon (Freddy Malins), Deanna Dunagan (Julia Morkan), Neil Friedman (Mr. Browne), Rob Hancock (Michael), Sara Minton (Mrs. Malins), Christen Paige (Rita, Young Julia), John Reeger (Gabriel Conroy), Hollis Resnik (Molly Ivors), Paula Scrofano (Gretta Conroy), Ana Sferruzza (Lily), Kathy Taylor (Kate Morkan), Stephen Wallem (Bartell D'Arcy)

THE ROMANCE CYCLE; PART I: CYMBELINE, PART II: PERICLES by William Shakespeare; Directed and Adapted by Charles Newell; Scenic Designer, John Culbert; Associate Scenic Designer, Jack K. Magaw; Costume Design, Linda Roethke; Lighting Design, Michelle Habeck; Sound Designers, Joshue Horvath, Lindsay Jones and Andre Pluess; March 28–June 1, 2003; Cast: Guy Adkins (British Lord, Cornelius, Pericles), Lance Stuart Baker (Posthumus, Simonides), Kati Brazda (Helen, Cerimon), McKinley Carter (Pisanio, Thaisa), Chaon Cross (Caius Lucius, Posthumus's Mother, Marina), Will Dickerson (Cymbeline, Knight, Boult), Neil Friedman (Belarius, Frenchman, Helicanus), Kate Fry (Imogen, Dionyza), Warren Jackson (Philario, Posthumus's Father, Thaliard, Knight, Leonine), Timothy Edward Kane (Cloten, Cleon, First Fisherman, Knight), Kymberly Mellen (Queen, Antiochus's Daughter, Second Fisherman, Lychorida, Pandor), Braden Moran (Arviragus, Knight), Chuck Stubbings (Guiderius, Third Fisherman, Knight, Lysimachus), Jay Whittaker (Iachimo, Antiochus, Marshal of Pentapolis, Bawd)

David Silverman, Allen Gilmore in *Scapin* PHOTO BY MICHAEL BROSILOW

Jay Whittaker, Kate Fry, members of the Company of *The Romance Cycle*
PHOTO BY MICHAEL BROSILOW

DALLAS THEATER CENTER

Kalita Humphreys Theater and Arts District Theater

Dallas, Texas
FORTY-FOURTH SEASON

Artistic Director, Richard Hamburger; Peter Culman, Consulting Managing Director; Mark Hadley, Interim Managing Director

OF MICE AND MEN by John Steinbeck; Director, Richard Hamburger; Scenic Design, John Coyne: Costume Design, Miguel Angel Huidor; Lighting Design, Marcus Doshi; Sound Design, Fitz Patton; Stage Manager, M. William Shiner; September 4–29, 2002; Cast: Adam Bartley (Whit), Brett Bock (Carlson), Dane Knell (Candy), Stanley Wayne Mathis (Crooks), Derek Phillips (Curley), Robert Prentiss (Slim), Sean Runnette (Lennie), Jerry Russell (The Boss), Lorca Simons (Curley's wife), Todd Weeks (George)

BE AGGRESSIVE by Annie Weisman; Director, Claudia Zelevansky; Scenic Designer, Alexander Dodge; Costume Designer, Linda Cho; Lighting Designer, Matthew Richards; Sound Designer, Geoff Zink; Stage Manager, Terry Tittle Holman; Cheer Consultant, Joel Ferrell; Dramaturg, Allison Horsley; October 16–November 10, 2002; Cast: Camille Bulliard (Cheer Chorus), Laura Heisler (Hannah), Lisa Lloyd (Cheer Chorus), Ali Marsh (Laura), Howard Pinhasik (Phil), Elizabeth Rothan (Judy), Jeanine Serralles (Leslie), Laurel Whitsett (Cheer Chorus)

A CHRISTMAS CAROL by Charles Dickens, adapted by Preston Lane and Jonathan Moscone; Director, Jenny Lord; Set Designer, Narelle Sissons; Costume Designer, Katherine B. Roth; Lighting Designer, Marcus Doshi: Sound Designer, Bruce Richardson; Choreographer, David Shimotakahara; Pianist/Musical Director, Jeff Lankov; Composer (original music) Kim Sherman; Stage Manager, M.William Shiner; November 29–December 29, 2003; Cast: Akin Babtunde (Marley, Mr. Fezziwig, Ensemble), Laurie Bulaoro (Lily, Charitable Woman, Ensemble), Joel Ferrell (Charitable Man, Dick Wilkins, Topper, Ensemble), Bob Hess (Bob Cratchit, Joe, Ensemble), Rick Leal (Fred, Ensemble), Lisa Lloyd (Fan, Debtor's Wife, Ensemble), Liz Mikel (Christmas Present, Mrs. Fezziwig, Ensemble), Thomas Penn (Young Scrooge, Debtor, Ensemble), Elizabeth Rothman (Mrs. Cratchit, Cynthia, Ensemble), Michael Rodko (Scrooge), Jessica Turner (Belle, Ensemble), Julie Williams (CharitableWoman, Ensemble)

THE REAL THING by Tom Stoppard; Director, Stan Wojewodski, Jr.: Set Designer, John Coyne, Costume Designer, Linda Fisher; Lighting Designer, Stephen Strawbridge; Composer/Sound Design, Bruce Richardson; Dramaturg, Allison Horsley; Vocal Coach, Barbara Sommerville; Stage Manager, M. William Shiner; January 15–February 9, 2003; Cast: James Crawford (Max), Julia Gibson (Charlotte), Chuck Huber (Brodie), Martin Kildare (Henry), Katie MacNichol (Annie), Daniel Magill (Billy), Shanna Riddle (Debbie)

BIG LOVE by Charles Mee; Director, Richard Hamburger; Costume Designer, Linda Cho; Scenic Designers, Office for Metropolitan Architecture, Amale Andraos, Dan Wood, Rem Koolhaas, Associate Scenic Designer, Alexander Dodge: Lighting Designer, Marcus Doshi; Sound Designer, David Budries; Fight Director, Colleen Kelly; Dramaturg, Allison Horsley; Stage Manager, M. William Shiner; February 26–March 23, 2003; Cast: Remy Auberjonois (Nikos), Franca Barchiesi (Bella, Elanor), Mark Alan Gordon (Piero, Leo), Adrian LaTourelle (Constantine), Miriam A. Laube (Lydia), Markus Lloyd (Oed), Kate Nowlin (Thyona), Lorca Simons (Olympia), Daniel Talbott (Giuliano), Ensemble: Jennifer Bronstein, Benjamin Lutz, Brian J. Smith, Melody Stacy.

FULLY COMMITTED by Becky Mode; Director, Daniel Goldstein; Scenic Designer, James Noone; Costume, Barbara Hicks; Lighting Designer, Frances Aronson; Sound Designer, Zach Moore; Stage Manager, Andrew D. Haver; April 9–May 4, 2003; Cast: Ethan Sandler (Sam Peliczowski) (And all other 36 characters).

Adam Justin Dietrich, Liz Mikel, Sonny Franks, Tom Key, B. Hayden Oliver in *Cotton Patch Gospel* PHOTO BY LINDA BLASE/SUELLEN FITSIMMONS

COTTON PATCH GOSPEL by Tom Key and Russell Treyz; Director/Choreographer, Joel Ferrell; Musical Director, M. Michael Fauss; Scenic Designer, Peter Hicks; Costume Designer, Barbara Hicks; Sound Designer, Ryan Mansfield; Co-Author, Russell Treyz; Composer/Lyricist, Harry Chapin; Dramaturg, Allison Horsley; Stage Manager, M. William Shiner; April 22–May 25, 2003; Cast: Keron L. Jackson (Soloist, Ensemble); Tom Key (Matthew and others); Liz Mikel (Soloist, Ensemble); Musician/Ensemble: Adam Justin Dietrich, Sonny Franks, George Merritt, B. Hayden Oliver, Willy Welch

GEORGIA SHAKESPEARE FESTIVAL

Atlanta, Georgia
SEVENTEENTH SEASON

Producing Artistic Director, Richard Garner; Managing Director, Philip J. Santora; Education Director, Kathleen McManus

TWO GENTLEMEN OF VERONA by William Shakespeare; Director, Tim Ocel; Set/Costume Design, B. Modern; Lighting Design, Ken Yunker; Sound Design, Brian Kettler; Vocal Director, Michael Monroe; Choreographer, Troy Inman; Dramaturg, Alice Benston; June 14–August 11, 2002; Cast: Hudson Adams (Eglamour, Ensemble), Janice Akers (Lucetta), Cynthia Barrett (Julia), Rob Cleveland (Speed), Scott Cowart (Outlaw, Ensemble), Jessie Dougherty (Woman, Ensemble), Evan Enderle (Outlaw, Ensemble), Chris Ensweiler (Thurio, Ensemble), Bruce Evers (Host, Antonio), Tommy Gomez (Launce), Chris Kayser (Duke), Joe Knezevich (Outlaw, Ensemble), Park Krausen (Sylvia), Daniel May (Valentine), Nathan Crocker (Outlaw, Ensemble), Allen O'Reilly (Panthino, Ensemble), Gamal Palmer (Outlaw, Ensemble), Brad Sherrill (Proteus)

DEATH OF A SALESMAN by Arthur Miller; Director, Vincent Murphy; Set/Costume Design, Lesley Taylor; Lighting Design, Mike Post; Sound Design, Brian Kettler; Dramaturg, Walter Bilderback; June 28–August 9, 2002; Cast: Hudson Adams (Stanley), Janice Akers (Linda Loman), Cynthia Barrett (Miss Forsyth), Carolyn Cook (The Woman), Jessie Dougherty (Jenny), Evan Enderle (Waiter), Chris Ensweiler (Bernard), Tommy Gomez (Charley), Chris Kayser (Ben), Park Krausen (Letta), Daniel May (Biff Loman), Tim McDonough (Willy Loman), Allen O'Reilly (Howard), Brad Sherrill (Happy)

MERRY WIVES OF WINDSOR by William Shakespeare; Director, Tom Markus; Set Design, Joe Varga; Lighting Design, Mike Post; Costume Design, Sydney Roberts; Sound Design, Brian Kettler; Dramaturg, Bob Hornblack; July 12–August 10, 2002; Cast: Hudson Adams (Mr. Page), Janice Akers (Mrs. Page), Damon Boggess (Simple), Rob Cleveland (Bardolf), Carolyn Cook (Mrs. Ford), Scott Cowart (Slender), Teresa DeBerry (Mistress Quickly), Jessie Dougherty (Ensemble), Evan Enderle (Town Crier), Chris Ensweiler (Dr. Caius), Bruce Evers (Falstaff), Tommy Gomez (Pistol), Chris Kayser (Mr. Ford), Joe Knezevich (Nym), Park Krausen (Ann Page), Daniel May (Rugby), Tim McDonough (Shallow), Nathan Crocker (Robert), Aidan O'Reilly (Walter), Allen O'Reilly (Hugh Evans), Evan O'Reilly (Robin), Gamal Palmer (John), Brad Sherrill (Fenton), Al Stilo (Host)

THE TAMING OF THE SHREW by William Shakespeare; Director, Richard Garner; Set Design, Kat Conley; Lighting Design, Mike Post; Costume Design, Sydney Roberts; October 11–November 3, 2002; Cast: Jen Apgar (Bianca), Damon Boggess (Hortensio) Jonathan Davis (Grumio), Chris Ensweiler (Pedant, Haberdasher), Bruce Evers (Baptista, Sugarsop), Joe Knezevich (Biondello, Curtis), Daniel May (Lucentio), Michele McCullough (Widow, Tailor), Allen O'Reilly (Gremio, Nathaniel, Vincentio), Saxon Palmer (Petruchio), Daniel Pettrow (Tranio), Gabra Zackman (Kate)

Janice Akers, Tim McDonough in *Death of a Salesman* PHOTO BY TOM MEYER

Daniel May, Taylor Dooley, Damon Boggess in *The Taming of the Shrew* PHOTO BY TOM MEYER

GEVA THEATRE CENTER

Rochester, New York
THIRTIETH SEASON

Mark Cuddy, Artistic Director; John Quinlivan, Managing Director; Nan Hildebrandt, Executive Director

COOKIN' AT THE COOKERY: THE MUSIC AND TIMES OF ALBERTA HUNTER Written and Directed by Marion J. Caffey; Musical Supervision and Arrangements, Danny Holgate; Musical Director, George Caldwell; Scenic and Lighting Design, Dale Jordan; Costume Design, Marilyn A. Wall; Sound Design, Josh Navarro; Casting Consultants, Elissa Meyers and Paul Fouquet; Stage Manager, Kirsten Brannen; Assistant Stage Manager, Joel Markus; Dance Captain, Debra Walton; Mainstage; September 3–October 6, 2002; Cast: Ann Duquesnay (Alberta Hunter), Debra Walton (Narrator) Band: George Caldwell (Musical Director, Keyboard), Joe Battaglia (Guitar), Rodney Harper (Percussion), Cliff Kellem (Bass) Understudy: LaVon Fisher (Alberta Hunter, Narrator)

PROOF by David Auburn; Director, Mark Cuddy; Scenic Design, Scott Bradley; Costume Design, B. Modern; Lighting Design, Kirk Bookman; Music Composer, Gregg Coffin; Sound Associate, Dan Roach; Casting, Elissa Meyers and Paul Fouquet; Stage Manager, Joel Markus; Assistant Stage Manager, Kirsten Brannen; Mainstage; October 15–November 17, 2002; Cast: Maria Dizzia (Catherine), Greg Mullavey (Robert), Courtney Peterson (Claire), Peter Smith (Hal)

BILLY BISHOP GOES TO WAR Written and Composed by John Gray in collaboration with Eric Peterson; Director, Christopher Gurr; Scenic Design, Gary Jacobs; Costume Design, B. Modern; Lighting Design, Marcus Doshi; Sound Design, Dan Roach; Dramaturg, April Donahower; Stage Manager, Frank Cavallo; The Nextstage; November 12–December 8, 2002; Cast: Richard Todd Adams (Billy Bishop, Piano Player), Tom Frey (Billy Bishop, Piano Player)

A CHRISTMAS CAROL by Charles Dickens; Adaptor, Richard Hellesen; Music and Lyrics, David de Berry; Director, Mark Booher; Scenic Design, Ramsey Avery; Costume Design, B. Modern; Lighting Design, Kendall Smith; Music Direction, Gregg Coffin; Choreography, Meggins Kelley; Assistant Director, Suzanne Tyler; Assistant Lighting Design, Derek Madonia; Sound Associate, Dan Roach; Stage Manager, Kirsten Brannen; Assistant Stage Manager, Joel Markus; Casting, Elissa Meyers and Paul Fouquet; Dance Captain, Kerry Neel; Mainstage; November 29–December 29, 2002; Cast: Trevor Bachman (Turkey Boy, Ignorance, Schoolboy), Guy Bannerman (Subscription Gentleman, Mr. Fezziwig, Belle's Husband, Guest), Stephanie Benkert (Baker's Helper, Book Vendor), Teressa Byrne (Maid, Parent, Miss Fezziwig, Sister-in-Law, Charwoman), Mitchell Canfield (Ebenezer the Child, Edward Cratchit), Devin Dunne Cannon (Longsong Seller, Miss Fezziwig), Robin Chadwick (Ebenezer Scrooge), Jenna Cole (Mrs. Cratchit, Ghost of Christmas Past), Julia Ann Devine (Fan, Rich Girl), Matthew Erickson (Labourer, Schoolboy, Suitor, Delivery Boy), John Gardiner (Tailor, Parent, Italian Teacher, Ebenezer the Young Man), Katie Germano (Belinda Cratchit, Schoolboy, Belle's Daughter), Lauren Gilray (Baker's Helper, Book Vendor), Jamey Hood (Maid, Parent, Belle, Martha Cratchit), Rebecca Elizabeth Isenhart (Fan, Rich Girl), Brett Jones (Ebenezer the Child, Edward Cratchit), Collin Jones (Turkey Boy, Ignorance, Schoolboy), Robert B. Kennedy (Marley, Old Joe, Beer Seller), Allison Lynch (Beggar Child, Schoolboy, Sleigh Puller), Stephen Muterspaugh (Labourer, Schoolboy, Ebenezer the Apprentice, Peter Cratchit), Kerry Neel (Fred's Wife, Maid, Parent, Miss Fezziwig, Laundress, Dance Captain), David Nevell (Fred, Labourer, Parent, Dick Wilkins, Undertaker's Man), Melinda Parrett (Tailor's Wife, Mrs. Fezziwig, Belle the Matron, Guest), Rebecca Rand (Want, Schoolboy, Grocer's Kid), Adam Rath (Labourer, Schoolboy, Suitor, Wreath Seller), Kathryn Rebholz (Belinda Cratchit, Schoolboy, Belle's Daughter), Brian Runbeck (Bob Cratchit, Fiddler), Giannina Spano (Want, Schoolboy), Aaron Sperber (Beggar Child, Schoolboy, Sleigh Puller), Erik Stein (Ghost of Christmas Present, Subscription Gentleman, Baker, Parent), René Thornton, Jr. (Topper, Labourer, Clerk, Ghost of Christmas Yet to Come), Carolyn Ruth Vernon (Tiny Tim, Schoolboy), Rachel Wallace (Longsong Seller, Miss Fezziwig), Allie Waxman (Tiny Tim, Schoolboy)

BRIGHTON BEACH MEMOIRS by Neil Simon; Director, Tim Ocel; Scenic Design, Erhard Rom; Costume Design, B. Modern; Lighting Design, Kendall Smith; Sound Associate, Dan Roach; Stage Manager, Joel Markus; Assistant Stage Manager, Kirsten Brannen; Dramaturg, Marge Betley; Casting, Elissa Meyers and Paul Fouquet; Mainstage; January 7–February 9, 2003; Cast: Dana Powers Acheson (Nora), Kathleen Burke (Laurie), Mitchell Greenberg (Jack), Bryant Richards (Stanley), Barbara Sims (Blanche), Dennis Staroselsky (Eugene)

MEET ME INCOGNITO by James Still; Director/Musical Director/Composer/Choreographer, Christopher Gurr; Scenic Design, Gary Jacobs; Costume Design, Amanda Doherty; Lighting Design, Derek Madonia; Sound Design, Dan Roach; Stage Manager, Alison Eastwood; Big Theatre for Little People; January 21–February 2; Cast: Matthew Erickson, Jamey Hood, Anita Loomis, Nicole Mangi, Stephen Muterspaugh

36 VIEWS by Naomi Iizuka; Director, Chay Yew; Scenic Design, Daniel Ostling; Costume Design, Lydia Tanji; Lighting Design, Mary Louise Geiger; Composer, Nathan Wang; Sound Associate, Dan Roach; Stage Manager, Kirsten Brannen; Assistant Stage Manger, Joel Markus; Casting, Elissa Meyers and Paul Fouquet; Mainstage; February 18–March 23, 2003; Cast: Elisabeth Adwin (Elizabeth Newman-Orr), Melody Butiu (Claire Tsong), Harry Carnahan (Darius Wheeler), Maile Holck (Setsuko Hearn), Gregory Patrick Jackson (John Bell), Alan Nebelthau (Owen Matthiassen)

LOBBY HERO by Kenneth Lonergan; Director, Skip Greer; Scenic Design, Rob Koharchik; Costume Design, Amanda Doherty; Lighting Design, Kendall Smith; Sound Design, Dan Roach; Assistant Director, Joanna Schmitt; Casting, Elissa Meyers and Paul Fouquet; Stage Manager, Frank Cavallo; The Nextstage; March 18–April 13, 2003; Cast: Morgan Davis (Dawn), Rodney Hicks (William), Lucas Papaelias (Jeff), Coleman Zeigen (Bill)

THEOPHILUS NORTH by Matthew Burnett; Director, Mark Cuddy; Scenic and Costume Design, G.W. Mercier; Lighting Design, Ann G. Wrightson; Composer, Gregg Coffin; Choreographer, Terry Berliner; Dramaturg, Marge Betley; Casting, Elissa Meyers and Paul Fouquet; Stage Manager, Joel Markus; Assistant Stage Manager, Kirsten Brannen; Mainstage; April 1–May 4, 2003; Cast: Edward James Hyland (Father, Josiah Dexter, Herman Augustus Bell, Dr. James Bosworth, Ensemble), Michael Laurino (Bill Wentworth, Charles Fenwick, George Granberry, Ensemble), Valerie Leonard (Hannah, Millicent Fenwick, Myra Granberry, Mrs. Sarah Bosworth, Ensemble), Siobhán Mahoney (Eloise Fenwick, Diana Bell, Ensemble, through April 9), Ari Meyers (Eloise Fenwick, Diana Bell, Ensemble, April 10 through close), Matthew Floyd Miller (Theophilus North), Andrew Polk (Henry Simmons, Hilary Jones, Willis, Ensemble), Lynn Stenmetz (Mother, Mrs. Cranston, Cora Cummings, Ensemble)

PANADERO: THE BAKER'S TALE by José Cruz González; Director, Graham Whitehead; Scenic Design, Edie Whitsett; Puppet Design, Douglas N. Paasch; Costume Design, Rebecca Akins; Lighting Design, Derek Madonia; Composer, Zarco Guerrero; Sound Design, Benjamin Monrad; Stage Manager, Catharine Shappell; Big Theatre for Little People; April 29–May 11, 2003; Cast: Carlton Franklin (Panadero, Modesto, Commandante Boots, Tirado, God of Lightning, El Sol), Jeff Goodman (Pepito), Christina Romano (Abuela, Madre, Ridiculo, Little Girl, Footsteps, Sergeant Boots, Arm, Nose, Eye, Luna, Baby Manatee, Great Sea Tortuga)

1776: AMERICA'S PRIZE WINNING MUSICAL Music and Lyrics by Sherman Edwards; Book, Peter Stone; Director, Mark Cuddy; Scenic and Costume Design, G.W. Mercier; Lighting Design, Phil Monat; Sound Design, Lindsay Jones; Musical Director, Don Kot; Musical Sequences, Gregg Coffin; Assistant Director, Dawn Naser; Production Dramaturg, Jean Gordon Ryon; Casting, Elissa Meyers and Paul Fouquet; Stage Manager, Kirsten Brannen; Assistant Stage Manager, Joel Markus; Mainstage; May 14–July 6, 2003; Cast: John Bolton (Richard Henry Lee), Brigid Brady (Abigail Adams), James Brennan (John Adams), Lance Bryant (Leather Apron), Greg Byrne (Caesar Rodney), Mario Cabrera (Rev. John Witherspoon), Chet Carlin (Andrew McNair), Brian Clickner (James Wilson), Steve Covey (Lewis Morris), Dick Decareau (Robert Livingston), Bill DeMetsenaere (George Read), Matthew Erickson (Courier), Skip Greer (John Hancock), Christopher Gurr (Edward Rutledge), Ken Harrington (Dr. Josaiah Bartlett), Munson Hicks (Col. Thomas McKean), Jens Hinrichsen (Dr. Lyman Hall), Liam Kaas-Lentz (Painter), Lew Lloyd (Samuel Chase), Jeffrey Alan Miller (Joseph Hewes), Crista Moore (Martha Jefferson), Tim Ocel (Charles Thomson), Remi Sandri (John Dickinson), David Silberman (Ben Franklin), Dick St. George (Stephen Hopkins), Jeff Williams (Roger Sherman), Steve Wilson (Thomas Jefferson)

SEPTEMBER SHOES by José Cruz González; Director, Michael John Garcés; Scenic Design, Troy Hourie; Costume Design, Meghan Healey; Lighting Design, Kirk Bookman; Sound Design, Rob Kaplowitz; Assistant Director, Evan Cummings; Casting, Elissa Meyers and Paul Fouquet; Stage Manager, Joel Markus; The Nextstage; June 3–22, 2003; Cast: David Anzuelo (Huilo), Maria Elena Ramirez (Gail), Socorro Santiago (Cuki, Lily Chu), Jaime Tirelli (Alberto), Alicia Velez (Ana)

HUNTINGTON THEATRE COMPANY

In residence at Boston University
Boston, Massachusetts
SIXTEENTH SEASON

Managing Director, Michael Maso; Artistic Director, Nicholas Martin; General Manager, Jill Pearson, Production Manager, Todd Williams

A MONTH IN THE COUNTRY adapted by Brian Friel, from Ivan Turgenev; Director, Nicholas Martin; Scenic Design, Alexander Dodge; Costume Design, Michael Krass; Lighting Design, Jeff Croiter; Sound Design, Jerry Yager; Casting Director, James Calleri; Production Stage Manager, Kelley Kirkpatrick; Stage Manager, David H. Lurie; Stage Manager, Tiffany N. Thetard September 6–October 6, 2002; Cast: Mark Setlock (Herr Schaaf), Melinda Lopez (Lizaveta Bogdanovna), Alice Duffy (Anna Islayeva), Jennifer Van Dyck (Natalya Petrovna), Stacy Fischer (Katya), James Joseph O'Neil (Michel Rakitin), Ben Fox (Aleksey Belyayev), Barlow Adamson (Matvey), Jeremiah Kissel (Ignaty Shpigelsky), Jessica Dickey (Vera Aleksandrovna), Tom Bloom (Arkady Islayev), Tom Lacy (Afanasy Bolshintsov)

MARTY Book by Rupert Holmes; Music by Charles Strouse; Lyrics by Lee Adams; Based on the screenplay by Paddy Chayefsky and on the United Artists film; Director, Mark Brokaw; Choreography, Rob Ashford; Musical Director, Eric Stern; Orchestrations, Don Sebesky and Larry Hochman; Scenic Design, Robert Jones; Costume Design, Jess Goldstein; Lighting Design, Mark McCullough; Sound Design, Kurt Eric Fischer; Casting Director, Tara Rubin; Production Stage Manager, James FitzSimmons; Stage Manager, Thomas M. Kauffman; World premiere; October 18–November 24; Cast: John C. Reilly (Marty), Cheryl McMahon (Mrs. Fusari), Jim Bracchitta (Angie), Alexander Gemignani (Tilio, Bandleader), Marilyn Pasekoff (Aunt Catherine), Jennifer Frankel (Virginia), Evan Pappas (Thomas), Frank Aronson (Patsy), Joey Sorge (Joe), Robert Montano (Ralph), Matt Ramsey (Leo), Tim Douglas (Bartender), Michael Allosso (Father DiBlasio), Barbara Andres (Mrs. Pilletti), Kate Middleton (Mary Feeney), Anne Torsiglieri (Clara), Michael Walker (Mr. Ryan), Tim Douglas (Andy), Kent French (Keegan), Shannon Hammons (Rita), Jim Augustine, Bethany J. Cassidy (Dance hall patrons)

THE BLUE DEMON Written and Directed by Darko Tresnjak; Music by Michael Friedman; Scenic Design, David P. Gordon; Costume Design, Linda Cho; Lighting Design, Rui Rita; Sound Design, Kurt Kellenberger; Casting Director, James Calleri; Production Stage Manager, Thomas M. Kauffman; Stage Manager, David H. Lurie; World premiere; January 3–February 2, 2003

THE HUNCHBACK'S TALE Cast: Roxanna Hope (Scheherazade), Darius de Haas (Jeweler), Tom Titone (Tailor), Matt Ramsey (Scrivener), Kirk McDonald (Jester), Gregory Derelian (Sultan), Paul Cortez (Executioner), Mehera Blum, Lauren Hatcher, Mariessa Portelance (Three Concubines), Michael Cohen, Sean-Michael Hodge-Bowles, Ben Sands (Three Imperial Guards), Gabriel Boyers, Gunnard Dobozé, Kareem Roustom, Mike Wiese (Four Musicians)

THE TAILOR'S TALE Cast: Brian Sgambati (Husband), Anna Belknap (Wife), Tom Flynn (Wizard), Kirk McDonald (Servant), Mehera Blum, Lauren Hatcher, Mariessa Portelance (Three Rabbis), Dara Fisher (Sultan of Akra)

THE SCRIVENER'S TALE Cast: Tom Flynn (King), Brian Sgambati (Prince), Matt Ramsey (Chancellor), Anna Belknap (Princess), Paul Cortez (Puppeteer), Dara Fisher (Witch), Mehera Blum, Lauren Hatcher, Mariessa Portelance (Three Mourners)

THE JEWELER'S TALE Cast: Brian Sgambati (Beggar), Mehera Blum, Lauren Hatcher, Mariessa Portelance (Three Virgins), Kirk McDonald (Peddler), Tom Flynn (Old Sultan), Dara Fisher (Vizier), Anna Belknap (Last Virgin)

BREATH, BOOM by Kia Corthron; Directed by Michael John Garcés; Scenic Design, Adam Stockhausen; Costume Design, Karen Perry; Lighting Design, Kirk Bookman, Sound Design and Original Music, Martin Desjardins; Fight Director, Rick Sordelet; Casting Director, James Calleri; Production Stage Manager, Thomas M. Kauffman; Stage Manager David H. Lurie March 7–April 6; Cast: Kellee Stewart (Prix), Zabryna Guevara (Angel), Carla J. Hargrove (Malika), Dwandra Nickole (Comet), Edwin Lee Gibson (Jerome), Jacqui Parker (Mother), Tawanna Benbow (Cat), Katrina Toshiko (Fuego), Chinasa Ogbuagu (Shondra), Jan Leslie Harding (Denise), Tawanna Benbow (Girl), Chinasa Ogbuagu (Pepper), Ramona Alexander (Jupiter), Carla J. Hargrove (Jo), Katrina Toshiko (Jo's Friend), Carla J. Hargrove (Fight Captain)

SPRINGTIME FOR HENRY by Benn Levy; Directed by Nicholas Martin; Scenic Design, James Noone; Costume Design, Michael Krass; Lighting Design, David Weiner; Sound Design, Kurt Kellenberger; Casting Director, James Calleri; Production Stage Manager, Stephen M. Kaus; Stage Manager, David H. Lurie; Stage Manager, Laura J. MacNeil May 16–June 15; Cast: Christopher Fitzgerald, Jessica Stone, Jeremy Shamos, Mia Barron

Marco Verna, Larry McCauley in *Over the River and Through the Woods*

ILLINOIS THEATRE CENTER

Park Forest, Illinois
TWENTY-SEVENTH SEASON

Etel Billig, Producing Director; Jonathan R. Billig, Associate Producer; James Corey. Production Manager; Howard Hahn, Business Manager; Alexandra Murdoch, Administrative Associate; Tony Mendoza, Artistic Associate.

BUS STOP by William Inge; Directed by Etel Billig; September 27–October 13, 2002; Cast: Shan Goodsell, Daren Dusenske, Mary Mulligan, Gary Rayppy, Christopher Merrill, Katie Kneeland, Sam Nykaza-Jones, Steve Misetic

OVER THE RIVER AND THROUGH THE WOODS by Joe Dipietro; Directed by Judy Rossignuolo-Rice; November 1–17, 2002; Cast: Marco Verna, Larry McCauley, Diane Dorsey, Etel Billig, M. Nunzio Cancilla, Katie Kneeland

Mary Mulligan, Lolly Trauscht in *Stevie*

BEGUILED AGAIN: THE SONGS OF RODGERS & HART Directed by Pete Thelen; December 6–22, 2002; Cast: Tim Resash, Carmen Severino, John B. Boss, Makeba Pace, Daren Dusenske, Regina Leslie

ANCESTRAL VOICES by A.R. Gurney; Directed by Etel Billig & Tony Mendoza; January 10–26, 2003; Cast: Robin Trevino, Bernard Rice, Judy Rossignuolo-Rice, Gary Rayppy, Etel Billig

MASTER HAROLD...AND THE BOYS by Athol Fugard; Directed by Etel Billig; February 14–March 2, 2003; Cast: Charles Glenn, Ansa Akyea, Joe Binder

STEVIE by Hugh Whitemore; Directed by David Perkovich; March 21–April 6, 2003; Cast: Mary Mulligan, Lolly Trauscht, David Perkovich

QUILTERS by Molly Newman and Barbara Damashek; Directed by Etel Billig; April 25–May 11, 2003; Cast: Laura Whyte, Dawn DeVries, Mary Jane Guymon, Siobhan Sullivan, Allison Weiss, Regina Leslie, Maria Barwegen.

The Company of *Quilters*

LA JOLLA PLAYHOUSE

La Jolla, California
TWENTIETH SEASON

Artistic Director, Des McAnuff; Managing Director, Terrence Dwyer; Associate Artistic Director, Shirley Fishman

TARTUFFE by Molière; English verse by Richard Wilbur; Director, Des McAnuff; Scenic Design, Robert Brill; Costume Design, Jess Goldstein; Lighting Design, Chris Parry; Sound Design, Robbin E. Broad; May 14–June 16, 2002; Cast: Jonathan Adams (Cléante), Nadia Bowers (Mariane), Paget Brewster (Dorine), John Campion (Madame Pernelle), Mike Genovese (Monsieur Loyal), John Getz (Orgon), Michael Keyloun (Laurent), Dikla Marshall (Flipote), Jefferson Mays (Tartuffe), David McMahon, Alex Smith, John Staley (Police Officers and servants), Jim Parsons (Valère), Klea Scott (Elmire), Jimmi Simpson (Damis)

FEAST OF FOOLS by Geoff Hoyle; Original Music, Gina Leishman; Director, Richard Seyd; Scenic Design, Patrick Larsen; Costume Design, Mary Larson; Lighting Design, David Lee Cuthbert; June 11–July 14, 2002; Cast: Geoff Hoyle (The Fool), Gina Leishman (The Musician)

WHEN GRACE COMES IN by Heather McDonald; Director, Sharon Ott; Scenic Design, Daniel Ostling; Costume Design, Frances Kenny; Lighting Design, Michael Chybowski; Original Music & Sound Design, David Van Tieghem; World Premiere; July 30–September 1, 2002; Cast: Jane Beard (Margaret Grace Braxton), Tommy Fleming (Claw Braxton), Mary Frances McClay (Doune Braxton), Shannon Fitzpatrick (Halley Braxton), Mark Alan Gordon (Simon, Paleontologist, Fabrizio Nacarelli), Mark Chamberlin (Senator Bill Braxton), Stephanie Berry (Roz Lapinski), Anne Gee Byrd (Belle, The Italian Restorer)

WINTERTIME by Charles L. Mee; Director, Les Waters; Scenic Design, Annie Smart; Costume Design, Christal Weatherly; Lighting Design, Robert Wierzel; Sound Design, Matthew Spiro; Movement, Jean Isaacs; World premiere; August 13–September 15, 2002; Cast: Emily Donahoe (Ariel), Daoud Heidami (Jonathan), Randy Danson (Maria), François Giroday (François), Nicholas Hormann (Frank), Tom Nelis (Edmund), Lauren Klein (Bertha), Lola Pashalinski (Hilda), Bruce McKenzie (Bob), Michi Barall (Dr. Jacqueline Benoit)

I THINK I LIKE GIRLS Written and Directed by Leigh Fondakowski; Scenic Design, Ryan Palmer; Costume Design, Liam O'Brien; Lighting Design, David Lee Cuthbert; Sound and Video Design, Casi Pacilio; Additional Music, Jana Losey; Movement, Jean Isaacs; Additional Movement, Sarah Crowell; Page to Stage Project; September 3–21, 2002; Cast: Zina Camblin (Chanel, Nkeka, Rochelli), Kathleen Mary Carthy (Colleen, Laura, Melissa), Dikla Marshall (Interviewer), Barbara Pitts (Mom, Dad, Mary, Kate, Carla, Anne), Amy Resnick (Jen, Sis, Zackie, Becky, Spider), Kelli Simpkins (Daphne, Adrianne, Terrie)

ADORATION OF THE OLD WOMAN by José Rivera; Director, Jo Bonney; Scenic Design, Neil Patel; Costume Design, Emilio Sosa; Lighting Design, Chris Akerlind; Sound Design, Darron West; World Premiere; September 17–October 20, 2002; Cast: Marisol Padilla Sanchez (Adoracion), Ivonne Coll (Doña Belen), Tamara Mello (Vanessa), Gary Perez (Ismael), John Ortiz (Cheo)

PETER & WENDY from the novel by J.M. Barrie; Adapted and Produced by Liza Lorwin; Designed by Julie Archer; Music by Johnny Cunningham; Director, Lee Breuer; Costumes, Sally Thomas; Sound Design, Edward Cosla; Associate Light Design, Steven L. Shelley; Fight Direction, B.H. Barry; Film Direction, Andrew Moore; Additional Puppetry Direction, Basil Twist, Jane Catherine Shaw; Lyrics, Johnny Cunningham, J.M. Barrie, Lee Breuer, Liza Lorwin; September 27–November 10, 2002; Cast: Karen Kandel (Narrator), Basil Twist with Sharon Provost, Sam Hack (Peter), Jane Catherine Shaw with Jenny Subjack, Lute Breuer (Hook), Sam Hack also Jane Catherine Shaw, Jessica Chandlee Smith, Sarah Provost, Jenny Subjack (Nana), Jane Catherine Shaw with Jenny Subjack, Jessica Chandlee Smith (Jane), Jane Catherine Shaw (Peter's Shadow), Sarah Provost with Jessica Chandlee Smith (Smee), Jessica Chandlee Smith (The Neverbird), Preston Foerder (Puppeteer Understudy), Johnny Cunningham (Fiddle, Vocals), Lisa Moscatiello (Singer), Jay Ansil (Celtic Harp, Guitar), Mirella Murray (Accordian), Susan Craig Winsberg (Flutes), Jay Peck (Percussion, Live Sound Effects)

Jefferson Mays, members of the Company of *Tartuffe* PHOTO BY KEN HOWARD

Bernie Sheredy, Erika Thomas in *Fallen* PHOTO BY DAVID A. ROGERS

Frank Deal, Angela Reed in *Women Who Steal* PHOTO BY DAVID A. ROGERS

Baylen Thomas, Elisabeth S. Rogers in *The Pavillion* PHOTO BY DAVID A. ROGERS

MERRIMACK REPERTORY THEATRE

Lowell, Massachusetts
TWENTY-FOURTH SEASON

Artistic Director, Charles Towers; Managing Director, Lisa Merrill-Burzak

FALLEN by Craig Warner; Director, Charles Towers; Scenic Designer, Bill Clarke; Costume Designer, Deborah Newhall; Lighting Designer, Dan Kotlowitz; World Premiere; September 6–September 29, 2002; Cast: Christopher McHale (Jim), Monique Fowler (Georgie), Erika Thomas (Hannah), Alexander Pascal (Pascal), Angela Bullock (Selina), Bernie Sheredy (Billy)

THE WOMAN IN BLACK by Stephen Mallatratt; Director, Charles Towers; Scenic Designer, John McDermott; Costume Designer, Gordon DeVinney; Lighting Designer, John Ambrosone; Sound Designer, Ben Emerson; October 11–November 3, 2002; Cast: Philip Pleasants (Actor), Harry Carnahan (Kipps), Liz Robbins (The Woman)

SANDERS FAMILY CHRISTMAS Written by Connie Ray; Conceived by Alan Bailey; Musical Arrangements, John Foley and Gary Fagin; Director, Alan Bailey; Scenic Designer, Peter Harrison; Costume Designer, Jeanette deJong; Lighting Designer, Tayva Pew; November 29–December 22, 2002; Cast: Robert Olsen (Mervin Oglethorpe), Tess Hartman (June Sanders), Bobby Taylor (Burl Sanders), Angela Brinton (Denise Sanders), B. Hayden Oliver (Dennis Sanders), Jo Ann Cunningham (Vera Sanders), Jason Edwards (Stanley Sanders)

OLD WICKED SONGS by Jon Marans; Director, Martin L. Platt; Scenic/Costume Designer, Bill Clarke; Lighting Designer, Tom Sturge; January 3–26, 2003; Cast: David Rogers (Professor Josef Mashkan), Mark Boyett (Stephen Hoffman)

WOMEN WHO STEAL by Carter W. Lewis; Director, Martha Banta; Scenic Designer, Eric Renschler; Costume Designer, Deborah Newhall; Lighting Designer, Neal M. Kerr; February 7–March 2, 2003; Cast: Paula Plum (Peggy), Angela Reed (Karen), Frank Deal (Man)

THE DRAWER BOY by Michael Healey; Director, Charles Towers; Scenic Designer, Judy Gailen; Costume Designer, Martha Hally; Lighting Designer, John Ambrosone; March 14–April 6, 2003; Cast: Ross Bickell (Morgan), Dennis Robertson (Angus), Steven Boyer (Miles)

THE PAVILION by Craig Wright; Director, Brendon Fox; Scenic Designer, Anna Louizos; Costume Designer, Erika Lilienthal; Lighting Designer, Jennifer Setlow; Sound Designer, Ben Emerson; April 18–May 11, 2003; Cast: Jonathan Tindle (The Narrator), Baylen Thomas (Peter), Elisabeth S. Rodgers (Kari)

OLD GLOBE THEATRE

San Diego, California
SIXTY-SEVENTH SEASON

Karen Carpenter, Associate Artistic Director; Craig Noel, Executive Director; Douglas C. Evans, Managing and Producing Director; Interim Managing Director, Artistic Director, Jack O'Brien

STONES IN HIS POCKETS by Marie Jones; Director, Ian McElhinney; Scenic Design, Jack Kirwan; Lighting Design, James C. McFetridge; Production Stage Manager, Zoya Kachadurian; Stage Manager, D. Adams; Technical Supervisor, Brian Lynch; Old Globe Thetare, February 3–March 16, 2002; Cast: Bronson Pinchot, Christopher Burns

Bronson Pinchot, Christopher Burns in *Stones in His Pockets* PHOTO BY NOBBY CLARK

COMPLEAT FEMALE STAGE BEAUTY by Jeffrey Hatcher; Director, Mark Lamos; Scenic Design, Michael Yeargan; Costume Design, Jess Goldstein; Lighting Design, York Kennedy; Original Music, Michael Roth; Sound Design, Paul Peterson; Dramaturge, Scott Horstien; Fight Director, Steve Rankin; Voice and Dialect Coach, Jan Gist; Stage Managers, D. Adams, Joel Rosen; Assistant to the Director, Ben Klein; Assistant to the director, Jennifer Vellenga; Assistant Stage Manager, Tracy Skoczelas; Assistant Scenic Design, David Ledsinger; Assistant Costume Design, Charlotte Devaux-Shields; Assistant Lighting Design, David Cuthbert; Assistant to the Fight Director, Wayne Kohanek; Movement Consultant, Bonnie Johnson; Old Globe Theatre; March 31–April 27, 2002; Cast: David Cromwell (Samuel Pepys), Robert Petkoff (Edward Kynaston), Jonathan Fried (Thomas Betterton), Antonie Knoppers (Male Emilia), Quentin Maré (George Villiars, Duke of Buckingham), Laura Heisler (Maria), Ryan Dunn (Lady Meresvale), Christine Marie Brown (Miss Frayne), Steve Hendrickson (Sir Charles Sedley), Krista Hoeppner (Margaret Hughes), Kwana Martinez (Nell Gwynn), Tom Hewitt (Charles II), David McCann (Sir Peter Lely), Ryan Dunn (Mistress Revels), D'Vorah Bailey (Courtier), Deb Heinig (Mrs. Elizabeth Barry, Courtier), Brian Ibsen (Ruffian, Courtier), Antonie Knoppers (Ruffian, Drunk, Courtier), Lucas Caleb Rooney (Ruffian, Thug, Courtier, Sir Thomas Pelligrew) Understudies: Antonie Knoppers (Edward Kynaston), Lucas Caleb Rooney (Thomas Betterton), Christopher Gottschalk (Samuel Pepys), Jeffrey Brick (Villars), Michele Vazquez (Maria), Deborah Heinig (Lady Meresvale),

D'Vorah Bailey (Miss Frayne), Christopher Gottschalk (Sir Charles Sedley), Eleanor O'Brien (Margaret Hughes), Brian Ibsen (Charles II), Nanka Sturgis (Nell Gwynn), Jeffrey Brick (Hyde), Jeffrey Brick (Sir Peter Lelley), Deborah Heinig (Mistress Revels)

SMASH Adapted by Jeffrey Hatcher; Director, Karen Carpenter; Scenic Design, Scott Bradley; Costume Design, Robert Wojewodski; Lighting Design, Aaron Copp; Sound Design, Paul Peterson; Voice and Dialect Coach, Jan Gist; Stage Manager, Joel Rosen; Assistant Stage Manager, Tracy Skoczelas; Assistant to the Director, Luke Sandler; Production Assistant, Libby Campbell; Assistant Scenic Design, David Ledsinger; Assistant Costume Design, Charlotte Devaux-Shields; Assistant Lighting Design, Criag Dettman; Period Movement Consultant, Bonnie Johnson; Old Globe Theatre; May 26–July 6, 2002; Cast: Charles Borland (Sidney Trefusis), Jennifer Roszell (Henrietta Jansenius), Jack Ryland (Mr. Jansenius), Michele Vazquez (Gertrude Lindsay), Emmelyn Thayer (Jane Carpenter), Priscilla Allen (Miss Wilson), Michael Kary (Chichester Erskine), Paul Benedict (Lumpkin), Laurel Moglen (Agatha Wylie), Eric Martin Brown (Sir Charles Brandon) Understudies: Jeffrey Brick (Lumpkin), David Raphael D'Agostini (Mr. Jansenius), Christopher Gottschalk (Chichester Erskine), Michael Kary (Sir Charles Brandon), Eleanor O'Brien (Miss Wilson), Nanka Sturgis (Gertrude Lindsay, Jane Carpenter), Javen Tanner (Sidney Trefusis), Emmelyn Thayer (Henrietta Jansenius), Michele Vazquez (Agatha Wylie)

BETRAYAL by Harold Pinter; Director, Karen Carpenter; Scenic Design, Robin Sanford Roberts; Costume Design, Charlotte Devaux-Shields; Lighting Design, Aaron M. Copp; Sound Design, Paul Peterson; Voice and Dialect Coach, Jan Gist; Stage Manager, Joel Rosen; Assistant Scenic Design, David Ledsinger; Cassius Carter Centre Stage; January 27–March 10, 2002; Cast: Pamela J. Gray (Emma), Daniel Freedom Stewart (Jerry), Christopher Randolph (Robert), Dimiter D. Marinov (The Waiter) Understudies: Emmelyn Thayer (Emma), Christopher Gottschalk (Robert), Antonie Knoppers (Jerry), David D'Agostini (The Waiter)

(CONTINUED ON NEXT PAGE)

Emmelyn Thayer, Jennifer Roszell, Michele Vazquez, Charles Borland, Laurel Moglen in *Smash* PHOTO BY CRAIG SCHWARTZ

(CONTINUED FROM PREVIOUS PAGE)

MEMOIR by John Murrell; Director, Joseph Hardy; Scenic and Costume Design, Robert Morgan; Lighting Design, Trevor Norton; Sound Design, Karl Mansfield; Stage Manager, Raúl Moncada; Assistant Stage Manager, Tracy Skoczelas; Assistant Scenic Design, David Ledsinger; Voice and Dialect Coach, Jan Gist; Cassius Carter Centre Stage; March 24–May 5, 2002; Cast: Katherine McGrath (Sarah Bernhardt), Jonathan McMurtry (Georges Pitou) Understudies: Emmelyn Thayer (Sarah Bernhardt), David D'Agostini (Georges Pitou)

AN INFINITE ACHE by David Schulner; Director, Brendon Fox; Scenic Design, Yael Pardess; Costume Design, Holly Poe Durbin; Lighting Design, Jennifer Setlow; Sound Design, Paul Peterson; Stage Manager, Raúl Moncada; Assistant Scenic Design, David Ledsinger; Assistant Costume Design, Shelly Williams; Production Assistant, James Feinberg; Voice and Dialect Coach, Jan Gist; Cassius Carter Centre Stage; May 19–June 30; Cast: Samantha Quan (Hope), James Waterston (Charles) Understudies: D'Vorah Bailey (Hope), Brian Ibsen (Charles)

THE TAMING OF THE SHREW by William Shakespeare; Director, John Rando; Scenic Design, Ralph Funicello; Costume Design, Lewis Brown; Lighting Design, York Kennedy; Sound Design, Christopher Walker; Dramaturge, Dakin Matthews; Fight Director, Steve Rankin; Voice and Dialect Coach, Jan Gist; Stage Manager, D. Adams; Assistant Stage Manager, Caren Heintzelman; Assistant Director, Kira Simiring; Assistant Scenic Design, David Ledsinger; Assistant to the Set Designer, Jeff Stander; Assistant Costume Design, Shelly Williams; Assistant Lighting Design, Jason Bieber; Lowell Davies Festival Theatre; June 29–August 4, 2002; Cast: Dakin Matthews (Baptista), Elizabeth Heflin (Katherine), Laura Heisler (Bianca), Jeffrey Nording (Petruccio), Arnie Burton (Grumio), Jack Banning (Curtis), Jonathan McMurtry (gremio), Michael Mastro (Hortensio), Remy Auberjonois (Lucentio), Rainn Wilson (Tranio), Jeffrey Brick (Biondello), Keith Jochim (Vincentio), John Seidman (A Pedant), Eleanor O'Brien (A Widow), Jack Banning (A Tailor), Brian Ibsen (A Haberdasher), Christopher Gottschalk (Messenger, Joseph), Antonie Knoppers (Nicholas), David Raphael D'Agostini (Nathaniel), Nanka Sturgis (Sugarsop), D'Vorah Bailey (Phoebe) Understudies: Keith Jochim (Baptista), Jeffrey Brick (Grumio, Tranio, Nicholas, Officer), Christopher Gottschalk (Hortensio), Brian Ibsen (Petruccio), D'Vorah Bailey (Katherine), Lucas Caleb Rooney (Gremio, Baptista's Servant), Nanka Sturgis (Bianca), David D'Agostini (Vincentio), Anotonie Knoppers (Lucentio, Biondello), Michael Kary (Curtis, Tailor, Pedant, Haberdasher)

FAITH HEALER by Brian Friel; Director, Seret Scott; Scenic Design, Robin Sanford Roberts; Costume Design, Lewis Brown; Lighting Design, David Lee Cuthbert; Sound Design, Paul Peterson; Voice and Dialect Coach, Jan Gist; Stage Manager, Raúl Moncada; Assistant Costume Design, Shelly Williams; Production Assistant, Michelle Cruz; Cassius Carter Centre Stage; July 14–August 25, 2002; Cast: Michael Rudko (Frank), Lizbeth Mackay (Grace), Tim Donoghue (Teddy) Understudies: Michael Kary (Frank), Eleanor O'Brien (Grace), Christopher Gottschalk (Teddy)

Laura Heisler, Dakin Matthews, Michael Mastro, Jonathan McMurtry in *The Taming of the Shrew* PHOTO BY CRAIG SCHWARTZ

ALL MY SONS by Arthur Miller; Director, Richard Seer; Scenic Design, David Ledsinger; Costume Design, Charlotte Devaux-Shields; Lighting Design, Trevor Norton; Sound Design, Paul Peterson; Stage Manager, Joel Rosen; Assistant Stage Manager, Tracy Skoczelas; Assistant to the Director, David Riesenberg; Assistant Scenic Design, Amanda Stephens; Assistant Lighting Design, Kurt Doemelt; Voice and Dialect Coach, Jan Gist; Studio Teacher, Randal McEndree; Old Globe Theatre; July 21–August 31, 2002; Cast: Daniel J. Travanti (Joe Keller), Russ Anderson (Dr. Jim Bayliss), Lucas Caleb Rooney (Frank Lubey), Caren Browning (Sue Bayliss), Deborah Annette Heinig (Lydia Lubey), Brian Hutchinson (Chris Keller), Zev Lerner (Bert), James Patterson (Bert), Robin Pearson Rose (Kate Keller), Melinda Page Hamilton (Ann Deever), Javen Tanner (George Deever) Understudies: Lucas Caleb Rooney (Joe Keller), David Raphael D'Agostini (Dr. Jim Bayliss), Michael Kary (Frank Lubey), Michele Vazquez (Sue Bayliss, Lydia Lubey), Javen Tanner (Chris Keller), Emmelyn Tanner (Kate Keller), Deborah Annette Heinig (Ann Deever), Brian Ibsen (George Deever)

Brian Hutchison, Daniel J. Travanti, Robin Pearson Rose, Melinda Page Hamilton in *All My Sons* PHOTO BY CRAIG SCHWARTZ

BEYOND THERAPY by Christopher Durang; Director, Brendon Fox; Scenic Design, Anna Louizos; Costume Design, Holly Poe Durbin; Lighting Design, Chris Rynne; Sound Design, Lindsay Jones; Movement, Faith Jensen Ismay; Stage Manager, Raúl Moncada; Voice Consultant, Jan Gist; Assistant Scenic Design, Amanda Stephens; Assistant Costume Design, Cindy Kinnard; Production Assistant, Michelle Cruz; Directing Intern, K.J. Swanson; Cassius Carter Centre Stage; September 14–October 20, 2002; Cast: Anna Cody (Prudence), Alma Cuervo (Charlotte), Adam Edwards (Bob), Matthew Montelongo (Bruce), Javen Tanner (Andrew), Paul Michael Valley (Stuart) Understudies: Deborah Heinig (Prudence), Jennifer Lynn McMillin (Charlotte), Neil Shah (Bob), Lucas Caleb Rooney (Bruce), Roderic Brogan (Andrew), Javen Tanner (Stuart)

IMAGINARY FRIENDS by Nora Ephron; Music, Marvin Hamlisch; Lyrics, Craig Carnelia; Director, Jack O'Brien; Scenic Design, Michael Levine; Costume Design, Robert Morgan; Lighting Design, Kenneth Posner; Sound Design, Jon Weston; Video Production Design, Jan Harley; Orchestrations, Torrie Zito; Conductor, James Vukovich; Production Stage Manager, Evan Ensign; Stage Manager, Joel Rosen; Stage Manager, Jim Wooley; Music Director, Ron Melrose; Choreography, Jerry Mitchell; Associate Director, Matt August; Associate Choreographer, Jim Osorno; Assistant Scenic Design, San Diego, Amanda Stephens; Assistand Scenic Design, New York, Kip Marsh; Assistant Costume Design, Charlotte Devaux-Shields, Michelle Short; Lighting Draftperson, Michele Disco; 1st Lighting Assistant, Laura Dubin; 2nd Lighting Assistant, Travis Richardson; SDCF Traube Fellow, Eli Gonda; Production Assistant, David Humphrey; Follow-Spot Operators, Jason Bieber, Shawn Sagady; Deck Electrician, Tom Lucenti; Orchestra: James Vukovich, Conductor, Keyboards; Gary Scott (Sax,Clarinet, Flute, Oboe, English Horn); Thomas Nygaard (Trumpet, Flugel Horn), Robert Johnston (Trombone,Tuba), Byron Delto (Guitar, Banjo), Ted Hughart (Bass), Jeff Dalrymple (Drums, Mallets) Old Globe Theatre; September 29–November 3, 2002; Cast: Swoosie Kurtz (Lillian Hellman), Cherry Jones (Mary McCarthy), Harry Groener (The Man), Anne Allgood (Abby Kaiser & Others), Bernard Dotson (Leo & Others), Rosena M. Hill (Smart Woman Soloist & Others), Gina Lamparella (Sarah Lawrence & Others), Dirk Lumbard (Fact & Others), Peter Marx (Fiction & Others), Perry Ojeda (Vic & Others), Karyn Quackenbush (Fizzy & Others), Anne Pitoniak (A Woman) Understudies: Contance Barron (Standby for Lillian Hellman & Mary McCarthy), Dirk Lumbard (Understudy for The Man), Anne Allgood (Understudy for The Woman), Jim Osorno (Male Swing), Melanie Vaughan (Female Swing)

THE SANTALAND DIARIES by David Sedaris; Adapted by Joe Mantello; Director, Brendon Fox; Scenic Design, David Ledsinger; Costume Design, Charlotte Devaux-Shields; Lighting Design, Trevor Norton; Original Music and Arrangements, James Vukovich; Sound Design, Paul Peterson; Stage Manager, Raúl Moncada; Production Assistant, Krisine Hummel-Rosen; Cast: Arnie Burton (The Writer)

PERICLES by William Shakespeare; Director, Darko Tresnjak; Scenic Design, Ralph Funicello; Costume Design, Linda Cho; Lighting Design, York Kennedy; Sound Design, Jerry Yager; Dramaturge, Dakin Matthews; Movement, Bonnie Johnston; Voice and Diction, Jan Gist; Stage Manager, D. Adams; Assistant Stage Manager, Tracy Skoczelas; Assistant Director, Enda O. Breadon; Assistant Scenic Design, Amanda Stephens; Assistant Costume Design, Shelly Williams; Assistant Lighting Design, Jason Bieber; Assistant to the Scenic Designer, Jeff Stander; Assistants to Ms. Johnston, Marilyn Green, Deborah Annette Heinig; Cast: Ned Schmidtke (Gower, as Chorus), Wynn Harmon (Antiochus), Michele Vazquez (Daughter of Antiochus), Gareth Saxe (Thaliard), Michael James Reed (Pericles), Charles Janasz (Helicanus), Christian Jasper, David Raphael D'Agostini, Christopher Gottschalk (Lords of Tyre), Brian Ibsen, Michael Kary, Antonie Knoppers, Gareth Saxe (Sailors of Tyre), Andrew Borba (Cleon), Joanna Glushak (Dionyza), Nisi Sturgis (Philoten), Gareth Saxe (Leonine), Liam Craig, Michael Kary, Gregor Paslawsky (Three Fisherman), Wynn Harmon (Simonides), Emmelyn Thayer (Thaisa), Dara Fisher, Gareth Saxe (Marshals), D'Vorah Bailey, Eleanor O'Brien, Nisi Sturgis, Michele Vazquez (Ladies of the Court), Andrew Borba, Jeffrey Brick, Brian Ibsen, Antonie Knoppers (Visiting Knights), Eleanor O'Brien (Lychorida), Gregor Paslawsky (Cerimon), Liam Craig (Philemon), Dara Fisher (Diana), Wynn Harmon (Pander), Dara Fisher (Bawd), Liam Craig (Boult), Christian Casper (Lysimachus) Anna Belknap (Marina) Understudies: D'Vorah Bailey (for Jennifer Stewart), Nisi Sturgis (for Anna Belknap), Brian Ibsen (for Andrew Borba), Roderic Brogan (for Jeffrey Brick), Antonie Knoppers (for Christian Casper), Brian Ibsen (for Liam Craig), Michael Newman (for David Raphael D'Agostini), Eleanor O'Brien (for Dara Fisher), D'Vorah Bailey (for Joanna Glushak), Michael Doyle (for Christopher Gottschalk), Michael Kary (for Wynn Harmon), Michael Newman (for Brian Ibsen), Michael Kary (for Charles Janasz), Michael Doyle (for Michael Kary), Roderic Brogan (for Antonie Knoppers), Karen Zippler (for Eleanor O'Brien), Jeffrey Brick (for Gregor Paslawsky), Christopher Gottschalk (for Michael James Reed), Jeffrey Brick (for Gareth Saxe), David Raphael D'Agostini (for Ned Schmidtke), Jennifer Stewart (for Nisi Sturgis), Michele Vazquez (for Emmalyn Thayer), Karen Zippler (for Michele Vazquez)

Anna Cody, Alma Cuervo, Adam Edwards, Paul Michael Valley, Matthew Montelongo in *Beyond Therapy* PHOTO BY SANDY HUFFAKER

PAPER MILL PLAYHOUSE

Millburn, New Jersey

Executive Producer, Angelo Del Rossi; Associate Producer, Roy Miller; Associate Director, Mark S. Hoebee; Press, Charlie Siedenburg/Jeff O'Keefe; Casting, Alison Franck; Stage Managers, Kevin Frederick, Alison Harma, Chris Jamros, Tom Jeffords

MISS SAIGON Music, Claude-Michel Schonberg; Lyrics, Richard Maltby, Jr., and Alain Boublil; Director, Mark S. Hoebee; Musical Director, Tom Helm; Choreography, Darren Lee; Set, Michael Anania; Costume Coordinator, Gail Baldoni; Lighting Design, F. Mitchell Dana; Sound Design, Duncan Robert Edwards and David F. Shapiro; Cast: Kevin Gray (The Engineer), Dina Lynne Morishita (Kim), Roxanne Taga (Kim: Sat, Sun matinees), Aaron Ramey (Chris), Alan H. Green (John), Steven Eng (Thuy), Kate Baldwin (Ellen), Adrienne Sam (Gigi), Naomi Nalzaro, Galen Ng (Tam), Cristina Ablaza, Randy B. Ballesteros, Bernie Blanks, Kevin M. Burrows, Paul Canaan, Terrence McKinley Clowe, Francis J. Cruz, Christopher Davis, Dexter Echiverri, Richard Feng Zhu, Kelly Fong, Samantha Futerman, Megumi Haggerty, Michael Hunsaker, Joanne Javien, Spencer C. Jones, Mark Ledbetter, Kathy Nejat, Mayumi Omagari, Whitney Osentoski, Bobby Pestka, Diane Veronica Phelan, Freddy Ramirez, Summer Tiana Sablan, Michael Vea, and Lisa Yuen

ANNIE Book, Thomas Meehan; Music, Charles Strouse; Lyrics, Martin Charnin; Director, Greg Ganakas; Choreographer, Linda Goodrich; Musical Director, Tom Helm; Scenic Design, Michael Anania; Lighting, F. Mitchell Dana; Sound, Duncan Robert Edwards and David F. Shapiro; Costumes, Jimm Halliday; Cast: Sarah Hyland (Annie), Rich Hebert (Daddy Warbucks), Catherine Cox (Miss Hannigan), Crista Moore (Grace Farrell), Jim Walton (Rooster Hannigan), Tia Speros (Lily St. Regis), Eric Michael Gillett (FDR), Buster (Sandy), Ivana Grace (Duffy), Molly Jobe (Pepper), Ashlee Keating (Tessie), Chiara Navarra (Kate), Jacklyn Neidanthal (Molly), Stacey Rose Richman (Swing), Addison Timlin (July), Brynn Williams (Swing), John Paul Almon, Colin Cunliffe, Montego Glover (Star To Be), Tripp Hanson (Bert Healy), Ken Kantor, Jody Madaras, Anna McNeely, Karyn Overstreet, Larissa Shukis, A.J. Sullivan, Jennifer Taylor, Tom Treadwell

BLUE a play with jazz by Charles Randolph-Wright; Music, Nona Hendryx; Director, Sheldon Epps; Sets, James Leonard Joy, Costume Design, Debra Bauer, Lighting Design, Michael Gilliam, Sound Design, Francois Bergeron; Cast: Leslie Uggams (Peggy Clark), Michael McElroy (Blue Williams), Chris Butler (Samuel Clark III), Willie C. Carpenter (Samuel Clark, Jr.), Amentha Dymally (Tillie Clark), Jovun Fox (Young Reuben Clark), Jacques C. Smith (Reuben Clark), Felicia Wilson (LaTonya Dinkins), Robert Scott Daye, Marjorie Johnson, Robert Lee Taylor Devon, Malik Backford, Jennifer Hunter

ROMEO AND BERNADETTE, A BROOKLYN MUSICAL Book and Lyrics, Mark Saltzman; Director, Mark Waldrop; Sets, Michael Anania, Costume Design, Miguel Angel Huidor; Lighting Design, F. Mitchell Dana Musical Director, Bruce W. Coyle. Cast: Adam Monley (Romeo), Natalie Hill (Bernadette Penza), Andy Karl (Brooklyn Guy, Dino Del Canto), Rosie De Candia (Brooklyn Girl, Donna Dubacek), Emily Zacharias (Camille Penza), Charles Pistone (Sal Penza), Andrew Varela (Tito Titone), Vince Trani (Lips), David Brummel (Don Del Canto), John Paul Almon (Enzo Aliria, Officer, Father Keneely, Arden, Donna's Father, Viola Duke, Roz), Christina D'Orta, Sal Sabella, Dante A. Sciarra

CAMELOT Book and Lyrics, Alan Jay Lerner; Music, Frederick Loewe; Director/Choreographer, Robert Johanson; Musical Direction by Tom Helm; Scenic Design, Michael Anania; Costume Design Thom Heyer; Lighting Design, F. Mitchell Dana; Cast: Brent Barrett (King Arthur), Glory Crampton (Guenevere), Matt Bogart (Lancelot), George S. Irving (Merlin, Pellinore), Barrett Foa (Mordred), Enrique Acevedo, Jacquelyn Baker, Bernie Blanks, Christy Boardman, Paul Canaan, Christopher Carl, Michael Gerhart, Tara Lynne Khaler, Ryan Malyar, Greg Mills, Michael Minarik, Diane Veronica Phelan, Abe Reynold, Larissa Shukis, Daniel Spiotta, Matt Stokes, Jeff Stone, Catherine Walker, Jennifer Hope Wills, and Matthew Karl Yoder, Nicholas Druzbanski, Garret Gallinot, Gus Gallinot, David Jastrab, Tim Lynch, Benjamin Rosenbach, Javier Woodard, Michael Yoson

GREASE Book, Music, Lyrics Jim Jacobs and Warren Casey; Director, Mark S. Hoebee; Choreographer, Jeffrey Amsden; Music Direction, Vicki Carter; Scenic Design, James Fouchard; Costume Design, Gregory A. Poplyk; Lighting Design, F. Mitchell Dana; Sound Design, Duncan Robert Edwards and David F. Shapiro; Cast: Enrique Acevedo (Johnny Casino), Clyde Alves (Sonny), Jordan Ballard (Marty), Steven Bogard (Vince Fontaine, Teen Angel), Justin Bohon (Doody), Colin Cunliffe, Brenda Cummings (Miss Lynch), Jenn Goodson, Becky Gulsvig (Patty Simcox), Stacey Harris, Andy Karl (Danny Zuko), Leslie Kritzer (Rizzo), John Jeffrey Martin (Kenickie), Benjie Randall (Roger), Heather Jane Rolff (Jan), Sarah Stiles (Frenchy), Noah Weissberg (Eugene), Jennifer Hope Wills (Sandy)

Brent Barrett, Glory Crampton in *Camelot* PHOTO BY JERRY DALIA

PITTSBURGH PUBLIC THEATER

Pittsburgh, Pennsylvania
TWENTY-EIGHTH SEASON

Ted Pappas, Artistic Director; Stephen Klein, Managing Director

MUCH ADO ABOUT NOTHING by William Shakespeare; Director, Ted Pappas; Scenic Design, James Noone; Costume Design, David R. Zyla; Lighting Design, Frances Aronson; Music Composer, Michael Moricz; Sound Design, Zach Moore; Casting, Patricia A. McCorkle; Production Stage Manager, Ruth E. Kramer; Assistant Stage Manager, Julie A. Barkovich; O'Reilly Theater; September 26–October 27, 2002; Cast: Michael McKenzie (Don Pedro), Jarrod Fry (Claudio), Douglas Harmsen (Benedick), Daniel Krell (Don John), Michael Greenwood (Balthasar), Randall Newsome (Borachio), Doug Mertz (Conrade), Andy Place (Soldier), Edward James Hyland (Leonato), Joe Warik (Anotonio), Stina Nielsen (Hero), Deirdre Madigan (Beatrice), David Crawford (Friar Francis), John Ahlin (Dogberry), John Seidman (Verges), Nick Ruggeri (Seacoal), Rajesh Bose (Oatcake), John Yost (Watchman), Michael Greenwood (Sexton), Elena Passarello (Margaret), Terry Wickline (Ursula), Elena Alexandratos (Waiting-woman) Understudies: Elena Alexandratos (Margaret, Ursula), Rajesh Bose (Claudio, Don John), David Crawford (Leonato, Antonio), Michael Greenwood (Don Pedro), Lara Hillier (Hero), Doug Mertz (Benedick), Elena Passarello (Beatrice), Andy Place (Balthasar, Sexton, Friar, Watchman, Oatcake, Seacoal), Nick Ruggeri (Dogberry, Verges), John Yost (Borachio, Conrade)

MAN OF LA MANCHA Book by Dale Wasserman; Music, Mitch Leigh, Lyrics, Joe Darion; Director and Choreographer, Ted Pappas; Scenic Design, James Noone; Costume Design, Gabriel Barry; Lighting Design, Kirk Bookman; Sound Design, Zach Moore; Orchestrations, Christopher Jahnke; Fight Choreographer, Shaun J. Rolly; Casting, Mark Simon; Production Stage Manager, Ruth E. Kramer; Assistant Stage Manager, Julie A. Barkovich; Musical Director, F. Wade Russo; Dance Captain, Mark Martino; Fight Captain, Todd M. Kryger; O'Reilly Theater; January 30–March 2, 2003; Cast: Brian Sutherland (Don Quixote, Miguel de Cervantes), Avery Saltzman (Sancho Panza, Manservant), Tari Kelly (Aldonza), Jeffrey Howell (The Innkeeper, Governor), Daniel Krell (Dr. Carrasco, Duke), Tim Salamandyk (The Padre), Laura Yen Solito (Antonia), Gina Ferrall (The Housekeeper), Larry Daggett (The Barber), Erik Nelson (Pedro), Greg Roderick (Anselmo), Dan Conville (José), Mark Martino (Captain of the Inquisition, Juan), Howard Kaye (Paco), Todd M. Kryger (Tenorio), Terry Wickline (Maria), Cindy Marchionda (Fermina), Cindy Marchionda, Larry Daggett, Todd M. Kryger (The Moors) Orchestra: F. Wade Russo (Conductor, Keyboards), Marie-Claude B. Driscoll (Horn), Christopher D. Hart (Trumpet), R.J. Heid (Percussion), George Hoydich (Reeds), Ken Karsh (Guitar), Phil Koval (Bassoon and Clarinet), Heidi Pandolfi (Oboe and English Horn), John Hall (Orchestra Personnel Manager) Understudies: Larry Daggett (Quixote, Cervantes), Cindy Marchionda (Aldonza, Antonia), Greg Roderick (Sancho, The Barber), Todd M. Kryger (The Padre), Terry Wickline (The Housekeeper), Erik Nelson (The Innkeeper, Governor), Mark Martino (Dr. Carrasco), Howard Kaye (Anselmo, Captain of the Inquisition)

THE DRAWER BOY by Michael Healey; Directed by Marshall W. Mason; Scenic Design, David Potts; Costume Design, Jennifer Von Mayrhauser; Lighting Design, Phil Monat; Music Composer, Peter Kater; Sound Design, Joe Pino; Assistant Director, Rand Mitchell; Casting, Rich Cole; Production Stage Manager, Fred Noel; Assistant Stage Manager, Alison Paleos; O'Reilly Theater; March 13–April 13, 2003; Cast: Jimmie Ray Weeks (Angus), Tom Atkins (Morgan), Jamie Bennett (Miles)

THE PIANO LESSON by August Wilson; Director, Israel Hicks; Scenic Design, Michael Brown; Costume Design, Christine Field; Lighting Design, Ann G. Wrightson; Sound Design, Zach Moore; Production Stage Manager, Mark C. Sharp; Assistant Stage Manager, Julie A. Barkovich; O'Reilly Theater; April 24–May 25, 2003; Cast: Terry Alexander (Doaker), Harvy Blanks (Boy Willie), Michael Eaddy (Lymon), Kim Staunton (Berniece), Shaquela Davis, Kaitlyn Findley (Maretha), Terrence Riggins (Avery), Charles Weldon (Wining Boy), January Murelli (Grace)

DIRTY BLONDE by Claudia Shear; Director, Ted Pappas; Scenic Design, Anne Mundell; Costume Design, David R. Zyla; Lighting Design, David F. Segal; Sound Design, Zach Moore; Music Director, Tom Frey; Casting, Mark Simon; Original song *Dirty Blonde*, Bob Stillman; Production Stage Manager, Fred Noel; Assistant Stage Manager, Alison Paleos; O'Reilly Theater; June 5–July 6, 2003; Cast: Tom Frey (Frank Wallace, Ed Hearn, others), Ryan Dunn (Jo, Mae), Lucas Caleb Rooney (Charlie, others)

DRIVING MISS DAISY by Alfred Uhry; Director, Pamela Berlin; Scenic Design, Michael Schweikardt; Costume Design, Amela Baksic; Lighting Design, Rui Rita; Original Music Composed by Robert Waldman; Sound Design, Zach Moore; Casting, Janet Foster; Production Stage Manager, Fred Noel; Assistant Stage Manager, Alison Paleos; O'Reilly Theater; November 7–December 8, 2002; Cast: Rosemary Prinz (Daisy Werthman), Jay Patterson (Boolie Werthan), Roger Robinson (Hoke Coleburn)

PLAYHOUSE ON THE GREEN

Bridgeport, Connecticut
FIFTH SEASON

Janet Granger-Happ, Executive Director; Kenneth Williams, Managing Director; Patricia Blaufuss, Press Representative

ARSENIC AND OLD LACE by Joseph Kesselring; Director, Christian Saint-Girard; October 3–27, 2002 Cast: Joan Copeland, Mia Dillon, Wendy Allyn, George Bass, Frank Calamaro, Joseph Culliton, James Glenn, Steve Kalarchian, Damien Langan, Randall B. Mix, Robert Watts

BABES IN TOYLAND Music by Victor Herbert; Book & Lyrics, Glen MacDonough; Director/Choreographer, Christian Saint-Girard; November 21–December 31, 2002; Cast: Michael Brelsford, Linda Cameron, Matthew Darling, Georgia Feroce, Lauren Gruet, Joel Harrington, Adam Hetrick, Stephen G. Humes, William Koch, Douglas LeLand, Caci Massaro, Andrea A. McCullough, Anthony Morelli, Ken Parker, Brendan Quinn, Brittany Ross, J. Brandon Savage, Krystie Seese, Rebecca Simon, Daniel Robert Sullivan

SLEUTH by Anthony Shaffer; Director, Terence Lamude; Scenic Design, Harry Feiner; February 6–March 2, 2003; Cast: Keir Dullea, Benim Foster

AIN'T MISBEHAVIN' Director, Saundra McClain; Choreographer, Byron Easley; Musical Director, Ron Metcalf; April 10–May 18, 2003; Cast: James Alexander, Rosena M. Hill, Danette E. Sheppard, Charles E. Wallace, Carla Woods

PORTLAND CENTER STAGE

Portland, Oregon
TWENTY-NINTH SEASON

Artistic Director, Chris Coleman; Executive Assistant, Lisa Sanman-Smith

MUCH ADO ABOUT NOTHING by William Shakespeare; Director, Chris Coleman; Scenic Design, Robert Pyzocha; Costume Design, Deb Trout; Lighting Design, Diane Ferry Williams; Sound Design, Jen Raynak; Choreographers, Jamey Hampton and Ashley Roland; Composer, Clark Taylor; September 24–October 20, 2002; Cast: Tobias Anderson (Antonio, Verges), Jim Iorio (Benedick), Debera-Ann Lund (Ursula, First Watch), Torrey Cornwell (Margaret, Conrade), Effie Johnson (Beatrice), Michael O'Connell (Don Pedro, Fourth Watch), Kevin Corstange (Don John), Albert Jones (Claudio), Ted Rosium (Borachio, Friar Francis, Bartender), Katherine Cunninghmam-Eves (Hero), Michael Kevin (Leonato), Charles Leggett (Dogberry, Messenger, Bartender), Steve Wilkerson (Balthasar, Second Watch, Sexton, Messenger, Bartender, Dance Captain)

TRUE WEST by Sam Shepard; Director, Henry Godinez; Scenic Design, Christopher Acebo; Costume Design, Jeff Cone; Lighting Design, Rita Pietraszek; Sound Design, Jen Raynak; Fight Director, John Armour; October 29–November 17, 2002; Cast: Mark D. Espinoza (Austin), Carole Gutierrez (Mom), Rene Rivera (Lee), Ted Rosium (Saul)

THE SANTALAND DIARIES by David Sedaris, adapted by Joe Mantello, with **A CHRISTMAS MEMORY** by Truman Capote; Director, Neel Keller; Scenic Design, Allen Moyer; Costume Design, Jeff Cone; Lighting Design, Don Crossley; Sound Design, Jen Raynak; December 3–December 22, 2002; Cast: Steve Wilkerson (David Sedaris, Truman Capote)

WHO'S AFRAID OF VIRGINIA WOOLF? by Edward Albee; Director, Nancy Keystone; Scenic Design; Douglas D. Smith; Costume Design, Jeff Cone; Lighting Design, Don Crossley; Sound Design, Jen Raynak; Fight Choreographer, John Armour; January 14–February 9, 2003; Cast: Kevin Corstange (Nick), Nicole Marks (Honey), Allen Nause (George), Margo Skinner (Martha)

OUTRAGE by Itamar Moses; Director, Chris Coleman; Scenic Design, Klara Zieglerova; Costume Design, Miranda Hoffman; Lighting Design, Daniel Ordower; Sound Design, Jen Raynak; West Coast Premiere, February 18–March 9, 2003; Cast: Christopher Burns (Rivnine, Agathon), Kevin Corstange (Plato, Grad Student #2, Critic #1, Chorus), David Cromwell (Lomax, Aristophanes), Robert Dorfman (Brecht, Galileo), Jeffrey Jason Gilpin (Brett, Alcibiades, Vorai, Critic #3, Chorus), Kate Levy (Kale, Oracle, Grad Student #3, Critic #4, Chorus), Kelly Talent (Laura, Critic #2, Chorus), Steve Wilkerson (Menocchio, Grad Student #1, Chorus)

MAN AND SUPERMAN by George Bernard Shaw; Director, Chris Coleman; Assistant Director, Christine Menzies; Scenic Design, Klara Zieglerova; Costume Design, Sydney Roberts; Lighting Design, Kirk Bookman; Sound Design, Jen Raynak; March 25–April 13, 2003; Cast: Kelly Allen Boulware (Hector Malone), Scott Coopwood (Henry Straker), David Crowe (Octavius Robinson), Gray Eubank (Mr. Malone), Peter Ganim (Jack Tanner), Linda Williams Janke (Miss Ramsden), Michael Kevin (Roebuck Ramsden), Zoaunne Leroy (Mrs. Whitefield), Debera-Ann Lund (Parlor Maid), Sarah Overman (Violet Robinson), Jessica Walling (Ann Whitefield)

PRINCE MUSIC THEATER

Philadelphia, Pennsylvania
NINETEENTH SEASON

Marjorie Samoff, Producing Artistic Director; Joseph M. Farina, Managing Director

IT'S BETTER WITH A BAND Lyrics by David Zippel; Music by Cy Coleman, Marvin Hamlisch, Wally Harper, Doug Katsaros, Alan Menken, David Pomeranz, Jonathan Sheffer, Michael Skloff, Bryon Sommers, Matthew Wilder; Scenic Design, Ray Klausen; Costume Design, Mark Mariani; Lighting Design, Michael Gilliam; Sound Design, Nick Kourtides; Production Stage Manager, Scott P. McNulty; Orchestrations and Music Direction, Christopher Marlowe; Directed by Joe Leonardo; Presented by arrangement with Susan Dietz and Roger Gindi. September 18–October 6, 2002. World Premiere September 21, 2002; Cast: John Barrowman, Judy Blazer, Marva Hicks, Sally Mayes

PAL JOEY Music by Richard Rodgers; Lyrics by Lorenz Hart. Book by John O'Hara. Scenic Design, Luke Hegel-Cantarella; Costume Designer, Mark Mariani; Lighting Design, Michael Lincoln; Sound Design, Nick Kourtides; Production Stage Manager, Scott P. McNulty; Casting Director, Janet Foster; Choreographer, Myra Bazell; Music Director, Lawrence Goldberg; Production Supervisor, Laurence Maslon November 2–17, 2002 Opening night November 9, 2002; Cast: Christine Andreas and featuring David Bailey, Tara Bruno, Anne Connors, Trent Dawson, Lesley M. Faigin, Susann Fletcher, Darren Fuller, Jenn Harris, Danielle Herbert, Zebediah K. Homison, Christa Justus, Colin E. Liander, Kelly McCormick, Tim Moyer, Wi-Moto Nyoka, Samuel Antonio Reyes.

PETER PAN & WENDY: THE ADVENTURES OF THE LOST BOYS Music by George Stiles; Lyrics, Anthony Drewe; Book, Willis Hall; Based on J. M. Barrie's original play by kind permission of Great Ormond St. Children's Hospital; Scenic Design, Fred Kinney; Costume Design, Loyce Arthur; Lighting Design, Howell Binkley; Sound Design, Nick Kourtides; Orchestrator, John Cameron; Production Stage Manager, Lori Aghazarian; Associate Lighting Designer, Burke J. Wilmore; Casting Director, Janet Foster; Dramaturg, Julie Felise Dubiner; Assistant Music Director, Eric Ebbenga; Choreographer, Myra Bazell; Music Director, Louis F. Goldberg; Director, Ted Sperling December 11–29, 2002 American Premiere: December 18, 2002; Cast: Nakia Dillard, Romain Frugé, Rita Gardner, Joanna Glushak, Colin Hanlon, Christopher Innvar, Michael Longoria, Tafari Nobles-El, Wi-Moto Nyoka, John O'Hara, Jay Parks, Erica Piccininni, Christopher Sapienza, Louis Shaw, Jacob A. Toth, Basil Beyah, Ally Doman, Cole Doman, Caitlyn Ebbenga, Kerry Gilbert, Gideon Glick, Shane Grant, Earl Harris, Tyler Horn, Rickey Ketchmore, Elizabeth S. Marmon, Jasmine Morrow, Morgan Morrow, Mason Quilty, Samuel Snider, Alee Spadoni, Michaela Tomcho, Vladimir Versailles.

AMBASSADOR SATCH: THE LIFE AND TIMES OF LOUIS ARMSTRONG Co-written by James P. Mirrione and André De Shields; Scenic Design, Dana Kenn; Costume Design, Mark Mariani; Lighting Design, Burke J. Wilmore, Production Stage Manager, Scott P. McNulty; Assistant Music Director, Paul Grant; Choreography and Musical Staging, Mercedes Ellington; Music Director and Arranger, Terry Waldo; Production Supervisor, Laurence Maslon; Cast: André De Shields, Harriett D. Foy. Ambassador Satch has been cooperatively produced and developed by the Prince Music Theater, Helen Hayes Theatre Company, and Queens Theatre in the Park. February 26–March 9, 2003.

GREEN VIOLIN: MARC CHAGALL AND THE SOVIET YIDDISH THEATER Book & Lyrics by Elise Thoron; Conceived by Rebecca Bayla Taichman and Elise Thoron; Music & Orchestrations by Frank London; Associate Artistic Director, Ted Sperling; Scenic & Costume Design, Marina Draghici; Lighting Design, Jane Cox; Sound Design, Nick Kourtides; Production Manager, Jim Griffith, Casting Director, Janet Foster; Production Stage Manager, Lori Aghazarian; Artistic Associate, Laurence Maslon; Choreography, David Dorfman; Musical Direction, Arrangements & Preparation, Steven M. Bishop; Directed by Rebecca Bayla Taichman; April 26–May 18, 2003 World Premiere May 3, 2003; Cast: Eric Bradley, David Cale, Jeanine Durning, Raúl Esparza, Joseph Poulson, Mark Price, Keith Reddin, Hal Robinson, Kate Suber, Bruce Turk, Max Zorin. Produced in Association with Musical Theatre Works, Thomas Cott, Artistic Director. Music and Yiddish Consultant Zalmen Mlotek, Artistic Director, Folksbiene Yiddish Theatre

John Altieri, Charley the Dog in *The Two Gentleman of Verona* PHOTO BY TOM CHARGIN

SAN JOSÉ REPERTORY THEATRE

San José, California
TWENTY-THIRD SEASON

Artistic Director, Timothy Near; Managing Director, Alexandra Urbanowski

THE DRAWER BOY by Michael Healey; Director, John McCluggage; Set Design, Michael Olich; Costume Design, B. Modern; Lighting Design, Lap-Chi Chu; Sound Design, Jeff Mockus; Assistant Director, Codie Fitch; Casting Director, Bruce Elsperger; New York Casting, Paul Russell; Los Angeles Casting, Julia Flores; Stage Manager, Jenny R. Friend; West Coast Premiere, August 31–September 29, 2002; Cast: Dion Anderson (Morgan), Bob Morrisey (Angus), Sheffield Chastain (Miles)

THE WIND CRIES MARY by Philip Kan Gotanda; Director, Eric Simonson; Set and Lighting Design, Kent Dorsey; Costume Design, Lydia Tanji; Sound Design, Jeff Mockus; Dramaturg, Tom Bryant; Casting Director, Bruce Elsperger; New York Casting, Rush and Super Casting; Los Angeles Casting, Julia Flores; Stage Manager, Bruce Elsperger; World Premiere, October 19–November 17, 2002; Cast: Thomas Vincent Kelly (Raymond Pemberthy), Joy Carlin (Auntie Gladys), Tess Lina (Eiko Hanabi), Allison Sie (Rachel Auwinger), Sab Shimono (Dr. Nakada), Stan Egi (Miles Katayama).

THE TWO GENTLEMEN OF VERONA by William Shakespeare; Director, Jeff Steitzer; Set Design, Drew Boughton; Costume Design, B. Modern; Lighting Design, Dawn Chiang, Original Music, Roberta Carlson; Sound Design, Jeff Mockus; Casting Director, Bruce Elsperger; Los Angeles Casting, Julia Flores; Filmmaker, Mark Larson; Stage Manager, Jenny R. Friend; December 7, 2002–January 12, 2003; Cast: Andrew Heffernan (Valentine), T. Edward Webster (Proteus), Andy Murray (Speed), Amanda Duarte (Julia), Maureen McVerry (Lucetta, Outlaw #1), Tom Blair (Antonio, Outlaw #3). Roberto Guajardo (Panthino, Outlaw #2), John Altieri (Launce), Charley the Dog (Crab), Jennifer Lee Taylor (Silvia), Remi Sandri (Thurio), Benjamin Stewart (Duke of Milan), Chris Ayles (Eglamour), Zach Hummell, Nick Spangler, Dale Stahl, Taylor Valentine.

David Pichette, Maureen McVerry, Sheila O'Neill Ellis, Peter Van Norden in *The Odd Couple* PHOTO BY TOM CHARGIN

Ric Salinas, Richard Montoya, Herbert Siguenza in *Culture Clash in AmeriCCa*
PHOTO BY TOM CHARGIN

CULTURE CLASH IN AMERICCA Created, Written and Performed by Culture Clash; Director, Tony Taccone; Set and Lighting Design, Alexander V. Nicols; San Jose Sound Design, Jeff Mockus; Original Costume Design, Donna Marie; Original Sound Design, Matthew Spiro and Culture Clash; Stage Manager, Cynthia Cahill; January 31–March 2, 2003; Cast: Culture Clash (Richard Montoya, Ric Salinas and Herbert Siguenza).

HUMPTY DUMPTY by Eric Bogosian; Director, John McCluggage; Set Design, Douglas Rogers; Costume Design, B. Modern; Lighting Design, Lap-Chi Chu; Sound Design, Steve Schoenbeck; Casting Director, Bruce Elsperger; New York Casting, Harriet Bass; Los Angeles Casting, Julia Flores; Stage Manager, Jenny R. Friend; West Coast Premiere, March 22–April 20, 2003; Cast: Elizabeth Hanly Price (Nicole), Saxon Palmer (Max), Andy Murray (Nat), Louis Lotorto (Troy), Amy Brewczyski (Spoon).

THE ODD COUPLE by Neil Simon; Director, Timothy Near; Set Design, William Bloodgood; Costume Design, Shigeru Yaji; Lighting Design, Robert Perry; Sound Design, Jeff Mockus; Casting Director, Bruce Elsperger; Dialect Coach, Lynne Soffer; Stage Manager, Jenny R. Friend; May 24–June 22, 2003; Cast: John McCluggage (Speed), Colin Thomson (Murray), Michael Butler (Roy), Howard Swain (Vinnie), Peter Van Norden (Oscar Madison), David Pichette (Felix Ungar), Sheila O'Neill Ellis (Gwendolyn Pigeon), Maureen McVerry (Cecily Pigeon).

COOKIN' AT THE COOKERY Writer, Director and Choreographer, Marion J. Caffey; Musical Supervision and Arrangements, Danny Holgate; Musical Director, George Caldwell; Original Scenic Design, Dale F. Jordan; Lighting Design, Dale F. Jordan; Original Costume Design, Marilyn A. Wall; Sound Design, Steve Schoenbeck; Original Sound Design, Marion J. Caffey; Wig and Hair Design, Bettie O. Rogers; Casting Director, Bruce Elsperger; Stage Manager, Jessica Berlin; Cast: Ann Duquesnay (Alberta Hunter), Janice Lorraine (Narrator). Musicians: George Caldwell (Keyboard), Oliver Harris (Guitar), Mel Nelson (Bass), Joe Hodge (Percussion).

SOUTH COAST REPERTORY

Costa Mesa, California
THIRTY-NINTH SEASON

Producing Artistic Director, David Emmes; Artistic Director, Martin Benson; Paula Tomei, Managing Director

MAJOR BARBARA by George Bernard Shaw; Director, Martin Benson; Scenic Design, Ralph Funicello; Costume Design, Shigeru Yaji; Lighting Design, Chris Parry; Composer, Karl Fredrik Lundeberg; October 11–November 17, 2002; Cast: Daniel Blinkoff (Charles Lomax), Kandis Chappell (Lady Britomart), JD Cullum (Adolphus Cusins), Nike Doukas (Barbara Undershaft), Richard Doyle (Peter Shirley), John Hines (Stephen Undershaft), Hal Landon Jr. (Bilton), Michael Louden (Snobby Price), Jane Macfie (Rummy Mitchens), Leo Marks (Bill Walker), Dakin Matthews (Andrew Undershaft), Martha McFarland (Mrs. Baines), Denise Tarr (Jenny Hill), Don Took (Morrison), Shian Velie (Sarah Undershaft)

THE VIOLET HOUR by Richard Greenberg; Director, Evan Yionoulis; Scenic Design, Christopher Barreca; Costume Design, Candice Cain; Lighting Design, Donald Holder; Original Music & Sound Design, Michael Yionoulis; World Premiere; November 5–24, 2002; Cast: Kate Arrington (Rosamund Plinth), Mario Cantone (Gidger), Michelle Hurd (Jessie Brewster), Hamish Linklater (John Pace Seavering), Curtis Mark Williams (Dennis McCleary)

A CHRISTMAS CAROL by Charles Dickens; Adaptation, Jerry Patch; Director, John-David Keller; Music Director, Dennis Castellano; Choreographer, Linda Kostalik; Scenic Design, Cliff Faulkner and Tom Buderwitz; Costume Design, Dwight Richard Odle; Lighting Design, Donna and Tom Ruzika; Sound Design, Garth Hemphill; November 30–December 24, 2002; Cast: Julia Coffey (Lena, Belle, Scavenger), Jonathan del Arco (Undertaker, Young Ebenezer), Richard Doyle (Spirit of Christmas Past, Gentleman), John-David Keller (Solicitor, Gentleman), Art Koustik (Joe, Mr. Fezziwig), Timothy Landfield (Spirit of Christmas Present), Hal Landon Jr., (Ebenezer Scrooge); Joshua Brownie Lash (Puppeteer, Mr. Topper); Martha McFarland (Mrs. Fezziwig, Solicitor); Scott Most (Thomas Shelley); Devon Raymond (Mrs. Crachit); Howard Shangraw (Fred, Gentleman); Hisa Takakuwa (Toy Lady, Sally, Scavenger); Don Took (Marley, Spirit of Christmas Yet-To-Come); Phillip C. Vaden (Constable, Wreath Seller, Young Jacob Marley, Poulterer); Shian Velie (Elizabeth Shelley, Pursued Maiden); David Whalen (Bob Crachit); Jeffrey Budner, Kelly Ehlert, Stephanie Finney, Patrick Gleason, Zan Gray, Austin Koustik, Geena Lovato, Amy Lashmet, Hayley Palmaer, Joseph Reed, Aliza Segal, Steven Siglin, Elise St. Clair, Luke Tagle, Casey Wianecki, Alison Wexler

LA POSADA MAGICA written by Octavio Solis; Music by Marcos Loya; Director, Diane Rodriguez; Musical Director, Marcos Loya; Choreographer, Linda Kostalik; Scenic Design, Christopher Acebo; Costume Design, Shigeru Yaji; Lighting Design, Lonnie Alcaraz; December 13–24, 2002; Cast: Denise Blasor (Consuelo, Widow), Sol Castillo (Refugio, Buzzard), Crissy Guerrero (Mom, Mariluz), Carla Jimenez (Caridad, Widow), Marcos Loya (Musician, Ensemble), Lorenzo Martinez (Musician, Ensemble), Mauricio Mendoza (Papi, Jose Cruz), Miguel Najera (Horacio), Kevin Sifuentes (Eli, Bones, Lauro), Tiffany Ellen Solano (Gracie)

PROOF by David Auburn; Director, Michael Bloom; Scenic Design, Tom Buderwitz; Costume Design, Maggie Morgan; Lighting Design, York Kennedy; Original Music & Sound Design, Mitch Greenhill; January 3–February 9, 2003; Cast: Emily Bergl (Catherine), Richard Doyle (Robert), Christina Haag (Claire), James Waterston (Hal)

INDIAN SUMMER by Richard Hellesen; Composer, Michael Silversher; Director, John-David Keller; Choreographer, Sylvia Turner; Scenic and Costume Design, Angela Balogh Calin; World Premiere; January 15–May 30, 2003; Cast: Christopher Lorenz (Koo-Nance), Peter McDaid (Jeff), Scott Most (Father), Hisa Takakuwa (Mother)

THE CARPETBAGGER'S CHILDREN by Horton Foote; Director, Martin Benson; Scenic and Costume Design, Angela Balogh Calin; Lighting Design, Paulie Jenkins; Sound Design, Mitch Greenhill; West Coast Premiere; January 28–February 16, 2003; Cast: Linda Gehringer (Sissie), Nan Martin (Grace Anne), Robin Pearson Rose (Cornelia)

TWO GENTLEMEN OF VERONA by William Shakespeare; Director, Mark Rucker; Scenic Design, Darcy Scanlin; Costume Design, Joyce Kim Lee; Lighting Design, Geoff Korf; Composer/Sound Design, Aram Arslanian; February 21–March 30, 2003; Cast: Guilford Adams (Thurio), Jennifer Elise Cox (Julia), Gregory Crane (Valentine), Nealy Glenn (Silvia), Erik Johnson (Eglamour), John-David Keller (Outlaw), Hal Landon Jr. (Panthino, Outlaw), Preston Maybank (Duke of Milan, Outlaw), Martha McFarland (Host, Outlaw), Daniel T. Parker (Speed), Scott Soren (Proteus), Don Took (Antonio, Outlaw), Travis Vaden (Launce), Rachel Dara Wolfe (Lucetta, Outlaw), Matt Demeritt, Katie Hall, Mandy Schmeider, Phillip C. Vaden

RELATIVELY SPEAKING by Alan Ayckbourn; Director, David Emmes; Scenic and Costume Design, Nephelie Andonyadis; Lighting Design, Lonnie Alcaraz; March 18–April 13, 2003; Cast: Richard Doyle (Philip), Jennifer Dundas (Ginny), Linda Gehringer (Sheila), Douglas Weston (Greg)

INTIMATE APPAREL by Lynn Nottage; Director, Kate Whoriskey; Scenic Design, Walt Spangler; Costume Design, Catherine Zuber; Lighting Design, Scott Zielinski; Sound Design, Lindsay Jones; Composer, Reginald Robinson; Arranger/Piano Coach, William Foster McDaniel; World Premiere co-produced with CenterStage (Baltimore); April 11–May 18, 2003; Cast: Sue Cremin (Mrs. Van Buren), Erica Gimpel (Mayme), Steven Goldstein (Mr. Marks), Kevin Jackson (George Armstrong), Brenda Pressley (Mrs. Dickson), Shané Williams (Esther)

(CONTINUED ON NEXT PAGE)

(CONTINUED FROM PREVIOUS PAGE)

THE INTELLIGENT DESIGN OF JENNY CHOW by Rolin Jones, Director, David Chambers; Scenic Design, Christopher Barreca; Costume Design, Dunya Ramicova; Lighting Design, Chris Parry; Composer/Sound Design, David Budries; World Premiere; April 29–May 18, 2003; Cast: Daniel Blinkoff (Todd, A Boy), Melody Butiu (Jennifer Marcus), JD Cullum (Preston, Terrence, Col. Hubbard, Dr. Yakunin, Voice of Computer Translator), Linda Gehringer (Adele Hartwick, Mrs. Zhang), April Hong (Jenny Chow), William Frances McGuire (Mr. Marcus, Mrs. Zhang)

Daniel Blinkoff, Melody Butiu in *The Intelligent Design of Jenny Chow* PHOTO BY KEN HOWARD

THE DRAWER BOY by Michael Healey; Director, Martin Benson; Scenic Design, James Youmans; Costume Design, Sylvia Rognstad; Lighting Design, John Philip Martin; Sound Design, Karl Fredrik Lundeberg; May 23–June 29, 2003; Cast: J. Todd Adams (Miles), Hal Landon Jr. (Morgan), Jimmie Ray Weeks (Angus)

STAMFORD THEATRE WORKS

Stamford, Connecticut
FIFTEENTH SEASON

Producing Director, Steve Karp; General Manager, Larry Frenock; Press Representative, Patricia Blaufuss

FULLY COMMITTED by Becky Mode; Director, Steve Karp; Scenic Design, Patrick McCluskey September 18–October 6, 2002; Cast: Athena Karkanis

SPINNING INTO BUTTER by Rebecca Gilman; Director, Doug Moser; Scenic Design, Patrick McCluskey; November 6–24, 2002; Cast: Danielle Di Vecchio (Sarah), Ivan Quintanilla (Patrick), Scott Kealey (Ross), George C. Hosmer (Dean Strauss), Sarah Peterson (Dean Kenney), Michael Waldron (Mr. Meyers), Edward Walsh (Greg)

A LESSON BEFORE DYING by Romulus Linney (Based on the novel by Ernest J. Gaines); Director, Patricia R. Floyd; Scenic Design, Richard Ellis; January 29–February 16, 2003; Cast: Patrick Moltane (Paul), Sharon Hope (Miss Emma), Royce Johnson (Grant), Darryl Gibson (Jefferson), Melissa Maxwell (Vivian), Hardy Rawls (Sheriff), Adam Wade (Reverend Ambrose)

SYNCOPATION by Allan Knee; Director, Doug Moser; Scenic Design, Richard Ellis; April 23–May 11, 2003; Cast: Sam Guncler (Henry Ribolow), Krista Braun (Anna Bianchi)

OVER THE RAINBOW: THE MUSIC OF HAROLD ARLEN Musical Director, David Bishop, Stage Director, Shawn Churchman; Scenic Design, Patrick McCluskey; June 11–29, 2003; Cast: Inga Ballard, David Coolidge, Andy Gale, Dominique Plaisant, Zakiya Young

SYRACUSE STAGE

Syracuse, New York
THIRTIETH SEASON

Artistic Director, Robert Moss; Producing Director Jim Clark

M. BUTTERFLY by David Henry Hwang; Directed by Robert Moss; Set Design by Michael Brown; Costume Design, Laura LaVon, Lighting Design, Dawn Chiang, Sound Design, Jonathan Herter; Stage Manager, Stuart Plymesser; September 18–October 12, 2002; Cast: Sun Mee Chomet (Chin, Suzuki, Shu Fang), Peter Davies (Toulon, Man #1, Judge), Genevieve Elam (Renee), Allen Fitzpatrick (Rene Gallimard), J LaRue (Song Liling), PJ Sosko (Marc, Man #2, Consul Sharpless), Lynne Wintersteller (Helga), Jordan Bass, Tara D'Antonio, Ignacio Serricchio, Kristi Williamson (Kurogo)

JITNEY by August Wilson; Directed by Timothy Douglas; Set Design, Paul Owen; Costume Design, Randall Klein; Lighting Design, Jane Hall; Sound Design,Vincent Olivieri; Stage Manager, Michele Ferguson; October 24–November 10, 2002; Cast: Pascale Armand (Rena), Doug Brown (Turnbo), Johnny Lee Davenport (Doub), Chuma Hunter Gault (Youngblood), Tyrone Mitchell Henderson (Philmore),William Charles Mitchell (Fielding), Charles Parnell (Booster), Ray Anthony Thomas (Stealy), Charles Weldon (Becker)

WEST SIDE STORY Based on a conception of Jerome Robbins; Book by Arthur Laurents, Music by Leonard Bernstein, Lyrics by Stephen Sondheim; Directed and Choreographed by Anthony Salatino; Musical Direction by Dianne Adams McDowell; A Syracuse Stage and S. U. Drama Department collaboration; Set Design, Troy Hourie; Costume Design, Randall Klein; Lighting Design, A. Nelson Ruger; Sound Design, Jonathan Herter; Stage Manager, Stuart Plymesser; November 29, 2002–January 5, 2003; Cast: Noah Aberlin (Shark, Pepe), Jordan Bass (Jet, Baby John), Josh Bradecich (Shark, Toro), Diane Cammarata (Shark, Teresita), Natalie Cortez (Maria), Lauren Creel (Shark, Francisca), Nicole Dupras (Jet, Clarice), Brett Essenter (Shark, Luis), Izetta Fang (Anita), Michael Gillis (Tony), Caroline Gulde (Shark, Margarita), Lauren Haughton (Shark, Estella), Kristin Hoesl (Jet, Velma), Paul James (Shark, Chino), Greg King (Jet, Action), Erin Kukla (Shark, Rosalia), Clarence Leggett (Shark, Anxious), Heidi Lembke (Shark, Consuelo), Nick Lichtenberg (Officer Krupke), George M. Livengood (Riff), Emily Mattheson (Jet, Anybody's), Marissa McGowan (Jet, Graziella), Eric Miller (Lt. Schrank, Glad Hand), Missy Morrison (Jet, Minnie), Cory Pattak (Shark, Juano), Michael Penna (Jet, Diesel), Jill Samuel (Jet, Pauline) Robb Sapp (Snowboy) Matthew Stucky (Jet, Big Deal), Renee Threatte (Shark, Esperanzit), David Villella (Bernardo), Booker T. Washington (Doc), Stuart Williams (Jet, A-Rab), Kristi Williamson (Jet, Sandra)

David Villella, Izetta Fang in *West Side Story* PHOTO BY OTTAVIANO

BACKSLIDING IN THE PROMISED LAND by Michele Lowe; Directed by Robert Moss; Set Design, Adam Stockhausen; Costume Design, Nanzi Adzima; Lighting Design, Matthew Frey; Sound Design, Jonathan Herter; Stage Manager, Michelle Ferguson; World premiere; January 15–February 2, 2003; Cast: Jacqueline Brookes (Enid), Suzanne Grodner (Mimi), Munson Hicks (Herman), Anne Penner (Naomi), Judith Roberts (Ludmilla); Tommy Schrider (Saul, Janitor), Kelly Trumbull (Jenny, Nurse), Alex Friedman (Leo), Ryan Ferguson (Leo)

THE CRUCIBLE by Arthur Miller; Revisioning of classic: Cast primarily with African-Americans Directed by Timothy Douglas; Set Design, Tony Cisek; Lighting Design, Michael Gilliam; Costume Design, Tracy Dorman; Sound Design, Jonathan Herter; Stage Manager, Stuart Plymesser; February 19–March 22, 2003; Cast: Cynthia Addai-Robinson (Abigail), Emily Agy (Betty Parris), Inga Ballard (Ann Putnam, Sarah Good), Marsha Stephanie Blake (Tituba), Doug Brown (Cheever), Johnny Lee Davenport (Thomas Putnam), Ariel Dupas (Girl of Salem), Richard Harris (Francis Nurse), Tyrone Mitchell Henderson (Rev. Parris), Malcolm Ingram (Giles Corey), Tamara E. Johnson (Mary Warren), Rachel Leslie (Elizabeth Proctor), Larry John Meyers (Reverend John Hale), Markiss Simpson (Willard), Kim Sullivan (Danforth), Ray Anthony Thomas (John Proctor), Renee Threatte (Mercy Lewis), Jane Welch (Rebecca Nurse)

COPENHAGEN by Michael Frayn; Directed by Michael Donald Edwards; Set Design, Andrew Lieberman; Lighting Design, Les Dickert; Costume Design, Kaye Voyce; Sound Design, Jonathan Herter; Stage Manager, Michelle Ferguson April 2–April 20, 2003; Cast: John Leonard Thompson (Heisenberg), Nancy Snyder (Margrethe), Paul Whitworth (Bohr)

SUCH SMALL HANDS by Tina Howe (commissioned by Syracuse Stage specifically for Ms. Franz); Directed by Robert Moss; Set Design, Donald Eastman; Costume Design, Michael Krass; Lighting Design, Chris Dallos; Sound Design, Jonathan Herter; Stage Manager, Stuart Plymesser; World premiere; April 30–May 25, 2003; Cast: Elizabeth Franz

TRINITY REPERTORY COMPANY

Providence, Rhode Island

THIRTY-NINTH SEASON

Artistic Director, Oskar Eustis; Managing Director, Edgar Dobie

THE SKIN OF OUR TEETH by Thornton Wilder; Director Amanda Dehnert; Scenic Design, David Jenkins; Costume Design, William Lane; Lighting Design, John Ambrosone; Sound Design, Peter Sasha Hurowitz; September 6–October 13, 2002; Cast: William Damkoehler (Mr. Antrobus), Phyllis Kay (Mrs. Antrobus), Stephen Thorne (Henry Antrobus), Rachael Warren (Sabina), Stephen Berenson, Janice Duclos, Mauro Hantman, Brian McEleney, Dan Welch, J. Fitz Harris, Claire Lewis

CLOUD NINE by Caryl Churchill; Director Tony Taccone; Scenic Design, Loy Arcenas, Costume Design, William Lane; Lighting Design, James Vermeulen; Sound Design, Matt Spiro; September 20–November 13, 2002; Cast: Timothy Crowe (Clive, Cathy), Danny Scheie (Betty, Gerry), Matthew Boston (Joshua, Edward), Angela Brazil (Edward, Victoria), Cynthia Strickland (Maud), Amy Van Nostrand (Ellen, Mrs. Saunders, Lin), Fred Sullivan Jr. (Harry Bagley, Martin)

Janice Duclos, Nehassaiu deGannes, William Damkoehler, Rachael Warren, Phyllis Kay in *The Skin of Our Teeth* PHOTO BY T. CHARLES ERICKSON

Cynthia Strickland, Timothy Crowe in *Cloud Nine* PHOTO BY T. CHARLES ERICKSON

Matthew Velina, Kyle Brown, Janice Duclos, Laurel Pecchia, Brian McEleney in *A Christmas Carol* PHOTO BY T. CHARLES ERICKSON

A CHRISTMAS CAROL by Charles Dickens; Adaptation, Adrian Hall and Richard Cumming; Music and Lyrics, Richard Cumming; Director, Mark Sutch; Musical Director, Amanda Dehnert; Scenic Design, Beowulf Boritt; Costume Design, William Lane; Lighting Design, Deb Sullivan; Sound Design, Peter Sasha Hurowitz; November 16–December 28, 2002; Cast: Jay Bragan, Sarah Dimuro, Janice Duclos, Andy Gaukel, Eric Greenlund, Mauro Hantman, Neil Hellegers, Phyllis Kay, Brian McEleney, Maya Parra, Alexa Palmer, Fred Sullivan Jr., Rachael Warren, Kevin Fallon, Rachel Maloney, Chris Turner, Christopher Brady, Kyle Brown, Arista Ely, Ari Itkin, Barret LaPlante, Evan Lourenco, Laurel Astri Pecchia, Thomas Pfanstiel, Stacey Peloquin, Tyler Perry, Patrick Saunders, Matthew Velino, Stephen Berenson, Angela Brazil, Seth Compton, Melissa D'Amico, William Damkoehler, Nehassaiu deGannes, J. Fitz Harris, Joseph Foss, David Rabinow, Paul Ricciardi, Cynthia Strickland, Dan Welch, Angela Williams, Claire Lewis, Chris Lussier, Lili Chase-Lubitz, Melanie Chitwood, Seth Chitwood, Kevin Coccio, Danielle Darling, Charlotte Forcht, Leah Kenney, Drew Kline, Brianna McBride, Collin McCarron, David Mizzoni, Dakota Pimentel

COPENHAGEN by Michael Frayn; Director, Oskar Eustis; Scenic and Lighting Design, Eugene Lee; Costume Design, William Lane; Sound Design, Peter Sasha Hurowitz; December 6, 2002–January 19, 2003; Cast: Stephen Thorne (Werner Heisenberg), Timothy Crowe (Niels Bohr), Anne Scurria (Margrethe Bohr)

Fred Sullivan Jr., Stephen Thorne in *Stones in His Pockets* PHOTO BY T. CHARLES ERICKSON

Angela Brazil, Cynthia Strickland, Phyllis Kay in *Nickel and Dimed* PHOTO BY T. CHARLES ERICKSON

STONES IN HIS POCKETS by Marie Jones; Director Brian McEleney; Scenic Design, Michael McGarty; Costume Design, William Lane; Lighting Design, John Ambrosone; Sound Design, Peter Sasha Hurowitz; February 22–April 6, 2003; Cast: Fred Sullivan Jr., Stephen Thorne

THE WDUM FAMILY RADIO HOUR Writer and Director, Bill Harley; World Premiere; March 8, 15, and April 5, 2003; Cast: Anitra Brooks, Bill Harley, Keith Munslow, Kenny Raskin, Valerie Remillard

(CONTINUED ON NEXT PAGE)

NICKEL & DIMED by Joan Holden, Adapted from the book by Barbara Ehrenreich; Director, Kevin Moriarty; Scenic Design, Beowulf Boritt; Costume Design, William Lane; Lighting Design, Jeff Croiter; Sound Design, Peter Sasha Hurowitz; January 31–March 9, 2003; Cast: Cynthia Strickland, Angela Brazil, Mauro Hantman, Phyllis Kay, Barbara Meek, Maya Parra, Eric Fontana

Andrea C. Ross, Fred Sullivan Jr. in *Annie* PHOTO BY T. CHARLES ERICKSON

(CONTINUED FROM TRINITY REPERTORY COMPANY)

ANNIE Book by Thomas Meehan; Music by Charles Strouse; Lyrics by Martin Charmin; Director, Amanda Dehnert; Scenic Design, David Jenkins; Costume Design, William Lane; Lighting Design, Bryon Winn; Choreographer, Sharon Jenkins; Sound Design, Peter Sasha Hurowitz; April 25–June 8, 2003; Cast: Andrea C. Ross (Annie), Fred Sullivan Jr.(Oliver Warbucks), Janice Duclos (Miss Hannigan), Lola (Sandy), Drew Battles, Melissa D'Amico, William Damkoehler, Wilkie Ferguson III, Scott Franco, Mauro Hantman, Lori Holmes, Phyllis Kay, Matthew LaBlanca, Brian McEleney, Patrick Pettys, Erick Pinnick, Miriam Silverman, Denise Summerford, Myxy Tyler, Dan Welch, Angela Williams, Kyle Brown, Joy Williams, Maia Chao, Brianna McBride, Amy Esposito, Amber Johnson, Daniella Gould, Claire Lewis, Tiia Groden, Erin Maughan, Patti Laliberte, Siara Padilla, Shannon Hartman, Johanna Wickemeyer, Abby Rose, Kevin Fallon, Chris Lussier, Tim Robertson, Jessie Darrell

THE LONG CHRISTMAS RIDE HOME by Paula Vogel; Director, Oskar Eustis; Scenic Design, Loy Arcenas; Costume Design, William Lane; Lighting Design, Pat Collins; Choreographer, Donna Uchizono; Sound Design, Darron L. West; Puppet Design, Basil Twist; World premiere; May 16–June 29, 2003; Cast: Angela Brazil (Claire), Timothy Crowe (Man), Sean Martin Hingston (Minister), Anne Scurria (Woman), Stephen Thorne (Stephen), Rachael Warren (Rebecca), Joshua Boggioni, Joanna Cole, Virginia Eckert, Andy Gaukel, Maya Parra, Paul Ricciardi, Sumie Kaneko

Angela Brazil, Ann Scuria, Stephen Thorne in *The Long Christmas Ride Home*
PHOTO BY T. CHARLES ERICKSON

RICHARD III by William Shakespeare; Director, Amanda Dehnert; Fight Choreographer, Craig Handel; Sound Design, Peter Sasha Hurowitz; May–August, 2003; Cast: Noah Brody (Rivers, Mayor), Andy Grotelueschen (Buckingham), Claire Karpen (Lady Anne), Mariah Sage Leeds (Queen Margaret), Sean McConaghy (Clarence, Prince Edward, Richmond), Niambi Nataki (Queen Elizabeth), Brian Platt (Catesby, King Edward), Ben Steinfeld (Richard III, Duke of Gloucester)

MUCH ADO ABOUT NOTHING by William Shakespeare; Director, Maria Goyanes; Sound Design, Peter Sasha Hurowitz; June–August, 2003; Cast: Noah Brody (Benedick), Andy Grotelueschen (Dogberry, Don John), Claire Karpen (Margaret, Verges), Mariah Leeds (Beatrice), Sean McConaghy (Claudio), Niambi Nataki (Hero), Brian Platt (Leonato), Ben Steinfeld (Friar, Borachio)

WALNUT STREET THEATRE

Philadelphia, Pennsylvania

TWENTIETH SEASON

Producing Artistic Director, Bernard Havard; Managing Director, Mark D. Sylvester

SHE LOVES ME Book, Joe Masteroff; Music, Jerry Bock; Lyrics, Sheldon Harnick; Based on a play by Miklos Laszlo; Original Orchestrations, Don Walker; Adapted by Frank Matosich, Jr.; Director/Choreographer, James Brennan; Music Director, Edward Reichert; Set Designer, Charles S. Kading; Costume Designer, Colleen McMillan; Lighting Designer, Jeffrey S. Koger; September 3–October 20, 2002; Mainstage; Cast: Bill Bateman (Sipos); Chip Klose (Arpad); Linda Romanoff (Ilona); David Hess (Kodaly); Jeffrey Coon (Georg); Larry Raiken (Maraczek); Brigid Brady (Amalia); John-Charles Kelly (Headwaiter); Linsay Chambers, Christopher DeAngelis, Mary Martello, Jesse Padgett, Joyce A. Presutti, Rebecca Robbins, Alecia Robinson, Ed Romanoff, Brian J. Swasey

THE SOUND OF MUSIC Book, Howard Lindsay & Russel Crouse; Music, Richard Rodgers; Lyrics, Oscar Hammerstein II; Director, Charles Abbott; Choreographer, Andrew Glant-Linden; Music Director, Sherman Frank; Set Designer, John Farrell; Costume Supervisor, Colleen McMillan; Lighting Designer, Jeffrey S. Koger; Sound Designer, P.J. Stasuk; November 5, 2002–January 5, 2003; Mainstage Cast: Luann Aronson (Maria); James Brennan (Von Trapp); Ann Arvia (Mother Abbess); Mary Martello (Elsa); John-Charles Kelly (Max); Sharon Alexander; Nick Baker; Andie Belkoff; Kathryn Brunner; Gillian Burke; Rachel Cohen; Jeffrey Coon; Rob DelColle; Kevin DeYoe; Jeremy R. Dueh; Maureen Francis; Zachary Freed; Lee Golden; Melissa Joy Hart; Carly Hawkins; Benjamin Kanes; Scott Langdon; AJ Luca; Victoria Masteller; Barbara McCullough; Joyce Moody; Ryan Musik; Joyce A. Presutti; Roxanne Quilty; Taylor Quilty; Christine Robertson; Ed Romanoff; Donna M. Ryan; Dan Schiff; Bobby Steggert; Jamie Lynn Udinson; Arianna Vogel; Denise Whealan; Alyse Wojciechowski; Adrienne Young

BRIGHTON BEACH MEMOIRS by Neil Simon; Director, Frank Ferrante; Set Designer, David P. Gordon; Costume Designer, Colleen McMillan; Lighting Designer, Troy A. Martin-O'Shia; Sound Designer, Scott Smith; January 14–March 2, 2003; Mainstage; Cast: Jennifer Alimonti (Nora); Lisbeth Bartlett (Blanche); Jesse Bernstein (Eugene); Scott Greer (Stanley); Tom McCarthy (Jack); Ellen Tobie (Kate); Alyse Wojciechowski (Laurie)

THE VOYSEY INHERITANCE by Harley Granville-Barker; Director, Malcolm Black; Set & Lighting Designer, Paul Wonsel; Costume Designer, Hilary Corbett; Musical Composition, Laura Burton; March 11–April 27, 2003; Mainstage; Cast: Paxton Whitehead (Mr. Voysey); Blair Williams (Edward); Ian D. Clark (Peacy); Grace Gonglewski (Alice); Michael Lombard (George Booth); Ian Merrill Peakes (Hugh); Ted Pejovich (Booth); Alicia Roper (Beatrice); Sharon Alexander; Jennifer Alimonti; Neale Anthony DiMento; Lorraine Foreman; J. Andrew Keitch; Louis Lippa; Sally Mercer; Sara Pauley; Hayden Saunier; Dan Schiff

Ana Maria Andricain in *Evita* PHOTO BY COY BUTLER

Michael Lombard, Paxton Whitehead in *The Voysey Inheritance* PHOTO BY GERRY GOODSTEIN

EVITA Lyrics, Tim Rice; Music, Andrew Lloyd Webber; Director, Bruce Lumpkin; Choreographer, Richard Stafford; Musical Director, Louis F. Goldberg; Set Designer, John Farrell; Costume Designer, Colleen McMillan; Lighting Designer, Jeffrey S. Koger; Sound Designer, Scott Smith. May 6–July 6, 2003; Mainstage; Cast: Ana Maria Andricain (Eva); Jeffrey Coon (Che); Scott Holmes (Peron); Vincent D'Elia (Magaldi); Christina DeCicco (Peron's Mistress); Kristine Fraelich (Eva Alternate); Gillian Burke, Renee Chambers, Anne Connors, Natalie Cortez, Gregory Daniels, Christopher DeAngelis, Michelle Gaudette, Mollie Hall, David Jackson, J. Andrew Keitch, David Kent, Scott Langdon, Michael McKee, Rebecca Robbins, Dan Schiff, Eadie Scott, Jonathan Stahl, Michael Susko, Bill Van Horn

(CONTINUED ON NEXT PAGE)

(CONTINUED FROM PREVIOUS PAGE)

THE LAST FLAPPER by William Luce; Director, Frank Burd; Set Designer, Kirsten Poizanski; Costume Designer, Karla Irwin; Lighting Designer, Shelley Hicklin; Sound Designer, Nick Rye. January 7–19, 2003; Studio on 3; Cast: Grace Gonglewski (Zelda Fitzgerald)

Grace Gonglewski in *The Last Flapper* PHOTO BY COY BUTLER

WRONG FOR EACH OTHER by Norm Foster; Director, Marcia Tratt; Set Designer, Glen W. Sears; Costume Designer, Kelly Pantzlaff; Lighting Designer, Robb Anderson; Sound Designer, Matthew Callahan, February 4–16, 2003; Studio on 3; Cast: Deborah Seif (Norah); Russ Widdall (Rudy)

THE LAKE by Robert Caisley; Director, Richard M. Parison, Jr.; Set Designer, Todd Edward Ivins; Costume Designer, Colleen McMillan; Lighting Designer, Troy Martin-O'Shia; Sound Designer, J. Hagenbuckle. March 4–16, 2003; Studio on 3; Cast: Juliette Dunn (Nicola); Dan Olmstead (Martin); Seth Reichgott (Alec); Jeremy Webb (Liam)

SUMMONS TO SHEFFIELD by Will Stutts; Director, Will Stutts; Set Designer, Virginia Jarvis; Costume Designer, Mary Folino; Lighting Designer, Shelley Hicklin; Sound Designer, John Mock. April 1–13, 2003; Studio on 3; Cast: Mollie Hall (Diane); Will Stutts (Ben); Maureen Torsney-Weir (Luara-Lucille); Adam Way (Wren); Susan Wilder (Sarah)

JACQUES BREL IS ALIVE AND WELL AND LIVING IN PARIS English Lyrics & Additional Material by Eric Blau & Mort Shuman; Based on Brel's Lyrics & Commentary; Music by Jacques Brel; Director, Brian Feehan; Musical Director, Mark Yurkanin; Set Designer, Ander Longenderfer; Costume Designer, Naomi Katz; Lighting Designer, Shelley Hicklin. April 29–June 8, 2003; Studio on 3; Cast: Jennifer Governor; Melissa Joy Hart, Jay Montgomery, Christopher Sapienza

YALE REPERTORY THEATRE

New Haven, Connecticut
THIRTY-SEVENTH SEASON

James Bundy, Artistic Director; Victoria Nolan, Managing Director; Mark Bly, Associate Artistic Director

MEDEA/MACBETH/CINDERELLA Conceived by Bill Rauch; Adapted by Bill Rauch and Tracy Young from Euripides' *Medea* as translated by Paul Roche; Music and Lyrics, Shishir Kurup; William Shakespeare's *Macbeth* and Rodgers & Hammerstein's *Cinderella* with Music by Richard Rodgers, Book and Lyrics, Oscar Hammerstein; *Medea* songs arranged, orchestrated, and recorded by David Markowitz with Shishir Kurup; Nurse's opening speec translator, Brendan Kennelly; Director, Bill Rauch and Tracy Young; Choreographer, Sabrina Peck; Music Director, Steven Argila; Set Design, Rachel Hauck; Costume Design, David Zinn; Lighting Design, Jennifer Tipton; Sound Design, David Budries; Fight Direction, Rick Sordelet; Vocal Coach, Walton Wilson; Dramaturgs, Mark Bly and Christine Evangelisto; Stage Manager, Karen Quisenberry; University Theatre; September 20–October 12, 2002; Cast: Caroline Stefanie Clay (Medea), Stefani Cvijetic (Portia), David Paul Francis (Banquo), Jennifer Griffin (Jason, Chorus of Corinthian Women), Alaina Reed Hall (Godmother), Chavon Aileen Hampton (Medea's Son I, II), Latrice Hampton (Medea's Son I), Jayne Houdyshell (Nurse), Peter Howard (Macduff), Kimberly JaJuan (Queen), Peter Kim (Prince), Ryan King (Third Witch, Rebel, Murderer), Jennifer Lim (Joy), Horace A. Little (Duncan), Derek Lucci (First Witch, Rebel, Murderer, Doctor), Peter Macon (Malcolm), Heather Mazur (Cinderella), Christopher Liam Moore (Lady Macbeth), Kate A. Mulligan (Chorus Leader), Adam O'Byrne (Second Witch, Rebel, Murderer), April Ortiz (Stepmother), Maulik Pancholy (Fleance), Daniel T. Parker (Stage Manager), Stephen Pelinski (Macbeth), Joan Schirle (Tutor, Creon, Chorus of Corinthian Women), Staysha Liz Silva (Medea's Son II), Christopher Spencer Wells (King) Musicians: Andrew Byrne (Conductor), Daine Orson (Musician), David Wonsey (Musician) Understudies: Christianna Nelson (Queen), Anita Gandhi (Medea), Bianca Jones (Portia), Adam Saunders (Banquo), Mozhan Navabi (Jason, Chorus), Maulik Pancholy (Macduff), Amanda Cobb (Nurse, Chorus), Jacob Knoll (Prince), Jeffrey Barry (Third Witch, Rebel, Murderer), Stephen Moore (Duncan), Amanda Cobb (Joy), Allen Read (First Witch, Rebel, Murderer, Doctor), LeRoy McClain (Malcolm), Gabrielle Castini (Cinderella), Ryan King (Lady MacBeth), Mikelle Johnson (Chorus Leader), Jeffrey Withers (Second Witch, Rebel, Murderer), Mozhan Navabi (Stepmother), Jedadiah Schultz (Fleance), David Bardeen (Stage Manager), Peter Macon (Macbeth), Bianca Jones (Godmother), Christianna Nelson (Tutor, Creon, Chorus), Lucas Howland (King)

BREATH, BOOM by Kia Corthron; Director, Michael John Garcés; Scenic Design, Wilson Chin; Costume Design, China Lee; Lighting Design, Torkel Skjaerven; Sound Design, Martin Desjardins; Fight Choreography, Rick Sordelet; Dramaturg, Emmy Grinwis; Stage Manager, Elena M. Maltese; Casting, Johson-Liff Associates, Ltd. Yale University Theatre; October 25–November 16, 2002; Cast: Opal Alladin (Prix), Donna Duplantier (Cat), Saidah Arrika Ekulona (Mother), Jan Leslie Harding (Denise), Carla J. Hardgrove (Malika, Socks), Phyllis Johnson (Jupiter), Billy Eugene Jones

(Jerome, Corrections Officer), Afi McClendon (Comet), Tijuana T. Ricks (Pepper, Officer Dray, Jo's Friend), Heather Alicia Simms (Angel), Kellee Stewart (Shondra, Jo), Marilyn Torres (Fuego, Girl) Understudies: Tijuana T. Ricks (Prix), Phyllis Johnson (Cat, Shondra, Jo), Arshenna Hines (Mother), Kristin Fiorella (Denise), Bianca Jones (Malika, Socks, Jupiter), Jordan Mahome (Jerome, Corrections Officer), Tamara Malawitz (Angel, Comet, Pepper), Robyn Ganales (Fuego)

FIGHTING WORDS by Sunil Thomas Kuruvilla; Director, Liz Diamond; Scenic Design, Marie Davis-Green; Costume Design, Meredith Palin; Lighting Design, Scott Bolman; Sound Design, Karl Mansfield; Dramaturg, Linda Bartholomai; Dialect Coach, Pamela Prather; Boxing Coach, Ray Velez; Stage Manager, Christine Collins; Casting, Johnson-Liff Associates, Ltd.; Yale Repertory Theatre; November 15–December 21, 2002; Cast: Emma Bowers (Peg), Meg Brogan (Nia), Jayne Houdyshell (Mrs. Davies) Understudies: Heather Lea Anderson (Peg), Maryne Young (Nia), Stefani Katarina Cvijetic (Mrs. Davies)

(CONTINUED ON NEXT PAGE)

Christopher Liam Moore, members of the Company of *Medea/Macbeth/Cinderella*
PHOTO BY JOAN MARCUS

Donna Duplantier, Opal Alladin in *Breath, Boom*

Meg Brogan, Jayne Houdyshell, Emma Bowers in *Fighting Words*

(CONTINUED FROM PREVIOUS PAGE)

THE PSYCHIC LIFE OF SAVAGES by Amy Freed; Director, James Bundy; Scenic Design, Young Ju Baik; Costume Design, Corrine Larson; Lighting Design, Torkel Skjaerven; Sound Design, Sten Severson; Dramaturg, Emily V. Shooltz; Vocal Coach, Pamela Prather; Fight Director, Rick Sordelet; Stage Manager, Laura MacNeil; Casting, Johnson-Liff Casting, Ltd. Yale Repertory Theatre; February 14–March 8, 2003; Cast: Fiona Gallagher (Sylvia Fluellen), Robyn Ganeles (Rebecca, Kit-Kat, Student, Party Guest), Meg Gibson (Anne Bittenhand), John Hines (Ted Magus), Bill Klux (Interviewer, Tito, Student, Party Guest), Will Marchetti (Dr. Robert Stoner), Phyllis Somerville (Emily Dickinson, Vera)

THE TAMING OF THE SHREW by William Shakespeare; Director, Mark Lamos; Choreography, Seán Curran; Scenic Design, Leiko Fuseya; Costume Design, Wade Laboissonniere; Lighting Design, Scott Bolman; Sound Design, David Budries; Dramaturgs, Mark Bly and John J. Hanlon; Vocal Coach, Beth McGuire; Fight Director, Rick Sordelet; Stage Manager, Lisa Porter; Casting, Andrew M. Zerman; Yale Repertory Theatre; March 21–April 12, 2003; Cast: Bryant Mason (Lucentio), Trindy Sandoval (Tranio), Lazaro Perez (Baptista), Jesse J. Perez (Gremio), Ramón de Ocampo (Kate), Charles Daniel Sandoval (Hortensio), Caesar Samayoa (Bianca), Tom Lee (Biondello), Joseph Urla (Petruchio), Orlando Pabotoy (Grumio), Jordan Mahome (Curtis), Rey Lucas (Clemente), LeRoy James McClain (Pedro), Stephen Moore (José), Adam Saunders (Guillermo), Adam Richman (Sugarsop), Derek Lucci (Pedant), Thom Rivera (Tailor, Vincentio), Anthony Manna (Lusty Widow), Jesse Gabbard (Boy) Understudies: Jacob Blumer (Kate); Rey Lucas (Petruchio), Derek Lucci (Baptista), Jordan Mahome (Gremio), Anthony Manna (Grumio), LeRoy James McClain (Hortensio, Lusty Widow), Stephen Moore (Biondello, Curtis); Adam Richman (Lucentio), Adam Saunders (Pedant, Tranio), Carlos M. Tesoro (Bianca, Tailor, Vincentio)

THE BLACK MONK by David Rabe, based on the novella by Anton Chekhov; Directed by Daniel Fish; Scenic Design, Christine Jones; Costume Design, Jane Greenwood; Lighting Design, Stephen Strawbridge; Sound Design, Leah Gelpe; Choreography, Peter Pucci; Music Director, Vicki Shaghoian; Vocal Coach, Walton Wilson; Dramaturg, Carrie Hughes; Stage Manager, Karen Quisenberry; Assistant Stage Manager, Christine Collins; Casting, Andrew Zerman; Yale Repertory Theatre; May 9–June 1, 2003; Cast: Sam Waterston (Yegor Semyonitch Pesotsky), Jenny Bacon (Tanya), Thomas Jay Ryan (Andrei Vasilich Kovrin), Leo Leyden (Orlov), Paul Mullins (Mikhail), Nancy Anderson (Nadia), Haynes Thigpen (Yakov), Christopher McCann (The Black Monk), Pamela Nyberg (Varvara Nikolaevna), Nancy Anderson, Matthew Martin, Paul Mullins, Haynes Thigpen, Jeffrey Withers (Workers, Guests, Ensemble) Understudies: Adam O'Byrne (Pesotsky), Mikelle Johnson (Tanya), Jacob Knoll (Kovrin), Lucas Howland (Orlov, Worker), Amanda Cobb (Nadia, Ensemble), Kevin Rich (Mikhail, Ensemble), Jeffrey Withers (Yakov, Ensemble), Ryan King (The Black Monk), Anita Gandhi (Varvara), Allen Read (Ensemble)

Sam Waterston, Thomas Jay Ryan in *Black Monk* PHOTO BY JOAN MARCUS

Caesar Samayoa, Ramon de Ocampo in *Taming of the Shrew*

AWARDS

2003 THEATRE WORLD AWARD WINNERS

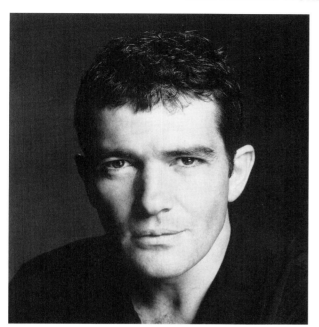

Antonio Banderas of *Nine*

Tammy Blanchard of *Gypsy*

Thomas Jefferson Byrd of *Ma Rainey's Black Bottom*

Jonathan Cake of *Medea*

Victoria Hamilton of *A Day in the Death of Joe Egg*

Clare Higgins of *Vincent in Brixton*

Jackie Hoffman of *Hairspray*

Mary Stuart Masterson of *Nine*

John Selya of *Movin' Out*

Daniel Sunjata of *Take Me Out*

Jochum ten Haaf of *Vincent in Brixton*

Marissa Jaret Winokur of *Hairspray*

SPECIAL THEATRE WORLD AWARDS

Peter Filichia, Treasurer of Theatre World Awards, Inc., and Master of Ceremonies of the Theatre World Awards ceremony, for Outstanding Stewardship of the Theatre World Awards ceremony

Ben Hodges, Associate Editor of Theatre World, Board member of the Theatre World Awards, Inc., and Executive Producer of the Theatre World Awards, for Outstanding Stewardship of the Theatre World Awards ceremony

59TH ANNUAL
THEATRE WORLD AWARDS PRESENTATION

Studio 54; Monday, June 2, 2003

Created in 1944 by *Theatre World* founders Daniel Blum, Norman MacDonald, and John Willis to coincide with the first release of *Theatre World*, the now fifty-nine-year-old definitive pictorial and statistical record of the American theatre, the Theatre World Awards are the oldest awards given for debut performances in New York City, as well as one of the oldest honors bestowed on New York actors.

A committee of New York drama critics currently joins longtime *Theatre World* editor John Willis in choosing six actors and six actresses for the Theatre World Award, who have distinguished themselves in Broadway and Off-Broadway productions during the past theatre season. Occasionally, Special Theatre World Awards are also bestowed on performers, casts, or others who have made a particularly lasting impression on the New York theatre scene.

The Theatre World Award "Janus" statuette is an original bronze sculpture in primitive-modern style created by internationally recognized artist Harry Marinsky. It is adapted from the Roman myth of Janus, god of entrances, exits, and all beginnings, with one face appraising the past and the other anticipating the future. It is cast and mounted on marble in the Del Chiaro Foundry in Pietrasanta, Italy.

Theatre World Awards Board members:

Tom Lynch, President
Marianne Tatum, Vice President
Patricia Elliott, Secretary
Peter Filichia, Treasurer
David Birney
Ben Hodges
Walter Willison

The Theatre World Awards are voted on by the following committee of New York drama critics:

Clive Barnes (*New York Post*), Peter Filichia (*Theatermania.com*), Harry Haun (*Playbill*), Ben Hodges (*Theatre World*), Frank Scheck (*The Hollywood Reporter*), Michael Sommers (*Newark Star Ledger*), Douglas Watt (*The Daily News*), John Willis (*Theatre World*), and Linda Winer (*Newdsay*)

Master of Ceremonies, Peter Filichia

Executive Producer, Ben Hodges

Associate editor of *Theatre World* and Theatre World Awards executive producer, Ben Hodges

2003 Theatre World Award winner Victoria Hamilton with fellow *A Day in the Death of Joe Egg* cast members Eddie Izzard and Dana Ivey

2003 Theatre World Award winners Tammy Blanchard (*Gypsy*) and Daniel Sunjata (*Take Me Out*)

Brad Hampton and Laura Hagan with associate editor of *Theatre World* and Theatre World Awards executive producer, Ben Hodges

Theatre World Award presenter and previous winner Eddie Izzard

2003 Theatre World Award winner Thomas Jefferson Byrd

2003 Theatre World Award winner Antonio Banderas (*Nine*), with former Theatre World winner and presenter, Linda Hart

Dana Ivey with *Theatre World* editor John Willis

Previous Theatre World Award winners and 2003 presenters Harvey Fierstein, Brian Stokes Mitchell, and Linda Hart

Theatre World Award winner Marissa Jaret Winokur (*Hairspray*)

Special entertainment for the ceremony courtesy of Stephanie D'Abruzzo and John Tartaglia of *Avenue Q*

Theatre World Award winner Clare Higgins (*Vincent in Brixton*)

Theatre World Award winner Tammy Blanchard with previous Theatre World Award winner, presenter, and fellow *Gypsy* cast member, Bernadette Peters

2003 presenters and previous Theatre World Award winners Patricia Elliott, Elizabeth Ashley, Harvey Fierstein, Brian Stokes Mitchell, and Linda Hart

Previous Theatre World Award winners and 2003 presenters Elizabeth Ashley and Harvey Fierstein

Master of Ceremonies and Treasurer of the Theatre World Awards, Peter Filichia

Previous Theatre World Award winners and 2003 presenters Danielle Ferland and Lewis J. Stadlen

Theatre World Award winner Antonio Banderas

Ben Hodges with previous winner and Secretary of the Theatre World Awards, Patricia Elliott

Theatre World Award winner John Selya (*Movin' Out*)

Theatre World editor John Willis

Entertainer Stephanie D'Abruzzo

Previous Theatre World Award winner and 2003 presenter, Tovah Feldshuh

2003 Theatre World Award winner Victoria Hamilton (*A Day in the Death of Joe Egg*)

John Willis and previous Theatre World Award winner Marianne Tatum, with 2003 Theatre World Award presenters

Lucie Arnaz

Marlon Brando

Nell Carter

James Earl Jones

PREVIOUS THEATRE WORLD AWARD RECIPIENTS

1944–45: Betty Comden, Richard Davis, Richard Hart, Judy Holliday, Charles Lang, Bambi Linn, John Lund, Donald Murphy, Nancy Noland, Margaret Phillips, John Raitt

1945–46: Barbara Bel Geddes, Marlon Brando, Bill Callahan, Wendell Corey, Paul Douglas, Mary James, Burt Lancaster, Patricia Marshall, Beatrice Pearson

1946–47: Keith Andes, Marion Bell, Peter Cookson, Ann Crowley, Ellen Hanley, John Jordan, George Keane, Dorothea MacFarland, James Mitchell, Patricia Neal, David Wayne

1947–48: Valerie Bettis, Edward Bryce, Whitfield Connor, Mark Dawson, June Lockhart, Estelle Loring, Peggy Maley, Ralph Meeker, Meg Mundy, Douglass Watson, James Whitmore, Patrice Wymore

1948–49: Tod Andrews, Doe Avedon, Jean Carson, Carol Channing, Richard Derr, Julie Harris, Mary McCarty, Allyn Ann McLerie, Cameron Mitchell, Gene Nelson, Byron Palmer, Bob Scheerer

1949–50: Nancy Andrews, Phil Arthur, Barbara Brady, Lydia Clarke, Priscilla Gillette, Don Hanmer, Marcia Henderson, Charlton Heston, Rick Jason, Grace Kelly, Charles Nolte, Roger Price

1950–51: Barbara Ashley, Isabel Bigley, Martin Brooks, Richard Burton, Pat Crowley, James Daley, Cloris Leachman, Russell Nype, Jack Palance, William Smithers, Maureen Stapleton, Marcia Van Dyke, Eli Wallach

1951–52: Tony Bavaar, Patricia Benoit, Peter Conlow, Virginia de Luce, Ronny Graham, Audrey Hepburn, Diana Herbert, Conrad Janis, Dick Kallman, Charles Proctor, Eric Sinclair, Kim Stanley, Marian Winters, Helen Wood

1952–53: Edie Adams, Rosemary Harris, Eileen Heckart, Peter Kelley, John Kerr, Richard Kiley, Gloria Marlowe, Penelope Munday, Paul Newman, Sheree North, Geraldine Page, John Stewart, Ray Stricklyn, Gwen Verdon

1953–54: Orson Bean, Harry Belafonte, James Dean, Joan Diener, Ben Gazzara, Carol Haney, Jonathan Lucas, Kay Medford, Scott Merrill, Elizabeth Montgomery, Leo Penn, Eva Marie Saint

1954–55: Julie Andrews, Jacqueline Brookes, Shirl Conway, Barbara Cook, David Daniels, Mary Fickett, Page Johnson, Loretta Leversee, Jack Lord, Dennis Patrick, Anthony Perkins, Christopher Plummer

1955–56: Diane Cilento, Dick Davalos, Anthony Franciosa, Andy Griffith, Laurence Harvey, David Hedison, Earle Hyman, Susan Johnson, John Michael King, Jayne Mansfield, Sara Marshall, Gaby Rodgers, Susan Strasberg, Fritz Weaver

1956–57: Peggy Cass, Sydney Chaplin, Sylvia Daneel, Bradford Dillman, Peter Donat, George Grizzard, Carol Lynley, Peter Palmer, Jason Robards, Cliff Robertson, Pippa Scott, Inga Swenson

1957–58: Anne Bancroft, Warren Berlinger, Colleen Dewhurst, Richard Easton, Tim Everett, Eddie Hodges, Joan Hovis, Carol Lawrence, Jacqueline McKeever, Wynne Miller, Robert Morse, George C. Scott

1958–59: Lou Antonio, Ina Balin, Richard Cross, Tammy Grimes, Larry Hagman, Dolores Hart, Roger Mollien, France Nuyen, Susan Oliver, Ben Piazza, Paul Roebling, William Shatner, Pat Suzuki, Rip Torn

1959–60: Warren Beatty, Eileen Brennan, Carol Burnett, Patty Duke, Jane Fonda, Anita Gillette, Elisa Loti, Donald Madden, George Maharis, John McMartin, Lauri Peters, Dick Van Dyke

1960–61: Joyce Bulifant, Dennis Cooney, Sandy Dennis, Nancy Dussault, Robert Goulet, Joan Hackett, June Harding, Ron Husmann, James MacArthur, Bruce Yarnell

1961–62: Elizabeth Ashley, Keith Baxter, Peter Fonda, Don Galloway, Sean Garrison, Barbara Harris, James Earl Jones, Janet Margolin, Karen Morrow, Robert Redford, John Stride, Brenda Vaccaro

1962–63: Alan Arkin, Stuart Damon, Melinda Dillon, Robert Drivas, Bob Gentry, Dorothy Loudon, Brandon Maggart, Julienne Marie, Liza Minnelli, Estelle Parsons, Diana Sands, Swen Swenson

1963–64: Alan Alda, Gloria Bleezarde, Imelda De Martin, Claude Giraud, Ketty Lester, Barbara Loden, Lawrence Pressman, Gilbert Price, Philip Proctor, John Tracy, Jennifer West

1964–65: Carolyn Coates, Joyce Jillson, Linda Lavin, Luba Lisa, Michael O'Sullivan, Joanna Pettet, Beah Richards, Jaime Sanchez, Victor Spinetti, Nicolas Surovy, Robert Walker, Clarence Williams III

1965–66: Zoe Caldwell, David Carradine, John Cullum, John Davidson, Faye Dunaway, Gloria Foster, Robert Hooks, Jerry Lanning, Richard Mulligan, April Shawhan, Sandra Smith, Leslie Ann Warren

1966–67: Bonnie Bedelia, Richard Benjamin, Dustin Hoffman, Terry Kiser, Reva Rose, Robert Salvio, Sheila Smith, Connie Stevens, Pamela Tiffin, Leslie Uggams, Jon Voight, Christopher Walken

1967–68: David Birney, Pamela Burrell, Jordan Christopher, Jack Crowder (Thalmus Rasulala), Sandy Duncan, Julie Gregg, Stephen Joyce, Bernadette Peters, Alice Playten, Michael Rupert, Brenda Smiley, Russ Thacker

1968–69: Jane Alexander, David Cryer, Blythe Danner, Ed Evanko, Ken Howard, Lauren Jones, Ron Leibman, Marian Mercer, Jill O'Hara, Ron O'Neal, Al Pacino, Marlene Warfield

1969–70: Susan Browning, Donny Burks, Catherine Burns, Len Cariou, Bonnie Franklin, David Holliday, Katharine Houghton, Melba Moore, David Rounds, Lewis J. Stadlen, Kristoffer Tabori, Fredricka Weber

1970–71: Clifton Davis, Michael Douglas, Julie Garfield, Martha Henry, James Naughton, Tricia O'Neil, Kipp Osborne, Roger Rathburn, Ayn Ruymen, Jennifer Salt, Joan Van Ark, Walter Willison

1971–72: Jonelle Allen, Maureen Anderman, William Atherton, Richard Backus, Adrienne Barbeau, Cara Duff-MacCormick, Robert Foxworth, Elaine Joyce, Jess Richards, Ben Vereen, Beatrice Winde, James Woods

1972–73: D'Jamin Bartlett, Patricia Elliott, James Farentino, Brian Farrell, Victor Garber, Kelly Garrett, Mari Gorman, Laurence Guittard, Trish Hawkins, Monte Markham, John Rubinstein, Jennifer Warren; Special Award: Alexander H. Cohen

1973–74: Mark Baker, Maureen Brennan, Ralph Carter, Thom Christopher, John Driver, Conchata Ferrell, Ernestine Jackson, Michael Moriarty, Joe Morton, Ann Reinking, Janie Sell, Mary Woronov; Special Award: Sammy Cahn

1974–75: Peter Burnell, Zan Charisse, Lola Falana, Peter Firth, Dorian Harewood, Joel Higgins, Marcia McClain, Linda Miller, Marti Rolph, John Sheridan, Scott Stevensen, Donna Theodore; Special Award: Equity Library Theatre

1975–76: Danny Aiello, Christine Andreas, Dixie Carter, Tovah Feldshuh, Chip Garnett, Richard Kelton, Vivian Reed, Charles Repole, Virginia Seidel, Daniel Seltzer, John V. Shea, Meryl Streep; Special Award: *A Chorus Line*

1976–77: Trazana Beverley, Michael Cristofer, Joe Fields, Joanna Gleason, Cecilia Hart, John Heard, Gloria Hodes, Juliette Koka, Andrea McArdle, Ken Page, Jonathan Pryce, Chick Vennera; Special Award: Eva LeGallienne

1977–78: Vasili Bogazianos, Nell Carter, Carlin Glynn, Christopher Goutman, William Hurt, Judy Kaye, Florence Lacy, Armelia McQueen, Gordana Rashovich, Bo Rucker, Richard Seer, Colin Stinton; Special Award: Joseph Papp

1978–79: Philip Anglim, Lucie Arnaz, Gregory Hines, Ken Jennings, Michael Jeter, Laurie Kennedy, Susan Kingsley, Christine Lahti, Edward James Olmos, Kathleen Quinlan, Sarah Rice, Max Wright; Special Award: Marshall W. Mason

1979–80: Maxwell Caulfield, Leslie Denniston, Boyd Gaines, Richard Gere, Harry Groener, Stephen James, Susan Kellermann, Dinah Manoff, Lonny Price, Marianne Tatum, Anne Twomey, Dianne Wiest; Special Award: Mickey Rooney

1980–81: Brian Backer, Lisa Banes, Meg Bussert, Michael Allen Davis, Giancarlo Esposito, Daniel Gerroll, Phyllis Hyman, Cynthia Nixon, Amanda Plummer, Adam Redfield, Wanda Richert, Rex Smith; Special Award: Elizabeth Taylor

1981–82: Karen Akers, Laurie Beechman, Danny Glover, David Alan Grier, Jennifer Holliday, Anthony Heald, Lizbeth Mackay, Peter MacNicol, Elizabeth McGovern, Ann Morrison, Michael O'Keefe, James Widdoes; Special Award: Manhattan Theatre Club

1982–83: Karen Allen, Suzanne Bertish, Matthew Broderick, Kate Burton, Joanne Camp, Harvey Fierstein, Peter Gallagher, John Malkovich, Anne Pitoniak, James Russo, Brian Tarantina, Linda Thorson; Special Award: Natalia Makarova

1983–84: Martine Allard, Joan Allen, Kathy Whitton Baker, Mark Capri, Laura Dean, Stephen Geoffreys, Todd Graff, Glenne Headly, J.J. Johnston, Bonnie Koloc, Calvin Levels, Robert Westenberg; Special Award: Ron Moody

1984–85: Kevin Anderson, Richard Chaves, Patti Cohenour, Charles S. Dutton, Nancy Giles, Whoopi Goldberg, Leilani Jones, John Mahoney, Laurie Metcalf, Barry Miller, John Turturro, Amelia White; Special Award: Lucille Lortel

1985–86: Suzy Amis, Alec Baldwin, Aled Davies, Faye Grant, Julie Hagerty, Ed Harris, Mark Jacoby, Donna Kane, Cleo Laine, Howard McGillin, Marisa Tomei, Joe Urla; Special Award: Ensemble Studio Theatre

1986–87: Annette Bening, Timothy Daly, Lindsay Duncan, Frank Ferrante, Robert Lindsay, Amy Madigan, Michael Maguire, Demi Moore, Molly Ringwald, Frances Ruffelle, Courtney B. Vance, Colm Wilkinson; Special Award: Robert DeNiro

1987–88: Yvonne Bryceland, Philip Casnoff, Danielle Ferland, Melissa Gilbert, Linda Hart, Linzi Hately, Brian Kerwin, Brian Mitchell, Mary Murfitt, Aidan Quinn, Eric Roberts, B.D. Wong; Special Awards: Tisa Chang, Martin E. Segal

1988–89: Dylan Baker, Joan Cusack, Loren Dean, Peter Frechette, Sally Mayes, Sharon McNight, Jennie Moreau, Paul Provenza, Kyra Sedgwick, Howard Spiegel, Eric Stoltz, Joanne Whalley-Kilmer; Special Awards: Pauline Collins, Mikhail Baryshnikov

1989–90: Denise Burse, Erma Campbell, Rocky Carroll, Megan Gallagher, Tommy Hollis, Robert Lambert, Kathleen Rowe McAllen, Michael McKean, Crista Moore, Mary-Louise Parker, Daniel von Bargen, Jason Workman; Special Awards: Stewart Granger, Kathleen Turner

1990–91: Jane Adams, Gillian Anderson, Adam Arkin, Brenda Blethyn, Marcus Chong, Paul Hipp, LaChanze, Kenny Neal, Kevin Ramsey, Francis Ruivivar, Lea Salonga, Chandra Wilson; Special Awards: Tracey Ullman, Ellen Stewart

1991–92: Talia Balsam, Lindsay Crouse, Griffin Dunne, Larry Fishburne, Mel Harris, Jonathan Kaplan, Jessica Lange, Laura Linney, Spiro Malas, Mark Rosenthal, Helen Shaver, Al White; Special Awards: *Dancing at Lughnasa* Company, Plays for Living

1992–93: Brent Carver, Michael Cerveris, Marcia Gay Harden, Stephanie Lawrence, Andrea Martin, Liam Neeson, Stephen Rea, Natasha Richardson, Martin Short, Dina Spybey, Stephen Spinella, Jennifer Tilly. Special Awards: John Leguizamo, Rosetta LeNoire

1993–94: Marcus D'Amico, Jarrod Emick, Arabella Field, Adam Gillett, Sherry Glaser, Michael Hayden, Margaret Illman, Audra Ann McDonald, Burke Moses, Anna Deavere Smith, Jere Shea, Harriet Walter

1994–95: Gretha Boston, Billy Crudup, Ralph Fiennes, Beverly D'Angelo, Calista Flockhart, Kevin Kilner, Anthony LaPaglia, Julie Johnson, Helen Mirren, Jude Law, Rufus Sewell, Vanessa Williams; Special Award: Brooke Shields

1995–96: Jordan Baker, Joohee Choi, Karen Kay Cody, Viola Davis, Kate Forbes, Michael McGrath, Alfred Molina, Timothy Olyphant, Adam Pascal, Lou Diamond Phillips, Daphne Rubin-Vega, Brett Tabisel; Special Award: *An Ideal Husband* Cast

1996–97: Terry Beaver, Helen Carey, Kristin Chenoweth, Jason Danieley, Linda Eder, Allison Janney, Daniel McDonald, Janet McTeer, Mark Ruffalo, Fiona Shaw, Antony Sher, Alan Tudyk; Special Award: *Skylight* Cast

1997–98: Max Casella, Margaret Colin, Ruaidhri Conroy, Alan Cumming, Lea Delaria, Edie Falco, Enid Graham, Anna Kendrick, Ednita Nazario, Douglas Sills, Steven Sutcliffe, Sam Trammel; Special Awards: Eddie Izzard, *Beauty Queen of Leenane* Cast

1998–99: Jillian Armenante, James Black, Brendan Coyle, Anna Friel, Rupert Graves, Lynda Gravatt, Nicole Kidman, Ciaran Hinds, Ute Lemper, Clarke Peter, Toby Stephens, Sandra Oh; Special Award: Jerry Herman

1999–2000: Craig Bierko, Everett Bradley, Gabriel Byrne, Ann Hampton Callaway, Toni Collette, Henry Czerny, Stephen Dillane, Jennifer Ehle, Philip Seymour Hoffman, Hayley Mills, Cigdem Onat, Claudia Shear

2000–2001: Juliette Binoche, Macaulay Culkin, Janie Dee, Raúl Esparza, Kathleen Freeman, Devin May, Reba McEntire, Chris Noth, Joshua Park, Rosie Perez, Joely Richardson, John Ritter; Special Awards: Seán Campion, Conleth Hill

2001–2002: Justin Bohon, Simon Callow, Mos Def, Emma Fielding, Adam Godley, Martin Jarvis, Spencer Kayden, Gretchen Mol, Anna Paquin, Louise Pitre, David Warner, Rachel Weisz

Major Theatrical **Awards**

AMERICAN THEATRE WING'S ANTOINETTE PERRY "TONY" AWARDS

The 57th annual Tony Awards are presented in recognition of distinguished achievement in the Broadway theater. The 2002–2003 Tony Awards Nominating Committee (appointed by the Tony Awards Administration Committee), included: Maureen Anderman, actor; Price Berkley, publisher; Ira Bernstein, manager; Robert Calley, administrator; Schuyler G. Chapin, executive; Veronica Claypool, manager; Betty Corwin, archivist; Gretchen Cryer, composer; Merle Debuskey, press; Edgar Dobie, manager; David Marshall Grant, actor; Micki Grant, composer; Julie Hughes, casting; Betty Jacobs, consultant; Robert Kamlot, manager; David Lindsay-Abaire, playwright; Theodore Mann, producer; Gilbert Parker, agent; Shirley Rich, casting; David Richards, journalist; Aubrey Reuben, photographer; Arthur Rubin, producer; Judith Rubin, executive; Bill Schelble, press; Meg Simon, casting; Sister Francesca Thompson, educator; Rosemarie Tichler, casting; Jon Wilner, producer

BEST PLAY (award goes to both author as well as producer): *Take Me Out* by Richard Greenberg; produced by Carole Shorenstein Hays, Frederick DeMann, the Donmar Warehouse and the Public Theater

Nominees: *Enchanted April* by Matthew Barber; produced by Jeffrey Richards, Richard Gross/Ellen Berman/Les Goldman, Raymond J. and Pearl Berman Greenwald, Irving Welzer, Jerry Frankel, Terry E. Schnuck, Frederic B. Vogel, Dori Berinstein/Barrie and Jim Locks/Dramatic Forces; *Say Goodnight, Gracie* by Rupert Holmes; produced by William Franzbau, Jay H. Harris, Louise Westergaard, Larry Spellman, Elsa Daspin Haft, Judith Resnick, Anne Gallagher, Libby Adler Mages/Mari Glick, Martha R. Gasparian, Bruce Lazarus, Lawrence S. Toppall, Jae French; *Vincent in Brixton* by Nicholas Wright; produced by Lincoln Center Theater, André Bishop, Bernard Gersten, The Royal National Theatre, Ambassador Theatre Group Ltd, Maidstone Productions, Robert Fox Ltd., Elliot F. Kulick, Incidental Coleman Tod, the Shubert Organization

BEST MUSICAL (award goes to producer): *Hairspray* produced by Margo Lion, Adam Epstein, the Baruch-Viertel-Routh-Frankel Group, James D. Stern/Douglas L. Meyer, Rick Steiner/Frederic H. Mayerson, SEL and the Gordon/Frost Organization, New Line Cinema, Clear Channel Entertainment, Allan S. Gordon/Elan V. McAllister, Dede Harris/Morton Swinsky, John and Bonnie Osher

Nominees: *Amour* produced by the Shubert Organization, Jean Doumanian Productions, Inc., USA Ostar Theatricals; *A Year With Frog and Toad* produced by Bob Boyett, Adrianne Lobel, Michael Gardner, Lawrence Horowitz, Roy Furman, Scott E. Nederlander, the Children's Theatre Company; *Movin' Out* produced by James L. Nederlander, Hal Luftig, Scott E. Nederlander, Terry Allen Kramer, Clear Channel Entertainment, Emanuel Azenberg;

BEST BOOK OF A MUSICAL: Mark O'Donnell and Thomas Meehan, *Hairspray*

Nominees: Didier van Cauwelaert, with English adaptation by Jeremy Sams, *Amour*; Willie Reale, *A Year With Frog and Toad;* David Henry Hwang, *Flower Drum Song*

BEST ORIGINAL SCORE (music and lyrics): Marc Shaiman (music), Scott Wittman and Marc Shaiman (lyrics), *Hairspray*

Nominees: Robert Reale (music) and Willie Reale (lyrics), *A Year With Frog and Toad*; Michael Legrand (music) and Didier van Cauwelaert, with English adaptation by Jeremy Sams (lyrics), *Amour*; Jeff Blumenkrantz, Bob Stillman, Jason Robert Brown, Danny Arena, Sara Light, Lauren Lucas, Jerry Silverstein, Martie Maguire, Wayland D. Holyfield, Bob Lee House, Carl L. Byrd, Pevin Byrd Munoz, Luke Reed, Roger Brown, Jerry Chestnut, Marcus Hammon, Clint Black, James Hayden Nicholas, Tommy Connors, Skip Ewing, Charles Daniels, Tom Crain, Fred Edwards, Taz DiGregorio, Jim Marshall, Charlie Hayward, Wanda Mallette, Patti Ryan, Ronnie Dunn and Bob Morrison (music and lyrics), *Urban Cowboy*

BEST REVIVAL OF A PLAY (award goes to producer): *Long Day's Journey Into Night* produced by David Richenthal, Max Cooper, Eric Falkenstein, Anthony and Charlene Marshall, Darren Bagert, Kara Medoff, Lisa Vioni, Gene Korf

Nominees: *A Day in the Death of Joe Egg* produced by Roundabout Theatre Company, Todd Haimes, Ellen Richard, Julia C. Levy, Sonia Friedman Productions; *Dinner at Eight* produced by Lincoln Center Theater, André Bishop, Bernard Gersten; *Frankie and Johnny in the Clair de Lune* produced by the Araca Group, Jean Doumanian Productions, USA Ostar Theatricals, Jam Theatricals, Ray and Kit Sawyer

BEST REVIVAL OF A MUSICAL (award goes to producer): *Nine*, produced by Roundabout Theatre Company, Todd Haimes, Ellen Richard, Julia C. Levy

Nominees: *Gypsy*, produced by Robert Fox, Ron Kastner, Roger Marino, Michael Watt, Harvey Weinstein, WWLC; *La Bohéme* produced by Jeffrey Seller, Kevin McCollum, Emanuel Azenberg, Bazmark Live, Bob and Harvey Weinstein, Korea Pictures/Doyun Seol, Jeffrey Sine/Ira Pittelman/Scott E. Nederlander, fox Searchlight Pictures; *Man of La Mancha* produced by David Stone, Jon B. Platt, Susan Quint Gallin, Sandy Gallin, Seth M. Siegel, USA Ostar Theatricals, Mary Lu Roffe

BEST SPECIAL THEATRICAL EVENT: *Russell Simmons's Def Poetry Jam* on Broadway produced by Russell Simmons, Stan Lathan, Jonathan Reinis, Richard Martini, Larry Magid, Allen Spivak, Kimora Lee Simmons, Jeffrey Chartier, Stacy Carter, Island Def Jam Music Group

Nominees: *Bill Maher: Victory Begins at Home* produced by Eric Krebs, Jonathan Reinis, CTM Productions, Anne Strickland Squadron, Michael Viner, David and Adam Friedson, Allen Spivak/Larry Magid, M. Kilburg Reedy; *The Play What I Wrote* produced by David Pugh, Joan Cullman, Mike Nichols, Hamilton South, Charles Whitehead, Stuart Thompson; *Prune Danish* produced by Jyll Rosenfeld, Jon Stoll

BEST PERFORMANCE BY A LEADING ACTOR IN A PLAY: Brian Dennehy, *Long Day's Journey Into Night*

Nominees: Brian Bedford, *Tartuffe*; Eddie Izzard, *A Day in the Death of Joe Egg*; Paul Newman, *Our Town*; Stanley Tucci, *Frankie and Johnny in the Clair de Lune*

(CONTINUED FROM PREVIOUS PAGE)

BEST PERFORMANCE BY A LEADING ACTRESS IN A PLAY:
Vanessa Redgrave, *Long Day's Journey Into Night*

Nominees: Jayne Atkinson, *Enchanted April*; Victoria Hamilton, *A Day in the Death of Joe Egg*; Clare Higgins, *Vincent in Brixton*; Fiona Shaw, *Medea*

BEST PERFORMANCE BY A LEADING ACTOR IN A MUSICAL:
Harvey Fierstein, *Hairspray*

Nominees: Antonio Banderas, *Nine*; Malcolm Gets, *Amour*; Brian Stokes Mitchell, *Man of La Mancha*; John Selya, *Movin' Out*

BEST PERFORMANCE BY A LEADING ACTRESS IN A MUSICAL:
Marissa Jaret Winokur, *Hairspray*

Nominees: Melissa Errico, *Amour*; Mary Elizabeth Mastrantonio, *Man of La Mancha*; Elizabeth Parkinson, *Movin' Out*; Bernadette Peters, *Gypsy*

BEST PERFORMANCE BY A FEATURED ACTOR IN A PLAY: Denis O'Hare, *Take Me Out*

Nominees: Thomas Jefferson Byrd, *Ma Rainey's Black Bottom*; Philip Seymour Hoffman, *Long Day's Journey Into Night*; Robert Sean Leonard, *Long Day's Journey Into Night*; Daniel Sunjata, *Take Me Out*

BEST PERFORMANCE BY A FEATURED ACTRESS IN A PLAY:
Michelle Pawk, *Hollywood Arms*

Nominees: Christine Ebersole, *Dinner at Eight*; Linda Emond, *Life (x) 3*; Kathryn Meisle, *Tartuffe*; Marian Seldes, *Dinner at Eight*

BEST PERFORMANCE BY A FEATURED ACTOR IN A MUSICAL:
Dick Latessa, *Hairspray*

Nominees: Michael Cavanaugh, *Movin' Out*; John Dossett, *Gypsy*; Corey Reynolds, *Hairspray*; Keith Roberts, *Movin' Out*

BEST PERFORMANCE BY A FEATURED ACTRESS IN A MUSICAL: Jane Krakowski, *Nine*

Nominees: Tammy Blanchard, *Gypsy*; Mary Stuart Masterson, *Nine*; Chita Rivera, *Nine*; Ashley Tuttle, *Movin' Out*

BEST SCENIC DESIGN: Catherine Martin, *La Bohéme*

Nominees: John Lee Beatty, *Dinner at Eight*; Santo Loquasto, *Long Day's Journey Into Night*; David Rockwell, *Hairspray*

BEST COSTUME DESIGN: William Ivey Long, *Hairspray*

Nominees: Gregg Barnes, *Flower Drum Song*; Catherine Martin and Angus Strathie, *La Bohéme*; Catherine Zuber, *Dinner at Eight*

BEST LIGHTING DESIGN: Nigel Levings, *La Bohéme*

Nominees: Donald Holder, *Movin' Out*; Brian MacDevitt, *Nine*; Kenneth Posner, *Hairspray*

BEST CHOREOGRAPHY: Twyla Tharp, *Movin' Out*

Nominees: Robert Longbottom, *Flower Drum Song*; Jerry Mitchell, *Hairspray*; Melinda Roy, *Urban Cowboy*

BEST DIRECTION OF A PLAY: Joe Mantello, *Take Me Out*

Nominees: Laurence Boswell, *A Day in the Death of Joe Egg*; Robert Falls, *Long Day's Journey Into Night*; Deborah Warner, *Medea*

BEST DIRECTION OF A MUSICAL: Jack O'Brien, *Hairspray*

Nominees: David Leveaux, *Nine*; Baz Luhrmann, *La Bohéme*; Twyla Tharp, *Movin' Out*

BEST ORCHESTRATIONS: Billy Joel and Stuart Malina, *Movin' Out*

Nominees: Nicholas Kitsopoulos, *La Bohéme*; Jonathan Tunick, *Nine*; Harold Wheeler, *Hairspray*

SPECIAL TONY AWARD FOR LIFETIME ACHIEVEMENT IN THE THEATRE: Cy Feuer

REGIONAL THEATRE TONY AWARD: The Children's Theatre Company, Minneapolis, Minnesota

Past Tony Award Winners

Awards listed are Best Play followed by Best Musical, and as awards for Best Revival and the subcategories of Best Revival of a Play and Best Revival of a Musical were instituted, they are listed respectively.

1947: No award given for musical or play **1948:** Mister Roberts (play) **1949:** Death of a Salesman, Kiss Me, Kate (musical) **1950:** The Cocktail Party, South Pacific **1951:** The Rose Tattoo, Guys and Dolls **1952:** The Fourposter, The King and I **1953:** The Crucible, Wonderful Town **1954:** The Teahouse of the August Moon, Kismet **1955:** The Desperate Hours, The Pajama Game **1956:** The Diary of Anne Frank, Damn Yankees **1957:** Long Day's Journey into Night, My Fair Lady **1958:** Sunrise at Campobello, The Music Man **1959:** J.B., Redhead **1960:** The Miracle Worker, Fiorello! tied with The Sound of Music **1961:** Becket, Bye Bye Birdie **1962:** A Man for All Seasons, How to Succeed in Business Without Really Trying **1963:** Who's Afraid of Virginia Woolf?, A Funny Thing Happened on the Way to the Forum **1964:** Luther, Hello Dolly! **1965:** The Subject Was Roses, Fiddler on the Roof **1966:** The Persecution and Assassination of Marat as Performed by the Inmates of the Asylum of Charenton Under the Direction of the Marquis de Sade, Man of La Mancha **1967:** The Homecoming, Cabaret **1968:** Rosencrantz and Guildenstern Are Dead, Hallelujah Baby! **1969:** The Great White Hope, 1776 **1970:** Borstal Boy, Applause **1971:** Sleuth, Company **1972:** Sticks and Bones, Two Gentlemen of Verona **1973:** That Championship Season, A Little Night Music **1974:** The River Niger, Raisin **1975:** Equus, The Wiz **1976:** Travesties, A Chorus Line **1977:** The Shadow Box, Annie **1978:** Da, Ain't Misbehavin', Dracula (innovative musical revival) **1979:** The Elephant Man, Sweeney Todd **1980:** Children of a Lesser God, Evita, Morning's at Seven (best revival) **1981:** Amadeus, 42nd St., The Pirates of Penzance **1982:** The Life and Adventures of Nicholas Nickelby, Nine, Othello **1983:** Torch Song Trilogy, Cats, On Your Toes **1984:** The Real Thing, La Cage aux Folles, Death of a Salesman **1985:** Biloxi Blues, Big River, Joe Egg **1986:** I'm Not Rappaport, The Mystery of Edwin Drood, Sweet Charity **1987:** Fences, Les Misérables, All My Sons **1988:** M. Butterfly, The Phantom of the Opera, Anything Goes **1989:** The Heidi Chronicles, Jerome Robbins' Broadway, Our Town **1990:** The Grapes of Wrath, City of Angels, Gypsy **1991:** Lost in Yonkers, The Will Rogers' Follies, Fiddler on the Roof **1992:** Dancing at Lughnasa, Crazy for You, Guys and Dolls **1993:** Angels in America: Millenium Approaches, Kiss of the Spider Woman,

Anna Christie **1994:** Angels in America: Perestroika (play), Passion (musical), An Inspector Calls (play revival), Carousel (musical revival) **1995:** Love! Valour! Compassion!, Sunset Boulevard, Show Boat, The Heiress **1996:** Master Class, Rent, A Delicate Balance, King and I **1997:** Last Night of Ballyhoo, Titanic, A Doll's House, Chicago **1998:** Art, The Lion King, View from the Bridge, Cabaret **1999:** Side Man, Fosse, Death of a Salesman, Annie Get Your Gun **2000:** Copenhagen, Contact, The Real Thing, Kiss Me, Kate **2001:** Proof, The Producers, One Flew Over the Cuckoo's Nest, 42nd Street **2002:** Edward Albee's The Goat, or Who Is Sylvia?, Thoroughly Modern Millie, Private Lives, Into the Woods

VILLAGE VOICE OBIE AWARDS

48th annual; For outstanding achievement in Off- and Off-Off-Broadway theater:

Performance: Kathleen Chalfant, Daniel Davis, Christine Ebersole, Valerie Mahaffey, Lynn Redgrave, Brenda Wehle, *Talking Heads*; Mos Def, *Fucking A*; Rosemary Harris, *All Over*; Ty Jones, J. Kyle Manzay, *The Blacks: A Clown Show*; Stephen Mellor, *Bitter Bierce, Or the Friction We Call Grief*; Edward Norton, *Burn This*; Jim Norton, *Dublin Carol*; Denis O'Hare, *Take Me Out*; Jason Petty, *Hank Williams: Lost Highway*; Simon Russell Beale, *Uncle Vanya*; Fiona Shaw, *Medea*; Barry Del Sherman, *The Mystery of Attraction*

Direction: Emily Mann, *All Over*; Deborah Warner, *Medea*

Sustained Excellence in Lighting Design: Kenneth Posner

Set Design: Anthony Ward, *Uncle Vanya*

Costume Design: Kimberly Glennon, *The Blacks: A Clown Show*

Sound Design: Whit MacLaughlin, *The Fab 4 Reach the Pearly Gates*

Mask Design: Anne Lommel, *The Blacks: A Clown Show*

Lifetime Achievement: Mac Wellman

Special Citations: Art Acuña, Loy Arcenas, Lonnie Carter, Ramon de Ocampo, Ron Domingo, Jojo Gonzalez, Orlando Pabotoy, Ralph Peña, *The Romance of Magno Rubio*; Brooklyn Academy of Music International Programming; Lisa D'Amour, Katie Pearl, Kathy Randels, *Nita and Zita*; David Greenspan, *She Stoops to Comedy*; Morgan Jenness for Longtime Support of Playwrights; John Kani, Winston Ntshona, *The Island*; Erika Munk, for editing *Theater*; Ellen Maddow, Paul Zimet, Diane Beckett, Gary Brownlee, Randolph Curtis Rand, Steven Rattazzi, Tina Shepard, Louise Smith, Nic Ularu, Kiki Smith, Carol Mullins, Karinne Keithley, "Blue" Gene Tyranny, *Talking Band's Painted Snake in a Painted Chair*

Grants: Collapsible Hole, Galapagos, The Immigrant Theatre Project

Ross Wetzsteon Award: Soho Think Tank's Ice Factory Series at the Ohio Theater

Past Obie Best New Play Winners

1956: Absalom, Absalom **1957:** A House Remembered **1958:** no award given **1959:** The Quare Fellow **1960:** no award given **1961:** The Blacks **1962:** Who'll Save the Plowboy? **1963**: no award given **1964:** Play **1965:** The Old Glory **1966:** The Journey of the Fifth Horse **1967:** no award given **1968:** no award given **1969:** no award given **1970:** The Effect of Gamma Rays on Man-in-the-Moon Marigolds **1971:** House of Blue Leaves **1972:** no award given **1973:** The Hot L Baltimore **1974:** Short Eyes **1975:** The First Breeze of Summer **1976:** American Buffalo, Sexual Perversity in Chicago **1977:** Curse of the Starving Class **1978:** Shaggy Dog Animation **1979:** Josephine **1980:** no award given **1981:** FOB **1982:** Metamorphosis in Miniature, Mr. Dead and Mrs. Free **1983:** Painting Churches, Andrea Rescued, Edmond **1984:** Fool for Love **1985:** The Conduct of Life **1986:** no award given **1987:** The Cure, Film Is Evil, Radio Is Good **1988:** Abingdon Square **1989:** no award given **1990:** Prelude to a Kiss, Imperceptible Mutabilities in the Third Kingdom, Bad Benny, Crowbar, Terminal Hip **1991:** The Fever **1992:** Sight Unseen, Sally's Rape, The Baltimore Waltz **1993:** no award given **1994:** Twilight: Los Angeles 1992 **1995:** Cyrptogram **1996:** Adrienne Kennedy **1997:** One Flea Spare **1998:** Pearls for Pigs and Benita Canova **1999:** no award given **2000:** no award given **2001:** The Syringa Tree **2002:** no award given **2003:** no award given

DRAMA DESK AWARDS

48th annual; For outstanding achievement in the 2002–2003 season, voted on by an association of New York drama reporters, editors and critics from nominations made from a committee:

New Play: *Take Me Out*

New Musical: *Hairspray*

Revival of a Play: *Long Day's Journey Into Night*

Revival of a Musical: *Nine*

Book: Mark O'Donnell, Thomas Meehan, *Hairspray*

Composer: Marc Shaiman, *Hairspray*

Lyricist: Scott Wittman, Marc Shaiman, *Hairspray*

Music in a Play: Willy Schwarz, *Metamorphoses*

Actor in a Play: Eddie Izzard, *A Day in the Death of Joe Egg*

Actress in a Play: Vanessa Redgrave, *Long Day's Journey Into Night*

Featured Actor in a Play: Denis O'Hare, *Take Me Out*

Featured Actress in a Play: Lynn Redgrave, *Talking Heads*

Actor in a Musical: (tie) Antonio Banderas, *Nine*; Harvey Fierstein, *Hairspray*

Actress in a Musical: Marissa Jaret Winokur, *Hairspray*

Featured Actor in a Musical: Dick Latessa, *Hairspray*

Featured Actress in a Musical: Jane Krakowski, *Nine*

Solo Performance: Tovah Feldshuh, *Golda's Balcony*

Director of a Play: Robert Falls, *Long Day's Journey Into Night*

Director of a Musical: Jack O'Brien, *Hairspray*

Choreography: Twyla Tharp, *Movin' Out*

Orchestrations: Harold Wheeler, *Hairspray*

Set Design of a Play: John Lee Beatty, *Dinner at Eight*

Set Design of a Musical: Catherine Martin, *La Bohéme*

Costume Design: William Ivey Long, *Hairspray*

Lighting Design: Nigel Levings, *La Bohéme*

Sound Design: Acme Sound Partners, *La Bohéme*

Unique Theatrical Experience: *The Exonerated*

OUTER CRITICS CIRCLE AWARDS

53rd annual; For outstanding achievement in the 2002–2003 season, voted on by critics in out-of-town periodicals and media:

Broadway Play: *Take Me Out*

Off-Broadway Play: *The Exonerated*

Revival of a Play: *A Day in the Death of Joe Egg*

Actor in a Play: Eddie Izzard, *A Day in the Death of Joe Egg*

Actress in a Play: Jayne Atkinson, *Enchanted April*

Featured Actor in a Play: Denis O'Hare, *Take Me Out*

Featured Actress in a Play: Linda Emond, *Life (x) 3*

Director of a Play: Joe Mantello, *Take Me Out*

Broadway Musical: *Hairspray*

Off-Broadway Musical: *A Man of No Importance*

Revival of a Musical: *Nine*

Actor in a Musical: Antonio Banderas, *Nine*

Actress in a Musical: Marissa Jaret Winokur, *Hairspray*

Featured Actor in a Musical: Dick Latessa, *Hairspray*

Featured Actress in a Musical: Jane Krakowski, *Nine*

Director of a Musical: Jack O'Brien, *Hairspray*

Choreography: Twyla Tharp, *Movin' Out*

Scenic Design: Catherine Martin, *La Bohéme*

Costume Design: William Ivey Long, *Hairspray*

Lighting Design: Nigel Levings, *La Bohéme*

Solo Performance: Frank Gorshin, *Say Goodnight, Gracie*

John Gassner Playwriting Award: Matthew Barber, *Enchanted April*

Special Achievement Award: Ensemble performance, the cast of *Talking Heads*

PULITZER PRIZE AWARD WINNERS FOR DRAMA

1918: *Why Marry?* by Jesse Lynch Williams **1919:** no award **1920:** *Beyond the Horizon* by Eugene O'Neill **1921:** *Miss Lulu Bett* by Zona Gale **1922:** *Anna Christie* by Eugene O'Neill **1923:** *Icebound* by Owen Davis **1924:** *Hell-Bent for Heaven* by Hatcher Hughes **1925:** *They Knew What They Wanted* by Sidney Howard **1926:** *Craig's Wife* by George Kelly **1927:** *In Abraham's Bosom* by Paul Green **1928:** *Strange Interlude* by Eugene O'Neill **1929:** *Street Scene* by Elmer Rice **1930:** *The Green Pastures* by Marc Connelly **1931:** *Alison's House* by Susan Glaspell **1932:** *Of Thee I Sing* by George S. Kaufman, Morrie Ryskind, Ira and George Gershwin **1933:** *Both Your Houses* by Maxwell Anderson **1934:** *Men in White* by Sidney Kingsley **1935:** *The Old Maid* by Zoe Atkins **1936:** *Idiot's Delight* by Robert E. Sherwood **1937:** *You Can't Take It with You* by Moss Hart and George S. Kaufman **1938:** *Our Town* by Thornton Wilder **1939:** *Abe Lincoln in Illinois* by Robert E. Sherwood **1940:** *The Time of Your Life* by William Saroyan **1941:** *There Shall Be No Night* by Robert E. Sherwood **1942:** no award **1943:** *The Skin of Our Teeth* by Thornton Wilder **1944:** no award **1945:** *Harvey* by Mary Chase **1946:** *State of the Union* by Howard Lindsay and Russel Crouse **1947:** no award **1948:** *A Streetcar Named Desire* by Tennessee Williams **1949:** *Death of a Salesman* by Arthur Miller **1950:** *South Pacific* by Richard Rodgers, Oscar Hammerstein II, and Joshua Logan **1951:** no award **1952:** *The Shrike* by Joseph Kramm **1953:** *Picnic* by William Inge **1954:** *The Teahouse of the August Moon* by John Patrick **1955:** *Cat on a Hot Tin Roof* by Tennessee Williams **1956:** *The Diary of Anne Frank* by Frances Goodrich and Albert Hackett **1957:** *Long Day's Journey into Night* by Eugene O'Neill **1958:** *Look Homeward, Angel* by Ketti Frings **1959:** *J.B.* by Archibald MacLeish **1960:** *Fiorello!* by Jerome Weidman, George Abbott, Sheldon Harnick, and Jerry Bock **1961:** *All the Way Home* by Tad Mosel **1962:** *How to Succeed in Business Without Really Trying* by Abe Burrows, Willie Gilbert, Jack Weinstock, and Frank Loesser **1963:** no award **1964:** no award **1965:** *The Subject Was Roses* by Frank D. Gilroy **1966:** no award **1967:** *A Delicate Balance* by Edward Albee **1968:** no award **1969:** *The Great White Hope* by Howard Sackler **1970:** *No Place to Be Somebody* by Charles Gordone **1971:** *The Effect of Gamma Rays on Man-in-the-Moon Marigolds* by Paul Zindel **1972:** no award **1973:** *That Championship Season* by Jason Miller **1974:** no award **1975:** *Seascape* by Edward Albee **1976:** *A Chorus Line* by Michael Bennett, James Kirkwood, Nicholas Dante, Marvin Hamlisch, and Edward Kleban **1977:** *The Shadow Box* by Michael Cristofer **1978:** *The Gin Game* by D.L. Coburn **1979:** *Buried Child* by Sam Shepard **1980:** *Talley's Folly* by Lanford Wilson **1981:** *Crimes of the Heart* by Beth Henley **1982:** *A Soldier's Play* by Charles Fuller **1983:** *'night, Mother* by Marsha Norman **1984:** *Glengarry Glen Ross* by David Mamet **1985:** *Sunday in the Park with George* by James Lapine and Stephen Sondheim **1986:** no award **1987:** *Fences* by August Wilson **1988:** *Driving Miss Daisy* by Alfred Uhry **1989:** *The Heidi Chronicles* by Wendy Wasserstein **1990:** *The Piano Lesson* by August Wilson **1991:** *Lost in Yonkers* by Neil Simon **1992:** *The Kentucky Cycle* by Robert Schenkkan **1993:** *Angels in America: Millenium Approaches* by Tony Kushner **1994:** *Three Tall Women* by Edward Albee **1995:** *Young Man from Atlanta* by Horton Foote **1996:** *Rent* by Jonathan Larson **1997:** no award **1998:** *How I Learned to Drive* by Paula Vogel **1999:** *Wit* by Margaret Edson **2000:** *Dinner with Friends* by Donald Margulies **2001:** *Proof* by David Auburn **2002:** *Topdog/Underdog* by Suzan Lori-Parks **2003:** *Anna in the Tropics* by Nilo Cruz

NEW YORK DRAMA CRITICS CIRCLE AWARD WINNERS

2003 New York Drama Critics' Circle Committee: President, Charles Isherwood (*Variety*), Clive Barnes (*The New York Post*), Jeremy Carter (*The New York Sun*), David Cote (*Time Out New York*), Michael Feingold (*The Village Voice*), Robert Feldberg (*The Bergen Record*), John Heilpern (*The New York Observer*), Howard Kissel (*Daily News*), Michael Kuchwara (*The Associated Press*), Jacques le Sourd (*Gannett Journal News*), Ken Mandelbaum (*Broadway.com*), David Sheward (*Back Stage*), Michael Sommers (*The Star-Ledger/Newhouse Papers*), Donald Lyons (*The New York Post*), Frank Scheck (*The Hollywood Reporter*), John Simon (*New York*), Linda Winer (*Newsday*), Jason Zinoman (*Time Out New York*), Richard Zoglin (*Time*)

Awards listed are in the following order: Best American Play, Best Foreign Play, Best Musical, and Best Regardless of Category, which was instituted during the 1962–1963 award season:

1936: Winterset **1937:** High Tor **1938:** Of Mice and Men, Shadow and Substance **1939:** The White Steed **1940:** The Time of Your Life **1941:** Watch on the Rhine, The Corn Is Green **1942:** Blithe Spirit **1943:** The Patriots **1944:** Jacobowsky and the Colonel **1945:** The Glass Menagerie **1946:** Carousel **1947:** All My Sons, No Exit, Brigadoon **1948:** A Streetcar Named Desire, The Winslow Boy **1949:** Death of a Salesman, The Madwoman of Chaillot, South Pacific **1950:** The Member of the Wedding, The Cocktail Party, The Consul **1951:** Darkness at Noon, The Lady's Not for Burning, Guys and Dolls **1952:** I Am a Camera, Venus Observed, Pal Joey **1953:** Picnic, The Love of Four Colonels, Wonderful Town **1954:** Teahouse of the August Moon, Ondine, The Golden

Apple **1955:** Cat on a Hot Tin Roof, Witness for the Prosecution, The Saint of Bleecker Street **1956:** The Diary of Anne Frank, Tiger at the Gates, My Fair Lady **1957:** Long Day's Journey into Night, The Waltz of the Toreadors, The Most Happy Fella **1958:** Look Homeward Angel, Look Back in Anger, The Music Man **1959:** A Raisin in the Sun, The Visit, La Plume de Ma Tante **1960:** Toys in the Attic, Five Finger Exercise, Fiorello! **1961:** All the Way Home, A Taste of Honey, Carnival **1962:** Night of the Iguana, A Man for All Seasons, How to Succeed in Business without Really Trying **1963:** Who's Afraid of Virginia Woolf? **1964:** Luther, Hello Dolly! **1965:** The Subject Was Roses, Fiddler on the Roof **1966:** The Persecution and Assassination of Marat as Performed by the Inmates of the Asylum of Charenton under the Direction of the Marquis de Sade, Man of La Mancha **1967:** The Homecoming, Cabaret **1968:** Rosencrantz and Guildenstern Are Dead, Your Own Thing **1969:** The Great White Hope, 1776 **1970:** The Effect of Gamma Rays on Man-in-the-Moon Marigolds, Borstal Boy, Company **1971:** Home, Follies, The House of Blue Leaves **1972:** That Championship Season, Two Gentlemen of Verona **1973:** The Hot L Baltimore, The Changing Room, A Little Night Music **1974:** The Contractor, Short Eyes, Candide **1975:** Equus, The Taking of Miss Janie, A Chorus Line **1976:** Travesties, Streamers, Pacific Overtures **1977:** Otherwise Engaged, American Buffalo, Annie **1978:** Da, Ain't Misbehavin' **1979:** The Elephant Man, Sweeney Todd **1980:** Talley's Folley, Evita, Betrayal **1981:** Crimes of the Heart, A Lesson from Aloes, Special Citation to Lena Horne, The Pirates of Penzance **1982:** The Life and Adventures of Nicholas Nickleby, A Soldier's Play, (no musical) **1983:** Brighton Beach Memoirs, Plenty, Little Shop of Horrors **1984:** The Real Thing, Glengarry Glen Ross, Sunday in the Park with George **1985:** Ma Rainey's Black Bottom, (no musical) **1986:** A Lie of the Mind, Benefactors, (no musical), Special Citation to Lily Tomlin and Jane Wagner **1987:** Fences, Les Liaisons Dangereuses, Les Misérables **1988:** Joe Turner's Come and Gone, The Road to Mecca, Into the Woods **1989:** The Heidi Chronicles, Aristocrats, Largely New York (special), (no musical) **1990:** The Piano Lesson, City of Angels, Privates on Parade **1991:** Six Degrees of Separation, The Will Rogers Follies, Our Country's Good, Special Citation to Eileen Atkins **1992:** Two Trains Running, Dancing at Lughnasa **1993:** Angels in America: Millenium Approaches, Someone Who'll Watch Over Me, Kiss of the Spider Woman **1994:** Three Tall Women, Anna Deavere Smith (special) **1995:** Arcadia, Love! Valour! Compassion!, Special Award: Signature Theatre Company **1996:** Seven Guitars, Molly Sweeny, Rent **1997:** How I Learned to Drive, Skylight, Violet, Chicago (special) **1998:** Pride's Crossing, Art, Lion King, Cabaret (special) **1999:** Wit, Parade, Closer, David Hare (special) **2000:** Jitney, James Joyce's The Dead, Copenhagen **2001:** The Invention of Love, The Producers, Proof **2002:** Edward Albee's The Goat, or Who is Sylvia?, Special citation to Elaine Stritch for Elaine Stritch at Liberty **2003:** Take Me Out, Talking Heads, Hairspray

LUCILLE LORTEL AWARDS

Presented by the League of Off-Broadway Theatres and Producers

The 2003 awards committee consisted of David Cote, Mark Dickerman, Susan Einhorn, Beverly Emmons, George Forbes, Charles Isherwood, Walt Kiskaddon, Sheila Mathews, Gerald Rabkin, Mark Rossier, Marc Routh, Donald Saddler, Tom Smedes, David Stone, Anna Strasberg, Barbara Wolkoff

Play: *Take Me Out*, by Richard Greenberg

Musical: *Avenue Q*, music and lyrics by Robert Lopez and Jeff Marx, book by Jeff Whitty

Revival: *Fifth of July*, by Lanford Wilson, produced by Signature Theatre Company

Actor: Daniel Sunjata, *Take Me Out*

Actress: Tovah Feldshuh, *Golda's Balcony*

Featured Actor: Denis O'Hare, *Take Me Out*

Featured Actress: Jan Maxwell, *My Old Lady*

Direction: Joe Mantello, *Take Me Out*

Choreography: Devanand Janki, *Zanna, Don't*

Scenery: Alexander Dodge, *Observe the Sons of Ulster Marching Towards the Somme*

Costumes: Michael Bottari and Ronald Case, *Shanghai Moon*

Lighting: Donald Holder, *Observe the Sons of Ulster Marching Towards the Somme*

Sound: Brett Jarvis, *Avenue Q*

Body of Work: Vineyard Theatre

Lifetime Achievement: Stephen Sondheim

Edith Olivier Award: Marian Seldes

Unique Theatrical Experience: *The Exonerated*

Past Lucille Lortel Award Winners

Awards listed are Outstanding Play and Outstanding Musical, respectively, since inception

1986: *Woza Africa!*; no musical award **1987:** *The Common Pursuit*; no musical award **1988:** no play or musical award **1989:** *The Cocktail Hour*; no musical award **1990:** no play or musical award **1991:** *Aristocrats*; *Falsettoland* **1992:** *Lips Together, Teeth Apart*; *And the World Goes 'Round* **1993:** *The Destiny of Me*; *Forbidden Broadway* **1994:** *Three Tall Women*; *Wings* **1995:** *Camping with Henry & Tom*; *Jelly Roll!* **1996:** *Molly Sweeney*; *Floyd Collins* **1997:** *How I Learned to Drive*; *Violet* **1998:** (tie) *Gross Indecency* and *The Beauty Queen of Leenane*; no musical award **1999:** *Wit*; no musical award **2000:** *Dinner With Friends*; *James Joyce's The Dead* **2001:** *Proof*; *Bat Boy. The Musical* **2002:** *Metamorphoses*; *Urinetown*

AMERICAN THEATRE CRITICS/STEINBERG NEW PLAY AWARDS AND CITATIONS

New Play Citations

1977: *And the Soul Shall Dance* by Wakako Yamauchi **1978:** *Getting Out* by Marsha Norman **1979:** *Loose Ends* by Michael Weller **1980:** *Custer* by Robert E. Ingham **1981:** *Chekhov in Yalta* by John Driver and Jeffrey Haddow **1982:** *Talking With* by Jane Martin **1983:** *Closely Related* by Bruce MacDonald **1984:** *Wasted* by Fred Gamel **1985:** *Scheherazade* by Marisha Chamberlain

New Play Awards

1986: *Fences* by August Wilson **1987:** *A Walk in the Woods* by Lee Blessing **1988:** *Heathen Valley* by Romulus Linney **1989:** *The Piano Lesson* by August Wilson **1990:** *2* by Romulus Linney **1991:** *Two Trains Running* by August Wilson **1992:** *Could I Have This Dance* by Doug Haverty **1993:** *Children of Paradise: Shooting a Dream* by Steven Epp, Felicity Jones, Dominique Serrand, and Paul Walsh **1994:** *Keely and Du* by Jane Martin **1995:** *The Nanjing Race* by Reggie Cheong-Leen **1996:** *Amazing Grace* by Michael Cristofer **1997:** *Jack and Jill* by Jane Martin **1998:** *The Cider House Rules, Part II* by Peter Parnell **1999:** *Book of Days* by Lanford Wilson

ATCA/Steinberg New Play Awards and Citations

2000: *Oo-Bla-Dee* by Regina Taylor; Citations: *Compleat Female Stage Beauty* by Jeffrey Hatcher; *Syncopation* by Allan Knee **2001:** *Anton in Show Business* by Jane Martin; Citations: *Big Love* by Charles L. Mee; *King Hedley II* by August Wilson **2002:** *The Carpetbagger's Children* by Horton Foote; Citations: *The Action Against Sol Schumann* by Jeffrey Sweet; *Joe and Betty* by Murray Mednick **2003:** *Anna in the Tropics* by Nilo Cruz; Citations: *Recent Tragic Events* by Craig Wright; *Resurrection Blues* by Arthur Miller

ASTAIRE AWARDS

22nd annual; For excellence in dance and choreography, administered by the Theatre Development Fund and selected by a committee comprising Douglas Watt (Chairman), Clive Barnes, Howard Kissel, Michael Kuchwara, Donald McDonagh, Richard Philip, Charles L. Reinhart, and Linda Winer:

Choreography: Twyla Tharp, *Movin' Out*

Female Dancer: Elizabeth Parkinson, *Movin' Out*

Male Dancer: John Selya, *Movin' Out*

Lifetime Achievement: Chita Rivera

CARBONELL AWARDS

28th annual; For outstanding achievement in South Florida theater during the 2002–2003 season.

New Work: *The Box Boomerang*, by Ivonne Azurdia

Ensemble: *Constant Star*, produced by Florida Stage

Production of a Play: *Constant Star*

Director of a Play: Michael Hall, *Fortune's Fool*

Actor in a Play: John Felix, *Fortune's Fool*

Actress in a Play: Laura Turnbull, *Crimes of the Heart*

Supporting Actor in a Play: David Kwiat, *Dirty Blonde*

Supporting Actress in a Play: Mayhill Fowler, *The Last Schwartz*

Production of a Musical: *Floyd Collins*, produced by the Actors Playhouse

Director of a Musical: David Arisco, *Floyd Collins*

Actor in a Musical: Tally Sessions, *Floyd Collins*

Actress in a Musical: Laura Turnbull, *Blood Brothers*

Supporting Actor in a Musical: John Paul Almon, *Romeo and Bernadette*

Supporting Actress in a Musical: Irene Adjan, *Blood Brothers*

Musical Direction: Eric Alsford, *Floyd Collins*

Choreography: Reggie Whitehead, *Zombie Prom*

Scenic Design: Gene Seyffer, *Floyd Collins*

Lighting: Stuart Reiter, *Floyd Collins*

Costumes: Mary Lynne Izzo, *Big Bang*

Sound: Nate Rausch, *Floyd Collins*

Non-Resident Productions

Production: *The Lion King*

Actress: Paulette Ivory, *Aida*

Actor: Jeremy Kushnier, *Aida*

Director: Julie Taymor, *The Lion King*

Special Achievement Award: Nilo Cruz and the New Theatre, *Anna in the Tropics*

George Abbott Award: Alex W. Dreyfoos, Carl L. Mayhue and Robert B. Lichie, Jr.

Howard Kleinberg Award: Elizabeth Boone

Ruth Foreman Award: Dorothy Willis

Bill Hindman Award: David Kwiat

CLARENCE DERWENT AWARDS

58th annual; Given to a female and male performer by Actors Equity Association, based on work in New York that demonstrates promise.

Kerry Butler; Denis O'Hare

CONNECTICUT CRITICS CIRCLE AWARDS

13th annual; For outstanding achievement in Connecticut theater during the 2002–2003 season:

Production of a Play: Yale Repertory Theatre, *Medea/Macbeth/Cinderella*

Production of a Musical: Goodspeed Musicals, for *Me and My Girl*

Actress in a Play: Annalee Jefferies, *The Night of the Iguana*

Actor in a Play: (tie) Leon Addison Brown, *Master Harold…and the Boys*, James Colby, *Night of the Iguana*

Actress in a Musical: Josie de Guzman, *The King and I*

Actor in a Musical: Hunter Bell, *Me and My Girl*

Direction of a Play: Bill Rauch and Tracy Young, *Medea/Macbeth/Cinderella*

Direction of a Musical: Scott Schwartz, *Me and My Girl*

Choreography: Lisa and Gary McIntyre, *Swing!*

Set Design: Jeff Cowie, *The Night of the Iguana*

Lighting Design: Robert Wierzel, *Wintertime*

Costume Design: Christal Weatherly, *Wintertime*

Sound Design: Christopher A. Granger, *A Lesson Before Dying*

Ensemble Performance: James Alexander, Rosena M. Hill, Danette E. Shepard, Charles E. Wallace and Carla Woods, *Ain't Misbehavin'*

Road Show: Stamford Center of the Arts for *bobrauschenbergamerica*

Debut Award: Royce Johnson, *A Lesson Before Dying*

Special Award: International Festival of Arts and Ideas, *Translations*

Tom Killen Memorial Award: John G. Rowland, Governor of the State of Connecticut

DRAMA LEAGUE AWARDS

69th annual; For distinguished achievement in the American theater:

Play: *Take Me Out*
Musical: *Hairspray*
Revival of a Play or Musical: *A Day in the Death of Joe Egg*
Performance: Harvey Fierstien, *Hairspray*
Julia Hansen Award for Excellence in Directing: Joe Mantello
Achievement in Musical Theatre: Twyla Tharp
Unique Contribution to Theater: Roundabout Theatre Company

DRAMATIST GUILD AWARDS

Elizabeth Hull-Kate Warriner Award (to the playwright whose work deals with social, political or religious mores of the time): Dael Orlandsmith, *Yellowman*
Frederick Loewe Award for Dramatic Composition: Jerry Herman
Flora Roberts Award: Jonathan Reynolds
Lifetime Achievement: Neil Simon

ELLIOTT NORTON AWARDS

21st annual; For outstanding contribution to the theater in Boston, voted by a Boston Theater Critics Association selection committee comprising Terry Byrne, Carolyn Clay, Iris Fanger, Joyce Kullhawik, Jon L. Lehman, Bill Marx, Ed Siegel and Caldwell Titcomb:

New Play: Ronan Noone, The Blowin' of Baile Gall, at Boston Playwrights' Theatre
Norton Prize: Jeremiah Kissel
Large Visiting Company: *Medea*, produced by Broadway in Boston, at the Wilbur Theatre
Small Visiting Company: *A New War*, from Wellfleet Harbor Actors Theater
Large Resident Company: *Highway Ulysses*, produced by American Repertory Theatre
Small Resident Company: *Betrayal*, produced by Nora Theatre Company
Local Fringe Company: *Spinning Into Butter*, produced by The Theatre Cooperative
Solo Performance: Annette Miller, *Golda's Balcony*
Musical Productions: *Bat Boy: The Musical*, produced by SpeakEasy Stage Company
Actor: Large company: Arliss Howard, *Uncle Vanya*; Small company: Bill Meleady, *Howie and the Rookie, The Lepers of Baile Baiste,* and *The Blowin' of Baile Gall*
Actress: Large company: Fional Shaw, *Medea*; Small company: Laura Latreille, *The Shape of Things*; Fringe company: Naeemah A. White-Peppers, *Bee-Luther-Hatchee, Chain*
Director: Large company: Anne Bogart, *La Dispute*; Small company: Paul Daigneault, *Passion, Bat Boy: The Musical*
Set design: Large company: David P. Gordon, *The Blue Demon*; Small company: Richard Chambers, *The Blowin' of Baile Gall*
Guest of Honor: Brian Dennehy

GEORGE FREEDLEY MEMORIAL AWARD

For the best book about live theater published in the United States the previous year; 2002 winner:

Ridiculous! The Life and Times of Charles Ludlam, by David Kaufman

GEORGE JEAN NATHAN AWARD

For dramatic criticism; 2001–2002 winner:

Daniel Mendolsohn

GEORGE OPPENHEIMER AWARD

To the best new American playwright, presented by *Newsday*; 2003 winner:

Tom Dowlin, *Corner Wars*

HELEN HAYES AWARDS

19th annual; Presented by the Washington Theatre Awards Society in recognition of excellence in Washington, D.C., theater.

Resident Productions

Play: *Hamlet*, produced by Synetic Theater
Musical: *Sweeney Todd*, produced by the Kennedy Center
Lead Actress, Musical: Christine Baranski, *Sweeney Todd*
Lead Actor, Musical: Rick Hammerly, *Hedwig and the Angry Inch*
Lead Actress, Play: Holly Twyford, *The Shape of Things*
Lead Actor, Play: John Cohn, *The Taste of Fire*
Supporting Actress, Musical: Lori Tan Chinn, *South Pacific*
Supporting Actor, Musical: Ted L. Levy, *Hot Mikado*
Supporting Actress, Play: Nancy Robinette, *The Little Foxes*
Supporting Actor, Play: Michael Ray Escamilla, *Recent Tragic Events*
Director, Play: Paata Tsikurishvili, *Hamlet*
Director, Musical: (tie) Christopher Ashley, *Sweeney Todd*; Toby Orenstein, *Jekyll & Hyde: The Musical*
Set Design, Play or Musical: (tie) James Kronzer, *Shakespeare, Moses and Joe Papp*; Hugh Landwehr, *The Little Foxes*
Costume Design, Play or Musical: Jelena Vukmirovic, Marie Schneggenburger, *Mississippi Pinocchio*
Lighting Design, Play or Musical: Howell Binkley, *Sweeney Todd*
Sound Design, Play or Musical: Mark K. Anduss, *Tiny Alice*
Musical Direction, Play or Musical: Rob Berman, *Sunday in the Park With George*
Choreography: Ilona Kessell, *Damn Yankees*

Non-Resident Productions

Production: *Lypsinka! The Boxed Set*, produced by the Studio Theatre
Lead Actress: Sarah Jones, *Surface Transit*
Lead Actor: Brian Stokes Mitchell, *Man of La Mancha*
Supporting Performer: Kelli Fournier, *Aida*
Charles MacArthur Award for Outstanding New Play: *Shakespeare, Moses, and Joe Papp*, by Ernie Joselovitz
Charles MacArthur Award for Outtstanding New Musical: *Polk County*, by Zora Neale Hurston and Dorothy Waring, adapted by Kyle Donnelly and Cathy Madison, music by Stephen Wade

HENRY HEWES DESIGN AWARDS

For outstanding design originating in the U.S., selected by a committee comprising Jeffrey Eric Jenkins (chair), Tish Dace, Glenda Frank, Mario Fratti, Randy Gener, Mel Gussow, Henry Hewes, Joan Ungaro; 2003 winners:

Scenic Design: John Lee Beatty, *Book of Days, Dinner at Eight, My Old Lady, Tartuffe*

Lighting Design: Brian MacDevitt, *Frankie and Johnny in the Clair de Lune*

Costume Design: Jane Greenwood, *Tartuffe*; Catherine Zuber, *Dinner at Eight, Tartuffe*

Unusual Effects: Production Design: Richard Foreman, *Panic (How to Be Happy!)*

JOSEPH JEFFERSON AWARDS

34th annual; For achievement in Chicago theater during the 2002–2003 season, given by the Jefferson Awards Committee in 28 competitive categories.

Resident Productions

New Work: *The Liquid Moon*, by John Green; *Waiving Goodbye*, by Jamie Pachino

New Adaptation: *Rosa Lublin*, by Robin Chaplik; *The Visit*, Terrence McNally, John Kander, Fred Ebb

Production of a Play: Writers Theatre, *The Price*

Production of a Musical: Chicago Shakespeare Theater, *Pacific Overtures*

Director of a Play: David Cromer, *The Price*

Director of Musical: Gary Griffin, *Pacific Overtures*

Director of a Revue: Joshua Funk, *Holy War, Batman! or The Yellow Cab of Courage*

Actor in a Principal Role, Play: John Sierros, *Dylan*

Actress in a Principal Role, Play: Lusia Strus, *Go Away-Go Away*

Actor in a Supporting Role, Play: Guy Adkins, *Misaillance*

Actress in a Supporting Role, Play: Peggy Roeder, *Indian Ink*

Actor in a Principal Role, Musical: Joseph Anthony Foronda, *Pacific Overtures*

Actress in a Principal Role, Musical: Kate Fry, *My Fair Lady*

Actor in a Supporting Role, Musical: Kevin Gudahl, *Pacific Overtures*

Actress in a Supporting Role, Musical: Marilynn Bogetich, *My Fair Lady*

Actor in a Revue: Keegan-Michael Key, *Holy War, Batman! or The Yellow Cab of Courage*

Ensemble: *The Laramie Project*, produced by Next Theatre

Scenic Design: James Schuette, *The Royal Family*

Costume Design: Mariann Verheyen, *As You Like It*

Lighting Design: Diane Ferry Williams, *Miss Saigon*

Sound Design: Duncan Robert Edwards, *Miss Saigon*

Choreography: David H. Bell, Lainie Sakakura, *Damn Yankees*

Original Music: Alaric Jans, *The Tempest*

Musical Direction: Tom Murray, *Pacific Overtures*

Non-Resident Productions

Production: Fox Searchlight Pictures, Lindsay Law, Thomas Hall, *The Full Monty*

Actor in a Principal Role: John Leguizamo, *Sexaholix...a Love Story*

Actress in a Principal Role: Bob Stillman, *Dirty Blonde*

Lifetime Achievement: Mike Nussbaum

Special Awards

The City of Chicago and **Lois Weisberg**, Cultural Affairs commissioner: "For extraordinary support and service to the theater community in Chicago"

Maggie Daley: For "energetic promotion of theater in Chicago."

Citations Wing Awards

30th annual; For outstanding achievement in professional productions during the 2002–2003 season of Chicago theaters not operating under union contracts:

Productions: *Awake and Sing*, produced by Timeline Theatre Company; *Machinal*, produced by The Hypocrites

Productions (musical): *The Secret Garden*, produced by Circle Theatre; *Sunday in the Park With George*, produced by Pegasus Players

Ensemble: *Awake and Sing; Around the World in 80 Days*, Lifeline Theatre; *Machinal, Nana*, Trap Door Theatre

Directors: (play): Louis Contey, *Awake and Sing*; Sean Graney, *Machinal*; Dorothy Milne, *Around the World in 80 Days*; (musical): Gareth Hendee, *Sunday in the Park With George*

New Work: Stephen Clark, *Stripped*; Robert Kroon, *Vintage Red and the Dust of the Road*

New Adaptation: John Hildreth, *Around the World in 80 Days*; Jim Lasko, *Seagull*

Actress in a Principal Role: (play): Mechelle Moe, *Machinal*

Actor in a Principal Role: (play): P.J. Powers, *Hauptmann*; Charlie Clark, *Company*; Joel Sutliffe, *Sunday in the Park With George*

Actress in a Supporting Role: (play): Corryn Cummins, *Hot L Baltimore*; Liz Fletcher, *Golden Boy*; (musical): Rebecca Finnegan, *Company*; Suzanne Genz, *A New Brain*; Sarah Swanson, *The Secret Garden*; Megan Van De Hey, *A New Brain*

Actor in a Supporting Role: (play): Rich Baker, *Awake and Sing*; Robert Kauzlaric, *Around the World in 80 Days*; Derrick Nelson, *The Royal Hunt of the Sun*; George W. Seegebrecht, *Taking Steps*; (musical): Henry Michael Odum, *The Fantasticks*

Scenic Design: Alan Donahue, *Around the World in 80 Days*; Noelle C.K. Hathaway, *Awake and Sing*; Stephanie Nelson, *Salao: the Worst Kind of Unlucky*

Costume Design: Michael Growler, *Sunday in the Park With George*; Thomas K. Kieffer, *Tartuffe*; Jeffrey Kelly, *The Secret Garden*

Lighting Design: Heather Graff and Richard Peterson, *Machinal*

Sound Design: Victoria Delorio, *Around the World in 80 Days*; Joseph Fosco, *Machinal*

Choreography: Kevin Bellie, *A New Brain*; Katrina Williams Brunner, *Company*

Original Music: Andre Pluess, *Knives in Hens*

Musical Direction: Eugene Dizon, *Company*

Puppet Design: Lisa Barcy, Jesse Mooney-Bullock, *Salao: the Worst Kind of Unlucky*

Special Award (for "creative energy and leadership in bringing diverse communities into Chicago theater for the pleasure and edification of its audiences"): David G. Zak

JOSEPH KESSELRING PRIZE

National Arts Club member Joseph Otto Kesselring was born in New York in 1902. He was an actor, author, producer, and playwright. Mr. Kesselring died in 1967, leaving his estate in a trust which terminated in 1978 when the life beneficiary died. A bequest was made to the National Arts Club "on condition that said bequest be used to establish a fund to be known as the Joseph Kesselring Fund, the income and principal of which shall be used to give financial aid to playwrights, on such a basis of selection and to such as the National Arts Club may, in it's sole discretion, determine."

A committee appointed by the president and the governors of the National Arts Club administers the Kesselring Prizes. It approves monetary prizes annually to playwrights nominated by qualified production companies whose dramatic work has demonstrated the highest possible merit and promise and is deserving of greater recognition, but who as yet has not received prominent national notice or acclaim in the theater. The winners are chosen by a panel of judges who are independent of the Club. In addition to a cash prize, the first prize winner also receives a staged reading of a work of his or her choice. The Kesselring Prize Committee: O. Aldon James, Stanley Morton Ackert III, Arnold J. Davis, Michael Parva, Jason deMontmorency, Dary Derchin, Alexandra Roosevelt Dworkin, John T James, Raymond Knowles.

2003: Bridget Carpenter **2002:** Melissa James Gibson **2001:** David Lindsay-Abaire **2000:** David Auburn **1999:** Heather McDonald **1998:** Kira Obolensky **1997:** No Award **1996:** Naomi Wallace **1995:** Amy Freed, Doug Wright **1994:** Nicky Silver **1993:** Anna Deavere Smith **1992:** Marion Isaac McClinton **1991:** Tony Kushner **1990:** Elizabeth Egloff, Mel Shapiro **1989:** Jo Carson **1988:** Diane Ney **1987:** Paul Schmidt **1986:** Marlane Meyer **1985:** Bill Elverman **1984:** Philip Kan Gotanda **1983:** Lynn Alvarez **1982:** No Award **1981:** Cheryl Hawkins **1980:** Susan Charlotte

Honorable Mentions

2003: Lynn Nottage **2002:** Lydia Diamond **2001:** Dael Orlandersmith **2000:** Jessica Hagedorn **1999:** Stephen Dietz **1998:** Erik Ehn **1997**: Kira Obolensky, Edwin Sanchez **1996:** Nilo Cruz **1993:** Han Ong **1992:** Jose Rivera **1991:** Quincy Long, Scott McPherson **1990:** Howard Korder **1989:** Keith Reddin **1988:** Jose Rivera, Frank Hogan **1987:** Januzsz Glowacki **1986:** John Leicht **1985:** Laura Harrington **1983:** Constance Congdon **1981:** William Hathaway **1980:** Carol Lashof

KENNEDY CENTER

Honors

25th annual; For distinguished achievement by individuals who have made significant contributions to American culture through the arts:

James Earl Jones; James Levine; Chita Rivera; Paul Simon; Elizabeth Taylor

Mark Twain Prize

6th annual; For American humor:

Lily Tomlin

M. ELIZABETH OSBORN AWARD

Presented to an emerging playwright by the American Theatre Critics Association; 2003 winner:

John Walch, *The Dinosaur Within*

NEW YORK UNIVERSITY MUSICAL THEATRE HALL OF FAME

Housed at the New York University Frederick Loewe Theatre, the New York University Musical Theatre Hall of Fame honors the composers, lyricists, and performers who originated and contributed to this quintessential American art form. Musical theatre is one of New York City's great gifts to world culture; we celebrate this vital heritage and encourage its transmission to the next generation by periodically inducting new members into the Hall of Fame.

Inducted **November 10, 1993** George Gershwin, composer; Ira Gershwin, lyricist; Oscar Hammerstein, lyricist, bookwriter; Jerome Kern, composer; Alan Jay Lerner, lyricist, bookwriter; Frederick Loewe, composer; Richard Rodgers, composer; Ethel Merman, performer **November 16, 1994** Irving Berlin, composer, lyricist; Mary Martin, performer; Cole Porter, lyricist; E.Y. "Yip" Yarburg, lyricist, composer **November 13, 1995** Harold Arlen, composer; Leonard Bernstein, composer; Eubie Blake, composer; Lorenz Hart, lyricist, bookwriter **November 11, 1996** Abe Burrows, Bookwriter, director; George M. Cohan, composer, lyricist, playwright, producer, director, performer; Dorothy Fields, lyricist, bookwriter; Frank Loesser, composer, lyricist, bookwriter; Harold Jacob Rome, composer, lyricist **November 10, 1999** Jerry Herman, composer, lyricist

The New York University Musical Theatre Hall of Fame Award is presented in recognition of musical theatre greats whose lives and work have contributed to sustaining this vital American art form.

1993 Carol Channing, performer; Jule Styne, composer **1994** Gwen Verdon, performer; George Abbott, director, bookwriter, producer; Betty Comden and Adolph Green, lyricists, bookwriters **1995** Burton Lane, composer; Jerome Robbins, director, choreographer **1996** John Kander, composer; Fred Ebb, lyricist

NATIONAL MEDALS OF THE ARTS

For individuals and organizations who have made outstanding contributions to the excellence, growth, support, and availability of the arts in the United States, selected by the President of the United States from nominees presented by the National Endowment; 2002 winners:

Florence Knoll Bassett; Trisha Brown; Uta Hagen; Lawrence Halprin; Al Hirschfeld; George Jones; Ming Cho Lee; Phillippe de Montebello; William "Smokey" Robinson, Jr.

NEW DRAMATISTS LIFETIME ACHIEVEMENT AWARD

To an individual who has made an outstanding artistic contribution to the American theater; 2002 winner:

August Wilson

OVATION AWARDS

Established in 1989, the L.A. Stage Alliance Ovation Awards are Southern California's premiere awards for excellence in theatre; 2003 winners:

World Premiere Play: *Gem of the Ocean,* by August Wilson, produced by Center Theater Group/Mark Taper Forum; *La Gioconda,* by Randy Sherman, produced by Stages Theatre Center and The Collective; *War Music,* by Bryan Davidson, produced by Playwrights' Arena and Echo Theatre Company

World Premiere Musical: *Songs My Mother Taught Me,* Mitzie and Ken Welch, and Lorna Luft, produced by Canon Theatricals

Lead Actor in a Play: David Paladino, *The Island*; Norbert Weisser, *Times Like These*

Lead Actress in a Play: Beth Grant, *The Trials and Tribulations of a Trailer Trash Housewife*; Laurie O'Brien, *Times Like These*

Lead Actor in a Musical: David Engel, *Crazy for You*

Lead Actress in a Musical: Connie Champagne, *Judy's Scary Little Christmas*

Featured Actor in a Play: James Farentino, *Boy Gets Girl*

Featured Actress in a Play: Nancy Linehan Charles, *Toys in the Attic*

Featured Actor in a Musical: Larry Cedar, *She Loves Me*

Featured Actress in a Musical: Sally Struthers, *Mame*

Solo Performance: Geraldine Hughes, *Belfast Blues*

Ensemble Performance: Cast of August Wilson's *Gem of the Ocean*; Cast of *La Gioconda*; Cast of *War Music*

Director of a Play: Randy Schulman, *La Gioconda*; Ken Sawyer, *The Woman in Black*

Director of a Musical: Edgar Landa, *Animal Farm*

Choreographer: Sergio Trujillo, *Empire A New American Musical*

Musical Direction: Colin R. Freeman, *Songs My Mother Taught Me*

Production from a Touring Company: *The Search for Signs of Intelligent Life in the Universe,* Tomlin and Wagner Theatricalz

Play (smaller theatre): *The Woman in Black*; (larger theatre): *Toys in the Attic*

Musical (smaller theatre): *Animal Farm*; (larger theatre): *Anything Goes*

Set Design (smaller theatre): Desma Murphy, *The Woman in Black*; (larger theatre): David Gallo, August Wilson's *Gem of the Ocean*; John Lee Beatty, *Morning's at Seven*

Lighting Design: (smaller theatre): Robert L. Smith, *The Woman in Black*; Jeremy Pivnick, *War Music*; (larger theatre): Donald Holder, August Wilson's *Gem of the Ocean*

Sound Design: (smaller theatre): David B. Marling, Ken Sawyer, *The Woman in Black*; (larger theatre): Dan Moses Schreier, August Wilson's *Gem of the Ocean*

Costume Design: (smaller theatre): Delcie Adams, Nina Ameri, *La Gioconda*; Shon LeBlanc, *The Women*; (larger theatre): Constanza Romero, August Wilson's *Gem of the Ocean*

James A. Doolittle Award for Leadership in the Theatre: Ed Waterstreet, Co-founding director of Deaf West Theatre

The Career Achievement Award: Gordon Davidson, Artistic director of the Center Theatre Group/Mark Taper Forum, Producing director of Center Theatre Group/Ahmanson Theatre's subscription season

RICHARD RODGERS AWARDS

For staged readings of musicals in nonprofit theaters, administered by the American Academy of Arts and Letters and selected by a jury including Stephen Sondheim (chairman), Lynn Ahrens, Jack Beeson, William Bolcom, John Guare, Sheldon Harnick, Richard Maltby, Jr., and Robert Ward; 2003 winners:

The Tutor, Maryrose Wood and Andrew Gerle; *Once Upon a Time in New Jersey*, Susan DiLallo and Stephen Weiner; *The Devil in the Flesh*, Jeffrey Lunden and Arthur Perlman

ROBERT WHITEHEAD AWARD

For outstanding achievement in commercial theatre producing, bestowed on a graduate of the fourteen-week Commercial Theater Institute Program who has demonstrated a quality of production exemplified by the late producer, Robert Whitehead.

The Commercial Theater Institute, Frederic B. Vogel, director, is the nation's only formal program which professionally trains commercial theatre producers. It is a joint project of the League of American Theatres and Producers, Inc., and Theatre Development Fund.

2001–2003: No Award **2000:** Anne Strickland Squadron **1999:** Eric Krebs **1998:** Liz Oliver **1997:** Marc Routh **1996:** Randall L. Wreghitt **1995:** Kevin McCollum **1994:** Dennis Grimaldi **1993:** Susan Quint Gallin; Benjamin Mordecai

SUSAN SMITH BLACKBURN PRIZE

25th annual; For women who have written works of outstanding quality for the English-speaking theater:

Dael Orlandersmith, *Yellowman*
Honorable Mention: Bryony Lavery, *Frozen*

THE THEATER HALL OF FAME

The Theater of Hall of Fame was created in 1971 to honor those who have made outstanding contributions to the American theater in a career spanning at least twenty-five years, with at least five major credits.

The following were honorees inducted January 27, 2003:

John Lee Beatty; Stockard Channing; Larry Gelbart; Bernard Gersten; Tammy Grimes; Frank Langella; David Mamet; Jean Stapleton

George Abbott; Maude Adams; Viola Adams; Stella Adler; Edward Albee; Theoni V. Aldredge; Ira Aldridge; Jane Alexander; Mary Alice; Winthrop Ames; Judith Anderson; Maxwell Anderson; Robert Anderson; Julie Andrews; Margaret Anglin; Jean Anouilh; Harold Arlen; George Arliss; Boris Aronson; Adele Astaire; Fred Astaire; Eileen Atkins; Brooks Atkinson; Lauren Bacall; Pearl Bailey; George Balanchine; William Ball; Anne Bancroft; Tallulah Bankhead; Richard Barr; Philip Barry; Ethel Barrymore; John Barrymore; Lionel Barrymore; Howard Bay; Nora Bayes; Samuel Beckett; Brian Bedford; S.N. Behrman; Norman Bel Geddes; David Belasco; Michael Bennett; Richard Bennett; Robert Russell Bennett; Eric Bentley; Irving Berlin; Sarah Bernhardt; Leonard Bernstein; Earl Blackwell; Kermit Bloomgarden; Jerry Bock; Ray Bolger; Edwin Booth; Junius Brutus Booth; Shirley Booth; Philip Bosco; Alice Brady; Bertolt Bercht; Fannie Brice; Peter Brook; John Mason Brown; Robert Brustein; Billie Burke; Abe Burrows; Richard Burton; Mrs. Patrick Campbell; Zoe Caldwell; Eddie Cantor; Morris Carnovsky; Mrs. Leslie Carter; Gower Champion; Frank Chanfrau; Carol Channing; Ruth Chatterton; Paddy Chayefsky; Anton Chekhov; Ina Claire; Bobby Clark; Harold Clurman; Lee. J. Cobb; Richard L. Coe; George M. Cohan; Alexander H. Cohen; Jack Cole; Cy Coleman; Constance Collier; Alvin Colt; Betty Comden; Marc Connelly; Barbara Cook; Katherine Cornell; Noel Coward; Jane Cowl; Lotta Crabtree; Cheryl Crawford; Hume Cronym; Russel Crouse; Charlotte Cushman; Jean Dalrymple; Augustin Daly; E.L. Davenport; Gordon Davidson; Ossie Davis; Ruby Dee; Alfred De Liagre Jr.; Agns DeMille; Colleen Dewhurst; Howard Deitz; Dudley Digges; Melvyn Douglas; Eddie Dowling; Alfred Drake; Marie Dressler; John Drew; Mrs. John Drew; William Dunlap; Mildred Dunnock; Charles Durning; Eleanora Duse; Jeanne Eagles; Fred Ebb; Florence Eldridge; Lehman Engel; Maurice Evans; Abe Feder; Jose Ferber; Cy Feuer; Zelda Fichandler; Dorothy Fields; Herbert Fields; Lewis Fields; W.C. Fields; Jules Fischer; Minnie Maddern Fiske; Clyde Fitch; Geraldine Fitzgerald; Henry Fonda; Lynn Fontanne; Horton Foote; Edwin Forrest; Bob Fosse; Rudolf Friml; Charles Frohman; Robert Fryer; Athol Fugard; John Gassner; Peter Gennaro; Grace George; George Gershwin; Ira Gershwin; John Gielgud;W.S. Gilbert; Jack Gilford; William Gillette; Charles Gilpin; Lillian Gish; John Golden; Max Gordon; Ruth Gordon; Adolph Green; Paul Green; Charlotte Greenwood; Joel Grey; George Grizzard; John Gaure; Otis L. Guernsey Jr.; Tyrone Guthrie; Uta Hagan; Lewis Hallam; T. Edward Hambleton; Oscar Hammerstein II; Walter Hampden; Otto Harbach; E.Y. Harburg; Sheldon Harnick; Edward Harrigan; Jed Harris; Julie Harris; Rosemary Harris; Sam H. Harris; Rex Harrison; Kitty Carlisle Hart; Lorenz Hart; Moss Hart; Tony Hart; June Havoc; Helen Hayes; Leland Hayward; Ben Hecht; Eileen Heckart; Theresa Helburn; Lillian Hellman; Katherine Hepburn; Victor Herbert; Jerry Herman; James A. Herne; Henry Hewes; Al Hirschfeld; Raymond Hitchcock; Hal Holbrook; Celeste Holm; Hanya Holm; Arthur Hopkins; De Wolf Hopper; John Houseman; Eugene Howard;

(CONTINUED ON NEXT PAGE)

(CONTINUED FROM THEATER HALL OF FAME)

Leslie Howard; Sidney Howard; Willie Howard; Barnard Hughes; Henry Hull; (Josephine Hull; Walter Huston; Earle Hyman; Henrik Ibsen; William Inge; Bernard B. Jacobs; Elise Janis; Joseph Jefferson; Al Jolson; James Earl Jones; Margo Jones; Robert Edmond Jones; Tom Jones; Jon Jory; Raul Julia; John Kander; Garson Kanin; George S. Kaufman; Danny Kaye; Elia Kazan; Gene Kelly; George Kelly; Fanny Kemble; Jerome Kern; Walter Kerr; Michael Kidd; Richard Kiley; Sidney Kingsley; Florence Klotz; Joseph Wood Krutch; Bert Lahr; Burton Lane; Lawrence Langner; Lillie Langtry; Angela Lansbury; Charles Laughton;

Arthur Laurents; Gertrude Lawrence; Jerome Lawrence; Eva Le Gallienne; Ming Cho Lee; Robert E. Lee; Lotte Lenya; Alan Jay Lerner; Sam Levene; Robert Lewis; Beatrice Lillie; Howard Lindsay; Frank Loesser; Frederick Loewe; Joshua Logan; Pauline Lord; Lucille Lortel; Alfred Lunt; Charles MacArthur; Steele McKaye; Rouben Mamoulian; Richard Mansfield; Robert B. Mantell; Frederic March; Nancy Marchand; Julia Marlowe; Ernest H. Martin; Mary Martin; Raymond Massey; Siobhan McKenna; Terrence McNally; Helen Menken; Burgess Meredith; Ethel Merman; David Merrick; Jo Mielziner; Arthur Miller; Marilyn Miller; Liza Minnelli; Helena Modjeska; Ferenc Molnar; Lola Montez; Victor Moore; Robert Morse; Zero Mostel; Anna Cora Mowatt; Paul Muni; Tharon Musser; George Jean Nathan; Mildred Natwick; Nazimova; James M. Nederlander; Mike Nichols; Elliot Norton; Sean O'Casey; Cliiford Odets; Donald Oenslager; Laurence Olivier; Eugene O'Neill; Jerry Orbach; Geraldine Paige; Joseph Papp; Osgood Perkins; Bernadette Peters; Molly Picon; Harold Pinter; Luigi Pirandello; Christopher Plummer; Cole Porter; Robert Preston; Harold Prince; Jose Quintero; Ellis Rabb; John Raitt; Tony Randall; Michael Redgrave; Ada Rehan; Elmer Rice; Lloyd Richards; Ralph Richardson; Chita Rivera; Jason Robards; Jerome Robbins; Paul Robeson; Richard Rodgers; Will Rogers; Sigmund Romberg; Harold Rome; Lillian Russell; Donald Saddler; Gene Saks; William Saroyan; Joseph Schildkraut; Harvey Schmidt; Alan Schnider; Gerald Shoenfeld; Arthur Schwartz; Maurice Schwartz; George C. Scott; Marian Seldes; Irene Sharaff; George Bernard Shaw; Sam Shepard; Robert F. Sherwood; J.J. Shubert; Lee Shubert; Herman Shumlin; Neil Simon; Lee Simonson; Edmund Simpson; Otis Skinner; Maggie Smith; Oliver Smith; Stephen Sondheim; E.H. Sothern; Kim Stanley; Maureen Stapleton; Frances Sternhagen; Roger L. Stevens; Isabelle Stevenson; Ellen Stewart; Dorothy Stickney; Fred Stone; Tom Stoppard; Lee Strasburg; August Strindberg; Elaine Stritch; Charles Strouse; Jule Styne; Margaret Sullivan; Arthur Sullivan; Jessica Tandy; Laurette Taylor; Ellen Terry; Tommy Tune; Gwen Verdon; Robin Wagner; Nancy Walker; Eli Wallach; James Wallack; Lester Wallack; Tony Walton; Douglas Turner Ward; David Warfield; Ethel Waters; Clifton Webb; Joseph Weber; Margaret Webster; Kurt Weill; Orson Welles; Mae West; Robert Whitehead; Oscar Wilde; Thorton Wilder; Bert Williams; Tennessee Williams; Landford Wilson; P.G. Wodehouse; Peggy Wood; Alexander Woollcott; Irene Worth; Teresa Wright; Ed Wynn; Vincent Youmans; Stark Young; Florenz Zeigfeld; Patricia Zipprodt

Founders Award

Established in 1993 in honor of Earl Blackwell, James M. Nederlander, Gerald Oestreicher and Arnold Weissberger, the Theater Hall of Fame Founders Award is voted by the Hall's board of directors to an individual for his of her outstanding contribution to the theater:

1993: James M. Nederlander **1994:** Kitty Carlisle Hart **1995:** Harvey Sabinson **1996:** Henry Hewes **1997:** Otis L. Guernsey Jr. **1998:** Edward Colton **1999**: no award **2000:** Gerard Oestreicher, Arnold Weissberger **2001:** Tom Dillon **2002:** No Award

Margo Jones Citizen of the Theater Medal

Presented annually to a citizen of the theater who has made a lifetime commitment to theater in the United States and has demonstrated an understanding and affirmation of the craft of playwriting:

1961: Lucille Lortel **1962:** Michael Ellis **1963:** Judith Rutherford Marechal; George Savage (university award) **1964:** Richard Barr, Edward Albee & Clinton Wilder; Richard A. Duprey (university award) **1965:** Wynn Handman; Marston Balch (university award) **1966:** Jon Jory; Arthur Ballet (university award) **1967:** Paul Baker; George C. White (workshop award) **1968:** Davey Marlin-Jones; Ellen Stewart (workshop award) **1969:** Adrian Hall; Edward Parone & Gordon Davidson (workshop award) **1970:** Joseph Papp **1971:** Zelda Fichandler **1972:** Jules Irving **1973:** Douglas Turner Ward **1974:** Paul Weidner **1975:** Robert Kalfin **1976:** Gordon Davidson **1977:** Marshall W. Mason **1978:** Jon Jory **1979:** Ellen Stewart **1980:** John Clark Donahue **1981:** Lynne Meadow **1982:** Andre Bishop **1983:** Bill Bushnell **1984:** Gregory Mosher **1985:** John Lion **1986:** Lloyd Richards **1987:** Gerald Chapman **1988:** no award **1989:** Margaret Goheen **1990:** Richard Coe **1991:** Otis L. Guernsey Jr. **1992:** Abbot Van Nostrand **1993:** Henry Hewes **1994:** Jane Alexander **1995:** Robert Whitehead **1996:** Al Hirschfield **1997:** George C. White **1998:** James Houghton **1999:** George Keathley **2000:** Eileen Heckart **2001:** Mel Gussow **2002:** Emilie S. Kilgore

WILLIAM INGE THEATRE FESTIVAL AWARD

22nd annual; For distinguished achievement in American theater:

Romulus Linney

New Voice: Theresa Rebeck

Longest Running Shows on **Broadway**

LONGEST RUNNING SHOWS
ON BROADWAY

When the musical or play version of a production is in question, it is so indicated, as are revivals. *Plays that were still playing as of May 31, 2003.

CATS
7,485 performances
Opened October 7, 1982; Closed September 10, 2000

LES MISÉRABLES
6,680 performances
Opened March 12, 1987; Closed May 18, 2003

PHANTOM OF THE OPERA*
6,397 performances
Opened January 26, 1988

A CHORUS LINE
6,137 performances
Opened July 25, 1975; Closed April 28, 1990

OH! CALCUTTA (REVIVAL)
5,959 performances
Opened September 24, 1976; Closed August 6, 1989

MISS SAIGON
4,097 performances
Opened April 11, 1991; Closed January 28, 2001

BEAUTY AND THE BEAST*
3,719 performances
Opened April 18, 1994

42ND STREET
3,486 performances
Opened August 25, 1980; Closed January 8, 1989

GREASE
3,388 performances
Opened February 14, 1972; Closed April 13, 1980

FIDDLER ON THE ROOF
3,242 performances
Opened September 22, 1964; Closed July 2, 1972

LIFE WITH FATHER
3,224 performances
Opened November 8, 1939; Closed July 12, 1947

Sarah Jessica Parker, Kim Fedena, Donna Graham, Dorothy Loudon, Robyn Finn, Danielle Brisebois, Diana Barrows in *Annie*, 1977 PHOTO BY MARTHA SWOPE

TOBACCO ROAD
3,182 performances
Opened December 4, 1933; Closed May 31, 1941

RENT*
2,951 performances
Opened April 29, 1996

HELLO, DOLLY!
2,844 performances
Opened January 16, 1964; Closed December 27, 1970

CHICAGO (MUSICAL, REVIVAL)*
2,723 performances
Opened November 19, 1996

MY FAIR LADY
2,717 performances
Opened March 15, 1956; Closed September 29, 1962

ANNIE
2,377 performances
Opened April 21, 1977; Closed January 22, 1983

THE LION KING*
2,345 performances
Opened November 13, 1977

MAN OF LA MANCHA
2,328 performances
Opened November 22, 1965; Closed June 26, 1971

ABIE'S IRISH ROSE
2,327 performances
Opened May 23, 1922; Closed October 21, 1927

OKLAHOMA!
2,212 performances
Opened March 31, 1943; Closed May 29, 1948

CABARET (REVIVAL)*
2,125 performances
Opened March 19, 1998

SMOKEY JOE'S CAFÉ
2,036 performances
Opened March 2, 1995; Closed January 16, 2000

PIPPIN
1,944 performances
Opened October 23, 1972; Closed June 12, 1977

SOUTH PACIFIC
1,925 performances
Opened April 7, 1949; Closed January 16, 1954

THE MAGIC SHOW
1,920 performances
Opened May 28, 1974; Closed December 31, 1978

DEATHTRAP
1,793 performances
Opened February 26, 1978; Closed June 13, 1982

GEMINI
1,788 performances
Opened May 21, 1977; Closed September 6, 1981

HARVEY
1,775 performances
Opened November 1, 1944; Closed January 15, 1949

DANCIN'
1,774 performances
Opened March 27, 1978; Closed June 27, 1982

LA CAGE AUX FOLLES
1,761 performances
Opened August 21, 1983; Closed November 15, 1987

HAIR
1,750 performances
Opened April 29, 1968; Closed July 1, 1972

THE WIZ
1,672 performances
Opened January 5, 1975; Closed January 29, 1979

BORN YESTERDAY
1,642 performances
Opened February 4, 1946; Closed December 31, 1949

THE BEST LITTLE WHOREHOUSE IN TEXAS
1,639 performances
Opened June 19, 1978; Closed March 27, 1982

CRAZY FOR YOU
1,622 performances
Opened February 19, 1992; Closed January 7, 1996

AIN'T MISBEHAVIN'
1,604 performances
Opened May 9, 1978; Closed February 21, 1982

MARY, MARY
1,572 performances
Opened March 8, 1961; Closed December 12, 1964

EVITA
1,567 performances
Opened September 25, 1979; Closed June 26, 1983

THE VOICE OF THE TURTLE
1,557 performances
Opened December 8, 1943; Closed January 3, 1948

JEKYLL & HYDE
1,543 performances
Opened April 28, 1997; Closed January 7, 2001

BAREFOOT IN THE PARK
1,530 performances
Opened October 23, 1963; Closed June 25, 1967

William Thomas Jr., Gene Barry, John Weiner in *La Cage aux Folles*, 1983
PHOTO BY MARTHA SWOPE

BRIGHTON BEACH MEMOIRS
1,530 performances
Opened March 27, 1983; Closed May 11, 1986

DREAMGIRLS
1,522 performances
Opened December 20, 1981; Closed August 11, 1985

MAME (MUSICAL)
1,508 performances
Opened May 24, 1966; Closed January 3, 1970

GREASE (REVIVAL)
1,503 performances
Opened May 11, 1994; Closed January 25, 1998

SAME TIME, NEXT YEAR
1,453 performances
Opened March 14, 1975; Closed September 3, 1978

ARSENIC AND OLD LACE
1,444 performances
Opened January 10, 1941; Closed June 17, 1944

THE SOUND OF MUSIC
1,443 performances
Opened November 16, 1959; Closed June 15, 1963

ME AND MY GIRL
1,420 performances
Opened August 10, 1986; Closed December 31, 1989

HOW TO SUCCEED IN BUSINESS WITHOUT REALLY TRYING
1,417 performances
Opened October 14, 1961; Closed March 6, 1965

HELLZAPOPPIN'
1,404 performances
Opened September 22, 1938; Closed December 17, 1941

THE MUSIC MAN
1,375 performances
Opened December 19, 1957; Closed April 15, 1961

FUNNY GIRL
1,348 performances
Opened March 26, 1964; Closed July 15, 1967

MUMMENSCHANZ
1,326 performances
Opened March 30, 1977; Closed April 20, 1980

AIDA*
1,324 performances
Opened March 23, 2000

ANGEL STREET
1,295 performances
Opened December 5, 1941; Closed December 30, 1944

LIGHTNIN'
1,291 performances
Opened August 26, 1918; Closed August 27, 1921

PROMISES, PROMISES
1,281 performances
Opened December 1, 1968; Closed January 1, 1972

THE KING AND I
1,246 performances
Opened March 29, 1951; Closed March 20, 1954

CACTUS FLOWER
1,234 performances
Opened December 8, 1965; Closed November 23, 1968

SLEUTH
1,222 performances
Opened December 8, 1965; Closed October 13, 1973

Keith Baxter, Anthony Quayle in *Sleuth*, 1970

TORCH SONG TRILOGY
1,222 performances
Opened June 10, 1982; Closed May 19, 1985

1776
1,217 performances
Opened March 16, 1969; Closed February 13, 1972

EQUUS
1,209 performances
Opened October 24, 1974; Closed October 7, 1977

SUGAR BABIES
1,208 performances
Opened October 8, 1979; Closed August 28, 1982

GUYS AND DOLLS
1,200 performances
Opened November 24, 1950; Closed November 28, 1953

AMADEUS
1,181 performances
Opened December 17, 1980; Closed October 16, 1983

CABARET
1,165 performances
Opened November 20, 1966; Closed September 6, 1969

MISTER ROBERTS
1,157 performances
Opened February 18, 1948; Closed January 6, 1951

ANNIE GET YOUR GUN
1,147 performances
Opened May 16, 1946; Closed February 12, 1949

GUYS AND DOLLS (REVIVAL)
1,144 performances
Opened April 14, 1992; Closed January 8, 1995

THE SEVEN YEAR ITCH
1,141 performances
Opened November 20, 1952; Closed August 13, 1955

BRING IN 'DA NOISE, BRING IN 'DA FUNK
1,130 performances
Opened April 25, 1996; Closed January 19, 1999

BUTTERFLIES ARE FREE
1,128 performances
Opened October 21, 1969; Closed July 2, 1972

PINS AND NEEDLES
1,108 performances
Opened November 27, 1937; Closed June 22, 1940

PLAZA SUITE
1,097 performances
Opened February 14, 1968; Closed October 3, 1970

FOSSE
1,092 performances
Opened January 14, 1999; Closed August 25, 2001

THEY'RE PLAYING OUR SONG
1,082 performances
Opened February 11, 1979; Closed September 6, 1981

GRAND HOTEL (MUSICAL)
1,077 performances
Opened November 12, 1989; Closed April 25, 1992

KISS ME, KATE
1,070 performances
Opened December 30, 1948; Closed July 25, 1951

DON'T BOTHER ME, I CAN'T COPE
1,065 performances
Opened April 19, 1972; Closed October 27, 1974

THE PAJAMA GAME
1,063 performances
Opened May 13, 1954; Closed November 24, 1956

SHENANDOAH
1,050 performances
Opened January 7, 1975; Closed August 7, 1977

ANNIE GET YOUR GUN (REVIVAL)
1,046 performances
Opened March 4, 1999; Closed September 1, 2001

THE TEAHOUSE OF THE AUGUST MOON
1,027 performances
Opened October 15, 1953; Closed March 24, 1956

DAMN YANKEES
1,019 performances
Opened May 5, 1955; Closed October 12, 1957

CONTACT
1,010 performances
Opened March 30, 2000; Closed September 1, 2002

NEVER TOO LATE
1,007 performances
Opened November 26, 1962; Closed April 24, 1965

BIG RIVER
1,005 performances
Opened April 25, 1985; Closed September 20, 1987

THE WILL ROGERS FOLLIES
983 performances
Opened May 1, 1991; Closed September 5, 1993

ANY WEDNESDAY
982 performances
Opened February 18, 1964; Closed June 26, 1966

SUNSET BOULEVARD
977 performances
Opened November 17, 1994; Closed March 22, 1997

A FUNNY THING HAPPENED ON THE WAY TO THE FORUM
964 performances
Opened May 8, 1962; Closed August 29, 1964

THE ODD COUPLE
964 performances
Opened March 10, 1965; Closed July 2, 1967

ANNA LUCASTA
957 performances
Opened August 30, 1944; Closed November 30, 1946

KISS AND TELL
956 performances
Opened March 17, 1943; Closed June 23, 1945

SHOW BOAT (REVIVAL)
949 performances
Opened October 2, 1994; Closed January 5, 1997

DRACULA (REVIVAL)
925 performances
Opened October 20, 1977; Closed January 6, 1980

BELLS ARE RINGING
924 performances
Opened November 29, 1956; Closed March 7, 1959

THE MOON IS BLUE
924 performances
Opened March 8, 1951; Closed May 30, 1953

BEATLEMANIA
920 performances
Opened May 31, 1977; Closed October 17, 1979

PROOF
917 performances
Opened October 24, 2000; Closed January 5, 2003

THE ELEPHANT MAN
916 performances
Opened April 19, 1979; Closed June 28, 1981

KISS OF THE SPIDER WOMAN
906 performances
Opened May 3, 1993; Closed July 1, 1995

LUV
901 performances
Opened November 11, 1964; Closed January 7, 1967

THE WHO'S TOMMY
900 performances
Opened April 22, 1993; Closed June 17, 1995

CHICAGO (MUSICAL)
898 performances
Opened June 3, 1975; Closed August 27, 1977

APPLAUSE
896 performances
Opened March 30, 1970; Closed July 27, 1972

CAN-CAN
892 performances
Opened May 7, 1953; Closed June 25, 1955

Roberta Keith, Myrna White, Judy Alexander, Lisa James, Zero Mostel in *A Funny Thing Happened...*, 1962 PHOTO BY FRED FEHL

CAROUSEL
890 performances
Opened April 19, 1945; Closed May 24, 1947

I'M NOT RAPPAPORT
890 performances
Opened November 19, 1985; Closed January 17, 1988

HATS OFF TO ICE
889 performances
Opened June 22, 1944; Closed April 2, 1946

FANNY
888 performances
Opened November 4, 1954; Closed December 16, 1956

CHILDREN OF A LESSER GOD
887 performances
Opened March 30, 1980; Closed May 16, 1982

FOLLOW THE GIRLS
882 performances
Opened April 8, 1944; Closed May 18, 1946

KISS ME, KATE (MUSICAL, REVIVAL)
881 performances
Opened November 18, 1999; Closed December 30, 2001

CITY OF ANGELS
878 performances
Opened December 11, 1989; Closed January 19, 1992

THE PRODUCERS*
875 performances
Opened April 19, 2001

CAMELOT
873 performances
Opened December 3, 1960; Closed January 5, 1963

I LOVE MY WIFE
872 performances
Opened April 17, 1977; Closed May 20, 1979

THE BAT
867 performances
Opened August 23, 1920; Unknown closing date

MY SISTER EILEEN
864 performances
Opened December 26, 1940; Closed January 16, 1943

Amy Spanger, Michael Berresse in *Kiss Me, Kate*, 1999 PHOTO BY JOAN MARCUS

42ND STREET (REVIVAL)*
861 performances
Opened May 2, 2001

NO, NO, NANETTE (REVIVAL)
861 performances
Opened January 19, 1971; Closed February 3, 1973

RAGTIME
861 performances
Opened January 18, 1998; Closed January 16, 2000

SONG OF NORWAY
860 performances
Opened August 21, 1944; Closed September 7, 1946

CHAPTER TWO
857 performances
Opened December 4, 1977; Closed December 9, 1979

A STREETCAR NAMED DESIRE
855 performances
Opened December 3, 1947; Closed December 17, 1949

BARNUM
854 performances
Opened April 30, 1980; Closed May 16, 1982

COMEDY IN MUSIC
849 performances
Opened October 2, 1953; Closed January 21, 1956

RAISIN
847 performances
Opened October 18, 1973; Closed December 7, 1975

BLOOD BROTHERS
839 performances
Opened April 25, 1993; Closed April 30, 1995

YOU CAN'T TAKE IT WITH YOU
837 performances
Opened December 14, 1936; Unknown closing date

LA PLUME DE MA TANTE
835 performances
Opened November 11, 1958; Closed December 17, 1960

THREE MEN ON A HORSE
835 performances
Opened January 30, 1935; Closed January 9, 1937

THE SUBJECT WAS ROSES
832 performances
Opened May 25, 1964; Closed May 21, 1966

BLACK AND BLUE
824 performances
Opened January 26, 1989; Closed January 20, 1991

THE KING AND I (REVIVAL)
807 performances
Opened April 11, 1996; Closed February 22, 1998

INHERIT THE WIND
806 performances
Opened April 21, 1955; Closed June 22, 1957

ANYTHING GOES (REVIVAL)
804 performances
Opened October 19, 1987; Closed September 3, 1989

TITANIC
804 performances
Opened April 23, 1997; Closed March 21, 1999

NO TIME FOR SERGEANTS
796 performances
Opened October 20, 1955; Closed September 14, 1957

FIORELLO!
795 performances
Opened November 23, 1959; Closed October 28, 1961

WHERE'S CHARLEY?
792 performances
Opened October 11, 1948; Closed September 9, 1950

THE LADDER
789 performances
Opened October 22, 1926; Unknown closing date

FORTY CARATS
780 performances
Opened December 26, 1968; Closed November 7, 1970

LOST IN YONKERS
780 performances
Opened February 21, 1991; Closed January 3, 1993

THE PRISONER OF SECOND AVENUE
780 performances
Opened November 11, 1971; Closed September 29, 1973

M. BUTTERFLY
777 performances
Opened March 20, 1988; Closed January 27, 1990

THE TALE OF THE ALLERGIST'S WIFE
777 performances
Opened November 2, 2000; Closed September 15, 2002

OLIVER!
774 performances
Opened January 6, 1963; Closed November 14, 1964

Alton Fitzgerald White, Darlesia Cearcy in *Ragtime*, 1998 PHOTO BY CATHERINE ASHMORE

THE PIRATES OF PENZANCE (REVIVAL, 1981)
772 performances
Opened January 8, 1981; Closed November 28, 1982

THE FULL MONTY
770 performances
Opened October 26, 2000; Closed September 1, 2002

WOMAN OF THE YEAR
770 performances
Opened March 29, 1981; Closed March 13, 1983

MY ONE AND ONLY
767 performances
Opened May 1, 1983; Closed March 3, 1985

SOPHISTICATED LADIES
767 performances
Opened March 1, 1981; Closed January 2, 1983

BUBBLING BROWN SUGAR
766 performances
Opened March 2, 1976; Closed December 31, 1977

INTO THE WOODS
765 performances
Opened November 5, 1987; Closed September 3, 1989

STATE OF THE UNION
765 performances
Opened November 14, 1945; Closed September 13, 1947

STARLIGHT EXPRESS
761 performances
Opened March 15, 1987; Closed January 8, 1989

THE FIRST YEAR
760 performances
Opened October 20, 1920; Unknown closing date

BROADWAY BOUND
756 performances
Opened December 4, 1986; Closed September 25, 1988

YOU KNOW I CAN'T HEAR YOU WHEN THE WATER'S RUNNING
755 performances
Opened March 13, 1967; Closed January 4, 1969

TWO FOR THE SEESAW
750 performances
Opened January 16, 1958; Closed October 31, 1959

JOSEPH AND THE AMAZING TECHNICOLOR DREAMCOAT (REVIVAL)
747 performances
Opened January 27, 1982; Closed September 4, 1983

DEATH OF A SALESMAN
742 performances
Opened February 10, 1949; Closed November 18, 1950

FOR COLORED GIRLS WHO HAVE CONSIDERED SUICIDE/WHEN THE RAINBOW IS ENUF
742 performances
Opened September 15, 1976; Closed July 16, 1978

SONS O' FUN
742 performances
Opened December 1, 1941; Closed August 29, 1943

CANDIDE (MUSICAL VERSION, REVIVAL)
740 performances
Opened March 10, 1974; Closed January 4, 1976

GENTLEMEN PREFER BLONDES
740 performances
Opened December 8, 1949; Closed September 15, 1951

THE MAN WHO CAME TO DINNER
739 performances
Opened October 16, 1939; Closed July 12, 1941

NINE
739 performances
Opened May 9, 1982; Closed February 4, 1984

CALL ME MISTER
734 performances
Opened April 18, 1946; Closed January 10, 1948

VICTOR/VICTORIA
734 performances
Opened October 25, 1995; Closed July 27, 1997

WEST SIDE STORY
732 performances
Opened September 26, 1957; Closed June 27, 1959

HIGH BUTTON SHOES
727 performances
Opened October 9, 1947; Closed July 2, 1949

Susan Strasberg in *The Diary of Anne Frank*, 1955 PHOTO BY FRED FEHL.

FINIAN'S RAINBOW
725 performances
Opened January 10, 1947; Closed October 2, 1948

CLAUDIA
722 performances
Opened February 12, 1941; Closed January 9, 1943

THE GOLD DIGGERS
720 performances
Opened September 30, 1919; Unknown closing date

JESUS CHRIST SUPERSTAR
720 performances
Opened October 12, 1971; Closed June 30, 1973

CARNIVAL!
719 performances
Opened April 13, 1961; Closed January 5, 1963

THE DIARY OF ANNE FRANK
717 performances
Opened October 5, 1955; Closed June 22, 1955

A FUNNY THING HAPPENED ON THE WAY TO THE FORUM (REVIVAL)
715 performances
Opened April 18, 1996; Closed January 4, 1998

I REMEMBER MAMA
714 performances
Opened October 19, 1944; Closed June 29, 1946

TEA AND SYMPATHY
712 performances
Opened September 30, 1953; Closed June 18, 1955

JUNIOR MISS
710 performances
Opened November 18, 1941; Closed July 24, 1943

FOOTLOOSE
708 performances
Opened October 22, 1998; Closed July 2, 2000

LAST OF THE RED HOT LOVERS
706 performances
Opened December 28, 1969; Closed September 4, 1971

THE SECRET GARDEN
706 performances
Opened April 25, 1991; Closed January 3, 1993

COMPANY
705 performances
Opened April 26, 1970; Closed January 1, 1972

SEVENTH HEAVEN
704 performances
Opened October 30, 1922; Unknown closing date

GYPSY (MUSICAL)
702 performances
Opened May 21, 1959; Closed March 25, 1961

THE MIRACLE WORKER
700 performances
Opened October 19, 1959; Closed July 1, 1961

THAT CHAMPIONSHIP SEASON
700 performances
Opened September 14, 1972; Closed April 21, 1974

URINETOWN*
700 performances
Opened September 20, 2001

THE MUSIC MAN (MUSICAL, REVIVAL)
698 performances
Opened April 27, 2000; Closed December 30, 2001

DA
697 performances
Opened May 1, 1978; Closed January 1, 1980

CAT ON A HOT TIN ROOF
694 performances
Opened March 24, 1955; Closed November 17, 1956

LI'L ABNER
693 performances
Opened November 15, 1956; Closed July 12, 1958

THE CHILDREN'S HOUR
691 performances
Opened November 20, 1934; Unknown closing date

PURLIE
688 performances
Opened March 15, 1970; Closed November 6, 1971

DEAD END
687 performances
Opened October 28, 1935; Closed June 12, 1937

THE LION AND THE MOUSE
686 performances
Opened November 20, 1905; Unknown closing date

WHITE CARGO
686 performances
Opened November 5, 1923; Unknown closing date

DEAR RUTH
683 performances
Opened December 13, 1944; Closed July 27, 1946

EAST IS WEST
680 performances
Opened December 25, 1918; Unknown closing date

COME BLOW YOUR HORN
677 performances
Opened February 22, 1961; Closed October 6, 1962

THE MOST HAPPY FELLA
676 performances
Opened May 3, 1956; Closed December 14, 1957

MAMMA MIA!*
677 performances
Opened October 18, 2001

DEFENDING THE CAVEMAN
671 performances
Opened March 26, 1995; Closed June 22, 1997

THE DOUGHGIRLS
671 performances
Opened Dec. 30, 1942; Closed July 29, 1944

THE IMPOSSIBLE YEARS
670 performances
Opened October 13, 1965; Closed May 27, 1967

IRENE
670 performances
Opened November 18, 1919; Unknown closing date

BOY MEETS GIRL
669 performances
Opened November 27, 1935; Unknown closing date

THE TAP DANCE KID
669 performances
Opened December 21, 1983; Closed August 11, 1985

BEYOND THE FRINGE
667 performances
Opened October 27, 1962; Closed May 30, 1964

WHO'S AFRAID OF VIRGINIA WOOLF?
664 performances
Opened October 13, 1962; Closed May 16, 1964

BLITHE SPIRIT
657 performances
Opened November 5, 1941; Closed June 5, 1943

A TRIP TO CHINATOWN
657 performances
Opened November 9, 1891; Unknown closing date

THE WOMEN
657 performances
Opened December 26, 1936; Unknown closing date

BLOOMER GIRL
654 performances
Opened October 5, 1944; Closed April 27, 1946

THE FIFTH SEASON
654 performances
Opened January 23, 1953; Closed October 23, 1954

RAIN
648 performances
Opened September 1, 1924; Unknown closing date

WITNESS FOR THE PROSECUTION
645 performances
Opened December 16, 1954; Closed June 30, 1956

CALL ME MADAM
644 performances
Opened October 12, 1950; Closed May 3, 1952

JANIE
642 performances
Opened September 10, 1942; Closed January 16, 1944

THE GREEN PASTURES
640 performances
Opened February 26, 1930; Closed August 29, 1931

AUNTIE MAME (PLAY VERSION)
639 performances
Opened October 31, 1956; Closed June 28, 1958

A MAN FOR ALL SEASONS
637 performances
Opened November 22, 1961; Closed June 1, 1963

JEROME ROBBINS' BROADWAY
634 performances
Opened February 26, 1989; Closed September 1, 1990

THE FOURPOSTER
632 performances
Opened October 24, 1951; Closed May 2, 1953

THE MUSIC MASTER
627 performances
Opened September 26, 1904; Unknown closing date

TWO GENTLEMEN OF VERONA (MUSICAL VERSION)
627 performances
Opened December 1, 1971; Closed May 20, 1973

THE TENTH MAN
623 performances
Opened November 5, 1959; Closed May 13, 1961

THE HEIDI CHRONICLES
621 performances
Opened March 9, 1989; Closed September 1, 1990

IS ZAT SO?
618 performances
Opened January 5, 1925; Closed July 1926

ANNIVERSARY WALTZ
615 performances
Opened April 7, 1954; Closed September 24, 1955

THE HAPPY TIME (PLAY VERSION)
614 performances
Opened January 24, 1950; Closed July 14, 1951

Joan Allen, Boyd Gaines in *The Heidi Chronicles*, 1989 PHOTO BY GERRY GOODSTEIN

SEPARATE ROOMS
613 performances
Opened March 23, 1940; Closed September 6, 1941

AFFAIRS OF STATE
610 performances
Opened September 25, 1950; Closed March 8, 1952

OH! CALCUTTA!
610 performances
Opened June 17, 1969; Closed August 12, 1972

STAR AND GARTER
609 performances
Opened June 24, 1942; Closed December 4, 1943

THE MYSTERY OF EDWIN DROOD
608 performances
Opened December 2, 1985; Closed May 16, 1987

THE STUDENT PRINCE
608 performances
Opened December 2, 1924; Unknown closing date

SWEET CHARITY
608 performances
Opened January 29, 1966; Closed July 15, 1967

BYE BYE BIRDIE
607 performances
Opened April 14, 1960; Closed October 7, 1961

RIVERDANCE ON BROADWAY
605 performances
Opened March 16, 2000; Closed August 26, 2001

IRENE (REVIVAL)
604 performances
Opened March 13, 1973; Closed September 8, 1974

SUNDAY IN THE PARK WITH GEORGE
604 performances
Opened May 2, 1984; Closed October 13, 1985

ADONIS
603 performances
Opened ca. 1884; Unknown closing date

BROADWAY
603 performances
Opened September 16, 1926; Unknown closing date

PEG O' MY HEART
603 performances
Opened December 20, 1912; Unknown closing date

MASTER CLASS
601 performances
Opened November 5, 1995; Closed June 29, 1997

STREET SCENE (PLAY)
601 performances
Opened January 10, 1929; Unknown closing date

FLOWER DRUM SONG
600 performances
Opened December 1, 1958; Closed May 7, 1960

KIKI
600 performances
Opened November 29, 1921; Unknown closing date

A LITTLE NIGHT MUSIC
600 performances
Opened February 25, 1973; Closed August 3, 1974

ART
600 performances
Opened March 1, 1998; Closed August 8, 1999

AGNES OF GOD
599 performances
Opened March 30, 1982; Closed September 4, 1983

DON'T DRINK THE WATER
598 performances
Opened November 17, 1966; Closed April 20, 1968

WISH YOU WERE HERE
598 performances
Opened June 25, 1952; Closed November 28, 1958

SARAFINA!
597 performances
Opened January 28, 1988; Closed July 2, 1989

A SOCIETY CIRCUS
596 performances
Opened December 13, 1905; Closed November 24, 1906

ABSURD PERSON SINGULAR
592 performances
Opened October 8, 1974; Closed March 6, 1976

A DAY IN HOLLYWOOD/A NIGHT IN THE UKRAINE
588 performances
Opened May 1, 1980; Closed September 27, 1981

THE ME NOBODY KNOWS
586 performances
Opened December 18, 1970; Closed November 21, 1971

THE TWO MRS. CARROLLS
585 performances
Opened August 3, 1943; Closed February 3, 1945

KISMET (MUSICAL VERSION)
583 performances
Opened December 3, 1953; Closed April 23, 1955

GYPSY (MUSICAL VERSION, REVIVAL)
582 performances
Opened November 16, 1989; Closed July 28, 1991

BRIGADOON
581 performances
Opened March 13, 1947; Closed July 31, 1948

DETECTIVE STORY
581 performances
Opened March 23, 1949; Closed August 12, 1950

NO STRINGS
580 performances
Opened March 14, 1962; Closed August 3, 1963

BROTHER RAT
577 performances
Opened December 16, 1936; Unknown closing date

BLOSSOM TIME
576 performances
Opened September 29, 1921; Unknown closing date

PUMP BOYS AND DINETTES
573 performances
Opened February 4, 1982; Closed June 18, 1983

SHOW BOAT
572 performances
Opened December 27, 1927; Closed May 4, 1929

THE SHOW-OFF
571 performances
Opened February 5, 1924; Unknown closing date

SALLY
570 performances
Opened December 21, 1920; Closed April 22, 1922

JELLY'S LAST JAM
569 performances
Opened April 26, 1992; Closed September 5, 1993

GOLDEN BOY (MUSICAL VERSION)
568 performances
Opened October 20, 1964; Closed March 5, 1966

ONE TOUCH OF VENUS
567 performances
Opened October 7, 1943; Closed February 10, 1945

THE REAL THING
566 performances
Opened January 5, 1984; Closed May 12, 1985

HAPPY BIRTHDAY
564 performances
Opened October 31, 1946; Closed March 13, 1948

LOOK HOMEWARD, ANGEL
564 performances
Opened November 28, 1957; Closed April 4, 1959

MORNING'S AT SEVEN (REVIVAL)
564 performances
Opened April 10, 1980; Closed August 16, 1981

THE GLASS MENAGERIE
561 performances
Opened March 31, 1945; Closed August 3, 1946

I DO! I DO!
560 performances
Opened December 5, 1966; Closed June 15, 1968

WONDERFUL TOWN
559 performances
Opened February 25, 1953; Closed July 3, 1954

THE LAST NIGHT OF BALLYHOO
557 performances
Opened February 27, 1997; Closed June 28, 1998

ROSE MARIE
557 performances
Opened September 2, 1924; Unknown closing date

STRICTLY DISHONORABLE
557 performances
Opened Sept. 18, 1929; Unknown closing date

SWEENEY TODD, THE DEMON BARBER OF FLEET STREET
557 performances
Opened March 1, 1979; Closed June 29, 1980

THE GREAT WHITE HOPE
556 performances
Opened October 3, 1968; Closed January 31, 1970

A MAJORITY OF ONE
556 performances
Opened February 16, 1959; Closed June 25, 1960

THE SISTERS ROSENSWEIG
556 performances
Opened March 18, 1993; Closed July 16, 1994

SUNRISE AT CAMPOBELLO
556 performances
Opened January 30, 1958; Closed May 30, 1959

TOYS IN THE ATTIC
556 performances
Opened February 25, 1960; Closed April 8, 1961

JAMAICA
555 performances
Opened October 31, 1957; Closed April 11, 1959

STOP THE WORLD—I WANT TO GET OFF
555 performances
Opened October 3, 1962; Closed February 1, 1964

FLORODORA
553 performances
Opened November 10, 1900; Closed January 25, 1902

NOISES OFF
553 performances
Opened December 11, 1983; Closed April 6, 1985

ZIEGFELD FOLLIES (1943)
553 performances
Opened April 1, 1943; Closed July 22, 1944

DIAL "M" FOR MURDER
552 performances
Opened October 29, 1952; Closed February 27, 1954

GOOD NEWS
551 performances
Opened September 6, 1927; Unknown closing date

PETER PAN (REVIVAL)
551 performances
Opened September 6, 1979; Closed January 4, 1981

HOW TO SUCCEED IN BUSINESS WITHOUT REALLY TRYING (REVIVAL)
548 performances
Opened March 23, 1995; Closed July 14, 1996

LET'S FACE IT
547 performances
Opened October 29, 1941; Closed March 20, 1943

MILK AND HONEY
543 performances
Opened October 10, 1961; Closed January 26, 1963

WITHIN THE LAW
541 performances
Opened September 11, 1912; Unknown closing date

PAL JOEY (REVIVAL)
540 performances
Opened January 3, 1952; Closed April 18, 1953

THE SOUND OF MUSIC (REVIVAL)
540 performances
Opened March 12, 1998; Closed June 20, 1999

WHAT MAKES SAMMY RUN?
540 performances
Opened February 27, 1964; Closed June 12, 1965

THE SUNSHINE BOYS
538 performances
Opened December 20, 1972; Closed April 21, 1974

WHAT A LIFE
538 performances
Opened April 13, 1938; Closed July 8, 1939

CRIMES OF THE HEART
535 performances
Opened November 4, 1981; Closed February 13, 1983

DAMN YANKEES (REVIVAL)
533 performances
Opened March 3, 1994; Closed August 6, 1995

THE UNSINKABLE MOLLY BROWN
532 performances
Opened November 3, 1960; Closed February 10, 1962

THE RED MILL (REVIVAL)
531 performances
Opened October 16, 1945; Closed January 18, 1947

RUMORS
531 performances
Opened November 17, 1988; Closed February 24, 1990

A RAISIN IN THE SUN
530 performances
Opened March 11, 1959; Closed June 25, 1960

GODSPELL
527 performances
Opened June 22, 1976; Closed September 4, 1977

FENCES
526 performances
Opened March 26, 1987; Closed June 26, 1988

THE SOLID GOLD CADILLAC
526 performances
Opened November 5, 1953; Closed February 12, 1955

BILOXI BLUES
524 performances
Opened March 28, 1985; Closed June 28, 1986

IRMA LA DOUCE
524 performances
Opened September 29, 1960; Closed December 31, 1961

THE BOOMERANG
522 performances
Opened August 10, 1915; Unknown closing date

FOLLIES
521 performances
Opened April 4, 1971; Closed July 1, 1972

ROSALINDA
521 performances
Opened October 28, 1942; Closed January 22, 1944

THE BEST MAN
520 performances
Opened March 31, 1960; Closed July 8, 1961

CHAUVE-SOURIS
520 performances
Opened February 4, 1922; Unknown closing date

BLACKBIRDS OF 1928
518 performances
Opened May 9, 1928; Unknown closing date

THE GIN GAME
517 performances
Opened October 6, 1977; Closed December 31, 1978

SUNNY
517 performances
Opened September 22, 1925; Closed December 11, 1926

VICTORIA REGINA
517 performances
Opened December 26, 1935; Unknown closing date

FIFTH OF JULY
511 performances
Opened November 5, 1980; Closed January 24, 1982

HALF A SIXPENCE
511 performances
Opened April 25, 1965; Closed July 16, 1966

THE VAGABOND KING
511 performances
Opened September 21, 1925; Closed December 4, 1926

THE NEW MOON
509 performances
Opened September 19, 1928; Closed December 14, 1929

THE WORLD OF SUZIE WONG
508 performances
Opened October 14, 1958; Closed January 2, 1960

THE ROTHSCHILDS
507 performances
Opened October 19, 1970; Closed January 1, 1972

ON YOUR TOES (REVIVAL)
505 performances
Opened March 6, 1983; Closed May 20, 1984

SUGAR
505 performances
Opened April 9, 1972; Closed June 23, 1973

SHUFFLE ALONG
504 performances
Opened May 23, 1921; Closed July 15, 1922

UP IN CENTRAL PARK
504 performances
Opened January 27, 1945; Closed January 13, 1946

CARMEN JONES
503 performances
Opened December 2, 1943; Closed February 10, 1945

SATURDAY NIGHT FEVER
502 performances
Opened October 21, 1999; Closed December 30, 2000

THE MEMBER OF THE WEDDING
501 performances
Opened January 5, 1950; Closed March 17, 1951

PANAMA HATTIE
501 performances
Opened October 30, 1940; Closed January 13, 1942

PERSONAL APPEARANCE
501 performances
Opened October 17, 1934; Unknown closing date

BIRD IN HAND
500 performances
Opened April 4, 1929; Unknown closing date

ROOM SERVICE
500 performances
Opened May 19, 1937; Unknown closing date

SAILOR, BEWARE!
500 performances
Opened September 28, 1933; Unknown closing date

TOMORROW THE WORLD
500 performances
Opened April 14, 1943; Closed June 17, 1944

The Company of *Saturday Night Fever*, 1999

Andy Blankenbuhler, Sean Palmer, James Carpinello, Richard H. Blake, Paul Castree of *Saturday Night Fever*, 1999 PHOTOS BY JOAN MARCUS

Longest Running Shows **Off-Broadway**

LONGEST RUNNING SHOWS
OFF-BROADWAY

*Plays that were still playing as of May 31, 2003.

THE FANTASTICKS
17,162 performances
Opened May 3, 1960; Closed January 13, 2002

PERFECT CRIME*
6,672 performances
Opened April 5, 1987

TUBES*
5,805 performances
Opened November 17, 1991

TONY 'N' TINA'S WEDDING
4,914 performances
Opened May 1, 1987; Closed May 18, 2003

STOMP*
3,883 performances
Opened February 27, 1994

NUNSENSE
3,672 performances
Opened December 12, 1985; Closed October 16, 1994

I LOVE YOU, YOU'RE PERFECT, NOW CHANGE*
2,836 performances
Opened August 1, 1996

THE THREEPENNY OPERA
2,611 performances
Opened September 20, 1955; Closed December 17, 1961

FORBIDDEN BROADWAY 1982–87
2,332 performances
Opened January 15, 1982; Closed August 30, 1987

LITTLE SHOP OF HORRORS
2,209 performances
Opened July 27, 1982; Closed November 1, 1987

GODSPELL
2,124 performances
Opened May 17, 1971; Closed June 13, 1976

VAMPIRE LESBIANS OF SODOM
2,024 performances
Opened June 19, 1985; Closed May 27, 1990

DE LA GUARDA*
1,952 performances
Opened June 16, 1998

JACQUES BREL
1,847 performances
Opened October 1, 1992; Closed February 7, 1997

FOREVER PLAID
1,811 performances
Opened May 20, 1990; Closed June 12, 1994

VANITIES
1,785 performances
Opened August 6, 1928; Unknown closing date

NAKED BOYS SINGING*
1,622 performances
Opened July 22, 1999

YOU'RE A GOOD MAN, CHARLIE BROWN
1,597 performances
Opened March 7, 1967; Closed February 14, 1971

THE BLACKS
1,408 performances
Opened May 4, 1961; Closed September 27, 1964

THE VAGINA MONOLOGUES
1,105 performances
Opened October 3, 1999; Closed January 26, 2003

Jane Galloway, Susan Merson, Kathy Bates in *Vanities*, 1976

ONE MO' TIME
1,372 performances
Opened October 22, 1979; Closed 1982–83 season

GRANDMA SYLVIA'S FUNERAL
1,360 performances
Opened October 9, 1994; Closed June 20, 1998

LET MY PEOPLE COME
1,327 performances
Opened January 8, 1974; Closed July 5, 1976

Thais Clark, Topsy Chapman, Sylvia "Kuumba" Williams in *One Mo' Time*, 1979

LATE NITE CATECHISM
1,115 performances
Opened October 4, 1995; Closed May 18, 2003

DRIVING MISS DAISY
1,195 performances
Opened April 15, 1987; Closed June 3, 1990

THE HOT L BALTIMORE
1,166 performances
Opened September 8, 1973; Closed January 4, 1976

I'M GETTING MY ACT TOGETHER AND TAKING IT ON THE ROAD
1,165 performances
Opened May 16, 1987; Closed March 15, 1981

LITTLE MARY SUNSHINE
1,143 performances
Opened November 18, 1959; Closed September 2, 1962

STEEL MAGNOLIAS
1,126 performances
Opened November 17, 1987; Closed February 25, 1990

EL GRANDE DE COCA-COLA
1,114 performances
Opened February 13, 1973; Closed April 13, 1975

THE PROPOSITION
1,109 performances
Opened March 24, 1971; Closed April 14, 1974

THE DONKEY SHOW*
1,103 performances
Opened January 26, 1999

OUR SINATRA
1,096 performances
Opened December 8, 1999; Closed July 28, 2002

BEAU JEST
1,069 performances
Opened October 10, 1991; Closed May 1, 1994

TAMARA
1,036 performances
Opened November 9, 1989; Closed July 15, 1990

ONE FLEW OVER THE CUCKOO'S NEST (REVIVAL)
1,025 performances
Opened March 23, 1971; Closed September 16, 1973

THE BOYS IN THE BAND
1,000 performances
Opened April 14, 1968; Closed September 29, 1985

FOOL FOR LOVE
1,000 performances
Opened November 27, 1983; Closed September 29, 1985

OTHER PEOPLE'S MONEY
990 performances
Opened February 7, 1989; Closed July 4, 1991

CLOUD 9
971 performances
Opened May 18, 1981; Closed September 4, 1983

SECRETS EVERY SMART TRAVELER SHOULD KNOW
953 performances
Opened October 30, 1997; Closed February 21, 2000

SISTER MARY IGNATIUS EXPLAINS IT ALL FOR YOU & THE ACTOR'S NIGHTMARE
947 performances
Opened October 21, 1981; Closed January 29, 1984

YOUR OWN THING
933 performances
Opened January 13, 1968; Closed April 5, 1970

CURLEY MCDIMPLE
931 performances
Opened November 22, 1967; Closed January 25, 1970

LEAVE IT TO JANE (REVIVAL)
928 performances
Opened May 29, 1959; Closed 1961–62 season

HEDWIG AND THE ANGRY INCH
857 performances
Opened February 14, 1998; Closed April 9, 2000

FORBIDDEN BROADWAY STRIKES BACK
850 performances
Opened October 17, 1996; Closed September 20, 1998

WHEN PIGS FLY
840 performances
Opened August 14, 1996; Closed August 15, 1998

THE MAD SHOW
831 performances
Opened January 9, 1966; Closed September 10, 1967

SCRAMBLED FEET
831 performances
Opened June 11, 1979; Closed June 7, 1981

THE EFFECT OF GAMMA RAYS ON MAN-IN-THE-MOON MARIGOLDS
819 performances
Opened April 7, 1970; Closed June 1, 1973

OVER THE RIVER AND THROUGH THE WOODS
800 performances
Opened October 5, 1998; Closed September 3, 2000

A VIEW FROM THE BRIDGE (REVIVAL)
780 performances
Opened November 9, 1965; Closed December 11, 1966

THE BOY FRIEND (REVIVAL)
763 performances
Opened January 25, 1958; Closed 1961–62 season

TRUE WEST
762 performances
Opened December 23, 1980; Closed January 11, 1981

FORBIDDEN BROADWAY CLEANS UP ITS ACT!
754 performances
Opened November 17, 1998; Closed August 30, 2000

ISN'T IT ROMANTIC
733 performances
Opened December 15, 1983; Closed September 1, 1985

DIME A DOZEN
728 performances
Opened June 13, 1962; Closed 1963–64 season

THE POCKET WATCH
725 performances
Opened November 14, 1966; Closed June 18, 1967

THE CONNECTION
722 performances
Opened June 9, 1959; Closed June 4, 1961

THE PASSION OF DRACULA
714 performances
Opened September 28, 1977; Closed July 14, 1979

Nicolas Surovy, John Pankow in *Cloud 9*, 1981 <small>PHOTO BY PETER CUNNIGHAM</small>

LOVE, JANIS
713 performances
Opened April 22, 2001; Closed January 5, 2003

ADAPTATION & NEXT
707 performances
Opened February 10, 1969; Closed October 18, 1970

OH! CALCUTTA!
704 performances
Opened June 17, 1969; Closed August 12, 1972

SCUBA DUBA
692 performances
Opened November 11, 1967; Closed June 8, 1969

THE FOREIGNER
686 performances
Opened November 2, 1984; Closed June 8, 1986

THE KNACK
685 performances
Opened January 14, 1964; Closed January 9, 1966

FULLY COMMITTED
675 performances
Opened December 14, 1999; Closed May 27, 2001

THE CLUB
674 performances
Opened October 14, 1976; Closed May 21, 1978

THE BALCONY
672 performances
Opened March 3, 1960; Closed December 21, 1961

PENN & TELLER
666 performances
Opened July 30, 1985; Closed January 19, 1992

DINNER WITH FRIENDS
654 performances
Opened November 4, 1999; Closed May 27, 2000

AMERICA HURRAH
634 performances
Opened November 7, 1966; Closed May 5, 1968

OIL CITY SYMPHONY
626 performances
Opened November 5, 1987; Closed May 7, 1989

THE COUNTESS
618 performances
Opened September 28, 1999; Closed December 30, 2000

HOGAN'S GOAT
607 performances
Opened March 6, 1965; Closed April 23, 1967

BEEHIVE
600 performances
Opened March 30, 1986; Closed August 23, 1987

THE TROJAN WOMEN
600 performances
Opened December 23, 1963; Closed May 30, 1965

THE SYRINGA TREE
586 performances
Opened September 14, 2000; Closed June 2, 2002

THE DINING ROOM
583 performances
Opened February 24, 1982; Closed July 17, 1982

KRAPP'S LAST TAPE & THE ZOO STORY
582 performances
Opened August 29, 1960; Closed May 21, 1961

THREE TALL WOMEN
582 performances
Opened April 13, 1994; Closed August 26, 1995

THE DUMBWAITER & THE COLLECTION
578 performances
Opened January 21, 1962; Closed April 12, 1964

FORBIDDEN BROADWAY 1990
576 performances
Opened January 23, 1990; Closed June 9, 1991

DAMES AT SEA
575 performances
Opened April 22, 1969; Closed May 10, 1970

THE CRUCIBLE (REVIVAL) (TRANSFER)
571 performances
Opened March 14, 1990; Closed May 13, 1990

THE ICEMAN COMETH (REVIVAL)
565 performances
Opened May 8, 1956; Closed 1957–58 season

FORBIDDEN BROADWAY 2001: A SPOOF ODYSSEY
552 performances
Opened December 6, 2000; Closed February 6, 2002

THE HOSTAGE (REVIVAL) (TRANSFER)
545 performances
Opened October 16, 1972; Closed October 8, 1973

WIT
545 performances
Opened October 6, 1998; Closed April 9, 2000

WHAT'S A NICE COUNTRY LIKE YOU DOING IN A STATE LIKE THIS?
543 performances
Opened July 31, 1985; Closed February 9, 1987

FORBIDDEN BROADWAY 1988
534 performances
Opened September 15, 1988; Closed December 24, 1989

GROSS INDECENCY: THE THREE TRIALS OF OSCAR WILDE
534 performances
Opened September 5, 1997; Closed September 13, 1998

FRANKIE AND JOHNNY IN THE CLAIR DE LUNE
533 performances
Opened December 4, 1987; Closed March 12, 1989

SIX CHARACTERS IN SEARCH OF AN AUTHOR (REVIVAL)
529 performances
Opened March 8, 1963; Closed June 28, 1964

ALL IN THE TIMING
526 performances
Opened November 24, 1993; Closed February 13, 1994

FORBIDDEN BROADWAY: 20TH ANNIVERSARY CELEBRATION*
526 performances
Opened March 20, 2002

OLEANNA
513 performances
Opened October 3, 1992; Closed January 16, 1994

MENOPAUSE THE MUSICAL*
512 performances
Opened April 4, 2002

MAKING PORN
511 performances
Opened June 12, 1996; Closed September 14, 1997

THE DIRTIEST SHOW IN TOWN
509 performances
Opened June 26, 1970; Closed September 17, 1971

HAPPY ENDING & DAY OF ABSENCE
504 performances
Opened June 13, 1965; Closed January 29, 1967

GREATER TUNA
501 performances
Opened October 21, 1982; Closed December 31, 1983

A SHAYNA MAIDEL
501 performances
Opened October 29, 1987; Closed January 8, 1989

THE BOYS FROM SYRACUSE (REVIVAL)
500 performances
Opened April 15, 1963; Closed June 28, 1964

BIOGRAPHICAL DATA

Aderer, Konrad Born July 7, 1968 in NYC. Graduate NYU. 1996 Debut OB in *Cymbeline* followed by *Venice Preserv'd, Fuenteovejuna.*

Ahearn, Daniel Born August 7, 1948 in Washington, DC. Attended Carnegie Mellon U. Debut 1981 OB in *Woyzek* followed by *Brontosaurus Rex, Billy Liar, Second Prize, Two Months in Leningrad, No Time Flat, Hollywood Scheherazade, Better Days, Joy Solution, Making Book, Flight, As You Like It.*

Ancheta, Susan Born January in Hololulu, HI. Graduate SMU. 1997 debut OB in *Shanghai Lil's,* Bdwy 1997 in *Miss Saigon;* followed by *Flower Drum Song.*

Anthony, Eric Born December 10 in Baltimore MD. Graduate Carver Center for the Arts and Technology and Arena Players, Inc. Bdwy credits: *Hairspray, The Lion King.*

Aranas, Raul Born October 1, 1947 in Manilla, P.I. Graduate Pace U. Debut 1976 OB in *Savages* followed by *Yellow is My Favorite Color, 49, Bullet Headed Birds, Tooth of the Crime, Teahouse, Shepard Sets, Cold Air, La Chunga, The Man Who Turned into a Stick, Twelfth Night, Shogun Macbeth, Boutique Living, Fairy Bones, In the Jungle of Cities,* Bdwy in *Loose Ends* (1978), *Miss Saigon, King and I, Flower Drum Song.*

Ari, Robert (Bob) Born July 1, 1949 in New York, NY. Graduate Carnegie Mellon U. Debut 1976 OB in *Boys from Syracuse* followed by *Gay Divorce, Devour the Snow, Carbondale Dreams, Show Me Where the Good Times Are, CBS Live, Picasso at the Lapin Agile, Twelfth Night, Baby Anger, Names, June Moon, Pieces of the Sky, Jolson & Co.*

Atkinson, Jayne Born February 18, 1959 in Bournemouth, England. Graduate Northwestern U., Yale U. Debut 1986 OB in *Bloody Poetry* followed by *Terminal Bar, Return of Pinocchio, The Art of Success, The Way of the World, Appointment with a High Wire Lady, Why We Have a Body, How I Learned to Drive,* Bdwy in *All My Sons* (1987) followed by *Ivanov,* followed by *Our Town, 2002*

Auberjonois, Rene Born June 1, 1940 in NYC. Graduate Carnegie Inst. With LC Rep in *A Cry of Player, King Lear, and Twelfth Night,* Bdwy in *Fire* (1969), *Coco, Tricks, The Good Doctor, Break a Leg, Every Good Boy Deserves Favor, Big River, Metamorphosis, City of Angels, Don Juan in Hell in Concert, BAM Co. in The New York Idwa, Three Sisters, The Play's the Thing, Julius Caesar, Dance of the Vampires.*

Baker, Becky Ann (formerly Gelke). Born February 17, 1953 in Ft. Knox, KY. Graduate W. KY. U. Bdwy debut 1978 in *Best Little Whorehouse in Texas* followed by *Streetcar Named Desire* (1988), *Titanic,* OB in *Altitude Sickness, John Brown's Body, Chamber Music, To Whom It May Concern, Two Gentlemen of Verona, Bob's Guns, Buzzsaw Berkeley, Colorado Catechism, Jeremy Rudge, Laura Dennis, June Moon, The Most Fabulous Story Ever Told, Shanghai Moon.*

Banderas, Antonio Born August 10, 1960 in Malaga Spain. Graduate of Art Dramatic National School in 1978. Bdwy debut in *Nine, 2003.*

Barnes, Ezra Born January 22, 1963 in Brooklyn, NY. Graduate Amherst Col. Natl. Theatre Cons. Debut 1998 OB in *Richard II, Far and Wide, 2003.*

Barnes, Lisa Born March 5, 1957 in Pasadena, CA. Graduate USC. Debut 1983 OB in *Midsummer Night's Dream* followed by *Domino Courts, Life on Earth, Quick-Change Room, Rapt.*

Bast, Stephanie Born October 4, 1972 in Seoul, Korea. Graduate Allentown Col. Debut 1995 OB in *Schoolhouse Rock,* Bdwy 1995 in *Christmas Carol* (MSG) followed by *Miss Saigon, King David, Scarlet Pimpernel, Nine.*

Bean, Reathel Bom August 24, 1942 in Missouri. Graduate Drake U. OB in *America Hurrah, San Francisco's Burning, Love Cure, Henry IV, In Circles, Peace, Journey of Snow White, Wanted, The Faggot, Lovers, Not Back with the Elephants, The Art of Coarse Acting, The Trip Back Down, Hunting Cockroaches, Smoke on the Mountain, Avow,* Bdwy in *Doonesbury* (1983), *Big River, Inherit the Wind, Chicago, Our Town.*

Bean, Shoshana Born September 1, 1977 in Olympia, WA. Graduate of University of Cincinnati, the College Conservatory of Music. Bdwy debut in *Hairspray.*

Becker, Rob Born in San Jose, CA in 1956. Bdwy debut 1995 in *Defending the Caveman.*

Bedford, Brian Born February 16, 1935 in Morley, England. Attended RADA. Bdwy debut 1960 in *Five Finger Exercise* followed by *Lord Pengo, The Private Ear, The Astrakhan Coat, Unknown Soldier and His Wife, Seven Descents of Myrtle, Jumpers, Cocktail Party, Hamlet, Private Lives, School for Wives, The Misanthrope, Two Shakespearean Actors, Timon of Athens, Moliere Comedies, London Assurance, Tartuffe* OB in *The Knack, The Lunatic, the Lover and the Poet, Much Ado About Nothing, The Miser*

Benanti, Laura Born 1980 in Kinnelon, NJ. Attended NYU. Bdwy debut 1999 in *Sound of Music, Nine.*

Bern, Mina Born May 5, 1920 in Poland. Bdwy debut 1967 in *Let's Sing Yiddish* followed by *Light Lively and Yiddish, Sing Israel Sing, Those Were the Days,* OB in *The Special, Old Lady's Guide to Survival, Blacksmith's Folly, Yentl*

Billman, Sekiya Born April 18, 1968 in Los Angeles, CA. Graduate UCLA. Bdwy debut 1996 in *Miss Saigon.* OB in *Shanghai Moon, Shanghai Moon.*

Birdsong, Mary Born April 18 in Tallahassee, Fla. OB *Big River, The Janet Lame Film Festival, The Respectable Race, Judy Speaks!, Palm Beach: the Musical, People Are Wrong, TheCompleatWorksofWllmShkspr, Adult Entertainment.*

Blankenbuehler, Andy Born March 7, 1970 in Cincinnati, OH. Attended SMU. Bdwy debut 1993 in *Guys and Dolls* followed by *Steel Pier, Big, Fosse, Man of LaMancha.*

Block, Larry Born October 30, 1942, in NYC. Graduate URI. Bdwy debut 1966 in *Hail Scrawdyke,* followed by *La Turista, Wonderful Town* (NYCO), OB in *Eh?, Fingernails Blue as Flowers, Comedy of Errors, Coming Attractions, Henry IV Part 2, Feuhrer Bunker, Manhattan Love Songs, Souvenirs, The Golem, Responsible Parties, Hit Parade, Largo Desolato, The Square Root of 3, Young Playwrights Festival, Hunting Cockroaches, Two Gentlemen of Verona, Yellow Dog Contract, Temptation, Festival of 1 Acts, Faithful Brethren of Pitt Street, Loman Family Picnic, One of the All-Time Greats, Pericles, Comedy of Errors, The Work Room, Don Juan in Chicago, Him, Devil Inside, Uncle Philip's Coat, Evolution.*

Eric Anthony

Shoshana Bean

Laura Bell Bundy

Shawna Casey

Bloom, Tom Born November 1, 1944 in Washington, D.C. Graduate Western MD. Col., Emerson Col. OB debut 1989 in *Widow's Blind Date*, followed by *A Cup of Coffee, Major Barbara, A Perfect Diamond, Lips Together Teeth Apart, Winter's Tale, The Guardsman, Stray Cats, Arms and the Man,* Bdwy debut 1995 in *Racing Demo, Winter's Tale.*

Bobbie, Walter Born November 18, 1945 in Scranton, PA. Graduate U. Scranton, Catholic U. Bdwy debut 1971 in *Frank Merriwell*, followed by *The Grass Harp, Grease, Tricks, Going Up, History of the American Film, Anything Goes, Getting Married, Guys and Dolls,* OB in *Drat!, She Loves Me, Up from Paradise, Goodbye Freddy, Cafe Crown, Young Playwrights '90, Polish Joke.*

Bogardus, Stephen Born March 11, 1954 in Norfolk, VA. Graduate Princeton U. Bdwy debut 1980 in *West Side Story* followed by *Les Miserables, Grapes of Wrath, Falsettos, Allegro, (Encores), Love! Valour! Compassion!* (also OB), *Sweet Adeline, King David, High Society,* OB in *Genesis, March of the Falsettos, In Trousers, Feathertop, No Way to Treat a Lady, Falsettoland, Umbrellas of Cherbourg, Man of La Mancha.*

Bostnar, Lisa Born July 19 in Cleveland, OH. Attended Case Western U. OB in *Far and Wide*

Bove, Mark Born January 9, 1960 in Pittsburgh, PA. Bdwy debut in *West Side Story* (1980) followed by *Woman of the Year, Chorus Line, Kiss of the Spider Woman, The Life, Urban Cowboy.*

Burkett, Shannon Born in New Jersey. Graduate NYU. Bdwy debut 2000 in *The Ride Down Mt. Morgan,* OB in *Endpapers* followed by *Cavedwellers* then *Endpapers.*

Busch, Charles Born August 23, 1954 in Hartsdale, NY. Graduate Northwestern U. Debut OB 1985 in *Vampire Lesbians of Sodom* followed by *Times Square Angel, Psycho Beach Party, Lady in Question, Red Scare on Sunset, Charles Busch Revue, You Should Be So Lucky, Flipping My Wig,* all of which he also wrote, *Swingtime Canteen* (co-writer), *Shanghai Moon.*

Brennan, Tom Born April 16, 1926 in Cleveland, OH. Graduate Oberlin, Western Reserve U. 1958 debut in *Synge Trilogy* followed by *Between Two Thieves, East, All in Love, Under Milk Wood, Evening* with James Purdy, *Golden Six, Pullman Car Hiawatha, Are You Now or Have You Ever, Diary of Anne Frank, Milk of Paradise, Transcendental Love, Beaver Coat, The Overcoat, Summer, Asian Shade, Inheritors, Paradise Lost, Madwoman of Chaillot, Time of Your Life, Dead Man's Apartment,* Bdwy in *Play Memory, Our Town, The Miser.*

Brown, P.J. Born November 5, 1956 in Staten Island, NYC. Graduate Boston Col. Debut 1990 OB in *Othello* followed by *America Dreaming, Waiting for Lefty, Soldier's Play, Burning Blue* Bdwy in *Grapes of Wrath* (1990).

Bundy, Laura Bell Born April 10, 1981 in Euclid Ohio. Graduate of NYU. Bdwy debut in *Hairspray.* OB *Ruthless, the Musical.*

Burkett, Shannon Born in New Jersey. Graduate NYU. Bdwy debut 2000 in *The Ride Down Mt. Morgan* followed by OB *Cavedweller.*

Burton, Arnie Born September 22, 1958 in Emmett, ID. Graduate U.AZ. Bdwy debut 1983 in *Amadeus,* OB in *Measure for Measure, Major Barbara, Schnitzler One Acts, Tartuffe, As You Like It, Ghosts, Othello, Moon for the Misbegotten, Twelfth Night, Little Eyolf, Mollusc, Venetain Twins, Beaux Stratagem, King Lear, Winter's Tale, When Ladies Battle, Barber of Seville, Mere Mortals, Cymbeline, The Last Sunday in June.*

Butler, Kerry Born in Brooklyn, NY. Graduate Ithaca. Bdwy debut 1993 in *Blood Brothers* followed by *Beauty and the Beast, Hairspray.*

Cain, William Born May 27, 1931 in Tuscaloosa, AL. Graduate U. Wash., Catholic U. Debut 1962 OB in *Red Roses for Me,* followed by *Jericho Jim Crow, Henry V, Antigone, Relatively Speaking, I Married an Angel in Concert, Buddha, Copperhead, Forbidden City, Fortinbras,* Bdwy in *Wilson in the Promise Land* (1970), *You Can't Take It with You, Wild Honey, The Boys in Autumn, Mastergate, A Streetcar Named Desire, The Heiress, Delicate Balance, Endpapers.*

Callaway, Liz Born April 13, 1961 in Chicago, IL. Debut 1980 OB in *Godspell,* followed by *The Matinee Kids, Brownstone, No Way to Treat a Lady, Marry Me a Little, 1-2-3-4-5,* Bdwy in *Merrily We Roll Along* (1981), *Baby, The Three Musketeers, Miss Saigon, Cats, Fiorello (Encores), Merrily We Roll Along in Concert.*

Gilles Chiasson

Michael Cone

Vanessa Conlin

Patricia Corbett

Camp, Joanne Born April 4, 1951 in Atlanta, GA. Graduate Fl. Atlantic U., Geo. Wash. U. Debut 1981 OB in *The Dry Martini*, followed by *Geniuses* for which she received a Theatre World Award, *June Moon, Painting Churches, Merchant of Venice, Lady from the Sea, The Contrast, Coastal Disturbances, The Rivals, Andromache, Electra, Uncle Vanya, She Stoops to Conquer, Hedda Gabler, Heidi Chronicles, Importance of Being Earnest, Medea, Three Sisters, Midsummer Night's Dream, School for Wives, Measure for Measure, Dance of Death, Two Schnitzler One-Acts, Tartuffe, Lips Together Teeth Apart, As You Like It, Moon for the Misbegotten, Phaedra, Little Eyolf, Beaux Stratagem, King Lear, Life Is a Dream, Winter's Tale, When Ladies Battle, The Guardsman, Candida*, Bdwy in *Heidi Chronicles* (1989), *Sisters Rosensweig, Last Night of Ballyhoo, Dinner at Eight*.

Casey, Shawna Born in San Diego, CA. Graduate of Cinema and Communication Arts. OB debut in *Joe & Betty*. Los Angeles theatre work: *Moe's Lucky 7, Each Day Dies, Children of Herakles, Party Mix, Secret of Success, The Brat, I Hate!, The Conception*.

Chalfant, Kathleen Born January 14, 1945 in San Francisco, CA. Graduate Stanford U. Bdwy debut 1975 in *Dance with Me* followed by *M. Butterfly, Angels in America, Racing Demon*, OB in *Jules Feiffer's Hold Me, Killings on the Last Line, The Boor, Blood Relations, Signs of Life, Sister Mary Ignatius Explains it All, Actor's Nightmare, Faith Healer, All the Nice People, Hard Times, Investigation of the Murder in El Salvador, 3 Poets, The Crucible, The Party, Iphigenia and Other Daughters, Cowboy Pictures, Twelve Dreams, Henry V, Endgame, When It Comes Early, Nine Armenians, Phaedra in Delurium, Far Away*.

Charles, Walter Bom April 4, 1945 in East Stroudsburg, PA. Graduate Boston U. Bdwy debut 1973 in *Grease*, followed by *1600 Pennsylvania Avenue, Knickerbocker Holiday, Sweeney Todd, Cats, La Cage aux Folles, Aspects of Love, Me and My Girl, 110 in the Shade* (NYCO), *Christmas Carol, Boys From Syracuse*.

Chernov, Hope Born June 13 in Philadelphia, PA. Graduate Temple U, U CA/Irvine. Debut 1996 OB in *Barber of Seville* followed by *Venice Preserv'd, As Bees in Honey Drown, Richard II, Miss Julie, School for Scandal, Julius Caesar.*

Chiasson, Gilles *Rent, Scarlet Pimpernel, Civil War, La Boheme.*

Colin, Margaret Born May 26, 1957 in Brooklyn, NY. OB in *Sight Unseen, Aristocrats, Psychopathia Sexualis*, Bdwy debut 1997 in *Jackie* for which she received a Theatre World Award; *Day in the Death of Joe Egg*, '03.

Cone, Michael Born October 7, 1952 in Fresno, CA. Graduate UWash. Bdwy debut 1980 in *Brigadoon* followed by *Christmas Carol*, OB in *Bar Mitzvah Boy, The Rink, Commedia Tonite!, La Boheme.*

Conlin, Vanessa Born April 26 in Amarillo TX Graduate of the University Arts in Philadelphia, Manhattan School of Music, Boston University. Bdwy debut in *La Boheme.*

Connell, Gordon Born March 19, 1923 in Berkley, CA. Graduate UCal, NYU. Bdwy debut 1961 in *Subways are for Sleeping* followed by *Hello Dolly!, Lysistrata, Human Comedy* (also OB), *Big River*, OB in *Beggars Opera, Butler Did It, With Love and Laughter, Deja Review, Good Doctor, Comedians.*

Conroy, Jarlath Born September 30, 1944 in Galway, Ire. Attended RADA. Bdwy debut 1976 in *Comedians*, followed by *The Elephant Man, Macbeth, Ghetto, The Visit, On the Waterfront*, OB in *Translations, The Wind that Shook the Barley, Gardenia, Friends, Playboy of the Western World, One-Act Festival, Abel & Bela/Architect, The Matchmaker, Henry V, A Man of No Importance.*

Converse, Frank Born May 22, 1938 in St. Louis, MO. Attended Carnegie-Mellon U. Bdwy debut 1966 in *First One Asleep Whistle* followed by *The Philadelphia Story, Brothers, Design for Living, A Streetcar Named Desire*, OB in *House of Blue Leaves, Lady in the Dark in Concert*. Bdwy in *Our Town*, '03.

Conway, Kevin Born May 29, 1941 in NYC. Debut 1968 in *Muzeeka* followed by *Saved, Plough and the Stars, One Flew Over the Cuckoo's Nest, When You Comin' Back Red Ryder?, Long Day's Journey into Night, Other Places, King John, Other People's Money, Man Who Fell in Love with His Wife, Ten Below*, Bdwy in *Indians* (1969), *Moonchildren, Of Mice and Men, Elephant Man, On the Waterfront, Dinner at Eight*.

Corbett, Patricia Born February 2, 1940 in No. Hollywood, CA. attended UCLA Opera School. Bdwy debut in *La Boheme 2002.*

Crosby, B.J. Born November 23, 1952 in New Orleans, LA. Bdwy debut 1995 in *Smokey Joe's Café*, followed by *Harlem Song.* (OB).

Holly Cruikshank   Stephanie D'Abruzzo   John Epperson   Pascale Faye

Cruikshank, Holly Born in Scottsdale AZ June 18, 1973. Graduate of North Carolina School of the Arts. *Will Rogers Follies* (Bdwy debut), *Hello Dolly, A Funny Thing Happened on the Way to the Forum, Fosse, Contact, Movin' Out*

D'Abruzzo, Stephanie Born in Pittsburgh PA. Bdwy debut in *Avenue Q*, OB: *Carnival (Encores!)*

Dafoe, Willem Born July 22, 1955. Has performed with OB's Wooster Group since 1977. OB in *Hairy Ape, Brace Up!*

Danson, Randy Born April 30, 1950 in Plainfield NJ. Graduate Carnegie-Mellon U. Debut 1978 OB in *Gimme Shelter* followed by *Big and Little, Winter Dancers, Time Steps, Casualties, Red and Blue, Resurrection of Lady Lester, Jazz Poets at the Grotto, Plenty, Macbeth, Blue Window, Cave Life, Romeo and Juliet, One-Act Festival, Mad Forest, Triumph of Love, The Treatment, Phaedra, Arts & Leisure, The Devils, The Erinyes, First Picture Show, Portia Coughlan, 8 Days (Backward).*

Darlow, Cynthia Born June 13, 1949 in Detroit, MI. Attended NCSch of Arts, Penn State U. Debut 1974 OB in *This Property Is Condemned* followed by *Portrait of a Madonna, Clytemnestra, Unexpurgated Memoirs of Bernard Morgandigler, Actor's Nightmare, Sister Mary Ignatius Explains.., Fables for Friends, That's It Folks!, Baby with the Bath Water, Dandy Dick, Naked Truth, Cover of Life, Death Defying Acts, Mere Mortals, Once in a Lifetime, Til the Rapture Comes,* Bdwy in *Grease* (1976), *Rumors, Prelude to a Kiss* (also OB), *Sex and Longing, Hank Williams' Lost Highway.* OOB: *Happy Birthday*

Davis, Mary Bond Born June 3, 1958 in Los Angeles, CA. Attended Cal. State U./Northridge, LACC. Debut 1985 in *Trousers* followed by *Hysterical Blindness, Scapin,* Bdwy in *Mail* (1988), *Jelly's Last Jam, Hairspray*

Day, Jamie Born in Decatur, IL. Graduate of Northern Kentucky University. OB debut in *Debbie Does Dallas.*

Dee, Ruby Born October 27, 1923 in Cleveland, OH. Graduate Hunter Col. Bdwy debut in *Jeb* (1946) followed by *Anna Lucasta, Smile of the World, Long Way Home, Raisin in the Sun, Purlie Victorious, Checkmates* (1988), OB in *World of Sholom Aleichem, Boesman and Lena, Wedding Band, Hamlet, Take It from the Top, Checkmates* (1995), *My One Good Nerve, A Last Dance for Sybil.*

Dennehy, Brian Born July 9, 1938 in Bridgeport, CT. Debut 1988 OB in *Cherry Orchard* followed by Bdwy 1995 in *Translations* followed by *Long Day's Journey into Night (2003)*

DeMunn, Jeffrey Born April 15, 1947 in Buffalo, NY. Graduate Union Col. Debut 1975 OB in *Augusta* followed by *A Prayer for My Daughter, Modigliani, Chekhov Sketchbook, Midsummer Night's Dream, Total Abandon, Country Girl, Hands Of Its Enemy, One Shoe Off, Gun-Shy,* Bdwy in *Comedians* (1976), *Bent, K2, Sleight of Hand, Spoils of War, Our Town.*

Diaz, Natascia Born January 4, 1970 in Lugano, Switzerland. Graduate Carnegie-Mellon U. Debut 1993 OB in *Little Prince* followed by *I Won't Dance.* Bdwy debut in *Man of La Mancha*

Dillon, Mia Born July 9, 1955 in Colorado Springs, CO. Graduate Penn State U. Bdwy debut 1977 in *Equus,* followed by *Da, Once a Catholic, Crimes of the Heart, The Corn is Green, Hay Fever, The Miser,* OB in *The Crucible, Summer, Waiting for the Parade, Crimes of the Heart, Fables for Friends, Scenes from La Vie de Boheme, Three Sisters, Wednesday, Roberta in Concert, Come Back Little Sheba, Venna Notes, George White's Scandals, Lady Moonsong, Mr. Monsoon, Almost Perfect, The Aunts, Approximating Mother, Remembrance, Lauren's Whereabouts, New England, With and Without, Cape Cod Souvenirs, Our Town.*

Dilly, Erin Born May 12, 1972 in Royal Oak, MI. Graduate U. MI. OB debut 1999 in *Things You Shouldn't Say Past Midnight,* Bdwy in *Follies 2001, Boys from Syracuse.*

Drew, Sarah Bdwy debut in *Vincent in Brixton* (02) for which she won Theatre World Award

Duell, William Born August 30, 1923 in Corinth, NY. Attended Il. Wesleyan Yale. OB 1962 in *Portrait of the Artist as a Young Man/Barroom Monks,* followed by *A Midsummer Night's Dream, Henry IV, Taming of the Shrew, The Memorandum Threepenny Opera, Loves of Cass Maguire, Romance Language, Hamlet, Henry IV (I & 11), On the Bum,* Bdwy in *A Cook for Mr. General, Ballad of the Sad Cafe, Ilya Darling, 1776, Kings, Stages, Inspector General, Marriage of Figaro, Our Town, A Funny Thing...(1996). Comedians* (2003)

Duncan, Sandy Born February 20, 1946 in Henderson, TX. Attended Len Morris Col. Debut 1965 in CC's revivals of *The Music Man, Carousel, Finnian's Rainbow, The Sound of Music, Wonderful Town, Life With Father,* also OB in *Ceremony of Innocence,* for which she received a Theatre World Award, followed by *Your Own Thing,* Bdwy in *Canterbury Tales* (1969), followed by *Love is a Time of Day, The Boy Friend* (1970), *Peter Pan* (1979), *5-6-7-8-Dance, My One and Only, Chicago, The Fourth Wall.*

Dutton, Charles S. Born January 30, 1951 in Baltimore, MD. Graduate Yale. Debut 1983 OB in *Richard III* followed by *Pantomime, Fried Chicken and Invisibility, Splendid Mummer,* Bdwy in *Ma Rainey's Black Bottom* for which he received a Theatre World Award, *Piano Lesson, St. Louis Woman (Encores).*

Dysart, Eric Born in Cleveland Ohio. Bdwy debut in *Hairspray.*

Ebersole, Christine Born February 21, 1953 in Park Forest, IL. Attended AADA. Bdwy debut in *Angel Street* (1976) followed by *I Love My Wife, On the 20th Century, Oklahoma!, Camelot, Harrigan and Hart, Getting Away with Murder, Dinner at Eight.* OB in *Green Pond, Three Sisters, Geniuses, Good as New.*

Emerson, Michael Born 1955 in Cedar Rapids, IA. Graduate Drake U, U AL. Debut 1997 OB in *Gross Indecency* followed by *Only the End of the World*

Emond, Linda Born May 22, 1959 in New Brunswick, NJ. Graduate U of WA. Debut 1996 OB in *Nine Armenians* followed by *Dying Gaul,* Bdwy in *1776* (1997) followed by *Life (x) 3.*

Epperson, John Born 1956 in Hazelhurst, MS. Debut 1988 OB in I *Could Go on Lypsynching,* followed by *The Fabulous Lypsinka Show, Lypsinka! A Day in the Life!, As I Lay Lip-Synching.*

Esparza, Raul Born October 24, 1970 in Wilmington, DE. Graduate NYU. Bdwy debut 2000 in *The Rocky Horror Show,* OB in *Comedians.*

Esposito, Giancarlo Born April 26, 1958 in Copenhagen, Denmark. Bdwy debut in *Maggie Flynn* (1968) followed by *Me Nobody Knows, Lost in the Stars, Seesaw, Merrily We Roll Along, Don't Get God Started, 3 Penny Opera, Sacrilege,* OB in *Zooman and the Sign* for which he received a 1981 Theatre World Award, *Keyboard, Who Loves the Dancer, House of 0., Do Lord Remember Me, Balm in Gilead, Anchorman, Distant Fires, The Root, Trafficking in Broken Hearts, Merrily We Roll Along*

Evans, Venida Born September 2, 1947 in Ypsilanti, MI. Attended Fisk U. Debut 1981 OB in *Tarbuckle* followed by *Ladies, Dinah Washington Is Dead, Ground People, East Texas, 900 Oneonta, Little Ham* Bdwy in *Amen Corner* (1983)

Falco, Edie Born July 5, 1963 in Brooklyn, NYC. Graduate SUNY/Purchase. OB in *Fabulous Beast, The Way, Side Man* for which she received a 1998 Theatre World Award., *Frankie and Johnny in the Clair du Lune.*

Faye, Pascale Born January 6, 1964 in Paris, France. Bdwy debut in *Grand Hotel* (1991) followed by *Guys and Dolls, Victor Victoria, Once Upon a Mattress* (1996). *Movin'Out.*

Feldshuh, Tovah Born December 28, 1953 in New York City. Graduate Sarah Lawrence Col., U. Minn. Bdwy debut 1973 in *Cyrano* followed by *Dreyfus in Rehearsal, Rodgers and Hart, Yentl* for which she received a Theatre World Award, *Sarava, Lend Me a Tenor,* OB in *Yentl the Yeshiva Boy, Straws in the Wind, Three Sisters, She Stoops to Conquer, Springtime for Henry, The Time of Your Life, Children of the Sun, The Last of the Red Hot Lovers, Mistress of the Inn, A Fierce Attachment, Custody, Six Wives, Hello Muddah Hello Faddah, Best of the West, Awake and Sing, Tovah: Out of Her Mind, Tovah in Concert, Names, Tallulah's Party, Golda's Balcony* (OB and Bdwy)

Ferland, Danielle Born January 31, 1971 in Derby, CT. OB debut 1983 in *Sunday in the Park with George,* followed by *Paradise, Young Playwrights Festival, Camp Paradox, Uncommon Women and Others, In Circles, Tartuffe,* Bdwy debut 1984 in *Sunday in the Park with George, Into the Woods,* for which she received a Theatre World Award, *A Little Night Music* (NYCO/LC), *Crucible, A Little Hotel on the Side, A Year with Frog and Toad*

Fierstein, Harvey Born June 6, 1954 in Brooklyn, NY. Graduate Pratt Inst. Debut 1971 OB in *Pork,* followed by *International Stud, Figures in a Nursery, Haunted Host, Pouf Positive, This Is Not Going to Be Pretty, Fagtime,* Bdwy in *Torch Song Trilogy* (1982) for which he won a Theatre World Award, *Safe Sex* (also OB), *Hairspray.*

Figueroa, Rona Born March 30, 1972 in San Francisco, CA. Attended UC/Santa Cruz. Bdwy debut in *Miss Saigon* (1993).followed by *Nine* (2003); OB in *Caucasian Chalk Circle*

Fleming, Eugene Born April 26, 1961 in Richmond, VA. Attended NC Sch of Arts. Bdwy in *Chorus Line* followed by *Tap Dance Kid, Black and Blue, High Rollers, DuBarry Was a Lady* (Encores), *Swinging on a Star, Street Corner Symphony,* OB in *Voorhas, Dutchman, Ceremonies in Dark Old Men, Freefall, Call the Children Home.*

Ford, Jennie Born November 13 in Saskatchewan, Canada. Bdwy: *Ragtime, The Music Man, Sweet Smell of Success, Dance of the Vampires.*

Foret, Nicole Born December 17, 1974 in New Orleans, LA. Bdwy *Urban Cowboy*

Fowler, Scott Born March 22, 1967 in Medford, MA Bdwy *Brigadoon, Ain't Broadway Grand, The Red Shoes, Jerome Robbins Broadway, Swing, Movin'Out.*

French, Arthur Born in New York City and attended Brooklyn Col. Debut 1962 OB in *Raisin' Hell in the Sun* followed by *Ballad of Bimshire, Day of Absence, Happy Ending, Brotherhood, Perry's Mission, Rosalee Pritchett, Moonlight Arms, Dark Tower, Brownsville Raid, Nevis Mountain Dew, Julius Caesar, Friends, Court of Miracles, The Beautiful LaSalles, Blues for a Gospel Queen, Black Girl, Driving Miss Daisy, The Spring Thing, George Washington Slept Here, Ascension Day, Boxing Day Parade, A Tempest, Hills of Massabielle, Treatment, As You Like It, Swamp Dwellers, Tower of Burden, Henry VI, Last Street Play, Out of the South, Fly,* Bdwy in *Ain't Supposed to Die a Natural Death, The Iceman Cometh, All God's Chillun Got Wings, Resurrection of Lady Lester, You Can't Take It with You, Design for Living, Ma Rainey's Black Bottom, Mule Bone, Playboy of the West Indies, A Last Dance for Sybil.*

Jennie Ford

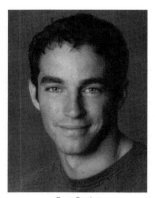

Scott Fowler

T.J. Gambrel

Erica Getto

Friedman, Peter Born April 24, 1949 in NYC. Debut 1971 OB in *James Joyce Memorial Theatre* followed by *Big and Little, A Soldier's Play, Mr. and Mrs., And a Nightingale Sang, Dannis, The Common Pursuit, Marathon '88, The Heidi Chronicles, Hello Again, The Loman Family Picnic, My Old Lady* Bdwy in *The Visit, Chemin de Fer, Love for Love, Rules of the Game, Piaf!, Execution of Justice, The Heidi Chronicles, Tenth Man.*

Gabriel, Gene Born August 27, 1970 in NYC. Graduated North Bergen High School, New Jersey. Bdwy debut: *Take Me Out.* OB *Making Scenes, The Groove Thing, Theatre Sports, I'm OK, You're OK.*

Galantich, Tom Born in Brooklyn, NY. Debut 1985 OB in *On the 20th Century,* followed by *Mademoiselle Colombe, Doll's Life,* Bdwy in *Into the Woods* (1989), *City of Angels*

Gallagher, Helen Born in 1926 in Brooklyn, NY. Bdwy debut in *Seven Lively Arts* (1947) followed by *Mr. Strauss Goes to Boston, Billion Dollar Baby, Brigadoon, High Button Shoes, Touch and Go, Make a Wish, Pal Joey, Guys and Dolls, Finian's Rainbow, Oklahoma!, Pajama Game, Bus Stop, Portofino, Sweet Charity, Mame, Cry for Us All, No No Nanette, A Broadway Musical, Sugar Babies,* OB in *Hothouse, Tickles by Tucholsky, Misanthrope, I Can't Keep Running in Place, Red Rover, Tallulah, Flower Palace, Tallulah Tonight, Riders to the Sea, Art, Life, & Show-Biz, A Non-Fiction Play.*

Gallagher, John Jr. Born June 17, 1984 in Wilmington, DE. OB debut 2000 in *Current Events, Kimberly Akimbo* (2003)

Gambrel, T.J. Born January 1, 1971 in Corpus Christi, TX. Graduated The Neighborhood Playhouse School of Theatre. OOB *Hallelujah Breakdown.*

Garrick, Barbara Born February 3, 1962 in NYC. Debut 1986 OB in *Today I Am a Fountain Pen* followed by *Midsummer Night's Dream, Rosencrantz and Guildenstern Are Dead, 8 Days (Backwards), Winter's Tale* Bdwy in *Eastern Standard* (1988, also OB), *Small Family Business, Stanley*

Garrison, David Born June 30, 1952 in Long Branch, NJ. Graduate Boston U. Debut 1976 OB in *Joseph and the Amazing Technicolor Dreamcoat* followed by *Living at Home, Geniuses, It's Only a Play, Make Someone Happy, Family of Mann, I Do I Do* (1996), *8 Days (Backwards)* Bdwy in *History of the American Film* (1978), *Day in Hollywood/A Night in the Ukraine, Pirates of Penzance, Snoopy, Torch Song Trilogy, One Touch of Venus* (Encores), *Titanic, Strike Up the Band* (Encores) .

Gaston, Lydia Born April 15, 1959 in NYC. Bdwy debut in *Jerome Robbins' Bdwy* (1990) followed by *Shogun, Miss Saigon, Red Shoes, King and I,* OB in *Rita's Resources* (1995) followed by *Cambodia Agonistes, Fuenteovejuna.*

Gerety, Peter Born May 17, 1940 in Providence, RI. Attended URI, Boston U. Debut 1964 OB in *In The Summer House* followed by *Othello, Baal, Six Characters in Search of an Author, Johnny Pye, Fucking A.* Bdwy in *The Hothouse* (1982), *Conversations with My Father.*

Gerroll, Daniel Born October 16, 1951 in London, England. Attended Central School of Speech and Drama. Debut 1980 OB in *Slab Boys* followed by *Knuckle/Translations,* for which he received a Theatre World Award, *The Caretaker, Scences from La Vie De Boheme, The Knack, Terra Nova, Dr. Faustus, Second Man, Cheapside, Bloody Poetry, Common Pursuit, Woman in Mind, Poet's Corner, Film Society, Emerald City, Arms and the Man, One Shoe Off, The Holy Terror, Three Birds Alighting on a Field, Loose Knit, Psychopathia Sexualis, Importance of Being Earnest, Madhouse in Goa, Scotland Road, The Shaughraun,* Bdwy in *Plenty, The Homecoming* (1991), *High Society, Shanghai Moon*

Getto, Erica Born August 23, 1993 in Chicago IL Bdwy debut (understudy Joe) *A Day in the Death of Joe Egg.*

Glenn, Eileen Born December 14, 1960 in Dover NJ. Graduate of University of Tennessee. OB *Uncle Vanya* (2003)

Gomez, David Eric Born July 7, 1971 in Dayton Ohio. Bdwy: *Contact, Movin'Out.*

Eileen Glenn

Paul Goodwin-Groen

Justin Greer

Ann Harada

Goodwin, Deidre Born September 15, 1969 in Oklahoma City, OK. Attended Southwest MI St. U. Bdwy debut 1998 in *Chicago*, followed by *Jesus Christ Superstar, The Rocky Horror Show, The Boys from Syracuse, Nine*.

Goodwin-Groen, Paul Born August 31, 1967 in St. Charles, IL. Graduate of Brandeis U. and Wheaton Col. Bdwy debut 2003 in *La Boheme*.

Graham, Enid Born February 8 in TX. Graduate Juilliard. Bdwy debut 1998 in *Honour*, OB in *Look Back in Anger, Crimes of the Heart. Dinner at Eight*.

Grant, Kate Jennings Born March 23, 1970 in Elizabeth, NJ. Graduate U. of PA, Juilliard. Bdwy debut 1997 in *American Daughter*, followed by *Hard Feelings*, OB in *Wonderland, Hard Feelings, Radiant Baby*.

Greenspan, David Born 1956 In Los Angeles, CA. OB in *Phaedra, Education of Skinny Spyz, Boys in the Band, Moose Mating, Second Hand Smoke, Sueño, Alien Boy, Small Craft Warnings, Saved or Destroyed, Lipstick Traces, The Wax*, Bdwy in *Hairspray*.

Greer, Justin Born January 25, 1973 in Buffalo NY. Graduate of Carnegie Mellon Univ. Bdwy: *Hercules Summer Spectacular, Annie Get Your Gun, Seussical, Urban Cowboy*, OB: *Just US Boys*.

Grimes, Tammy Born January 30, 1934 in Lynn, MA. Attended Stephens College, Neighborhood Playhouse. Debut 1956 OB in *Littlest Revue* followed by *Clerambord, Molly Trick, Are You Now Or..., Father's Day, A Month in the Country, Sunset, Waltz of the Toreadors, Mlle. Colombe, Tammy in Concert, After the Ball, Stories of Women, 24 Evenings of Wit and Wisdom*, Bdwy in *Look After Lulu* (1959) for which she received a Theatre World Award, *The Unsinkable Molly Brown, Private Lives, High Spirits, Rattle of a Simple Man, The Only Game in Town, Musical Jubilee, California Suite, Tartuffe, Pal Joey in Concert, 42nd Street, Orpheus Descending*.

Groener, Harry Born September 10, 1951 in Augsburg, Germany, Graduate U. Washington. Bdwy debut in *Oklahoma!* (1979) for which he received a Theatre World Award, followed by *Oh, Brother!, Is There Life After High School?, Cats, Harrigan 'n' Hart, Sunday in the Park with George, Sleight of Hand, Crazy for You*, OB in *Beside the Seaside, Twelve Dreams, Picasso at the Lapin Agile*.

Hall, George Born November 19, 1916 in Toronto, Canada. Attended Neighborhood Playhouse. Bdwy debut 1946 in *Call Me Mister* followed by *Lend an Ear, Touch and Go, Live Wire, The Boy Friend, There's a Girl in My Soup, An Evening with Richard Nixon, We Interrupt This Program, Man and Superman, Bent, Noises Off, Wild Honey, Abe Lincoln in Illinois, The Boys from Syracuse* OB in *The Balcony, Ernest in Love, A Round with Rings, Family Pieces, Carousel, The Case Against Roberta Guardino, Marry Me!, Arms and the Man, The Old Glory, Dancing for the Kaiser, Casualties, The Sea Gull, A Stitch in Time, Mary Stuart, No End of Blame, Hamlet, Colette Collage, The Homecoming, And a Nightingale Sang, The Bone Ring, Much Ado about Nothing, Measure for Measure, The Doctor's Dilemma, The Crucible, Merry Wives of Windsor, Flea in Her Ear*.

Halston, Julie Born December 7, 1954 in New York. Graduate Hofstra U. Debut OB 1985 in *Times Square Angel* followed by *Vampire Lesbians of Sodom, Sleeping Beauty or Coma, The Dubliners, Lady in Question, Money Talks, Red Scare on Sunset, I'll Be the Judge of That, Lifetime of Comedy, Honeymoon Is Over, You Should Be So Lucky, This Is Not Going to Be Pretty, The Butter and Egg Man*. Bdwy in *Boys from Syracuse* (Encores!).

Hamilton, Josh Born in NYC. Attended Brown U. OB in *Women and Wallace, Korea, As Sure As You Live, Four Corners, Eden Cinema, A Joke, Sons and Fathers, Wild Dogs, Suburbia, Wonderful Time, This Is Our Youth, As Bees in Honey Drown, Evolution*.

Hammer, Ben Born December 8, 1925 in Brooklyn, NY. Graduate Brooklyn College. Bdwy debut 1955 in *Great Sebastians* followed by *Diary of Anne Frank, Tenth Man, Mother Courage, The Deputy, Royal Hunt of the Sun, Colda, Broadway Bound, Three Sisters*, OB in *The Crucible, Murderous Angels, Richard III, Slavs!, 24 Evenings of Wit and Wisdom, A Last Dance for Sybil*.

Hammer, Mark Born April 28, 1937 in San Jose, CA. Graduate Stanford U., Catholic U. Debut 1966 OB in *Journey of the Fifth Horse* followed by *Witness for the Prosecution, Cymbeline, Richard III, Taming of the Shrew, As You Like It, Henry VI, Twelve Dreams, Henry VIII, Problem Child, Criminal Genius, More Stately Mansions, Our Lady of 121st Street*. Bdwy in *Much Ado about Nothing* (1972).

Robb Hillman

Andy Hoey

Jackie Hoffman

Brian Lee Hunyh

Harada, Ann Born in Honolulu, Hawaii. Graduate of Brown Univ. Bdwy in *M. Butterfly, Suessical, Avenue Q*. OB in *The Wonderful O, FalsettoLand, America Dreaming, Avenue Q, The Moment When.*

Harman, Paul Born July 29, 1952 in Mineola, NY. Graduate Tufts U. Bdwy debut 1980 in *It's So Nice to Be Civilized* followed by *Les Miserables, Chess, Candide, Triumph of Love*, OB in *City Suite, Sheik of Avenue B, Decline of the Middle West, Showtune.*

Harner, Jason Butler Born October 9 in Elmira, NY. Graduate VCU, NYU. OB debut in *Henry VIII*, followed by *Macbeth, An Experiment with an Air Pump, Juno and the Paycock, Crimes of the Heart, Observe the Sons of Ulster.*

Harris, Rosemary Born September 19, 1930 in Ashby, Eng. Attended RADA. Bdwy debut 1952 in *Climate of Eden* for which she received a Theatre World Award, followed by *Troilus and Cressida, Interlock, The Disenchanted, The Tumbler*, with APA in *The Tavern, School for Scandal, The Sea Gull, Importance of Being Earnest, War and Peace, Man and Superman, Judith and You Can't Take It with You, Lion in Winter, Old Times, Merchant of Venice, Streetcar Named Desire, Royal Family, Pack of Lies, Hay Fever, An Inspector Calls, Delicate Balance*, OB in *New York Idea, Three Sisters, The Sea Gull, 24 Evenings of Wit and Wisdom.*

Harris, Cynthia Born in NYC. Graduate Smith Col. Bdwy debut 1963 in *Natural Affection* followed by *Any Wednesday, Best Laid Plans, Company, Greenwich Village Follies, Madwoman of Chaillot, Too Clever by Half*. OOB in *Happy Birthday*

Higgins, Clare Bdwy debut in *Vincent in Brixton* (2003)

Hillman, Robb Born February 4, 1975 in Portland OR. Graduate of Univ. of CA at Irvine. Bdwy debut *La Boheme.*

Hindman, James Born March 25, 1960 in Detroit, MI. Attended Eastern MI U, Graduate Neighborhood Playhouse. Debut 1983 OB in *Promenade* followed by *Hello Muddah, Hello Faddah, Merrily We Roll Along, Wonder Years, A Man of No Importance*. Bdwy in *City of Angels* (1989) followed by *Grand Night for Singing, Once upon a Mattress, 1776* .

Hirsch, Judd Born March 15, 1935 in NYC. Attended AADA. Bdwy debut 1966 in *Barefoot* in the Park followed by *Chapter Two, Talley's Folly, I'm Not Rappaport* (also OB), *Conversations with My Father, A Thousand Clowns*, OB in *On the Necessity of Being Polygamous, Scuba Duba, Mystery Play, The Hot l Baltimore, Prodigal, Knock Knock, Life and/or Death, Talley's Folly, Sea Gull, Below the Belt.*

Hoey, Andy Born April 4, 1979. Graduate of Dartmouth Coll. OB in *Julius Caesar*

Hoffman, Jackie Born November 11, 1960. Graduate of NYU, New York. OB *One Woman Shoe, Incident at Cobbler's Knob, Imitation of Imitation of Life, The Children's Hour, Jackie's Kosher Christmas, 55 Minutes of Pure Hatred, Straight Jacket, Book of Liz* (Obie Award) *Jackie Hoffman's Valentine's Day Massacre*, Bdwy debut in *Hairspray.*

Hoffman, Philip Seymour Born July 23, 1967 in Fairport, NY. OB in *Food and Shelter, The Skriker, Defying Gravity, Shopping and Fucking* Bdwy debut in *Long Day's Journey Into Night*

Hostetter, Curt (Formerly Curtis) Born December 16, 1953 in Harrisburg, PA. Graduate Messiah Col. Debut 1977 OB in *My Life* followed by *Romeo and Juliet, The Contrast, Hamlet, Richard III, Retribution, The Phoenician Women*

Hoxie, Richmond Born July 21, 1946 in NYC. Graduate Dartmouth Col., LAMDA. Debut 1975 OB in *Straw for an Evening* followed by *The Family, Landscape with Waitress, 3 from the Marathon, The Slab Boys, Vivien, Operation Midnight Climax, The Dining Room, Daddies, To Gillian on Her 37th Birthday, Dennis, Traps, Sleeping Dogs, Equal Wrights* EST *Marathon '93, Dolphin Project, Rain, Slice of Life, Vienna: Lusthaus*

Huff, Neal Born in NYC. NYU Graduate. Debut 1992 OB in *Young Playwrights Festival* followed by *Joined at the Head, Day the Bronx Died, Macbeth, House of Yes, Class 1-Acts, Saturday Mourning Cartoons, Troilus and Cressida, Tempest, From Above, The Seagull: 1990, The Hamptons*. Bdwy debut in *Take Me Out.*

Hunyh, Brian Lee Born January 23, 1980. in Portland ME. Graduate Ithaca College. OB in *Uncle Vanya, Henry V.*

Rachel Isaac

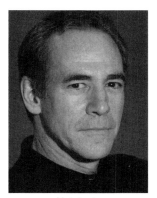
Mark Jacoby

Tim Jerome

Joseph Jonas

Hyman, Earle Born October 11, 1926 in Rocky Mount, NC. Attended New School, Am. Th. Wing. Bdwy debut 1943 in *Run Little Chillun,* followed by *Anna Lucasta, Climate of Eden, Merchant of Venice, Othello, Julius Caesar, The Tempest, No Time for Sergeants, Mr. Johnson,* for which he received a Theatre World Award, *St. Joan, Hamlet, Waiting for Godot, The Duchess of Malfi, Les Blancs, The Lady from Dubuque, Execution of Justice, Death of the King's Horseman, The Master Builder,* OB in *The White Rose and the Red, Worlds of Shakespeare, Jonah, Life and Times of J. Walter Smintheus, Orrin, The Cherry Orchard, House Party, Carnival Dreams, Agamemnon, Othello, Julius Caesar, Coriolanus, Pygmalion, Richard II, East Texas Hot Links, Merchant of Venice, A Last Dance for Sybil.*

Ierardi, Robert Born November 4, 1961 in Southington, CT. Debut 1987 OB in *The Trial* followed by *Hamlet, Three Sisters, The Rehearsal, Importance of Being Earnest, Rockland County No Vaudeville, Play, Peanut, 24 Evenings of Wit and Wisdom.*

Isaac, Rachel Born September 28, 1974, South Wales, U.K. B.A. in Theatre Studies Bdwy debut in *Medea.*

Isola, Kevin Born January 27, 1970 in Ft. Irwin, CA. Graduate Duke U., NYU. Debut 1995 in *Wasp and Other Plays* followed by *Venus, The World Over*

Ivey, Dana Born August 12 in Atlanta, GA. Graduate Rollins Col., LAMDA. Bdwy debut in Macbeth (LC-1981) followed by *Present Laughter, Heartbreak House, Sunday in the Park with George, Pack of Lies, Marriage of Figaro, Major Barbara, Indiscretions, Last Night of Ballyhoo, Sex and Longing, A Day in the Death of Joe Egg.* OB in *Call from the East, Vivien, The Uneasy Chair, Quartermaine's Terms, Baby with the Bath Water, Driving Miss Daisy, Wenceslas Square, Love Letters, Hamlet, Subject Was Roses, Beggars in the House of Plenty, Kindertransport*

Izzard, Eddie Born February 7, 1962 in Aden, Yemen. Attended Sheffield U. OB Debut 1998 in *Dress To Kill,* for which he won a Theatre World Award, followed by *Glorious.* Bdwy debut in *A Day in the Death of Joe Egg.*

Jacoby, Mark Born May 21, 1947 in Johnson City, TN. Graduate GA State U., FL State U., St. John's U. Debut 1984 OB in *Bells Are Ringing,* Bdwy in *Sweet Charity* for which he received a 1986 Theatre World Award, *Grand Hotel, The Phantom of the Opera, Show Boat, Ragtime, Man of La Mancha*

Jerome, Timothy Born December 29, 1943 in Los Angeles, CA. Graduate Ithaca Col. Bdwy debut 1969 in *Man of La Mancha,* followed by the *Rothschilds. Creation of the World..., Moony Shapiro Songbook, Cats, Lost in Yonkers, Me and My Girl, Grand Hotel, La Boheme.* OB in *Beggars Opera, Pretzels, Civilization and Its Discontents, Little Prince, Colette Collage, Room Service, Romance in Hard Times, Petrified Prince.*

Jonas, Joseph Born August 15, 1989 in Casa Grande, AZ. Bdwy debut in *La Boheme.*

Jones, Cherry Born November 21, 1956 in Paris, TN. Graduate Carnegie-Mellon. Debut 1983 OB in *The Philanthropist,* followed by *He and She, The Ballad of Soapy Smith, The Importance of Being Earnest, I Am a Camera, Claptrap, Big Time, A Light Shining in Buckinghamshire, The Baltimore Waltz, Goodnight Desdemona, And Baby Makes 7, Desdemona, Pride's Crossing,* Bdwy in *Stepping Out* (1986), *Our Country's Good, Angels in America, The Heiress, Night of the Iguana, Imaginary Friends*

Jones, Simon Born July 27, 1950 in Wiltshire, Eng. Attended Trinity Hall. NY debut 1984 OB in *Terra Nova* followed by *Magdalena in Concert, Woman in Mind, Privates on Parade, Quick-Change Room, You Never Can Tell,* Bdwy in *The Real Thing* (1984), *Benefactors, Getting Married, Private Lives, Real Inspector Hound/5 Minute Hamlet, School for Scandal, Herbal Bed* OOB in *Happy Birthday*

Keating, Charles Born October 22, 1941 in London, Eng. Bdwy debut 1969 in *Arturo Ui* followed by *House of Atreus, Loot, A Man of No Importance.* OB in *Ounce of Prevention, Man for All Seasons, There Is a Dream Dreaming Us, What the Butler Saw, Light Up the Sky, Pygmalion, You Never Can Tell .*

Kimbrough, Charles Born May 23, 1936 in St. Paul, MN. Graduate Ind. U., Yale U. Bdwy debut 1969 in Cop Out followed by Company, Love for Love, Rules of the Game, Candide, Mr. Happiness, Same Time Next Year, Sunday in the Park with George, Hay Fever, OB in All for Love, Struts and Frets, Troilus and Cressida, Secret Service, Boy Meets Girl, Drinks before Dinner, Dining Room, Later Life, Sylvia, The Fourth Wall.

King, Nicolas Born July 26, 1991 in Westerly, RI. Bdwy debut 2000 in *Beauty and the Beast,* followed by *A Thousand Clowns, Hollywood Arms.*

Kirk, Justin Born May 28, 1969 in Salem, OR. OB debut 1990 in *The Applicant*, followed by *Shardston, Loose Ends, Thanksgiving, Lovequest Live, Old Wicked Songs, June Moon, Ten Unknowns, The World Over*, Bdwy in *Any Given Day* (1993), *Love! Valour! Compassion!* (also OB).

Kittrell, Michelle Born December 16, 1972 in Cocoa Beach, FL. OB debut 1993 in *Girl of My Dreams*, followed by *New Yorkers, Joseph and the Amazing Technicolor Dreamcoat*, Bdwy debut 2000 in *Seussical, Urban Cowboy*.

Kliban, Ken Born July 26, 1943 in Norwalk, CT. Graduate U. Miami, NYU. Bdwy debut 1967 in *War and Peace* followed by *As Is, Stanley*, OB in *War and Peace, Puppy Dog Tails, Istanbul, Persians, Home, Elizabeth the Queen, Judith, Man and Superman, Boom Boom Room, Ulysses, Mr. Pim Passes By, Far and Wide*.

Knight, James Born March 3, 1973. in Mt. Clemens, MI. Graduate of Western Michigan and Univ. of Missouri. OB debut in *Far and Wide*.

Knight, T.R. Born Minneapolis, MN. OB debut 1999 in *Macbeth*, followed by *This Lime Tree Bower, The Hologram Theory, The Right Way to Sue, Scattergood*, Bdwy in *Tartuffe*.

Koenig, Jack Born May 14, 1959 in Rockville Centre, NY. Graduate Columbia U. Debut 1991 OB in *Grand Finale* followed by *Misalliance, Cymbeline, American Plan, Mad Forest, Not about Heroes, Trip to the Beach, Three Days of Rain*. OOB in *Happy Birthday*.

Krakowski, Jane Born September 11, 1968 in New Jersey. Debut 1984 OB in *American Passion* followed by *Miami, A Little Night Music*, Bdwy in *Starlight Express* (1987), *Grand Hotel, Face Value, Company* (1995), *One Touch of Venus* (Encores), *Tartuffe: Born Again, Once Upon a Mattress* (1996), *Nine*.

Lambert, Mikel Sarah Born in Spokane, WA. Graduate Radcliffe, RADA. After much work in England, debut 1996 OB in *900 Oneonta* followed by *Cyrano, Private Battles, Three Cornered Moon*

Lange, Anne Born June 24, 1953 in Pipestone, MN. Attended Carnegie-Mellon U. Debut 1979 OB in *Rats Nest* followed by *Hunting Scenes from Lower Bavaria, Crossfire, Linda Her and the Fairy Garden, Little Footsteps, Hotel Play, 10th Young Playwrights Festival, Jeffrey, Family of Mann, 12 Dreams, All My Sons, Dinner at Eight*, Bdwy in *The Survivor* (1981), *Heidi Chronicles, Holiday*.

Lansbury, David Born February 25, 1961 in NYC. Attended Conn. Col., Circle in the Sq Th Sch, Central Sch of Speech/Drama, London. Debut 1989 OB in *Young Playwrights Festival* followed by *Advice from a Caterpillar, Progress, Hapgood, Principality of Sorrows, Pride's Crossing, Comedians*. Bdwy in *Heidi Chronicles* (1990).

Lavin, Linda Born October 15, 1939 in Portland, ME. Graduate Wm. & Mary Col. Bdwy debut 1962 in *A Family Affair* followed by *Riot Act, The Game Is Up, Hotel Passionata, It's a Bird It's Superman!, On a Clear Day You Can See Forever, Something Different, Cop-Out, Last of the Red Hot Lovers, Story Theatre, The Enemy Is Dead, Broadway Bound, Gypsy* (1990), *Sisters Rosensweig, Diary of Anne Frank, Hollywood Arms*. OB in *Wet Paint* (1965) for which she received a Theatre World Award, *Death Defying Acts, Cakewalk* .

Leeds, Jordan Born November 29, 1961 in Queens, NY. Graduate SUNY Binghamton. Bdwy debut 1987 in *Les Miserables*, followed by *Sunset Blvd.*, OB in *Beau Jest, Angel Levine, Jest a Second, Fishkin Touch, I Love You You're Perfect Now Change*

Leonard, Robert Sean Born February 28, 1969 in Westwood, NJ. Debut 1985 OB in *Sally's Gone She Left Her Name*, followed by *Coming of Age in Soho, Beach House, Young Playwrights Festival-And the Air Didn't Answer, When She Danced, Romeo and Juliet, Pitching to the Star, Good Evening, Great Unwashed, Principality of Sorrows, Below the Belt, You Never Can Tell, Fifth of July* Bdwy 1985 in *Brighton Beach Memoirs* followed by *Breaking the Code, Speed of Darkness, Candida, Philadelphia Here I Come, Arcadia, Invention of Love* (Tony Award, Best Supporting Actor), *Long Days Journey Into Night*.

Lenox, Adriane Born September 11, 1956 in Memphis, TN. Graduate Lambuth Col. Bdwy debut 1979 in *Ain't Misbehavin'*, followed by *Dreamgirls*, OB in *Beehive, Merrily We Roll Along, America Play, Identical Twins from Baltimore, Dinah Was, Cavedweller*

Leung, Telly Born January 3, 1980 in Brooklyn NY. Graduate Carnegie Mellon Univ. Bdwy debut in *Flower Drum Song*

Lieber, Mimi Bdwy debut 2002 in *I'm Not Rappaport*.

Ligon, Kevin Born May 17, 1961 in Dallas, TX. Graduate SMU. Debut 1988 OB in *The Chosen* followed by *Forbidden Broadway, Requiem for William*, Bdwy in *Secret Garden* (1991), *Boys from Syracuse (Encores), 1776* .

Linehan, Rosaleen Born January 6, 1937 in Dublin, Ire. Graduate U. Dublin. Bdwy debut in *Dancing at Lughnasa* (1991), OB in *Mother of all the Behans* (1994), *Tartuffe*

Lisi, Joe Born September 9, 1950 in NYC. Graduate of NY Ints. of Tech. OB and Bdwy debut in *Take Me Out*

Liu, Allen Born September 22, 1975 in Taipei Taiwan. Graduate Univ. of Virginia and UC Irvine. Bdwy debut in *Flower Drum Song*.

LeStrange, Philip Born May 9, 1942 in the Bronx, NY. Graduate Catholic U., Fordham U. Debut 1970 OB in *Getting Married* followed by *Erogenous Zones, Quilling of Prue, Front Page, Six Degrees of Separation, Dinner at Eight*. Bdwy in *A Small Family Business* (1992), *Guys and Dolls, Rose Tattoo, Last Night of Ballyhoo, Kiss Me Kate*

Lloyd, John Bedford Born January 2, 1956 in New Haven, CT. Graduate Williams Col., Yale. Debut 1983 OB in *Vieux Carre*, followed by *She Stoops to Conquer, The Incredibly Famous Willy Rivers, Digby, Rum and Coke, Trinity Site, Richard 11, Some Americans Abroad Flaubert's Latest, Good Will, Tartuffe* Bdwy in *Some Americans Abroad* (1990).

Long, Jodi Born in New York, NY. Graduate SUNY Purchase. Bdwy debut 1962 in *Nowhere to Go But Up*, followed by *Loose Ends, Bacchae, Getting Away with Murder, Flower Drum Song*, OB in *Fathers and Sons, Family Devotions, Rohwer, Tooth of the Crime, Dream of Kitamura, Midsummer Night's Dream, Madame de Sade, The Wash, Golden Child, Red, Old Money*.

Lopez, Carlos Born May 14, 1963 in Sunnyvale, CA. Attended CalStU/Hayward. Debut 1987 OB in *Wish You Were Here*, followed by Bdwy in *The Pajama Game* (NYCO-1989), *A Chorus Line, Grand Hotel, Guys and Dolls, Grease, Wonderful Town* (NYCO), *Man of La Mancha*

James Knight

Joe Lisi

Sean Matic

Michael McCormick

Lopez, Priscilla Born February 26, 1948 in The Bronx, NY. Bdwy debut in *Breakfast at Tiffany's* (1966) followed by *Henry Sweet Henry, Lysistrata, Company, Her First Roman, Boy Friend, Pippin, Chorus Line* (also OB), *Day in Hollywood Night in the Ukraine, Nine,* OB in *What's a Nice Country Like You..., Key Exchange, Buck, Extremities, Non Pasquak, Be Happyfor Me, Times and Appetites of Toulouse Lautrec, Marathon '88, Other People's Money, Antigone in NY, Class Mothers '68.*

Luker, Rebecca Born 1961 in Helena, AL. Graduate U Montevello. Bdwy debut in *Phantom of the Opera* followed by *Secret Garden, X(NYCO), Show Boat, Boys from Syracuse* (Encores), OB in *Jubilee, Music in the Air, No No Nanette, Trouble in Tahiti, Gay Divorce, Sound of Music* (1998), *Can't Let Go.*

Lynch, Tertia Born May 22, in Long Island NY. Graduate of Marymount Coll. and NYU. OB in *The Picture of Dorian Gray, Hank Williams: Lost Highway.*

Mack, Victoria Born September 26, 1979 in New Jersey. Graduate of Barnard College. OB debut *Far and Wide*

Maier, Charlotte Born January 29, 1956 in Chicago, IL. Graduate Northwestern U. Debut 1984 OB in *Balm in Gilead* followed by *Gunplay, Last Girl Singer, Dinner at Eight,* Bdwy in *Abe Lincoln in Illinois* (1993), *Picnic* (1984).

Mardirosian, Tom Born December 14, 1947 in Buffalo, NY. Graduate U. Buffalo. Debut 1976 OB in *Gemini* followed by *Grand Magic, Losing Time, Passione, Success and Succession, Groud Zero Club, Cliffhanger, Cap and Bells, Normal Heart, Measure for Measure, Largo Desolato, Good Coach, Subfertile, Oh Captain, Butter and Egg Man.* Bdwy in *Happy End* (1977), *Magic Show, My Favorite Year.*

Markell, Jodie Born April 13, 1959 in Memphis, TN. Attended Northwestern U. Debut 1984 OB in *Balm in Gilead* followed by *Carring School Children, UBU, Sleeping Dogs, Machinal, Italian American Reconciliation, Moe's Lucky 7, La Ronde, House of Yes, Saturday Mourning Cartoons, Flyovers, Easter, Clash by Night, Snakebit, Kimberly Akimbo.*

Martin, Lucy Born February 8, 1942 in NYC. Graduate Sweet Briar Col. Debut 1962 OB in *Electra,* followed by *Happy as Larry, Trojan Women, Iphigenia in Aulis, Wives, Cost of Living, Substance of Fire, Private Battles,* Bdwy in *Shelter* (1973) *Children of a Lesser God, Pygmalion, The Sisters Rosensweig, A Day in the Death of Joe Egg, Hollywood Arms.*

Matic, Sean Born July 22, 1970 in NYC. Graduate of Univ. of Hawaii. OB in *The Uninvited Guest, The Novelist.*

Matthews, Liesel Bdwy debut 2003 in *Vincent in Brixton* for which she won a Theatre World award.

Maxwell, Jan Born November 20, 1956 in Fargo, ND. Graduate Moorhead St. U. Bdwy debut 1990 in *City of Angels,* followed by *Dancing at Lughnasa, Doll's House, Sound of Music, The Dinner Party,* OB in *Everybody Everybody, Hot Feet, Light Years to Chicago, Ladies of the Fortnight, Two Gentlemen of Verona, Marriage Fool, Oedipus Private Eye, Inside Out, The Professional, My Old Lady*

Mayes, Sally Born August 3 in Livingston, TX. Attended U. Houston. Bdwy debut 1989 in *Welcome to the Club,* for which she received a Theatre World Award, followed by *She Loves Me, Urban Cowboy,* OB in *Closer Than Ever, Das Barbecue, Marry Me a Little.*

Mayo, Don Born October 4, 1960 in Chicago, IL. Graduate Loyola U. Debut 1988 OB in *Much Ado about Nothing,* followed by *Christina Alberta's Father,* Bdwy in *Wizard of Oz (MSG)* followed by *Scarlet Pimpernel, Man of La Mancha* (2002).

McCallum, David Born September 19, 1933 in Scotland. Attended Chapman Col. Bdwy debut 1968 in *Flip Side,* followed by *California Suite, Amadeus,* OB debut in *After the Prize,* followed by *The Philanthropist, Ghosts, Nasty Little Secrets, Communicating Doors, Julius Caesar, Time and Again, Comedians.*

McCormick, Michael Born July 24, 1951 in Gary, IN. Graduate Northwestern U. Bdwy debut 1964 in *Oliver!,* followed by *Kiss of the Spider Woman, 1776, Marie Christine, Kiss Me Kate, A Man of No Importance* OB in *Coming Attractions, Tomfoolery, Regard of Flight, Charlotte's Secret, Half A World Away, In a Pig's Valise, Arturo Ui, Scapin, Mafia on Prozac.*

McDermott, Sean Born October 23, 1961 in Denver, CO. Attended Loretto Heights. Debut 1986 on Bdwy in *Starlight Express* followed by *Miss Saigon, Falsettos,* OB in *New Yorkers, Boys in the Band, Call the Children Home.*

Lué McWilliams   Kathryn Meisle   Nicholas Mongiardo-Cooper   Nathan Morgan

McDonough, Ann Born Portland, ME. Graduate Towson State U. Debut 1975 OB in *Trelawney of the Wells, Secret Service, Boy Meets Girl, Scribes, Uncommon Women, City Sugar, Fables for Friends, The Dining Room, What I Did Last Summer, The Rise of Daniel Rocket, The Middle Ages, Fighting International Fat, Room Service, The Spring Thing, Dinner at Eight,* Bdwy in *Abe Lincoln in Illinois* (1993).

McDonough, J. M Born April 1, 1946 in Baltimore, MD. Graduate U. of the South. OB debut 1999 in *The Made Man,* followed by *Descent, Sweeney Todd, Ten Little Indians.*

McDormand, Frances Born in 1958 in Illinois. Yale graduate. Debut 1983 OB in *Painting Churches,* followed by *On the Verge, The Swan, Oedipus, Far Away,* Bdwy in *Awake and Sing* (1984), *A Streetcar Named Desire* (1988), *The Sisters Rosensweig.*

McGrath, Matt Born June 11, 1969 in NYC. Attended Fordham U. Bdwy debut in *Working* (1978) followed by *Streetcar Named Desire,* OB in *Dalton's Back* (1989), *Amulets Against the Dragon Forces, Life During Wartime, The Old Boy, Nothing Sacred, The Dadshuttle, Fat Men in Skirts, A Fair Country, Minutes from the Blue Route, What Didn't Happen.*

McGrath, Michael Born September 25, 1957 in Worcester, MA. OB debut 1988 in *Forbidden Bdwy,* followed by *Coconuts, Forbidden Hollywood, Louisiana Purchase, Secrets Every Smart Traveler Should Know, Exactly Like You, Game Show, Butter and Egg Man,* Bdwy in *My Favorite Year* (1992), *Goodbye Girl, DuBarry Was a Lady* (Encores), *Swinging on a Star,* for which he received a 1996 Theatre World Award, *Boys from Syracuse* (Encores), *Little Me.*

McGuire, Mitchell Born December 26, 1936 in Chicago, IL. Attended Goodman Theatre Sch., Santa Monica City Col. OB in *The Rapists,* (1966), *Go Go God is Dead, Waiting for Lefty, The Bond, Guns to Carrar, Oh! Calcutta!, New York! New York!, What a Life!, Butter and Egg Man, Almost in Vegas, Festival of 1-Acts, Prime Time Punch Line, The Racket, Endpapers.*

McLachlan, Roderick Born September 9, 1960 in Detroit, MI. Graduate Northwestern U. Bdwy debut in *Death and the King's Horseman* (LC-1987) followed by *Our Town, Real Inspector Hound, Saint Joan, Timon in Athens, Government Inspector, Holiday,* OB in *Madame Bovary, Julius Caesar, Oh Hell!, Hauptmann, Make Up Your Mind, Edmond, Clean, Home Therapy Kit, Cyrano, Observe the Sons of Ulster.*

McWilliams, Lué Born June 12 in Phil. PA. Graduate of Univ. of Vermont and Harvard. OB debut in *Hallelujah Breakdown.*

Meisle, Kathryn Born June 7 in Appleton, WI. Graduate Smith Col., UNC Chapel Hill. OB debut 1988 in *Dandy Dick,* followed *by Cahoots, Othello, As You Like It* (CP), *Brutality of Fact, The Most Fabulous Story Ever Told, What You Get and What You Expect, Old Money,* Bdwy in *Racing Demon* (1995), *The Rehearsal, London Assurance, Tartuffe.*

Mendillo, Stephen Born October 9, 1942 in New Haven, CT. Graduate Colo. Col., Yale U. Debut 1973 OB in *Nourish the Beast* followed by *Gorky, Time Steps, The Marriage, Loot, Subject to Fits, Wedding Band, As You Like It, Fool for Love, Twelfth Night, Grotesque Lovesongs, Nowhere, Portrait of My Bikini, Country Girl, Last Yankee, Ivanov, Black Ink, Red Devil Battery Sign, Minutes from the Blue Route, Ivanov, From Above,* Bdwy in *National Health* (1974), *Ah! Wilderness, View from the Bridge, Wild Honey, Orpheus Descending, Guys and Dolls, Our Town.*

Merkerson, S. Epatha Born November 28, 1952 in Saginaw, MI. Graduate Wayne State U. Debut 1979 OB in *Spell #7* followed by *Home, Puppetplay, Tintypes, Every Goodbye Ain't Gone, Hospice, The Harvesting, Moms, Lady Day at Emerson's Bar and Grill, 10th Young Playwrights Festival, Fear Itself, Fucking A* Bdwy in *Tintypes* (1982), *Piano Lesson.*

Mills, Elizabeth Born August 3, 1967 in San Jose, CA. Attended San Jose St. U. Bdwy debut 1993 in *Ain't Broadway Grand,* followed by *Crazy for You, DuBarry was a Lady* (Encores), *Kiss Me Kate, Boys from Syracuse,* OB in *A Connecticut Yankee in King Arthur's Court* (CC).

Mitchell, Brian Stokes (formerly Brian Mitchell) Born October 31, 1957 in Seattle, WA. Bdwy debut 1988 in *Mail,* for which he received a Theatre World Award, followed by *Oh Kay!, Jelly's Last Jam, Kiss of the Spider Woman, Kiss Me Kate, Man of La Mancha* (2002), OB in *Do Re Mi.*

Marcus Nance

Daniel Neer

Mark Nelson

Drew Perkins

Mitchell, Gregory Born December 9, 1951 in Brooklyn, NY. Graduate Juilliard, Principle with Eliot Feld Ballet before Bdwy debut in *Merlin* (1983) followed by *Song and Dance, Phantom of the Opera, Dangerous Games, Aspects of Love, Man of La Mancha* (1992), *Kiss of the Spider Woman, Chronicle of a Death Foretold, Steel Pier, Man of La Mancha* (2002), OB in *Kicks* (1961), *One More Song One More Dance, Young Strangers, Tango Apasionado.*

Molaskey, Jessica Born in Waterbury, CT. Bdwy debut in *Oklahoma!* (1980), *Chess, Cats, Les Miserables, Crazy for You, Tommy, Dream,* OB in *Weird Romance* (1991), *Songs for a New World, A Man of No Importance.*

Mongiardo-Cooper, Nicholas Born September 9, 1980 in New York, NY. Graduate NYU. OB debut 2002 in *Julius Caesar*

Moran, Martin Born December 29, 1959 in Denver, CO. Attended Stanford U., Amer. Conservatory Theatre. OB debut 1983 in *Spring Awakening,* followed by *Once on a Summer's Day, 1-2-3-4-5, Jacques Brel Is Alive* (1992), *Bed and Sofa, Floyd Collins, Fallen Angles, A Man of No Importance,* Bdwy in *Oliver!* (1984), *Big River, How to Succeed in Business Without Really Trying* (1995), *Titanic, Cabaret, Bells Are Ringing.*

Morgan, Lee Born July 21, 1961 in Shreveport, LA. Graduate Centenary Col. of LA. Bdwy debut 1993 in *Tommy,* OB in *Heat Lightning.*

Morgan, Nathan Born November 28, 1990 in Rhinebeck, NY. Still a student. Bdwy in *LA Boheme.* OB in *Dora the Cat (2002)*

Murray, Brian Born October 9, 1939 in Johannesburg, SA. OB debut 1964 in *The Knack,* followed by *King Lear, Ashes, Jail Diary of Albie Sachs, Winter's Tale, Barbarians, The Purging, Midsummer Night's Dream, Recruiting Officer, Arcata Promise, Candide in Concert, Much Ado About Nothing, Hamlet, Merry Wives of Windsor, Travels with My Aunt, Entertaining Mr. Sloane, Molly Sweeney, The Entertainer, Da, Mud River Stone, Misalliance, Long Day's Journey into Night, Spreadeagle, The Butterfly Collection, The Play about the Baby, Scattergood,* Bdwy in *All in Good Time* (1965), *Rosencrantz and Guildenstern Are Dead, Sleuth, Da, Noises Off, Small Family Business, Black Comedy, Racing Demon, Little Foxes, Twelfth Night, Uncle Vanya.*

Mustillo, Louis Born May 28, 1958 in Buffalo, NY. Graduate AADA. OB in *Blessed Event, Circumstances, Bartenders.*

Nance, Marcus Born March 12, 1964 in Carmel, CA. Graduate UC Fresno. Bdwy debut 2003 in *La Boheme.*

Naughton, Keira Born June 3, 1971 in New Haven, CT. Graduate Skidmore Col., NYU. Bdwy debut in *Three Sisters,* OB debut in *All My Sons,* followed by *Tesla's Letters, Hotel Universe, Uncle Jack, Snapshots 2000, Evolution.*

Neer, Daniel Born February 12, 1967 in Bellevue, OH. Graduate the OH State U., Royal Acad. Of Music, U. of MI. Bdwy debut 2003 in *La Boheme.*

Nelson, Mark Born September 26, 1955 in Westwood, NJ. Graduate Princeton U. Debut 1977 OB in *The Dybbuk* followed by *Green Fields, The Keymaker, Common Pursuit, Cabaret Verboten, Flaubert's Latest, Picasso at the Lapin Agile, June Moon, As Bees in Honey Drown, Vienna Lusthaus,* Bdwy in *Amadeus* (1981), *Brighton Beach Memoirs, Biloxi Blues, Broadway Bound, Rumors, A Few Good Men, Three Sisters, The Invention of Love.*

Nelson, Sarah Jane Born in Little Rock, AR. Attended Skidmore Col. Bdwy in *Swing!* followed by *The Green Bird,* OB in *Radiant Baby.*

Nixon, Marni Born February 22 in Altadena, CA. Attended LACC, U.S. Cal., Pasadena Playhouse. Bdwy debut 1952 in *The Girl in Pink Tights,* followed by *My Fair Lady* (1964), OB in *Thank Heaven for Lerner and Loewe, Taking My Turn, Opal, Romeo and Juliet, Requiem for William.*

Nobbs, Keith Born 1979 in Kingswood, TX. Attended Columbia U. OB in *Stupid Kids, Fuddy Meers, Four, Dublin Carol*

Norton, Edward Born August 18, 1969 in Boston, MA. Graduate Yale U. Debut 1992 OB in *Waiting for Lefty,* followed by *Lovers, Italian American Reconciliation, Bring Me Smiles, Bible Burlesque, Fragments, Burn This.*

Norton, Jim Born January 4, 1938 in Dublin, Ireland. Bdwy debut 1999 in *The Weir,* OB 2000 in *Juno and the Paycock, Dublin Carol.*

Noth, Chris Born November 13, 1957 in Madison, WI. Graduate Yale U., attended Marlborough Coll., Neighborhood Playhouse. OB in *Patronage, Arms and the Man, Kentucky Cycle, What Didn't Happen.,* Bdwy in *The Best Man* (2000),

Orbach, Ron Born March 23, 1952 in Newark, NJ. Graduate Rider Col. Debut 1985 OB in *Lies and Legends,* followed by *Philistines, Skin of Our Teeth, Mrs. Dally Has a Lover,* Bdwy in *Laughter on the 23rd Floor* (1993), *Pal Joey* (Encores).

Oreskes, Daniel Born in New York, NY. Graduate U. PA., LAMDA. OB debut 1990 in *Henry IV,* followed by *Othello, 'Tis Pity She's a Whore, Richard II, Henry VI, Troilus and Cressida, Quills, Missing/Kissing, The Devils, Mrs. Peter's Connections, Julius Caesar* Bdwy debut 1992 in *Crazy He Calls Me,* followed by *Electra, Aida.*

Paley, Petronia Born May 31 in Albany, GA. Graduate Howard U. OB debut 1972 in *Us vs. Nobody,* followed by *Cherry Orchard, The Corner, Three Sisters, Frost of Renaissance, Long Time Since Yesterday, Telltale Heart, Trial of One Short-Sighted Black Woman, A Last Dance for Sybil* Bdwy debut 1975 in *First Breeze of Summer.*

Park, Joshua Born November 26, 1976 in North Carolina. Attended NC Sch. of the Arts. Bdwy debut 2001 in *Tom Sawyer,* OB in *A Celtic Christmas.*

Patton, Charlotte Born June 12 in Danville, KY. Attended U. Cincinnati, OB in *The New Living Newspaper, The Problem, The Bad Penny, The Happy Journey from Trenton to Camden, You've Changed, Montage, Delicate Dangers, The Street, My Mother's a Baby Boy.* OOB in *Labor Day.*

Pawk, Michele Born November 16, 1961 in Pittsburgh, PA. Graduate CCCM. Bdwy debut 1988 in *Mail,* followed by *Crazy for You, Cabaret, Seussical, Hollywood Arms* (Tony Award, Best Supporting Actress in a Play), OB in *Hello Again, Decline of the Middle West, john & jen, After the Fair.*

Payton-Wright, Pamela Born November 1, 1941 in Pittsburgh, PA. Graduate Birmingham So.Col., RADA. Bdwy debut 1967 in *Show-Off,* followed by *Exit the King, Cherry Orchard, Jimmy Shine, Mourning Becomes Electra, Glass Menagerie (1975), Romeo and Juliet, Night of the Iguana, M. Butterfly, Garden District,* OB in *Effect of Gamma Rays..., The Crucible, The Seagull, Don Juan, In the Garden, Richard III, Til the Rapture Comes, What You Get and What You Expect, Fifth of July.*

Perez, Rosie Born September 4, 1966 in Brooklyn, NY. OB debut 2001 in *The Vagina Monologues,* followed by *A Midsummer Night's Dream, Union City New Jersey, Where Are You, References to Salvador Dali Make Me Hot.* Bdwy debut 2003 in *Frankie & Johnny in the Claire de Lune.*

Perkins, Drew Born April 13, 1953 in Cincinati, OH. Graduate U. of Denver, Webster U. OB debut 2002 in *Hank Williams: Lost Highway.*

Perkins, Patti Born July 9 in New Haven, CT. Attended AMDA. OB debut 1972 in *The Contrast,* followed by *Fashion, Tuscaloosa's Calling Me, Patch, Shakespeare's Cabaret, Maybe I'm Doing It Wrong, Fabulous LaFontaine, Hannah 1939, Free Zone, New Yorkers, A Man of No Importance,* Bdwy in *All Over Town* (1974), *Shakespeare's Cabaret, The Full Monty.*

Pinkins, Tonya Born May 30, 1962 in Chicago Il. Attended Carnegie-Mellon U. Bdwy debut in *Merrily We Roll Along* (1981) followed by *Jelly's Last Jam, Chronicle of a Death Foretold, Play On!,* OB in *Five Points, Winter's Tale, An Ounce of Prevention, Just Say No, Mexican Hayride, Young Playwrights '90, Approximating Mother, Merry Wives of Windsor, Merrily We Roll Along in Concert, Caroline or Change (2003)*

Pittu, David Born April 4, 1967 in Fairfield, CT. Graduate NYU. Debut 1987 OB in *Film is Evil: Radio is Good* followed by *Five Very Live, White Cotton Sheets, Nothing Sacred, Stand-In, The Lights, Three Postcards, Dangerous Corner, Sympathetic Magic, Once in a Lifetime, The Fourth Wall,* Bdwy in *Tenth Man* (1989).

Pope, Peggy Born May 15, 1929 in Montclair, NJ. Attended Smith Col. Bdwy in *Doctor's Dilemma,* followed by *Volpone, Rose Tattoo, Harvey, School for Wives, Dr. Jazz,* OB in *Muzeeka, House of Blue Leaves, New Girl in Town, Romeo and Juliet, Wasp and Other Plays, Stonykill Lookout, Avow, 24 Evenings of Wit & Wisdom .*

Porter, Billy Born September 21, 1969 in Pittsburgh, PA. Graduate Carnegie Mellon U. OB debut 1989 in *Romance in Hard Times,* followed by *Merchant of Venice, Songs for a New World, Radiant Baby* Bdwy debut 1991 in *Miss Saigon,* followed by *Five Guys Named Moe, Grease, Miss Saigon.*

Prince, Faith Born August 5, 1957 in Augusta, GA. Graduate U. of Cincinnati. OB debut 1981 in *Scrambled Feet,* followed by *Olympus on My Mind, Groucho, Living Color, Bad Habits, Falsettoland, 3 of Hearts, The Torchbearers, Ancestral Voices, A Man of No Importance,* Bdwy in *Jerome Robbins' Broadway* (1989), *Nick & Nora, Guys and Dolls* (1992), *Fiorello* (Encores), *What's Wrong with This Picture, DuBarry Was a Lady* (Encores), *King and I, Little Me, James Joyce's The Dead, Bells Are Ringing.*

Pankow, John Born 1955 in St. Louis, MO. Attended St. Nichols Sch. of Arts. OB debut 1980 in *Merton of the Movies,* followed by *Slab Boys, Forty Deuce, Hunting Scenes from Lower Bovaria, Cloud 9, Jazz Poets at the Crotto, Henry V, North Shore Fish, Two Gentlemen of Verona, Italian American Reconciliation Aristocrats, Ice Cream with Hot Fudge, EST Marathon '92, Tempest* (CP), *Baby Anger, Measure for Measure, Barbara's Wedding* (CP), Bdwy in *Amadeus* (1981), *The Iceman Cometh, Serious Money.*

Pellegrino, Susan Born June 3, 1950 in Baltimore, MD. Attended CC San Francisco, CA St. U. OB debut 1982 in *Wisteria Trees,* followed by *Steel on Steel, Master Builder, Equal Wrights, Come as You Are, Painting Churches, Marvin's Room, Glory Girls, Minor Demons, Blood Orange, I'm Coming in Soon,* Bdwy in *Kentucky Cycle* (1994), *Present Laughter, View from the Bridge, Imaginary Friends.*

Pitoniak, Anne Born March 30, 1922 in Westfield, MA. Attended U. NC Women's Col. Debut 1982 OB in *Talking With,* followed by *Young Playwrights Festival, Phaedra, Steel Magnolias, Pygmalion, The Rose Quartet, Batting Cage, Last of the Thorntons,* Bdwy debut 1983 in *'night, Mother,* for which she received a 1983 Theatre World Award, followed by *The Octette Bridge Club, Picnic, Amy's View, Uncle Vanya, Imaginary Friends.*

Redgrave, Vanessa Born January 30, 1937 in London, Eng. Attended Central School of Speech and Drama. Bdwy debut 1976 in *Lady from the Sea* followed by *Orpheus Descending* (1989), *Prophets & Heroes, Long Day's Journey Into Night* OB in *Vita and Virginia, Anthony and Cleopatra.*

Rees, Roger Born May 5, 1944 in Wales. Graduate Glade School of Fine Art. Bdwy debut 1975 in *London Assurance* followed by *Nicholas Nickleby* (1981), *Red Shoes* (previews only), *Indiscretions, The Rehearsal,* OB in *End of the Day* (1992), *The Misanthrope, A Man of No Importance.*

Reid, Michael "Mikey" Born December 30, 1992 in Bronx, NY. OB debut 2003 in *The Winter's Tale*

Remo, Melissa Born September 5, 1990 in Staten Island, NY. Bdwy in *Miss Saigon,* followed by *King & I, La Boheme.*

Melissa Remo

Justin Robertazzi

Struan Rodger

David Runco

Rickman, Allen Lewis Born February 4, 1960 in Far Rockaway, NY. Attended Brooklyn Col. OB debut 1988 in *Faithful Brethren of Pitt Street*, followed by *Dr. Dietrich's Process, The Big Winner, Tony 'n' Tina's Wedding, Theda Bara and the Frontier Rabbi, A Klezmer's Tale, Far and Wide*.

Robertazzi, Justin Born August 20, 1990 in Englewood, NJ. OB in *Amahl and the Night Visitors*, Bdwy in *La Boheme*.

Robertson, Scott Born January 4, 1954 in Stanford, CT. Bdwy debut 1976 in *Grease*, followed by *The Pajama Game* (LC), *Damn Yankees* (1994), *Boys from Syracuse*, OB in *Scrambled Feet, Applause, A Lady Needs a Change, A Baker's Audition, She Loves Me, Secrets of a Lava Lamp, Love in Two Countries*.

Robinson, Andrew Born February 14, 1942 in NYC. Graduate New School, LAMA. Debut 1967 OB in *Macbird*, followed by *Cannibals, Futz, Young Master Dante, Operation Sidewinder, Subject to Fits, Mary Stuart, Narrow Road to the Deep North, In the Belly of the Beast, Vienna: Lusthaus*, Bdwy in *Any Given Day* (1993).

Rodger, Struan Born in Manchester, England. Attended Central School of Speech and Drama. Bdwy debut 2002 in *Medea*.

Rogers, Michael Born December 8, 1954 in Trinidad. Attended LIU, Yale U. OB debut 1974 in *Elena*, followed by *Chiaroscuro, Forty Deuce, Antigone, Julius Caesar, Insufficient Evidence, Othello, Young Playwrights '90, Salt, Troilus and Cressida, Julius Caesar* (2003).

Rossetter, Kathryn (a.k.a. Kathy). Born July 31 in Abington, PA. Graduate Gettysburg Col. Debut 1982 OB in *After the Fall*, followed by *The Incredibly Famous Will Rivers, A Midsummer Night's Dream, How to Say Goodbye, The Good Coach, Love Lemmings, The White Bear, Black Snow, The Mount of AHA, Hold Please*, Bdwy in *Death of a Salesman* (1984).

Rubin-Vega, Daphne Born November 18, 1968 in Panama. Bdwy debut 1996 in *Rent* (also OB), for which she received a 1996 Theatre World Award, followed by *Rocky Horror Show*, OB in *Two Sisters and a Piano, Gum, Fucking A, Free to be You and Me*

Runco, David Born November 1 in NYC. Graduate of Queens College. OOB in *The Moon of the Caribbees, Paul Westerberg, The Widow's Blind Date, Cleveland, No Mother to Guide Her, The Uninvited Guest*.

Salata, Gregory Born July 21, 1949 in New York, NY. Graduate Queens Col. Bdwy debut 1975 in *Dance with Me*, followed by *Equus, Bent*, OB in *Piaf: A Remembrance, Sacraments, Measure for Measure, Subject of Childhood, Jacques and His Master, Androcles and the Lion, Madwoman of Chaillot, Beauty Part, Heartbreak House, Filumena, Boy Meets Girl, The Admirable Crichton, Endpapers*.

Salguero, Sophia Born July 5, 1972 in Ann Arbor, MI. Graduate Carnegie Mellon U. Debut 1995 OB in *I Was Looking at the Ceiling* followed by *Green Bird, On the Town, Call the Children Home*, Bdwy 1996 in *Juan Darien*.

Sarsgaard, Peter Born March 7, 1971 in Scott A.F.B., IL. Graduate WA U. Debut 1995 OB in *Laura Dennis* followed by *Kingdom of Earth, Burn This*.

Schoeffler, Paul Born November 21, 1958 in Montreal, Canada. Graduate U.CA/Berkley, Carnegie Mellon, U. Brussels. Debut 1988 OB in *Much Ado About Nothing* followed by *Cherry Orchard, Carnival, Doll's Life, No Way to Treat a Lady*, Bdwy in *Cyrano the Musical* (1993), *Peter Pan, Nine*.

Seldes, Marian Born August 23, 1928 in New York, NY. Attended Neighborhood Playhouse. Bdwy debut 1947 in *Media*, followed by *Crime and Punishment, That Lady, Town Beyond Tragedy, Ondine, On High Ground, Come of Age, Chalk Garden, Milk Train Doesn't Stop Here Anymore, The Wall, Gift of Time, Delicate Balance, Before You Go, Father's Day, Equus, The Merchant, Deathtrap, Boys from Syracuse* (Encores), *Ivanov, Ring Round the Moon*, OB in *Different, Ginger Man, Mercy Street, Isadora Duncan Sleeps with the Russian Navy, Painting Churches, Gertrude Stein and Companion, Richard II, The Milk Train Doesn't Stop…, Bright Room Called Day, Another Time, Three Tall Women, The Torchbearers, Dear Liar, The Butterfly Collection, The Play About the Baby, Dinner at Eight*.

Setlock, Mark Born June 26, 1968 in Cleveland, OH. Graduate Kent St. U., Am Rep Th/Harvard. OB debut 1995 in *Don Juan in Chicago*, followed by *Fully Committed, The Last Sunday in June*, Bdwy debut 1996 in *Rent*.

Shaw, Fiona Born July 10, 1955 in Cork, Ire. Attended RADA. Debut 1996 OB in *The Waste Land* for which she received a 1997 Theatre World Award. Bdwy in *Medea*.

Juliet Smith

Martín Solá

Felix Solis

Allyson Tucker

Shelton, Sloane Born March 17, 1934 in Asheville, NC. Attended Bates Col., RADA. Bdwy Debut 1967 in *Imaginary Invalid* followed by *Touch of the Poet, Tonight at 8:30, I Never Sang for My Father, Sticks and Bones, Runner Stumbles, Shadow Box, Passione, Open Admission, Orpheus Descending,* OB in *Androcles and the Lion, The Maids, Basic Training of Pavlo Hummel, Play and Other Plays, Julius Caesar, Chieftans, Passione, Chinese Viewing Pavilion, Blood Relations, Great Divide, Highest Standard of Living, Flower Palace, April Snow, Nightingale, Dearly Departed, Other People's Money, Dog Opera, Importance of Being Earnest, Not Waving, Dinner at 8.*

Shipley, Sandra Born February 1 in Rainham, Kent, Eng. Attended New Col. of Speech and Drama, London U. OB debut 1988 in *Six Characters in Search of an Author,* followed by *Big Time, Kindertransport, Venus, Backward Glance, Phaedra in Delirium, Arms and the Man, The Clearing, Once Around the City, Only the End of the World,* Bdwy 1995 in *Indiscretions,* followed by *Deep Blue Sea, Vincent in Brixton.*

Shively, Ryan Born August 2, 1971 in Springfield, OH. Graduate Purdue U., U. Findlay. OB debut 1997 in *All My Sons,* followed by *Macbeth, It Just Catches* Bdwy debut 1997 in *1776,* followed by *The Man Who Came to Dinner.*

Skinner, Emily Born June 29, 1970 in Richmond, VA. Graduate Carnegie Mellon U. Bdwy debut 1994 in *Christmas Carol* (MSG) followed by *Jekyll & Hyde, Side Show, The Full Monty,* OB in *Watbanaland, James Joyce's The Dead, Dinner at Eight.*

Smith, Juliet Born in Denver, CO. Attended NYU, Nat'l Theatre Conservatory, Denver. Debut OB 2003 in *Hank Williams: Lost Highway.*

Smith-Cameron, J. Born September 7 in Louisville, KY. Attended FL St U. Bdwy debut in *Crimes of the Heart* (1982) followed by *Wild Honey, Lend Me a Tenor, Our Country's Good, Real Inspector Hound, 15 Minute Hamlet, Tartuffe,* OB in *Asian Shade, The Knack, Second Prize: Two Weeks in Leningrad, Great Divide, Voice of the Turtle, Women of Manhattan, Alice and Fred, Mi Vida Loca, Little Egypt, On the Bum, Traps/Owners, Desdemona, Naked Truth, Don Juan in Chicago, Blue Window, As Bees in Honey Drown.*

Solá, Martín Born November 16, 1968 in Bronx, NY. Graduate FI State U., U. of IL. Bdwy debut 1996 *King and I* followed by *La Boheme.*

Solis, Felix Born September 17, 1971 in New York, NY. Graduate Marymount Col. Debut OB 1997 in *Under a Western Sky,* followed by *Our Lady of 121st St.*

Spivak, Alice Born August 11, 1935 in Brooklyn, NY. Debut 1954 OB in *Early Primrose* followed by *Of Mice and Men, Secret Concubine, Port Royal, Time for Bed, House of Blue Leaves, Deep Six the Briefcase, Selma, Ferry Tales, Temple, A Backer's Audition, Group One Acts, Chaim's Love Song, A Last Dance for Sybil.*

Stackpole, Dana Born February 25, 1966 in Misawa, Japan. Bdwy debut 1994 in *Carousel, Movin' Out.*

Stern, Cheryl Born July 1, 1956 in Buffalo, NY. Graduate Northwestern U. OB debut 1984 in *Daydreams,* followed by *White Lies, Pets, That's Life!, I Love You You're Perfect, Now Change, Game Show, Requiem for William.*

Stevens, Jodi Born April 24 in Summit, NJ. Graduate PA St. Debut OB in *My Name Is Pablo Picasso* followed by *27 Wagons Full of Cotton, Antigone, Meet Him, Bodyshop, Cardenio, Gender Wars,* Bdwy in *Jekyll & Hyde* (1997), *Urban Cowboy.*

Stovall, Count Born January 15, 1946 in Los Angeles, CA. Graduate U CA. Debut 1973 OB in *He's Got a Jones* followed by *In White America, Rashomon, Sidnee Poet Heroical, A Photo, Julius Caesar, Coriolanus, Spell #7, Jail Diary of Albie Sachs, To Make a Poet Black, Transcendental Blues, Edward II, Children of the Sun, Shades of Brown, American Dreams, Pantomime, Stovall, Telltale Heart, Fear Itself, Scapin, A Last Dance for Sybil,* Bdwy in *Inacent Black*(1981), *Philadelphia Story.*

Taylor, Myra (Lucretia) Born July 9, 1960 in Ft. Motte, SC. Graduate Yale U. OB debut 1985 in *Dennis,* followed by *The Tempest, Black Girl, Marathon 86, Phantasie, Walking the Dead, I Am a Man, Marathon Dancing, Come Down Burning, American Clock, Force Continuum,* Bdwy in *A Streetcar Named Desire* (1987), *Mule Bone, Chronicle of a Death Foretold, Electra, Macbeth, Nine.*

Ten Haaf, Jochum Bdwy debut 2003 in *Vincent in Brixton* for which he received a Theatre World Award.

Thompson, Jennifer Laura Born December 5, 1969 in Southfield, MI. Graduate U. MI, AADA. OB debut 1994 in *A Doll's Life,* followed by *Urinetown,* Bdwy debut 1998 in *Strike Up the Band* (Encores). OOB in *Happy Birthday*

Daniel C. Webb

Nicholas Wuehrmann

Remy Zaken

David Zayas

Tirrell, Barbara Born November 24, 1953 in Nahant, MA. Graduate Temple U., Webber-Douglas Acad. OB debut 1977 in *Six Characters in Search of an Author*, followed by *Cyrano, Romeo and Juliet, Louis Quinse, Day Out of Time, King Lear, Oedipus Texas, Father West, Leaving Queens, A Man of No Importance*, Bdwy in *Annie* (1997).

Tucker, Allyson Born August 14 in Milwaukee, WI. Graduate Brown U. OB debut 1985 in *De Obeah Man*, Bdwy debut 1989 in *Oh Kay!*, followed by *Will Rogers Follies, Ragtime, Follies 2001, Man of La Mancha*(2002).

Turturro, John Born February 28, 1957 in Brooklyn, NY. Graduate SUNY/New Paltz, LaU. Debut 1984 OB in *Danny and the Deep Blue Sea* for which he received a Theatre World Award, followed by *Men Without Dates, Chaos and Hard Times, Steel on Steel, Tooth of the Crime, Of Mice and Men, Jamie's Gang, Marathon 86, The Bald Soprano/The Leader, La Puta Vita Trilogy, Italian American Reconciliation, Arturo Ui, The Normal Heart* (benefit reading), Bdwy in *Death of a Salesman* (1984) followed by *Waiting for Godot, Life (x) 3*.

Urbaniak, James Born September 17, 1963 in Bayonne, NJ. OB debut 1988 in *Giants of the Mountain*, followed by *The Universe, Imaginary Invalid, South, Mamba's Daughters, Lipstick Traces, The World Over*.

Vaughan, Melanie Born September 18 in Yazoo City, MS. Graduate LA St U. Bdwy debut 1976 in *Rex* followed by *Sunday in the Park with George, On the 20th Century, Music Is, Starlight Express, Most Happy Fella* (1992), *Imaginary Friends*, OB in *Canterbury Tales, Big City Rhythm*.

Vereen, Ben Born October 10, 1946 in Miami, FL. OB debut 1965 in *Prodigal Son*, Bdwy in *Sweet Charity, Golden Boy, Hair, Jesus Christ Superstar*, for which he received a 1972 Theatre World Award, *Pippin, Grind, Jelly's Last Jam, Christmas Carol* (MSG) *I'm Not Rappaport* (2002).

Vida, Richard Born March 15, 1963 in Hartford, CT. Graduate S. Ct. State U. Bdwy debut 1994 in *The Best Little Whorehouse Goes Public*, OB in *Little Ham*.

Vidnovic, Martin Born January 4, 1948 in Falls Church, VA. Graduate Cinn. Consv. Of Music. Debut 1972 OB in *The Fantasticks* followed by *Lies and Legends, Showtune*, Bdwy in *Home Sweet Homer* (1976), *King and I* (1977), *Oklahoma!* (1979), *Brigadoon* (1980), *Baby, Some Enchanted Evening*(also OB), *Guys and Dolls* (1994), *King David*.

Vig, Joel Born December 27, 1952 in Freeport, IL. Graduate U. of ND. OB debut 1992 in *Ruthless!*, Bdwy in *Hairspray*.

Vlastnik, Frank Born May 30, 1965 in Pru, IL. Graduate IL, Wesleyan U. Bdwy debut 1996 in *Big*, followed by *A Year with Frog and Toad*, OB in *Oy!, Saturday Night Fever*.

Webb, Daniel C. Born January 30, 1977 in Oklahoma City, OK. Graduate Oklahoma City U. Bdwy debut 2002 in *La Boheme*.

Weller, Frederick Born April 18, 1966 in New Orleans, LA. Graduate U NC/Chapel Hill, Juilliard. Bdwy debut 1991 in *Six Degrees of Separartion* followed by *The Rehearsal, Little Foxes, Take Me Out*, OB 1997 in *Plunge* .

Wellman, John Born April 17, 1965 in Baltimore, MD. Graduate U.MD., Temple U. Debut OB 1994 in *King Lear*, followed by *Terminal Hip, The Miser, Requiem for William*.

West, Michael Born July 4, 1960 in Atlanta, GA. Graduate Boston U., GA. St. U. OB debut 1993 in *Whoop Dee Doo*, followed by *Live from the Betty Ford Center, Forbidden Hollywood, When Pigs Fly, Forbidden Bdwy Cleans Up Its Act, Almost Live from the Betty Ford Clinic*.

Whaley, Frank Born July 20, 1963 in Syracuse, NY. Graduate SUNY/Albany. Debut 1986 OB in *Tigers Wild*, followed by *The Years, Good Evening, Veins and Thumbtacks, Hesh, Great Unwashed*.

White, Amelia Born September 14, 1954 in Nottingham, England. Attended London Central School. Debut 1984 OB in *The Accrington Pals*, for which she received a Theatre World Award, followed by *American Bagpipes, Once in a Lifetime, Butter and Egg Man* Bdwy in *Crazy for You* (1992), *The Heiress*(1995).

White, Jacob Garrett Born December 14, 1976 in New York,NY. Graduate U. of Cincinnati Conservatory of Music. OB debut 1988 in *Cymbeline*, followed by *Julius Caesar*.

White, Julie Born June 4, 1962 in San Diego, CA. Attended Fordham U. OB debut 1988 in *Lucky Stiff*, followed by *Just Say No, Early One Evening, Stick Wife, Marathon '91, Spike Heels, The Family of Mann, Dinner With Friends, Barbra's Wedding*.

Wilkof, Lee Born June 25, 1951 in Canton, OH. Graduate U. of Cincinnati. OB debut 1977 in *Present Tense*, followed by *Little Shop of Horrors*, *Holding Patterns*, *Angry Housewives*, *Assassins*, *Born Guilty*, *Treasure Island*, *Golden Boy*, *Names*, *Waiting for Lefty*, *Mizlansky*, *Zilinsky*, *The Stumbling Tongue*, *Oy!*, *Do Re Mi*, *Arsenic and Old Lace* (CC), Bdwy in *Sweet Charity* (1986), *Front Page*, *She Loves Me*, *Kiss Me Kate*, *Boys from Syracuse*.

Wilson, C.J. OB debut 1994 in *The Merry Wives of Windsor*, Bdwy debut 2000 in *Gore Vidal's The Best Man* followed by *Long Day's Journey Into Night*.

Wilson, Danelle Eugenia Born August 23, 1987 . OB in *No Niggers, No Jews, No Dogs*. Bdwy in *Hairspray*

Wolf, Scott Born 1968 in West Orange, NJ. Bdwy debut 1999 in *Side Man*. OB in *The Sons of Ulster*.

Wong, B.D. Born October 24, 1962 in San Francisco, CA. Debut 1981 OB in *Androcles and the Lion* followed by *Applause*, *The Tempest*, *Language of Their Own*, *As 1000 Cheer*, *Shanghai Moon*. Bdwy in *M. Butterfly*, for which he received a Theatre World Award, *Face Value*, *You're a Good Man Charlie Brown*.

Wright, Chloe Born in the UK, graduate of the Guild Hall School of Music & Drama. Bdwy debut in *La Boheme*.

Wuehrmann, Nicholas Born June 18, 1961 in Perth Amboy NJ. Graduate of James Madison Univ. and Kent State Univ. OB in *El Greco*, *Hallellujah Breakdown*.

Wynkoop, Christopher Born December 7, 1943 in Long Branch, NJ. Graduate AADA. Debut 1970 OB in *Under the Gaslight*, followed by *And So to Bed Cartoons for a Lunch Hour*, *Telecast*, *Fiorello!*, *The Aunts*, *Moonlight*, *American Clock*, *BAFO*, Bdwy in *Whoopee!* (1979) *City of Angels*, *Anna Christie*, *Long Day's Journey into Night*

Zaken, Remy Born May 9, 1989 in Norwalk, CT. OB in *Radiant Baby*.

Zayas, David Born in Bronx, NY. OB debut 2002 *in Our Lady of 121st St*. OB in *Jesus Hopped the A Train*, *In Arabia We'd All Be Kings*.

Zien, Chip Born March 20, 1947 in Milwaukee, WI. Attended U. Penn. OB in *You're a Good Man Charlie Brown*, followed by *Kadish*, *How to Succeed...*, *Dear Mr. G.*, *Tuscaloosa's Calling*, *Hot L Baltimore*, *El Grande de Coca Cola*, *Split*, *Real Life Funnies*, *March of the Falsettos*, *Isn't It Romantic*, *Diamonds*, *Falsettoland*, *Imaginary Life*, *A New Brain*, Bdwy in *All Over Town* (1974), *The Suicide*, *Into the Woods*, *Grand Hotel*, *Falsettos*, *Boys from Syracuse*.

Zorich, Louis Born February 12, 19 in Chicago, IL. Attended Roosevelt U. OB in *Six Characters in Search of an Author*, *Crimes and Crimes*, *Henry V*, *Thracian Horses*, *All Women Are One*, *The Good Soldier Schweik*, *Shadow of Heroes*, *To Clothe the Naked*, *A Memory of Two Mondays*, *They Knew What They Wanted*, *The Gathering*, *True West*, *The Tempest*, *Come Day Come Night*, *Henry IV Parts 1 & 2*, *The Size of the World*, *On A Clear Day You Can See Forever* (CC), Bdwy in *Becket*, *Moby Dick*, *The Odd Couple*, *Hadrian VII*, *Moonchildren*, *Fun City*, *Goodtime Charley*, *Herzl*, *Death of a Salesman*, *Arms and the Man*, *The Marriage of Figaro*, *She Loves Me*, *Follies 2001*, *Ma Rainey's Black Bottom*.

OBITUARIES
June 1, 2002–May 31, 2003

Gretchen Davidson Adamson, 77, Chicago-born actress, died August 2, 2002, in Los Angeles following a long illness. Seen early in life in radio work with Mercury Theatre on the Air and later in life in several television commercials, she made her 1937 Broadway debut in *Many Mansions*, followed by *The American Way* and *The Return of the Vagabond*. Touring company credits include *Showboat*, *The Man Who Came to Dinner* with Alexander Wolcott and *My Sister Eileen*. The wife of five-time Oscar-nominated lyricist Harold Adamson, she administered his music catalog after his death, was an active member of ASCAP, and also served as secretary as well as a member of the board of directors of the Songwriters Guild of America. She is survived by a son, grandson, daughter-in-law, granddaughter-in-law, and stepdaughter.

Mary Todd Andrews, 86, Santa Monica, California-born actress, died January 17, 2003, in Palm Springs, California, of Alzheimer's disease. A long-time performer at the Pasadena Playhouse, she also appeared in several national tours with her husband, actor Dana Andrews, including *The Glass Menagerie*, *Morning's at Seven*, and *Gaslight*. Children from her marriage survive.

Cholly Atkins (Charles Sylvan Atkinson), 89, Pratt City, Alabama-born dancer/choreographer, died April 19, 2003, in Las Vegas, Nevada, of pancreatic cancer. An early vaudeville performer with groups such as the Rhythm Pals, he was later a choreographer for performers at the Apollo Theater and Cotton Club in the 1940's, and also performed on tour as a dancer with Count Basie and Louis Armstrong. As half of the duo of Coles and Atkins, he virtually defined "class act," the term for a routine distinguished by deceptively easy dignity, and was an early teacher to Sammy Davis, Jr. He also choreographed for groups such as the June Taylor Dancers, The Supremes and Gladys Night and the Pips. Broadway credits include *Gentleman Prefer Blondes* and *Black and Blue*, for which he won a Tony Award for choreography in 1989. He was awarded a fellowship from the National Endowment for the Arts in 1993 to record his memoirs and tour colleges teaching choreography and dance. Survivors include his wife of nearly 40 years, Maye Harrison Anderson, grandchildren, and others.

Pepsi Bethel (Alfred Bethel), 83, Greensboro, North Carolina-born jazz-dance performer/teacher/choreographer, died August 30, 2002, in the Bronx, New York, of cardiopulmonary arrest. A dancer at the Savoy Ballroom in Harlem in the 1930's, he eventually developed expertise over a wide variety of dance steps, from the cakewalk to the aerial Lindy. He performed with the Mura Dehn Jazz Ballet before founding his own troupe in the 1960's, the Pepsi Bethel Authentic Jazz Dance Theater, which performed African, folk, social, and African-American dance. The Bethel and Dehn dance troupes were chosen by the United States State Department in 1969 to perform in nine African countries as cultural emissaries. Broadway credits as a performer include *Kwamina*, and as choreographer and/or consultant include *One Mo' Time* and *Jelly Roll*. He staged *An Evening with Charles Cook and Friends* in 1984 at Aaron Davis Hall, and was a production consultant for *Sing Hallelujah!*, a 1987 gospel musical at the Village Gate. His choreography has been performed by the Jiving Lindy Hoppers and the companies of Charles Moore and Joan Miller. In 1980 he was honored as a choreographer in *Celebration of Men in Dance* at the Thelma Hill Performing Arts Center in Brooklyn. No immediate survivors.

Maria Bjornson, 53, Paris-born set and costume designer, died December 13, 2002, in London of undisclosed causes. A Tony Award winner for both her set and costume designs for *Phantom of the Opera*, Broadway credits also include *Aspects of Love*. She designed extensively for opera, ballet, and theater throughout the world, and began her career at the Glasgow Citizens Theater, where she designed thirteen productions. She later designed for the Scottish Opera, the English National Opera, and Royal Shakespeare Company.

Cathy Blaser, Cleveland, Ohio-born stage manager, died April 12, 2003, in New York City following a long battle with cancer. Her Broadway credits include *Mastergate*, *Penn & Teller*, *Whose Life Is It Anyway?*, and *Ain't Misbehavin'*. Off-Broadway credits include *Family Secrets*, and national tour credits include *Penn and Teller*, *Children of a Lesser God* and *Whose Life Is It Anyway*. She has also been production manager of special events such as the "7th on Sixth" fashion shows, Earth Day events, and serving as stage manager for the millennium New Year's Eve celebration in Times Square. She was also responsible for conceiving and publishing the first Stage Managers Directory and Theatrical Sourcebook.

Mel Bourne (Melvin Bourne), 79, Chicago-born production designer, died January 14, 2003, in New York City of a heart attack. Broadway credits include *Seventeen* (asst. to Stewart Chaney), *The Male Animal* (scenic design), *Seagulls Over Sorrento* (scenic and lighting design), *My Darlin' Aida* (asst. to Lemuel Ayers), *End as a Man* (scenic design). An apprentice at the Papermill Playhouse and having attended Yale School of Drama, he also assisted legendary theatrical designer Robert Edmund Jones before beginning a career as a film production designer facilitated by Woody Allen, which brought him three Oscar nominations. He was also prolific in television production design. Survivors include three sons, Travis, Timothy, a film producer, and Tristan, an art director, and five grandchildren.

Eddie Bracken (Edward Vincent Bracken), 87, Astoria, Queens, New York-born actor, died November 14, 2002, in Montclair, New Jersey, from surgery complications. An early protégé of George Abbott, Broadway credits include *The Lady Refuses*, followed by *The Drunkard*, *Life's Too Short*, *So Proudly We Hail*, *Iron Men*, *What a Life*, *Too Many Girls*, *The Seven Year Itch*, *Shinbone Alley*, *Beg, Borrow, or Steal*, *How to Make a Man*, *The Odd Couple*, *Hello, Dolly!* (Tony nomination), and *Sugar Babies*. A veteran of many national tours, he is perhaps best known for his 35 film roles and television career which spanned 60 years, beginning with the Preston Sturges comedies of the 1940's. He also logged 15,000 performances on the Papermill Playhouse stage. Actress Constance "Connie" Nickerson Bracken, his wife of 62 years, preceded him in death by three months, and survivors include three daughters, two sons, nine grandchildren, and two great-grandchildren.

Fritzi Burr, 78, Philadelphia, Pennsylvania-born actress, died January 17, 2003, in Fort Myers, Florida, of natural causes. In a career spanning seven decades beginning as a comedian with the East Coast Little Theater circuit and in sketches with the legendary vaudeville team of Smith and Dale, her Broadway credits include *I Can Get It for You Wholesale*, *Once Upon a Mattress*, *The Family Way*, and *Funny Girl*. National touring companies include *Fiddler on the Roof* and *Norman, Is That You?* with Milton Berle. She is perhaps best known for her roles in television and film. Survivors include sisters Temmi Saltzman and Shirley Turteltaub, brother-in-law/multihyphenate Saul Turteltaub, a niece, Dr. Nita Salzman, nephews Bennett Salzman and Adam Turteltaub, and producer-director, Jon Turteltaub. Husband and longtime friend Aaron Hyman preceded her in death in 1995.

Eddie Braken

Vinnette Carroll

Nell Carter

Peggy Conklin

Vinnette Carroll, 80, Jamaica-born actress/playwright/writer/director, died November 5, 2002, in Fort Lauderhill, Florida, of complications from diabetes and heart disease. The first African-American woman to direct a production on Broadway (*Don't Bother Me, I Can't Cope*), she also garnered a Tony nomination for her work on that production. Other Broadway credits include *A Small War on Murray Hill* (actress), *Jolly's Progress* (actress), *Trumpets of the Lord* (producer/director), *Your Arms Too Short to Box with God* (conceived/directed), and *But Never Jam Today*. Off-Broadway credits include *Moon Over a Rainbow Shawl* (actress, Obie Award). She also directed and starred in a critically acclaimed production of Langston Hughes's *Prodigal Son*, which toured Europe, and founded the Urban Arts Corps in 1967, which produced dozens of shows out of a space on W. 20th St. In 1967 she won an Emmy Award for her contributions to *Beyond the Blues*, a televised dramatization of selections by black poets, and in the late 1980's she founded The Vinnette Carroll Repertory Theatre in Fort Lauderdale, Florida, devoted to featuring work by minority playwrights and actors. She is perhaps best known for her work in television and film. Survivors include her sister, Dorothy Carroll Hudgins, of Manhattan, New York.

Nell Carter (Nell Hardy), 54, Birmingham, Alabama-born actress/singer, died January 23, 2003, in Beverly Hills, California, from complications of diabetes. A Tony Award winner as best featured actress in a musical for her work in *Ain't Misbehavin'*, her other Broadway credits include *Soon*, *Dude*, the special benefit *Angela Lansbury: A Celebration*, and *Annie*. Other theater credits include *Hello Dolly!*, *Hair*, *Don't Bother Me, I Can't Cope*, *Jesus Christ Superstar*, and *Bubbling Brown Sugar*. An Emmy winner for the television version of *Ain't Misbehavin'*, she was nominated two more times for the award for her work on *Gimme a Break!*, for which she is best remembered. Other television credits include work on a soap opera and an appearance on the acclaimed PBS special *Baryshnikov on Broadway*. Survivors include her daughter, Tracy, and two sons, Joshua and Daniel.

Don Chastain, 66, Oklahoma City, Oklahoma-born actor/screenwriter, died August 9, 2002, in Los Angeles of colon cancer. Broadway credits include *It's a Bird…It's a Plane…It's Superman*, *No Strings*, *Dance a Little Closer*, *42nd St.*, and *Parade*. He also penned the 1978 film *The Mafu Cage* starring Lee Grant and Carol Kane. An Emmy nominee for his work on television, he is best remembered for his work in that medium.

Kathleen Claypool (Kathleen Claypool Meyer), 85, actress, died May 5, 2003, in Cornwall, Pennsylvania from longtime hip surgery complications. Claiming to have appeared onstage in every state in the United States with the exception of Alaska, she shared an Obie Award with the ensemble of *Curtains* in 1998. Production designer for 17 years for Plays for Living, she also did a two-year stint as Betty Meeks in Larry Shue's *The Foreigner* at the Astor Place Theater. She made several independent film appearances and worked in radio early in her career. Survivors include a son, daughter-in-law, grandson, and several nieces and nephews.

Janet Collins, 86, New Orleans, Louisiana-born ballerina, died March 28, 2003, in Fort Worth, Texas. The first African-American ballerina to perform at the Metropolitan Opera, she was one of only a few African-American women to become prominent in American classical ballet. She made her Broadway debut in 1950 in *Out of This World*. In 1951 she performed lead roles in *Aida*, *Carmen*, and danced in *La Gioconda* and *Samson and Delilah* at the Met in New York City, and she also appeared in several film musicals.

Peggy Conklin, 96, Dobbs Ferry, New York-born actress, died March 18, 2003, in Naples, Florida. She made her Broadway debut in 1929 in *The Little Show*, followed by *His Majesty's Car*, *Purity*, *Old Man Murphy*, *Hot Money*, *Mademoiselle*, *The Party's Over*, *The Ghost Writer*, *The Pursuit of Happiness*, *The Petrified Forest* with Humphrey Bogart, *Co-respondent Unknown*, *Yes, My Darling Daughter*, *Casey Jones*, *Miss Swan Expects*, *Mr. And Mrs. South*, *Feathers in a Gale*, *Alice in Arms*, *The Wisteria Trees*, *Picnic*, and *Howie*. She was also the veteran of five films made in the 1930's. Survivors include a son, daughter, and three grandchildren.

Joel Craig, 58, St. Louis, Missouri-born actor, died April 8, 2003, in Vancouver, British Columbia, where he was being treated for a heart ailment. Making his Broadway debut in 1967 in *Rosencrantz and Guildenstern are Dead*, that was followed by *A Patriot for Me*, *Conduct Unbecoming*, *Vivat! Vivat Regina!*, *Going Up*, and *Dance a Little Closer*.

Keene Curtis (Keene Holbrook Curtis), 79, Salt Lake City, Utah-born actor, died October 13, 2002, in Bountiful, Utah, of complications from Alzheimer's disease. A Tony Award winner in 1971 as best featured actor in a musical for his work in *The Rothschilds*, Broadway credits as a production stage manager include *The Dark is Light Enough*, *The Desk Set*, *Nude With Violin*, *Present Laughter*, *The Firstborn*, *Look After Lulu*, *Much Ado About Nothing*, *Silent Night*, and *Lonely Night*. Broadway acting credits include *You Can't Take It With You*, *The School for Scandal*, *Right You Are If You Think You Are*, *The Wild Duck*, *War and Peace*, *Pantagleize*, *The Cherry Orchard*, *The Cocktail Party*, *The Misanthrope*, *Cock-A-Doodle Dandy*, *Hamlet*, *A Patriot for Me*, *Division Street*, *Night Watch*, *Via Galactica*, *Annie*, *La Cage aux Folles*, and *White Liars & Black Comedy*. Best known for his long running role as the snippy restaurant owner John Allen Hill on the television sitcom *Cheers*, he also appeared in many other television and film roles. No immediate survivors.

Ira Eaker, 80, New York City-born co-founder and co-publisher of *Back Stage*, the weekly showbiz newspaper, died June 26, 2002, in Florida, following surgery. In 1960 he created *Back Stage* with Allen Zwerdling, Eaker serving as co-publisher and advertising director, and Zwerdling serving as co-publisher and editor. Over the next quarter century, they built the national weekly into the consummate trade publication for the working performer in America. The first issue was released on December 2, 1960, a sixteen page weekly selling for twenty-five cents, touting the promise to offer readers "a new, complete service weekly for the entertainment industry." *Back Stage* opened a West Coast office in 1975, with Eaker serving as liaison to the Los Angeles branch. Eventually, the paper expanded coverage to Chicago, New England, and Florida as television commercial production began to grow in those areas. *Back Stage* was sold to Billboard Publications, Inc. in 1986, but Eaker stayed on as consultant for another two and a half years, until June, 1989. He is survived by his wife of 55 years, Lee Eisenberg, son, Dean, daughter, Sherry Eaker (current editor in chief of *Back Stage*), a sister, and two grandchildren.

Mary Ellis (May Belle Elsas), 105, New York City-born actress, died in London on January 30, 2003. She made her Broadway debut in 1922 in *The Merchant of Venice*, followed by *Merry Wives of Gotham*, *Rose-Marie*, *The Dybbuk*, *The Romantic Young Lady*, *The Humble*, *The Crown Prince*, *The Taming of the Shrew*, *$12,000*, *Meet the Prince*, *Becky Sharp*, *Children of Darkness*, and *Jewelry Robbery*. She was a singer with the New York Metropolitan Opera with important roles such as Mityl in *The Blue Bird*. She could also be seen in such movies as *All the King's Horses*, *Paris in Spring*, *The Magic Box*, and *The 3 Worlds of Gulliver*, and after the 1930's, appeared in numerous theatrical and musical productions exclusively in England. No immediate survivors.

Sylvia Regan Ellstein (Sylvia Hoffenberg), 94, New York City-born actress/author, died January 18, 2003 in New York City. She made her Broadway debut as a performer in 1926 in *We Americans*, followed by *The Waltz of Dogs*. Broadway credits as a writer include *Poppa*, *Morning Star*, *Great to Be Alive!*, *The Fifth Season*, and *Zelda*. Survivors include three brothers.

Rolf Fjelde, 76, Brooklyn, New York-born translator/playwright/teacher, died September 10, 2002, in White Plains, New York. His fluent and authoritative translations of 12 major prose plays (including *A Doll's House* and *Hedda Gabler*), are regularly performed at theaters throughout the United States. His translation of *Peer Gynt* was staged successfully at C.S.C. Repertory Off-Broadway in 1981. A founding editor of *The Yale Poetry Review*, he taught drama at Pratt Institute for over 40 years, as well as having taught at the Julliard School. He was founding president of The Ibsen Society of America and editor of its newsletter. In 1991, he was awarded the Norwegian Royal Medal of St. Olaf. He is survived by his wife, Cristel, daughter, Michelle Andrea Fjelde-Burke, of Charlestown, Massachussets, two sons, Eric and Christopher, both of Hartsdale, New York, and two grandchildren.

Irving Foy, 94, actor, died April 20, 2003. The last surviving member of the *Seven Little Foys* vaudeville act which criss-crossed America from 1912 to 1928, he began performing by popping out of a large carpetbag carried onstage by his father, whom he would imitate, and would eventually tug offstage. Later in life he ran a series of movie theaters in Albuquerque, New Mexico, as well as a drive-in movie theater. The 1955 Bob Hope and James Cagney vehicle *The Seven Little Foys* was based on his and his brothers' vaudevillian life. Survivors include four sons and four grandchildren.

Betsy Friday, 44, Chapel Hill, North Carolina-born actress/director/producer/fundraiser, died July 16, 2002, in New York City from complications of a bone marrow transplant. She made her Broadway debut in 1980 in *Best Little Whorehouse in Texas*, followed by *Bring Back Birdie*, *The Secret Garden*, and *She Loves Me*. Off-Broadway credits include *I Ought to Be in Pictures*, *Smile*, and *Ace of Diamonds*. A dancer and the veteran of many television commercials, she also organized the concert group the Broadway Tenors, as well as directed at Actor's Repertory Co. in Washington, DC, the 40th anniversary gala at Lincoln Center, and other benefits. She was a fundraising consultant for the North Carolina School for the Arts, the University of North Carolina, Georgetown University, London's Almeida Theater Co., the Phyllis Newman Women's Health Initiative, Santa Clara University, North Carolina State University, and New York's Professional Children's School. She was president of a company that invested in and/or co-produced such Broadway shows as *Hamlet* starring Ralph Fiennes, and *How to Succeed in Business Without Really Trying* with Matthew Broderick, among others. Survivors include her parents, two sisters, a niece, and a nephew.

Keene Curtis

Ira Eaker

Cliff Gorman

Dolores Gray

Jack Gelber, 71, Chicago-born playwright, died May 9, 2003, in Manhattan, New York, of Waldenstrom's macroglobulinemia, a cancer of the blood. Best known for 1959's *The Connection*, performed at the Living Theater and which sent a shockwave through contemporary theater with its realism, it was eventually seen as innovative in style, substance, and language. *The Connection* won Obie Awards for best new play, best new production, and an award for one of its actors. It became the signature piece of the Living Theater, which was founded by Judith Malina and her husband, Julian Beck. Also a theater director and teacher, he penned more than 10 other plays, including *The Apple*, *Square in the Eye*, *The Cuban Thing* (which he directed on Broadway), *Sleep*, *Barbary Shore* (which he adapted from the Norman Mailer novel), and *Rehearsal*. Plays which he directed include *The Kitchen* by Arnold Wesker, *The Kid* by Robert Coover, *Seduced*, by Sam Shepard, and Fanz X. Kroetz's *Farmyard*. In 1964 his novel *On Ice* was published. He also taught at Columbia University, Brooklyn College, and in the Actors program at the New School University. He is survived by his wife, Carol, son, Jed, of Manhattan, New York, daughter, Amy, of Brooklyn, New York, and two brothers, Jules, of Scottsdale, Arizona, and David, of Austin, Texas.

Clark Gesner, 64, Augusta, Maine-born composer/lyricist, died July 23, 2002, in New York City of a heart attack, at the Princeton Club, of which he was a member. His *You're a Good Man, Charlie Brown* was the breakaway hit of 1967, opening at the 179 seat Theater 80 in the East Village, and going on to run for nearly 1,600 performances, spawned six national tours, and countless productions at high schools, colleges, and community theaters across the country. It also performed on Broadway in 1971, and was revived again in 1999. Other Broadway credits include *The Utter Glory of Morrissey Hall*, and performances in regional theatres including *1776*, *Lend Me a Tenor*, and *Carnival!* He also contributed songs to *The Jell-O is Always Red*, a revue performed by the York Theater Company in 1998. Survivors include his nieces, Amber Gesner, of Philadelphia, Pennsylvania, and Page Gesner, and a nephew, Eli Gesner.

William Glover, 91, New York City-born theatre critic, died December 21, 2002, in Manhattan, New York. Beginning in 1960, he reviewed theater for the Associated Press for18 years, covering Broadway, Off-Broadway, and theater in 28 states and 20 countries. When he retired in 1978, *Variety* reported that his reviews had appeared in 1,700 American newspapers. He began his career at the Asbury Press and was city editor for four years before joining The Associated Press. He was a former president of the New York Drama Critics Circle and was on the Tony Award nominating committee.

Cliff Gorman, 65, Queens, New York-born actor, died September 5, 2002, in Manhattan, New York, of leukemia. A Tony Award winner as best actor for his performance as Lenny Bruce in 1971's *Lenny*, other Broadway credits include *Chapter Two*, (Tony nomination) *Doubles*, and *Social Security*. He also son an Obie Award for his role in 1967's groundbreaking *Boys in the Band*, a role which he repeated in the 1970 film version. He was a veteran of many television and film roles, which include 1975's *Rosebud*, 1992's *Night and the City*, and *Ghost Dog: The Way of the Samurai*, in 1999. He is survived by his wife, Gayle.

Dolores Gray, 78, Chicago-born actress, died June 26, 2002, in Manhattan, New York, of a heart attack. She made her Broadway debut in 1944 in *Seven Lively Arts*, followed by *Are You With It?*, *Annie Get Your Gun*, *Two on the Aisle*, *Carnival in Flanders* (Tony Award, Best Actress in Musical), *Destry Rides Again*, *Sherry!*, *Jules Friends at the Palace*, and *42nd St.* Off-Broadway credits include *Money Talks* in 1990. She was the veteran of many films, including *Kismet* with Sebastian Cabot, *It's Always Fair Weather* with Gene Kelly, *The Opposite Sex* with June Allyson, and *Designing Woman* with Gregory Peck and Lauren Bacall, as well as many theatrical productions in England. Credited with keeping a crowd of 1,504 people calm while fire broke out in the Imperial Theater on May 28, 1959, she continued singing *Anyone Would Love You* louder and louder while stage hands fought the flames backstage. Survivors include a stepdaughter.

Adolph Green

James Gregory

Richard Harris

Wendy Hiller

Adolph Green, 87, Brooklyn, New York-born playwright and lyricist, died October 24, 2002, in Manhattan, New York, of natural causes. The dedication in the Volume 52, 1995–96 edition of *Theatre World* reads, "With boundless admiration, appreciation, and gratitude, this volume is dedicated to performers, playwrights, lyricists, and Broadway's longest-running collaborators: Betty Comden and Adolph Green. Their words have adorned numerous musicals, have been rewarded with many 'Tony' nominations, and are the recipients of several." The winner of five Tony Awards with his writing partner, Betty Comden, for *Wonderful Town*, *On the Twentieth Century* (one for book, one for lyrics), *Hallelujah, Baby!*, and *The Will Rogers Follies*, other Broadway credits to which he contributed either in whole or in part include *Billion Dollar Baby*, *Two on the Aisle*, *Peter Pan*, *Bells Are Ringing*, *Say, Darling*, *A Party with Betty Comden and Adolph Green*, *An Evening with Yves Montand*, *Do Re Mi*, *Subways are for Sleeping*, *Dylan*, *Fade Out-Fade In*, *Applause*, *Lorelei*, *The Madwoman of Central Park West*, *Singin' in the Rain*, *Barbara Cook: A Concert for the Theatre*, *Jerome Robbins' Broadway*, *A Doll's Life*, *Elaine Stritch at Liberty*, and *Barbara Cook's Broadway*, as well as many associated revivals. Beginning as writers and performers with The Revuers, which included Judy Holliday in their gigs at the Village Vanguard in 1939, his collaboration with Ms. Comden was the longest such partnership in the history of the theatre, totaling more than 60 years. Their screenplays include *The Barkleys of Broadway*, the 1958 classic *Singin' in the Rain*, as well as *Auntie Mame*, among many other films. In addition to the theatre, Comden and Green performed their material many times on television, film, and in nightclubs. Their many enduring classic songs include *Make Someone Happy*, *Just in Time*, *The Party's Over*, *Never Never Land*, and *New York, New York*. Survivors include his wife, actress Phyllis Newman, son, Adam, and daughter, Amanda, all of Manhattan, New York.

James Gregory, 90, Bronx, New York-born actor, died September 16, 2002, in Sedona, Arizona. Broadway credits include *Key Largo*, *The Man with Blond Hair*, *In Time to Come*, *Autumn Hill*, *Dream Girl*, *All My Sons*, *Death of a Salesman*, *Dinosaur Wharf*, *Collector's Item*, *Dead Pigeon*, *Fragile Fox*, and *The Desperate Hours*. Best known for his role as Inspector Luger on the television sitcom *Barney Miller*, he performed that role for eight years. His numerous film credits include *Clambake*, *Sons of Katie Elder*, and *The Manchurian Candidate* (1962). He is survived by his wife, Anne.

George Haimsohn, 77, St. Louis, Missouri-born writer/lyricist, died January 17, 2003, in New York City of a massive aneurysm. His 1968 Off-Broadway show *Dames at Sea* led to a Theatre World Award for actress Bernadette Peters and launched her career, as well as became a staple of community and regional theatres across the country. Other musicals include *Now, Zing!* and *Johnny American*, and he illustrated three books for college students, *The Portable Hamlet*, *The Bedside Faust*, and *Inside Romeo and Juliet*. He was also a lifelong resident of Greenwich Village, where he worked as a professional photographer calling himself Plato, as well as wrote ads, gay fiction, and limericks. He is survived by a sister, Dolores Fox, of Santa Clarita, California.

George Hall, 85, Toronto, Canada-born actor, died October 21, 2002, in Hawthorne, New York, following a stroke. He made his Broadway debut in 1946 in *Call Me Mister*, followed by *Lend and Ear*, *Touch and Go*, *The Boy Friend*, *There's a Girl in My Soup*, *An Evening With Richard Nixon and…*, *We Interrupt This Program…*, *Man and Superman*, *Bent*, *the Stitch in Time*, *Noises Off*, *A Moon for the Misbegotten*, *Wild Honey*, *Abe Lincoln in Illinois*, and *The Boys from Syracuse*. He was a graduate of the Neighborhood Playhouse and performed in vaudeville acts early in his career. He also performed in several films and on television. No immediate survivors.

Jonathan Harris (Jonathan Charasuchin), 87, Bronx, New York-born actor, died October 27, 2002, in Los Angeles of a blood clot. Broadway credits include *Heart of a City*, *A Flag is Born*, *The Madwoman of Chaillot*, *The Grass Harp*, *Hazel Flagg*, and *The Teahouse of the August Moon*. He appeared in 16 productions as a repertory member of the Millpond Playhouse in Roslyn, NY, and was the veteran of many television and film productions. He is best known for his role as Dr. Smith on the 1960's sitcom *Lost in Space*. Survivors include his wife of 64 years, Gertrude, son, Richard, two grandchildren, and two sisters, Rosalie and Allene.

Richard Harris, 72, Limerick, Ireland-born actor, died October 25, 2002, in London of lymphatic cancer. Appearing on Broadway and in a major national tour of *Camelot*, he will forever be remembered for his role as King Arthur in the film version of that musical. Other stage appearances include Arthur Miller's *A View from the Bridge* and Luigi Pirandello's *Man, Beast, and Virtue*, as well as many other productions in England. The veteran of over 70 films, among his most memorable are 1963's *This Sporting Life* (Academy Award nomination, Cannes Best Actor Award), *The Guns of Navarone*, *Mutiny on the Bounty*, *A Man Called Horse*, the first two *Harry Potter* films, *Hawaii*, *Unforgiven*, *The Molly Maguires*, and *The Field* (Academy Award, Golden Globe nominations). He also made several notable television appearances. Survivors include three sons from his first marriage to Elizabeth Rees-Williams, including the actor, Jared Harris.

James Hazeldine, 55, British-born actor, died December 17, 2002, in London of undisclosed causes. Broadway credits include 1985's *Strange Interlude* with Glenda Jackson, as well as 1999's *The Iceman Cometh*. A veteran of the Royal Shakespeare Company, he performed there as Troilus in *Troilus and Cressida*, as John Clare in Edward Bond's *Fool*, as well as the role of Alcibiades in *Timon of Athens*. He also appeared in several television and film roles.

Frankie Hewitt (Frankie Teague), 71, Oklahoma-born artistic director, died February 28, 2003, in Washington, D.C., of cancer. As founder and producing artistic director of the Ford's Theatre Society, she produced over 150 productions in 35 years, including the 1971 world premiere of *Don't Bother Me, I Can't Cope*, an eighteen month run of *Godspell* that opened in 1972, and other success included *Elmer Gantry*, *Your Arms Too Short to Box With God*, and two James Whitmore one-man shows, *Give 'Em Hell, Harry*, and *Will Rogers' USA*. She was also executive producer of over 15 network television shows broadcast from the theatre, and received the National Humanities Medal in 2002. Survivors include two daughters, several grandchildren, and a sister.

Wendy Hiller (Dame Wendy Hiller), 90, Bramhall, Cheshire, England-born stage, screen, and television actress, died May 14, 2003, at her home in Beaconsfield, England. Broadway credits include *Love on the Dole*, *The Heiress*, *A Moon for the Misbegotten* (Tony nomination), *Flowering Cherry*, and *The Aspern Papers*. She was hand chosen by George Bernard Shaw to star in his *St. Joan* as well as his *Pygmalion*, before he also selected her to star in the film of the latter as well as in *Major Barbara*. One of the most admired of all British actresses, she won an Academy Award for the 1958 film *Separate Tables*. She made her motion picture debut in 1937 in *Lancashire Luck*, followed by her Oscar-nominated performance in *Pygmalion*. Her other films include *Major Barbara*, *I Know Where I'm Going*, *Outcast of the Islands*, *Something of Value*, *How to Murder a Rich Uncle*, *Sons and Lovers*, *Toys in the Attic*, *A Man for All Seasons* (Oscar nomination), *Murder on the Orient Express*, *Voyage of the Damned*, *The Elephant Man*, *Making Love*, and *The Lonely Passion of Judith Hearne*. In 1975, Queen Elizabeth II named her a Dame of the British Empire. Survivors include her son and daughter, from her marriage to writer Ronald Gow (who died in 1993).

Al Hirschfeld (Albert Hirschfeld), 99, St. Louis, Missouri-born artist, died January 20, 2003, in New York City of heart failure. The dedication in the Volume 39, 1982–1983 edition of *Theatre World* reads, "To Albert Hirschfeld— who since 1925 has applied his genius, satirical wit and humor, and love of performers, to recording theatrical history with uniquely irreverent line drawings that are deservedly known as masterpieces." Unique unto himself, Hirschfeld's caricatures of Broadway stars numbered over 10,000, and became legendary, as did he, in a career that spanned more than 70 years and most productions of the twentieth century. He was best known for his caricatures which appeared in the drama pages of *The New York Times*, but his work appeared as well in *The New York Herald*, in books and in other publications, and is in the collections of many museums including the Metropolitan Museum of Art, the Museum of Modern Art, the Whitney Museum of Modern Art in New York, and in his hometown at the St. Louis Art Museum. Early in life he studied in New York at the Arts League and traveled to London and Paris to study painting, drawing, and sculpture, and his other artwork often incorporated his experiences in traveling throughout the South Pacific and Japan. His will most remembered for his portrayals of everyone from Charlie Chaplin to Nathan Lane, including those of Ray Bolger, Barbra Streisand, Woody Allen, Carol Channing, Ethel Merman, Liza Minelli, among scores of others. When his daughter, Nina, was born in 1945, he began incorporating her name multiple times into his drawings, which were hidden from obvious view. This became his signature, and was so effective that the military began using the drawings to train their bomber pilots to spot their targets. His published collections include 1970's *The World of Hirschfeld* and *The American Theatre as Seen by Hirschfeld*, and in 1951 he wrote and illustrated *Show Business is No Business*. He collaborated with humorist S.J. Perelman on *Westward Ha! Or, Around the World in 80 Clichés*, and with Ogden Nash and Vernon Duke on the short-lived musical *Sweet Bye and Bye*. Additional illustrations include those in *Harlem*, by William Saroyan, and *Treadmill to Oblivion*, by Fred Allen. In 1991 he received a tribute from the U.S. Postal Service, which for the first time put an artist's name on a booklet of stamps. He followed that in 1994 with stamps honoring silent film stars. He won a Special Tony Award in 1975 for having immortalized Broadway and its stars (one of two Special Tonys he received in his lifetime), and in 1984 he was the first recipient of the Brooks Atkinson Award. He was named a New York City Landmark in 1996 by the New York City Landmark Commission, and a 1996 documentary titled *The Line King* chronicled his life and career, and received an Academy Award nomination. He was the most celebrated artist in the theatre, and on what would have been his 100th birthday, June 21, 2003, Jujamcyn Theaters renamed the Martin Beck theatre in his honor. He posthumously received the National Medal of the Arts in 2003, and was also elected to the American Academy of Arts and Letters that same year. His wife of 52 years, Dolly Haas Hirschfeld, who also served as his social director and adviser, survives him, as does his daughter, Nina Hirschfeld, of Austin, Texas, grandson, Matthew, granddaughter, Margaret, both of Austin, Texas, and two stepsons, Jonathan Kerz of Larchmont, New Jersey, and Antony Kerz, of Rocky Hill, Connecticut.

Al Hirschfeld

Joy Hodges

Kim Hunter

Adele Jergens

Joy Hodges, 88, Des Moines, Iowa-born actress/singer, died January 19, 2003, in Palm Desert, California. Responsible for helping Ronald Reagan get a contract with Warner Brothers, her Broadway credits include *I'd Rather Be Right*, *The Odds on Mrs. Oakley*, *Nellie Bly*, and *No, No, Nanette*. The veteran of more than a dozen films, she was also a vocalist and singer, appearing with well-known figures such as Ozzie Nelson, and the Glenn Miller Orchestra during World War II.

Richard Horner, 82, Portland, Oregon-born producer, died December 28, 2002, in Palm Springs, California. In more than 50 years as a producer, company manager, and consultant, he worked on more than 150 Broadway and Off-Broadway productions, receiving six Tony Award nominations. He founded and co-owned the Coronet Theater Corp. in the 1960's and 70's with Lester Osterman, presiding over several Broadway houses, including the 46th Street Theater (now the Richard Rodgers), the Helen Hayes, and the Morosco Theatres, the latter two of which were razed in the early 1980's to create the Marriot Marquis Hotel. Broadway credits include *The Curious Savage* (stage manager), *The Dark is Light Enough*, *Damn Yankees*, *Debut*, *Blue Denim*, *Goldilocks*, *The Nervous Set*, *Tenderloin*, *Show Girl*, *How to Succeed in Business Without Really Trying*, *New Faces of 1962*, *The Aspern Papers*, *A Funny Thing Happened on the Way to the Forum*, *High Spirits*, *Do I Hear a Waltz?*, *The Yearling*, *It's a Bird…It's a Plane…It's Superman*, *I Do! I Do!*, *Forty Carats*, *Hadrian VII*, *1776*, *Borstal Boy*, *The Rothschilds*, *Hay Fever*, *Home*, *No, No, Nanette*, *And Miss Reardon Drinks a Little*, *Butley*, *The Changing Room*, *The Women*, *Crown Matrimonial*, The *Moon for the Misbegotten*, *Will Rogers' U.S.A.*, *Equus*, *Sizwe Banzi is Dead*, *The Island*, *Rodgers and Hart*, *The Norman Conquests*, *The Royal Family*, *Rockabye Hamlet*, *Let My People Come*, *The Innocents*, *The Eccentricities of a Nightingale*, *Something Old, Something New*, *A Party With Betty Comden and Adolph Green*, *The Shadow Box*, *Bully*, *Da*, *The Crucifer of Blood*, *Once a Catholic*, *The Lady from Dubuque*, *Harold and Maude*, *Mister Lincoln*, *Happy New Year*, *Passione*, *A Life*, *Othello*, *Do Black Patent Leather Shoes Really Reflect Up?*, *Ghosts*, *The Man Who Had Three Arms*, *The Flying Karamasov Brothers*, and *Doubles*. During the 1980's he served as an executive producer of the Jones Beach Marine Theatre. He is survived by his wife, former actress Lynne Stuart, two sons and two daughters, a sister, and three grandchildren.

Kim Hunter (Janet Cole), 79, Detroit, Michigan-born actress, died September 11, 2002, in New York City of a heart attack. Best known for her Broadway and screen portrayal of Stella in *A Streetcar Named Desire*, the latter of which earned her an Academy Award as best supporting actress, her other Broadway credits include *Darkness at Noon*, *The Chase*, *The Children's Hour*, *The Tender Trap*, *Write Me a Murder*, *Weekend*, *The Penny Wars*, *The Women*, *To Grandmother's House We Go*, and *An Ideal Husband*. Off-Broadway credits include *Come Slowly Eden*, *All is Bright*, *Cherry Orchard*, *When We Dead Awaken*, *Territorial Rites*, *Faulkner's Bicycle*, *Man and Superman*, *Murder of Crows*, *Eye of the Beholder*, *The Visit*, *Driving Miss Daisy*, and *The Madwoman of Chaillot*. Beginning her career in regional theatre at such venues as the Pasadena Playhouse, she survived being blacklisted in the 1950's after *Streetcar* and returned to appear in several *Planet of the Apes* movies as Dr. Zira, and made numerous television performances, for which she received two Emmy nominations. Other film credits include *Tender Comrade* with Ginger Rogers, *Deadline, U.S.A.* with Humphrey Bogart, *Anything Can Happen* with José Ferrer, *Storm Center* with Bette Davis, *The Young Stranger*, *Bermuda Affair*, and *Money, Women, and Guns*. She is survived by her daughter, Kathryn Emmett, of Stamford, Connecticut, and Sean Robert Emmett, also of Stamford, Connecticut, and six grandchildren. Her husband, actor Robert Emmett, died in 2000.

Eddie Jaffe (Edward Jaffe), 89, Duluth, Minnesota-born press agent, died March 25, 2003, in Bronx, New York, following a long illness. Beginning his career as a columnist for *The New York Telegram*, he eventually went into publicity work, working first with vaudeville and burlesque acts, and later in theatre, television, film and sports. His clients included Margie Hart, Jackie Gleason, Victor Borge, Marlene Dietrich, Joe Namath, the Shah of Iran, John Wayne, Martha Mitchell, and Claus von Bulow, along with movie studios, television networks, large corporations, and government agencies. He is survived by his daughter, Jordan Jaffe, of Alexandria, Virginia.

Adele Jergens, 84, Brooklyn, New York-born model/actress, died November 22, 2002, in Camarillo, California. Broadway credits include *Leave It to Me!*, *DuBarry Was a Lady*, *Banjo Eyes*, and *Star and Garter*. Beginning her career as a model, she also worked as a Rockette before appearing in such films as *The Day the World Ended*, *A Thousand and One Nights*, *Armored Car Robbery*, *The Treasure of Monte Cristo*, and *The Big Chase*. Her husband of forty-two years, actor Glenn Langan, died in 1991. No immediate survivors.

Michael Jeter

Susan Johnson

Vinnie Liff

Rusty Magee

Michael Jeter, 50, Lawrenceburg, Tennessee-born actor, died May 30, 2003, in Los Angeles of natural causes. He made his Broadway debut in 1978 in *Once in a Lifetime*, and won a Theatre World Award for his performance in *G. R. Point*. In 1990, he received the Tony, Outer Critics, and Drama Desk Awards, as well as the Clarence Derwent Prize for his role as a dying clerk who visits Berlin for one last fling in *Grand Hotel*. Off-Broadway credits include Caryl Churchill's *Cloud 9*, *Greater Tuna*, and *The Master and Margarita*. He also spent a year as a guest artist at Arena Stage in Washington, D.C. He was a regular on the television program *Sesame Street* since 2000, and won a 1992 Emmy Award as best supporting actor for his role as football coach Herman Stiles opposite Burt Reynolds on the sitcom *Evening Shade*. He was nominated for the Emmy twice more for his work on that program, as well as two more times for his guest roles on *Picket Fences* and *Chicago Hope*. He compiled a long list of film appearances, including roles in *Hair*, *Ragtime*, *The Money Pit*, *Tango & Cash*, *Miller's Crossing*, *The Fisher King*, *Waterworld*, *Air Bud*, *Patch Adams*, *Mouse Hunt*, *The Green Mile*, and *Welcome to Collinwood*. He is survived by his life partner, Sean Blue, his parents, Dr. William and Virginia Jeter of Lawrenceburg, Tennessee, brother, William K. Jeter, and four sisters, Virginia Anne Barham, Amanda Parsons, Emily Jeter, and Larie Wicker.

Susan Johnson (Marilyn Jean Johnson), 75, Columbus, Ohio-born actress, died February 24, 2003, in Carmichael, California, of emphysema and congestive heart failure. A Theatre World Award winner for her role in 1956's *The Most Happy Fella*, other Broadway credits include *Carnival of Flanders*, *Carefree Heart*, *Brigadoon*, *Buttrio Square*, *Oh, Captain!*, *Whoop-Up*, and *Donnybrook!* A former chorus girl at Radio City Music Hall, she also appeared in regional theatres as well as on several audio recordings. She is survived by her daughter, Corianne Dann, and three granddaughters.

Jean Kerr (Jean Collins Kerr), 80, Scranton, Pennsylvania-born playwright/author, died January 5, 2003, in White Plains, New York, of pneumonia. Along with her husband, drama critic Walter Kerr, Broadway credits include *Song of Bernadette*, *Touch and Go*, *King of Hearts* (with Eleanor Brooke and directed by Walter Kerr), and *Goldilocks*. Her solo credits include *Jenny Kissed Me*, *Mary, Mary* (which became one of the longest running productions of the 1960's with over 1,500 performances), *Poor Richard*, *Finishing Touches*, *Lunch Hour*, and contributions to *John Murray Anderson's Almanac*. She was also the author of the novels *Please Don't Eat the Daisies*, which was adapted into a film and a television sitcom, *The Snake Has All the Lines*, *Penny Candy*, as well as *How I Got to Be Perfect*, a collection of humorous essays. Survivors include sons Colin of Port Jefferson, NY, John of Portland, Maine, Gregory of Coopersburg, Pennsylvania, and Gilbert of Ponte Vedra Beach, Florida, daughter Kitty of Arlington, Massachusetts, brothers Hugh Collins of Meriden, Connecticut, and Frank Collins of Ardmore, Pennsylvania, and eleven grandchildren. Her husband, Walter Kerr, died in 1996, and the former Ritz Theater on Broadway is named in his honor.

Frederick Knott, 86, Hankow, China-born playwright, died December 17, 2002, at his home in Manhattan, New York. The author of a total of three plays—*Write Me a Murder*, *Dial M for Murder*, and *Wait Until Dark*—the latter two of which were made into successful films, he is survived by his wife, Ann Hilary Knott, a son, Dr. Anthony Frederick Knott, of Kayenta, Arizona, and two grandsons.

Marvin A. Krauss, 74, Bronx, New York-born general manager of nearly 100 Broadway shows, died October 22, 2002, in New York City of a bacterial infection. Beginning his career as a production stage manager, his numerous Broadway credits in that capacity include *A Story for a Sunday Evening*, *Christophe Columb*, *Volpone*, *Le Misanthrope*, *Les Nuits de la Colere/Feu la Mere de Madame*, *Intermezzo*, *Le Chien du Jardinier/Les Adieux*. Broadway credits as a general manager include *The Happiest Girl in the World*, *Sherry!*, *Butterflies Are Free*, *Minnie's Boys*, *Gypsy*, *Summer Brave*, *The Magic Show*, *Children! Children!*, *Something's Afoot*, *An Evening with Diana Ross*, *Godspell*, *Bing Crosby on Broadway*, *American Buffalo*, *Beatlemania*, *The Merchant*, *Dancin'*, *King of Hearts*, *Platinum*, *The Goodbye People*, *Up in One*, *King Richard III*, *The Madwoman of Central Park West*, *Gilda Radner: Live from New York*, *Bette! Divine Madness*, *Teibele and Her Demon*, *Frankenstein*, *Broadway Follies*, *Woman of the Year*, *Can-Can*, *Wally's Café*, *Dreamgirls*, *Little Johnny Jones*, *Seven Brides for Seven Brothers*, *The Poison Tree*, *Rock and Roll! The First 5,000 Years*, *Merlin*, *Aznavour*, *Dreamgirls*, *La Cage aux Folles*, *The Rink*, *Rags*, *Mort Sahl on Broadway!*, *Don't Get God Started*, *Rodney Dangerfield on Broadway!*, *Oba Oba*, *Romance/Romance*, *Legs Diamond*, *Dangerous Games*, *Grand Hotel*, *Peter Pan*, *The Will Rogers Follies*, *Moscow Circus: Cirk Valentin*, *Private Lives*, *Camelot*, *The Twilight of the Golds*, *Any Given Day*, *Passion*, *A Tuna Christmas*, *Comedy Tonight*, *Indiscretions*, *Patti Lupone on Broadway*, *Sacrilege*, *Getting Away With Murder*, *Taking Sides*, *Annie*, *Steel Pier*, *The Life*, *The Herbal Bed*, and *The Ride Down Mt. Morgan*. He also managed concerts and events featuring celebrities including Frank Sinatra, Liza Minnelli, and Count Basie. Survivors include his wife, Elaine, daughters Robin Plevener, Anne Krauss, of Amherst, Massachusetts, and Nina Krauss Herter, of Forest Hills, Queens, New York, aunt, Irene Gold, of Manhattan, and a brother, Richard Krauss, of Manhattan.

Louis Larusso II, 67, Hoboken, New Jersey-born playwright, died February 22, 2003, in Jersey City, New Jersey, of bladder cancer. The author of scores of plays, his Broadway credits include *Lamppost Reunion* (Tony and Drama Desk nominations), *Wheelbarrow Closers*, and *Knockout*. Off-Broadway credits include *Marlon Brando Sat Right Here* and *Sweatshop*. Other credits include *Vespers Eve* (DramaLogue Award), *Stooplife*, and *Sea Mother's Son*. He worked on the books of several musicals, including *Dreamgirls*, *Platinum*, and *Broadway Babies*, and contributed to the screenplay of *Saturday Night Fever* as well as completed 14 commissioned screenplays of his own. His honors include the Jean Dalrymple Lifetime Achievement Award as well as a caricature residing on a wall at Sardi's. Survivors include a son, Louis III.

Florence Lessing, 86, actress/dancer, died September 5, 2002, in Manhattan, New York, of kidney failure. Beginning her career as a part of a trio including Jack Cole and Anna Austin performing at the Rainbow Room, she then appeared in many concert stage productions choreographed by contemporaries like Doris Humphrey. She also choreographed much of her own work, and founded the New York Academy of Ballet, which operated from 1960 to 1991. Broadway credits include *Windy City*, *Kismet*, and *Sailor Beware*, and she also appeared in several movie musicals, including *Moon Over Miami* with Betty Grable and *Just for You* starring Bing Crosby and Jane Wyman. Survivors include her husband, Tito Enrique Canepa, son Eric Canepa, and daughter, Dr. Cathy Canepa of White Plains, New York.

Robert P. Lieb, 88, Pelham, New York-born actor, died September 28, 2002, from complications of intestinal surgery. Broadway credits include *Mr. And Mrs. North*, *Harvey*, *O'Daniel*, *Two Blind Mice*, and *Inherit the Wind*. His numerous appearances on television and film include roles in *The Graduate*, *Myra Breckenridge*, and *The Parallax View*. Survivors include his wife of 56 years, Ina, three daughters, and two grandsons.

Vincent "Vinnie" Liff, 52, casting director, died February 25, 2003, in New York City of brain cancer. Along with his business partner Geoffrey Johnson in the New York office of Johnson-Liff, he was one of the most respected, productive, and prestigious theatrical casting directors during the last 30 years. His first Broadway credit came in 1975 with *The Wiz*, followed by such productions as *Ain't Misbehavin'*, *Dreamgirls*, *Night and Day*, *Indiscretions*, *Morning's at Seven*, *Cats*, *Les Misérables*, *The Phantom of the Opera*, *Miss Saigon*, *Dreamgirls*, *The Elephant Man*, *Equus*, *Amadeus*, *The Dresser*, *Contact*, and *The Producers*. He was also a mentor to many aspiring producers, casting directors, and actors early in their careers, from Scott Rudin to Tara Rubin, to Gary Beach and Peter Gallagher. Survivors include his partner, Ken Yung, father, George, of Fort Lauderdale, Florida, brother, Stephen, of Jamaica Plains, Massachusetts, sister, Martha Liff-Smith, of Londonderry, New Hampshire, and an uncle, Samuel (Biff) Liff, an agent at the William Morris Agency.

James Luisi, 73, New York City-born actor, died June 7, 2002, in Los Angeles of cancer. Broadway credits include *Alfie*, *Do I Hear a Waltz?*, *Sweet Charity*, *Soldiers*, and *Zorba*. An Emmy Award winner for the role of George Washington in the *First Ladies' Diaries: Martha Washington* on television, he is best known for his work in that medium. He returned to the stage later in life, winning the Valley Theater League Award for best director of a new play for his work in the San Fernando Valley section of Los Angeles, California. He is survived by his wife of 41 years, the former Georgia Phillips, daughter, Jamie Swartz of Los Angeles, California, brother, Jerry Luisi, of Dallas, Texas, and two grandchildren.

Edith Lutyens (Edith Lutyens Bel Geddes), 95, Brussels, Belgium-born costume designer, died August 16, 2002, in Hudson, New York. From her New York costume shop, she helped create costumes for several Ballet Theater productions, among them Antony Tudor's *Dim Luster*, and Jerome Robbins's *Fancy Free*. A producer of the 1947 Broadway production of Gian Carlo Menotti's *Medium* and *Telephone*, she was also associated with Cheryl Crawford and Eva Le Galliene and the American Repertory Theatre. Her Broadway costume design credits include *As You Like It*, *Two on the Aisle*, *The Shrike*, *The Grass Harp*, *The Crucible*, *A Girl Can Tell*, *Wedding Breakfast*, *Do You Know the Milky Way?*, *Giants, Sons of Giants*, *A Gift of Time*, *Dear Me, The Sky is Falling*, *Too True to Be Good*, *Bicycle Ride to Nevada*, and *The Deputy*. No immediate survivors.

Rusty Magee (Benjamin Rush Magee), 47, Washington-born composer/actor/lyricist, died February 16, 2003, in Manhattan, New York, of colon cancer. A 1993 New York Outer Critics Circle Award winner for the music and lyrics for an adaptation of Molière's *Scapin*, he also appeared as a comedian and entertainer at venues such as the West Bank Café. He was the music director of Manhattan's Irish Repertory Theater, and was associated with Moonwork, a downtown troupe known for its spirited adaptations of the classics. He composed music for *The Green Heart*, presented at the Manhattan Theater Club in 1996, and for *Flurry Tale*, the children's Christmas opera performed in 1999 by American Opera Projects at Lincoln Center. He wrote the music for the Moonwork production of *What You Will*, an adaptation of Shakespeare's *Twelfth Night*, as well as for Moonwork's farcical reworking of *A Midsummer Night's Dream* in 1999. He created the score for Frank McCourt's history in song, *The Irish…and How They Got That Way*, and arranged music for *The House of Blue Leaves* on Broadway in 1986. His first musical, *1919: A Baseball Opera*, was produced at Yale Repertory, where he worked for three years as a music consultant early in his career. Survivors include his wife, the actress Alison Fraser, son, Nathaniel, mother, Bettie Morris Magee of Natick, Massachusetts, and two brothers, Kenneth, of Portland, Oregon, and James, of Natick, Massachusetts.

Tom Mallow, 71, Carlsbad, New Mexico-born producer, died June 6, 2002, in Deerfield, Florida, of complications of Alzheimer's disease. Beginning in the 1960's, Mr. Mallow produced more than 60 Broadway shows on the "bus and truck" circuit-touring productions that crisscross the country, stopping in small cities and towns. Road shows which he produced include *Hello, Dolly!*, *Sweeney Todd*, *Cabaret*, *A Chorus Line*, and *La Cage aux Folles*. His Broadway production credits include *No Sex Please, We're British* in 1973, and he was co-producer with the Shubert Organization of the Broadway revivals and touring productions of *Your Arms Too Short to Box With God* in 1980 and *The Wiz* in 1984. American Theater Productions, his production company founded with partner James Janek, was innovative in expanding the territory of the touring circuit, incorporating previously unsaturated markets in states such as North Dakota, Kentucky, and Florida. Highly respected within the industry for its professionalism, American Theater Productions eventually included a transportation company to give them greater control of movement of production materials across the country. Survivors include his wife, Jan, daughters Catherine, of Niwot, Colorado, Pamela, of Ho Ho Kus, New Jersey, and Jill, of Boca Raton, Florida, seven grandchildren, and sister, Virginia Ann Close, of Denver, Colorado.

Anne Burr McDermott, 84, died February 1, 2003, in Old Lyme, Connecticut. Broadway credits include Orson Welles's staging of *Native Son*, followed by *Plan M*, *Dark Eyes*, *Lovers and Friends*, *While the Sun Shines*, *The Hasty Heart*, *O'Daniel*, *Detective Story*, *The Gambler*, and *Mert & Phil*. She also appeared in many radio and television roles. She is survived by her daughter, Maggie McDermott-Walsh, of Bernardsville, New Jersey, two sons, Burr, of Boston, Massachusetts, and Michael, of Beijing, China, as well as five grandchildren.

Tanya Moiseiwitsch, 88, London-born set and stage designer, died February 18, 2003, in London. Founding designer of the Stratford Festival, she also designed its Festival Theater Stage, which became a model for other thrust stages in North America and Britain. She worked at the Westminster Theater, the Royal Academy of Dramatic Art, the Abbey Theater in Dublin, and the Duchess Theater on the West End, before her first collaboration with the Stratford Festival's artistic director, Tyrone Guthrie, at the Old Vic, in 1945. She created variations of her thrust stage for the Crucible Theater in England, as well as for the Guthrie Theater in Minneapolis, Minnesota, where she served as principal designer for the first twelve productions. Her designs also influenced the stages of the Vivian Beaumont Theater in Lincoln Center, the Olivier Theater at the National Theater in London, and the Swan Theater at Stratford-Upon-Avon in England, among others. She was also on occasion the simultaneous designer of stage sets and costumes, including those for more than 40 productions at the Stratford Festival. Her designs also include those for television, including the BBC. In 1976 she was honored by Queen Elizabeth II with the title commander of the British Empire, and at the time of her death she was an associate director laureate at the Stratford Festival. She is survived by a brother and a stepsister.

Karen Morley (Mildred Linton), 93, Ottumwa, Iowa-born actress, died March 8, 2003, in Woodland Hills, California, of pneumonia. Her Broadway credits include *The Walrus and the Carpenter*, *Hedda Gabler*, and *Little Darling*. Off-Broadway credits include *The Banker's Daughter*. Her many appearances in film include *Mata Hari* with Greta Garbo, *Arsene Lupin* with John Barrymore, and *Dinner at Eight* with Jean Harlow, as well as films with Lionel Barrymore, Wallace Beery and Boris Karloff. Her refusing to name names at a Congressional hearing into her possible involvement with the Communist Party effectively ended her career in that medium. Survivors include two grandsons, a granddaughter, a great-grandson, and a great-granddaughter.

Wesley Naylor, 44, Hattiesburg, Mississippi-born composer, died August 25, 2002, in Brooklyn, New York, of undisclosed causes. Serving for 25 years as director of the historic Bethany Baptist Church in the Bedford-Stuyvesant section of Brooklyn, New York, he was the musical director for *Mama, I Want to Sing*, adding his own compositions to the existing score, the result of which became one of the longest running Off-Broadway shows in history, with 2,213 performances. Off-Broadway credits also include *Mama, I Want to Sing II*, and *Born to Sing!* He also played and arranged gospel music for gospel greats such as Shirley Caesar, Cee Cee Winans, and Aretha Franklin. Survivors include his brother, Wendell, of Memphis, Tennessee, mother, Nareatha Woullard Naylor, of Jackson, Mississippi, father, Walter Jerome Naylor, of Hattiesburg, Mississippi, sister, Frances Johnson, of Jackson, Mississippi, and two other brothers, Walley Naylor, of Madison, Mississippi, and Rashad Naylor, of New York, New York.

Duncan Noble (Duncan McGillvary), 80, Vancouver, British Columbia-born dancer/teacher, died August 5, 2002, in Winston-Salem, North Carolina. Broadway credits include *Something for the Boys*, *One Touch of Venus*, *On the Town*, and *Annie Get Your Gun*. Also a dancer with Ballet Theater (as American Ballet Theater was then known), he was also a member of the Ballet Russe do Monte Carlo and Valerie Bettis's modern dance group. He partnered with Bettis in several of her productions, including 1948's *As I Lay Dying*. He choreographed and directed for several theater groups, including the Pittsburgh Playhouse and the Papermill Playhouse in New Jersey. He joined the faculty of the North Carolina School for the Arts in 1965, working there at least part-time until just before his death, and was a guest teacher for Netherlands Dance Theater, the Basel Ballet, the Hungarian State Ballet of Budapest, and the Alberta Ballet, among others. He was also an on-site visitor for the National Endowment of the Arts. In 1982 he directed *Jazz Is*, a touring production originating at the North Carolina School of the Arts which traced the history of jazz. No immediate survivors.

Sherle North (Gladynne Sherle Treihart), 85, Newark, New Jersey-born dancer/actress, died August 14, 2002, in Los Angeles of pulmonary complications. Broadway credits include *Tis of Thee*, *If the Shoe Fits*, *You Can't Sleep Here*, and *What Killed Vaudeville*. She also made several film appearances, and worked in vaudeville and kiddie burlesque shows early in her career. Survivors include her son, Steven, daughter, Elissa, granddaughter, Olivia, and longtime companion, painter John Kalamaras.

Lore Noto, 79, Brooklyn, New York-born actor/producer, died July 8, 2002, in Forest Hills, New York, following a long battle with cancer. He made his Off-Broadway debut as an actor in 1940 in *The Master Builder*, followed by *Chee Chee*, *Time Predicted*, *Bomb Shelter*, *Armor of Light*, *Truce of the Bear*, *Shake Hands with the Devil*, and *The Fantasticks* (continuously from 1972 to 1990). As *The Fantasticks*' producer, he brought the show to the Sullivan Playhouse on May 3, 1960, where, with over 17,162 performances, it eventually became the longest running musical in history and garnered both an Obie Award and Special Tony Award. Survivors include his wife of 55 years, Mary, three sons, Thad, of Gary, Tennessee, Anthony, of Manhattan, Jody, of Vancouver, Washington, daughter Janice, of Ossining, New York, and seven grandchildren.

Vera Dunn O'Connor, 89, actress, died July 11, 2002, in Fort Lauderdale, Florida. Performing in her youth with vaudevillian parents, she appeared early on in George M. Cohan's *Zander the Great*, followed by Broadway credits including *Lieber Augustin*, *Stolen Fruit*, and *Anything Goes*. She also appeared in *Leave It to Me* with Mary Martin and Sophie Tucker, as well as in the1920's and 1930's with vaudeville dancers Benny Davis and Georgie Jessel. She is survived by a son and grandson.

Phil Oesterman, 64, director/producer, died July 30, 2002, in Fort Myers, Florida, of heart failure. An early mentor for Tommy Tune, he was associate director of *My One and Only*, *The Will Rogers Follies*, and *The Best Little Whorehouse Goes Public*, as well as associate producer of *Tommy Tune Tonight!*, all Tune projects. In addition, Broadway credits include *Let My People Come*, as well as *Urban Cowboy*, which he was directing on route to Broadway at the time of his death. He also directed Yoko Ono's *New York Rock* Off-Broadway. He is survived by life partner Nakies Constantinou.

Jason Opsahl, 39, Savannah, Georgia-born actor/singer, died October 25, 2002, of cardiac arrest, following a long battle with brain cancer. Broadway credits include *The Will Rogers Follies*, *Grease*, *Once Upon a Mattress*, *The Full Monty*, and the special benefit performance of *Dreamgirls*. He was also the veteran of many regional theatre and major theme park productions. Active in fundraising for Broadway Cares/Equity Fights AIDS (BC/EFA), he worked on all 12 *Broadway Bares* strip show fundraising events for that organization.

Felice Orlandi, 78, Italy-born actor, died May 21, 2003, in Studio City, California, of lung cancer. Beginning his career at Circle in the Square under the direction of José Quintero, he made his Broadway debut in *Romeo and Juliet*, followed by *The Girl on the Via Flaminia*, *All in One*, *Brigadoon*, and *Diamond Orchid*. Other credits include *27 Wagons Full of Cotton* opposite Maureen Stapleton, which also featured actress Alice Ghostley, to whom he was married for 52 years. He also appeared in numerous television programs and roles in film including *Never Love a Stranger*, *Bullitt*, *They Shoot Horses, Don't They?*, *Another 48 Hours*, and *Catch-22*. Survivors include his wife, Ms. Ghostley.

Lester Osterman, 88, Brooklyn, New York-born producer/theatre owner, died January 28, 2003, in Norwalk, Connecticut. A three-time Tony Award winner for his productions of *A Moon for the Misbegotten*, *Da*, and *The Shadow Box*, other Broadway credits either alone or with longtime producing partner Richard Horner include *Mr. Wonderful*, *Candide*, *Miss Lonelyhearts*, *Say, Darling*, *The Great God Brown*, *A Loss of Roses*, *The Cool World*, *Tenderloin*, *Face of a Hero*, *Show Girl*, *How to Succeed in Business Without Really Trying*, *Isle of Children*, *A Funny Thing Happened on the Way to the Forum*, *High Spirits*, *Fade Out-Fade In*, *Something More*, *Do I Hear a Waltz?*, *The Yearling*, *It's a Bird…It's a Plane…It's Superman*, *Dinner at Eight*, *I Do! I Do!*, *Weekend*, *Forty Carats*, *Hadrian VII*, *1776*, *The Rothschilds*, *Hay Fever*, *Home*, *No, No, Nanette!*, *And Miss Reardon Drinks a Little*, *Butley*, *The Changing Room*, *The Women*, *Crown Matrimonial*, *Will Rogers' USA*, *Sizwe Banzi Is Dead*, *The Island*, *Rodgers and Hart*, *Chicago*, *The Norman Conquests*, *The Royal Family*, *Rockabye Hamlet*, *Let My People Come*, *The Innocents*, *The Eccentricities of a Nightingale*, *Something Old, Something New*, *The Shadow Box*, *Da*, *The Crucifer of Blood*, *Knockout*, *Once a Catholic*, *Strider*, *Watch on the Rhine*, *The Lady from Dubuque*, *Mister Lincoln*, *Happy New Year*, *Charlie and Algernon*, *Passione*, *A Life*, *Perfectly Frank*, *The Five O'Clock Girl*, *The Survivor*, *The Moony Shapiro Songbook*, *I Won't Dance*, and *Execution of Justice*. At one point his company owned largest number of theatres of the so-called "independent owners," including the Eugene O'Neill, the 46th St. (now Richard Rodgers), and the Alvin theatres. He also managed the Helen Hayes and Morosco theatres until their demolition to make way for the Marriot Marquis Hotel on Times Square. In addition to his New York theatrical ventures, he produced several television programs and London theatrical productions, and at one time was in partnership with composer Jule Styne in a company called On Stage Productions. He is survived by his wife of 66 years, Marjorie K. Osterman, of Southport, Connecticut, daughter, Patricia Thackeray, of Manhattan, six grandchildren, and two great-grandchildren.

William Packard, 69, playwright/teacher/poet, died November 3, 2002, in New York City of natural causes. In a career that spanned nearly 50 years, his plays include *The Killer Thing, The Funeral, The Marriage,* and *War Play,* along with three collections of one-act plays, *Psychotherapy of Everyday Life, Threesome,* and *Behind the Eyes.* He was the author of the textbooks *The Art of the Playwright* and *The Art of Screenwriting,* published six volumes of poetry, and was the founder in 1969 of the *New York Quarterly,* the highly respected and influential poetry magazine. He was a past vice-president of the Poetry Society of America, co-director of the Hofstra Writers Conference for seven years, awarded with a Frost Fellowship in 1957, and was honored in 1980 with a reception at the White House for distinguished American poets. No immediate survivors.

Irving Phillips, 83, Newark, New Jersey-born stagehand/propmaster, died November 2, 2002, in New York City of renal failure brought on by congestive heart failure. In a career which spanned over 40 years, Broadway credits include *Man of La Mancha* starring Richard Kiley, *Death of a Salesman* starring Dustin Hoffman, *Sly Fox* starring George C. Scott, and *That Championship Season* starring Charles Durning, as well as the musical *Jennie,* starring Mary Martin. He worked on the television program *Sesame Street* from its first airing and for the next 19 years, and early in his career built sets for NBC and ABC.

Robert Randolph, 76, Centerville, Iowa-born set designer, died March 2, 2003, in Palm Springs, California, of heart failure. A Tony nominee for his scenic designs of *Bye Bye Birdie, Sweet Charity, Anya, Skyscraper, Golden Rainbow, Applause,* and *Porgy and Bess,* his many other Broadway design credits include *The Saint of Bleecker Street* (scenic/costume design), *The Desperate Hours* (costume design), *Small War on Murray Hill* (asst. to Aronson), *Ziegfeld Follies of 1957* (asst. to Dubois), *Heartbreak House* (asst. to Ben Edwards), *The Wall* (asst. to Mr. Bay), *Tenderloin* (asst. to Mr. Beaton), *How to Succeed in Business Without Really Trying* (scenic/lighting design), *Bravo Giovanni* (scenic/lighting design), *Calculated Risk* (scenic design), *Little Me* (scenic/lighting design), *Sophie* (scenic/lighting design), *Foxy* (scenic/lighting design), *Any Wednesday, Funny Girl* (scenic/lighting design), *Something More!* (scenic/lighting design), *Minor Miracle, Xmas in Las Vegas* (scenic/lighting design), *It's a Bird...It's a Plane...It's Superman!* (scenic/lighting design), *Walking Happy* (scenic/lighting design), *Sherry!* (scenic/lighting design), *Henry, Sweet Henry* (scenic/lighting design), *How to Be a Jewish Mother, Golden Rainbow* (scenic/lighting design), *A Teaspoon Every Four Hours* (scenic/lighting design), *Angela* (scenic/lighting design), *Ari* (scenic design), *70 Girls 70* (scenic/lighting design), *No Hard Feelings* (scenic/lighting design), *Good Feelings* (scenic design), *Words & Music* (scenic design), *Gypsy* (scenic/lighting design), *We Interrupt This Program...* (scenic design), *The Norman Conquests* (scenic/lighting design), *Little Johnny Jones* (scenic design), *Seven Brides for Seven Brothers* (scenic design), *Parade of Stars Playing the Palace.* During the 1964–1965 season, he had 11 shows running on Broadway, and in the 1970's he became bi-coastal, becoming set designer for Edwin Lester at L.A. Civic Light Opera and San Francisco Light Opera. His credits also include several Tony broadcasts, Liza Minelli's first television special, *Liza with a Z,* and 1985's *Night of 100 Stars.* Survivors include his life partner, Charles Guthrie, and a niece, Susan Luke, of Urbandale, Iowa.

Claibe Richardson, mid-70s, Louisiana-born composer, died January 5, 2003, in New York City of cancer. Broadway credits to which he contributed scores and/or incidental music include *The Grass Harp, The Royal Family, The Philadelphia Story,* and *The Curse of an Aching Heart.*

Mel Rodnon, 74, Iowa-born performer/musical contractor/coordinator/consultant/supervisor, died January 1, 2003. Broadway credits as either a musical contractor, supervisor, consultant, coordinator, or performer include *The Rothschilds, Jesus Christ Superstar, Pippin, Anthony Newley/Henry Mancini, Chicago, The Mikado, The Pirates of Penzance, H.M.S. Pinafore, Porgy and Bess, On the Twentieth Century, Bruce Forsyth on Broadway!, The 1940's Radio Hour, The Moony Shapiro Songbook, The Life and Adventures of Nicholas Nickleby, Cats, All's Well that Ends Well, My One And Only, Much Ado About Nothing, Cyrano de Bergerac, Leader of the Pack, Singin' in the Rain, Song and Dance, Les Misérables, The Phantom of the Opera, Romance/Romance, Carrie, Aspects of Love,* and *Dream.* During the 1988–1989 season, he had the unlikely distinction of engaging orchestras for eight Broadway shows running concurrently, and was a longtime member of André Gregory's Manhattan Project, having joined that group in 1966. He also appeared in Shakespearean works with Joseph Papp and as well as in several films.

Lois S. Rosenfield, 78, Chicago-born producer, died May 25, 2003, in Glencoe, Illinois, of cancer. With husband Maurice, her partner in their theatrical production company, Rosenfield Productions, she produced Broadway credits including *Barnum, The Glass Menagerie,* and *Singing' in the Rain,* the latter of which they also produced in London, England. Off-Broadway credits include *The Road to Mecca* and *Falsettoland,* as well as producing *Other People's Money* in Chicago, Illinois. She is survived by her husband, Maurice, sons James, of Santa Fe, New Mexico, and Andrew, of Lake Forest, Illinois, brothers, Howard and Donald Fried, and four grandchildren.

Ted Ross, 68, Zanesville, Ohio-born actor, died September 2, 2002, in Dayton, Ohio, of complications of a stroke sustained in 1998. A Tony Award winner as best featured actor in a musical for his portrayal of The Cowardly Lion in 1975's *The Wiz,* other Broadway credits include *Buck White, Purlie,* and *Raisin.* Best known for his work on television and in film, his numerous screen appearances include *Arthur, Ragtime, Amityville II, Police Academy, Stealing Home,* and *The Fisher King,* as well as recurring roles on the sitcoms *The Cosby Show* and *A Different World.*

Martha Scott (Martha Ellen Scott), 90, Jamesport, Missouri-born actress, died May 28, 2003, in Van Nuys, California. In a career that spanned more than 60 years, Broadway credits include originating the role of Emily Webb in Thornton Wilder's *Our Town* (which garnered her an Academy Award nomination as best actress for the subsequent film version), *Foreigners*, *The Willow and I*, *Soldier's Wife*, *It Takes Two*, *Design for a Stained Glass Window*, *The Number*, *The Male Animal*, *The Remarkable Mr. Pennypacker*, *Cloud 7*, *A Distant Bell*, *The Tumbler*, *The 49th Cousin*, *The Subject Was Roses*, *The Skin of Our Teeth*, *First Monday in October*, and *The Crucible*. With Henry Fonda and Robert Ryan she formed the Plumstead Playhouse, which produced classical revivals with all-star casts in New York and later, under the name the Plumstead Theater, in Los Angeles. Film credits include *The Howards of Virginia*, *Cheers for Miss Bishop*, *One Foot in Heaven*, *In Old Oklahoma*, *So Well Remembered*, *The Desperate Hours*, *The Ten Commandments*, *Sayonara*, *Ben-Hur*, *Airport 1975*, *The Turning Point*, and *Doin' Time on Planet Earth*. Her many television roles include Sue Ellen Ewing's mother on *Dallas*, Bob Newhart's mother on *The Bob Newhart Show*, and Lindsay Wagner's guardian on *The Bionic Woman*. She is survived by her son, Scott Alsop, two daughters, Mary Powell Harpel and Kathleen Powell, and her brother, Charles Scott. Her second and 52 year marriage to Pulitzer Prize-winning composer/musician Mel Powell ended with his death in 1998.

Scott Shukat, 66, agent/manager, died January 9, 2003, in New York City of cancer. Beginning his career as a booker for the William Morris Agency, he farmed out talent to such television programs as *The Mitch Miller Show* and *The Jimmy Dean Show*. He eventually became a full agent, representing such personalities as Peter Allen, Don McClean, the group Sly and the Family Stone, orchestrator Peter Matz, and comedienne Joan Rivers. In 1972 he opened his own office, The Shukat Company, which represented Off-Broadway's *Free to Be You and Me*, among other properties. Survivors include his wife, Evelyn, son, Jonathan, and parents, as well as a brother, sister, and their families.

Marjorie Slaiman (Marjorie Lawler), 77, Bronx, New York-born costume designer, died September 13, 2002, in Washington, D.C., of complications from heart surgery. In her 26-year career as costume designer at Arena Stage, she designed thousands of costumes for more than 130 productions, including the world premiere of *The Great White Hope* in 1967. Her credits there also include *Our Town* and *Inherit the Wind* (which both eventually toured the Soviet Union). She began her career designing costumes for the Shakespeare Theater Festival in Washington during the 1960's, and Broadway credits include Arthur Kopit's *Indians*, Studs Terkel's *Working*, and Elie Wiesel's *Zalmen, or the Madness of God*. She won the first Helen Hayes Award for costume design for *Man and Superman* in 1985, and was nominated for seven more Hayes awards before her retirement in 1993. She is survived by four children, Gary, of Mclean, Virginia, Donald, of Columbus, Ohio, Lauren, of New York, New York, and Tracey Barrentine of Annandale, Virginia, five brothers, John Lawler of Yonkers, New York, Lawrence Lawler of Mamaroneck, New York, Robert Lawler of Seaford, New York, Brendan Lawler of Katonah, New York, and James Lawler of Staten Island, four sisters, Therese Lawler Stevenson of Bedford, New York, Kathleen Lawler Gerard of Cortlandt Manor, New York, Patricia Lawler Odell of Parlin, New Jersey, and Joan Lawler Cirone of San Luis Obispo, California, and six grandchildren.

Rod Steiger (Rodney Stephen Steiger), 77, Westhampton, New York-born actor, died July 9, 2002, in Los Angeles of pneumonia and kidney failure. A veteran of the American Theatre Wing and the Actors Studio, Broadway credits include *An Enemy of the People*, *Night Music*, *Seagulls Over Sorrento*, *Rashomon*, and *Moby Dick*. An Academy Award winner for his performance as a Southern sheriff in *In the Heat of the Night*, other films include *Teresa*, *On the Waterfront* (Academy Award nomination), *The Big Knife*, *Oklahoma!*, *The Court-Martial of Billy Mitchell*, *Jubal*, *The Harder They Fall*, *Back from Eternity*, *Across the Bridge*, *The Unholy Wife*, *Run of the Arrow*, *Cry Terror*, *Al Capone*, *Seven Thieves*, *The Mark*, *13 West Street*, *The Longest Day*, *Convicts Four*, *Doctor Zhivago*, *The Pawnbroker* (Academy Award nomination), *The Loved One*, *No Way to Treat a Lady*, *The Sergeant*, *Three Into Two Won't Go*, *The Illustrated Man*, *Waterloo*, *Happy Birthday*, *Wanda June*, *The Heroes*, *Duck, You Sucker*, *A Fistful of Dynamite*, *Loly Madonna XXX*, *Hennessy*, *W.C. Fields and Me*, *Portrait of a Hitman*, *F.I.S.T.*, *Love and Bullets*, *The Amityville Horror*, *Cattle Annie and Little Britches*, *Klondike Fever*, *The Chosen*, *The Naked Face*, *The Kindred*, *American Gothic*, *The January Man*, *The Twilight Murders*, *Men of Respect*, *The Ballad of the Sad Café*, *The Player*, *The Specialist*, *Carpool*, *Shiloh*, *Truth or Consequences, N.M.*, *Body and Soul*, *End of Days*, *Shiloh 2: Shiloh Season*, *Crazy in Alabama*, and *The Hurricane*. He made frequent appearances on television, and won an Emmy Award in 1958 for his work on *The Lonely Wizard*. Survivors include his wife, Joan Benedict, daughter, Anna Justine Steiger, from his marriage to actress Claire Bloom, and son, Michael Winston, from his marriage to singer Paula Ellis.

Elaine Anderson Steinbeck, 88, Austin, Texas-born stage manager/producer/philanthropist, died April 27, 2003, in New York City and had a home in Sag Harbor, New York. One of the first women to achieve the position of stage manager on Broadway, her credits there include *Mr. Sycamore* and *Oklahoma!*, and in stage managing, organizing, and supervising the national tour of *Othello* with Paul Robeson, she became one of the first women to work in those capacities. The wife of author John Steinbeck, following his death in 1968 she worked to keep his work in print as well as promoted books about him. She was also active in the Steinbeck Research Center at San José University in California, and in 1996 donated an archive of more than 200 letters sent to Steinbeck by John F. Kennedy, Harry S. Truman, Carl Sandburg, Alice B. Toklas, Ingrid Bergman, and others. She was also a board member of the Bay Street Theater in Sag Harbor, New York. She is survived by her daughter from her first marriage to actor Zachary Scott, Waverly Scott Kaffaga, of New York, New York, stepson, Thomas Steinbeck, four grandchildren, and two sisters, Jean Boone of New York, New York, and Frances Atkinson of Tuscaloosa, Alabama.

Martha Scott

Rod Steiger

Irene Worth

Vera Zorina

Peter Stone (Peter Joshua, Pierre Marton), 73, writer, died April 26, 2003, in New York City of pulmonary fibrosis. He also had a home in Amagansett, on Long Island. A three-time Tony Award winner for best book of a musical for *1776*, *Woman of the Year*, and *Titanic*, other Broadway credits include *Kean*, *Skyscraper* (Tony nomination), *Two by Two*, *Sugar*, *Full Circle*, *My One and Only* (Tony nomination), *The Will Rogers Follies* (Tony nomination), and *Annie Get Your Gun*. The first writer to win the Tony, Emmy, and Academy Awards, he won the latter for *Father Goose* in 1964. Other screenplays include *Charade*, *Mirage*, *Arabesque*, *Who Is Killing the Great Chefs of Europe?*, and *Just Cause*. Screen adaptations for film include *Sweet Charity* and *The Taking of Pelham One, Two, Three*, as well as the adaptation of *Androcles and the Lion* for television and *Some Like It Hot* for the stage. He won his Emmy Award for a 1962 episode of *The Defenders*. He is survived by his wife, Mary, and a brother, David, of Los Angeles, California.

Alan Tagg, 74, Sutton-in-Ashfield, England-born scenic designer, died November 4, 2002, in London. Known for his detailed sets for the National Theater, the Chichester Festival, the Royal Shakespeare Company, and many of Alan Ackybourn's West End plays, he earned a nomination in the London Theater Critics' annual awards for his work on the Royal Shakespeare Company's acclaimed 1970 revival of *London Assurance*. Broadway credits include *Look Back in Anger*, *The Entertainer*, *All in Good Time*, *Black Comedy/White Lies* (Tony nomination), *London Assurance*, *The Constant Wife*, *The Kingfisher*, *Whose Life is it Anyway?*, *Corpse!*, and *Lettice and Lovage*. He is survived by his longtime partner, as well as a brother.

Lynne Thigpen (Lynne Redmond), 54, Joliet, Illinois-born stage, screen, and television actress, died March 12, 2003, in Los Angeles of a cerebral hemorrhage. A Tony Award winner for Wendy Wasserstein's *An American Daughter*, other Broadway credits include *The Magic Show*, *The Night That Made America Famous*, *Working*, *But Never Jam Today*, *Tintypes* (Tony nomination), *Fences*, and *A Month of Sundays*. *Fences* also brought her a Los Angeles Drama Critics Circle Award. Off-Broadway credits include *Balm in Gilead*, *Jar in the Floor*, and *Boesman and Lena*, the last two of which earned her Obie Awards. She was working on the television series *The District* at the time of her death, and is perhaps best known for her role as host of the PBS kid shows *Where in the World is Carmen Sandiego?* and *Where in Time is Carmen Sandiego?* Other television credits include *Thirtysomething* and *L.A. Law*, and the Hallmark Hall of Fame movies *Night Ride Home* and *The Boys Next Door*. Her motion pictures include *Godspell*, *Tootsie*, *Sweet Liberty*, *Running on Empty*, *Lean on Me*, *Bob Roberts*, *The Paper*, *The Insider*, *Novocaine*, and *Anger Management*. No reported survivors.

Joseph A. Walker, 67, playwright/teacher, died January 25, 2003, from complications of a stroke. A Tony Award winner in 1974 for penning *The River Niger*, which was developed into a film two years later starring James Earl Jones and Cicely Tyson. Other honors include a 1973 Obie Award, a Dramatists Guild Award, and a Guggenheim Fellowship. His other works include the musical *King Buddy Bolden*, and in later years he served as a professor of theatre at Rutgers University as well as director for numerous productions the Philadelphia, Pennsylvania area.

William Warfield, 82, Helena, Arkansas-born actor/singer, died August 25, 2002, in Chicago of complications of a broken neck suffered in a fall a month prior. Broadway credits include *Set My People Free* and *Regina*, as well as major tours of *Call Me Mister*, *Porgy and Bess*, and *Showboat*. In addition to his several very prominent audio recordings, he also taught at the University of Illinois at Champaign-Urbana in 1975, and joined the faculty of Northwestern University in 1994. Divorced following his marriage to singer Leontyne Price from 1952 to 1972, survivors include his brothers, Vern and Thaddeus, both of Rochester, New York.

Robert Whitehead, 86, prolific and universally respected Montreal, Canada-born producer, died June 15, 2002, in Pound Ridge, New York, of cancer. A Tony Award winner for his productions of *A Man for All Seasons*, the 1984 revival of *Death of a Salesman*, *Master Class*, and the recipient of a Special Lifetime Achievement Tony Award in 2002, his numerous other Broadway credits either in whole or part, (often with partner Roger L. Stevens), include *Cure For Matrimony*, *Medea*, *Crime and Punishment*, *The Member of the Wedding*, *Night Music*, *Mrs. McThing*, *Golden Boy*, *Four Saints in Three Acts*, *Sunday Breakfast*, *The Time of the Cuckoo*, *The Emperor's Clothes*, *The Remarkable Mr. Pennypacker*, *The Confidential Clerk*, *Portrait of a Lady*, *The Flowering Peach*, *Bus Stop*, *The Skin of Our Teeth*, *A View From the Bridge*, *Joyce Grenfell Requests the Pleasure….* *Tamburlaine the Great*, *Separate Tables*, *Major Barbara*, *The Sleeping Prince*, *The Waltz of the Toreadors*, *A Hole in the Head*, *Orpheus Descending*, *The Day the Money Stopped*, *The Visit*, *A Touch of the Poet*, *Goldilocks*, *The Man in the Dog Suit*, *The Cold Wind and the Warm*, *Much Ado About Nothing*, *The Conquering Hero*, *Midgie Purvis*, *After The Fall*, *Foxy*, *Marco Millions*, *But For Whom Charlie*, *The Physicists*, *The Changeling*, *Incident at Vichy*, *Tartuffe*, *Where's Daddy?*, *The Prime of Miss Jean Brodie*, *The Price*, *Sheep on the Runway*, *Old Times*, *The Creation of the World and Other Business*, *Finishing Touches*, *Cat on a Hot Tin Roof*, *A Matter of Gravity*, *1600 Pennsylvania Avenue*, *A Texas Trilogy: Lu Ann Hampton Laverty Oberlander*, *A Texas Trilogy: Oldest Living Graduate*, *No Man's Land*, *Bedroom Farce*, *Carmelina*, *Betrayal*, *Lunch Hour*, *The West Side Waltz*, *Lillian*, *The Petition*, *A Few Good Men*, *Artist Descending a Staircase*, *The Speed of Darkness*, *Park Your Car in Harvard Yard*, and *Broken Glass*. Broadway credits as a performer include *Mr. Big* and *Heart of a City*. An enthusiastic supporter of national as well as international playwrights with whom he found his greatest successes on the stage, he was responsible for five plays on Broadway during 1957 alone. He served with Elia Kazan as the first head of Lincoln Center Theater, and also served as a trustee of the Theatre Development Fund from 1985 to 1992, as well as from 1993 to present, and was the Honorary President of TDF's Chairman's Council at the time of his death. He was a Trustee of the Actors' Fund since 1979, a vice-president since 1993, a member of the Edwin Forrest Society, and was awarded The Actors' Fund Medal in 1994. In 1993, the Commercial Theater Institute created the Robert Whitehead Award to honor "outstanding achievement in commercial theatre producing." A cousin of the late actor Hume Cronyn, survivors include his wife, the actress Zoe Caldwell, and two sons, theatre critic Sam Whitehead, and Charlie Whitehead, who works in theatrical production.

Eleanor "Siddy" Wilson, 93, Chester, Pennsylvania-born actress, died May 31, 2002, in Williamstown, Massachusetts. Broadway credits include *Watch on the Rhine*, *The Eagle Has Two Heads*, *The Silver Whistle*, *The Wayward Saint*, and *Weekend* (Tony nomination). Off-Broadway credits include *Dandelion Wine* and *The Villa of Madame Vidac* in 1959. She also performed in seasons at Houston's Alley Theater, Milwaukee Rep, and Arena Stage in Washington, D.C., as well as on radio and on television, and with the USO in W.W.II. A veteran of the Berkshire Playhouse, she performed in 25 productions there beginning with *Junior Miss* in 1947.

Paul Zindel, 66, Staten Island, New York-born writer, best known for adapting to film his 1971 Broadway play *The Effect of Gamma Rays on Man-in-the-Moon Marigolds*, died March 27, 2003 in New York City, of cancer. The play won a 1970 best American play Obie Award, as well as the 1971 Pulitzer Prize. Other Broadway credits include *And Miss Reardon Drinks a Little*, *The Secret Affairs of Mildred Wild*, and *Ladies at the Alamo*. In addition to his novels for children including *The Pigman*, *My Darling*, *My Hamburger*, *I Never Loved Your Mind*, *Pardon Me*, *You're Stepping on My Eyeball*, *Confessions of a Teenage Baboon*, and *The Undertaker's Gone Bananas*, he also worked on the scripts for *Up the Sandbox*, *Mame*, *Maria's Lovers*, *Runaway Train*, and *Let Me Hear You Whisper*. He is survived by a daughter, Lizabeth Zindel, a son, David, of Los Angeles, California, and a sister, Betty Hagen, of Edison, New Jersey.

Vera Zorina (Eva Brigitta Hartwig), 86, Berlin-born dancer/actress, best known for the ballets she appeared in that were choreographed by her first husband, George Balanchine, died on April 9, 2003 at her home in Santa Fe, New Mexico, of natural causes. Broadway credits include *I Married an Angel*, *Louisiana Purchase*, *Dream With Music*, *The Tempest*, *A Temporary Island*, and *On Your Toes*. She appeared in a handful of movies including *The Goldwyn Follies*, *On Your Toes* (repeating her role from the London stage production), *Louisiana Purchase*, *Star Spangled Rhythm*, and *Follow the Boys*. She is survived by a son from her marriage to CBS Records president Goddard Lieberson; her third husband, harpsichordist Paul Wolfe; and three granddaughters.

INDEX

A

Aaron, Joyce 144
Aaron, Randy 141
Aarone, Donnell 93
Abadie, William 159
Abbott, Charles 231
Abbott, George 27
Abdala, Enrique 38
Aberlin, Noah 227
Abingdon Theatre Company 139
Ablaza, Cristina 220
Abner, Devon 183
Abraham, F. Murray 124
Abrams, Arthur 178
Abrams, Richarda 147
Abrons, Richard 176
Abtahi, Ornid 191
Acadine, Sophie 163
Access Theater 139
Acchione, Amy 187
Accidental Activist, The 145
Accidental Nostalgia 170
Acebo, Christopher 199, 222, 225
Acevedo, Dacyl 150
Acevedo, Enrique 220
Acheson, Dana Powers 151, 211
Acheson, Matthew 149
Acito, Tim 102, 167
Ackerman, Emily 184, 185
Ackerman, Joan 141
Ackerman, Loni 180
Ackermann, Joan 192
Ackroyd, David 144
Acme Sound Partners 29, 38, 58, 91, 92, 128, 197
Acting Company, The 139
Actor's Playground Theatre, The 139
Actors' Playhouse 111
Actors Collective, The 111

Actors Company Theatre, The (TACT) 139
Actors Playhouse 139
Act of Contrition 140
Acuna, Art 151
Acuna, Arthur T. 187
Adair, Arthur Maximillian 171, 172
Adams, Candi 37, 42, 93, 98, 131
Adams, D. 217, 218, 219
Adams, Guilford 225
Adams, Hudson 210
Adams, J.B. 66
Adams, J. Todd 226
Adams, Jonathan 215
Adams, Kevin 47, 101, 109, 128, 179, 197, 206
Adams, Lee 213
Adams, Paul 143
Adams, Richard Todd 156, 211
Adams, Sarah 39
Adams, Ty 143
Adams, Victoria 183
Adamson, Barlow 213
Adamson, Eve 149
Adamson, Gretchen Davidson 313
Adamy, Paul 71
Addai-Robinson, Cynthia 227
Adderley, Konrad 129
Addictions 146
Addinall, Caroline 205
Addison, Debbie L. 188
Addona, Emily 72
Aderer, Konrad 149, 293
Adilifu, Kamau 124
Adilman, Marci 92
Adkins, David 185
Adkins, Guy 208
Adler, Jay 53, 132

Adler, Joanna P. 175
Adopt a Sailor 160
Adoration of the Old Woman 215
Adult Entertainment 98
Adwin, Elisabeth 212
Adyanthaya, Aravind Enrique 170
Adzima, Nanzi 227
Aeschylus 158
Afro-Bradley, Henry 152
After 161
Agee, Martin 54
Aghazarian, Lori 223
Agnes, M. 68
Aguilar, Ruth 155
Agy, Emily 227
Ah, Wilderness! 200
Aharanwa, Maechi 144
Ahearn, Daniel 163, 293
Ahlin, John 221
Ahlstedt, Borje 123
Ahmanson Theatre 196
Ahnquist, Jordan 146
Ahrens, Lynn 160
Ai, Angela 147
Aibel, Douglas 179
Aida 65
Aidem, Betsy 143
Aiello, Danny 98
Ain't Misbehavin' 222
Ainsley, Paul 197
Airaldi, Remo 186
Air Raid 153
Aitchison, John 199
Aitken, Bobby 71, 196
Aizawa, Akiko 186
Ajanaku, Nkechi 205
Akalaitis, JoAnne 208
Akashi, Yoko 149

Akerlind, Christopher 179, 186, 215
Akers, Janice 210
Akesson, Hans 123
Akins, Rebecca 212
Akyea, Ansa 214
Alagic, Tea 154
Alai, Dean 145
Alan, Todd 193
Albach, Carl 39
Albee, Edward 132, 183, 222
Alberto, Henry 141
Albery, Donald 204
Albom, Mitch 97
Albrecht, Timothy 95
Alcaraz, Lonnie 225
Alcaraz, Roberto 199
Alchemists, The 156
Alda, Alan 84
Alden, Howard 180
Alden, Terrie Richards 180
Aldermann, Lisa 188
Aldous, Brian 112, 180
Aldrich, Tamara 190
Aldridge, Amanda 188, 189
Aldridge, Heather 139
Aldridge, Tamela 144
Alers, Karmine 74
Alers, Yassmin 74
Alessandrini, Gerard 110
Alex, Timothy J. 37
Alexander, Adinah 49
Alexander, Cheryl 93
Alexander, James 222
Alexander, Jessica 148
Alexander, Jill 57
Alexander, Julie 172
Alexander, Kevin 151
Alexander, Leslie 71
Alexander, Musashi 47
Alexander, Neil 48

Alexander, Sharon 231
Alexander, Stephan 71, 111
Alexander, Taro 112
Alexander, Terry 206, 221
Alexander, Zakiyyah 175
Alexandra's Web 157
Alexandratos, Elena 221
Alhadeff, Mark 154, 200
Ali, Hisham 185
Alifante, Nicole 145
Alimonti, Jennifer 231
Alioto, Alexander 139
Alive 160
Alkalae, Nina 97
Alladin, Opal 233
Allagree, Andrew 32
Allen, Chad 97
Allen, Douglas 172
Allen, Fred 197
Allen, Glenn 111
Allen, Joe 95
Allen, Lewis 23
Allen, Low Sandra 29
Allen, Morgan 175
Allen, Peter 99
Allen, Philip G. 196, 198
Allen, Priscilla 217
Allen, Scott 100
Allen, Thomas Michael 95
Allen, Tyrees 65
Allen, Woody 106
Allers, Roger 70
Alley, David Brian 204, 205
Alley, Lindsey 33
Alley Theatre 183
Allgood, Anne 42, 124, 219
Alliance Theatre Company 196
Allison, Dorothy 130
Allosso, Michael 213
Alltop, Michael 152, 168
Allyn, David 156

Allyn, Wendy 143, 222
All My Sons 187, 218
All Over Revival 132
All the World's a Stage 152
Alma and Mrs. Woolf 141
Almon, John Paul 220
Almos, Carolyn 154
Almos, Matt 154
Almost Blue 139
Almost Full Circle at the Guggenheim 143
Almost Grown Up 149
Almost Live from the Betty Ford Clinic 146
Aloha Flight 243 148
Alonso, Valerie 109
Alpert, Herb 92
Alsford, Eric 193
Alter, Eric 143
Altered Stages 140
Alterman, Glenn 143
Altheide, Eric 200
Altieri, John 224
Altman, Chelsea 126
Altman, Jane 143, 153
Altman, Jason 155
Altman, Sean 178
Altmeyer, Timothy 57
Altomare, Lisa 147
Alvarez, Gabriel Enrique 129
Alvarez, Lynne 176
Alves, Clyde 220
Alvin, Farah 60
Amas Musical Theatre 93, 167
Ambassador Satch: The Life and Times of Louis Armstrong 223
Ambassador Theatre Group Ltd. 48
Ambrosone, John 183, 216, 228, 229
American Airlines Theatre 27, 44, 52, 53
American Buffalo 185
American Conservatory Theatre 184
American Dreams: Lost and Found 139
American Globe Theatre 140
American Living Room, The 148
American Ma(u)l 147
American Magic 140
American Menu 176
American Repertory Theatre 186
American Theatre of Actors, The 140
Ames, Craig D. 195
Ames, Jonathan 176
Ami, Shoshana 163
Amieva, Sophie 171

Amory, Kate Kohler 147
Amour 10, 30
Amram, Adira 142
Amsden, Jeffrey 220
Anania, Michael 220
Anastassakis, Yiannis 97
Ancestral Voices 214
Ancheta, Susan 29, 293
Anders, Mark 194
Anders, Wynne 143, 153
Anderson, Cletus 203
Anderson, Dennis 40, 59
Anderson, Dion 224
Anderson, Frank 147
Anderson, Heather Lea 233
Anderson, Maxwell L. 150
Anderson, Michael 148, 196
Anderson, Nancy 94, 234
Anderson, Paul 96
Anderson, Robb 232
Anderson, Russ 155, 218
Anderson, Sergia 180
Anderson, Stephen Lee 51
Anderson, Stig 71, 196
Anderson, Tobias 222
Andersson, Benny 71, 196
Andino, Paolo 200
Andonyadis, Nephelie 225
Andos, Randy 42, 54
Andraos, Amale 209
Andreano, Liliana 146
Andreas, Christine 223
Andres, Barbara 150, 213
Andres, Ryan 39
Andress, Carl 168
Andress, Rosemary K. 157
Andrews, Dwight 45
Andrews, George Lee 72
Andrews, Lindsey 205
Andrews, Marnie 143
Andrews, Mary Todd 313
Andric, Ivo 171
Andricain, Ana Maria 66, 231
And My Friend 160
Angela, Sharon 151
Aniello, Chris 180
Anna Christie 159
Anna in the Tropics 170
Annie 220, 230
Anonymous Remailers 161
Anouilh, Jean 139
Anschutz, Sue 60
Anselm, Monica 180
Ansil, Jay 215
Anspacher Theater 128, 129
Anthem 161
Anthony, Eric 26, 293
Anthony, Morris 112
Anthony, Stephen G. 103, 151, 206

Antigone 97, 145
Antigone's Red 161
Antonia, Kathleen 185
Antonio, Jose 156
Antunovich, Lynn 157
Anything's Dream 146
Anzuelo, David 212
An Ice Cream Man for All Seasons 144
An Infinite Ache 200, 218
Apathy, Christina 205
Apfel, Wesley 143
Apgar, Jen 210
Apollo Theater 92, 102, 104
Apollo Theater Foundation 92
Aponte, Justin 178
Appel, Peter 146
Apple 152
Appleton, Bev 187
Appleyard, Russ 191
Aquilina, Corinne 110, 111
Aquiline, Carlyn Ann 203
Aquino, Amy 199
Aquino, Jessica 142
Araca Group 24, 76, 96
Arana-Downs, Ruben 195
Aranas, Raul 293
Arand, Christine 38, 39
Aravena, Michelle 196
Arber, Gyda 143
Arbuckle, Sean 110, 139
Arcelus, Sebastian 74
Arcenas, Loy 125, 127, 151, 228, 230
Archer, Julie 173, 215
Arc Light Theatre 140
Arden Theatre Company 187
Arditti, Paul 123, 130
Arena, Danny 49
Argila, Steven 233
Argument, The 170, 174
Arhelger, Joan 191
Ari, Robert 94, 293
Arias, Joey 156
Arkin, Anthony 23
Arkin, Matthew 190
Arko, Brenda 93
Arlen, Harold 124
Armand, Pascale 186, 227
Armitage, Robert M. 65
Armoroso, Amorika M. 158
Armour, John 222
Armstrong, Karen 43, 69
Armstrong, Mark 148
Armstrong, William 173
Arnold, David A. 97
Arnold, Joseph 144
Arnold, Michael 67, 69
Arnold, Tex 196
Arnone, John 198

Arnov, Michael 159
Aronow, Scott 99
Aronson, Billy 74, 168
Aronson, Frances 179, 209, 221
Aronson, Frank 213
Aronson, Letty 106
Aronson, Luann 231
Around the World in 80 Days 188
Arredondo, Rosa Evangelina 92
Arrington, Kate 225
Arruda, Chris 147
Arsenic And Old Lace 222
Arslanian, Aram 225
Ars Nova Theater 140
"Art" 204
Arthur, Loyce 223
Arvanitis, Nikos 97
Arvia, Ann 231
Arvin, Mark 32
Asbury, Donna Marie 68
Ascending Lulu 175
Aschenbrenner, Eric 150
Ascher, James 161
Ash, Kathryn 174
Ashford, Rob 27, 75, 213
Ashkenasi, Danny 172
Ashley, Elizabeth 18, 56
Ashman, Howard 66
Ashmanskas, Brooks 59
Askin, Peter 162, 197
Aspel, Brad 66, 69
Aspen Group 25
Asprey, Jason 147
Assadourian, Joseph 170
Astaire, Fred 99
Astor Place Theatre 112
As Long As We Both Shall Laugh 53
As You Like It 129, 163
Atens, Jim 109
Atherlay, John M. 66, 94
Atkins, Cholly 313
Atkins, Meredith 71
Atkins, Tom 221
Atkinson, Elizabeth 202, 203
Atkinson, Jayne 36, 56, 293
Atkinson, Kristin 172
Atkinson, Scot 188, 189
Atlantic Theater Company 99, 106, 167
Atlas, Ravil 124
Attias, Michael 154
Attractive Women on the Train, The 163
At a Plank Bridge 178
Auberjonois, Remy 209, 218
Auberjonois, Rene 40, 293
Auburn, David 194, 200, 206, 211, 225
Arnone, John 198

AuCoin, Kelly 141, 146
Augensen, René 184
Augesen, René 184, 185
August, Bille 153
August, Curtis 186
August, Ian 172
August, Matt 219
Augustin, Julio 159
Augustine, Jim 213
August Wilson's Gem of the Ocean 199
Aujla, Ravi 102
Aukin, Daniel 178
Auntie Mayhem 141
Aunt Pittipat in the Tower 160
Aural Fixation 43
Austin, Gary 152
Austin, Ivy 180
Austin-Williams, Jaye 161
Autobiography of God as Told by Mel Schneider, The 154
Autograph 50
Avenue Q 179
Avery, Alicia 145
Avery, Ramsey 211
Avery, Vance 67
Avila, John 199
Avni, Ron 133
Awata, Urara 173
Axelrod, Jane A. 29
Axen, Eric 157
Ayckbourn, Alan 225
Ayles, Chris 224
Ayme, Marcel 30
Azenberg, Emanuel 32, 38, 74
Azurdia, Richard 199

B
Babad, Herman 153
Babak, Cynthia 139
Babb, Zakia 172
Babe, Thomas 176
Babes in Toyland 222
Babson, Leila 99
Babtunde, Akin 209
Babylon, Guy 65
Bacalzo, Dan 140
Bacchae of Euripides: A Communion Rite, The 205
Bacharach, Burt 60
Bachman, Trevor 211
Backford, Malik 220
Backsliding in the Promised Land 227
Back Story 192
Bacon, Jenny 208, 234
Bacon, Mary 139, 146, 174, 194
Bacon, Roy 152
Baden, Leslie 92, 103, 104
Bader, Jenny Lyn 153

Badgen, Ron 141
Badgett, Will 148, 171
Bad Bugs Bite 171
Bad Women 148
Bae, Terrence 154
Baer, Stacy 180
Baeta, Virginia 145
Baeumler, Carolyn 160, 175, 201
Bageot, Karine 32
Bagert, Darren 62
Bag of Marbles 174
Baibussynova, Ulzhan 186
Baik, Young Ju 234
Bailegangaire 169
Bailey, Alan 216
Bailey, Beth 193
Bailey, Bill 97
Bailey, Christopher Eaton 124
Bailey, Christopher J. 176
Bailey, D'Vorah 217, 218, 219
Bailey, David 223
Bailey, Erika 152
Bailey, Kevin 70
Baiocchi, Frank 110
Baird, Chuck 198
Baird, Mary 191
Baisch, Maggie 48
Baitz, Jon Robin 199
Baker, Ali 184
Baker, Becky Ann 168, 293
Baker, Darrin 110
Baker, David 67
Baker, Denys 67
Baker, Douglas C. 196
Baker, Edward Allan 148, 158
Baker, Elna 172
Baker, Jacquelyn 220
Baker, Janelle 202
Baker, Lance Stuart 208
Baker, Larry 197
Baker, Mark 190
Baker, Max 176
Baker, Nick 231
Baker, Sarah 139
Baker, Simon 50
Baker, Travis 153
Baksic, Amela 92, 221
Bakunas, Steve 33
Balaban, Bob 95
Baldassari, Mike 53, 67
Baldauff, Julie 50, 186
Balderrama, Michael 49
Baldinu, Pichon 109
Baldoni, Gail 94, 220
Baldwin, Alec 160
Baldwin, Craig 128
Baldwin, Kate 75, 220
Balkwill, Dean 74
Ball, Erica 144
Ball, Jessica 146

Ballad of Mary O'Connor, The 160
Ballard, Inga 226, 227
Ballard, Jordan 220
Ballard, Kaye 192
Ballesteros, Randy B. 220
Ballou, Joan 188
Balmilero, Kime J. 71
Balzer, Julie Fei-Fan 158
Bamman, Gerry 175
Banda, A. Raymond 146
Banderas, Antonio 15, 54, 237, 293
Bandhu, Pun 149
Bang! 156
Bank, Jonathan 173
Bankerd, Lance 146
Banks, Michelle A. 198
Banks, Nedrah 192
Banks, Ronald M. 201
Bank Street Theatre 140
Bannerman, Guy 211
Banning, Jack 218
Bannister-Colon, Laurie 150
Bansavage, Lisa 193
Banta, Martha 194, 216
Baptizing Adam 156
Baquerot, Aliane 32
Bar, Hadas Gil 172
Barall, Michi 153, 161, 215
Baratta, Maria 145
Barbanell, Ari 150
Barbara Cook in Mostly Sondheim 196
Barbara Wolff Monday Night Reading Series, The 142
Barber, Matthew 56
Barberio, Gabriela 109
Barberry, Jess 146
Barbour, Thomas 159
Barboussi, Vasso 97
Barbra's Wedding 100
Barchiesi, Franca 145, 209
Bardeen, David 233
Barden, Alice 139
Bardwell, Gina 161
Barkan, Elizabeth 178
Barke, Tim 143
Barkely, Lynnette 195
Barker, Amy 147
Barkley, Lynnette 195
Barkovich, Julie A. 221
Barlett, Tom 32
Barlow, David 176
Barlow, John 32, 33, 40, 41, 45, 55, 57, 73, 75, 94, 95, 97, 101, 104
Barlow, Roxane 75

Barlow-Hartman 32, 33, 40, 41, 45, 55, 57, 75, 91, 94, 95, 97, 99, 101, 102, 104
Barnes, Clive 241
Barnes, Edward 190
Barnes, Ezra 173, 293
Barnes, Geoffrey 140
Barnes, Gregg 29, 180
Barnes, Leah Noel 204
Barnes, Lisa 147, 151, 293
Barnes, Paul 205
Barnes, William Joseph 47
Barnett, Bill 157
Barnett, Brigitte 171
Barnhart, Jen 179
Baron, Art 55
Baron, Evalyn 188, 189
Baron, Jeff 158
Barr, Drew 145
Barranca, Victor 178
Barreca, Christopher 225, 226
Barrett, Brent 68, 220
Barrett, Cynthia 210
Barrett, Joy 162
Barrett, Laurinda 139
Barricelli, Marco 184, 185
Barrie, J.M. 215, 223
Barrie-Wilson, Wendy 36
Barrier, Randee 155
Barrish, Seth 141
Barron, Amanda 147
Barron, Contance 219
Barron, Mia 130, 131, 174, 213
Barron, Steven L. 147
Barrowman, John 223
Barrow Group, The 141
Barry, B.H. 179, 215
Barry, Gabriel 221
Barry, James 192
Barry, Jeffrey 233
Barry, Paul 153
Barry-Hill, Eugene 70
Barsha, Debra 128
Barsky, Neil 155
Bart, Lionel 204
Bart, Roger 73
Bartenders 98
Bartenieff, Alexander 178
Barter Theatre 188
Bartholomai, Linda 233
Bartlett, Lisbeth 231
Bartlett, Rob 68
Bartley, Adam 209
Bartner, Robert G. 29, 45, 91
Barton, Bruce 143
Barton, Caitlin 140
Barton, Fred 133, 156
Bartosik, Steve 37
Bartow, Arthur 180
Baruch, Steven 94, 95

Baruch-Viertel-Routh-Frankel Group 25
Barwegen, Maria 214
Barzee, Anastasia 76
Basche, David Alan 146
Bashey, Ismail 176
Basil, John 140
Bass, George 222
Bass, Harriet 199, 224
Bass, Jordan 227
Bassett, J. Philip 25
Basset Table, The 148
Bast, Stephanie 54, 293
Bastock, Michael 159
Bateman, Bill 231
Bateman, Jeffrey 143
Bates, Alan 80
Bates, Jerome Preston 139, 158
Bates, Jessica 139
Bates, Keith 203
Bates, Larry 200
Bates, Stephen 111
Bath, Mykel 70
Batistick, Mike 170
Batman, Jack W. 56
Batnagar, Krish 156
Battaglia, Eve 95
Battaglia, Joe 211
Battaglia, Lynn 140
Battat, Jacob 159
Battersby, Charles 152
Battles, Drew 230
Battle of Black and Dogs 154
Batwin and Robin Productions 92, 103, 128, 196
Bauer, Beaver 185, 191
Bauer, C. Andrew 163
Bauer, Debra 220
Bauer, Jim 149
Bauer, Laura 24, 98, 106, 126
Bauer, Martin 109
Bauer, Matt 58, 59
Bauer, P. Seth 163
Bauer, Ruth 149
Bauman, Jessica 158
Baura, Gary 171
Bavan, Yolande 186
Baxter, Kalimi 161
Baxter, Robin 71
Baxter Stage 206, 207
Bayes, Christopher 208
Bayron, Harry 124
Baysic, Emy 196
Bay Street Theatre 190
Bazell, Myra 187, 223
Bazmark Live 38
Bazzle, Bradley 148
Bazzone, Mark 175
BBC America Comedy Live 97
Beach, David 76

Beach, Gary 73
Beach Radio 142
Beal, John 124
Beale, Simon Russell 123
Bean, Christa 206
Bean, Jeffrey 183
Bean, Noah 190
Bean, R. 68
Bean, Reathel 36, 293
Bean, Shoshana 26, 293
Beane, Douglas Carter 168
Beard, Alec 44
Beard, Jane 215
Beat 154
Beatty, John Lee 24, 43, 44, 68, 94, 124, 126, 177, 196
Beaubier, Jason 186
Beauregard, Jon 154
Beauty and the Beast 66
Beaver, Jerry 97
Beavers, Brandon 205
Beazer, Tracee 129
Beber, Neena 174
Bechtel, Erich 57
Beck, Bobby 188, 189
Beck, Emily 176
Becker, Rob 293
Beckett, Diane 171
Beckett, Samuel 144
Beckim, Chad 147
Beckler, Steven 25
Beckler, Steven Ted 66
Beckley, Carol 194
Beckwith, Eliza 168
Becoming Bernarda 177
Bedbound 169
Bedford, Brian 44, 293
Bedi, Purva 148
Bed among the Lentils 104
Beecher, James 176
Before Death Comes for the Archbishop 179
Beginning, The 140
Begleiter, Marcie 179
Begue, Nicole 205
Beguiled Again: The Songs of Rodgers & Hart 195, 214
Behn, Aphra 145
Beitzel, Robert 157, 174
Bekins, Richard 155, 163
Belasco, Mark 158
Belasco Theatre 24, 56
Belber, Stephen 100, 154, 159
Belcher, James 183
Belcon, Natalie Venetia 74, 179
Belgrader, Andrei 208
Belknap, Anna 213, 219
Belkoff, Andie 231
Bell, Barbara A. 195
Bell, David 153

Bell, Gail Kay 150
Bell, Glynis 159, 176
Bell, Jacob 205
Bell, Nancy 127
Bell, Neal 160
Bell, Yvonne Carlson 196
Bellamy, Brad 168
Bellazzin, Richard 150
Belles of the Mill 152
Bellingham, Rebecca 169
Belluso, John 175
Belton, Ian 154
Belton, Nicholas 131
Belver, Carla 187
Bel Geddes, Edith Lutyens 321
Bembridge, Brian Sidney 208
Ben-David, Adam 40
Benanti, Laura 54, 293
Benari, Neal 65
Benator, Andrew 141
Benbow, Tawanna 213
Bender, Patty 110
Bender, Paul 207
Bendul, Kristine 124
Benedict, Paul 217
Benesch, Vivienne 175
Benjamin, Ari 171
Benjamin, Maggie 74
Benjamin, P.J. 68, 192
Benkert, Stephanie 211
Benko, Tina 52, 150
Benn, Shamicka 205
Bennett, Alan 104
Bennett, Andrew 102
Bennett, Craig 196
Bennett, David 160, 175
Bennett, Jamie 139, 221
Bennett, Mark 44, 103, 179, 197
Bennett, Matthew 30
Bennett, Tim 193
Benoit, David 40
Benoit, John 172
Benson, Martin 225, 226
Benson, Peter 67, 124
Benson, Robin 200
Benson, Stephen 60
Benston, Alice 210
Bentley, Kenajuan 160, 161
Benton, Heather 186
Benz, Deena 93
Benzinger, Suzy 32, 98
Berc, Shelley 208
Berdini, Kevin 66
Berenson, Stephen 228, 229
Berg, Neil 91
Bergelson, Ilene 153
Bergen, Polly 67, 161
Berger, Jesse 147
Bergeron, Francois 220
Bergl, Emily 225

Bergman, Evan 140
Bergman, Ingmar 123, 204
Berinstein, Dori 75
Berkeley Repertory Theatre 191
Berkman, John 133
Berkow, Jay 94
Berkowitz, D. Michael 168
Berkowitz, Roy 143
Berkshire, Devon 158
Berkshire Theatre Festival 192
Berlin, Howard R. 56
Berlin, Irving 99
Berlin, Jeannie 98
Berlin, Jessica 224
Berlin, Pamela 92, 146, 221
Berlind, Roger 41
Berliner, Jay 124
Berliner, Terry 212
Berlinsky, Harris 149
Berlovitz, Sonya 191
Berman, Brooke 174
Berman, Ellen 56
Berman, Heather 157
Berman, Rob 125
Bermowitz, Arnie 163
Bermudez, Kina 178
Bern, Mina 293
Bernard Telsey Casting 25, 30,
    37, 38, 40, 56, 62, 98, 101,
    106, 186
Berneche, Alicia 167
Berney, Brig 74
Bernstein, Jesse 231
Bernstein, Jonathan 180
Bernstein, Leonard 161, 227
Bernstone, Jennifer 147
Bernzweig, Jay 148
Beroza, Janet 197
Berresse, Michael 68
Berry, Gabriel 130, 167, 186
Berry, Stephanie 215
Berstler, Becky 69
Bertolacci, Kevin 44
Bertran, Moe 140, 141
Bess, Abigail Zealey 168
Besterman, Brian 37
Besterman, Doug 75
Besterman, Douglas 73
Bethel, Pepsi 313
Betley, Marge 211, 212
Betrayal 217
Bettenbender, Ben 157
Beuerlein, Joseph 205
Beuscher, John 190
Bewilderness 97
Bewley, Sarah 162
*Bexley, Oh(!) Or, Two Tales of
    One City* 130
Beyah, Basil 223
Beyond Therapy 219

Beyond the Veil 152
Be Aggressive 209
Biagi, Michael 99
Biagi, Randall 99
Bianchi, Ed 148
Bianco, Christina 180
Biancomano, Frank 178
Biberi, James 139
*Bible: The Complete Word of
    God (Abridged), The* 200
Bickell, Ross 216
Bieber, Jason 218, 219
Biggers, Barbara 54
Biggs, Casey 124
Biggs, Jason 81
Biggs, Steven 205
Big Al 140
Big Love 209
*Big River: The Adventures of
    Huckleberry Finn* 198
Big Theatre for Little People
    211, 212
Bilderback, Walter 210
Bilecky, Scott 145
Billiau, Drew 187
Billie 170
Billig, Etel 214
Billig, Jonathan R. 214
Billig, Robert 37
Billington, Ken 40, 68, 124, 197
Billman, Sekiya 168, 293
Billy Bishop Goes to War 211
Bill Evans and Associates 23, 30,
    36, 61
*Bill Maher: Victory Begins at
    Home* 61
Bilton, Wendy 158
Binder, David 109
Binder, Jay 49, 69, 76, 94, 100,
    124, 197
Binder, Joe 214
Binion, Sandy 100
Binkley, Howell 33, 60, 103, 128,
    131, 203, 223
Binsley, Richard 71
Birdie Blue 203
Birdsong, Mary 98, 293
Birdy 179
Birdy's Bachelorette Party 145
Birkelund, Olivia 151
Birney, David 241
Biro 170
Bish, David 146
Bishoff, Joel 110
Bishop, André 43, 48, 125
Bishop, Barton 139
Bishop, David 226
Bishop, Stephen 133
Bishop, Steven M. 223
Bisno, Debbie 45

Bitetti, Bronwen 148
*Bitter Bierce, Or the Friction We
    Call Grief* 176
Bivins, Mary Lucy 189
Bixby, Jonathan 76, 185
Bixler, John 193
Bizarro Bologna Show, The 154
Bizjak, Amy 143
Bjornson, Dave 203
Björnson, Maria 72, 313
Black, Bill 205
Black, Brent 71
Black, Christopher 149
Black, Clint 49
Black, Deborah 191
Black, James 183
Black, Jeremy 142
Black, Lisa 171
Black, Malcolm 231
Black, Paul Vincent 185
Blackburn, Kyle 207
Blackman, Robert 103, 184, 206
Blacks: A Clown Show, The 144
Blackwell, Susan 150
Black Alert in Sarajevo 160
Black Ensemble Touring
    Company 104
Black Monk, The 234
Blair, Kelli 204
Blair, Tom 185, 224
Blaisdell, Kerrie 190
Blake, Marsha Stephanie 227
Blake, Patrick 95
Blake, Richard H. 65, 74
Blake, Stephanie 128
Blakesley, Darcy 144
Blanchard, Steve 66
Blanchard, Tammy 12, 58, 237,
    241
Blanco, Arian 156
Blanco, Michael 95
Blank, Jessica 95
Blank, Larry 73, 99
Blankenbuehler, Andy 37, 293
Blankenship, Hal 141, 143
Blankfort, Jase 179
Blanks, Bernie 220
Blanks, Harvy 221
Blase, Linda 105
Blaser, Cathy 313
Blasius, Chuck 141
Blasor, Denise 225
Blau, Eric 232
Blaufuss, Patricia 222, 226
Blazer, Judy 223
Bleckmann, Theo 167
Bleicher, Jonathan Andrew 66
Blessing, Lee 161, 175
Blessing in Disguise 159
Bless Me, Father 158

Blind Mouth Singing 170
Blinkoff, Daniel 225, 226
Blinn, David 124
Bliss 157
Blithe Spirit 190
Block, Dan 55
Block, Larry 147, 174, 293
Blommaert, Susan 129
Blood, Wayne 180
Bloodgood, William 191, 224
Blood Wedding 174
Bloom, Michael 225
Bloom, Tom 168, 213, 294
Blooming of Ivy, A 168
Blount, William 124
Blue 220
Blue, Pete 110
Blue/Orange 98
Blue Demon, The 213
Blue Flower 149
Blue Heaven 146
Blue Heron Arts Center 141
Blue Man Group 112
Blue Room 207
Blue Room, The 195
*Blue Sky Transmission: A
    Tibetan Book of the Dead*
    171
Bluhm, Anni 148
Blum, Daniel 241
Blum, Gerald 155
Blum, Joel 192
Blum, Mehera 213
Blumberg, Kate 106
Blume, Kathryn 145
Blumenfeld, Mara 167
Blumenkrantz, Jeff 49
Blumer, Jacob 234
Blunt, Ed 95
Bluteau, Lothaire 96
Bly, Mark 233, 234
Boardman, Christy 220
Bobbie, Walter 68, 127, 160,
    180, 294
Bobby, Anne 110
Bobgan, Raymond 171
Bobish, Randy 69
Boccato, Richard 155
Bocchetti, Mike 155
Bochenski's Brain 148
Bock, Adam 145
Bock, Brett 209
Bock, Jerry 231
Bockhorn, Craig 207
Bodd, Patrick 151
Bode, Raine 172
Bodeen, Michael 33, 45, 55,
    167, 183
Bodega Lung Fat 170
Boe, Alfred 38

Boesche, John 167
Boevers, Jessica 74
Bofill, Maggie 169, 177
Bogaev, Paul 65
Bogard, Steven 220
Bogardus, Janet 168
Bogardus, Stephen 37, 294
Bogart, Anne 186
Bogart, Dominic 178
Bogart, Matt 220
Boggess, Damon 210
Boggioni, Joshua 230
Bogin, Abba 180
Bogner, Dunia 147
Bogosian, Eric 176, 224
Bohjalian, Chris 205
Bohle, Ruppert 96, 201
Bohon, Justin 220
Boitel, Raphaelle 153
Bokhour, Ray 68
Bolden, Chris 192
Boll, Heinrich 172
Boll, Patrick 144, 178
Bollinger, Lee C. 102
Bolman, Scott 233, 234
Bolton, Guy 147
Bolton, John 212
Bolton Theatre 206, 207
Bonard, Mayra 109
Bond, Clint, Jr. 24, 68, 96
Bond, Jeff 174
Bond, Justin 144, 174
Bond, Will 186
Bondoc, Eric 201
Bonds, Rufus, Jr. 198
Boneau, Chris 38, 47, 65, 66,
    67, 69, 70, 98, 99, 105,
    106, 112, 126, 127
Boneau/Bryan-Brown 24, 27,
    29, 38, 44, 47, 50, 51, 52,
    53, 54, 58, 60, 71, 76, 96,
    98, 99, 100, 102, 105, 106,
    126, 127, 132
Bonet, Wilma 191
Bongiorno, Joe 39
Bonitto, Sondra M. 124
Bonner, Ann 172
Bonney, Jo 170, 174, 177, 215
*Boobs! The musical (The World
    According to Ruth Wallis)*
    106
Booher, Mark 211
Bookman, Kirk 168, 169, 200,
    211, 212, 213, 221, 222
Bookwalter, D. Martyn 196
Book of Days 177
Book of Job, The 172
Booth, Susan V. 196
Boothe, Cherise 144, 174, 192
Booth Theatre 23, 36

Bopp, Willi 123
Borba, Andrew 219
Borchard, Thomas 132
Borden, Walter 141
Borg, Christopher 143
Boris, Michael 205
Boritt, Beowulf 229
Boriu, Beowulf 103
Borland, Charles 217
Borle, Christian 30, 75, 125
Born, David 183
Borowka, Steve 146
Borowski, Michael S. 37, 42,
    98, 130, 131
Borrero, Camila 184
Borstelmann, Jim 73
Bortz, Daniel 123
Bos, Hannah 158
Bosch, Barbara 143, 155
Bosch, Michelle 55
Bosco, Nick 155
Bose, Rajesh 221
Bosley, James 153
Bosley, Tom 67
Boss, John B. 214
Bostic, Kathryn 199
Bostnar, Lisa 173, 294
Boston Marriage 128
Boston, Matthew 139, 151
Boston, Phyllis Kay 228
Boston area refugee youth 186
Boswell, Laurence 52
Botchan, Rachel 155
Botello, Kate 156
Bottari, Michael 168
Bottle, Caroline 150
Bottle Factory Theater Company,
    The 142
Boublil, Alain 220
Bougere, Teagle F. 168
Boughton, Drew 224
Boulevard X 152
Boulware, Kelly Allen 202, 222
Bourne, Mel 313
Boutrup, Jens Svane 158
Boutte, Duane 174
Bove, Linda 198
Bove, Mark 49, 294
Bovshow, Buzz 175
Bowcutt, Jason 201
Bowdan, Jack 49, 94
Bowditch, Rachel 172
Bowen, Alex 67
Bowen, Ann 152
Bowen, Chris 112
Bowen, Graham 59
Bower, Sharron 168
Bowers, Emma 141, 233
Bowers, Nadia 215
Bowersock, Karin 140

Bowery Poetry Club 142
Bowling, Alec Shelby 200
Bowman, Benjamin G. 32
Bowman, Margaret 103, 151,
    206
Bowman, Rob 197
Bowyer, Clodagh 169
Boxcar Children, The 187
Box of Pearls 179
Boyd, D'Ambrose 93
Boyd, Gregory 183
Boyd, Guy 143
Boyd, Julie 168, 174
Boyd, Ken 150
Boyd, Patrick 141
Boyer, Katherine Lee 36, 56
Boyer, Steven 23, 175, 216
Boyers, Gabriel 213
Boyett, Bob 40, 55
Boyett, Mark 216
Boykin, Nancy 187
Boyle, Cristin 180
Boyle, Seamus 156
Boys and Girls 115
Bozell, Tom 147
Braben, Eddie 50
Bracchitta, Jim 213
Bracco, Lorraine 160
Bracho, Pablo 183
Brack, Ryan 154
Bracken, Eddie 313
Bradbury, Stephen 205
Bradecich, Josh 227
Braden, John 36
Bradford, Josh 173, 178
Bradley, David 123
Bradley, Eric 223
Bradley, Everett 124
Bradley, Henry 144
Bradley, Neil 156
Bradley, Scott 203, 211, 217
Brady, Alexander 32
Brady, Brigid 212, 231
Brady, Charlie 196
Brady, Christopher 229
Brady, John E. 70
Brady, Jonathan 152
Brady, Patrick S. 73
Brady, Stephen A. 206
Brady, Steve 149
Braff, Zach 128
Bragan, Jay 229
Braithwaite, Kai 70
Brake, Brian 49
Bramble, Mark 69, 197
Branagh, Kenneth 50
Brancato, Joe 183
Brancoveanu, Eugene 38
Brand, Gibby 198
Brandt, Kirsten 175

Brannen, Kirsten 211, 212
Brantman, Jason 95
Brathwaite, Charlotte 171
Brathwaite, Jonathan 155
Braude, Oleg 172
Braun, Krista 226
Braunsberg, Andrew 40
Bravaco, Joe 188
Brawley, Lucia 151, 174
Braxton, Brenda 68, 93, 124
Braxton, Toni 65
Brazda, Kati 208
Brazil, Angela 228, 229, 230
Breadon, Enda O. 219
Bread and Circus 3099 172
Breaker, Daniel 147
Breath, Boom 213, 233
Brecht, Bertolt 96
Breckenridge, Rob 139, 173
Breckfield, Jeff 161
Breedlove, Gina 70
Breen, Patrick 199
Brehm, Justin 146
Brel, Jacques 232
Brelsford, Michael 222
Bremlette, Rebekka 49
Breneman, Ali 200
Brennan, James 212, 231
Brennan, Kathleen 167
Brennan, Tom 36, 294
Breuer, Lee 173, 215
Breuer, Lute 215
Breving, Andrew 148
Brevoort, Deborah 176
Brewczyski, Amy 224
Brewster, Paget 215
Breyer, Maria Emilia 112
Brice, Richard 59
Brick, Jeffrey 217, 218, 219
Bridge, Andrew 72
Briel, Joel 172
Brier, Kathy 91
Brigden, Tracy 202, 203
Briggs, David 168
Brighton Beach Memoirs
    211, 231
Bright Ideas 206
Briguccia, Vincent 143
Brill, Robert 67, 97, 98, 127, 215
Brimer, James 204
Briner, Allison 192, 205
*Bring In 'Da Noise, Bring In
    'Da Funk* 196
Brink-Washington, Daniel 147
Brinker, Patrick 187
Brinton, Angela 216
Brito, Silvia 177
Broad, Robbin E. 215
Broadhurst, Jeffrey 27
Broadhurst Theatre 49

Broadway Theatre 38
Broad Channel 105
Brock, Lee 141
Brockway, Stephen 133
Brocone, Genna 154
Brod, Broke 148
Broderick, Deirdre 171
Broderick, Matthew 73
Brody, Jonathan 111
Brody, Noah 230
Brogan, Meg 233
Brogan, Roderic 219
Brohn, William David 125
Brokaw, Chris 186
Brokaw, Mark 140, 160, 161, 213
Broken Head, A 160
Brolly, Brian 29, 45
Bromelmeier, Martha 110
Bronstein, Jennifer 209
Bronx Casket Company 148
Bronx Witch Project, The 170
Brooker, Meg 142, 155
Brookes, Jacqueline 227
Brooking, Fallon McDevitt 157
Brooklyn Academy of Music 123,
    167
Brooks, Adam 184
Brooks, Anitra 229
Brooks, Benjamin 58
Brooks, De Anne N. J. 208
Brooks, Donald L. 178
Brooks, Hal 139, 141
Brooks, Jeff 66
Brooks, Mel 73
Brooks, Taylor 139
Brooks Atkinson Theatre 41, 60,
    167
Broom, Louis 150
Brophy, John 102
Brothers Karamazov, Part 1, The
    147
Brouk, Tricia 145
Brourman, Michele 193
Brouwer, Peter 139
Brown, Benjamin Franklin 60, 92
Brown, Blair 127
Brown, Brennan 150, 160, 161,
    174
Brown, Camille M. 70
Brown, Charles 95
Brown, Christine Marie 217
Brown, Chuck 145
Brown, Cynthia 153
Brown, Danielle Melanie 156
Brown, David 100
Brown, David, Jr. 95, 163
Brown, Deborah 36
Brown, Doug 227
Brown, Eric Martin 217
Brown, Hallie 133

Brown, Irina 144
Brown, Jason Robert 49, 127, 161
Brown, Jeb 23
Brown, Jessica Leigh 54
Brown, John Francis 187
Brown, Judy 179
Brown, Katy 188
Brown, Keirin 145
Brown, Kyle 229, 230
Brown, Laura Grace 96, 168
Brown, Lewis 218
Brown, Luqman 170
Brown, Michael 95, 131, 221, 227
Brown, Michael Henry 174
Brown, P.J. 158, 294
Brown, Paul 37
Brown, Peter 95
Brown, Renee Monique 92
Brown, Robin Leslie 155
Brown, Roger 49
Brown, Ronald K. 132
Brown, Siobhan Juanita 139
Brown, Stephen 204
Brown, Sterling K. 96, 128
Brown, Tim 148
Browne, Christopher 149
Browne, Roscoe Lee 124
Browning, Amber K. 200
Browning, Caren 218
Brownlee, Addie 147
Brownlee, Gary 171
Brownson, Karmenlara 144
Brownstein, Norman 40
Brownstone 192
Broyles, Tracy 171
Bruce, Andrew 71, 196
Bruce, Claudia 171
Bruel, Kaya 167
Brumble, Stephen, Jr. 151
Brummel, David 167, 220
Bruneau, Tim 188
Brunell, Catherine 75
Brunner, Kathryn 231
Brunner, Michael 48, 125
Bruno, Lou 29
Bruno, Tara 223
Brustein, Robert 186
Brustofski, Larry 156
Bruton, Amanda 158
Bryan-Brown, Adrian 24, 27, 29, 44, 50, 51, 52, 53, 54, 58, 60, 65, 66, 67, 69, 70, 71, 76, 96, 100, 102, 112, 132
Bryant, Brienan 144
Bryant, Lance 212
Bryant, Lee 173, 205
Bryant, Shannon 178

Bryant, Tom 224
Bryant, Tommy 188
Bryll, Dee Anne 200
Buberman, Shalom 186
Buccaneer, The 156
Bucciarelli, Renee 150
Buchanan, Georgia 179
Buchanan, Linda 183
Buchholtz, Susan 192
Buchman, Allan 95
Buchner, Georg 145, 167
Buckley, Betty 125
Buckley, Candy 67
Buckley, Michael 133
Buckley, Patrick Michael 151
Buddeke, Kate 59
Buderwitz, Tom 225
Budin, Rachel 194
Budner, Jeffrey 225
Budries, David 209, 226, 233, 234
Buell, Bill 128, 151, 179
Buena Vista 65
Buffini, Moira 159
Buford, Bill 190
Buford, William 190
Buggeln, Samuel 154
Buicks 151
Bulaoro, Laurie 209
Bull, Ginevra 159
Bulliard, Camille 209
Bullins, Ed 144
Bullock, Angela 216
Bulos, Yusef 97
Bulosan, Carlos 151
Bunch, Elizabeth 150, 183
Bundy, James 233, 234
Bundy, Laura Bell 26, 294
Bunin, Keith 130
Bunn, David Alan 93
Bunsee, Antony 102
Buol, John Jay 140
Buonopane, Todd 147, 167
Burba, Blake 74
Burd, Frank 232
Burdett, Patricia 193
Burdette, Nicole 161
Burgess, Troy Allan 65
Burgi, Chuck 32
Burgoyne, Marissa 110
Burgoyne, Sidney J. 180
Burich, George 162
Burke, Christopher 163
Burke, Gillian 231
Burke, Kathleen 211
Burke, Marylouise 127
Burke, Mary Catherine 159, 178
Burke, Richard 162
Burke, Tim 111, 193

Burkell, Scott 142
Burkett, Shannon 92, 130, 294
Burkholder, Page 163
Burmester, Leo 49
Burnett, Carol 33
Burnett, Janinah 38, 39
Burnett, Matthew 212
Burnette, Dorsey, III 49
Burning Blue 158
Burns, Andrea 66
Burns, Christopher 217, 222
Burns, Heather 106
Burns, Niea 41
Burns, Ralph 68, 75, 124
Burns, Trad A. 171
Burn This 93
Burr, Fritzi 313
Burrell, Fred 132
Burrell, Ty 93, 175
Burridge, Hollis 42, 59
Burrows, Allyn 185
Burrows, Kevin M. 220
Burrows, Sidney, Jr. 185
Burson, Linda 152
Burstein, Danny 110
Burt, Courtney 204, 205
Burthwright, Karen 196
Burtka, David 58, 59
Burton, Arnie 105, 157, 218, 219, 294
Burton, DyShaun 146
Burton, Kate 80, 128
Burton, Laura 231
Burton, Matthew 94
Burward-Hoy, Ken 124
Burwell, Carter 173
Buscemi, Steve 96
Busch, Charles 168, 294
Bush, Bob 39
Bush, Nancy 111
Business Lunch in the Russian Tea Room 152
Bustamante, Billy 187
Buster 220
Buster, Diane Michelle 150
Bus Stop 214
Butelli, Louis 92
Butiu, Melody 212, 226
Butkus, Denis 139, 150
Butler, Chris 220
Butler, Gregory 68
Butler, Isaac 158
Butler, Kerry 26, 294
Butler, Michael 224
Butler, Paul 144
Butler, Tom 159
Butterell, Jonathan 54, 125
Butterfield, Judy 184
Butter and Egg Man, The 167
Butz, Norbert Leo 74, 151

Buurman, Jasper 171
Bye, Bye 174
Byers, Joe 139
Byk, Jim 29, 58, 76, 126, 127
Bynner, Witter 148
Byrd, Anne Gee 215
Byrd, Carl L. 49
Byrd, Thomas Jefferson 45, 237
Byrd-Munoz, Pevin 49
Byrne, Andrew 233
Byrne, Greg 212
Byrne, Pete 162
Byrne, Teressa 211
Byrnes, Brian 179
Byrnes, Michael 176
Byrnes, Tommy 32
Byron, Amanda 192
By Her Side 140

C
Caballero, Christophe 66
Cabaret 67
Cabrera, Mario 212
Cacioppo, P.J. 157
Caddick, David 72
Cadell, Selina 123
Cadiff, Andrew 192
Café a Go Go 142
Cafe A Go Go Theatre 142
Caffey, Marion J. 151, 211, 224
Cahill, Cynthia 224
Cahn, Danny 26
Cahn, Victor L. 162
Cahoon, Kevin 70
Cain, Candice 199, 225
Cain, Marie 111
Cain, William 92, 294
Caird, John 127
Caisley, Robert 232
Cake, Jonathan 41, 167, 237
Calamaro, Frank 222
Calaway, Belle 68
Caldwell, George 91, 211, 224
Caldwell, Jeff 208
Caldwell Theatre Company 193
Cale, David 154, 223
Calene-Black, Shelly 183
Calexico 186
Calhoun, Jeff 198
Calhoun, Matthew 146
Caliban, Richard 144
Calin, Angela Balogh 225
Call, Edward Payson 207
Callaghan, Sheila 148
Callahan, Matthew 232
Callaway, Liz 60, 294
Calleri, James 130, 131, 213
Callicutt, Jonathan 96
Call the Children Home 176
Calma, Franne 65

Calo, Peter 26
Calpito, Isaac 141
Calvello, Jessica 143, 157
Camacho, Blanca 177
Camblin, Zina 215
Camelot 220
Camera, John 155
Cameron, Bruce 124
Cameron, John 223
Cameron, Linda 222
Cameron, Rob 163
Cammarata, Diane 227
Camp, Joanne 43, 155, 295
Camp, Joshua 172
Campbell, Alan 177
Campbell, Alexi Kaye 102
Campbell, Almeria 145
Campbell, Annie 168
Campbell, Beatrice 194
Campbell, Christopher 145
Campbell, Cori Lynn 147
Campbell, Drae 144
Campbell, Jeff 71
Campbell, Justin 179
Campbell, Kirsten 41
Campbell, Libby 217
Campbell, Nell 54
Campbell, Rob 126
Campbell, Sarah 205
Campbell, Sekou 192
Campion, John 215
Campion, Kieran 36
Campo, Helen 40
Campo, John 124
Canaan, Paul 220
Canavan, Elizabeth 101, 151
Cancelmi, Louis 48
Cancilla, M. Nunzio 214
Cander, William 106
Canfield, Mitchell 211
Cani, Christine 101
Cannavale, Bobby 129
Cannistraro, Mark 143, 158
Cannon, Alice 179, 183
Cannon, Devin Dunne 211
Cannon, Jessica 142
Cannon, Paige 205
Canonico, Gerard 91
Canonigo, Rosanna 143
Cantler, Will 186
Cantler, William 98, 173
Cantone, Mario 160, 225
Cantor, Carolyn 143
Cantor, Daniel 97
Caparelliotis, David 126, 127
Capital Repertory Theatre 194
Capitol Steps: When Bush Comes to Shove 115
Caplan, Henry 148
Caplan, Matt 74

Capone, Joseph 150
Capone, Tony 124
Capote, Truman 124, 222
Capozzi, Darren 146
Capozzi, Joe 158
Capps, Lisa 194
Cap 21 Theater 142
Cara Lucia 173
Carden, Stuart 158
Cardinalli, Valentina 152
Cardona, Iresol 70
Carey, Jared T. 130
Carey, Jess 140
Carey, Tom 196
Caridad Svich 175
Carino, Joel 147, 149
Cariou, Len 124, 160
Carl, Christopher 220
Carlebach, Joshua 178
Carlin, Aviva Jane 149
Carlin, Chet 212
Carlin, Joy 224
Carlin, Tony 52, 71
Carlisle, Craig 160, 172
Carlson, Jeffrey 44, 81
Carlson, Richard 183
Carlson, Roberta 224
Carlson, Sandra 69
Carmello, Carolee 76, 125
Carmichael, Bill 71
Carmody, Brian 109
Carnahan, Harry 212, 216
Carnahan, Jim 27, 44, 51, 52,
    53, 54, 58, 60, 75, 104
Carnelia, Craig 42, 219
Caron, David 92
Carousel 180
Carpenter, Barnaby 125
Carpenter, Bridget 174
Carpenter, Cassandra 185
Carpenter, Dave 196
Carpenter, James 185
Carpenter, Karen 217
Carpenter, Willie C. 220
Carpetbagger's Children, The
    115, 225
Carr, Ann 158
Carr, Geneva 168
Carraasco, Roxane 68
Carrafa, John 40, 76, 185
Carrasco, Roxane 68
Carrasquillo, Julien A. 168
Carrick, William 40
Carrico, Stewart 155
Carroll, Barbara 43, 48, 125, 180
Carroll, John 124
Carroll, Kevin 47, 128
Carroll, Kristina 143
Carroll, Melissa 143
Carroll, Ronn 125

Carroll, Vinnette 314
Carrubba, Philip 102
Carson, Thomas 200
Carter, Brian 160
Carter, Caitlin 68, 124
Carter, Eric 147
Carter, Gerrard 49
Carter, Jeanine 161
Carter, John 132
Carter, Lisa 92
Carter, Lonnie 151
Carter, McKinley 208
Carter, Myra 132
Carter, Nell 314
Carter, Sam 148
Carter, Vicki 220
Carthy, Kathleen Mary 215
Carvajal, Celina 129
Carver, Brent 131
Casanova, Michael 180
Cascio, Anna Theresa 105
Case, Andrew 156
Case, Ronald 168
Casella, Carlos 109
Casey, Chan 159
Casey, Shawna 150, 295
Casey, Warren 220
Caskey, Kristin 75
Casper, Christian 219
Cassandra Song 160
Cassel, John 158
Cassidy, Bethany J. 213
Cassidy, Orlagh 146
Cassier, Brian 27, 54
Cassius Carter Centre Stage
    217, 218, 219
Castellano, Anthony 148
Castellano, Dennis 225
Castellanos, Teo 169
Castellino, Bill 193
Castillo, Raul 169
Castillo, Sol 225
Castillo Theatre 142
Castini, Gabrielle 233
Castle, Elowyn 175
Castle, Robert 159
Casto, Robert 186
Catanese, Ivana 167
Cataract 174
Catcall 145
Cates, Kristy 106
Cates, Michael 112
Catherine Filene Shouse New
    Play Series 205
Cathey, Reg E. 160
Cato, Anders 192
Catti, Christine 96, 110, 111
Cavallo, Frank 211, 212
Cavanaugh, Michael 32
Cavanaugh, Tom 76

Cavari, Jack 75
Cave, Lisa Dawn 33
Cave, Suzanne 102
Cave, Victoria Lecta 67
Cavedweller 130
Cavenaugh, Matt 49
Ceballo, Kevin 60
Cedano, Johnathan 143
Cedeno, Tony 205
Celebrating Sondheim 35
Celebre, Jaesun 133
Celik, Aysan 147, 159, 175
Cellario, Maria 162
Celtic Christmas, A 169
Cenci, Rob 195
Centenary Stage Company 105
Centeno, Francisco 26
Centers, David A. 200
CenterStage 225
Center for Jewish History 133
Center Stage 143
Center Theatre Group 29, 94,
    196, 198
Centlivre, Susannah 148
Century Center for the
    Performing Arts 94, 105, 130,
    143, 157
Ceraulo, Rich 29, 187
Cerezo, Antonio 172
Cerveris, Todd 145, 200
Cervone, Thomas 204
Cesa, Jamie 111
Chadwick, Robin 211
Chaikelson, Steven 70
Chaikin, Joseph 144
Chaisson, Gilles 161
Chait, Marcus 49
Chalfant, Kathleen 104, 295
Chalifore, Dianne 186
Chamberlain, Andrea 110
Chamberlain, Travis 148
Chamberlin, Aubrey 154
Chamberlin, Mark 215
Chambers, David 226
Chambers, Lindsey 147
Chambers, Linsay 231
Chambers, Renee 231
Champa, Russell H. 126
Champagne, Lenora 154
Champion, Gower 69, 197
Champlin, Donna Lynne 33, 131
Chan, Claire 29
Chan, Eric 29
Chan, Joanna 155
Chan, Jovinna 150
Chandler, Blaire 201
Chandler, David 172, 174, 175
Chanel, Tymberlee 192
Chang, Christina 161
Chang, Jennifer 153

Chani, Pushpinder 102
Chao, Maia 230
Chapadjiev, Sophia 148
Chapin, Harry 209
Chapman, Clay Mcleod 158
Chapman, Mo 97
Chappell, Kandis 225
Charasuchin, Jonathan 317
Charity That Began at Home,
    The 173
Charles, Leovina 70
Charles, Walter 27, 295
Charley the Dog 224
Charlston, Erik 124
Charmin, Martin 230
Charney, Jordan 139
Charnin, Martin 133, 180, 220
Chase, David 29, 124
Chase, Eric 143
Chase, Jennifer 124
Chase, Kristin Stewart 148, 157
Chase, Myles 71
Chase, Will 65, 74
Chase-Lubitz, Lili 229
Chashama 143
Chastain, Don 314
Chastain, Sheffield 224
Chatterton, John 152
Chavez Ravine 199
Chayefsky, Paddy 213
Chbosky, Stephen 197
Cheadle, Don 86
Cheat 179
Cheatham, Maree 196
Chekhov, Anton 123, 149, 234
Chekov, Anton 185, 186
Chen, Tina 178
Cheng, Kipp Erante 147
Chepulis, Kyle 176
Chernov, Hope 177, 179, 295
Cherns, Penelope 161
Chernus, Michael 174
Cherry, Ben 158
Cherry, Erin 144
Cherry, Jennifer 183
Cherry Lane Theatre 144
Chesnut, Jerry 49
Chester, Nora 139
Chestnut, Maurice 196
Cheung, Cindy 168, 174
Chianese, Dominic 96
Chiang, Dawn 224, 227
Chiasson, Gilles 38
Chicago 68
Chicoine, Susan 96
Child's Christmas In Wales, A
    169
Children Of Herakles, The 186
Childs, Casey 100, 176
Childs, Kirsten 124

Childs, Rebecca N. 200
Chin, Staceyann 34
Chin, Wilson 233
Chineses Art of Placement, The
    158
Chinese Tale, A 170
Chiodo, Louis 179
Chiodo, Thomas 94
Chipman, Kerry 175
Chip in the Sugar, A 104
Chisholm, Anthony 199
Chittick, Joyce 75
Chitwood, Melanie 229
Chitwood, Seth 229
Cho, Linda 209, 213, 219
Cho, Myung Hee 184
Choi, Marcus 29
Cholet, Blanche 143
Chomet, Sun Mee 227
Chong, Ping 170
Christensen, Tracy 100
Christian, Angela 75
Christian, Eric L. 68
Christmas Carol, A 183, 184,
    200, 209, 211, 225, 229
Christmas Memory, A 222
Christmas with the Crawfords
    156
Christopher, Sybil 190
Christopher, Thom 192
Christopher T. Washington
    Learns to Fight 140
Chu, Lap-Chi 176, 199, 224
Chu, Nancy S. 146, 154
Chu, Robert Lee 155
Chumley, Sophia 198
Chun, Marc 157
Church, Joseph 70
Church, Vernon 178
Churchill, Caryl 130, 228
Churchman, Shawn 226
Chybowski, Michael 128, 130,
    215
Cicci, Jason 155
Ciccone, Christine 171
Cilento, Wayne 65
Cimmet, Alison 156
Cincinnati Playhouse in the Park
    200
Cindy Tolan Casting 186
Cino, Maggie 148
Circle East 143
Circle in the Square 51
Cirie, Andrea 200
Cirque Jacqueline 156
Cirrius, Nebraska 152
Cisek, Tony 187, 227
Citygirl, Geeta 153
City Center 97
City Center Encores! 124

City Center Stage I 126, 127
City Center Stage II 126, 127
City of Dreams 152, 168
City Theatre 202
Ciulla, Celeste 155
Claar, E. Alyssa 40
Claire, Jessica 159
Clancy, Dan 140
Clancy, Elizabeth Hope 94, 202
Clancy, John 129
Clandestine Crossing 175
Clarence Brown Theatre at the
  University of Tennessee 204
Clark, CA. 47, 128
Clark, Carrie 188
Clark, Chris 190
Clark, H. 147
Clark, Ian D. 231
Clark, Jim 227
Clark, Nate 193
Clark, Tom 197
Clark, Victoria 67, 76, 180
Clark-Price, Stafford 149
Clarke, Bill 205, 206, 216
Clarke, Jeffrey 111
Clarke, Peter Philip 143
Clarke, Tanya 23
Clarkson, Scott 143
Classical Theatre Of Harlem 144
Classic Stage Company 168
Class Mothers '68 147
Claussen, Diane 208
Clay, Caroline 144
Clay, Caroline Stefanie 233
Clay, Chris 69
Clay, Paul 74
Clayburgh, Jill 95, 160
Clayburgh, Jim 173
Claypool, Kathleen 314
Clayton, Lawrence 132
Cleale, Lewis 30
Clear, Alison 186
Clear, Patrick 33
Cleary, Malachy 36
Clear Channel Entertainment
  25, 32, 40, 75
Cleevely, Gretchen 143, 145
Clemente Soto Velez Cultural
  Center (CSV) 144
Cleveland, Rob 210
Cleveland Play House 206
Cleveland Raining 174
Clickner, Brian 212
Clifford, Christen 160
Climate 143, 160
Cline, Gina E. 172
Cline, Nathan 158
Cline, Perry 29
Cloud Nine 228
Clowe, Terrence McKinley 220

Clowers, Michael 69
Clubbed Thumb 145
Clubland 174
Club El Flamingo 109
Cobb, Amanda 233, 234
Cobey, Derrick 187
Coble, Eric 206
Coccio, Kevin 229
Cochrane, Anthony 92
Cochrane, Brendan 170
Cochren, Felix E. 206
Coco 58
Cocooning 158
Coda 158, 168
Cody, Anna 207, 219
Cody, Jennifer 76, 96
Cody, Matthew J. 194
Coffey, Julia 225
Coffin, Gregg 211, 212
Coffman, David 167
Cohen, Adrian 194
Cohen, Benjamin Brooks 59
Cohen, Buzz 129
Cohen, Greg 180
Cohen, Jeff 163
Cohen, Jeri Lynn 185, 191
Cohen, Lynn 174, 186
Cohen, Lynne 39
Cohen, Michael 213
Cohen, Rachel 231
Cohen, Samuel 194
Cohen, Scott 161
Cohn, Charlotte 38
Cohn Davis Associates 92
Coiro, Rhys 43
Colacci, David 206
Colangelo, Anthony 54
Cole, Janet 319
Cole, Jenna 211
Cole, Joanna 230
Cole, Kimberly 189
Cole, Nora 186
Cole, Ralph, Jr. 111
Cole, Rich 221
Cole, Robert 45
Colella, Jenn 49
Coleman, Chad L. 163
Coleman, Chris 222
Coleman, Cy 223
Coleman, Dara 169
Coleman, David 92
Coleman, Nathan 188
Coleman, Rosalyn 176
Colin, Margaret 52, 97, 295
Coll, Ivonne 215
Colley-Lee, Myrna 206
Collins, Ashley Wren 186
Collins, Christine 233, 234
Collins, David 153
Collins, Grant 205

Collins, Janet 314
Collins, Joey 191
Collins, Owen 92
Collins, Pat 23, 93, 230
Collins, Rufus 52, 185
Colman, Steve 34
Coloff, Rachel 76
Colon, Oscar A. 169, 177
Colón-Zayas, Liza 101, 151
Color Mad Inc. 92
Colossus of Rhodes, The 185
Colston, Robert 178
Colt, Alvin 110
Colton, John 155
Coluca, Teddy 150
Columbia Artists Management
  112
Columbia Artists Theatricals
  196, 197
Comden, Betty 180
Comeau, Jessica 38
Comedians 176
Comedy of Errors, The 92
Come Light the Menorah 140
Comfort, Jane 30
Coming Together 161
Compleat Female Stage Beauty
  217
Complicite 96
Compton, J.C. 143
Compton, Seth 229
Comstock, Eric 118
Conard, Don 204
Conarro, Ryan 153
Condren, Conal 152
Cone, Jeff 222
Cone, Michael 38, 295
Congdon, Constance 161
Conklin, Peggy 314
Conlee, John Ellison 80, 167
Conley, Alexandra 178
Conley, Kat 210
Conley, Matt 163
Conley, Miyoko 201
Conlin, Vanessa 38, 295
Connections 178
Connell, Gordon 176, 295
Connelly, Brendan 172, 176
Connelly, John 39
Connelly Theatre 145
Conners, Tommy 49
Connery, Sean 204
Connington, Bill 171
Connolly, Ryan 172
Connors, Anne 223, 231
Connors, Julie 75
Connors, Michael 141, 147
Conolly, Patricia 56
Conroy, Jarlath 125, 295

Conroy, Jim 157
Constantine, Deborah 194
Constant Wife, The 185
Contact 79
Conti, Eva 37
Converse, Frank 36, 295
Conville, Dan 221
Conway, Kathryn 40
Conway, Kevin 43, 295
Coogan, Tracy 149
Cook, Barbara 83, 196
Cook, Carolyn 210
Cook, Julia 140
Cooke, Marty 204
*Cookin' at the Cookery: The
  Music and Times of Alberta
  Hunter* 151, 224, 211
Cooleen, Dolores 190
Coolidge, David 226
Coon, Jeffrey 231
Cooney, Deborah 186
Coonrod, Karin 179
Cooper, Cara 49
Cooper, Chuck 68, 91, 174
Cooper, Helmar Augustus 45
Cooper, Max 62
Cooper, Mindy 68
Cooper, Pamela 94
Cooper, Sean 38
Cooper-Hecht, Gail 176, 179
Coopwood, Scott 222
Copeland, Carolyn Rossi 91
Copeland, Dawn 143
Copeland, Joan 222
Copeland, Marissa 131
Copeland, Richard 132, 143
Copenhagen 227, 229
Copp, Aaron 111, 217
Corbett, Hilary 231
Corbett, Patricia 38, 295
Corbett, Winslow 200
Corbino, Maurizio 72
Corcoran, Tim 162
Cordle, Dan 195
Cordon, Christopher 208
Cordon, Susie 131
Corduner, Allen 176
Corenswet, David 187
Corey, James 214
Coriaty, Peter J. 150
Corker, John 74
Corman, Maddie 146
Cormican, Peter 169
Cornelia, Craig 160
Cornelisse, Tonya 158
Cornell, Heather 50
Cornell, Sarah 73
Corner Wars 147
Cornholed! 148
Cornwell, Eric 35
Cornwell, Jason 143

Cornwell, Torrey 222
Corn Corn 156
Corn Exchange 102
Corre, Bo 178
Correa, AnaMaria 169
Corren, Donald 105, 157
Corrigan, Kevin 145
Corstange, Kevin 222
Cort, Bud 160
Cortese, Drew 129
Cortez, Natalie 227, 231
Cortez, Paul 213
Corthron, Kia 160, 213, 233
Cortinas, Jorge Ignacio 170
Cort Theatre 33, 55
Corwin, John 126
Coseglia, Jared 147
Cosentino, Paul 139
Cosla, Edward 215
Cossa, Joanne 180
Cosson, Steve 170
Costa, Richard 67
Costabile, David 168
Costabile, Richard 132
Costantakos, Evangelia 38
Costelloe, David 169
Cote, Alison 132
Cote, Doug 150
Cott, Thomas 223
Cotter, Margaret 104
Cottle, Jason 198
Cotton, Keith 26
Cotton, Shamika 163
Cotton Patch Gospel 209
Cottrell, Richard 132, 143
Coughlin, Bruce 58, 76, 131
Coughlin, Ruth 175
Counter Girls 143
Countess, The 193
Courtney, Erin 170
Courtney, Philip 157
Courtyard Playhouse 111
Court Theatre 208
Cousens, Heather 127
Cousineau, Jorge 187
Cover, Bradford 207
Covey, Elizabeth 200
Covey, Steve 212
Coward, Noël 190
Cowart, Scott 210
Cowell, Matt 131
Cowie, Jeff 131, 183, 202
Cowles, Peggy 141
Cowley, Hannah 175
Cox, Catherine 220
Cox, Jane 100, 168, 176, 223
Cox, Jennifer Elise 225
Cox, Julie 124
Cox, Tim 156
Cox, Veanne 116

Coxe, Helen 168
Coyle, Bill 32, 73, 104
Coyle, Bruce W. 220
Coyne, John 209
Coyne, Sterling 162
Cozart, Stephanie 201
Cozior, Jimmy 92
Cozens, Dan 186
Crace, Jim 178
Craig, Deborah S. 140, 149, 174
Craig, Joel 314
Craig, Lawrence 38
Craig, Liam 179, 219
Crain, Tom 49
Cralle, Darin 188
Crampton, Glory 220
Crane, Gregory 225
Crane, Warren 23
Craven, Elizabeth 205
Craven, Kim 196
Crawford, David 221
Crawford, James 209
Crawford, Jared 196
Crawford, Kim 150
Crawford, Michael 40
Crawford, Richard 178
Craymer, Judy 71, 196
Crazy Girl, The 160
Crazy Locomotive, The 144
Creaghan, Dennis 193
Creative Artists Laboratory
   Theatre 145
Creative Battery 197
Creative Theatrics' Performance
   Team 163
Creek, Luther 125
Creel, Gavin 75
Creel, Lauren 227
Cremin, Sue 225
Creskoff, Rebecca 192
Cresswell, Luke 112
Crimson Productions 94
Criss Angel: Mindfreak 116
Crocker, Nathan 210
Croft, Paddy 139
Croiter, Jeff 100, 126, 176,
   194, 203, 213, 229
Crom, Rick 76
Croman, Dylis 124
Cromarty, Alice 28
Cromarty, Peter 28, 91, 111
Cromarty and Company 28, 91
Cromelin, Caroline 158
Cromer, Bruce 200
Cromie, Aaron 187
Cromwell, David 167, 217, 222
Cronin, Christopher T. 31, 51
Crooks, David 38
Croom, Gabriel A. 92
Croot, Cynthia 161

Crosby, B.J. 68, 92, 295
Cross, Chaon 208
Cross, Tim 158
Crossley, Don 222
Crouse, Russel 231
Crow, Laura 177
Crowe, David 222
Crowe, Timothy 228, 229, 230
Crowell, Sarah 215
Crowl, Jason 149
Crowley, Bob 65
Crowley, Dennis 52, 60, 102
Crowley, Kurt 186
Crowns 132
Crucible, The 79, 227
Crudup, Billy 80, 96
Cruikshank, Holly 32, 296
Cruise, Julee 129
Crumb, Ann 144
Crumbs from the Table of Joy
   206
Cruse, Andrew 154
Cruz, Francis J. 220
Cruz, Michael 151
Cruz, Michelle 218, 219
Cruz, Nilo 170
Cryer, Dan 109
Cryer, Suzanne 131
CTM Productions 61
Cuban Operator Please and
   Floating Home 156
Cucci, Tony 45
Cuccioli, Robert 97, 146
Cucuzza, Robert 154
Cuddy, Mark 211, 212
Cudia, John 72
Cuervo, Alma 67, 174, 219
Culbert, John 208
Culbreath, Lloyd 124
Culek, Robert 177
Cullen, David 72
Cullen, Sean 179, 183
Cullinan, Ivanna 150
Culliton, Joseph 222
Cullman, Joan 50, 204
Cullman, Trip 47, 105, 128, 157,
   170
Cullum, JD 225, 226
Cullum, John 76
Culman, Peter 209
Culpepper, Dan 124
Culturemart 149
Culture Clash 199, 224
Culture Clash in Americca 224
Culture Club 145
Culture Project, The 95
Cumming, Alan 163
Cumming, Richard 229
Cummings, Brenda 220
Cummings, Evan 212

Cummings, Jack, III 145
Cummings, Tim 24
Cummins, Stephanie 75
Cumpsty, Michael 56, 69
Cunliffe, Colin 220
Cunningham, Christina 96
Cunningham, John 30
Cunningham, Johnny 215
Cunningham, John C. 156
Cunningham, Jo Ann 141, 216
Cunningham, Michael 132
Cunningham, Sean 154
Cunningham, T. Scott 158
Cunninghmam-Eves, Katherine
   222
Curchak, Alia 205
Curran, Seán 131, 234
Curran, Shawn 155
Currie, Richard 202
Currier, Margaret A. 194
Curry, David 186
Curry, Michael 70
Curry, Rosa 92
Curtin, Catherine 160
Curtin, Jane 36
Curtis, Jeff 76
Curtis, Keene 315
Curve 171
Cushing, James 23
Cusick, Melissa 123
Cuskern, Dominic 155
Cusson, Ann-Marie 173
Cuthbert, David Lee 215, 217,
   218
Cutler, Joe 127
Cvijetic, Stefani Katarina 233
Cvitanov, Kevin 146
Cwikowski, Bill 168
Czarnecki, Julie 187
Czyz, Chris 205

D
D., Eva 104
D'Abruzzo, Stephanie 179, 296
Dadiani, Marika 172
Daedalus: A Fantasia of
   Leonardo Da Vinci 187
Dafoe, Willem 296
Daggett, Larry 221
D'Agostini, David Raphael 217,
   218, 219
D'Agrossa, Anna 148
Dahlquist, Gordon 174, 175
Daily, Dan 155
Daily, Paul 143
Daisey, Mike 119
Daisy in the Dreamtime 139
Daisy Mayme 155
Dakota Project, The 149
Daldry, Stephen 130

Dale, Jim 176
Dalen, Patricia 200
D'Alessandro, Franco 145
Daley, Sandra 174
Dalgleish, Jack M. 102
Dallas Summer Musicals, Inc. 29
Dallas Theater Center 209
Dallimore, Stevie Ray 130
Dallin, Howard 200
Dallos, Chris 97, 227
Dalrymple, Jeff 219
Dalton, Jill 152
Dalton, Nicholas 151
Dal Vera, Rocco 200
Damashek, Barbara 191, 214
d'Amboise, Charlotte 68
D'Ambrosio, Tom 25, 62, 132
D'Amico, Melissa 229, 230
Damkoehler, William 228, 229,
   230
D'Amour, Lisa 174, 175
Damutzer, Don 103
Dana, F. Mitchell 220
Danao, Julie P. 74
Dance of the Vampires 40
Dance Theater Workshop 145
Dancing on Moonlight 174
Dancing Princesses, The 163
d'Ancona, Miranda 159
Dandridge, Merle 74
Dandridge, Sarah 152
Dane, Taylor 65
Danford, James 193
Danger of Strangers 143
Daniele, Graciela 125, 132
Danieley, Jason 80
Danielian, Barry 32
Danielli, Gordon 105
Daniels, Charles 49
Daniels, Gregory 231
Daniels, Matt 152
Daniels, Nikki Renee 60
Daniels, Ron 200
Danielsen, Carl J. 194
Danis, Amy 94
Dannick, Jeff 194
Danson, Randy 191, 215, 296
D'Antonio, Tara 227
Dantuono, Michael 69
Danvers, Marie 124
D'Aquila, Fabio 109
Darby, Brigit 153
Darion, Joe 37, 221
Darling, Danielle 229
Darling, Matthew 222
Darlow, Cynthia 139, 296
Darnutzer, Don 185, 194, 206
Darragh, Anne 191
Darragh, Patch 36
Darrell, Jessie 230

Darrow, Nathan 144
Darweish, Kammy 102
Darwell Associates 68
Daryl Roth Theatre 109, 145
Das, Meneka 102
Davalos, David 187
D'Avanzo, Sylvia 39
Davenport, Robert 145
Davenport, Johnny Lee 227
Daves, Evan 33
Davey, Patrick 141
Davey, Shaun 125, 208
David, Angel 169
David, Hal 60
David, James 60
David, Keith 174, 191
Davidson, Derek 188, 189
Davidson, Gordon 29, 94,
   196, 198
Davidson, Jack 45
Davidson, Jeremy 192
Davidson, Melissa 188, 189
Davidson, Tonja Walker 56
Davies, Amanda 167
Davies, Irving 50
Davies, Lowell 218
Davies, Peter 227
Davies, Stephen Bel 168
Davila, Ivan 140, 141, 160, 161
Davis, Ben 38
Davis, Briana 155
Davis, Christopher 220
Davis, Daniel 104
Davis, Eisa 174, 175
Davis, Eric Dean 111
Davis, Helen 68
Davis, Helene 92
Davis, Jen Cooper 98
Davis, Jonathan 210
Davis, K.C. 174
Davis, Keith 144, 159, 163
Davis, Kristin 160
Davis, Lizzy Cooper 174, 186
Davis, Mark Allan 70
Davis, Marshall L., Jr. 196
Davis, Mary Bond 26, 296
Davis, Michael 198
Davis, Morgan 212
Davis, Mylika 161
Davis, Randy A. 92
Davis, Raquel 178
Davis, Roz 144
Davis, Shaquela 221
Davis, Todd 171
Davis, Vicki R. 173
Davis, Will 159
Davis-Green, Marie 233
Davolos, Sydney 54
Dawes, Bill 158
Dawn, Karalee 71

Dawson, Deanne 156
Dawson, Margaret 162
Dawson, Michelle 175
Dawson, Neil 144
Dawson, Trent 140, 175, 223
Day, Jamie 296
Day, Johanna 157
Day, Maryam Myika 69
Day, Tarissa 146
Day, Tom 154
Day, Wes 112
Daye, Robert Scott 220
Daykin, Judith E. 124
Days, Maya 65, 124
Day in the Death of Joe Egg, A
  16, 52, 238
Dazzle, The 185
D'Beck, Patti 198
Dead Man's Socks 151
Deaf West Theatre 198
Deakins, Lucy 179
Deal, Frank 216
Dealy, Bill 159, 178
Dean, Bradley 37
Dean, Charles 185, 191
DeAngelis, Christopher 231
Dearest Enemy 180
DeArmon, Eric 101
Dear Prudence 157
Death in Venice 151
Death of a Salesman 210
Death of Frank 154
Death of Tintagiles, The 148
Debbie Does Dallas 96
deBenedet, Rachel 54
DeBerry, Teresa 210
Deblinger, David 151, 174
DeBord, Jason 95
DeBoy, Paul 200
DeCamillis, Chris 186
Decareau, Dick 212
DeCarlo, Kenny 39
DeCaro, Matt 185
DeChristopher, Dave 142
DeCicco, Christina 231
Deck, Deanna 105
DeCorleto, Drew 151
DeCoux, Nathan 143
Dee, Ruby 296
Deering, J. Claude 180
Def, Mos 86, 129
deGannes, Nehassaiu 228, 229
DeGioia, Eric 75, 124
DeGonge-Manfredi, Marcy 180
Dehnert, Amanda 228, 229, 230
Dejesus, Ron 32
deJong, Jeanette 216
DeKaye, Aryn 109
Delacorte Theater 128
DelaCruz, Scott 94, 179

DeLaria, Lea 132
Delate, Brian 57
DelColle, Rob 231
deLeeuw, Meyer 142
DeLeon, Aya 156
Delgado, Emilio 156
Delgado, Judith 174
DelGaudio, Dennis 32
D'Elia, Vincent 231
Delillo, Don 141
Delinger, Larry 207
Delisco 65
Delto, Byron 219
del Arco, Jonathan 225
Del Corso, Geralyn 72
Del Guidice, Judy 158
Del Negro, Matthew 158
Del Prete, Mike 194
Del Rossi, Angelo 220
Del Sherman, Barry 163
Del Valle, Mayda 34
Del Valle, Melissa Delaney 169
DeMaio, Tommy 23
DeMann, Frederick 47
DeMann, Pilar 47
Demar, Jonathan 156
DeMarse, James 139
Demerritt, Matt 225
Demery, Brandon 98
DeMetsenaere, Bill 212
Demont, Lisa 168
Demon Baby 170
Dempsey, Michael 62
Dempster, Curt 168
DeMunn, Jeffrey 36, 296
Denithorne, Peg 143
Denley, William 188
Denman, Jeffry 73, 111, 147
Dennehy, Brian 5, 62, 296
Dent, John 37
Dent, Kelly 40
Denton, Dylan 41, 167
Dentone, Julieta 109
D'Entrone, Eric 158
Denuszek, Jason 208
Denzer, Chris 150
DeOni, Chris 174
Derasse, Domenic 124
Derelian, Gregory 213
DeRose, Teresa 72
Derrah, Thomas 186
Desai, Angel 168
Desanti, Michael J. 190
Descarfino, Charles 75
Desch, Brad 146
Design Your Kitchen 145
Desjardins, Martin 213, 233
deSpain, Brandon 150
Details 153
Dettman, Criag 217

Devaux-Shields, Charlotte 217, 218, 219
Devils of Loudun, The 171
Devine, Julia Ann 211
Devine, Nicholas 171
Devine, Sean 178
DeVinney, Gordon 200, 201, 216
Devlin, Es 52
Devon, Robert Lee Taylor 220
deVries, David 66
DeVries, Dawn 214
DeVries, Jon 179, 183
Dewar, Jenny 36
Dewhurst, Jeffrey 171
DeWitt, David 140, 143
DeWitt, Rosemarie 167
deWolf, Cecilia 168
DeWolf, Nat 47
Dey, Naleah 124
Deyle, John 76
DeYoe, Kevin 231
De La Guarda: Villa Villa 109
de Berry, David 211
De Camillis, Chris 186
De Candia, Rosie 220
de Ganon, Clint 26
de Guzman, Donna Sue 154
de Haas, Aisha 74
de Haas, Darius 213
De Jesus, Wanda 191
de Jong, Alexander 69
de la Fuente, Joel 149, 153
de Michele, Heather 148
de Ocampo, Ramón 151, 174, 234
De Shae, Ed 196
De Shields, André 80, 223
de Suze, Alexandra 124
de Vega, Lope 149
Diamond, Liz 233
Diana, Rachel 172
Dias, John 128
Dias, Romi 141
Diaz, Carlos 172
Diaz, David 200
Diaz, Natascia 37, 296
Dibble, Sean 171
Dibiasio, Matt 146
DiBuono, Toni 27, 145
Dick, Adam 151
Dick, Paul 151
Dickens, Charles 183, 184, 200, 209, 211, 225, 229
Dickerson, Brian 150
Dickerson, Nicole 185
Dickerson, Will 208
Dickert, Les 227
Dickey, Jessica 213

Dickinson, Shelly 74
Dickstein, Rachel 175
DiConcetto, Joseph 66
Dido (and Aeneas) 156
Diehl, John 150
Dietrich, Adam Justin 209
Dietz, Buck 133
Dietz, Ryan 171
Dietz, Steven 202
Dietz, Susan 45, 223
Diflo, Mick 176
Diggs, Taye 68
Dignan, Pat 172
DiGregorio, Taz 49
Dill, Sean 152
Dillard, Nakia 223
Dilliard, Marcus 191
Dillingham, Charles 29, 196, 198
Dillman, Laura 152
Dillon, Mia 36, 174, 222, 296
Dilly, Erin 27, 296
DiMaggio, Stephanie 175
DiMento, Neale Anthony 231
Dimetos 192
DiMilla, Paul 186
Dimino, Donna 146
Dimon, Elizabeth 193
DiMonda, Vic 171
Dimson Theatre 145
Dimuro, Sarah 229
DiMurro, Tony 142, 146
Dinelaris, Alexander 102, 167
Dini, Gary 170
Dinklage, Jonathan 60
Dinklage, Peter 147
Dinnerman, Amy 27, 44, 54, 132
Dinner at Eight 17, 43
DiNoia, Jennifer 196
Dionisio, Ma-Anne 29
DiPietro, Jay 155
Dipietro, Joe 110, 214
Dipteracon, Or Short Lived
  S*%t Eaters 172
Directors Company, The 146
Dirty Blonde 207, 221
Dirty Laundry 152
Dirty Story 151
Disco, Michele 219
Disney 70
Disorderly Conduct 161
DiVita, Diane 45, 91
Divorce Southern Style 189
Dixon, Beth 92, 185
Dixon, Brandon Victor 124
Dixon, Keith 132
Dixon, MacIntyre 58, 59
Dixon, Tami 143
Dizzia, Maria 211
Di Dia, Maria 68
Di Donna, Suzanne 148

Di Martino, Annie 144
Di Novelli, Donna 170
Di Vecchio, Danielle 226
Dlamini, Nomvula 70
Dlamini, Ntomb'khona 70
Dlugos, Gregory J. 54
Dmitriev, Alex 139
DMV Tyrant 152
Dobell, Curzon 179, 201
Dobie, Edgar 228
Dobozé, Gunnard 213
Dobrikow-O'Hep, Norma 193
Dobrish, Jeremy 144, 147
Dobrusky, Pavel 206
Dockery, Leslie 93, 150
Doctor, Bruce 27
Doctor Will See You Now, The
  152
Dodd, C. Sue 204
Dodge, Alexander 125, 194, 209, 213
Dodge, Anthony 190
Dodge, Marcia Milgrom 190
Dodger Management Group 100
Dodger Productions 66, 205
Dodger Stage Holding 35, 100, 197
Dodger Theatricals 69, 76
Dods, John 66
Doemelt, Kurt 218
Doers, Matthew 170
Doherty, Amanda 211, 212
Doherty, Denny 162
Doherty, Jeffrey Johnson 95
Doherty, Madeleine 73
Doherty, Sarah 187
Doherty, Vincent 102
Doi, Yuriko 201
Dokuchitz, Jonathan 27, 60
Dolan, Amy 69
Dolan, Donovan 154
Dolan, Judith 33, 146, 183, 184
Dold, Mark H. 168
Doll House, A 204
Doman, Ally 223
Doman, Cole 223
Domigues, Dan 186
Dominczyk, Dagmara 56
Domingo, Colman 147, 191
Domingo, Ron 151, 174
Domingues, Dan 186
Domoney, Kurt 147
Domski, Jude 158
Donaghy, Tom 187
Donahoe, Emily 215
Donahower, April 211
Donaldson, Martha 104, 130
Dondlinger, Mary Jo 169, 179
Donegan, James 133
Donen, Stanley 98

Donkey Show, The 109
Donmar Warehouse 123
Donna Paradise 156
Donnelly, Candice 104, 110, 124
Donnelly, Kyle 185
Donnelly, Terry 169
Donno, Pete 112
Donoghue, Tim 218
Donovan, Conor 36
Donovan, Sean 154
Donowaki, Kyoko 173
Don Juan 179
Dooley, Bill 187
Dooley, Paul 196
Doornbos, Jeffrey 112
Door Wide Open 142
DoPico, Madeleine Jane 145
Doran, Bathsheba 144
Doran, Carol F. 198, 199
Doran, Jesse 139
Doran, Tonya 71
Dorfman, David 223
Dorfman, Robert 222
Dorian, Stephanie 152
Dorman, Tracy 227
Dornfeld, Autumn 174
Dorsen, Annie 145
Dorsey, Court 171
Dorsey, Diane 214
Dorsey, Kent 185, 207, 224
D'Orta, Christina 220
Dory, Johnna 176
Doshi, Marcus 178, 209, 211
Doss, John 43
Dossett, John 58
Dostoevsky, Fyodor 147
Dos Passos, John 139
Dos Santos, Marivaldo 112
Dotson, Bernard 42, 219
Doty, Johnna 110
Dougherty, Christine 185, 207
Dougherty, Doc 105
Dougherty, Jessie 210
Douglas, Thomas Wesley 202
Douglas, Timothy 192, 203, 213, 227
Douglas Fairbanks Theatre 110, 146
Doukas, Nike 225
Douzos, Adriana 50, 69, 98, 99, 100
Dove, Lilith 156
Dowlin, Tim 147
Dowling, Bryn 73
Dowling, Cheryl 180
Dowling, Jocelyn 40
Dowling, Joe 44
Dowling, Joey 124
Dowling, Michael 192
Down, Katie 175

Downey, Gerald 153
Downey, Melissa 32
Downing, Michael B. 190
Down a Long Road 105
Down in the Depths 163
Doyle, Jim 156
Doyle, Kathleen 176
Doyle, Lori M. 60
Doyle, Michael 158, 219
Doyle, Richard 225
Doyle, Timothy 57
Dr. Jekyll and Mr. Hyde 207
DR2 Theatre 146
Draghici, Marina 223
Dragotta, Robert 29
Drake, David 145
Drake, Donna 106, 156
Dramatic Forces 29, 75
Dramaturg 98
Drama Dept. 168
Drance, George 172
Draper, Alex 92
Draper, David F. 184
Drapkin, Russel 99
Draves, J. Kevin 106
Drawer Boy, The 216, 221, 224, 226
Drawn and Quartered 169
Dreamworks 74
Dream a Little Dream 162
Dressel, Michael 56
Drew, Jeffrey 159
Drew, Sarah 48, 296
Drewe, Anthony 223
Drewes, Glenn 75, 124
Dreyblatt, Arnold 172
Dreyfuss, Meghann 71
Dreyfuss, Richard 95
DRG 110
Driffield, Joseph 167
Driscoll, Kermit 49
Driscoll, Marie-Claude B. 221
Driscoll, Ryan 133
Driver, Kip 158
Driving Miss Daisy 195, 221
Droznin, Andrei 186
Drummond, Scott 187
Drury Theatre 206, 207
Druzbanski, Nicholas 220
D'Souza, Laine 145
D'Souza, Neil 102
Duarte, Amanda 224
Duarte, Derek 206
Duarte, Myrna 178
Dubin, Al 69, 197
Dubin, Laura 219
Dubiner, Julie Felise 223
Dublin Carol 99
DuBoff, Jill B.C. 61, 179
DuBois, Peter 174

Dubreuil, Alexa 154
Dubrowsky, Kristin 143
DuChez, Liz 207
Duclos, Janice 228, 229, 230
Duclos, Matthew Janice 228
Dudding, Joey 59
Dudley, Anton 144
Dudu Fisher: Something Old, Something New 95
Dueh, Jeremy R. 231
Duell, William 176, 296
Duff, Brian 188
Duffield, Marjorie 163
Duffy, Alice 213
Duffy, Michelle 191
Duffy, Mike 180
Duffy, R. Ward 200
Duffy, Scott 140
Duffy Theatre, The 111
DuFord, Chip 206
Duggan, Annmarie 94
Duguay, Brian 67, 163
Dug Out 148
Duke, Cherry 124
Duke Theater, The 130, 131
Dullea, Keir 222
DuMaine, Rebecca 147
duMaine, Wayne 37
Dumas, Jennifer 111
Dunagan, Deanna 208
Duncan, Laura Marie 150
Duncan, Lindsay 84
Duncan, Sandy 176, 297
Duncan-Gibbs, Mamie 68
Dundas, Jennifer 225
Dundas, Shane 153
Dundon, Marie Bridget 150
Dunn, Erin 67
Dunn, Jennifer 147
Dunn, Juliette 232
Dunn, Lindsay 49
Dunn, Ronnie 49
Dunn, Ryan 217, 221
Dunn, Sally Mae 66
Dunn, Wally 59
Dunne, Carol 206
Dupas, Ariel 227
Duplantier, Donna 233
DuPont, Anne 139
Dupras, Nicole 227
Dupré, Chris Payne 65
Dupree, Lynette 196
Duprey, Leslie 148
Dupuis, John Michael 186
Duquesnay, Ann 151, 196, 211, 224
Duran, Sherrita 124
Durang, Christopher 152, 160, 202, 219
Durang Project: Five Short Plays,

The 152
Duras, Marguerite 145
Durbin, Holly Poe 218, 219
Durham, Nathan 129
Duricko, Erma 143
Durkee, Savitri 154
Durkin, Dave 155
Durkin, Todd Allen 153
Durning, Charles 96
Durning, Jeanine 223
Durran, Jacqueline 41
Dusenbury, Tom 153
Dusenske, Daren 214
d'Usseau, Arnaud 141
Dutton, Charles S. 45, 297
Duva, Christopher 148, 150, 174, 175
Duwon, Tony 104
Duykers, John 167
Dwyer, Terrence 215
Dybisz, Kenneth 60
Dyck, Jordan 162
Dygert, Denise 194
Dykstra, Brian 139
Dykstra, Ted 194
Dymally, Amentha 220
Dysart, Eric 26, 297
Dyszel, Bill 143

E
Eaddy, Michael 221
Eagan, Jason Scott 127
Eagar, Erin 149
Eakeley, Benjamin 156
Eaker, Ira 315
Eakes, Jenny 141
Early, Kathleen 169
Earth's Sharp Edge, The 172
Easley, Bill 92
Easley, Byron 222
East, Richard 71, 196
Easter, Allison 172
Eastman, Donald 194, 195, 227
Easton, Richard 125
Eastwood, Alison 211
East 13th Street Theatre 92
Eatfest 143
Eaves, Dashiell 125
Eaves, Obadiah 129
Ebb, Fred 67, 68, 192
Ebbenga, Caitlyn 223
Ebbenga, Eric 223
Ebersold, Scott 152, 174
Ebersole, Christine 43, 69, 104, 297
Echiverri, Dexter 220
Echoles, Rueben D. 104
Echols, Rick 184, 185
Eckert, Rinde 160, 186
Eckert, Virginia 230

Eddy, Rebecca 204, 205
Edel, Carrie 163
Edelstein, Barry 160, 168
Edelstein, Gordon 174
Edgar, David 207
Edge, Biff 204, 205
Edgerly, Corinne 145, 163
Edgerton, Annie 153
Edgerton, Nina 151
Edgewood Productions 98
Edington, Pamela 92
Edmunds, Kate 185
Edwards, Adam 219
Edwards, Alison 132
Edwards, Anderson 91
Edwards, Bill 152
Edwards, Duncan Robert 110, 220
Edwards, Fred 49
Edwards, Jason 153, 205, 216
Edwards, Jay 195
Edwards, Linda 205
Edwards, Luanne 170
Edwards, Michael Donald 227
Edwards, Sherman 189, 212
Effect of Gamma Rays on Man-in-the-Moon Marigolds, The 149
Effler, Charlie 205
Egan, John Treacy 73
Egan, Rich 178
Egan, Robert 191, 199
Eggers, Allison 180
Eggers, David 75
Egi, Stan 224
Ehlert, Kelly 225
Ehrenreich, Barbara 198, 229
Eidem, Bruce 59
Eigenberg, David 47
Eighteen 148
Einstein's Dreams 147
Eisenberg, Deborah 132
Eisenberg, Ned 150, 161
Eisenhauer, Peggy 30, 58, 67, 92, 132, 196, 197
Eisenman, Andrew 149
Eisenstein, Alexa 130
Eisloeffel, Elizabeth 201
Eisner, Morten 167
Ekeh, Onome 163
Ekulona, Saidah Arrika 160, 233
Elaine Stritch at Liberty 197
Elam, Genevieve 227
Elder, David 69
Eldredge, Lynn 111
Eleanore and Isadora: A Duet of Sorrows 179
Eleazar, Joshua 205
Elegies 125
Elegy 149

Elephant Man, The 80
Elevator 160
Elg, Taina 145
Elhai, Robert 70
Elice, Eric 98
Elkins, Doug 186
Elle 163
Ellett, Trey 74
Elliard, Leslie 174, 175
Ellington, Mercedes 223
Elliott, David 95
Elliott, Patricia 1, 241, 243, 244, 246
Elliott, Robert 200
Elliott, Scott 144, 176
Elliott, Shawn 175
Ellipsis 158
Ellis, Brad 110
Ellis, Mary 315
Ellis, Michael Shane 151
Ellis, Richard 226
Ellis, Scott 27, 60
Ellis, Sheila O'Neill 224
Ellison, Bill 59
Ellison, Nancy 98
Ellison, Todd 30, 69, 197
Ellman, Bruce 127
Ellsmore, Siho 149, 153
Ellstein, Sylvia Regan 315
Elly, James 208
Elrod, Carson 130
Elsas, May Belle 315
Elsen Associates, Inc. 202, 203
Elson, Elizabeth 155
Elsperger, Bruce 224
Ely, Arista 229
Ely, Christian 152
El Samahy, Nora 191
Emelson, Beth 98, 99, 106, 167
Emerick, Shannon 144
Emerson, Ben 216
Emerson, Michael 159, 297
Emery, Lisa 144
Emmes, David 225
Emmons, Beverly 186, 190
Emond, Linda 51, 96, 297
Emory, Linda Rodgers 180
Emrich, Kathleen 193
Enchanted April 18, 56
Enderle, Evan 210
Enders, Camilla 155
Endpapers 92
Endre, Lena 123
Endy, Alex 149
Eng, Steven 201, 220
Engel, David 175
Engelkes, Charlotte 123
England, Mel 159
Engle, Tod 154
Engler, Michael 104

English, Donna 110
Engquist, Richard 93
Ensemble Studio Theatre 168
Ensign, Evan 42, 219
Ensler, Eve 120, 160
Ensweiler, Chris 210
Entitled Entertainment 62, 93
Entriken, Dan 38, 39
Ephron, Nora 42, 219
Epperson, John 297
Epps, Sheldon 220
Epstein, Adam 25
Epstein, Alvin 97
Epstein, Donny 95
Erba, Edoardo 156
Ercan, Bora 205
Erendira 149
Ergo Entertainment 62, 95
Ericksen, Susan 206
Erickson, Matthew 211, 212
Erickson, Mike 196
Ernst, Robert 184, 185
Errico, Melissa 10, 30, 160, 180
Erwin, Jonathan 206
Esbjornson, David 94, 97
Escaler, Ernest De Leon 29
Escamilla, Michael Ray 174, 179
Esler, David 171
Esparza, Raúl 67, 176, 180, 223, 297
Esper, Michael 168
Espinosa, Al 128
Espinoza, Brandon 58, 59
Espinoza, Mark D. 222
Esposito, Amy 230
Esposito, Giancarlo 297
Essenter, Brett 227
Essman, Nina 37
Esterman, Laura 141
Estevez, Abilio 169
Estevez, Oscar 109
Estey, Suellen 197
Esther, Queen 92
Eterovich, Karen 156
Ethel Barrymore Theatre 42, 57
Etta Jenks 155
Eubank, Gray 222
Eugene O'Neill Theatre 54
Euripides 41, 148, 159, 163, 167, 186, 233
Eurydice 139
Eustis, Oskar 91, 228, 229, 230
Evan, Rob 40, 91
Evangelisto, Christine 233
Evans, Ben 110
Evans, Bill 110
Evans, Christine 148
Evans, David 29
Evans, Daviel 205
Evans, Dawn 141

Evans, Douglas C. 217
Evans, Jessma 147, 154
Evans, Joan 140
Evans, Leo Ash 147
Evans, Omar 147
Evans, Scott Alan 139
Evans, Venida 93, 297
Evered, Charles 160
Everhart, Kurt 139, 173
Evers, Bruce 210
Evett, Benjamin 186
Evita 231
Evolution 147
Ewell, Dwight 163
Ewin, Paula 162
Ewing, Skip 49
Excelsior 148
Excerpt from Return to the Upright Position 160
Exode 156
Exodus 160
Exonerated, The 95
Expat/Inferno 170, 174
Eyer, J. Austin 180
Eyre, Richard 48

F

Fabel, Kyle 139
Faber, Ron 144
Fabrizi, Chip M. 133
Fadale, Cristina 74
Fagan, Garth 70
Fagan, Valerie 110
Fagin, Gary 216
Faiella, Lori 163
Faigin, Lesley M. 223
Fairbairn, Bill 149
Fairchild, Diane D. 208
Fair Game 175, 203
Faith Healer 218
Falco, Edie 17, 24, 161, 297
Falcone, Terianne 152
Falkenstein, Eric 62
Fallen 216
Fallon, Kevin 229, 230
Fallon, Sharon 23
Falls, Robert 62, 65
Fandrei, Graham 38
Fang, Izetta 207
Fanning, Gene 147
Fantaci, Jim 98
Farazis, Takis 97
Farber, Gene 168
Farber, Seth 26
Faridany, Francesca 191
Farina, Joseph M. 223
Farkas, Michael 149
Farley, Leo 162
Farrar, Ann 158
Farrar, Thursday 65

Farrell, Erin 178
Farrell, I. Thecia 142
Farrell, John 231
Farrell, Larry 75
Farrell, Sean 99, 169
Farrell, Tim 175
Farrell, Tom Riis 96
Farrow, Kris 194
Far and Wide 173
Far Away 130
Fasbender, Bart 132
Fashion 152
Faster 157
Fatone, Joey 74
Faulkner, Cliff 225
Faulkner, Todd 158
Fauss, M. Michael 201, 209
Faust, Bobby 38
Faustus 152
Fay, Tom 110
Faye, Pascale 32, 297
Fazio, Santo 151
Feagan, Leslie 156
Fear and Friday Nights 155
Feast of Fools 215
Fechter, Steven 158
Federle, Tim 59
Feehan, Brian 232
Fegley, Michael 172
Feichtner, Vadim 125
Feiffer, Halley 144
Feil, Simon 146
Feinberg, Amy 149
Feinberg, James 218
Feiner, Harry 222
Feingold, Michael 123
Feist, Gene 67
Felciano, Manoel 67
Feldman, Aaron 151
Feldman, Lawrence 75, 124
Feldman, Melissa 101, 151
Feldman, Rachel 147
Feldman, Tibor 151
Feldshuh, Tovah 103, 180, 297
Feliciano, Gloria 191
Felix, John 193
Feltch, John 56
Felty, Janice 186
Feng, Han 170
Fenkart, Bryan 145
Fennell, Bob 37, 42, 93, 98, 112, 130, 131
Fennell, Denise 145
Ferber, Edna 43
Ferencz, George 172
Ferguson, Jesse Tyler 132
Ferguson, John Forrest 204, 205
Ferguson, Michele 227
Ferguson, Michelle 227
Ferguson, Ryan 227

Ferguson, Wilkie, III 230
Ferland, Danielle 11, 55, 153, 297
Ferm, Shayna 179
Fernandez, Peter Jay 91, 157
Fernandez-Coffey, Gabriela 153
Feroce, Georgia 222
Ferra, Max 169
Ferrall, Gina 221
Ferrante, Frank 231
Ferrara, Susan 150
Ferrell, Joel 209
Ferrieri, Tony 202, 203
Ferro, Rafael 109
Ferrone, Richard 139
Ferver, Jack 175
Feser, Craig 175
Festival Theatre 218
Fetherolf, Andrew 157
Feuchtwanger, Peter R. 61
Feuer, Donya 123
Feuerstein, Mark 192
Feydeau, Georges 200
Feyer, Daniel 156
Fiedler, John 190
Field, Barbara 187
Field, Christine 221
Field, Crystal 178
Fielding, Jonathan 145
Fields, Edith 150
Fields, Heather 49
Fields, Joseph 29
Field of Fireflies 148
Fierstein, Harvey 8, 26, 297
Fife, Michael 145
Fifth of July 177
Fifth, Rob 33, 40, 55, 101
Figueroa, Rona 54, 297
Filerman, Michael 101
Filichia, Peter 240, 241
Filloux, Catherine 175
Findlay, Diane J. 133
Findley, Kaitlyn 221
Fine, Rosemary 173
Fine, Stacy N. 188
Fineman, Carol R. 92, 103, 104, 128, 129
Finley, Felicia 65
Finn, Rob 33, 40, 55, 101
Finn, William 125
Finneran, Katie 67
Finney, Stephanie 225
Fiorella, Kristin 233
Firman, Linsay 174, 175
First Day of School 160
Firth, Katie 150, 159
Fisch, Irwin 55
Fischer, Allison 91
Fischer, Jeremy 204, 205
Fischer, Kurt Eric 74, 213

Fischer, Stacy 213
Fish, Daniel 168, 234
Fishelson, David 103
Fisher, Dara 213, 219
Fisher, Ellen 167
Fisher, Joe 174
Fisher, Joley 67
Fisher, Jules 30, 58, 92, 196, 197
Fisher, LaVon 211
Fisher, Linda 169, 173, 209
Fisher, Rick 130
Fisher, Rob 68, 124
Fisher, Robert 133
Fisher, Roy 188
Fisher, Wade 142
Fishman, Alan H. 167
Fishman, Carol 132
Fishman, Shirley 215
Fitch, Codie 224
Fitzgerald, Christopher 30,
    125, 213
Fitzgerald, David 141
Fitzgerald, Glenn 98
Fitzgerald, Julie 190
Fitzgerald, Kathy 73
Fitzgerald, Paul 96
Fitzgerald, Peter 23, 32, 49,
    69, 99, 100, 197
Fitzgerald, Shannon 178
Fitzgerald, T. Richard 66, 95,
    98, 197
Fitzgibbons, Mark 168
Fitzmaurice, Colm 124
Fitzpatrick, Allen 69, 176, 227
Fitzpatrick, Bettye 183
Fitzpatrick, Julie 141
Fitzpatrick, Michael 197
Fitzpatrick, Shannon 215
Fitzsimmons, Andrew 156
FitzSimmons, James 213
Fitzsimmons, Kelly Jean 152
Fitzwater, Anna 148
Five Frozen Embryos 154
Fjelde, Rolf 315
Flachsmann, Isabelle 69
Flack 152
Flaherty, Stephen 125, 160
Flanagan, Laura 160
Flanagan, Margiann 179
Flanagan, Pauline 169
Flanders, Kristin 179, 198
Flanery, Bridget 156
Flaningam, Louisa 139
Flashing Stream, The 159
Flateman, Charles 92
Flaten, Barbara 193
Flatt, Travis 205
Flea in Her Ear, A 200
Flea Theater, The 146
Fleischmann, Stephanie 174

Fleming, Adam 26
Fleming, Eugene 60, 176, 297
Fleming, Sam 91
Fleming, Tommy 215
Fletcher, Gregory 143, 153
Fletcher, Jim 172
Fletcher, Susann 223
Flintstone, Trauma 156
Floating World 158
Flodine, Dave 202
Flood, Karen 177
Florax, Peter 155
Flores, Julia 224
Flowering Peach, The 133
Flower Drum Song 29
Floyd, Carmen Ruby 132
Floyd, Patricia R. 176, 226
Floyd, Thayules K. 180
Flying Machine 178
Flynn, Laura James 169
Flynn, Tom 213
Foa, Barrett 220
Focareta, Darren E. 202
Fodor, Barbara 49
Fodor, Peter 49
Foerder, Preston 215
Fogarty, Brud 184, 185
Fogarty, Sharon 173
Fogel, Donna Jean 140, 141
Fois, Laura 151
Folden, Lewis 187
Foley 102
Foley, Eamon 58, 59
Foley, John 205, 216
Foley, Peter 160, 186
Foley, Sean 50
Folino, Mary 232
Folksbiene Yiddish Theatre 223
Followell, James 100
Folson, Eileen 40, 59
Folts, Barbara 66
Fondakowski, Leigh 215
Fondoukis, Kosmas 97
Fong, Kelly 220
Font, Vivia 162, 174
Fontaine, Jeff 111
Fontana, Eric 229
Foote, Hallie 183
Foote, Horton 183, 225
*Forbidden Broadway: 20th
    Anniversary Celebration* 110
Forcht, Charlotte 229
Ford, A. Jackson 200
Ford, Betsy 198
Ford, Jennie 49, 297
Ford, Mark Richard 74
Ford, Paul 35
Ford, Rachel 148
Ford, Stevie 188

Ford Center for the Performing
    Arts 69
Foreigner, The 192
Foreman, Lorraine 231
Foreman, Richard 154
Foret, Nicole 49, 297
Forman, Ken 155
Fornes, Maria Irene 178
Forrester, Sean 176
Forsman, Carl 150
Fortenberry, Philip 60
Fortin, Mark Alexandre 186
Fortunato, Sean 208
Fortune's Fool 80, 193
45th Street Theatre 146
45 Bleecker 147
42nd Street 69, 197
47th St. Playhouse 111
47th Street Theatre 97, 147
Foss, Joseph 229
Fosse, Bob 68
Foster, Benim 175, 222
Foster, Charles 171
Foster, Duane Martin 124
Foster, Flannery 155
Foster, Herb 190
Foster, Hunter 76
Foster, Janet 45, 221, 223
Foster, Kathryn 188
Foster, Norm 232
Foster, Sutton 75
Foucard, Alexandra 124
Fouchard, James 220
Fouquet, Paul 206, 207, 211, 212
Fournier, Kelli 65
14th Street Y 147
Fourth Sister, The 179
Fourth Wall, The 176
4/19(/95) 161
Fowler, Beth 66
Fowler, Bruce 70
Fowler, Molly 105
Fowler, Monique 216
Fowler, Rachel 139, 200
Fowler, Robert H. 73
Fowler, Scott 32, 297
Fox, Alan 57
Fox, Ben 36, 213
Fox, Brendon 216, 218, 219
Fox, Eamon 102
Fox, Josh 171
Fox, Jovun 220
Fox, Lori Haley 196
Fox, Robert 57, 58
Fox Searchlight Pictures 38
Fox Theatricals 75
Foy, Conor 199
Foy, Hariett D. 132
Foy, Harriett D. 174, 223
Foy, Irving 315

Fracher, Drew 200, 201
Fraelich, Kristine 231
Fragalid, Helle 153
Fraioli, David 147
Frame 312
Franciosa, Christopher 173
Francis, Cameron 159
Francis, David Paul 233
Francis, James 205
Francis, Juliana 175
Francis, Kevin 187
Francis, Maureen 231
Francis, Stacy 124
Franck, Alison 23, 220
Franco, Scott 230
Frandsen, Erick 194
Frank, Sherman 231
Frankel, Jennifer 213
Frankel, Jerry 56
Frankel, Richard 73, 94, 95, 112
Frankel-Baruch-Viertel-Routh
    Group, The 73
*Frankie and Johnny in the Clair
    de Lune* 17, 24
Franklin, Carlton 212
Franklin, Nicole 205
Franklin, Tara 192
Franklin Thesis, The 148
Frankovich, Emily 207
Franks, Sonny 209
Frantz, Marisa 178
Franz, Elizabeth 196, 227
Franzblau, William 28
Franzman, Jared 146
Fraser, Alison 168
Fraser, Jon 143
Fratti, Mario 54
Fratti, Valentina 144
Fraulein Else 191
Frayn, Michael 227, 229
Frederick, Kevin 220
Frederick, Patrick 139
Freed, Amy 234
Freed, Randall 190
Freed, Zachary 231
Freedman, Glenna 34, 49, 68,
    99, 110
Freedman, Katherine 163
Freedson, John 110
Freeman, Carroll 205
Freeman, Jonathan 69
Freeman, K. Todd 183
Freeman, Ryan 145
Freeman, Steven 180
Freeman, Tony 70, 100
Freer, Karen 145
Freitag, Barbara 49
Frelich, Phyllis 198
French, Arthur 144, 297
French, Jae 28

French, Kent 213
Frenkel, Ana 109
Frenock, Larry 226
Frey, Matthew 131, 206, 227
Frey, Tom 207, 211, 221
Fri, Sean 150
Friday, Betsy 315
Fried, Jonathan 185, 217
Fried, Joshua 149
Friedman, Alex 227
Friedman, Carrie 25, 62
Friedman, David 66
Friedman, Dee Dee 163
Friedman, Melissa 159
Friedman, Michael 170, 178,
    202, 213
Friedman, Neil 208
Friedman, Peter 94, 298
Friedman, Renata 153
Friedson, Adam 61
Friedson, David 61
Friel, Brian 123, 213, 218
Friel, Diedra 192
Friend, David 118
Friend, Jenny R. 224
Frimark, Merle 72
Frink, Arlene 150
Frisch, Peter 139
Frith, Christiane 205
Frith, Christopher 205
Fromm, Richard 139
From the Top 163
Frosk, John 124
Frugé, Romain 80, 223
Frugia, Todd 200
Fry, Jarrod 221
Fry, Kate 208
Fuchs, Ken 147
Fuchs, Michael 38, 40
Fucking A 129
Fugard, Athol 123, 192, 203, 214
Fugate, Rachael 204
Fujiyabu, Kaori 172
Fulbright, Peter 197
Fulham, Mary 171
Fuller, Dale 159
Fuller, Darren 223
Fuller, David 149
Fuller, Larry 142
Fuller, Penny 124
Fully Committed 194, 209, 226
Full Monty, The 80
Full Spectrum: A Techno-Theatre
    Experiment 168
Fumusa, Dominic 128
Funaro, Robert 155
Fundamental 148
Funeral Parlor 152
Funicello, Ralph 185, 218,
    219, 225

Funk, Andrew 167
Funteovejuna 149
Fuqua Slone Reisenglass Appraisal, The 143
Furman, Jay 92
Furman, Jill 98
Furman, Roy 40, 55, 98, 99
Furr, Teri 66
Fusco, Anthony 184, 185
Fuseya, Leiko 234
Futerman, Samantha 220
Future?, The 145
Fyfe, Jim 168
Fynsworth Alley 180

G

Gabara, Cornel 186
Gabbard, Jesse 234
Gabriel, Denise 205
Gabriel, Gene 47, 128, 298
Gabrielle, Maya 160
Gaffigan, Catherine 190
Gaffin, Arthur 54
Gagen, J.P. 207
Gagnon, David 124
Gailen, Judy 216
Gaines, Alexander Crowder 180
Gaines, Ernest J. 226
Gaines, Reg E. 196
Gajda, Lisa 49
Gajdusek, Karl 175, 203
Gajic, Olivera 100
Galantich, Tom 27, 298
Galassini, Sara 172
Gale, Andy 226
Gale, Gregory A. 185
Gale, Jack 124
Gale, James 169
Galilee, Clove 173
Galileo Galilei 167
Galin/Sandler 112
Galindo, Eileen 199
Galindo, Louis 174
Gall, Susan 186
Gallagher, Anne 28
Gallagher, Fiona 234
Gallagher, Helen 298
Gallagher, Jerry 93
Gallagher, John, Jr. 127, 298
Gallagher, Peter 160
Gallant Johnjoe, The 149
Galligan, Carol 142
Gallin, Sandy 37
Gallin, Susan Quint 37
Gallinot, Garret 220
Gallinot, Gus 220
Gallo, David 40, 45, 75, 199
Gallo, Glory 143
Gallo, Paul 37, 69, 197
Gallop, Mark 172

Gambatese, Jennifer 26, 55
Gamble, Julian 43, 176
Gambrel, T.J. 153, 298
Ganakas, Greg 220
Ganales, Robyn 233
Gandhi, Anita 233, 234
Gandy, Irene 56
Ganeles, Robyn 234
Ganier, Yvette 174, 199
Ganim, Peter 222
Ganio, Michael 206, 207
Gann, John 204
Gant, Mtume 157
Gantt, Leland 45, 174
Garayva, Gloria 175
Garcés, Michael John 160, 169, 170, 174, 212, 213, 233
Garcia, Alejandro 109
Garcia, Jesus 38
Garcia, Minerva 199
Garcia, Perry 169
Garcia, Roland 144
Garcia-Gelpe, Marina 154
Gardiner, John 211
Gardiner, Leah 174
Gardiner, Leah C. 203
Gardner, Angel 170
Gardner, Cecilia Hobbs 39
Gardner, Herb 23
Gardner, Kim 178
Gardner, Lisa 154
Gardner, Lori 139
Gardner, Michael 40, 55
Gardner, Rita 223
Garello, Lawrence 147
Gargani, Michael 145
Garin, Michael 194
Garman, Andrew 57, 161
Garment, Paul 76
Garner, Andre 93
Garner, Crystal 124
Garner, Patrick 132
Garner, Richard 210
Garner, Sandra 103
Garrett, Jack 153
Garrick, Barbara 168, 298
Garrison, David 298
Garrison, Gary 140
Garrison, Gregory 66
Garrison, Mary Catherine 96
Garrity, Jack 153, 193
Garvey-Blackwell, Jennifer 179
Garzia, Bernie 91
Gash, Kent 176, 201
Gasman, Ira 128
Gasparian, Martha R. 28
Gasteyer, Ana 127
Gaston, Lydia 149, 298
Gaston, Michael 52
Gates, Thomas J. 95

Gatton, Vince 156
Gaudette, Michelle 231
Gaughan, Jack 72
Gaughan, John 66
Gaukel, Andy 229, 230
Gault, Chuma Hunter 227
Gavigan, Jenna 59
Gaviria, Adriana 144
Gay, Jackson 156
Gaydos, Matthew 202
Gaylor, Angela 162
Gaynor, Bob 65
Gaysunas, Cheryl 201
Gehringer, Linda 225, 226
Geidt, Jeremy 186
Geiger, , Mary Louise 110
Geiger, Mary Louise 198, 212
Geis, Alexandra 142
Geissinger, Katie 38, 167
Geisslinger, Bill 191
Geither, Mike 171
Gelber, Jack 316
Gelber, Jordan 179
Geller, Marc 146
Gelormini, Bruno 159
Gelpe, Leah 234
Gemeinhardt, Brad 75
Gemignani, Alexander 213
General from America, The 179, 183
Generations, The 140
Genet, Jean 144, 163
Geneva 171
Geno, Erica 52
Genovese, Mike 215
Gentile, Autumn 200
Gentry, Ken 95
Genzlinger, Neil 154
George, Emmitt C. 154
George, Libby 141
George, Lovette 145, 192
George, Madeleine 175
George, Philip 110
George, Rhett G. 129
Georgia Shakespeare Festival 210
Geralis, Anthony 30
Gerckens, T.J. 167
Gereghty, Ruthanne 152
Gerety, Peter 129, 146, 298
Gerhart, Michael 220
Germano, Katie 211
Gerroll, Daniel 56, 168, 190, 298
Gershon, Gina 67
Gershwin, George 99, 147
Gershwin, Ira 147
Gersten, Bernard 43, 48, 125
Gersten, David 101
Gerstenberger, Emil 124
Gesner, Clark 316

Gets, Malcolm 10, 30, 115, 127
Gettelfinger, Sara 27, 54
Getto, Erica 298
Getz, John 215
Geva Theatre Center 211
Ghaffari, Mohammad 173
Ghassemi, Deligani Alaeaddin 173
Ghassemi, Mohammadreza 173
Ghedia, Mala 102
Ghir, Kulvinder 102
Ghosts 168
Giacalone, Johnny 129
Giacosa, Giuseppe 38
Giamatti, Paul 96
Gianfrancesco, Edward T. 93
Gianino, Antonia 103, 130
Gianino, Jack 133
Giannini, Maura 40, 59
Giannitti, Michael 195
Giarrizzo, Guy 143
Gibbons, Adrienne 73
Gibbons, Tessa 154
Gibbs, Jennifer 147, 150
Gibbs, Nancy Nagel 37
Gibbs, Sheila 70
Gibson, Darren 124
Gibson, Darryl 226
Gibson, Deborah 67
Gibson, Edwin Lee 213
Gibson, Julia 157, 159, 209
Gibson, Meg 234
Gibson, Michael 67
Gibson, William 103
Gibson-Clark, Tanya 176
Gien, Pamela 119, 201
Gifford, Sarah 158
Gigl, Aloysius 91
Gigliotti, Lauren Rose 202
Gilbert, James 146
Gilbert, Kerry 23
Gilbert, Sara 95
Gilbert and Sullivan 189
Gilbo, Robert 202
Gilburne, Jessica 93
Giles, Martin 202
Gilfry, Rodney 124
Gilger, Paul 100
Gill, Michael 72
Gill, Michel 168
Gill, Temple 29
Gillett, Eric Michael 220
Gilliam, Michael 110, 198, 199, 220, 223, 227
Gilliams, Ida 73
Gilliespie, Lisa P. Miller 186
Gillis, Graeme 168
Gillis, Michael 227
Gillman, Jason 192
Gilman, Rebecca 226

Gilman, Zachary 142
Gilmer, KJ 187
Gilmore, Allen 208
Gilpin, Jeffrey Jason 222
Gilray, Lauren 211
Gilsig, Jessalyn 177
Gimpel, Erica 225
Gin, Ray 196
Gindi, Roger 223
Gines, Christopher 118
Gines, Shay 146
Ginsberg, Allen 154
Ginzler, Robert 58
Gionson, Mel 149, 153
Giordano, Charles 180
Giordano, Tyrone 198
Girard, Stephanie 151, 192
Girl of 16, A 144
Giroday, François 215
Giron, Arthur 169
Girvin, Terri 143
Gist, Jan 217, 218, 219
Give Them Wings 160
Glaab, Caryl 112
Gladden, Dean R. 206
Gladis, Michael J.X. 174, 177
Gladstone, Ralph 186
Glant-Linden, Andrew 231
Glascock, Scott 159
Glass, Philip 167, 186
Glassberg, Marcalan 150
Glaszek, Andrew 156
Glaudini, John 91
Glean, Robert 74
Gleason, Patrick 225
Glenn, Charles 214
Glenn, Don Wilson 176
Glenn, Eileen 149, 150, 298
Glenn, James 222
Glenn, Nealy 225
Glick, Gideon 223
Glick, Mari 28, 56
Glick, Marian 75
Glimmer of Hope 143
Glore, John 199
Gloria Maddox Theatre 147
Glorioso, Bess Marie 24
Glotzer, Marcia A. 193
Glover, Brian P. 171
Glover, Keith 91, 174, 175
Glover, Montego 220
Glover, Savion 196
Glover, William 316
Glovinsky, Henry 156
Glowacki, Janusz 179
Glushak, Joanna 219, 223
Glynn, Carlin 183
Gnapp, Rod 184, 185
Goat Or Who Is Sylvia?, The 81, 183

God's Comic 172
God's Daughter 139
Godbout, John 206, 207
Godfadda Workout, The 116
Godfrey, Joe 158
Godineaux, Edgar 40
Godinez, Henry 222
Goding, Teresa L. 151
Godman, Kate 198
God and Mr. Smith 153
Goebbels, Heiner 123
Goede, Jay 11, 55, 153
Goekjian, Samuel V. 56
Going, John 200
Golay, Seth 151
Gold, Alice 158
Gold, Michael 178
Gold, Natalie 162
Golda's Balcony 103
Goldberg, Aileen 180
Goldberg, Janice 143
Goldberg, Jon-Erik 71
Goldberg, Lawrence 75, 223
Goldberg, Louis F. 223, 231
Goldberg, Marc 54
Goldberg, Max 178
Goldberg, Whoopi 45, 75, 92
Golden, Lee 231
Golden, Peg McFeeley 45
Goldenhersh, Heather 174
Golden Bear, The 178
Golden Theatre 48
Goldfarb, Abe 149, 158
Goldfarb, Sidney 148
Goldfeder, Laurie 41, 54
Goldfinger, Michael 96
Goldfrank, Lionel, III 56
Goldin, Igor 151
Goldman, Matt 112
Goldman, Nina 72
Goldoni, Carlo 177
Goldsberry, Olivia 206, 207
Goldsberry, Rene Elise 70
Goldschneider, Ed 76
Goldsmith, Oliver 155
Goldstein, Daniel 209
Goldstein, David 174
Goldstein, Jess 47, 56, 101, 103, 128, 206, 213, 215, 217
Goldstein, Steven 225
Goldstone, Bob 180
Goler-Kosarin, Lauren 66
Golub, Peter 94
Goluboff, Bryan 140
Gomex, Lino 124
Gomez, Carlos 199
Gomez, David 32
Gomez, David Eric 298
Gomez, Lino 37
Gomez, Marga 171

Gomez, Tommy 210
Gomez, Tommy A. 184, 185
Gonda, Eli 219
Gone Home 126
Gonglewski, Grace 187, 231, 232
Gonzalez, Aldrin 75
Gonzalez, Charlene 143
Gonzalez, Ching 167
Gonzalez, Jojo 129, 151
González, José Cruz 212
Gonzalez, Juan Carlos 74
Gonzalez, Mandy 40, 65
Gooch, Katherine 171
Good, John 142, 155
Good, Tara 175
Goodbrod, Gregg 75
Goode, Jennifer 38, 39
Goodman, Alfred 124
Goodman, Grant 147
Goodman, Henry 44, 73
Goodman, Jake 192
Goodman, Jeff 212
Goodman, John 96
Goodman, Paul Scott 154
Goodman, Robyn 101, 150
Goodrich, Joseph 148, 174
Goodrich, Linda 220
Goodsell, Shan 214
Goodson, Jenn 220
Goodun, Elfeigo N., III 104
Goodwin, Deidre 27, 54, 68, 299
Goodwin, Philip 44
Goodwin-Groen, Paul 38, 175, 299
Goranson, Alicia 168, 174, 179
Gordon, Aaron 144
Gordon, Allan S. 25, 74
Gordon, Carl 45
Gordon, Charles 27
Gordon, David P. 168, 179, 187, 213, 231
Gordon, Lana 70
Gordon, Mark Alan 209, 215
Gordon, Miriam 154
Gordon, Ricky Ian 131
Gordon, Seth 206
Gordon, Terri 163
Gorin, Stephanie 196
Gorman, Cliff 316
Gorrek, Matt 140
Gorshin, Frank 28
Gorski, Erin 192
Goss, Bick 145
Gotanda, Philip Kan 224
Gottesman, Yetta 150, 169, 175
Gottlieb, Jon 94, 196, 198, 199
Gottlieb, Lizzie 147
Gottschalk, Christopher 217, 218, 219
Gough, Shawn 125

Gould, Bonnie 205
Gould, Daniella 230
Gould, Erica 160
Gould, Richard 192
Gould, Robert 168
Governor, Jennifer 232
Govich, Milena 27
Goyanes, Maria 230
Goyette, Marie 123
Grace, Ivana 220
Grace, Jamie 188
Graduate, The 81
Grady, John 112
Graffeo, Marylee 110
Graham, Dion 174
Graham, Enid 43, 80, 299
Graham, Somer Lee 71
Graham-Handley, Emily 33
Gramercy Theatre 132
Gramm, Joseph Lee 154
Granata, Dona 30
Grande-Marchione, Frank 146
Grandin, Harley 184
Grandy, Marya 95
Grand Design, The 161
Granger-Happ, Janet 222
Grant, Calvin 74
Grant, Joan 141
Grant, Kate Jennings 129, 299
Grant, Paul 223
Grant, Robin 133
Grant, Shane 223
Grant, William H., III 176, 195, 206
Granville-Barker, Harley 231
Grappo, Connie 141
Grappone, Raymond 29
Grasmere 144
Gravatt, Lynda 132
Gravellese, Gerard 140
Gravens, David 175
Graves, Christopher 156
Graves, Michael 153
Graves, Rupert 80
Gravina, Damon 200
Gravitte, Debbie 180
Grawemeyer, J. 143
Gray, Damian 160
Gray, David Barry 125
Gray, Dolores 316
Gray, Douglas 104
Gray, John 211
Gray, Kevin 220
Gray, Matthew 178
Gray, Nicholas 148
Gray, Pamela 175
Gray, Pamela J. 217
Gray, Ritz 185
Gray, Zan 225
Graynor, Ari 132

Grease 220
Great Ormond St. Children's Hospital 223
Great Scott Productions 99
Greaves, Danielle Lee 26
Greber, Denise 172
Greco, Loretta 150, 184
Greco, Nick 145
Green, Adolph 161, 180, 317
Green, Alan H. 220
Green, Ashley 143
Green, Chris 149
Green, Cody 196
Green, Colton 139
Green, David 148, 180
Green, Frank 188, 189
Green, Jackie 24, 50, 58, 65, 67, 70, 71, 76, 96, 112, 126, 127
Green, Jessica 178
Green, Laura 73
Green, Marilyn 219
Green, William 153
Greenberg, Gordon 194
Greenberg, Julia 130
Greenberg, Mitchell 211
Greenberg, Richard 47, 128, 185, 225
Greenblatt, Richard 194
Greene, Graham 139
Greenfeld, Josh 172
Greenfield-Sanders, Timothy 170
Greenhill, Mitch 225
Greenhill, Susan 147
Greenidge, Kirsten 174
Greenlund, Eric 229
Greenspa, David 26
Greenspan, David 131, 154, 170, 171, 174, 299
Greenwald, Pearl Berman 56
Greenwald, Raymond J. 56
Greenwood, Jane 44, 57, 93, 125, 196, 234
Greenwood, Michael 221
Green Violin: Marc Chagall and the Soviet Yiddish Theater 223
Greer, D.M.W. 158
Greer, Justin 49, 299
Greer, Keith 143
Greer, Matthew 67
Greer, Scott 187, 231
Greer, Skip 212
Gregory, Chester, II 104, 208
Gregory, James 317
Greif, Michael 74, 129, 130
Grene, David 205
Grenfell, Katy 26
Grenier, Bernard 93
Grey, Jane 62, 98
Grey, Joel 161

Grice, Brian O. 92
Gridley, Steven 157
Grifasi, Joe 43
Griffin, Edward 149
Griffin, Gary 124
Griffin, Jennifer 233
Griffin, Sean 158
Griffin Productions 92
Griffith, Jim 110, 223
Griffith, Kristin 168, 173
Griffith, Natalie 43
Griffith, P.J. 180
Griffith, Sheila 61
Griffiths, Heidi 47, 128, 129
Griffiths, Trevor 176
Griggs, George 150
Grigolia-Rosenbaum, Jacob 156
Grigsby, Kimberly 128, 129
Grimaldi, James 159
Grimberg, Deborah 168
Grimes, Kenny 105
Grimes, Tammy 299
Grimm, David 174, 175
Grindrod, David 196
Grinwis, Emmy 233
Groag, Lillian 191
Groden, Tiia 230
Grodner, Suzanne 201, 227
Groener, Harry 42, 219, 299
Groeschel, Amy 162
Groff, Rinne 160
Groff, Steve 159
Gromada, John 56, 101, 131, 177, 183, 206
Grosjean, Mia 190
Gross, Richard 56
Gross, Yeeshas 95
Grossman, Henry 133
Grossman, Jason 186
Grossman, Larry 133
Grotelueschen, Andy 230
Ground Floor Theatre Fat Chance Productions, Inc. 147
Grove, Barry 126
Grové, Jessica 75
Groves, Kelly 154
Grubb, Roger Dean 189
Gruen, John 128
Gruer, Rachel 190
Gruet, Lauren 222
Grunberg, Klaus 123
Grunwald, Roger 142
Grupper, Adam 38, 39, 110
Gruss, Amanda 142
Guajardo, Roberto 224
Gualtieri, Tom 111
Guare, John 161, 191
Guerrero, Crissy 225
Guerrero, Zarco 212
Guettel, Mary Rodgers 180

Guevara, Zabryna 213
Guffey, Krista 188
Guilarte, Andrew 168
Guilbert, Ann 130
Guiles, Coats 38
Guirgis, Stephen Adly 101, 151
Guisinger, Nathan 150, 158
Gulan, Timothy 70
Gulde, Caroline 227
Gulla, Joe 140
Gulsvig, Becky 220
Guncler, Sam 94, 162, 226
Gundersheimer, Lee 154
Gunderson, Lauren 144
Gunhus, Eric 73
Gunn, Suzette 147
Gunning, Michael 41
Gurian, Daniel 143
Gurney, A.R. 146, 176 , 214
Gurr, Christopher 211, 212
Gurwitch, Annabelle 150
Gusman, Matthew 36
Gustern, Joe 72
Guthertz, Elisa 185
Gutierrez, Carole 222
Gutierrez, Gerald 43
Gutterman, Cindy 103
Gutterman, Jay 103
Guttman, Eddie 169
Guy, Jasmine 68
Guy, Larry 39
Guy, Rebecca 139
Guymon, Mary Jane 214
Guys, The 191
Guzzi, Ann 96
Gwinn, Marc 201
Gyllenhaal, Maggie 175
Gypsy 12, 13, 58, 237

H

H.A.M.L.E.T. 171
Haag, Christina 225
Haas, Lenny 187
Haase, Ashley Amber 40
Haasova, Monika 171
Habeck, Michelle 208
Haber, Julie 184, 185
Habitat 159
Hack, Sam 215
Hackett, Peter 206, 207
Hackler, Blake 156
Hadary, Jonathan 180
Hadden, John 142
Hadley, Jonathan 158, 169
Hadley, Mark 209
Hadsell, Devon Charisse 184
Haefner, Susan 75
Haft, Elsa Daspin 28
Hagenbuckle, J. 232

Hagerty, Julie 196
Haggerty, Megumi 220
Hahn, Howard 214
Hahn, Kristen 36
Haidle, Noah 149
Haimes, Todd 44, 52, 53, 54, 60, 67, 132
Haims, Nolan 153
Haimsohn, George 317
Haines, Todd 27
Hairspray 8, 25, 238, 239
Haiti 160
Halaska, Linda 98
Halbach, John 44
Hale, Tony 150
Hall, Adrian 229
Hall, Alaina Reed 233
Hall, Amy 124
Hall, Carlyle W., Sr. 37
Hall, Connie 171
Hall, Davis 159
Hall, Dennis Michael 91
Hall, Donei 186
Hall, George 27, 299, 317
Hall, Gretchen S. 145
Hall, Irma P. 203
Hall, Jake 178
Hall, Jane 227
Hall, John 221
Hall, John Keith 188, 189
Hall, Josephine 188, 189
Hall, Katie 225
Hall, Michael 193
Hall, Michaela 145
Hall, Michael C. 68
Hall, Mollie 231, 232
Hall, Rick 104
Hall, Willis 223
Hall, Wilson 172
Hallas, Brian 170
Hallelujah Breakdown 153
Hallett, Morgan 62
Halley, Elton P. 34
Halliday, Jimm 220
Halliday, Lynne 179
Hallqvist, Britt G. 123
Hally, Martha 216
Halstead, Carol 144, 147
Halston, Julie 59, 167, 299
Hamburger, Richard 209
Hamilton, Ann 167
Hamilton, Carrie 33
Hamilton, George 68
Hamilton, Josh 126, 147, 299
Hamilton, Mark Sage 141
Hamilton, Melinda Page 146, 218
Hamilton, Nicolai Dahl 153
Hamilton, Stephen 190

Hamilton, Tony 140, 141
Hamilton, Victoria 16, 52, 238, 241
Hamlet 183
Hamlet Machine 142
Hamlisch, Marvin 42, 133, 160, 219, 223
Hammad, Suheir 34
Hammel, Lori 110
Hammel, Tessa 188
Hammer, Ben 150, 299
Hammer, Mark 101, 151, 299
Hammerstein, James 110
Hammerstein, Oscar, II 29, 124, 180, 231, 233
Hammerstein Matinee: A Grand Night for Singing, A 180
Hammond, Thomas M. 179, 183
Hammons, Shannon 213
Hampton, Chavon Aileen 233
Hampton, Christopher 51, 179, 204
Hampton, Jamey 222
Hampton, Kate 145, 150
Hampton, Latrice 233
Hamrick, Joshua P. 204
Hamza, Jerry 103
Hanan, Stephen Mo 94
Hancock, Rob 208
Hand, Frederic 123
Handegard, A.J. 162
Handel, Craig 230
Handler, Evan 168
Hands 161
Hands Holding Hands 161
Handy, John 168
Hand of God, The 104
Hanemann, Heather 155
Hanes, Tyler 49
Haney, Michael Evan 200, 201
Hanig, Frank 204
Hankin, St. John 173
Hankla, Mark 178
Hank Williams: Lost Highway 151
Hanlon, Colin 223
Hanlon, John J. 234
Hannett, Juliana 38, 47, 52, 53, 105
Hannon, Allison 202
Hannon, Mary Ann 151
Hannon, Patti 117
Hannouche, Cherie 171
Hansen, Ann-Mari Max 167
Hansen, Anna Ryan 62
Hansen, Benedicte 153
Hansen, Randy 103
Hansen, Teri 27
Hanson, Alison 147

Hanson, Lars 174
Hanson, Marsh 144, 194
Hanson, Peter 27, 52, 67
Hanson, Suzan 186
Hanson, Tripp 27, 220
Hantman, Mauro 228, 229, 230
Happy Birthday 139
Happy Days 144
Haqq, Devin 163
Hara, Doug 82
Hara, Shinichiro 173
Harada, Ann 179, 300
Harada, Tamotsu 167
Haran, Mary Cleere 180
Harbaum, Bob 158
Harbour, David 177
Hardcastle, Terrell 193
Hardeman, Daria 93
Hardgrove, Carla J. 233
Hardie, Raymond 146
Harding, Jan Leslie 175, 213, 233
Hardwick, Mark 205
Hardy, John 188, 189
Hardy, Joseph 218
Hardy, K.J. 178
Hardy, Kevin 169
Hardy, Nell 314
Hare, David 195, 207
Hare, Jason 143, 153
Harelik, Mark 103, 151, 206
Harger, Brenda Bakker 168
Hargrove, Carla J. 213
Harker, James 66
Harlem Duet 141
Harlem Song 92
Harley, Bill 229
Harley, Jan 219
Harling, Robert 189
Harlow, Kristen 150
Harma, Alison 220
Harman, Paul 100, 300
Harmon, Wynn 190, 219
Harmsen, Douglas 221
Harner, Jason Butler 125, 300
Harnetiaux, Trish 158
Harnett, Daniel 160
Harnick, Aaron 24, 96
Harnick, Sheldon 180, 231
Harold Clurman Theatre 92, 111, 147
Haroun and the Sea of Stories 191
Harper, Francesca 124
Harper, Rodney 211
Harper, Wally 99, 223
Harran, Jacob 159
Harriell, Marcy 132
Harrill, Callie 188
Harrington, Alexander 147

Harrington, Delphi 139
Harrington, Joel 222
Harrington, Ken 212
Harrington, Nancy 50, 186
Harrington, Wendall K. 48, 99, 104
Harrington, Wren Marie 72
Harris, Alana 148
Harris, Alison 36
Harris, Conrad 54
Harris, Cynthia 139
Harris, Dede 25, 95
Harris, Derric 40, 124
Harris, Earl 223
Harris, Harriet 75, 160
Harris, J. Fitz 228, 229
Harris, James Berton 126
Harris, Jamie 176
Harris, Jared 127
Harris, Jay H. 28
Harris, Jenn 223
Harris, Jeremiah J. 66
Harris, Jonathan 317
Harris, Kristen 129
Harris, Neil Patrick 67, 160
Harris, Oliver 224
Harris, Paul 156
Harris, Rachel Lee 153
Harris, Rebecca 148
Harris, Richard 227, 318
Harris, Rosemary 132, 300
Harris, Roy 127, 196
Harris, Sam 73
Harris, Stacey 220
Harris, Timothy Scott 163
Harrison, Babo 169, 174
Harrison, Gregory 68
Harrison, Howard 71, 196
Harrison, Lanny 167
Harrison, Maryna 143
Harrison, Peter 216
Harrison, Stanley 159
Harrow, Lisa 151
Harry, Jackeé 27
Hart, Charles 72
Hart, Christopher D. 221
Hart, Jake 148
Hart, Linda 26
Hart, Lorenz 27, 180, 195, 223
Hart, Melissa Joy 169, 192, 231, 232
Hart, Moss 183
Hart, Nicolette 150
Hart, Perry 111
Hartenstein, Frank 38, 69
Hartford Stage 101
Harting, Carla 141
Hartley, Jan 42, 130, 170
Hartley, Mariette 67
Hartman, Karen 175

Hartman, Michael 32, 33, 40, 41, 45, 55, 57, 73, 75, 94, 97, 101, 104
Hartman, Mike 206
Hartman, Shannon 230
Hartman, Tess 216
Haruta, Atsushi 173
Harvey, Rita 91, 169
Harvey Theater 123
Harwood, Ronald 192
Hase, Thomas C. 201
Hasegawa, Kishiko 171
Hashimoto, Kunihiko 173
Hashirigaki 123
Hassler, Stacie May 142
Hastings, Edward 144
Hastings-Phillips, Amanda 184
Hatcher, Chuck 201
Hatcher, Jeffrey 97, 217
Hatcher, Lauren 213
Hatcher, Robert 163, 178
Hatley, Tim 48, 127
Hatt, Karen 171
Hatzis, Georgia 186
Hauck, Rachel 104, 179, 199, 233
Hauck, Steve 171
Haugen, Eric T. 91
Haughton, Lauren 227
Haughton, Stacey 93
Haun, Harry 241
Haun, Maggie 205
Hauptman, William 198
Havana Is Waiting 200
Havana Under The Sea 169
Havard, Bernard 231
Haver, Andrew D. 209
Havergal, Giles 151
Hawke, Ethan 161
Hawkes, Victor W. 76
Hawking, Judith 160, 174, 201
Hawkins, Carly 231
Hawkins, Peter 174
Hawkinson, Timothy 145
Hawks, Victor 76
Hawley, J. Malia 142
Hayden, John 44
Hayden, Michael 56, 67
Hayden, Sophie 190
Hayden, Tamra 195
Hayes, Bill 30, 60
Hayes, Drew 145
Hayes, Elizabeth 147
Hayes, Hugh 111
Hayes, Jack 72
Hayes, Lisa 150
Hayes, Mark D. 104
Hayes, Steve 193
Hayes, Walter 205
Haynes, Diana H. 188

Haynes, Kristoffer 170
Haynie, Jim 177
Hayon, Sarah 160
Hays, Carole Shorenstein 47
Hayward, Charlie 49
Haywood, Mindy 112
Hazeldine, James 318
Headley, Heather 65
Healey, Meghan 169, 212
Healey, Michael 216, 221, 224, 226
Healy, Ann Marie 145
Healy, Chris 172
Heartbeats 193
Heartbreak House 155
Hear No Evil, LLC 180
Heath, Robin 206, 207
Heather Brothers 142
Heaton, Kenneth 141
Heat Lightning 150
Heavy Mettle 152
Hebert, Rich 220
Hébert-Gregory, Kimberly 208
Hecht, Jessica 161, 175, 179, 190
Hecht, Paul 127, 192
Heckman, Richard 29, 124
Hedden, Brian 147
Hedges, John 188, 189
Hedley, Nevin 41, 197
Hedwig and the Angry Inch 203
Heffernan, Andrew 224
Heffron, Mike 200
Heflin, Elizabeth 183, 218
Hefti, Susan Kathryn 157
Hegel-Cantarella, Luke 223
Heggins, Amy 75
Heid, R.J. 221
Heidami, Daoud 215
Heifets, Victor 40
Heil, Michael 204
Heinemann, Larry 112
Heinig, Deborah Annette 217, 218, 219
Heinmann, Theresa 188
Heintzelman, Caren 218
Heinze, Roxane 156
Heird, Amanita 178
Heisler, Laura 145, 209, 217, 218
Helen: Queen of Sparta 172
Helen Hayes Theatre 28
Helen Hayes Theatre Company 223
Hellegers, Neil 229
Heller, Robert 57
Hellesen, Richard 211, 225
Hellman, Nina 175
Hellstrom, Emily 109
Hellyer, John 168
Helm, Tom 220

Helms, Barbara 95, 163
Hemingway, Carol 144
Hemingway, Ernest 144
Hemphill, Garth 184, 185, 225
Hendel, Ruth 101
Henderson, Joyce 41
Henderson, Kevin 139
Henderson, Luther 93
Henderson, Shirley 188
Henderson, Stephen McKinley 45
Henderson, Tate 148
Henderson, Tyrone Mitchell 227
Hendricks, James J. 151
Hendrickson, Steve 217
Hendrix, Leslie 33
Hendryx, Nona 220
Hendy, Jessica 30
Heney, Jessica 178
Henk, Annie 169, 177
Henley, Beth 160
Hennion, Gary 148
Henrique, Paulo 172
Henry, Buck 196
Henry, Neil 151
Henry, Vincent 129
Henry, Wayne 143
Henry Miller Theatre 35, 67, 76
Henry V 149, 150
Henry VI 150
Hensley, Schuler 180
Henze, Sheryl 124
Henzler, Oliver 186
Hepburn, Angus 149
Herald, Diana 111
Herber, Pete 95
Herbert, Danielle 223
Herbert, Victor 222
Herendeen, Ed 175
Here Arts Center 148
Herlinger, Karl 148, 175
Hermalyn, Joy 38
Herman, Darra 172
Herman, Jerry 100
Herman, Tim 143
Herman, Tom 146
Hermansen, Mary Ann 68
Hernandez, Jon-Michael 152
Hernandez, Juan Carlos 130, 140
Hernandez, Omar 156
Hernandez, Oscar 167
Hernández, Riccardo 92, 128, 130, 132, 186, 196, 197, 200
Heroes 152
Heron, Denis 180
Herrero, Mercedes 145, 146, 174, 175
Herrick, Peter 143
Herrington, Ben 76
Hersch, Fred 180

Hershey, Lowell 124
Herskovits, David 149
Herter, Jonathan 227
Hertzenberg, Kristen 193
Herwood, Patrick 111
Her Big Chance 104
Heslin, George 174
Hess, Bob 209
Hess, David 231
Hess, Gale 105
Hess, Nancy 68, 201
Hess, Rodger 95
Hessing, Laurel 178
Hester, Kimberly 73
Hester, Richard 58, 72
Hetrick, Adam 222
Hewitt, Frankie 318
Hewitt, Tom 27, 185, 217
Heyer, Thom 194, 195, 220
Hiatt, Dan 191
Hickey, Carol A. 156
Hickey, Tom 149
Hicklin, Shelley 232
Hickok, John 65, 158
Hickok, Molly 145
Hicks, Barbara 209
Hicks, Bryan 174, 190
Hicks, Daniel 178
Hicks, Dustin M. 200
Hicks, Israel 221
Hicks, Marva 91, 223
Hicks, Munson 212, 227
Hicks, Peter 209
Hicks, Rodney 212
Hicks, Sander 174, 175
Hidalgo, Allen 159
Higgins, Clare 7, 48, 238, 300
Higgins, John Patrick 184
Higgins, Patience 93
Highway Ulysses 186
High Priest of California 162
Hilaire, Christopher St. 194
Hilda 170
Hildebrandt, Erika 144
Hildebrandt, Nan 211
Hilferty, Susan 131, 179, 183
Hill, Alexander 192
Hill, Eric 192
Hill, Erin 76
Hill, John 26
Hill, Natalie 220
Hill, Raymond James 154
Hill, Roderick 174
Hill, Rosena M. 42, 219, 222
Hill, Ryan 167
Hill, Valerie 158
Hiller, Dame Wendy 318
Hiller, Wendy 318
Hilliard, Ryan 151, 153
Hillier, Lara 221

Hillier, Martin 190
Hillman, Richard 93, 102
Hillman, Robb 38, 300
Hillmer, Melissa 124
Hillson, Rebecca 205
Hime, Jeanne 155
Him and Her 154
Hindman, Earl 179
Hindman, James 180, 300
Hines, Arshenna 233
Hines, John 225, 234
Hines, Kay 172
Hines, Maurice 124
Hingle, Pat 190
Hingston, Sean Martin 230
Hinkle, Marin 179, 192
Hinks, Alison 146
Hinners, Carson 141
Hinrichs, Renata 147
Hinrichsen, Jens 212
Hinton, Michael 37
Hip-Flores, Richard 156
Hipkens, Robert 194
Hirata, Mikio 201
Hirota, Yuji 173
Hirsch, Barry J. 159
Hirsch, Gina 144, 171
Hirsch, Judd 23, 300
Hirschfeld, Al 318
His Wife 161
Hitchcock, Tony 155
Hiura, Ben 173
Hlengwa, Lindiwe 70
Hoak, Madeline 146
Hoch, Chris 66
Hochman, Larry 213
Hock, Robert 155
Hocking, Leah 40
Hodge, Joe 224
Hodge, Kate 206
Hodge, M. Pat 186
Hodge, Mike 174
Hodge-Bowles, Sean-Michael 213
Hodges, Ben 147, 240, 241
Hodges, Dale 200
Hodges, Joy 319
Hodges, Mary 150
Hoebee, Mark S. 220
Hoehler, Richard 152
Hoeppner, Krista 194, 217
Hoesl, Kristin 227
Hoey, Andy 179, 300
Hoff, Andrew J. 151
Hoffenberg, Sylvia 315
Hoffman, Constance 183
Hoffman, Ellen 66
Hoffman, Gavin 153
Hoffman, Gregory 184, 185, 191
Hoffman, Jackie 26, 238, 300

Hoffman, Jeffrey 191
Hoffman, Miranda 131, 222
Hoffman, Philip Seymour 62, 101, 151, 300
Hoffman, Susan R. 102
Hoffman, William 206
Hofmaier, Mark 163
Hofsiss, Jack 190
Hogan, Jonathan 177
Hogan, Michael 140
Hogan, Robert 131
Hogue, Rochelle 45
Hoiby, Lee 184
Holbrook, Curtis 129
Holcenberg, David 71
Holck, Maile 212
Hold, Please 141
Holden, Joan 198, 229
Holder, Donald 27, 32, 45, 70, 75, 125, 127, 199, 225
Holderness, Rebecca 147
Holgate, Danny 211, 224
Holgate, Ron 185
Holiday, Joel 147
Holland, Bruce 208
Holland, Greg 47
Holland, Kate 149
Hollander, Anita 172
Hollander, Owen 57
Hollenbeck, John 167
Holliday, Jennifer 68
Hollingshead, Megan 156
Hollis, Marnee 111
Hollman, Mark 76, 160, 185
Hollywood Arms 33
Holm, Celeste 180
Holman, Hunt 132
Holman, Terry Tittle 209
Holman, Tricia 205
Holmes, David 123
Holmes, Douglas 133
Holmes, Lori 230
Holmes, Prudence Wright 130
Holmes, Rick 67
Holmes, Rupert 28, 213
Holmes, Scott 231
Holmes, Wright 130
Holmstrom, Mary 139
Holsinger, Holly 171
Holt, Charles Paul 141
Holt, Lorri 185
Holum, Suli 172
Holyfield, Wayland D. 49
Homer, Brian 163
Homewrecker 175
Homison, Zebediah K. 223
Honda, Shuji 173
Honey Makers, The 168
Hong, April 226
Honnoll, Tim 146

Hood, Cynthia 144
Hood, Jamey 211
Hood, Stephen D. 207
Hoodwin, Rebecca 159, 178
Hooper, Laura 183
Hoover, Richard 177
Hoover, Roger 204
Hope, Paul 183
Hope, Roxanna 213
Hope, Sharon 226
Hope Bloats 168
Hopkins, Barbara Barnes 141
Hopkins, Billy 160
Hopkins, Cynthia 170
Hopkins, Karen Brooks 123, 167
Hopkins, Lisa 38
Hopkins, Robert Innes 96
Hopper, Tim 92
Hormann, Nicholas 215
Horn, Bill Van 231
Horn, Tyler 223
Hornback, Nancy 155
Hornberger, Ellen 39
Hornblack, Bob 210
Horner, John 204, 205
Horner, Richard 319
Horovitz, Israel 94, 156, 159, 161, 193
Horowitz, Jeffrey 179
Horowitz, Lawrence 40, 55
Horowitz, Susan N. 152
Horsford, Raquel 112
Horsley, Allison 209
Horstien, Scott 217
Horton, Damon 150
Horton, Greg 156
Horton, Ward 154
Horvath, Joshue 208
Horwatt, Linda 143
Horwitz, Andrew 156
Hosmer, George C. 226
Hosney, Doug 96
Hostetter, Curt 159, 300
Hotaling, Brian 111
Hottinger, Eric 147
Hoty, Dee 196
Houdyshell, Jayne 175, 233
Houfek, Nancy 186, 205
Houghton, James 93, 177
Hould-Ward, Ann 40, 66, 177
Hourglass, The 140
Hourie, Troy 97, 190, 212, 227
House, Bob Lee 49
House and Garden 116
House of Blue Leaves, The 191
House of Flowers 124
Houston, Lauren 205
Howard, Aimee 153
Howard, Anto 173
Howard, Arliss 186

Howard, Bryce Dallas 44, 129, 190
Howard, Celia 144
Howard, David S. 23
Howard, Ed 206
Howard, Heidi 148
Howard, Hollie 26
Howard, Jason 148
Howard, Kisha 65
Howard, Mark 208
Howard, Peter 68, 133, 233
Howard, Stuart 98
Howard Gilman Opera House 123
Howe, Tina 150, 161, 227
Howell, Jeffrey 202, 221
Howell, Michael W. 103, 151, 206
Howes, Benjamin 143, 155, 173
Howland, Jason 159
Howland, Lucas 233, 234
Hoxie, Richmond 146, 168, 300
Hoydich, George 221
Hoyle, Geoff 215
Hoyt, Lon 25, 26
Hoyt, Tom 40
Hsu, Emily 29
Hu, Ann 142
Huang, Wei 38
Hubbard, Amy 205
Hubbard, Kerrin 40
Huber, Chuck 209
Huber, David 150
Huber, Janet 132
Hudson, Chuck 155
Hudson, David Stewart 185
Hudson, Richard 70
Hudson, Scott 101
Hudson, Walter 192
Huff, Neal 6, 47, 128, 300
Huffman, Cady 73
Huffman, Tracey 172
Hughart, Ted 219
Hughes, Allen Lee 132
Hughes, Carrie 234
Hughes, Colleen 70
Hughes, Doug 160, 173
Hughes, Kenneth 142
Hughes, Langston 93
Hughes, Ted 156
Huidor, Miguel Angel 128, 200, 203, 209, 220
Hulce, Tom 104
Hull, Ashley 124
Hull, Mylinda 69, 110
Humbertson, Lisa 143
Humble Boy 127
Humes, Stephen G. 222
Hummel, Martin 93
Hummel-Rosen, Krisine 219

Hummell, Zach 224
Hummon, Marcus 49
Humphrey, David 219
Humphris, Caroline 123
Humpty Dumpty 224
Hunchback's Tale, The 213
Hune, Matt 183
Hung, Lyris 172
Hunsaker, Michael 220
Hunt, Alva 124
Hunt, Helen 51
Hunt, Mame 198
Hunt, Robert 106
Hunter, Adam 38, 110
Hunter, Holly 160
Hunter, Jennifer 220
Hunter, JoAnn M. 75
Hunter, Kim 319
Hunter, Tim 65
Hunter, Timothy 70
Huntington, Crystal 74
Huntington Theatre Company 213
Huntley, Paul 73, 196
Hunyh, Brian Lee 300
Hurd, Michelle 225
Hurley, Jimmy 141
Hurowitz, Peter Sasha 228, 229, 230
Hurt, Mary Beth 127
Hussa, Robyn 145
Husted, Patrick 174
Hustis, Jono 175
Hutcheson, Jessie 154
Hutchins, Amy 155
Hutchins, Reid 145
Hutchinson, Brian 218
Hutchinson, Chris 150
Hutchinson, Derek 41, 167
Hutchinson, Kelly 176
Hutchison, Chris 176
Hutton, Arlene 141, 175
Huxley, Aldous 171
Huynh, Brian Lee 149
Hwang, David Henry 29, 65, 186, 227
Hyatt, Jeffrey 111
Hyatt, Michael 126
Hygom, Gary N. 190
Hyland, Edward James 212, 221
Hyland, Sarah 220
Hyman, Charles 174
Hyman, Earle 301
Hyperion Theatricals 65
Hypothetical Theatre Company 149
Hyslop, David 51

I

Iacucci, Lisa 132

Ianculovici, Dana 40, 59
Ibroci, Astrit 141
Ibsen, Brian 217, 218, 219
Ibsen, Henrik 143, 159, 168, 204
Ice, Black 34
ICM Artists, Ltd. 97
Ierardi, Robert 301
Iggy Woo 170
Igrejas, Manuel 112
Iizuka, Naomi 212
Ikeda, Jennifer 129
Ilijevich, Eric 147
Illinois Theatre Center 214
Illuminating Veronica 174
Im, Jennie 172
Imaginary Friends 42, 219
Imhoff, Gary 110
Impact 160
Imperial Theatre 133
Importance of Being Earnest, The 149
I'm Not Rappaport 23
I'm Still Here 161
Inbar, Sara 71
Independent Presenters Network 75
Indian Summer 225
Informed Consent 143
Ing, Alvin 29
Ingalls, James F. 55, 106, 131, 179, 183, 185, 186
Inge, William 145, 214
Ingman, Matthew 39
Ingram, Malcolm 227
Inkley, Fred 27
Inman, Troy 210
Innvar, Christopher 175, 223
Inoue, Masahiro 167
Inside a Bigger Box 158
Insurrection: Holding History 192
Intar 169
Intar 53 Theater 111, 149
Intelligent Design of Jenny Chow, The 226
Intemann, E.D. 172
InterSchool Orchestras of New York Symphonic Band 180
Intiman Theatre World 198
Intimate Apparel 225
Intimate Shift 149
Inventing Van Gogh 202
In Love and Anger 174
In Real Life 126
In the Realm of the Unreal 148
In the Solitude of Cotton Fields 154
Iordanov, Krassin 154
Iorio, Jim 155, 222
Iphigenia 163
Iphigenia in Tauris 148

Ireland, Marin 130, 174, 175
Irish Arts 149
Irish Repertory Theatre 99, 169
Irving, Amy 160, 168
Irving, George S. 220
Irwin, Karla 232
Irwin, Robin 40
Isaac, Rachel 41, 301
Isaacs, Jean 215
Isaacson, Mike 75
I' Cook, Curtiss 70
Isenegger, Nadine 69
Isenhart, Rebecca Elizabeth 211
Isherwood, Christopher 67
Ishikawa, Takeshi 173
Island, The 123
Island Def Jam Music Group 34
Isler, Seth 116
Islington Entertainment 97
Ismay, Faith Jensen 219
Isola, Kevin 128, 130, 301
Israel, Robert 186
Is There a Doctor in the House?
     152
It's a . . . Mexican-Mormon 172
It's a Wonderful Lie 140
*It's Beginning to Look a Lot Like
     Murder!* 146
It's Better with a Band 223
Itkin, Ari 229
It Just Catches 144
Ivanek, Zeljko 98
Ivanovski, Goron 146
Iventosch, Nina 100
Ives, David 40, 124, 127
Ivey, Dana 52, 160, 190, 241,
     301
Ivey, Judith 176, 183
Ivins, Todd Edward 232
Izard, E. Ashley 187
Izquierdo, Michael X. 162
Izzard, Eddie 16, 52, 241, 301
I Am a Camera 67
I Am My Own Wife 131
*I Am Strong in the Face of
     Everything Except Nuclear
     War* 160
I Love Myself 152
*I Love New York—What's Your
     Excuse?* 152
*I Love You, You're Perfect, Now
     Change* 110
I Think I Like Girls 215
I Want You To 155

J
Jackie Wilson Story, The 104
Jacksina, Judy 95, 97, 98, 109
Jacksina Company Inc. 95, 97,
     98

Jackson, Anne 160
Jackson, Carter 36
Jackson, Christopher 70
Jackson, David 231
Jackson, Doug 105
Jackson, Gregory Patrick 212
Jackson, Jasmine 186
Jackson, Jason 92, 124
Jackson, Jovan 183
Jackson, Keron L. 209
Jackson, Kevin 225
Jackson, Mark Leroy 74
Jackson, Warren 208
Jacob, Abe 201
Jacob, Lou 174
Jacobs, Amy 24, 38, 47, 66, 69
Jacobs, Chelsea 205
Jacobs, Gary 211
Jacobs, Jim 220
Jacobs, Marian Lerman 91
Jacobs, Stefan 173
Jacoby, Mark 37, 301
*Jacques Brel Is Alive and Well
     and Living in Paris* 232
Jaeger, Darleen 163
Jaffe, Debbie 162
Jaffe, Eddie 319
Jaffe, Jill 124
Jah, Zainab 206
Jahi, Meena T. 70
Jahnke, Christopher 125, 221
Jain, Ravi 171
JaJuan, Kimberly 233
Jakobsson, Magnus 153
Jalali, Faezah 205
James, Amy 186
James, Ann C. 183
James, Diqui 109
James, Doug 205
James, Elmore 66
James, Elsie 149
James, Laurissa 143
James, Michael Guy 171
James, Nikki M. 124
James, Paul 227
James, Peter Francis 124, 199
James, Steven Anthony 185
James, Stu 74
James, Tomas 109
James, Tommy 196
James, Toni-Leslie 45, 91, 124,
     125, 132
James Joyce's The Dead 208
Jampolis, Neil Peter 110
Jamrog, Joseph 163
Jamros, Chris 220
Jam Theatricals 24, 96, 97
Janaki 158
Janasz, Charles 219
Jane's Exchange and North of

Providence 158
Janelli, Ronald 29, 59
Jane Street Theatre 96
Janke, Linda Williams 222
Janki, Devanand 102, 167
Jardine, Luke 123
Jarrett, Jennifer 189
Jarrow, Kyle 148
Jarvis, Brett 109, 179
Jarvis, Mitchell 95
Jarvis, Virginia 232
Jasper, Christian 219
Jasperson, Mary 153
Jastrab, David 220
Jaudes, Christian 29, 59
Javien, Joanne 220
Jay, Anjali 102
Jay-Alexander, Richard 95
Jaynes, Randall 112
Jay Binder Casting 32
Jazi, Esmaeil Arefian 173
Jazi, Hassan Aliabbasi 173
Jazi, Kamal Aliabbasi 173
Jazi, Majid Aliabbasi 173
Jean Cocteau Repertory 149
Jean Doumanian Productions,
     Inc. 24, 30
Jefferies, Annalee 131, 183
Jeffords, Tom 220
Jeffries, Susan 141, 155
Jelks, John Earl 199
Jellison, Marcy 171
Jenkins, Amanda 205
Jenkins, Capathia 60
Jenkins, David 199, 228, 230
Jenkins, Michael A. 29
Jenkins, Paulie 225
Jenkins, Sharon 230
Jennin, Byron 43
Jennings, Byron 179
Jennings, Ken 76
Jennings, Mikeah Ernest 140
Jensen, Erik 95, 161
Jensen, Julie 179
Jensen, Sarah Jayne 59
Jensen, Tim Douglas 156
Jensen, Tom 167
Jerins, Alana 175
Jerome, Timothy 38, 39, 301
Jerrnaine, Omar 145
Jerry Beaver and Associates 93
Jeske, Joel 152
Jesson, Belch-Paul 123
Jesurun, John 172
Jeter, Michael 320
Jeweler's Tale, The 213
Jewish Repertory Theatre 133
Jewsbury, Lovely 53
Jews Without Money 178
Jhung, Catherine 155

Jiggetts-Tivony, Shelby 196
Jiles, Jennifer 146
Jimenez, Carla 225
Jimenez, Robert M. 47, 128
Jitney 227
JoAnn, Ebony 45, 132
Jobe, Molly 220
Jobin, David 202
Jochim, Keith 218
Joe 176
Joel, Billy 32
Joel, Stephanie 102
Joey Shakespear 170
Joe and Betty 150
Johannes, Mark 94
Johanson, Robert 220
John, Elton 65, 70
Johnny 23 156
Johns, Ernest 149
Johnson, Addie 174, 175
Johnson, Alan 186
Johnson, Amber 230
Johnson, Birch 26
Johnson, Bonnie 217
Johnson, Carrie A. 151
Johnson, Catherine 71, 196
Johnson, Craig 75
Johnson, Denis 145
Johnson, Douglas 200
Johnson, Effie 222
Johnson, Erik 225
Johnson, Joyce 142
Johnson, Maree 192
Johnson, Marilyn Jean 320
Johnson, Marjorie 220
Johnson, Melody 72
Johnson, Mikelle 233, 234
Johnson, Natalie Joy 171
Johnson, Phyllis 233
Johnson, Richard T. 192
Johnson, Royce 226
Johnson, Susan 320
Johnson, Tamara E. 227
Johnson, Tom 140
Johnson-Liff & Zerman 72
Johnson-Liff Associates, Ltd 73,
     233
Johnson-Liff Casting, Ltd. 234
Johnston, Bonnie 219
Johnston, Cara 124
Johnston, Donald 69, 197
Johnston, Kristen 128
Johnston, Laura 158
Johnston, Owen, II 74
Johnston, Robert 219
John Houseman Studio Theatre
     98
John Houseman Theatre 93,
     102, 150
Johson-Liff Associates, Ltd. 233

Joines, Howard 29
Jokovic, Mirjana 185
Jolie, Danielle 124
Jolles, Susan 124
Jolson and Company 94
Jonas, Joseph 39, 301
Jonas, Phoebe 186
Jondon 102
Jones, Albert 222
Jones, Amanda 149
Jones, Austin 156
Jones, Bianca 233
Jones, Billy Eugene 233
Jones, Bill T. 170
Jones, Brett 211
Jones, Bryan C. 204
Jones, Camila 163
Jones, Charlotte 127
Jones, Cherry 42, 219, 301
Jones, Christine 93, 96, 168,
     177, 234
Jones, Christopher Joseph 169
Jones, Collin 211
Jones, Cynthia 198
Jones, Delise 150
Jones, Denis 68, 124
Jones, Dexter 197
Jones, Fateema 127
Jones, Gabrielle 196
Jones, Guiesseppe 204
Jones, Jeffrey M. 163
Jones, Jennifer 69
Jones, John Christopher 179
Jones, John Kevin 156
Jones, Julia P. 76
Jones, Lindsay 208, 212, 219,
     225
Jones, Lizzi 184
Jones, Marie 183, 217, 229
Jones, Michael 204
Jones, Nate 168
Jones, Robert 213
Jones, Robert Anthony 91
Jones, Rodney 92
Jones, Rolin 226
Jones, Ron Cephas 101, 151
Jones, Russell G. 101
Jones, Sarah 191
Jones, Simon 124, 139, 301
Jones, Spencer C. 220
Jones, Steven Anthony 184, 185
Jones, Terace 40
Jones, Toby 50
Jones, Ty 144
Jones, Vanessa A. 70
Jones, Vanessa S. 70
Joplin, Joneal 200
Jordan, Dale 189, 211
Jordan, Dale F. 224
Jordan, Don 143

Jordan, Shane 202
Joseph, Elbert 186
Joseph, Leonard 70
Joseph, Sandra 72
Josephs, Jennifer 70
Josephson, Erland 123
Joseph Papp Public Theater/
    New York Shakespeare
    Festival, The 170
Jose Quintero Theatre 150
Joshi, Abhijat 148
Joshua, Peter 326
Jovanovic, Jelena 171
Jovanovich, Brandon 124
Joy, James Leonard 200, 220
Joy, Michael 70
Joyce, Melba 180
Jubett, Joan 154
Judd, Fermon, Jr. 112
Judge, Daniel 124
Judson, Tom 197
Judy, James 175
Jue, Fancis 75
Jue, Francis 75, 201
Juhn, Paul 149, 154
Jules, Anny 128
Juliano, Lisa 102
Julia Sweeney: Guys and
    Babies, Sex and Gods 140
Julius Caesar 179
Jump/Cut 174
Jumper, Samantha 145
Jun, Paul 174
Junebug Symphony, The 153
Jurglanis, Marla 187
Justeson, Ryan 154
Justus, Christa 223
Just Us Boys 140
Jutras, Simon 43

K

K., Benja 176
Kaas-Lentz, Liam 212
Kabatznick, Brian 104
Kachadurian, Zoya 217
Kaczorowski, Peter 73, 94, 124
Kading, Charles S. 231
Kaefer, Kathleen 150
Kafele, Fatima 123
Kafka, Franz 150
Kagan, Diane 179
Kaikkonen, Gus 155, 173
Kainuma, Morris 40, 59
Kaiser, Joseph 38, 39
Kaiwi, Brant 156
Kakuk, Naomi 73
Kalarchian, Steve 222
Kalas, Janet 47, 128, 190
Kale, Bob 196
Kalember, Patricia 190

Kaling, Mindy 154
Kallins, Molly Grant 58, 59
Kamal, Joseph 43
Kaminsky, Sheila 172
Kamyshkova, Masha 204
Kandel, Karen 215
Kander, John 58, 67, 68, 192
Kane, David 27
Kane, Honour 175
Kane, Lyndsay Rose 140
Kane, Timothy Edward 208
Kaneko, Sumie 230
Kanes, Benjamin 231
Kang, M.J. 172
Kang, Tim 150
Kani, John 123
Kanor, Seth 175
Kanouse, Lyle 198
Kanter, Lynn 150
Kantor, Ken 220
Kanyok, Laurie 32
Kaokept, Adam Michael 175,
    187
Kaplowitz, Robert 93, 130, 212
Kapner, Sara 33
Karas, Ellen 185
Kardana-Swinsky Productions
    Inc. 103
Kardana Productions 68
Karel, Charles 147
Karen, Jamie 37
Karibalis, Curt 207
Karkanis, Athena 226
Karl, Alfred 98
Karl, Andy 220
Karlin, Julie 158
Karp, Steve 226
Karpel Group 109
Karpen, Claire 230
Karsh, Ken 221
Karslake, Daniel 38
Kary, Michael 217, 218, 219
Kashani, Dariush 160, 161
Kastner, Ron 51, 58, 104
Kata, Greg 180
Kata, Takeshi 105
Kater, Peter 221
Katigbak, Mia 149, 151
Katovich, Scout 184
Katsafados, Thodoros 97
Katsaros, Doug 223
Katsiadaki, Maria 97
Katz, Alan 194
Katz, Naomi 232
Katz, Natasha 29, 49, 65, 66,
    91, 99
Kauffman, Anne 170
Kauffman, Thomas M. 186, 213
Kaufman, Daniel 143, 153
Kaufman, George S. 43, 167, 183

Kaufman, Jason 186
Kaufman, Lynne 139
Kaufman, Moises 131
Kaufman, Shawn 169
Kaufmann, Thomas 186
Kaus, Stephen M. 167, 213
Kawahara, Karl 75
Kay, Phyllis 228, 229, 230
Kayden, Mildred 176
Kayden, Spencer 76, 180
Kaye, Bradley 110
Kaye, Howard 93, 192, 221
Kaye, Judy 71, 180
Kayser, Chris 210
Kazantzakis, Nikos 192
KazKaz, Rana 161
Keach, Stacy 199
Kealey, Scott 226
Keane, John B. 99
Keany, Paul 154
Kearney, Kristine A. 206
Kearney-Patch, Kate 179, 183
Keating, Ashlee 220
Keating, Charles 125, 301
Keating, John 149, 169, 185
Keefe, Anne 36
Keefe, Elizabeth 140
Keel-Huff, Sandra 150
Keeley, David W. 71
Keenan-Bolger, Celia 132
Keener, Catherine 93
Keen Company 150
Kegley, Elizabeth 186
Kehr, Donnie 65
Keigwin, Larry 40
Keister, Olivia 152
Keitch, J. Andrew 231
Keith, Larry 67, 139
Keithley, Karinne 171
Keith Sherman and Associates
    100
Kellem, Cliff 211
Kellenberger, Kurt 177, 213
Keller, Greg 147
Keller, Jeff 72
Keller, John-David 225
Keller, Michael 37, 40, 42, 58, 71
Keller, Neel 202, 222
Keller, Rod 198
Kellermann, Susan 177
Kelley, Meggins 211
Kelley, R.J. 27
Kellner, Jeff 148
Kellogg, Marjorie Bradley 200
Kelly, Alexa 157
Kelly, Christopher 200
Kelly, Colleen 209
Kelly, Daniel Hugh 199
Kelly, Daren 197
Kelly, David 191

Kelly, David Patrick 168
Kelly, EC 143
Kelly, Erica 148
Kelly, Francis 133
Kelly, George 155
Kelly, Glen 73
Kelly, Janie 155
Kelly, John-Charles 231
Kelly, Kristopher 111
Kelly, Lee 74
Kelly, Mickey 149
Kelly, Patti 202, 203
Kelly, Reade 141
Kelly, Stephen 145
Kelly, Tari 221
Kelly, Thomas Vincent 224
Kelpie Arts 29
Kemp, Sally 155
Kenaston, Tom 195
Kendall, Arnold 187
Kendall, Rebecca 143, 153
Kendrick, Louisa 66
Kenin, Sean 152
Kenn, Dana 91, 223
Kennedy, Chilina 196
Kennedy, Daniel Patrick 184
Kennedy, J. 169
Kennedy, James 146
Kennedy, Robert B. 211
Kennedy, Steve Canyon 25,
    65, 73
Kennedy, York 191, 217, 218,
    219, 225
Kennelly, Brendan 233
Kenney, Gabriel 184
Kenney, Leah 229
Kenny, Frances 215
Kenny, Gerard 142
Kent, David 231
Kent, Jonathan 37
Kent, Sean 158
Kenyon, Steven 124
Kenzler, Karl 43, 173
Keogh, Des 99
Kepros, Nicholas 179, 183
Kern, Joey 132
Kerouac 156
Kerpel, Gabriel 109
Kerr, E. Katherine 131
Kerr, Jean 320
Kerrigan, Patricia 50
Kesey, Ken 189
Kesler, Ian Reed 168
Kesselman, Wendy 151
Kesselring, Joseph 222
Kessler, Marc 99
Ketchmore, Rickey 223
Kettler, Brian 210
Kevin, Michael 222
Key, Tom 209

Keyes, Dave 49
Keyes, Katherine 38
Keylock, Joanna 99
Keyloun, Michael 215
Keyser, Brett 171
Keyser, Rhonda 155
Keystone, Nancy 222
Khalaf, Ramzi 192
Khaler, Tara Lynne 220
Khan, Shaheen 102
Khoulenjani, Asadollah
    Momenzadeh 173
Khoulenjani, Mohammadali
    Momenzadeh 173
Kiehn, Dontee 59, 69
Kiel, Larissa 153
Kievman, Melissa 175
Kievsky, Boris 148
Kiki & Herb: Coup de Theatre
    144
Kildare, Martin 209
Kilday, Ray 75
Kilgarriff, Patricia 44
Kilgore, John 97
Killenberger, Robert 102, 167
Killian, Scott 179
Killing Louise 142
Kim, Chung Sun 39
Kim, Peter 233
Kim, Randall Duk 29
Kim, Susan 168
Kim, Willa 169, 190
Kim, Youn 65
Kimball, Chad 131
Kimball, Dyana 152
Kimberly Akimbo 127
Kimble, Phil 146
Kimbrough, Charles 176, 301
Kimura, Mami 148
Kincaid, Ken 171
King, Alan 117
King, Brendan 40
King, Christopher 178
King, Denis 192
King, Ginifer 59
King, Greg 227
King, Nicolas 33, 301
King, Raymond A. 196
King, Ryan 233, 234
King, Woodie, Jr. 176
King, Zoë 186
Kingdom of Lost Songs, The 148
Kingsley, Mira 92
Kingwell, Jay 110
King and Queen of Planet
    Pookie, The 143
King Lear 144
Kinnard, Cindy 219
Kinney, Fred 223
Kinsherf, John 150

Kirby, Davis 27, 140
Kirchner, Jamie 180
Kirk, James T. 205
Kirk, Justin 130, 302
Kirk, Keith Byron 125
Kirk, Roger 69, 197
Kirkland, Dale 37
Kirkland, Keith 205
Kirkpatrick, Kelley 126, 213
Kirk Theatre 150
Kirstein, Ruth Priscilla 180
Kirsten, Amy 172
Kirwan, Jack 217
Kirwan, Larry 169
Kissel, Jeremiah 213
Kitchen, Heather M. 184
Kitsopoulos, Antonia 39
Kitsopoulos, Constantine 38
Kitsopoulos, Nicholas 38
Kitt, Tom 96
Kittredge, Ann 124
Kittrell, Michelle 49, 302
Kitty the Waitress 152
Kit Kat Club 67
Kit Marlowe 174
Kiwitt, Catherine Richardson 198
Kjellson, Ingvar 123
Kladitis, Manny 96
Klainer, Traci 31
Klaisner, Fred D. 92
Klaitz, Jay 186
Klapinski, Bridget 68, 109
Klapmeyer, Renée 69
Klapper, Stephanie 194, 195, 205
Klausen, Ray 198, 223
Klavan, Laurence 161
Kleiman, Lauren 145
Klein, Alisa 66, 75
Klein, Ben 217
Klein, Julia 139
Klein, Lauren 117, 215
Klein, Noah 147
Klein, Randall E. 168, 227
Klein, Stephen 221
Klein, Tanya 145
Kleinhans, Elysabeth 146
Kleinmann, Kurt 146
Klemperer, Jerusha 157
Kliban, Ken 173, 302
Klimzak, Michael 152
Kline, Carol 198
Kline, Drew 229
Klinger, Christopher 145
Klinger, Pam 66
Klose, Chip 231
Klug, Jan 171
Klux, Bill 234
Knapp, Emily 186
Knapp, Hannah 185

Knee, Allan 163, 226
Kneeland, Katie 214
Knell, Dane 209
Knezevich, Joe 210
Knight, Ann 204
Knight, James 173, 302
Knight, T.R. 44, 173, 175, 302
Knoll, Jacob 233, 234
Knopf, Robert 161
Knoppers, Anotonie 218
Knoppers, Antonie 217, 218, 219
Knott, Frederick 320
Knower, Zachary 147
Knowland, Matthew 142
Knowles, Michael 142
Knox, Leila 30, 125
Knox, Paul 143
Knutson, Tom 143, 147
Koch, Jeremy 151
Koch, Marilyn 190
Koch, Martin 71, 196
Koch, Ted 150
Koch, William 222
Kocher, Cynthia 45
Koehl, Coby 171
Koenig, Jack 139, 302
Kofman, Gil 140
Koger, Jeffrey S. 231
Kohanek, Wayne 217
Koharchik, Rob 212
Kohlhaas, Karen 128
Kohn, Christian 33
Kole, Hilary 118
Kolinski, Joe 145
Koltes, Bernard Marie 154
Koltes New York 2003: New
    American Translations 154
Komer, Chris 39
Komine, Lily 167
Kondoleon, Harry 130
Koniordou, Lydia 97
Kono, Ben 30
Kontouri, Niketi 97
Koob, Shannon 201
Kookept, Adam Michael 167
Koolhaas, Rem 209
Koonin, Brian 42, 55
Kopit, Arthur 54
Koplin, Russell Arden 100
Koppel, Nurit 23
Koprowski, John 155
Kopryanski, Karen 186
Korbee, Thomas, Jr. 100
Korea Pictures/Doyun Seol 38
Korey, Alix 68, 124
Korf, Gene 62
Korf, Geoff 225
Kornberg, Richard 25, 62,
    74, 109
Kornhaber, David 150

Koroly, Charles 123
Kosarin, Michael 66
Kosek, Kenny 169
Kosh, David 152
Kosis, Tom 29
Koskey, Monica 187
Kostalik, Linda 225
Kostival, Jessica 69
Kostroff, Gregory 97
Kosuzu, Masaki 173
Kot, Don 212
Koteas, Elias 160
Kotis, Greg 76, 160, 185
Kotler, Jill 156
Kotlowitz, Dan 200, 216
Kotsur, Troy 198
Koudal, Morten Thorup 167
Kourtides, Nick 223
Koustik, Art 225
Koustik, Austin 225
Kovacs, Michelle 150
Koval, Phil 221
Kovich, Matt 190
Kovner, Todd 154
Koym, Kimberlee 191
Kozoll, Rory 186
KPM Associates 99, 105
Kraft, Kevin 139
Krag, James 208
Kraine Theater 151
Krakowski, Fritz 40
Krakowski, Jane 15, 54, 302
Kramer, Julie 153
Kramer, Ruth E. 221
Kramer, Sara 143
Kramer, Terry Allen 32
Krane, David 37, 67
Krass, Michael 124, 168, 190,
    213, 227
Krause, Matthew 208
Krausen, Park 210
Krauss, Marvin A. 321
Kravitz, Zarah 172
Kreager, Jeb 187
Krebs, Eric 61, 93
Kreeger, Doug 142
Kreisler, Katie 191
Kreitzer, Carson 201
Kreitzer, Scott 32
Krell, Daniel 221
Krepos, Nicholas 139
Krich, Gretchen Lee 174
Krimbel, Jacob 188
Krinsky, Marc 151
Krishnamma, Ranjit 102
Kristel, Jackie 158
Kristina, Amy 171
Kritas Productions 97
Kritzer, Leslie 220
Krohn, Charles 183

Kronenberg, Bruce 95
Kroner, John 180
Kronzer, James 187
Krueger, Rich 160
Krummel, Jens Martin 159
Kruse, Mahlon 37
Krutoff, Glenn 147
Kryger, Todd M. 221
Kua, Kenway Hon Wai K. 201
Kubala, Michael 68
Kuchar, Dan 190
Kudisch, Marc 75, 124
Kuether, John 72
Kuhar, Elisa R. 180
Kuhn, Dave 40
Kuhn, Jeffrey 200
Kuhn, Kevin 125
Kukla, Erin 227
Kukoff, Bernie 110
Kulasinghe, Muni 172
Kulick, Brian 128, 151
Kulick, Elliott F. 48
Kulu, Faca 70
Kumar, Syreeta 102
Kunene, Ron 70
Kuney, Daniel 153
Kung, Yufen 93
Kunii, Masahiro 167
Kunimoto, Takeharu 173
Kunkle, Connie 180
Kunze, Michael 40
Kupiec, Keirsten 69
Kurisu-Chan 112
Kurlander, Gabrielle 142
Kuroda, Kathy 151
Kurtz, Swoosie 42, 219
Kurtzuba, Stephanie 183
Kurup, Shishir 233
Kuruvilla, Sunil Thomas 233
Kurze, Kevin 159
Kwapy, William 92
Kwiatkowski, John 156
Kya-Hill, Robert 159
Kyanko, Janine 189

L

L.J.Ganser 159
Labey, Russell 151
Labin, Ann 40, 59
LaBlanca, Matthew 230
Laboissonniere, Wade 102, 167,
    234
LaBute, Neil 160, 173
LAByrinth Theater Company 101,
    151
Labyrinth Theater Company 151
LaCause, Sebastian 68
Lacey, Maggie 36, 150
Lacey, Matthew 76
LaChanze 160
LaChiusa, Michael John 132,

160, 161
Lachowicz, Ted 98
Lacivita, Carman 145
Lackawanna Blues 184
Lacy, Kevin 28
Lacy, Tom 213
Ladd, Eliza 145
Ladies, The 170
Ladies of the Corridor, The 141
Ladutke, Rachel Rubin 152
Lady, Be Good 147
Lady of Letters, A 104
Laev, Jim 40
laFosse, Robert 176
Lagarce, Jean-Luc 159
Lagomarsino, Ron 190
Lahr, John 197
Laidlaw, Elizabeth 208
Laing, Robin 41, 167
Laird, Marvin 59
Lake, The 232
Lakeera 161
Lakis, Maggie 187
Laliberte, Patti 230
Lam, Nina Zoie 144
Lam, Serena 168
Lamb, Mary Ann 124
Lamb's Theatre 91, 105
Lambert, Jason 145
Lambert, Mikel Sarah 132, 150,
    302
Lambert, Molly 144
Lamberton, David 150
Lamia, Jenna 169
Lamm, Alessandra Corona 124
Lamm, Teri 159
Lamos, Mark 217, 234
Lamparella, Gina 42, 59, 219
Lampley, Oni Faida 141
Lamude, Terence 149, 222
LaMura, Mark 43
Lanciers, Barb 172
Landa, Edgar 199
Landau, Elie 95
Landau, Randall 37
Landau, Steven 198
Landecker, Amy 146, 195
Lander, David 131
Landers, Diane 146
Landers, Matt 154
Landes, Francine 185
Landesman, Rocco 73
Landfield, Matthew 139
Landfield, Timothy 225
Landon, Hal, Jr. 225, 226
Landon, Kendra Leigh 163
Landowne, Mahayana 152
Landwehr, Hugh 173
Land of the Dead 160
Lane, Nathan 73

Lane, Preston 209
Lane, Stewart F. 75
Lane, William 228, 229, 230
Lang, Matt 202
Lang, Philip J. 69, 197
Lang, William H. 110
Langan, Damien 222
Langdon, Scott 231
Lange, Alyson 39
Lange, Anne 43, 302
Langham, Joseph 105
Lanier, Laurice 38
Lankov, Jeff 209
Lansbury, David 176, 302
Lapine, James 30, 207
Lapira, Liza 163
LaPlante, Barret 229
Laporte, Stephane 151
Largay, Stephen 130
Larkin, Jennifer 145
Larkin, Peter 57
Larsen, Anika 102, 167
Larsen, Darrell 157
Larsen, Liz 154
Larsen, Patrick 215
Larsen, Ronnie 99
Larson, Corrine 234
Larson, Jonathan 74
Larson, Linda Marie 196
Larson, Mark 224
Larson, Mary 215
Larson, Peter 94, 192
Larsson, Stefan 123
LaRue, J 227
Lasana, Gyavira 178
Lash, Elissa 156
Lash, Joshua Brownie 225
Lashmet, Amy 225
Laskey, Margaux 143
Lasky, Becky 178
Last Child 148
Last Day 140
Last Flapper, The 232
Last of the Suns 151
Last One, The 160
Last Stand 163
Last Sunday in June, The 105, 157, 193
Last Train to Nibroc 141
Last Two Jews of Kabul, The 172
Last Year 161
Laszlo, Miklos 231
Latarro, Lorin 37
Later Lyrics 180
Latessa, Dick 26, 67
Late (A Cowboy Song) 145
Late Night, Early Morning 161
Late Night Catechism 117
Latham, Aaron 49

Lathan, Stan 34
Lathan, Tendaji 34
Lathon, Daryl 153
Lathroum, E. Tonry 188, 189
LaTourelle, Adrian 150, 209
Latta, Richard 93
Lattimore, Richard 205
Lattimore, Todd 69
Latus, James 128
Laube, Miriam A. 209
Lauer, Andrea 183
Lauer, Leo 151
Lauren, Ellen 186
Laurents, Arthur 58, 227
Lauria, Dan 191
Laurie, Piper 196
Laurino, Michael 212
Laurits, Eric 156
LaVecchia, Antoinette 127
Lavelle, Robert 57
Lavender, Daniel T. 151
LaVerdiere, Jamie 73
Lavin, Linda 33, 85, 302
Lavner, Steve 66
LaVon, Laura 227
Lawler, Marjorie 325
Lawler, Matthew 141
Lawrence, Blake 146
Lawrence, Darrie 139, 206
Lawrence, David H. 66, 69, 197
Lawrence, Elliot 180
Lawrence, Megan 76
Lawrence, Peter 37, 58
Lawrence, Sharon 68, 191
Laws, Heather 67
Lawson, David M. 111, 169
Lawson, Mandy 205
Lawson, Steve 161
Lawson, Whitney 204
Lawton, Anthony 187
Lay, Josh 205
Layng, Kathryn A. 144
Lazar, Paul 145
Lazarus, Bruce 28
La Boheme 14, 38
La Dispute 186
La Dolce Vita: Movie Songs of the 1960s 202
La Jolla Playhouse 215
La Mama Experimental Theatre Club (ETC) 170
La Musica 145
La Posada Magica 225
La Ronde 195, 207
la Vecchia, Antoinette 139
Leach, Kristina 144
Leal, Rick 209
Leal, Sharon 74
Leaming, Greg 200

Lear, Richard 111
Learned, Michael 132
Leavel, Beth 69
Leavengood, Bill 161
Leavitt, Michael 75
LeBouef, Clayton 176
LeBow, Will 186
Lecure, Bruce 193
Ledbetter, Mark 145, 220
Ledoux, Paul 162
Ledsinger, David 217, 218, 219
Lee, C.S. 149
Lee, C.Y. 29
Lee, China 233
Lee, Darren 75, 201, 220
Lee, Eugene 91, 229
Lee, Gihieh 125
Lee, Gypsy Rose 58
Lee, Heather 59
Lee, Heland 140
Lee, Hoon 29
Lee, Hyunjung 148
Lee, Jack 180
Lee, James Edward 153
Lee, Jeff 70
Lee, Jeffrey Yoshi 105
Lee, John 28
Lee, Joyce Kim 199, 225
Lee, Linda Talcott 66
Lee, Michelle 85
Lee, Sherri Parker 158, 179
Lee, Tina 149
Lee, Tom 172, 234
Lee, Tuck 40
Leebove, Patricia Harusame 171
Leech, Kitty 180
Leeds, Jordan 110, 302
Leeds, Mariah Sage 230
Leeves, Jane 67
LeFevre, Adam 71
Leftfield Productions 91
Legault, Anne 141
Leggett, Charles 222
Leggett, Clarence 227
Leggett, Will 191
Legrand, Michel 30
Leguillou, Lisa 24
Leguizamo, John 197
Lehl, Philip 183
Lehmann, Harold 149
Lehrer, Robert 146, 178
Lehrer, Scott 24, 68, 124, 125, 131, 132, 179, 183
Leichter, Aaron 103
Leigh, Mitch 37, 221
Leight, Warren 160
Leighton, John 169
Leighton, Richard 146, 155
Leiner, Matthew 33
Leishman, Gina 179, 215

Leitner, James 187
LeLand, Douglas 222
Lema, Julia 93
LeMaster, Jarret 198
Lemay, Harding 175
Lemenager, Nancy 147
Lemmeke, Ole 153
Lemon 34
Lenat, Jesse 129, 150
Lenat, Zachary 184
Lenhart, Leanna 195
Lenox, Adriane 130, 190, 302
Lenz, Matt 25
Leo, Melissa 175
Leonard, Dan 193
Leonard, John 102
Leonard, Katharine 26
Leonard, Robert Sean 62, 177, 302
Leonard, Valerie 212
Leonard, Wendy 190
Leonardo, Joe 223
Leonce and Lena 145
Leong, David S. 45
Leong, Philippe Cu 143
Leong, Terry 178
Leonhart, Jay 180
Lepard, John 177
Lepcio, Andrea 148
Lerch, Sara 124
Leritz, Lawrence 106
Lerner, Alan Jay 220
Lerner, Zev 218
Leroux, Gaston 72
Leroy, Zoaunne 222
Lesbian Pulporama! 148
Leshner, Lori 180
Leslie, Don 111
Leslie, Rachel 227
Leslie, Regina 214
Leslie, Sonya 70
Lesser, Sally 172
Lessing, Florence 321
Lessing, Gotthold 155
Lesson before Dying, A 226
Lester, Gideon 186
LeStrange, Philip 43, 302
Les Misérables 81
Letendre, Brian 49
Letscher, Brian 143
Lettre, Peter 144, 171
Lettuce, Hedda 99
Leung, Ken 75
Leung, Telly 29, 302
Levan, Martin 72
Leve, Harriet Newman 45, 112
Leveaux, David 54
Leverett, T. Doyle 200
Levering, Kate 69, 192

Levesque, Joe 156
Levin, Kate 180
Levine, Daniel C. 111
Levine, David 145, 174, 175, 176
Levine, Douglas 202
Levine, Jonathan 27
Levine, Lawrence 142, 155
Levine, Michael 42, 219
Levine, Peter 143
Levings, Nigel 38
Levinson, Brad 151
Levy, Aaron 98
Levy, Annie 150
Levy, Benn 213
Levy, Daniel 149
Levy, Julia C. 27, 44, 52, 53, 54, 60, 132
Levy, Kate 206, 222
Levy, Lisa 148
Levy, Philip 95
Lew, Jason 154
Lewandowski, Sheila 148
Lewis, Carter W. 216
Lewis, Claire 228, 229, 230
Lewis, Clea 106
Lewis, Ellen 50
Lewis, J. Barry 195
Lewis, Jeff 208
Lewis, Marcia 68
Lewis, Michael Shawn 72
Lewis, Norm 30
Lewis, Paul 111
Lewis, Peter 147
Lewis, Shannon 60
Lewis, Vicki 68
Lewkowitz, Jerry 162
Lexington Road Productions 40
Leyden, Leo 234
Leynse, Andrew 100, 176
Leyton-Brown, Allison 148
Le Passe-Muraille 30
LFG Holdings 40
Liander, Colin E. 223
Liao, Angela 150
Liao, Joanna 174
Libman, Daniel 141
Libman, Martha 176
Lichtenberg, Nick 227
Lieb, Robert P. 321
Lieber, Mimi 23, 175, 302
Lieberman, Amy 29, 196, 198, 199
Lieberman, Andrew 227
Life, Regge 195
Life (x) 3 51
Liff, Vincent "Vinnie" 321
Light, Judith 175
Light, Sara 49
Lightcap, Brenda 105
Lightman, Alan 147

Oliver! 204
Oliver, Anna R. 185, 191
Oliver, B. Hayden 209, 216
Oliver, Jennifer 196
Oliver, Wendy 66
Oliver-Watts, Guy 153
Oliveras, Maria 144
Olivieri, Vincent 227
Olivo, Karen 74
Olmstead, Dan 232
Olness, Kristin 67
Olsen, Chuck 39
Olsen, Jennifer 39
Olsen, Ralph 59
Olsen, Robert 216
Omagari, Mayumi 220
Onagan, Patty 70
One Dream Sound 91
One Festival, The 156
*One Flew over the Cuckoo's
    Nest* 189
One Million Butterflies 100
One Shot, One Kill 117
Ong, Han 153
Only the End of the World 159
Onodera, Kaori 172
OnStage Percussion 196
Ontiveros, Jesse 169
Ontiveros, Tom 95
Ontological Detective, The 141
Ontological Theatre 154
On Golden Pond 206
Opatrny, Matt 173
Opel, Nancy 76, 127
Opsahl, Jason 323
Orbach, Ron 40, 305
Orchard, Robert J. 186
Ordell, Darryl 74
Ordower, Daniel 222
Oreskes, Daniel 65, 176, 179,
    306
Orfeh 160
Origlio, Tony 93, 102, 105
Origlio Public Relations 93, 102,
    105
Orizondo, Carlos 177
Orlandersmith, Dael 126, 174
Orlandi, Felice 323
Orloff, Rich 140, 143, 153
Ornstein, Suzanne 124
Orphan on God's Highway 171
Orpheum Theatre 112
Orr, Laurie Ann 145
Orsini, Angelique 178
Orson, Daine 233
Ortado, Victor 154
Orth-Pallavicini, Nicole 141, 175
Ortiz, April 233
Ortiz, Deborah Louise 152

Ortiz, John 215
Orton, Kevin 201
Or Polaroids (Version 2.1) 148
Osborn, Paul 196
Osborne, Kevin 32
Oscar, Brad 73
Osentoski, Whitney 220
Oser, Harriet 193
Osgood, K. Winston 153
Osher, Bonnie 25
Osher, John 25
Osheroff, Joe 139
Oshima, Usaburo 173
Osian, Matte 96
Osorno, Jim 42, 219
Ost, Tobin 102, 167
Ostadazim, Sheila 150
Ostar Enterprises 33
Osterman, Lester 323
Ostling, Daniel 167, 212, 215
Ostroski, Mike 188, 189
Ostrowski, Andrew David 203
Other Line, The 160
Other Love 154
Other Side of the Closet, The
    143
Otis, John 171
Otis, Laura 154
Ott, Gustavo 170
Ott, Sharon 215
Ottiwell, Frank 185
Oulianine, Anik 75
Our Lady of 121st Street 101,
    151
Our Sinatra 118
Our Town 190
Outen, Denise Van 68
Outrage 222
Out of My Mind 148
Ouvert, Michael 47
Overbey, Kellie 126
Overcamp, David 172
Overman, Sarah 222
Overshown, Howard W. 126
Overstreet, Karyn 124, 220
Overton, Kenneth 124
Over Analysis 140
*Over the Rainbow: The Music of
    Harold Arlen* 226
*Over the River and through the
    Woods* 214
Owen, Paul 227
Owens, Dan 93
Owens, Destan 68
Owens, Frederick B. 37
Owens, Greg 188
Owens, Jon 27, 60
Owens, Robert Alexander 174,
    175
Owuor, Gilbert 186

OyamO 160
O Jerusalem 146

P

"Pure" Gospel Christmas, A 150
Paasch, Douglas N. 212
Pabotoy, Orlando 151, 234
Pace, Lee 179
Pace, Makeba 214
Pacek, Steve 187
Pacheco, Kim 150
Pacific Overtures 173, 187, 201
Pacilio, Casi 215
Pacino, Al 57, 96
Paciotto, Andrea 171
Packard, Kent Davis 172
Packard, William 324
Packett, Kila 123
Padding the Wagon 140
Paddywack 153
Padgett, Jesse 231
Padilla, Siara 230
Padla, Steven 65, 66, 71
Paeper, Eric 141
Paez, Gabriel 180
Page, Carolann 111
Page to Stage Project 215
Pagliano, Jeff 143
Pai, Ian 112
Paige, Amanda Ryan 167
Paige, Christen 208
Painted Snake in a Painted Chair
    171
Pair of Hands, A 148
Pakledinaz, Martin 27, 55, 60,
    75, 127
Pakman, Ben 39
Palace Theatre 65, 66
Paleos, Alison 221
Paley, Petronia 306
Palillo, Ron 154
Palin, Meredith 233
Palladino, Andrew 67
Palmaer, Hayley 225
Palmer, Alexa 229
Palmer, Carl 143, 147
Palmer, Chris 205
Palmer, Gamal 210
Palmer, Ryan 215
Palmer, Saxon 210, 224
Palminteri, Chazz 96
Paltrowitz, Adam 156
Pal Joey 223
Panadero: The Baker's Tale 212
Panaro, Hugh 72, 132
Panayotopoulos, Nikos 97
Pancholy, Maulik 233
Pandolfell, Lizabeth 190
Pandolfell, Michael 190
Pandolfi, Heidi 221

Pang, Andrew 159
Panic! (How to Be Happy!) 154
Pankow, John 100, 306
Panou, Themistoklis 97
Panson, Bonnie 40
Pantheon Theatre 155
Pantoliano, Joe 24
Pantzlaff, Kelly 232
Paoluccio, Tricia 96, 146
Papaelias, Lucas 212
Papagapitos, Chris 170
Paparella, Joe 196
Paper Armor 174
Paper Mill Playhouse 220
Pappas, Evan 213
Pappas, Justin 175
Pappas, Ted 221
Paradise, Grace 59
Paradise Theater Company 155
Paraiso, Nicky 172
Pardess, Yael 218
Pardoe, Tom 66
Parente, Greg 158
Parents Evening, The 144
Pareschi, Brian 55
Parham, Lennon 174
Parichy, Dennis 177, 200
Paris, Mikel 112
Pariseau, Kevin 110
Parison, Richard M. Jr. 232
Parisse, Annie 150
Park, Joshua 169, 306
Park, Scott 30
Parker, Chandler 129
Parker, Christian 98
Parker, Christina 150
Parker, Daniel T. 225, 233
Parker, Dorothy 141
Parker, Jacqui 213
Parker, Ken 222
Parker, Mary-Louise 84
Parker, Timothy Britten 160
Parkinson, Elizabeth 32
Parkinson, Scott 208
Parks, Jay 223
Parks, Suzan-Lori 129
Park Your Car in Harvard Yard
    193
Parnell, Charles 175, 227
Parnes, Joey 97
Parra, Maya 229, 230
Parrett, Melinda 211
Parrish, Robyne 158
Parry, Chris 104, 183, 191, 215,
    225, 226
Parry, Steve 50
Parry, William 58, 59
Parsons, Estelle 57, 82
Parsons, Jim 215
Parsons, Robert 185

Partington, Jonathan 207
Parts They Call Deep 144
Parttime Gods 147
Pascal, Adam 65
Pascal, Alexander 216
Pasekoff, Marilyn 213
Pashalinski, Lola 215
Pask, Scott 47, 54, 76, 109,
    128, 185
Paslawsky, Gregor 219
Pasquale, Steven 125
Passarello, Elena 202, 221
Passaro, Joseph 124, 139
Passaro, Michael J. 40, 55
Passengers 160
Passion 179
Patch, Jerry 225
Patchell, Debra 38
Patel, Neil 92, 98, 100, 173, 183,
    186, 201, 215
Patellis, Anthony 142
Paternite, Amy 180
Patinkin, Mandy 35
Patric, Jason 160, 161
Patrick, Leslie 146
Patrick, Michelle 56
Patsas, Yorgos 97
Pattak, Cory 227
Patterson, Billy "Spaceman" 91
Patterson, Chuck 206
Patterson, George Paco 104
Patterson, James 195, 218
Patterson, Jay 221
Patterson, Jimmie Lee 191
Patterson, Meredith 69
Patterson, Michael Craig 162
Patterson, Rebecca 145, 186
Patton, Charlotte 306
Patton, Fitz 53, 100, 126, 167,
    209
Patton, Jammie 144
Patton, Leland 55
Patton, Monica L. 93
Patton, Will 145
Paul, John 152
Paul, Meg 32
Pauley, Sara 231
Paulsen, Lair 203
Paulsen, Larry 168
Paulsen, Rick 207
Paulus, Diane 109
Paul Russell Casting 188, 189
Pavilion, The 216
Pavlopoulos, Lefteris 97
Pawk, Michele 33, 68, 306
Pawl, Christina 67
Paykin, Lanny 124
Payne, Casey 205
Payne, Herman 124
Payne, Robyn 70

Payton-Wright, Pamela 177, 306
Pazerski, Gayle 145
Peaco, Bobby 100
Peacock, Raphael 187
Peakes, Ian Merrill 187, 231
Peakes, Karen Elizabeth 187
Pearl, Katie 174, 175
Pearlman, Dina 150
Pearl Theatre Company, The 155
Pearson, Jill 213
Pearthree, Pippa 92
Pease, Robert 106
Peccadillo Theater Company 155
Pecchia, Laurel Astri 229
Peck, Erin Leigh 40
Peck, Jay 215
Peck, Nathan 40
Peck, Sabrina 233
Peden, Jennifer Baldwin 191
Peden, William 159
Pederson, Rose 198
Pedini, Rob 152
Peek, Brent 110
Peet, Amanda 161
Peg O' My Heart 169
Peiia, Ralph B. 174
Peil, Mary Beth 54
Peirano, Tomi 149
Pejovich, Ted 231
Pelegano, Jim 141
Pelican Theatre 155
Pelinski, Stephen 233
Pellegrini, Larry 159
Pellegrino, Susan 42, 306
Pellerano, Micki 154
Pellick, Andy 40
Peloquin, Stacey 229
Pelzig, Daniel 55, 124
Pemberton, Michael 23, 201
Pena, Ralph B. 151
Pendarvis, Sade 156
Pendleton, Austin 160
Penetrate the King 174
Penhall, Joe 98
Penn, Matthew 160
Penn, Stephane 148
Penn, Thomas 209
Penna, Michael 227
Penner, Anne 227
Pennington, Jesse 179, 183
Pennino, Anthony P. 156
Pentecost, Del 96
Pepe, Neil 98, 99, 106, 167
Peppas, Sophoclis 97
Pepper, Rick 141
Perez, Gary 174, 215
Perez, Jesse J. 174, 234
Perez, Lazaro 234
Perez, Luis 37, 68, 91
Perez, Paul Andrew 150

Perez, Rosie 24, 160, 168, 306
Perez, Sonny 140
Perfect Crime 111
Performance Space 122 176
Perhaps 140
Perich, Frank 155
Pericles 147, 186, 219
Perkins, Damian 65
Perkins, Drew 103, 151, 206, 306
Perkins, Kathy A. 126
Perkins, Patti 125, 127, 306
Perkins, Toi 178
Perkovich, David 214
Perlman, Max 106
Perloff, Carey 184, 185
Perloff-Giles, Nicholas 184
Perozo, Frank 177
Perri, Harvey 153
Perri, Michael 151
Perrineau, Harold, Jr. 98
Perrotta, Joe 51, 60, 97, 99, 106
Perry, Ernest, Jr. 203
Perry, Eugene 167, 186
Perry, Herbert 186
Perry, Karen 213
Perry, Lisa M. 154
Perry, Margarett 139
Perry, Robert 128, 132, 167, 224
Perry, Tara 143
Perry, Tyler 229
Persbrandt, Mikael 123
Persians 156
Pesce, Vince 124
Pessino, Maria 167
Pessyani, Attila 173
Pessyani, Khosrow 173
Pessyani, Setareh 173
Pestka, Bobby 220
Peter, Jaime St. 139
Peters, Bernadette 12, 58, 59
Peters, Clarke 68
Peters, Glenn 139, 154
Peterson, Courtney 211
Peterson, Eric 211
Peterson, Lisa 130, 179, 199
Peterson, Matt 27, 60
Peterson, Paul 217, 218, 219
Peterson, Sarah 226
Peter & Wendy 215
Peter and Vandy 155
Peter Pan & Wendy: The
   Adventures of the Lost Boys
   223
Pete Sanders Group 34, 49, 92,
   99
Petit, Lenard 145
Petkoff, Robert 217
Petrarca, David 55, 127, 153
Petrocelli, Richard 101, 151
Petrosino, Marc 149

Pet Sounds 123
Pettigrew, Shawyonia 95, 97
Pettrow, Daniel 210
Petty, Jason 103, 151, 206
Pettys, Patrick 230
Peveteaux, April 139
Pevsner, David 111
Pew, Tayva 216
Pfanstiel, Thomas 229
Pfeiffer, Matt 187
Pfisterer, Sarah 72
Phaedra in Delirium 175
Phantom of the Opera, The 72
Pharaoh, William 190
Phédre 208
Phelan, Aimee 154
Phelan, Andy 141
Phelan, Diane Veronica 220
Phelps, Darin 69
Phenomenon 149
Philippi, Michael 201
Philippou, Nick 163
Philipsen, Heidi E. 147
Philip Rinaldi Publicity 125
Phillip, Kathryn 178
Phillips, Barbara-Mae 72
Phillips, Bob 187
Phillips, David 125
Phillips, Derek 209
Phillips, Irving 324
Phillips, Jack 175
Phillips, Jacquie 95
Phillips, Mark A. 185
Phillips, Michael 172
Phillips, Patricia 38, 175
Phillips, Siân 94
Phillips, Thaddeus 172
Philoktetes 172
Phil Bosakowski Theatre 105,
   156
Phoenecican Women, The 159
Piano Lesson, The 221
Piccini, Cristy 178
Piccininni, Erica 139, 223
Piccione, Nancy 126, 127
Pichette, David 224
Pickart, Christopher 187
Pickering, Patrice 72
Pickle, John 124
Pickle, Judy 188
Pielmeier, John 161
Pierce, Cynthia 158
Pierre, Christophe 177
Pierson, Kyle 156
Pietraszek, Rita 222
Pietropinto, Angela 176
Pietrs, Roman 109
Pigg, Kendall 155
Piletich, Natasha 157
Pill, Alison 153

Pillow, Charles 42, 59
Pillow, Richard 36
Pimentel, Dakota 229
Pinchot, Bronson 217
Pine, Larry 176
Pinhasik, Howard 209
Pinheiro, Ilka Saddler 154
Pinkins, Tonya 124, 306
Pinnick, Erick 230
Pino, Joe 183, 202, 221
Pintauro, Dan 154, 158, 175
Pintauro, Joe 143, 158, 160
Pinter, Harold 217
Pinter, Mark 175
Pinti, Adam 146
Piper, Curtis August Thomas 186
Piper, Nicholas 139, 188, 189
Piper, Thomas 186
Piraro, Dan 154
Pirates & Pinafores: A
   Celebration of the Music
   and Lyrics of Gilbert and
   Sullivan 189
Piretti, Ron 155
Pisoni, Lorenzo 129
Pistone, Charles 220
Pitoniak, Anne 42, 219, 306
Pitre, Louise 71, 161
Pittelman, Ira 38, 94, 101
Pittman, Jamet 38
Pittman, Mike 205
Pittman, Reggie 93
Pitts, Barbara 215
Pittsburgh Public Theater 221
Pittu, David 167, 176, 306
Place, Andy 221
Placencia, Osvaldo 177
Plaisant, Dominique 226
Plantadit-Bageot, Karine 70
Platt, Brian 230
Platt, Jon B. 37, 110
Platt, Martin L. 216
Platt, Oliver 128
Platt, Sean 188
Plattsmier, Amanda 175
Playboy of the Western World,
   The 169
Playhouse on the Green 222
Playwrights Horizons 130
Playwright of the Western
   World, The 142
Play What I Wrote, The 50
Play Yourself 130
Pleasant, David 132
Pleasants, Philip 216
Plimpton, Martha 128
Ploss, Chad 194
Pluess, Andre 131, 208
Plum, Paula 216
Plummer, Joe 152

Plymesser, Stuart 227
Plymouth Theatre 62
Poet, Bruno 102
Poetics of Baseball, The 156
Poetri 34
Poisson, Michael 188, 189
Poitier, Raymond 112
Poizanski, Kirsten 232
Polan, Nina 177
Polanski, David 192
Polanski, Roman 40
Polaski, Miles 189
Pole, Jane 44
Polendo, Ruben 170
Poleshuck, Jesse 110
Polish Joke 127
Polk, Andrew 212
Polk, Matt 27, 44, 52, 53, 54,
   60, 132
Pollack, Charlie 76
Pollard, Jonathan 110
Pollin, Tera-Lee 49
Polseno, Robin 37
Polsky, Eric J. 158
Polunin, Siava 172
Polygram/Polydor 72
Pomahac, Bruce 133, 180
Pomeranz, David 223
Ponce, Ramona 171
Ponder, Nathan 204, 205
Pool, Carol 26
Poole, Richard 72
Poor Beast in the Rain 149
Pope, Eric 189
Pope, Manley 74
Pope, Peggy 306
Pope, Stephanie 68
Poplyk, Gregory A. 220
Pops 161
Porro, Susan 158
Portelance, Mariessa 213
Porter, Billy 129, 306
Porter, Cole 99, 144, 179
Porter, Kilbane 172
Porter, Lisa 234
Porter, Lloyd 147
Porter, Spence 162
Porterphiles 179
Portia 101, 151
Portland Center Stage 222
Portnow, Richard 106
Posey, Parker 177
Posillico, Cynthia 153
Posner, Aaron 187
Posner, Kenneth 25, 42, 129, 219
Pospisil, Craig 163
Post, Mike 210
Poster, Kim 45
Posterli, Tina 152
Pothier, Nancy 143

Potter, Betsey 176
Potter, Eric 111
Potting Shed, The 139
Potts, David 221
Potts, Michael 128, 160, 174, 186
Poulos, Jim 131
Poulsen, Emily 205
Poulson, Joseph 223
Poulton, Mike 193
Pourfar, Susan 105, 157, 174
Powell, Arabella 197
Powell, Arnell 196
Powell, Gary 123
Powell, J. Dakota 160
Powell, Janis 98
Powell, Katherine 185
Powell, Linda 174, 186
Powell, Marcus 176
Powell, Michael Warren 141, 161
Powell, Molly 139, 174, 175
Powell, Steve 154
Power, Alice 50
Powers, Andy 144
Powers, Dennis 184
Powers, Leslie 145
Prada, John 155
Prael, William 97, 139
Prasad, Shanti Elise 145
Prather, Pamela 233, 234
Pratt, Nina 95
Prayer, A 160
Prebilich, Nancy 205
Precious Stone 175
Preece, Lars 172
Preisser, Alfred 144
Prelude to a Kiss 147
Prendergast, James 139
Prendergast, Shirley 176
Prentiss, Robert 209
Press, Seymour Red 29, 124, 132, 197
Pressley, Brenda 225
Pressman, Kenneth 140
Preston, Carrie 175
Preston, Lisa 150
Preston, Wade 32
Presutti, Joyce A. 111, 231
Pretlow, Wayne W. 124
Preuss, Rob 71
Prewitt, Tom 170
Price, Elizabeth Hanly 224
Price, Lonny 49
Price, Mark 40, 71, 223
Price, Timothy 168
Priestley, J.B. 159
Prikryl, Sarah 183
Primary Stages 176
Primis, Theo 40

Prince, Akili 174
Prince, Charles 131
Prince, Faith 125, 306
Prince, Harold 33, 72
Prince, Warren "Chip" 39
Prince and the Pauper, The 91
Prince Hal 146
Prince Music Theater 223
Prinz, Rosemary 142, 221
Prinzo, Chris 71
Private Jokes, Public Places 172
Private Lives 84
Procaccino, Gregory 200
Producers, The 73
Producers Club, The 156
Promenade Theatre 94, 101
Proof 84, 194, 200, 206, 211, 225
Prosky, Andy 155, 201
Prospect Theater Company 156
Prosser, Peter 40, 59
Prosser, Sarah 32
Proust, Marcel 131
Prouty, Deane 59
Provost, Sarah 215
Provost, Sharon 215
Prud'homme, Julia 175
Pruitt, Jasika Nicole 142
Pruner, Linda 188
Prune Danish 31
Prymus, Ken 159, 175
Pryor, Peter 187
Psychic Life of Savages, The 234
Psychotherapy Live! 148
Publicity Office 37, 42, 93, 98, 130, 131
Public Relations 148
Pucci, Peter 234
Puccini, Giacomo 38
Puerto Rican Traveling Theater 177
Pugh, David 50, 204
Pugh, Regina 200
Pugh, Richard Warren 72
Pugliese, Frank 160, 161
Pula, Ramona 172
Pullman, Bill 81
Pulse Ensemble Theatre 157
Pumo, David 140, 141
Pump Boys and Dinettes 205
Puppetry of the Penis 118
Purcell, Douglas 124
Purdum, Corrie E. 206, 207
Purinton, Miles 151
Purl, Linda 191
Purnell, Kimberly "Q" 176
Purse, John 203
Purviance, Douglas 37
Pusz, Christy 43
Puzzo, Michael 151

Pyant, Paul 127
Pye, Tom 41, 167
Pyretown 175
Pytel, Janice 131
Pyzocha, Robert 222

Q
QED 84
Quackenbush, Anne 183
Quackenbush, Karyn 42, 110, 219
Quan, Samantha 168, 218
Quandt, Stephen 195
Quarles, Jason 171
Quartet 192
Queens Theatre in the Park 223
Queer @ Here Festival 148
Queer Carol, A 158
Quick and Dirty (A Subway Fantasy) 163
Quigley, Bernadette 146, 149
Quijas, Vanessa 162
Quilters 214
Quilty, Mason 223
Quilty, Roxanne 231
Quilty, Taylor 231
Quinlan, Michael 171
Quinlivan, John 211
Quinn 109
Quinn, Ardes 140
Quinn, Brendan 222
Quinn, Doug 71
Quinn, Patrick 159, 180
Quinn, Rosemary 148
Quintanilla, Ivan 226
Quirk, Brian 193
Quisenberry, Danielle 153
Quisenberry, Karen 233, 234

R
Rabe, David 234
Rabe, Lily 160
Rabinow, David 229
Rabson, Lawrence 32
Racey, Noah 75
Rachele, Rainard 140
Racine, Jean 208
Rada, Edward L. 196
Rada, Mirena 179
Radiant Baby 128
Radio Wonderland 149
Raetz, Elizabeth 184
Rafferty, Stephanie 172
Raffo, Heather 140
Rafter, Michael 75
Raiken, Larry 231
Rainer, Elizabeth 206
Raines, Ron 68
Rainey, Dana-Shavonne 92
Rainey, David 183

Rain Dance 177
Raiter, Frank 186
Rak, Rachelle 60
Rakosi, Samantha Massell 39
Ralph, Sheryl Lee 75
Ramey, Aaron 75, 220
Ramicova, Dunya 226
Ramin, Sid 58
Ramirez, Ana Tulia 169
Ramirez, Bardo S. 179
Ramirez, Freddy 220
Ramirez, Maria Elena 212
Ramirez, Rebeca 145
Ramos, Richard Russell 200
Ramsey, Kenna J. 74
Ramsey, Matt 213
Ramsey, Richard 183
Rand, Ian 74
Rand, Randolph Curtis 171
Rand, Rebecca 211
Rand, Ronald 144
Rand, Tom 167
Randall, Benjie 220
Randall, Jay 184
Randall, Tony 96
Randals, Kathy 175
Randell, Patricia 141, 158
Rando, John 40, 76, 127, 185, 218
Randoja, Karin 171
Randolph, Beverley 124
Randolph, Christopher 217
Randolph, Jim 23, 30, 36, 61, 110
Randolph, Robert 324
Randolph-Wright, Charles 220
Rankin, Steve 199, 217, 218
Raphael, Frederic 167
Raphael, Gerianne 192
Raphael, Gerrianne 156, 163
Raphel, David 169
Rapp, Adam 143, 157
Rapp, Anthony 143, 203
Rapt 147
Raree 174
Rasalingam, Selva 102
Rashad, Phylicia 199
Rasheed, Amen 144, 147
Rask, Julia 104
Raskin, Kenny 229
Rasmussen, Andrew 147
Rasmussen, Benjamin Boe 167
Ratajczak, Dave 60
Rath, Adam 211
Ratner, Brett 34
Ratner, Bruce C. 123
Ratray, Peter 111
Rattazzi, Steven 160, 171, 179, 201
Rattlestick Theatre 105, 157

Rauch, Bill 199, 233
Rauch, Matthew 177
Ravvin, Genna 186
Rawls, Hardy 226
Ray, Connie 216
Raymond, Devon 225
Raymond, Lisa 157
Raynak, Jen 222
Rayne, Stephen 183
Rayner, Martin 175
Rayppy, Gary 214
Rayson, Jonathan 55
Ray on the Water 148
RCA 67, 68
Read, Allen 233, 234
Reade, Simon 102
Reale, Robert 55, 153
Reale, Willie 55, 153
Really Useful Theatre Co., The 72
Real Thing, The 209
Reardon, Peter 76
Reaser, Elizabeth 168, 175
Rebholz, Kathryn 211
Rebhorn, James 43, 168
Reborn, James 82
Redbird 158
Reddin, Keith 139, 160, 183, 223
Reddy, Brian 43
Reddy, Gita 153
Redesign 160
Redgrave, Corin 179, 183
Redgrave, Lynn 104
Redgrave, Vanessa 5, 62, 306
Redmond, Lynne 326
Redsecker, John 124
Redwood, John Henry 161
Red and Tan Line 141
Red Hot Mama 118
Red Room, The 157
Reed, Angela 216
Reed, GW 156, 163
Reed, Joseph 225
Reed, Kevin 192
Reed, Kim 153
Reed, Luke 49
Reed, Maggie 175
Reed, Michael 40
Reed, Michael James 219
Reed, Rebecca 188
Reed, Vivian 206
Reeder, Ana 127
Reedy, M. Kilburg 61, 93
Reeger, John 208
Rees, Douglas 202
Rees, Roger 125, 306
Reese, Andrea 156
Regan, Suzanne 177
Reich, Seth 186
Reichard, Daniel 128

Reichel, Cara 156
Reichert, Edward 231
Reichgott, Seth 232
Reid, Catherine 185
Reid, Michael 159, 168, 306
Reid, T. Oliver 75
Reidy, David 163
Reilly, Ellen 143, 146
Reilly, John C. 213
Reilly, T.L. 162
Reim, Alyson 140
Reimer, M. Anthony 193
Reina, Christina 190
Reinders, Kate 58, 153
Reiner, Alysia 146
Reiners, Portia 151
Reingold, Jacquelyn 161, 168
Reinhardt, Les 185
Reinis, Jonathan 61
Reinking, Ann 60, 68, 124, 161
Reiser, Paul 106
Reissa, Eleanor 180
Reiter, Elizabeth 167
Reiter, Erin Brooke 72
Relatively Speaking 225
Releford, Starr 205
Rella, Concetta Rose 175
Remedios, David 186
Remembrance of Things Past 131
Remillard, Valerie 229
Remler, Pamela 59
Remo, Melissa 39, 306
Rempe, Frank 145
Remsen, Penny 205
Rene, Yves 144
Reni, Sam 133
Renschler, Eric 53, 216
Rent 74
Rentmeester, Ryan 144
Repplinger, Jill 145
Requiem for William 145
Resash, Tim 214
Resa Fantastiskt Mystick 154
Resistible Rise of Arturo Ui, The 96
Resnick, Amy 215
Resnick, Judith 28, 29
Resnik, Hollis 208
Resstab, Barbara 109
Restrepo, Federico 172
Reuben, Gloria 161
Reuning, Jonathan 143
Revelation Theater 97
Reverend Billy 154
Revill, William, III 205
Rey, Melanie 158
Reybold, Abe 195
Reyes, Erik 171
Reyes, Joselin 169

Reyes, Randy 171, 201
Reyes, Samuel Antonio 223
Reyes, Stephen 147
Reynaud, Jacques 167
Reynold, Abe 220
Reynolds, Brett W. 144
Reynolds, Corey 26
Reynolds, Graham 175
Reynolds, Lisa 36
Reza, Yasmina 51, 204
Rhapsody in Seth 139
Rhodes, Elizabeth 105, 168, 183
Rhodes, Ginette 147
Rhodes, Josh 49
Rhodes, Michael 163
Ribbon in the Sky 161
Ricciardi, Paul 229, 230
Riccomini, Raymond 54
Rice, Bernard 214
Rice, Tim 65, 66, 70, 231
Rich, Geoffrey 176
Rich, Jeremy 54
Rich, Kevin 234
Rich, Marian 142
Richard, Don 76
Richard, Ellen 27, 44, 52, 53, 54, 60, 67, 132
Richard, Jeffrey 100
Richard, Judine 26
Richards, Bryant 211
Richards, Devin 124
Richards, Jamie 168
Richards, Jeffrey 56
Richards, Lisa 36
Richards, Matthew 209
Richards, Walker 143
Richardson, Bruce 209
Richardson, Chad 74
Richardson, Claibe 324
Richardson, Desmond 60, 124
Richardson, Gisele 140, 145
Richardson, Kevin 68
Richardson, Travis 219
Richardson, Trevor 111
Richard III 230
Richard Kornberg and Associates 25, 130, 132
Richard Rodgers Theatre 32, 68
Richel, Stu 156
Richenthal, David 62
Richie, Chuck 206
Richman, Adam 234
Richman, Stacey Rose 220
Richmond, Robert 92, 153
Richter, Tom 152
Rickenberg, Dave 26
Rickman, Alan 84
Rickman, Allen Lewis 173, 307
Ricks, Tijuana T. 233
Ricky Jay on the Stem 118

Riddle, Shanna 209
Rideout, Leenya 67
Rideout, Vale 124
Riebe, Jeff 143
Riegel, Chara 184
Riemann, Katherine 185
Riesco, Armando 147, 161, 175
Riesenberg, David 218
Rifkin, Jay 70
Rigdon, Kevin 183
Rigg, Kate 161, 172
Riggins, Terrence 221
Riker, Jennifer 191
Riley, Eric 93
Riley, Ron 174, 175
Rimland, Renée 197
Rinaldi, Philip 43, 48, 125
Ring, Derdriu 169, 206
Ringle, Jilline 202
Ringwald, Molly 56, 67, 180
Rios, Michelle 37, 171
Ripplinger, Jody 65
Rising, Craig 159
Rita, Rui 56, 92, 183, 213, 221
Ritchey, Lee 154
Rittman, Trude 133
Ritual of Faith, A 151
Riva, Amadeo 159
Rivals, The 139
Rivera, Chita 54, 160
Rivera, Clea 174
Rivera, Eileen 153
Rivera, Elan 175
Rivera, Jose 160
Rivera, José 215
Rivera, Mira 178
Rivera, Primy 178
Rivera, Rene 222
Rivera, Thom 200, 234
Rivera, Thorn 168
Rivers, Ben 144
Riverside Drive 106
Rizner, Russ 124
Rizner, Russel L. 29
Rizzo, Jeff 197
Rno, Sung 174
Roach, Dan 211, 212
Roach, Kevin Joseph 112
Roach, Maxine 39
Roache, Michael 207
Robards, Jake 36
Robbins, Blake 161
Robbins, David 95
Robbins, Jerome 58, 227
Robbins, Kurt 95
Robbins, Liz 216
Robbins, Rebecca 124, 231
Robbins, Sanford 183
Robbins, Tom Alan 70
Roberson, Ken 92, 179

Robertazzi, Justin 39, 307
Roberto Zucco 154
Roberts, Alison 187
Roberts, Chris 161
Roberts, Dallas 93
Roberts, Daniel 140
Roberts, Jennifer Erin 155
Roberts, Jimmy 110
Roberts, Jonathan 70
Roberts, Jonno 47
Roberts, Judith 227
Roberts, Keith 32
Roberts, Marcia 29
Roberts, Rachael 145
Roberts, Robin Sanford 217, 218
Roberts, Samuel 140
Roberts, Sydney 210, 222
Roberts, Tony 85
Robertson, Christine 231
Robertson, Dennis 216
Robertson, Scott 27, 67, 307
Robertson, Tim 230
Robert Fox Ltd. 48
Robins, Laila 146
Robinson, Alecia 231
Robinson, Andrew 307
Robinson, Angela 129, 176
Robinson, Audrey 172
Robinson, Edward G. 102, 196
Robinson, Fatima 128
Robinson, Hal 223
Robinson, J.R. 111
Robinson, Julie Anne 174
Robinson, Leanne 200
Robinson, Mark Steven 152
Robinson, Mary B. 161, 168
Robinson, Michelle M. 68
Robinson, Ore 104
Robinson, R. David 158
Robinson, Rebecca 149
Robinson, Reginald 225
Robinson, Roger 221
Robinson, Romel 150
Robinson, Stacey 174
Robinson, Terrell 172
Robison, Blake 204
Roboff, Annie L. 49
Robustelli, Patrick 111
Roche, Billy 149
Roche, Paul 233
Rockwell, David 25
Rodarte, Randy 199
Rodarte, Scott 199
Roden, Nadine 196
Rodenborn, Ted 176
Roderick, Greg 221
Roderick, Ray 91, 110
Rodericks, Basil 140
Rodger, Struan 41, 167, 307
Rodgers, Elisabeth S. 216

Rodgers, Kami 143
Rodgers, Richard 27, 124, 133, 180, 195, 223, 231, 233
Rodgers & Daughters 180
Rodgers & Hammerstein 233
Rodgers and Hammerstein Organization 29
Rodgers in Yiddish 180
Rodgriguez, Jai 74
Rodko, Michael 209
Rodnon, Mel 324
Rodrigues, Tania 102
Rodriguez, Adrian 156
Rodriguez, Diane 199, 225
Rodriguez, Enrico 102
Rodriguez, Jai 74, 102
Rodriguez, Jake 185
Rodriguez, Nicholas 193
Rodriguez, Raymond 65
Rodwin, David 170
Roe, Alex 152
Roe, Kate 140
Roemer, Laura 158
Roethke, Linda 208
Roff, Brian 101
Roffe, Al 101, 151
Roffe, Mary Lu 37
Rogers, Ambere 196
Rogers, Bettie O. 224
Rogers, Brian 148
Rogers, David 216
Rogers, Douglas 224
Rogers, Mac 148
Rogers, Michael 179, 307
Rogers, Ninon 160
Rogers, Richard 29
Roggie, John 129
Roginsky, Michelle 184
Rognstad, Sylvia 226
Rohr, Beth Stiegel 131
Roland, Ashley 222
Rolff, Heather Jane 220
Rolle, John Livingstone 155
Rolly, Shaun J. 221
Rom, Erhard 211
Romance Cycle; Part I: Cymbeline, Part II: Pericles, The 208
Romance of Magno Rubio, The 151
Romano, Christina 212
Romano, Joe 199
Romanoff, Ed 231
Romanoff, Linda 231
Roman Nights 145
Romberg, Sigmund 124
Romeo and Bernadette, A Brooklyn Musical 220
Romeo and Juliet 205
Romero, Constanza 199

Romero, Elaine 179
Romick, James 72
Rommen, Ann-Christin 167
Romoff, Colin 180
Romoff, Linda 67
Romola and Nijinsky 176
Ronan, Brian 27, 60, 67
Ronnick, Bill 98
Rooks, Joel 28
Room 314 142
Rooney, Brian Charles 180
Rooney, Lucas Caleb 217, 218, 219, 221
Root, Frank 197
Roper, Alicia 231
Ropes, Bradford 69, 197
Rordam, Jeppe Dahl 167
Rosa, Billy 153, 180
Rosa, Ray Rodriguez 112
Rosato, Mary Lou 168
Rose, Abby 230
Rose, Erez 143
Rose, Fred 67
Rose, Gina 130
Rose, Philip 176
Rose, Richard 188, 189
Rose, Robin Pearson 218, 225
Rosen, Cherie 37
Rosen, Joel 42, 217, 218, 219
Rosen, Lauren 175
Rosen's Son 158
Rosenbach, Benjamin 220
Rosenberg, David 34
Rosenberg, Michael S. 168
Rosenberg, Roger 124
Rosenblum, Tamara 148
Rosenfeld, Jyll 31
Rosenfield, Lois S. 324
Roses in December 162
Rosium, Ted 222
Rosler, Larry 188
Rosoff, Wendy 69
Ross, Andrea C. 230
Ross, Blair 197
Ross, Brittany 222
Ross, Chris 188, 189
Ross, Jonathan Todd 142
Ross, Joye 40
Ross, Linda 183
Ross, Roshaunda 205
Ross, Stacy 185
Ross, Steve 180
Ross, Stuart 128
Ross, Ted 324
Rossellini, Isabella 160
Rossetter, Kathryn 141, 307
Rossignuolo-Rice, Judy 214
Rosswog, Joseph 148
Roszell, Jennifer 217
Roth, Daryl 41, 57, 92, 101,

104, 109
Roth, Jordan 109
Roth, Katherine B. 209
Roth, Michael 104, 191, 217
Roth, Robert Jess 66
Roth, Sarah Hewitt 26
Rothan, Elizabeth 209
Rothe, Lisa 159
Rothenberg, David 168
Rothman, Alyse Leigh 148, 149
Rothman, Carol 132
Rothman, Elizabeth 209
Roundabout Theatre Company 67, 104, 132
Rouse, Brad 203
Rouse, Elizabeth Meadows 207
Roustom, Kareem 213
Routh, Marc 94, 95, 112
Rovere, Craig 159
Rowan, Tom 168
Rowand, Nada 155
Rowe, Karen N. 188, 189
Rowe, Stephen 146
Rowland, Janice 192
Roy, Edward 143
Roy, Melinda 49
Royale Theatre 31, 45
Royal Dramatic Theatre of Sweden 123
Royal National Theatre 48, 123
Royce, Jim 196
Rozenblatt, David 40
Ruark, Joel K. 174
Rubber 152
Rubens, Herb 176
Rubenstein Associates Inc. 94, 124
Rubenstein Public Relations 196
Rubin, John Gould 101, 160
Rubin, Tara 71, 213
Rubin-Vega, Daphne 129, 307
Rubins, Josh 192
Rucker, Mark 225
Rudd, Paul 160
Ruderman, Jordin 109, 150
Rudetsky, Seth 139
Rudin, Scott 41
Rudko, Michael 218
Rueck, Fred 162
Ruede, Clay 29, 124
Ruehl, Mercedes 81
Ruf, Elizabeth 178
Ruf-Maldonado, Clara 178
Ruger, A. Nelson 227
Ruggeri, Nick 221
Ruggles, Brian 32
Ruhl, Sarah 145, 168
Ruhr-Triennale 186
Rum and Vodka 154
Runbeck, Brian 211

Runco, David 153, 307
Rundle, Erika 170
Runnette, Sean 209
Ruocco, John 160
Ruoti, Helena 203
Rupert, Michael 125
Ruppe, Diana 145
Ruscio, Elizabeth 199
Rush, Brian 155
Rush, Cindi 76
Rush, Joanna 133
Rush, Jo Anna 133
Rush, Michael S. 178
Rushdie, Salman 102, 191
Rushen, Jack 143
Rush and Super Casting 224
Rusinek, Roland 192
Russell, Brian Keith 184
Russell, Catherine 111
Russell, Deborah 185
Russell, Dylan 185
Russell, Francesca 184
Russell, Jay 50, 192
Russell, Jerry 209
Russell, Kirsten 148
Russell, Mark 176
Russell, Melissa 141
Russell, Monica 145
Russell, Paul 224
Russell, Ricky 179
Russell, Ron 159
Russell, Susan 72
Russell Simmons' Def Poetry Jam on Broadway 34
Russo, F. Wade 221
Russo, Peter 151
Russo, William 130, 131
Rust, Steve 205
Rustin, Sandy 110
Ruta, Ken 191
Rutherford, Stanley 158
Rutigliano, Danny 70, 124
Rutkovsky, Ella 27, 60
Ruzika, Donna 225
Ruzika, Tom 225
Ryan, Amanda 102
Ryan, Annie 102
Ryan, Bruce 34
Ryan, Dennis 190
Ryan, Donna M. 231
Ryan, Kate 145
Ryan, Kate Moira 130
Ryan, Leah 161, 172
Ryan, Patti 49
Ryan, Rand 202
Ryan, Randy 160
Ryan, Richard 40
Ryan, Roz 68
Ryan, Thomas Jay 234
Rychlec, Daniel 72

Rye, Nick 232
Ryland, Jack 217
Ryndak, Christine 203
Rynne, Chris 219
Ryon, Jean Gordon 212
Rzepski, Sonja 148

S

S., Albert 186
S.U. Drama Department 227
Saba, Sirine 102
Sabath, Bruce 146
Sabberton, Kenn 153
Sabel, Shelly 96, 129, 132
Sabella, D. 68
Sabella, Ernie 37
Sabella, Sal 220
Sablan, Summer Tiana 220
Sabo, Karen 188, 189
Sacharow, Lawrence 161
Sachon, Peter 123, 125
Sacks, Jonah 186
Sadler, Christopher 195
Sadler, Paul B., Jr. 72
Sadler, William 96
Sadoski, Thomas 179, 183
Saed, Zohra 170
Safan, Craig 193
Safdie, Oren 172
Safer, Daniel 154
Saffarianrezai, Morteza 173
Sagady, Shawn 219
Sage, Raymond 66
Sageworks 45
Sagona, Vincent 158
Said, Najla 153
Saietta, Bob 171
Saint, David 176
Saint-Girard, Christian 222
Saints and Singing 152
Saint She Ain't, A 192
Sainvil, Martin 76
Sainvil, Martine 24, 29
Saito, James 168, 201
Saito, Kirihito 173
Saivetz, Deborah 145, 174, 179
Sakakura, Lainie 29
Sakemoto, Akira 173
Salamandyk, Tim 221
Salamone, Louis S. 98
Saland, Ellen 156
Salata, Gregory 92, 139, 307
Salatino, Anthony 227
Saldivar, Matt 179
Sale, James 201
Sale, Jonathan 144
Salguero, Sophia 176, 307
Salinas, Ric 199, 224
Salkin, Eddie 27, 55
Sally Smells 143

Salmen, Tania 170
Salmon, Susan 41
Salmon-Wander, Ashley 158
Salome 57
Salome Sings the Blues 158
Salonga, Lea 29
Saltz, Amy 161
Saltzberg, Sarah 153
Saltzman, Avery 221
Saltzman, Mark 220
Salvati, Juan 204, 205
Salvatore, Alana 197
Salvatore, Matthew 39
Salzman, Thomas 193
Sam, Adrienne 220
Samayoa, Caesar 176, 234
Samoff, Marjorie 223
Sampliner, James 129
Sams, Casey 204
Sams, Jeremy 30
Samson, R.J. 112
Samuel, Jill 227
Samuel, Peter 73
Samuels, Jill 149
Samuel Beckett Theatre 105, 158
Sanabria, Marilyn 151, 153
Sananes, Adriana 177
Sanchez, Alba 170
Sanchez, Alex 124
Sanchez, Edwin 140, 161
Sanchez, K.J. 175
Sanchez, Marisol Padilla 215
Sanchez, Olga 198
Sandel, Joel 183
Sanders, Eileen 188
Sanders, Jay O. 95
Sanders, Pete 34, 49, 68, 110, 133
Sanders, Scott 197
Sanderson, Austin K. 176, 195
Sanders Family Christmas 216
Sande Shurin Theatre 158
Sandler, Ethan 209
Sandler, Luke 217
Sandoval, Charles Daniel 234
Sandoval, Trindy 234
Sandri, Remi 212, 224
Sandri, Thomas 72
Sands, Ben 213
Sandy, Solange 40, 124
Sanford, Tim 130, 131
Sanman-Smith, Lisa 222
Sans Cullotes in the Promised Land 174
Santaland Diaries, The 219, 222
Santana, Orlando 109
Santiago 197
Santiago, Maxx 140
Santiago, Saundra 54

Santiago, Socorro 212
Santiago, Tania 147
Santiago-Hudson, Ruben 184
Santora, Philip J. 210
Santos, Fiona 95
Santvoord, Van 169
Sanville, Guy 177
San José Repertory Theatre 224
San Jose Sound Design 224
Sapienza, Christopher 223, 232
Saporito, James 55
Sapp, Robb 102, 167, 227
Sarabande, Varese 110
Sarcoxie and Sealove 174
Sargent, Mark 156
Sargent, Stacey 92
Sarkar, Indrajit 140
Sarossy, Gyuri 123
Sarpola, Dick 76
Sarpola, Richard 124
Sarsgaard, Peter 307
Satalof, Stu 29, 124
Saturn's Wake 149
Saumanis, Kristina 190
Saunders, A. 68
Saunders, Adam 233, 234
Saunders, Patrick 229
Saunier, Hayden 231
Sauter, Eddie 133
Savage, Abby 159
Savage, J. Brandon 106, 222
Savage, Mark 111
Savages of Hartford, The 175
Savant, Joseph 66
Savelli, Jennifer 40, 124
Sawotka, Sandy 123
Sawyer, Kit 24
Sawyer, Ray 24
Saxe, Gareth 127, 219
Saxon, Carolyn 196
Sayama, Haruki 173
Say Goodnight, Gracie 28
Scanavino, Peter 144
Scanlan, Dick 75
Scanlin, Darcy 225
Scanlon, Patricia 168
Scapin 208
Scarpulla, John 32
Scarpulla, Stephen Scott 58, 59
Scattergood 173
Schachter, Beth 146
Schactman, Ken 147
Schadt, Timothy 54
Schaechter, Ben 111
Schaefer, Paul A. 131
Schaefer-Jeske, Juliet 152
Schafer, Scott 139
Schantz, Magin 144, 171
Schanzer, Jude 143
Scharf, Erik 194

Scharf, Katie 145
Scharf, Kenny 170
Schatz, Jack 29, 124
Schechner, Richard 172
Schechner, Saviana 172
Scheck, Frank 241
Schecter, Amy 98
Schedule Included: Matt and Ben 154
Scheib, Jay 154
Scheie, Danny 228
Schein, Omri 150
Scheine, Raynor 199
Scheitinger, Alexander 41
Schellenbaum, Tim 171, 172
Schenck, Margaret 184, 191
Schenck, Megan 69
Schertler, Nancy 185
Schiappa, John 47
Schiff, Dan 231
Schilke, Raymond D. 36, 112
Schimmel, John 205
Schirle, Joan 233
Schirner, Buck 187
Schiro, Chad L. 49
Schlackman, Marc 98
Schlecht, Ryan 198
Schlobohm, Eric 190
Schlossberg, Julian 98, 99
Schmeider, Mandy 225
Schmidt, Douglas W. 69, 183, 197
Schmidt, Erica 96, 129, 132, 144
Schmidt, Katherine 124
Schmidt, Paul 185, 208
Schmidt, Sara 40
Schmidtke, Ned 219
Schmitt, Eric-Emmanuel 151
Schmitt, Joanna 212
Schmoll, Ken Rus 170
Schnee, Jicky 155
Schneid, Megan 96
Schneider, Peter 65, 70
Schneider, Ted 168, 174
Schneiderman, L.J. 142
Schnirman, David 57
Schnitzler, Arthur 173, 191, 195, 207
Schnore, Ludis 140
Schnuck, Terry E. 56
Schoeffler, Paul 54, 307
Schoenbeck, Steve 224
Schoevaert, Marion 154
Scholl, Katherine 200
Schonberg, Claude-Michel 220
Schondorf, Zohar 39
Schooler, Luan 191
School for Greybeards 175
Schovanec, Shellie 73

Schrader, Benjamin 193
Schreiber, John 92, 197
Schreiber, Liev 160, 173
Schreiber, Terry 162
Schreier, Dan Moses 30, 128, 199
Schrider, Tommy 227
Schrock, Robert 111
Schroder, Erica 195
Schroeder, John 72
Schroeder, Meg Kelly 206
Schroeder, Wayne 91
Schubert, Allison 184
Schuette, James 186
Schuld, Susan 192
Schull, Rebecca 159
Schulman, Andrew 150
Schulman, Arlene 152
Schulman, Susannah 191
Schulner, David 200, 218
Schultz, Carol 155, 200
Schultz, Jedadiah 233
Schulz, Robert 186
Schumacher, Jon 154
Schumacher, Thomas 65, 70
Schuster/Maxwell 112
Schuttler, Harmony 173
Schuval, Michael 148
Schuyler, Peter 172
Schwab, Laurence 124
Schwartz, Andrew 29, 153
Schwartz, Chandra Lee 59
Schwartz, Clifford 65, 68
Schwartz, Mark 110
Schwartz, Robert Joel 176
Schwartz, Scott 103, 192
Schwartz, Susan L. 96
Schweikardt, Michael 95, 221
Schweizer, David 171
Schwiesow, Deirdre 156
Schworer, Angie L. 73
Sciaroni, Rayme 111
Sciarra, Dante A. 220
Sciotto, Eric 65
Scoones, Fiona 175
Scott, Alyssa 205
Scott, Christian 205
Scott, Eadie 231
Scott, Eric Dean 154
Scott, Gary 219
Scott, Jared 99
Scott, Jason 156
Scott, Kimberly J. 185
Scott, Klea 199, 215
Scott, Les 54
Scott, Martha 325
Scott, Rachel 184, 185
Scott, Seret 174, 218

Scott, Sherie René 65, 96
Scott, Wayne 147, 192
Scott-Flaherty, Alexa 158
Scott-Reed, Christa 93, 150
Screaming in the Wilderness 153
Scrivener's Tale 213
Scrofani, Aldo 196
Scrofano, Paula 208
Scruggs, James 148
Scurria, Anne 229, 230
SDog 171
Seal, Elizabeth 192
Sealed for Freshness 155
Seamon, Edward 155
Search for Signs of Intellingent Life in the Universe, The 197
Sears, Djanet 141
Sears, Glen W. 232
Sears, Joe 206
Seaton, Laura 124
Seattle Repertory Theatre, The 197
Seavey, Jordan 140
Seawell, Damon 185
Sebesky, Don 27, 29, 60, 99, 213
Sechrest, Ric 200
Second Skin 160
Second Stage 111
Second Stage Theatre 132
Sedaris, David 219, 222
Sedgwick, Rob 157
Seebald, Ed 160
Seed, The 140
Seehorn, Rhea 130
Seer, Richard 218
Seese, Krystie 222
Segal, Aliza 225
Segal, David F. 221
Segal, Tobias 187
Seiden, Jackie 150
Seiderman, Pamela 148
Seidman, John 218, 221
Seif, Deborah 232
Seiff, Carolyn 141
Seilber, Christopher 66
Seiver, Sarah 54
Seldes, Marian 43, 130, 307
Sell, Brian 192
Sella, Robert 115
Sellars, Lee 202
Sellars, Peter 186
Seller, Jeffrey 38, 74, 109
Sellon, Kim 66
Sellwood, Tom 147
Selma's Break and RX 154
Seltzer, Michael 59
Selya, John 9, 32, 239
SEL and GFO 25

Sembloh, Saycon 65
Sen, Nandana 159
Senor, Andy 74
Sensenig, E. Andrew 95
Senske, Rebecca 200
September Morning 160
September Shoes 212
Serban, Andrei 186
Serino Coyne, Inc. 73
Serralles, Jeanine 141, 209
Serrand, Dominique 191
Serricchio, Ignacio 227
Servitto, Matt 160
Sesma, Thom 37
Setaro, Keri 200
Setlock, Mark 74, 105, 157, 213, 307
Setlow, Jennifer 191, 216, 218
Setrakian, Ed 57
1776 189
1776: America's Prize Winning Musical 212
78th Street Lab 158
7–11 160
Severence, Michael 175
Severine, Nicole 147
Severino, Carmen 214
Severs, William 146
Severson, Sten 234
Sevy, Bruce K. 194
Sewell, Richard 155
Sexaholix…A Love Story 197
Sexton, Coleen 150
Sexton, Michael 130
Seyd, Richard 215
Seymour, C.C. 156
Seymour, Christina 133
Seymour, Nicole 139
Sferruzza, Ana 208
SFX Theatrical Group 73
Sgambati, Brian 213
Shaddow, Elena 54, 95
ShadowCatcher Entertainment 97
Shafer, Margaret 124
Shafer, Scott 139
Shaffer, Anthony 222
Shaffer, Henry 173
Shaffer, Jeremy 45, 57, 75, 91, 94, 95, 97
Shaffer, Molly 109
Shaffer, Zach 174
Shafir, Ariel 147
Shaghoian, Vicki 234
Shah, Neil 219
Shahinian, Sarah 180
Shaiman, Marc 25
Shain, Julie 141
Shakar, Martin 36

Shakespeare, William 92, 123, 128, 129, 140, 144, 147, 149, 150, 153, 155, 158, 162, 163, 167, 168, 179, 183, 186, 187, 188, 205, 208, 210, 218, 219, 221, 222, 224, 225, 230, 233, 234
Shakespeare Unplugged: The History Cycle 150
Shakman, Felicia Carter 172
Shalit, Willa 45
Shamblin, Jack 172
Shamieh, Betty 143, 160
Shamos, Jeremy 125, 208, 213
Shanahan, Mark 190
Shand, Kevin 109
Shandel, Milo 196
Shane, Hal 99
Shanet, Larry 178
Shanghai Gesture, The 155
Shanghai Moon 168
Shangraw, Howard 225
Shankel, Lynne 142
Shanks, Gabriel 140, 148
Shanks, Priscilla 146
Shanley, John Patrick 151, 160, 161
Shanman, Ellen 154
Shannon, Michael 145
Shannon, Sarah Solie 66
Shapiro, David F. 220
Shapiro, Doug 147
Shapiro, Raphael Odell 190
Shapiro, Ronald 23
Shapiro, Steve 193
Shappell, Catharine 212
Share, Elizabeth 196
Sharma, Kish 102
Sharp, Elliott 126
Sharp, John 145
Sharp, Jonathan 40
Sharp, Kim T. 139
Sharp, Mark C. 221
Sharp, Rebecca 148
Shattuck, Frank 153
Shattuck, Matthew 167
Shaud, Grant 106
Shaughnessy, Shannan 172
Shaw, David 147
Shaw, Fiona 41, 167, 307
Shaw, George Bernard 155, 222, 225
Shaw, Jane Catherine 176, 194, 215
Shaw, Louis 223
Shaw, Meryl Lind 184, 185
Shaw, Rob 26
Shayne, Sharron 150
Shayne, Tracy 68
She, Jessenia 205

Shead, Henry W., Jr. 112
Shear, Claudia 207, 221
Sheara, Nicola 143
Sheedy, Jaime 145
Sheehan, Kelly 69
Sheerin, Kelleia 49
Sheffer, Isaiah 180
Sheffer, Jonathan 223
Sheffey, George 161
Sheik, Duncan 128
Shell, Roger 39
Shelley, Carole 67
Shelley, Steven L. 215
Shelton, Sloane 43, 308
Shenker, Jenifer 102
Shepard, John 203
Shepard, Matthew 66
Shepard, Sam 222
Shepard, Tina 148, 171, 172
Shepardson, Dia 99
Shepherd, Suzanne 179
Sheppard, Danette E. 222
Sheppard, Julian 151
Shepperd, Drey 142
Sher, Bartlett 198
Sher, Erik 158
Sheredy, Bernie 216
Sheri, Bartlett 179
Sheridan, Richard Brinsley 139
Sherill, Brad 210
Sherlock Holmes and the Secret of Making Whoopee 154
Sherman, Andrew 96
Sherman, Elizabeth 141, 168
Sherman, Jonathan Marc 147, 154, 161
Sherman, Kim 209
Sherrill, Brad 210
Sherwood, Tony 196
She Loves Me 231
She Stoops to Comedy 131
She Stoops to Conquer 155
Shields, Brooke 67
Shim, Eric 168
Shimono, Sab 224
Shimotakahara, David 209
Shin, Eddie 168
Shindle, Kate 67
Shiner, M.William 209
Shinn, Christopher 131, 154, 161
Shipley, Michael 205
Shipley, Sandra 48, 159, 308
Shirley Herz Associates 110
Shively, Ryan 144, 308
Shoes 156
Shooltz, Emily V. 234
Shoppers Carried by Escalators into the Flames 145
Shor, Miriam 146, 177
Short, Melissa 145

Short, Michelle 219
Shorthouse, Dame Edith 40
Shortt, Paul 200
Showtune: The Words and Music Of Jerry Herman 100
Shpitalnik, Vladimir 205
Shriver, Lisa 30
Shubert Organization 30, 48
Shubert Theatre 58
Shue, Larry 192
Shukat, Scott 325
Shukis, Larissa 220
Shukla, Ami 145
Shulman, Lawrence Harvey 143
Shuman, Mort 232
Shumway, Susan 124
Shunpo 173
Shusterman, Tamlyn Brooke 69
Shutt, Christopher 96, 127
Shyre, Paul 139
Sia, Beau 34
Siccardi, Arthur 196
Siciliano, Adam 206
Sickles, Scott C. 163
Sicular, Robert 191
Sie, Allison 224
Sieber, Christopher 75
Siedenburg, Charlie 220
Siegel, Marv 154
Siegel, Rachel 192
Siegel, Seth M. 37
Sieger, Gary 49
Sieh, Kristen 176
Sifuentes, Kevin 225
Sigler, Jamie-Lynn 66
Siglin, Steven 225
Signals of Distress 178
Signature Theatre Company 177
Signor, Tari 173
Siguenza, Herbert 199, 224
Sikora, Megan 69, 75
Sikula, Dave 185
Silberman, Adam 38
Silberman, Brian 160
Silberman, David 212
Silcott, Thomas 196
Silence 159
Silent Piece 163
Sillerman, Robert F.X. 73
Silva, Donald 142, 174
Silva, Michael 143
Silva, Staysha Liz 233
Silver, Amy 178
Silver, H. Richard 157
Silver, Matthew 131
Silver, Mort 59
Silver, Nicky 27
Silver, Stephanie Ila 143
Silverman, Adam 52
Silverman, Antoine 49, 125

Silverman, David 208
Silverman, Leigh 174
Silverman, Miriam 230
Silverman, Ryan 196
Silversher, Michael 225
Silverstein, Jerry 49
Silverstone, Alicia 81
Silzer, Niesa D. 196
Sim, Keong 129
Simiring, Kira 218
Simkin, Toby 62
Simmons, Candy 156
Simmons, Gregory 141
Simmons, Kimora Lee 34
Simmons, Paulanne 178
Simmons, Rusell 34
Simms, Heather Alicia 45, 233
Simon, Alyssa 150
Simon, Christen 139
Simon, Dan Hendricks 144
Simon, Mark 33, 221
Simon, Neil 211, 224, 231
Simon, Rebecca 222
Simon, Richard 150
Simon, Roger Hendricks 144
Simonds, Dave 168
Simone 65
Simoneau, Marcel 159
Simons, E. Gray, III 192
Simons, Lake 149
Simons, Lorca 209
Simons, Ron 144, 163
Simonson, Eric 224
Simpatico, David 160
Simpkins, Kelli 215
Simpson, Ian 196
Simpson, Jim 146
Simpson, Jimmi 215
Simpson, Markiss 227
Simpson, Pete 112
Simpson, Ted 190, 194
Sims, Barbara 211
Sims, Bill, Jr. 184
Sims, Gregory 147
Sims, Laura 204
Sims, Marlayna 70
Sine, Jeffrey 38
Sinfully Rich 153
Singer, David S. 97
Singer, Gammy 176
Singer, Isaac Bashevis 150
Singlish 158
Siplak, Sarah 203
Siravo, Joseph 27, 168, 175
Sirugo, Carol 162
Sissons, Narelle 100, 101, 168, 201, 209
Siverls, Aynna 206
Six, Michelle R. 175, 200
Six of One Musical 142

Skiles, Sophia 171
Skinker, Sherry 43
Skinner, Emily 43, 124, 131, 308
Skinner, Margo 222
Skinner, Randy 69, 197
Skinner, Steve 74
Skin of Our Teeth, The 228
Skipitares, Theodora 172
Skjaerven, Torkel 233, 234
Skloff, Michael 223
Skoczelas, Tracy 217, 218, 219
Skura, Greg 163
Skybell, Steven 131
Skye, Iona 147
Skye, Robin 167
Skylab 160
Sky over Nineveh, The 148
Slag Heap 144
Slaight, Craig 184
Slaiman, Marjorie 325
Slanty Eyed Mama Rebirth of an Asian 172
Slater, Glenn 161
Slaton, Shannon 196
Sledge, Logan 144
Sleepers, The 154
Sleeping with Straight Men 99
Sleigh, Tom 152
Sleuth 222
Slezak, Victor 162
Slinkard, Jefferson 153, 163
Sloan, Peter 147
Slovacek, Randy 68
Slugocki, Lillian Ann 160
Slusar, Catharine K. 187
Slutforart a.k.a. Ambiguous Ambassador 170
Smagula, Jimmy 37
Smart, Annie 184, 191, 215
Smash 217
Smedes, Tom 111
Smell of the Kill, The 201
Smirnoff, Yakov 53
Smith, Alex 158, 215
Smith, Alice Elliot 34
Smith, Anna Deavere 198
Smith, Brian J. 209
Smith, Chris 146, 161
Smith, Craig 149
Smith, David B. 200
Smith, David Ryan 184, 185
Smith, Dennis 140, 161
Smith, Derek 70
Smith, Douglas D. 222
Smith, Effay Tio 205
Smith, Geddeth 125
Smith, Greg 32
Smith, Jacques C. 220
Smith, James E. 162
Smith, Jennifer 73, 142

Smith, Jessica Chandlee 159, 162, 215
Smith, Jonathan 42
Smith, Joseph 51, 104
Smith, Juliet 103, 151, 206, 308
Smith, Keith Randolph 174
Smith, Kendall 211, 212
Smith, Kiki 171
Smith, Larilu 169
Smith, Leslie L. 97
Smith, Levensky 70
Smith, Louise 167, 171
Smith, M. Ryan 189
Smith, Molly 160
Smith, Peter 105, 157, 211
Smith, Peter Matthew 26, 71, 74
Smith, Sam 124
Smith, Scott 231
Smith, Selina 154
Smith, Simba 205
Smith, T. Ryder 120, 131
Smith, Timothy Edward 65
Smith, Todd Michel 26
Smith, Vicki 207
Smith, Virginia Louise 44, 52
Smith, Warren 93
Smith, Willoughby 189
Smith-Cameron, J. 44, 308
Smits, Jimmy 128, 191
Smullens, Doug 187
Smythe, Ashi K. 70
Smythe, Debenham 111
Snedeker, Lourelene 193
Sneed, Terry 189
Snider, Samuel 223
Snider-Stein, Teresa 23
Sniffin, Allison 167
Snook, Dan 145, 179
Snow, Cherene 162
Snow, Chesney 155
Snow, Daniel 153
Snow, Jason 196
Snow, Tom 193
Snowdon, Ted 93, 105
Snow Angel 148
Snow White 163
Snyder, Dana 206
Snyder, Kelly 156
Snyder, Nancy 177, 227
Soar Like an Eagle 151
Sobel, Shepard 161
Sod, Ted 175
Soelistyo, Julyana 186
Soffer, Lynne 191, 224
Sofia, Steven 66
Soho Rep 178
Sola, Martin 38
Solá, Martín 308
Solano, Tiffany Ellen 225

Solis, Felix 101, 151, 168, 174, 308
Solis, Meme 169
Solis, Octavio 225
Solito, Laura Yen 221
Solomon, Andrew 160
Solovyeva, Ekaterina 38
Soloway, Leonard 49, 99
Somers, Asa 40
Somerville, Phyllis 168, 234
Somewhere Someplace Else 145
Some Enchanted Evening 180
Some Other Time 161
Sommers, Bryon 223
Sommers, Michael 208, 241
Sommerville, Barbara 209
Somogyi, Ilona 129, 130
Son, Diana 161
Sonderskov, Robert 159
Sondheim, Stephen 35, 58, 161, 173, 180, 187, 201, 227
Sonenberg, David 40
Song, Sue Jin 161
Song for Lachanze, A 160
Song of Singapore 194
Sonooka, Shintaro 173
Sony 73, 103
Sony Music 92
Son of Drakula 145
Soooo Sad 143
Sophocles 97, 145
Sordelet, Rick 23, 27, 40, 49, 66, 76, 91, 100, 168, 179, 201, 213, 233, 234
Soren, Scott 225
Sorge, Joey 213
Sorkin, Joan Ross 143
Soroka, Stephen 146
Sorrentini, Jamie 145
Sorrows and Rejoicings 203
Sosa, Emilio 128, 132, 215
Sosko, PJ 158, 227
Sosnow, Pat 66
Soto, Carlow 167
Soto, Letty 169
Souder, Jeannine 205
Soule, Samantha 43, 155
Soules, Dale 147, 187
Sound of a Voice, The 186
Sound of Music, The 231
Sourceworks Theatre 158
South, Hamilton 50
Southard, Elizabeth 72
South Coast Repertory 225
Soyinka, Wole 205
Spadoni, Alee 223
Spanger, Amy 68
Spangler, Nick 224
Spangler, Walt 33, 99, 128, 225
Spanish Girl 132

Spano, Giannina 211
Spano, Joe 191
Sparagen, Steve 111
Sparks, Don 169
Sparks, Johnny 141
Sparks, Paul 47, 174
Spear, Cary Anne 193, 203
Spear, Jamie 180
Speas, Bruce 204
Special Price for You, Okay? 161
Spectacle of Spectacles: The Clairvoyant Cabaret 171
Speier, Susanna 148
Spellman, Larry 28
Spence, Barbara J. 153
Spencer, Brant 147
Spencer, Keith 124
Spencer, Rebecca 124, 171
Sperber, Aaron 211
Speredakos, John 144, 146
Sperling, Ted 125, 223
Speros, Tia 220
Speth, Vii 39
Spialek, Hans 124
Spidel, Jonah 171
Spiller, Christopher M. 168
Spiller, Jennifer R. 168
Spinella, Stephen 36, 163
Spiner, Brent 51
Spinghel, Radu 38
Spinning into Butter 226
Spinosa, Tony 192
Spinozza, David 26
Spiotta, Daniel 220
Spiro, Matthew 191, 215, 224, 228
Spivak, Alice 308
Spivak, Allen 61
Spizzo, Christine 72
Split 151
Spon, Marian 123
Sposito, Dee 143
Spottag, Jens Jorn 167
Sprague, Ruslan 192
Sprecher, Ben 98
Spring, Robert 197
Springer, Gary 96
Springer/Chicoine Public Relations 96
Springtime for Henry 213
Springworks 2003 145
Spring Awakening 156
Squadron, Anne Strickland 61
Squire, Theresa 173, 178
Srok, Ben 205
SRU Productions LLC 106
Ssstoneddd 171
St. James Theatre 73
St. Clair, Elise 225
St. Clair, Richard 187

St. Cyr, Byron 180
St. George, Dick 212
St. Hilaire, Christopher 194, 195
St. Hilaire, Stephanie 142
St. Louis, David 92
St. Paul, Stephen 174
St. Paule, Irma 150
St. Pierre, Venise 202
Staats, Amy 168
Stackpole, Dana 32, 308
Stacy, Melody 209
Stadelmann, Matthew 143, 176
Stadlen, Lewis J. 73
Stafford, Richard 231
Stage Holding 69
Stahl, Dale 224
Stahl, Jonathan 231
Stahl, Mary Leigh 72
Staley, John 215
Staller, David 180
Stametz, Lee 207
Stamford Theatre Works 226
Stamos, John 67
Stan, Sebastian 145
Stancati, Frank 140
Stanczyk, Laura 76, 124
Stander, Jeff 218, 219
Stanescu, Saviana 172
Stanion, Karen 140
Stanley, Gordon 66
Stanton, Ben 130, 177
Stanton, Brooke 186
Stanton, Phil 112
Stanton, Robert 96
Stapleton, Jean 115
Starcrossed: A Quintet of Five Short Plays 158
Starcrossed Lovers 152
Staroselsky, Dennis 211
Starratt, Laura 204
Starrett, Pete 48, 112
Star Messengers 171
Stasuk, P.J. 231
Staton, Daniel C. 25
Stauffer, Scott 125
Staunton, Kim 221
Staunton, Noel 38
Steadman, Allison 204
Stearns, Donna 152
Steele, Erik 44
Steele, Kameron 167
Steele, Shayna 26, 74
Steel Magnolias 189
Stefanowicz, Janus 126
Steggert, Bobby 231
Steiger, Rick 128
Steiger, Rod 325
Stein, Adam 70
Stein, Andy 99
Stein, Douglas 179, 183, 201

Stein, Erik 211
Stein, Gertrude 123, 152
Stein, Jean 41
Stein, Joseph 192
Stein, Navida 156
Steinbeck, Elaine Anderson 325
Steinbeck, John 153, 209
Steinberg, Eric 151
Steinbruner, Gregory 178
Steindler, Catherine Baker 153
Steiner, Rick 25, 73
Steinfeld, Ben 230
Steinfeld, Dayna 143
Steinman, Jim 40
Steinmeyer, Jim 66
Steitzer, Jeff 224
Stella, Robert 186
Stenmetz, Lynn 212
Stephens, Amanda 218, 219
Stephens, Claudia 176, 200
Stephens, Darcy 98, 99
Stephens, James A. 169
Stephens, Lamont 139
Stephens, Mara 145
Stephens, Mark Edgar 192
Stephenson, Don 73, 180
Sterl, Tania 172
Sterlin, Jenny 159, 174, 176
Sterman, Andrew 27, 124
Stern, Cheryl 110, 145, 308
Stern, Daniel 100
Stern, Edward 160, 200, 201
Stern, Eric 213
Stern, James D. 25, 45, 73, 160
Stern, Jamison 133
Stern, Jenna 160, 175
Stern, Kathryn 160
Stern, Matthew Aaron 56
Sternbach, Gerald 193
Sternhagen, Frances 104, 160, 196
Sterrett, T.O. 40, 129
Stetor, Jennifer 69
Steve 161
Stevens, Alexandra 59
Stevens, Eric Sheffer 193, 200
Stevens, Fisher 161
Stevens, Graham 140
Stevens, Jodi 49, 308
Stevens, Robert 151
Stevens, Wass M. 145
Stevenson, Robert Louis 207
Stevens Advertising 186
Stevie 214
Stewart, Benjamin 224
Stewart, Daniel 154
Stewart, Daniel Freedom 144, 217
Stewart, Ellen 170
Stewart, Gwen 198

Stewart, Jennifer 219
Stewart, Kellee 213, 233
Stewart, Michael 69, 197
Stewart, Nicole 162
Stewart, Paul Anthony 168
Stewart, Peter 156
Stickney, Mollie 191
Stieb, Corey Tazmania 162
Stiers, David Ogden 66
Stiles, George 123, 223
Stiles, Julia 128
Stiles, Sarah 220
Stilgoe, Richard 72
Still, James 211
Still, Melly 102
Still, Peter John 179
Stillman, Bob 49, 221
Stilo, Al 210
Stinger, Laura Berlin 154
Stites, Kevin 54
Stith, Monica 178
Stock, Jennifer Sherron 150
Stockhausen, Adam 213, 227
Stoddard, Erin 69
Stoddard, Gerald 171
Stokes, Colin 110
Stokes, Matt 220
Stole, Mink 99
Stoll, Jill 31
Stollmack, Noele 167
Stomp 112
Stone, Angie 68
Stone, Daryl A. 177, 183
Stone, David 37
Stone, Doug 155
Stone, Elise 149
Stone, Greg 49
Stone, Jay 111
Stone, Jeff 220
Stone, Jessica 213
Stone, Peter 133, 189, 212, 326
Stoner, Ross 140
Stones in His Pockets 183, 217, 229
Stone Cold Dead Serious 143
Stoppard, Tom 184, 209
Stop All the Clocks 161
Storace, Greta 147
Storey, Tella 158
Storm, Doug 40
Storms, Jake 200
Stout, Marta 204, 205
Stout, Stephen 153
Stovall, Count 308
Stover, Laren 158
Stowe, Dennis 37, 111
Straiges, Tony 56, 101, 183, 206
Strand, Ashley 147
Straney, Paul 151
Strange, Dean 193

Stranger, The 170
Strange Fish 161
Stratakes, Glenn 188
Stratakes, Helen 188, 189
Stratford, Aoise 152
Strathairn, David 57, 168
Strathie, Angus 38
Stratton, Jay 155
Strauss, Edwin 76
Strauss, Georgia 148
Strawbridge, Stephen 209, 234
Streber, Ryan 168
Street, Lawrence 76
Street Corner Pierrot, A 172
Street of Useful Things, The 174
Stren, James D. 112
Strickland, Cynthia 228, 229
Strickstein, Robert C. 69
Strindberg, August 192
String Fever 168
Stritch, Billy 69, 180
Stritch, Elaine 197
Strobel, Guy 205
Strober, Rena 175
Strock, Bob 171
Stroman, Susan 73
Strome, Jenny 100
Stronach, Tami 178
Strong, Caroline 159
Strong, Mark 123
Strong as a Lion, Soft as Silk 161
Strouse, Charles 213, 220, 230
Stuart, Kelly 175
Stuart, Lisa Martin 92
Stuart, Maria 123
Stuart, Matty D. 153
Stubbings, Chuck 208
Stuckenbruck, Dale 39
Stucky, Matthew 227
Stude, Roger Dale 163
Studio 42 158
Studio on 3 232
Studio Theatre 159
Stuhlbarg, Michael 128, 174, 175
Stumm, Michael 154
Sturge, Tom 216
Sturgis, Nanka 217, 218
Sturgis, Nisi 219
Stutts, Will 232
Styer, Allan 153
Styler, Trudie 160
Styles, Joy 93
Styne, Jule 58
Su, Pei-Chi 203
Suarez, Antonio Edwards 200
Suber, Kate 223
Subjack, Jenny 215

Subway Series—The Subway 163
Svich, Caridad 160, 174, 175
Svilar, Gordana 208
Swados, Liz 172
Swain, Howard 224
Swan, Matthew 154
Swanigan, Troy 196
Swanson, K.J. 219
Swanson, Reedy 205
Swarm, Sally Ann 111
Swartz, Jerome 51
Swartz, Marlene 112
Swartz, Tami 193
Swasey, Brian J. 231
Swee, Amy 125
Swee, Christopher 125
Swee, Daniel 43, 48, 196
Sweeney, April 175
Sweeney, Julia 140
Sweet Smell of Success 85
Swenson, Todd 151
Swenson, Will 146, 150
Swinging Rodgers I, II, III 180
Swinsky, Morton 25, 38, 40, 45, 92, 95
Sykes, Kim 139
Sylvester, Mark D. 231
Sylvia, Abe 73
Symes, Weylin 156
Symphony Space 180
Synapse Theatre 159
Syncopation 226
Synge, J.M. 169
Syracuse Stage 227
Syringa Tree, The 119, 201
Szász, János 186
Szczepanski, John-Paul 95
Szücs, Edit 186
Szyz, Christopher M. 205

T

T. Schreiber Studio 162
T'Kaye, Eileen 97
Ta'Ziyeh of Hor, The 173
Tabb, Leni 178
Tabor, Philip 131
Tabori, George 96
Taccone, Tony 191, 224, 228
Taffe, Kelly 203
Taga, Roxanne 220
Tagano, Mia 194
Tagg, Alan 326
Tagle, Luke 225
Tague, Steve 187
Taichman, Rebecca Bayla 223
Tailor's Tale, The 213
Takahara, Yuka 71
Takahashi, Suzi 172
Takakuwa, Hisa 225
Takami, Janet 106

Subway Series—The Subway
Subway Series—The Subway
Suddaby, Anne 142
Suddeth, J. Allen 130
Sudduth, Kohl 47, 128
Sudduth, Skipp 106
Sudler, Elizabeth 190
Suga, Shigeko 172
Sugarman, David 30
Sugden, John W. 184
Sugg, James 187
Suh, Lloyd 168
Sullivan, A.J. 220
Sullivan, Daniel 23, 126, 196
Sullivan, Daniel Robert 222
Sullivan, Deb 229
Sullivan, Fred, Jr. 228, 229, 230
Sullivan, Kerry 171
Sullivan, Kim 227
Sullivan, KT 180
Sullivan, Nick 207
Sullivan, Patrick Ryan 66, 197
Sullivan, Siobhan 214
Sullivan, Susan 176
Sullivan, T.J. 36
Sullivan, Yaakov 147
Sulsona, Philip James 156
Sumbry-Edwards, Dormeshia 196
Summa, Don 25, 62, 74, 109, 130, 132
Summerford, Denise 230
Summerhays, Jane 67
Summerour, John 152
Summers, Lee 93
Summons to Sheffield 232
Sumonja, Drago 150
Sun, Burt 186
Sun, Nilaja 159
Sundown 188
Sunjata, Daniel 6, 47, 128, 239, 241
Sunup 152
Supple, Tim 102, 191
Surabian, Michael 149
Surface Transit 191
Survival of the Fetus 171
Surviving Grace 119
Susko, Michael 231
Sussel, Deborah 184, 185
Sussman, Ben 131, 208
Sutch, Mark 229
Sutcliffe, William 151
Sutherland, Brian 221
Sutherland, Diane 145
Suzuki, Boko 196

Takara, Yuka 29
Take Me Out 6, 47, 128, 239
Taking Steps Three Thirteen 170
Talbott, Daniel 200, 209
Talen, Bill 154
Talent, Kelly 222
Tale of the Allergist's Wife, The 85
Talking Heads 104
Talley's Folly 190
Tamaki, Yasuko 69
Tambella, Mark 172
Taming of the Shrew, The 210, 218, 234
Tanaka, Anne 168
Tanaka, Yumiko 123
Tandy, Madame Pat 170
Tangelson, Dario 144, 171
Tani, Akinori 173
Tanji, Lydia 112, 212, 224
Tanner, Emmelyn 218
Tanner, Javen 217, 218, 219
Tanner, Jill 56
Tanner, Vickie 139
Taphorn, Peggy 195
Tapia, Sheila 200
Tapper, Jeff 172
Tarallo, Barry 205
Tara Rubin Casting 29, 42, 196
Tarr, Denise 225
Tartaglia, John 179
Tartuffe 44, 215
Tassara, Carla 153
Tatad, Robert 29
Tate, Katrina 104
Tate, Umar 205
Tate Entertainment Group, Inc. 197
Tatgenhorst, Rob 205
Tatum, Bill 156, 163
Tatum, Marianne 241
Tauber, Michele 173
Taxi Caberet 156
Tayloe, Richard 143
Taylor, Bobby 216
Taylor, Candace 205
Taylor, Clark 222
Taylor, Clifton 173
Taylor, Dominic 175
Taylor, Giva 105
Taylor, Jackie 104
Taylor, Jennifer Lee 147, 220, 224
Taylor, Jonathan 69
Taylor, Juliet 50
Taylor, Kathy 208
Taylor, Lesley 210
Taylor, Lindsay Rae 153
Taylor, Mark Anthony 68
Taylor, Myra 308

Taylor, Myra Lucretia 54
Taylor, Regina 132
Taylor, Russel 154
Taylor, Samuel 124
Taylor, Shane 192
Taylor, Tara 205
Taylor-Shellman, Endalyn 65, 70
Taymor, Julie 70
Tazel, Erika 174
Tazewell, Paul 34, 92, 128, 196, 197, 201
Teague, Frankie 318
Tea at Five 101, 206
Tec, Roland 147
Tech Production Services, Inc. 196
Teddy Tonight! 139
Tedeschi, John 152
Tekosky, Valarie 104
Teller, Keith 163
Teller, Ryan Michael 139
Tellier, Jerry 69
Telsey, Bernard 65, 132, 173, 185
Tempest, The 155, 188
Temporary Help 97
Tena, Paul 99
Tenney, Jon 97
Tennyson, John Gentry 92
Ten Haaf, Jochum 308
Ten Unknowns 199
ten Haaf, Jochum 7, 48, 239
Tepe, Heather 13, 58
Tepper, Arielle 33, 40, 92
Terkel, Studs 139
Terrano, Susan 200
Terrazas, Elisa 149
Territory 142
Terror Eyes 160
Terruso, Gene 187
Terry, Audrey 111
Terry, Beatrice 148, 168
Terry, Robin 183
Terstriep, Tracy 73
Tesori, Jeanine 75
Tesoro, Carlos M. 234
Testa, Mary 69
Testani, Andrea J. 24, 131
Tester, Hans 173
Teti, Tom 187
Tetreault, Paul 183
Texarkan Waltz 150
Thacher, Andrew 140
Thacker, Kit 162
Thacker, Sloan 200
Thaiss, Jeffries 200
Thaler, Jordan 47, 128, 129
Tharp, Twyla 32
That's How I Say Goodbye 160
Thatcher, Ginger 55

That Damn Dykstra 139
That Day in September 155
Thau, Harold 97
Thayer, Emmelyn 217, 218, 219
Thayer, Maria 92, 174
TheaterDreams, Inc. 76
Theatersmith, Inc. 197
Theater for the New City 178
Theatre, Lyceum 50
Theatre 3 159
Theatre at Saint Peter's Church 100
Theatre at St. Peter's 159
Theatre for a New Audience 179
Theatre Four 110, 111
Theatre Royal Haymarket Productions 45
Theatrical Services, Inc. 196
Thelen, Pete 214
Theodorou, Andrew 99
Theophilus North 212
There Will Be a Miracle 160
Theroux, Justin 125
Thestrup, Ole 167
Thetard, Tiffany N. 213
Thiam, Samuel N. 65
Thibault, Anne 205
Thibodeau, Marc 37, 42, 72, 93, 98, 130, 131
Thierree, James 153
Thies, Howard 57
Thiessen, Vern 152
Thieves in the Temple: The Reclaiming of Hip Hop 156
Thigpen, Haynes 234
Thigpen, Lynne 326
Thinnes, Roy 157
13th Street Repertory Theatre 159
Thirty-Fourth and Dyer 161
36 Views 212
This Will Be the Death of Him 143
Thomalen, E. 150
Thomas, Baylen 216
Thomas, Brenda 142, 174
Thomas, Cori 168
Thomas, Dylan 169
Thomas, Erika 36, 216
Thomas, Jack 101
Thomas, Jay 106
Thomas, Katrina 158
Thomas, Keith Lamelle 92
Thomas, Marlo 160, 161
Thomas, Michael 180
Thomas, Ray 147
Thomas, Ray Anthony 227
Thomas, Robert L. 104
Thomas, Sally 215
Thomas, Sarah Megan 162

Thomas, Shelley 102, 167
Thompson, April Yvette 95
Thompson, Billy 91
Thompson, David 60, 68, 124
Thompson, E. Randy 154
Thompson, Ernest 206
Thompson, Fred 147
Thompson, Jenn 139
Thompson, Jennifer Laura 76, 132, 308
Thompson, John Leonard 227
Thompson, Judith 159
Thompson, Justin Ray 140
Thompson, Lea 67
Thompson, Louisa 178
Thompson, Mark 51, 71, 123, 196
Thompson, Raphael Nash 147
Thompson, Robert 44
Thompson, Stuart 50
Thompson, Trance 111
Thompson, Victoria 184
Thompson, Yvette 144
Thomson, Ole 224
Thorell, Clarke 26
Thorn, Chris 151, 159
Thorne, Callie 126
Thorne, Joan Vail 179
Thorne, Stephen 228, 229, 230
Thornton, Angela 190
Thornton, Christopher 175
Thornton, David 140, 168
Thornton, René, Jr. 205, 211
Thoron, Elise 223
Thoroughly Modern Millie 75
Thrasher, Mark 27, 60
Threatte, Renee 227
Three-Cornered Moon 150
3 O'Clock in Brooklyn 139
Three Sisters, The 185
3 Weeks after Paradise 159, 161
Throw 160
Thunderbird 174
Thunder Knocking on the Door 91
Thureen, Paul 158
Thwak! 153
Tiamfook, Marissa 144
Tiberghien, Lucie 159
Tichenor, Austin 200
Tichler, Rosemarie 128
Tiffany, Forrest Fraser, II 184
Tighe, John 180
Tighe, Susanne 29, 51, 69, 98, 99, 100, 106
Tilford, A. Michael 189
Tilford, Joseph P. 200
Till, Kevin Scott 150
Tilley, Bobby Frederick, II 167
Tillinger, John 28, 101, 206

Tillman, Ellis 49
Tillman, Gary 71
Tillman, Jimmy 104
Tillman, Rochele 143
Timbers, Alex 148
Times Square Theatre 159
Time and the Conways 159
Time Machine 2.0 152
Timlin, Addison 13, 58, 220
Timperman, Erika 130
Tindall, Blair 37, 124
Tindle, Jonathan 175, 216
Ting, Liuh-Wen 27, 54
Tiplady, Neil 112
Tipton, Betty 204
Tipton, Jennifer 130, 233
Tirelli, Jaime 212
Tisdale, Michael 191
Titcomb, Gordon 49
Titone, Tom 213
Titus, Jane 150
To, Rodney 151
Toan, Braden 37
Tobes, Bill 147
Tobie, Ellen 231
Tobin, David A. 150
Tobin, Kathleen 201
Tobolowsky, Stephen 196
TOC Productions 110
Tod, Incidental Colman 48
Today's Broadway 180
Todd, Jeffrey 140
Todd, John J. 32
Todd, Will 160
Todhunter, Jeffrey 204
Toibin, Fiana 62
Tolan, Cindy 55, 96
Tolan, R.J. 157
Tolins, Jonathan 105, 157, 193
Tomcho, Michaela 223
Tomei, Marisa 57, 160, 161
Tomei, Paula 225
Tomko, Daniel 203
Tomlin, Lily 197
Tomlinson, Sorrel 147
Tomlin and Wagner Theatricalz 197
Tommer, Michael 41
Tommy Tune: White Tie and Tails 99
Tongue Tied and Duty Free 175
Tonkonogy, Gertrude 150
Tony 'n' Tina's Wedding 119
Took, Don 225
Toolajian, Loren 93
Topdog/Underdog 86
Topol, Daniella 152
Toppall, Lawrence S. 28
Topping, John 153
Torcellini, Jamie 37

Toren, Nick 139, 150
Torke, Michael 168
Torn, Tony 142, 154
Torres, Joaquin 168
Torres, Maria 109, 167
Torres, Marilyn 233
Torres, Mario 112
Torres, Michelle 169
Torres-Yap, Fay 178
Torsiglieri, Anne 213
Torsney-Weir, Maureen 232
Toser, David 99, 169
Tosetti, Sara J. 95
Toshiko, Katrina 213
Toth, Jacob A. 223
Touch, Tony 197
Touchscape 148
TOURture Press & Marketing 196
Toussaint, Lorraine 191
Tower, Josh 70
Towers, Charles 216
Towler, Lorinne 161
Townsend, Glenn 187
Town Hall: Brave New World 160
Trabitz, Randee 176
Trade 144
Traffic 140
Trafficking in Broken Hearts 140
Traina, Anastasia 143
Trani, Vince 220
Trask, Stephen 130, 203
Tratt, Marcia 232
Trauscht, Lolly 214
Travanti, Daniel J. 218
Travis, David 159
Travis, Ken 92, 176, 178
Travis, Michele 148
Treadway, Erin 157
Treadway, Stephen 133
Treadwell, Tom 220
Treco, Gregory 167
Tree, The 158
Treherne, Nichola 71, 196
Treick, Joel 93
Treihart, Gladynne Sherle 323
Trentacosta, Joe 96
Trese, Adam 145, 176
Tresnjak, Darko 213, 219
Tresty, Steve 155
Trevens, Francine L. 150
Trevino, Robin 214
Treyz, Russell 155, 158, 209
Triad Theater 106
Triantaphyllopoulos, Kostas 97
Tribeca Playhouse 162
Trien, Cathy 59
Trinity Repertory Company 228
Trinkoff, Donna 167

Triple Happiness, The 174
Trip to Bountiful, The 183
Triska, Jan 186
Triumph of Love, The 149
Trivett, Nellie 188
Troche, Alfredo D. 171
Trojan Women, The 175
Troob, Danny 66
Trout, Deb 222
Trueblood, Paul 180
True Love Productions, Inc. 41
True West 222
Trumbo 162
Trumbo, Christopher 162
Trumbull, Kelly 227
Trunell, Christopher 142
Tse, Elaine 186
Tseng, Muna 170
Tsuchigane, Sonya 178
Tsuji, Yukio 57
Tsukuda, Saori 144
Tsutsui, Hideaki 168
Tuan, Alice 151, 170
Tubes 112
Tucci, Louis 179
Tucci, Stanley 17, 24, 161
Tucker, Allyson 37, 309
Tucker, Rachel Tecora 70
Tucker, Rob 187
Tuesdays With Morrie 97
Tufino, Pablo 177
Tuft, Sarah 160
Tulchin, Ted 91
Tullock, Devon 196
Tully, Pauline 163, 173
Tumor 148
Tuna Christmas, A 206
Tunick, Jonathan 54, 124, 197
Tunie, Tamara 176
Tureen, Rufus 174
Turgenev, Ivan 193, 213
Turhal, Ozlem 150
Turk, Bruce 223
Turner, Allyson 27, 60
Turner, Charles 144
Turner, Charles M., III 103
Turner, Chris 229
Turner, David 105, 157, 167
Turner, Jessica 209
Turner, Jessica D. 144
Turner, Michael 193, 205
Turner, Sylvia 225
Turnpike, Jerzy 180
Turpin, Pamela 189
Turturro, John 51, 161, 309
Tushingham, David 191
Tuthill, Patricia 124
Tuttle, Ashley 32
TV Music Publishing LLC, A 103
Twain, Mark 91, 198

Twelfth Night 123, 128, 187
Twelve Brothers 163
29th Street Rep 162
21 Dog Years: Doin' Time @Amazon.Com 119
Twiggy 190
Twine, Linda 55, 91, 132
Twist, Basil 215
Two-Five Media 180
Two by Two: The Richard Rodgers Centennial Concert 133
Two Gentlemen of Verona 210, 224, 225
Two Loves and a Creature 170
2 Pianos, 4 Hands 194
2001: An Oral History 160
Tyler, Myxy 230
Tyler, Suzanne 211
Typographer's Dream, The 145
Tyranny, "Blue" Gene 171
Tyson, David 172
Tyson, John 183

U

Ucedo, Maria 109
Uchizono, Donna 230
Udinson, Jamie Lynn 231
UE92/02 170
Uffelman, Jonathan 145
Uggams, Leslie 75, 91, 220
Ugurlu, Zishan 154
Uhry, Alfred 160, 195, 221
Ularu, Nic 171
Ulen, John 205
Ullian, Seth 125
Ullrich, Mattie 97, 168, 176, 179
Ullrich, William 54
Ulvaeus, Björn 71, 196
Uncle Dan 139
Uncle Vanya 123, 149, 186
Underneath the Lintel 120
Undesirable Elements/Secret History 170
Unger, Aaron Mostkoff 144, 171
Unicorn Theater 192
Uninvited Guest, The 153
Union City, New Jersey, Where Are You? 168
Union Square Theatre 93, 101, 151
Unity Fest 2002: Growing Up 140
Universal 196
Universal Casting 71
University of Michigan Musical Society 102
University Theatre 233
Unresolved: One-act Plays on Loss, Grief and Recovery 158
Until We Find Each Other 174

Upham, Ben 159
Up (The Man in the Flying Lawn Chair) 174
Urban, Carey 140
Urban, Edward 93
Urban, Ken 148
Urbaniak, James 130, 145, 309
Urbanowski, Alexandra 224
Urban Cowboy 49
Urban Stages 162
Urbi, Erwin G. 201
Urgent Fury 144
Urinetown 76, 185
Urla, Joseph 234
Urriquia, Melissa 201
USA: A Reading 139
USA Ostar Productions 24
USA Ostar Theatricals 30, 37, 40, 42
Usiatynski, Walter "Wally" 26
Utley, Byron 74
Utt, Rebecca 203

V

Vaccariello, Patrick 40, 58, 67
Vaden, Phillip C. 225
Vaden, Travis 225
Vagina Monologues, The 120
Vahanian, Ivy 207
Valdes-Aran, Ching 149, 151
Valencia, Carlos 169
Valentine, Taylor 224
Valladares, Mercy 156
Valle, Miriam Colon 177
Valles, Tony 156
Valley, Paul Michael 219
Valparaiso 141
Vanasse, Holly 186
Vanda 153
vanden Heuvel, Wendy 41, 141
Vanderbilt, Kip 93
Vandermeulen, Lynae 188
Vanderpoel, Mark 30
VanDevender, Kate 155
Vanstone, Hugh 51, 123
van Cauwelaert, Didier 30
Van Cleve, Emory 141
Van Curtis, Jeffrey 206
van den Berg, Klaus 204
van den Ende, Joop 69, 197
Van Der Beek, James 177
van der Schyff, Melissa 198
Van Driest, Carey 149, 150
Van Druten, John 67
Van Duyne, Elisa 69
Van Dyck, Jennifer 213
Van Giesen, Nicole 67
Van Laast, Anthony 71, 196
Van Name, J.J. 155
Van Norden, Peter 191, 224

Van Nostrand, Amy 228
Van Note, Jill 163
Van Tieghem, David 130, 173, 215
van Tonder, Michelle 170
Van Wagner, Peter 151
Van Why, Artie 155
Van Wieren, Astrid 196
Varbalow, Jennifer 168
Varela, Andrew 220
Varga, Joe 210
Vargas, Ovi 167
Varhola, Kim 29
Varia, Zubin 102
Variety Arts Theatre 92, 98
Varjas, Grant 142, 155
Varner, Kevin 178
Varon, Susan 141
Varveris, Stefanie 149
Vasan, Sheila 192
Vasen, Tim 130
Vasquez, Michele 217
Vassallo, Ed 151, 174
Vaughan, Melanie 42, 219, 309
Vaughn, Erika 69
Vaughn, Robert 192
Vavasseur, Kevin 148
Vazquez, Michele 217, 218, 219
Vazquez, Tory 176
Vazquez, Yul 175
VCX Ltd. 96
V-Day 143
Vea, Michael 220
Velez, Alicia 212
Velez, Jamie 145
Velez, Loraine 74
Velez, Ray 233
Velie, Shian 225
Velino, Matthew 229
Vellenga, Jennifer 217
Velvel, Kathryn 163
Venberg, Lorraine 202
Venitucci, Guido 139
Ventimiglia, John 96, 142
Ventouras, Phoebe 158
Ventura, Eliza 142
Verastique, Rocker 68
Vercelloni, Franca 178
Vereen, Ben 23, 309
Vergel, Fulvia 177
Vermeulen, James 101, 173, 177, 184, 228
Vermont Stage Company 205
Verna, Marco 214
Vernace, Kim 32, 66
Verne, Jules 188
Vernoff, Kaili 145
Vernon, Carolyn Ruth 211
Veronique 155
Versailles, Vladimir 223

Vertgalant 143
Vess, Stephen 188
Victims! Trust 139
Victory at Sea 180
Vida, Richard 93, 309
Vidnovic, Martin 100, 193, 309
Vieira, Davi 112
Vienna: Lusthaus (Revisited) 120
Viertel, Jack 124
Viertel, Tom 94, 95
Vietti, Alejo 105
Vig, Joel 26, 309
Vigorito, Nick 152
Vilanch, Bruce 111
Villabon, Luis 111
Village Light Opera Chorus 180
Village Theatre, The 162
Villalobos, Vanessa 153
Villar, Paula 193
Villella, David 227
Vincent, Christian 129
Vincent, Jerald 65
Vincents, Michelle 111
Vincent in Brixton 7, 48, 238, 239
Viner, Michael 61
Vineyard Theatre, The 179
Vinton, Chandler 203
Violet Hour, The 225
Vioni, Lisa 62
Vipond, Neil 92
Virgil 156
Virginia Theatre 29, 61
Viscomi, Jordan 58, 59
Vish, A.T. 203
Visitor, Nana 68
Vitale, Stephanie 180
Vitali, Carl 161
Vivian, John 74
Vivian Beaumont 43
Vizki, Morti 158
Vlastnik, Frank 11, 55, 153, 309
Vogel, Arianna 231
Vogel, Carlo 154
Vogel, Frederic B. 56
Vogel, Jerry 206
Vogel, Paula 230
Volckhausen, Alex Lyu 126
Vollmer, Lula 152
Volunteer, The 178
von Arnim, Elizabeth 56
Von Essen, Max 40
von Gerkan, Florence 123
von Hoffman, Nicholas 171
von Mayrhauser, Jennifer 132, 221
von Schiller, Friedrich 123
von Waldenburg, Raina 154
Vosburg, Jarron Edward 204
Vosburgh, Dick 192

Voyage of the Carcass 148
Voyce, Kaye 99, 168, 208, 227
Voysey Inheritance, The 231
Voytko, Kathy 54
Vrancovich, Estela 193
Vroman, Lisa 72
Vujosevic, Tatjana 162
Vukovic, Monique 155
Vukovich, James 219

W

Waara, Scott 198
Wackerman, Dan 141, 155
Wactor, Sheilynn 112
Wada, Emi 173
Waddington, Rona 184
Wade, Adam 23, 226
Wade, Bryan L. 195
Wade, Geoffrey 193
Wadsworth, Don 203
Wadsworth, Oliver 92, 175, 194
Wadsworth, Stephen 191
Wagman, Nela 161, 168
Wagner, Daniel MacLean 187
Wagner, Dawn 205
Wagner, Jane 197
Wagner, Jean 163
Wagner, Robin 29, 73
Wahl, Tom 193
Wailes, Alexandria 198
Waite, Todd 183
*Waiting for My Man (World
    Without End)* 142
Waiting for the Telegram 104
Waits, Tom 167
Wakely, Richard 102
Walbye, Kay 76
Waldman, Jennifer 150, 190
Waldman, Price 147, 179
Waldman, Robert 43, 221
Waldo, Terry 223
Waldron, Michael 226
Waldrop, Mark 220
Walford, Malinda 143, 147
Walker, Catherine 220
Walker, Chris 126
Walker, Christopher 218
Walker, Don 231
Walker, Gavin 156
Walker, Jon Patrick 96
Walker, Joseph A. 326
Walker, Michael 213
Wall, Marilyn A. 211, 224
Wall, Mary Ann 178
Wallace, Charles E. 92, 222
Wallace, Cynthia 36
Wallace, Deborah 144
Wallace, Greggory 185
Wallace, Gregory 184, 185
Wallace, Naomi 179

Wallace, Nathan 200
Wallace, Peter 192
Wallace, Rachel 211
Wallach, Eli 160, 161
Wallach, Tyler 161
Wallem, Stephen 208
Waller, Kenneth H. 72
Wallert, James 159
Walling, Jessica 222
Wallis, Ruth 106
Wallnau, Carl 105
Wallnau, Colleen Smith 105
Wall to Wall Richard Rodgers
    180
Walnut Street Theatre 231
Walrath, Luke 69
Walsh, Alice Chebba 29, 45
Walsh, Edward 226
Walsh, Enda 169
Walsh, Mary Ann 172
Walsh, Paul 184, 185
Walsh-Smith, Tricia 146
Walters, Travis 36
Walter Kerr Theatre 47
Walton, Bob 110
Walton, Debra 151, 211
Walton, Emma 190
Walton, Jim 220
Walton, Tony 23, 36, 190
Walt Disney Productions 66
Walt Disney Records 66
Walt Disney Theatrical
    Productions 70
Wanetik, Ric 94
Wang, Nathan 212
Wann, Jim 205
Warchus, Manhew 51
Ward, Anthony 58, 123
Ward, Bethe 72
Ward, Bruce 173
Ward, Buzz 200
Ward, Christopher 184
Ward, Elizabeth Caitlin 179, 208
Ward, Hilary 150, 163
Ward, Jennifer 156
Ward, Jim 200
Ward, Joseph 153
Ward, Lauren 124
Ward, Sharon 204
Ward, Steven 93
Wardell, Brandon 75
Ware, Bill 178
Warehouse, Donmar 128
Warfield, William 326
Warik, Joe 221
Warmen, Timothy 40
Warner, Amy 200
Warner, Christina L. 190
Warner, Craig 216
Warner, Deborah 41, 167

Warner, Gertrude Chandler 187
Warner, Neil 37
Warner, Sturgis 175, 177
Warren, David 100, 126
Warren, Harry 69, 197
Warren, Rachael 228, 229, 230
Warren, Thom Christopher 70
Warren-Gibson, David 68
Warren-Gray, Nicholas 140
Warshaw, Mike 69
Warwick, James 192
Washburn, Anne 170
Washington, Ajene 176
Washington, Booker T. 227
Washington, Krystal L. 74
Washington, Michael Benjamin
    71
Washington, Mindy 190
Washington, Rhonnie 184
Wassberg, Goran 123
Wasser, Alan 72
Wasserman, Dale 37, 189, 221
Wassum, Debra 178
Watanabe, , Kunio 173
Waterbury, Marsha 71
Waters, Daryl 92, 126, 196
Waters, Les 191, 215
Waterston, James 218, 225
Waterston, Sam 160, 234
Water Coolers 95
Watford, Myk 103, 151, 206
Watkins, Amanda 110
Watkins, Jamie 153
Watkins, Maurine Dallas 68
Watson, Emily 123
Watson, Robin 205
Watson-Davis, Myiia 74
Watt, Douglas 241
Watt, Michael 58
Watts, Robert 222
Wave 174
Waxman, Allie 211
Waxman Williams
    Entertainment 29, 96
Way, Adam 232
Wayth, Laura 186
Way Out, The 154
WDUM Family Radio Hour, The
    229
Weatherly, Christal 215
Weaver, Casey 153
Weaver, Deke 149
Weaver, Lori J. 112
Weaver, Marissa 205
Weaver, Sigourney 173
Weaver, Thom 203
Webb, Alex 92
Webb, Daniel C. 38, 309
Webb, Jeremy 139, 232
Webb, Kimberly Mark 184, 185

Webber, Andrew Lloyd 72, 231
Webber, Stephen 186
Weber, Carl 142
Weber, Jake 127
Weber, James 145
Weber, Steven 73
Weber, Suzanne 148
Weber, Terry 204, 205
Weber, Theresa 154
Webster, Douglas 180
Webster, J.D. 124
Webster, T. Edward 184, 191,
    224
Wedekind, Frank 156
Weeden, Bill 158
Weeks, Jimmie Ray 221, 226
Weeks, Todd 209
Weems, Andrew 145
Wegener, Jessica 204
Wehle, Brenda 104, 186
Wehrle, Elizabeth 128, 129
Weidman, John 173, 187, 201
Weigand, John 146
Weil, Melissa 110
Weil, Tim 74, 129
Weiman, Kate 147
Weinberger, Eric H. 147
Weincek, David 158
Weiner, David 43, 179, 186, 201,
    213
Weiner, Gregg 153
Weiner, Miriam 163
Weiner, Randy 109
Weinstein, Arnold 167
Weinstein, Bob 38, 73
Weinstein, Bruce H. 197
Weinstein, Harvey 38, 58, 73
Weir, DeeAnn 145
Weisberg, Noah 142
Weiser, Mark 152
Weiskopf, Walt 75
Weisman, Annie 141, 209
Weiss, Allison 214
Weissbard, A.J. 167
Weissberg, Noah 220
Weissler, Barry 68
Weissler, Fran 68
Weitman, Rebecca 151
Weitzenhoffer, Max 41
Weitzer, Jim 72
Weitzman, Ira 131
Welch, Christopher Evan 106,
    174
Welch, Dan 228, 229, 230
Welch, Jane 168, 227
Welch, Rainey 154
Welch, Willy 209
Weldon, Charles 221, 227
Weller, Frederick 6, 47, 128, 309
Weller, Michael 144, 151

Weller-Fahy, Johanna 172
Wellman, John 145, 309
Wellman, Mac 145, 146, 176
Wells, Christopher Spencer 175,
    233
Wells, Matthew 156
Welty, Tara 175
Welzer, Irving 56
Wendell, Courtenay 140
Wendland, Mark 129, 130
Wendt, Angela 74
Wendt, Roger 40, 59
Werner, Howard 28
Werner, Jennifer 53
Werner, Stewart 177
Wernke, John 151
Werther, Ken 196
Werthmann, Colleen 175
Wertz, Kimberlee 55
Wesbrooks, William 95
West, Ashley 139, 185
West, Cheryl L. 203
West, Darron L. 132, 186, 215,
    230
West, Matt 66
West, Merrill 69
West, Michael 102, 110, 146,
    309
WestBeth Entertainment 97
Westbrooks, Nyjah Moore 141
Westergaard, Louise 28
Weston, Douglas 225
Weston, Jon 42, 54, 75, 112,
    219
*Westport Country Playhouse
    Production of Our Town* 36
Westside Theatre 100
Westside Theatre Upstairs 110
Westside Theatre Downstairs
    162
West End Horror, The 190
West Pier 154
West Side Story 227
Wetherall, Jack 148, 174
Wever, Merritt 130
Wever, Russ 103, 151, 206
Wexler, Alison 225
We Never Knew Their Names
    161
Whalen, David 225
Whaley, Frank 140, 309
Whaley, Michael 106
Wharton, William 179
What's Inside the Egg? 149
What's Your Karma? 156
What Didn't Happen 131
What I Missed in the '80s 140
Whealan, Denise 231
Wheeler, Harold 25
Wheeler, Hugh 187, 201

Wheeler, Jedediah 41
Wheeler, Nathan Thomas 184
Wheeler, Sally 163
Wheeler, Susan 124
Wheetman, Dan 103
When Grace Comes In 215
When We Dead Awaken 143
Whidden, Amanda 206
Whisper 169
Whitaker, Mary 75
Whitaker, Paul 105
White, Al 199
White, Alecia 204, 205
White, Alice 173, 188, 189
White, Amelia 167, 309
White, Carl D. 111
White, Conor 168
White, George C. 161
White, J. Steven 93, 177, 179
White, Jacob Garrett 179, 309
White, Jennifer Dorr 159
White, Julie 100, 146, 309
White, Lilias 132
White, Margot 147
White, Michole Briana 129
White, Nathan 174
White, Randy 152, 174, 175
White, Rebecca 175
White, Richard E. T. 180, 185
White, Steve 112
White, Welker 163
Whitehead, Charles 50
Whitehead, Graham 212
Whitehead, Paxton 231
Whitehead, Robert 327
Whitehill, B.T. 168
Whitehurst, Scott 155
Whiteley, Ben 124
Whitemore, Hugh 214
White Bird Productions. Boro
    Tales: Brooklyn 163
White Russian 148
Whitney, Barbara 186
Whitney, Belinda 75, 124
Whitsett, Edie 212
Whitsett, Laurel 209
Whittaker, Jay 208
Whittinghill, Kevin 150
Whitty, Jeff 179
Whitworth, Paul 184, 227
Who's Afraid of Virginia Woolf?
    183, 222
Whores 175
Whoriskey, Kate 225
Whose Family Values! 176
*Who Are the People in Your
    Neighborhood?* 152
Whyte, Laura 214
Wianecki, Casey 225
Wickemeyer, Johanna 230

Wickline, Terry 221
Wicks, Michael 195
Wickwire, Alexis 150
Wiens, Wolfgang 167
Wierzel, Robert 215
Wiese, Mike 213
Wiesenfeld, Cheryl 104
Wiesner, Nicole 208
Wiest, Dianne 57
Wiggin, Tom 150
Wiggins, Jeremiah 200
Wilbur, Richard 44, 215
Wilde, Oscar 57, 149
Wilder, Matthew 140, 223
Wilder, Susan 232
Wilder, Thornton 36, 190, 228
Wiley, Amber 189
Wiley, Shonn 69
Wilfert, Sally 91
Wilkas, Matthew 105, 157
Wilkerson, John 124
Wilkerson, Steve 222
Wilkerson, Weston 204
Wilkes, Fiona 112
Wilkof, Lee 27, 310
Wilks, Talvin 170
Will, Ethyl 27, 59
Willeford, Charles 162
Willett, Chad 206
Willett, Mark 139
Williams, Angela 229, 230
Williams, Bill 191
Williams, Blair 231
Williams, Brynn 220
Williams, Cartier A. 196
Williams, Christopher 147
Williams, Craig 160, 161
Williams, Curtis Mark 225
Williams, Denise Marie 70
Williams, Diane Ferry 222
Williams, Garry 168
Williams, Jaston 206
Williams, Jeff 212
Williams, Jim 147
Williams, Jonathan Rhys 185
Williams, Joy 230
Williams, Julie 209
Williams, Juson 142
Williams, Karl 152
Williams, Kenneth 222
Williams, Larry, Jr. 205
Williams, M. Drue 176
Williams, Mel 147
Williams, Richard Neal 189
Williams, Ross 144
Williams, Roy 174
Williams, Schele 65
Williams, Shané 225
Williams, Shelly 218, 219
Williams, Stuart 227

Williams, Tennessee 191
Williams, Toby 91
Williams, Todd 213
Williams, Trevor 175
Williams, Virginia 163
Williamson, Elizabeth 185
Williamson, Jama 96, 132
Williamson, Kristi 227
Williamson, Laird 184, 185
Williamson, Laurie 124
Williamson, Zachary 169
Williford, Steven 160
Willinger, David 178
Willis, Dan 75
Willis, Haley 190
Willis, Jack 79, 96
Willis, John 241
Willis, Steve 140
Willison, Walter 133, 180, 241
Wills, Jennifer Hope 220
Wills, Ray 73
Will and the Ghost 152
Will the Sun Ever Shine Again?
    161
Wilmes, Gary 176
Wilmore, Burke J. 223
Wilson, Anna 109
Wilson, August 45, 144, 221,
    227
Wilson, Brian 123
Wilson, C.J. 62, 310
Wilson, Casey 178
Wilson, Chuck 29, 60
Wilson, Dana 192
Wilson, Danelle Eugenia 26, 310
Wilson, Darlene 29, 124
Wilson, Eleanor "Siddy" 327
Wilson, Erin Cressida 161
Wilson, Felicia 220
Wilson, Greg 190
Wilson, Jackie 104
Wilson, Joe, Jr. 93
Wilson, Lanford 93, 168, 177,
    190
Wilson, Lindsay 144
Wilson, Mark Elliot 185
Wilson, Mary Louise 196
Wilson, Matthew R. 162, 171
Wilson, Michael 56, 131, 161,
    183
Wilson, Moira 97
Wilson, Rainn 218
Wilson, Robert 167
Wilson, Ron 207
Wilson, Steve 212
Wilson, Walton 233, 234
Wilson, Wendy Barrie 36
Wiltse, David 97
Wimmer, Aaron 99
Winchester, Richard 156

Windheim, Bennett 146
Wind Cries Mary, The 224
Winer, Linda 241
Wing-Davey, Mark 160, 170, 201
Wink, Chris 112
Winkler, David 180
Winkler, Mark 111
Winkler, Richard 206, 207
Winn, Bryon 230
Winokur, Marissa Jaret 26, 239
Winsberg, Susan Craig 215
Winslow, Lawrence 144
Winston, Connie 148
Winter's Tale, The 168
Winternitz, Kathryn A. 200
Wintersteller, Lynne 180, 227
Wintertime 215
Winter Garden Theatre 71
Winther, Michael 129
Winton, David 157, 162
Winton, Graham 179
Wirth, Julius Rene 29
Wise, Paula 49
Wise, Scott 32, 202
Wiseman, Johanna 72
Wisker, Stephen 160
Wisniewski, Jim 153
Wisniski, Ron 194
Wisocky, Rebecca 145, 191
Withers, Brenda 154, 155
Withers, Jeffrey 233, 234
Witherspoon, Cindy 200
Witherspoon, Pilar 173
With a Song in My Heart 180
Witkiewicz, Stanislaw Ignacy
    144, 172
Witten, Dean 39
Witter, Terrence J. 68
Wittman, Scott 25
Wizeman, Bryan 155
Wochna, Janine 206
Wohl, David 43, 179
Wojciechowski, Alyse 231
Wojewodski, Robert 217
Wojewodski, Stan, Jr. 209
Wojyltko, Chris 143
Woldin, Judd 93
Wolf, Eugene 188, 189
Wolf, Jeffrey C. 153
Wolf, Rita 146
Wolf, Scott 125, 310
Wolfe, George C. 92, 128, 129,
    170, 196, 197
Wolfe, Isadora 192
Wolfe, Jordan 156
Wolfe, Rachel Dara 225
Wolfe, Wayne 33, 40, 41, 55,
    101
Wolk, James 200
Wolkowitz, Morton 112

Womack, Cornell 126
Womack, Mark 38
*Woman at a Threshold,
    Beckoning* 161
Woman from the Sea, The 162
Woman in Black, The 216
Woman vs. Superman 152
Womble, Terence 34, 49
Women's Project and
    Productions 176, 179
Women's Project Theatre 97
Women in Heat 143
Women of Lockerbie, The 176
Women Who Steal 216
Won, Allen 75
Wong, B.D. 168, 190, 310
Wong, Eunice 155, 174, 200
Wonka, Peter 189
Wonsel, Paul 231
Wonsey, David 233
Wood, Dan 209
Wood, David A. 66
Wood, Frank 33, 161, 190
Wood, Greg 187
Wood, Stephen Douglas 157
Woodall, Alaina 205
Woodall, April 205
Woodall, Sandra 185
Woodard, Charlayne 126
Woodard, Javier 220
Woodard, Larry 180
Woodbury, Richard 62
Woodell, Colin Todd 184
Woodell, Keelin Shea 184
Woodeson, Nicholas 116
Woodhead, Mindy 186
Woodiel, Paul 27, 60
Woodruff, Loretta Guerra 150
Woodruff, Robert 186
Woods, Allie 144
Woods, Carla 222
Woods, Yvonne 144, 179, 183
Woodward, Joanne 36
Woodward, Jonathan M. 199
Woolard, David C. 100, 109, 127,
    131, 183
Wooley, Jim 219
Wooley, Michael-Leon 124
Woolley, Jim 42, 58
Woolsey, Wysandria 66
Woolverton, Linda 65, 66, 70
Wooten, Jason 40
Wopat, Tom 69
Workshop Theater Company, The
    163
World Over, The 130
Worley, D. Matt 184
Wormsworth, James 151
Worm Day 146
Worsdale, Brian P. 180

Worster, Collin 200
Worth, Irene iii
Worth Street
    Theater Company 163
Woyasz, Laura 131
Woyzeck 167
Wrangler, Jack 160
Wray, Kate 72
Wreen, Peggy 180
Wreford, Catherine 69, 197
Wright, Amy 142
Wright, Chloe 14, 38, 310
Wright, Christopher 98
Wright, Craig 216
Wright, Doug 131
Wright, Erica 156
Wright, Frank, II 70
Wright, Jeffrey 86
Wright, Josh 186
Wright, Lynn 139
Wright, Nicholas 48
Wright, Samuel E. 70
Wright, Shawn 196
Wrightson, Ann G. 212, 221
Writer's Block 106
Wrong for Each Other 232
Wu, Jade 155
Wu, Mia 124
Wuehrmann, Nicholas 153, 310
WWLC 58
Wynkoop, Christopher 62, 310
Wynn, Doug 147
Wynne, Gene 176

Y
Yadegari, Shahrokh 186
Yaegashi, James 47, 128
Yager, Jerry 125, 130, 213, 219
Yaji, Shigeru 224, 225

Yajima, Mineko 29, 124
Yale Repertory Theatre 233, 234
Yale University Theatre 233
Yamada, Mayu 173
Yamagata, Aja M. 178
Yamamoto, Takanori 173
Yamashita, Kosuke 173
Yamauchi, Satomi 175
Yaney, Denise 126
Yang, Chiwang 171
Yang, Ericka 29
Yang, Wendy Meiling 154
Yankowitz, Susan 175
Yasunaga, Christine 70
Yeager, Kenton 204
Yeager, Matt 145
Yearby, Marlies 74
Yeargan, Michael 217
Year with Frog and Toad, A 11,
    55, 153
Yeaton, Dana 205
Yee, David 37, 139
Yee, Jenny 170
Yeh, Felice 149
Yeh, Ming 39
Yellin, Harriet 110
Yellowman 126, 174
Yerkes, Tamlyn Freund 60
Yershon, Gary 50, 51
Yeston, Maury 54
Yew, Chay 151, 160, 212
Yionoulis, Evan 225
Yionoulis, Michael 225
Yionulis, Evan 151
Yntena, Sylvia 145
Yoder, Matthew Karl 220
Yokastas 172
Yonka, Peter 188, 189
Yoo, Aaron 149

Yoo, Mia 186
York, Marshall 153
York, Nora 180
Yorkin, Bud 23
York Theatre Company 179
Yoshida, Keiko 146
Yoson, Michael 220
Yost, John 221
Youmans, James 126, 176, 226
Youmans, William 38
Young, Adrienne 142, 231
Young, Eric Jordan 60, 68, 132
Young, Karen 171, 179
Young, Maryne 233
Young, Nan 168
Young, Rebecca 106
Young, Sharon L. 70
Young, Tara 40
Young, Tracy 233
Young, Zakiya 226
Younger, Carolyn 158
Young Playwrights Festival 2002
    144
Your Call Is Important to Me 143
You Can't Take It with You 183
Ysamat, Vma 153
Yuen, Lisa 220
Yule, Maggie 191
Yulin, Harris 177
Yunker, Ken 210
Yurkanin, Mark 232
Yurman, Lawrence 124

Z
Zacarias, Karen 170
Zacharias, Emily 220
Zachry, Anne Louise 179
Zackman, Gabra 210
Zafiropoulou, Miranta 97

Zaitchik, Daniel 127
Zaken, Remy 129, 310
Zaki, Antony 102
Zaloom, Joe 45
Zaloom, Paul 176
Zambri, Catherine 148
Zamore, Simone 156
Zane, Billy 68
Zanna, Don't! 102, 167
Zaragoza, Gregory 133
Zaray, Nicole 172
Zarish, Janet 176
Zarle, Brandy 174
Zarret, Lee 192
Zayas, David 101, 151, 310
Zayas, Dean 177
Zazzali, Peter 139
Zee, Alexa 140
Zehra, Sameena 102
Zeigen, Coleman 212
Zeiler, Van 142
Zekaria, Richard Ezra 143
Zelevansky, Claudia 209
Zellnik, David 152, 168
Zellnik, Joseph 152
Zemsky, Craig 188
Zepp, Lori Ann 105
Zerman, Andrew M. 234
Zero Hour, The 175
Zes, Evan 139
Zeus, Jared 102, 167
Zhu, Richard Feng 220
Zhuravenko, Richard 176
Zickel, Mather 161
Zieglerova, Klara 100, 126, 169,
    197, 201, 222
Zielinski, Scott 168, 200, 225
Zielinski, William 187
Ziemba, Karen 175

Zien, Chip 27, 310
Ziman, Richard 127
Zimet, Paul 171, 175
Zimmer, Hans 70
Zimmer, Kim 139
Zimmerman, Guy 150
Zimmerman, Mark 196
Zimmerman, Mary 167
Zindel, Paul 149, 327
Zink, Geoff 209
Zinn, David 186, 233
Zinnato, Stephen 91, 163, 179
Zipay, Joanne 150
Zippel, David 223
Zipper Theater 163
Zippler, Karen 219
Zisa, Natalia 65
Zito, Torrie 42, 219
Zittel, Dan 193
Zizka, Blanka 126
Zollo, Frederick 45
Zorba 192
Zorich, Louis 45, 310
Zorin, Max 223
Zorina, Vera 327
Zorn, Danny 161
Zorn, John 149
Zuber, Catherine 43, 130, 173,
    179, 201, 225
Zubrycki, Robert 124
Zuniga, Rolando 145
Zweigbaum, Steven 73
Zyla, David R. 198, 221

JOHN WILLIS | Editor

John Willis has been editor-in-chief of both *Theatre World* and its companion series *Screen World* for over forty years. *Theatre World* and *Screen World* are the oldest definitive pictorial and statistical records of each American theatrical and foreign and domestic film season and are referenced daily by industry professionals, students, and historians worldwide.

Mr. Willis has also served as editor of *Dance World*, *Opera World*, *A Pictorial History of the American Theatre 1860–1985*, and *A Pictorial History of the Silent Screen*. Previously, he served as assistant to *Theatre World* founder Daniel Blum on *Great Stars of the American Stage*, *Great Stars of Film*, *A Pictorial History of the Talkies*, *A Pictorial History of Television*, and *A Pictorial Treasury of Opera in America*.

For the past forty years he has presided over the presentation of the annual Theatre World Awards. Begun in 1945 and presented by past winners, they are the oldest awards given to actors for a Broadway or Off-Broadway debut role. On behalf of Theatre World, Mr. Willis received a Special 2001 Tony Honor for "Excellence in the Theatre" and the 2003 Broadway Theatre Institute Lifetime Achievement Award, in addition to awards from Drama Desk, Lucille Lortel, the Broadway Theater Institute, National Board of Review, Marquis Who's Who Publications Board, and Milligan College. He has served on the nominating committees for the Tony Awards and the New York University Hall of Fame, and is currently on the board of the University of Tennessee Clarence Brown Theatre.

BEN HODGES | Associate Editor

As an actor, Ben has appeared in New York with the Barrow Group Theatre Company, Monday Morning Productions, Coyote Girls Productions, Jet Productions, New York Actors' Alliance, and Outcast Productions. Additionally, he has appeared in numerous productions presented by theatre companies which he founded, the Tuesday Group and Visionary Works. On film, he can be seen featured in *Macbeth: The Comedy*.

In 2001, he became director of development, then served as executive director for Fat Chance Productions, Inc., and the Ground Floor Theatre, a New York–based nonprofit theatre and film production company. *Prey for Rock and Roll* was developed by Fat Chance from their stage production into a feature film starring Gina Gershon, Drea de Matteo, and Lori Petty.

In 2003, frustrated with the increasingly daunting economic prospects involved in producing theatre on a small scale in New York, Ben founded NOOBA, the New Off-Off-Broadway Association, an advocacy group dedicated to representing the concerns of expressly Off-Off-Broadway producers in the public forum and in negotiations with other local professional arts organizations. He also serves on the New York Innovative Theatre Awards Committee, selecting outstanding Off-Off-Broadway individuals for recognition.

Ben served as an editorial assistant for many years on the 2001 Special Tony Honor Award–winning *Theatre World*, becoming the associate editor to John Willis in 1999. Also an assistant for many years to Mr. Willis for the prestigious Theatre World Awards, Ben was elected to the Theatre World Awards Board in 2002 and currently serves as the executive producer of the ceremony. He was presented with a Special Theatre World Award in 2003 for his ongoing stewardship of the event. He will also serve as executive producer for the 2005 LAMBDA Literary Awards ceremony.

Forbidden Acts, the first collected anthology of gay and lesbian plays from the span of the twentieth century, edited and with an introduction by Hodges, was published by Applause Theatre and Cinema Books in 2003 and was a finalist for the 2004 LAMBDA Literary Award for Drama. His tentatively titled *Producing for the Commercial Theatre*, edited with the Commercial Theater Institute's Frederic B. Vogel and including contributions from over twenty industry professionals, is anticipated as the comprehensive and definitive guide to theatrical production in the United States, to be released by Applause in 2006.

Ben also currently serves as executive director of The Learning Theatre, Inc., a nonprofit organization committed to incorporating theatre into the development of autistic and learning disabled children.

LUCY NATHANSON | Assistant Editor

Lucy Nathanson grew up in Manhattan, during a more heroic and innocent time. She studied fine arts at the High School of Music & Art, ballet at the School of American Ballet, and sculpture and painting at the Arts Students League. The genesis of her love of musical theatre, plays, and cultural performances of all types began at home, nurtured by her theatrical/motion picture press agent father and classical pianist mother. She currently works at the Open Center, a holisitic and world culture learning institution in New York City. She also freelances as an editor. Working for John Willis, Ben Hodges, and *Theatre World* has reinforced her belief that Art, beautifully shaped, can reshape lives.

EMMANUEL SERRANO | Assistant Editor

Emmanuel Serrano is the marketing and communications manager of Hudson Highland Group. He has a longstanding interest in the performing arts, having performed as a dancer professionally for many years, and he has a specific interest in the development and preservation of theatre and dance history. Prior to his tenure at Hudson Highland Group, he was the senior brand associate of the global branding team of Monster Worldwide (formerly known as TMP Worldwide). Mr. Serrano has also been an account executive with TMP's advertising and communications unit, where he managed the recruitment advertising campaigns of major accounts. He graduated from Boston University with a bachelor of arts degree in psychology and a minor in biology.

RACHEL WERBEL | Assistant Editor

Rachel has assisted on Theatre World and the Theatre World Awards for the past three years. She has also worked as an assistant to Ben Hodges and Robin Whitehouse, the executive and artistic directors, respectively, of Fat Chance Productions nonprofit theatre company and Fat Chance Films. She is a graduate of the American Academy of Dramatic Arts and currently a member of the Agency improv group. She has studied performance with the Barrow Group Theatre Company and Holly Mandel's Improvolution.

COLOPHON | Theatre World Volume 59

Typeset in Quark Express 6.0 on a Macintosh G5

Univers 47 Condensed Light, 8/10 points
Univers 67 Condensed Bold, 8/10 and 12/12 points

Printed on 60 lb. Sterling Ultra Web gloss stock
4-color process insert printed on 60 lb. Utopia II gloss stock

Interior design & layout by Pearl Chang
Cover design by Kristina Rolander
Art direction by Mark Lerner

Printed in the U.S.A.

SOUTH ORANGE PUBLIC LIBRARY

3 9507 00124122 2

WITHDRAWN

WITHDRAWN